D1282928

ANTHONY TROLLOPE

FRAMLEY PARSONAGE

In the course of the last century, Anthony Trollope's fictional county of Barset has become one of English literature's most 'real', most celebrated landscapes. FRAMLEY PARSONAGE – the fourth of his engrossing Barsetshire novels – concerns itself with the drastic misjudgements of an amiable but naive and overly ambitious young clergyman. Through its shrewd and excellent social comedy and subtle, sometimes wicked, grasp of political and ecclesiastical manoeuvering, Trollope brings a whole local universe to convincing and triumphant life.

EVERYMAN'S LIBRARY

EVERYMAN,
I WILL GO WITH THEE,
AND BE THY GUIDE,
IN THY MOST NEED
TO GO BY THY SIDE

ANTHONY TROLLOPE, 1815-1882

Framley Parsonage

with an Introduction by
Graham Handley

EVERYMAN'S LIBRARY

Alfred A. Knopf New York Toronto

171

THIS IS A BORZOI BOOK

PUBLISHED BY ALFRED A. KNOPF, INC.

First included in Everyman's Library, 1906

Typography by Peter B. Willberg

 Published in the United States by Alfred A. Knopf, Inc., New York, and simultaneously in Canada by Random House of Canada Limited, Toronto. Distributed by Random House, Inc., New York

ISBN 0-679-43133-0
LC 93-81320

Book Design by Barbara de Wilde and Carol Devine Carson

Printed and bound in Germany by
Mohndruck Graphische Betriebe GmbH, Gütersloh

FRAMLEY PARSONAGE

INTRODUCTION

Framley Parsonage, serialized in 1860–61, is the fourth novel in what has come to be known as the Barchester sequence, which began in 1855 with *The Warden* and concluded with the magisterial *The Last Chronicle of Barset*, published in 1867. The sequence evolved gradually out of its creator's initial vision of life in an English cathedral city, which came to him one day in the early 1850s as he surveyed the city of Salisbury from a nearby bridge, but Trollope had no grand strategy for his Barchester novels: they were not conceived in advance as a sequence, and despite the modest success of *Doctor Thorne*, published in 1859, he had no immediate plans to continue the series. We owe *Framley Parsonage* rather to the intervention of chance in the shape of the *Cornhill* magazine, a new monthly periodical launched in 1860 and edited by Trollope's literary idol, Thackeray.

In November 1859, shortly after his return from the West Indies, where he gathered the material for a travel book, Trollope began an Irish novel, *Castle Richmond*, which he offered to George Smith, the publisher of the new periodical. But Smith wanted 'an English story'; and flattered by a letter of praise from Thackeray, Trollope put *Castle Richmond* on one side and immediately began writing *Framley Parsonage* instead. The chance was fortunate for both the author and his publisher. *Framley Parsonage* fitted easily into the Barchester sequence. It was also a popular success and a considerable step forward in Trollope's development as a novelist.

Like *Doctor Thorne*, the new novel moves the centre of attention away from the bishop's palace and towards the families outside the city – though, as I shall indicate more fully later, the combination of old friends and new characters is one which Trollope enjoyed exploiting to the full. But *un*like his previous novels, *Framley Parsonage* first appeared as a serial, and this made a considerable difference. As always, Trollope moved quickly into his narrative stride: beginning the novel in early November, he had completed five instalments by the deadline set for the first (12 December). Half the book was finished by Christmas, giving him time to resume work on *Castle Richmond* which was published in May 1860. By then, Trollope had returned to *Framley Parsonage*. Writing at speed and revising as he went, he adapted easily and resourcefully to the serial form, learning how to shape his material to the medium and fashioning effective climaxes for each episode. Four chapters were published each month and the completed text gives hints of its serial origins.

Trollope was rewarded with the immediate enthusiasm of his readers. But although his revisions also suggest that he was intent on more than mere entertainment, such intentions were not apparent to his critics, and public esteem was more than matched by the hostility of reviewers. *The Examiner* declared that the author of *Framley Parsonage* had 'not a touch of original fancy', adding that he lacked 'any subtle or peculiar insight into character'. The reviewer found additionally that 'The weakest parts of the book are those which affect political satire', though he balances this with high praise for the presentation of Mr Crawley and Lady Lufton. The *Saturday Review* observed snidely that Trollope 'is a writer who is born to make the future of circulating libraries', and that 'he is far less of a novelist than a good diner-out', but then the *Saturday Review* had already lost some of its contributors – and perhaps its readers – to the lure of the *Cornhill*. *Framley Parsonage* was also seen as being deficient in construction: the *Westminster Review*, for example, thought it 'rather a series of anecdotes than a well-knit tale', having 'no evolution; the story progresses by constant aggregation of details; in this way novels may be manufactured like Manchester goods, and retailed at so much per yard . . .'

These strictures did not influence the sale of the *Cornhill* or the popularity of *Framley Parsonage*, but it is interesting to set them beside Trollope's own views of the novel, given many years later in *An Autobiography* (written 1875–6 but not published until 1883, after his death). The self-mocking tone which he often adopts when commenting on his own work is evident here: 'There was a little fox-hunting and a little tuft-hunting, some Christian virtue and some Christian cant. There was much Church, but more love-making. And it was downright honest love... Indeed I doubt whether such a character could be made more lifelike than Lucy Robarts. And I will say also that in this novel there is no very weak part, – no long succession of dull pages.' These are small claims, like the small criticisms referred to in the preceding paragraph. The fact is that *Framley Parsonage* is a carefully constructed novel, much more artistically coherent than Trollope's own throwaway remarks would have us believe, and in the following paragraphs I want to concentrate on this structure with particular reference to character and location and the evident principle of contrast which here as elsewhere characterizes Trollope's best work.

Framley Parsonage contains a number of new characters or characters who are brought into fuller focus from previous mention: we think immediately of Mr Crawley and Lady Lufton and Lucy Robarts, but we should also include the vacillating Mark Robarts and his strikingly loyal wife Fanny, the unquenchable Sowerby and the winningly outspoken Miss Dunstable. These and many others are seen against the 'established' characters, the ineffectual bishop, his domineering prelatess, the archdeacon and Mrs Grantly and their society-conquering and arctic daughter Griselda. Trollope cleverly deploys characters in private and in public in order to emphasize their essential differences. As early as the end of the fourth part in the *Cornhill*, Lord Lufton, despite his mother's innuendo, has already succumbed to Lucy Robarts: he tells her that he loves her, and is confused, frustrated, even angered, by her response. The result is a sequence charged with feeling:

> 'By heavens,' he said, 'I will take no such answer from you till you put your hand upon your heart, and say that you cannot love me.'
>
> 'Oh, why should you press me so, Lord Lufton?'
>
> 'Why, because my happiness depends upon it; because it behoves me to know the very truth. It has come to this, that I love you with my whole heart, and I must know how your heart stands towards me.' She had now again risen from the sofa, and was looking steadily in his face.
>
> 'Lord Lufton,' she said, 'I cannot love you,' and as she spoke she did put her hand, as he had desired, upon her heart.

'Then God help me! for I am wretched. Good-bye, Lucy,' and he stretched out his hand to her.

'Good-bye, my lord. Do not be angry with me.'

'No, no, no!' and without further speech he left the room and the house and hurried home . . . And when he was well gone – absolutely out of sight from the window – Lucy walked steadily up to her room, locked the door, and then threw herself on the bed. Why – oh! why had she told such a falsehood? Could anything justify her in a lie? was it not a lie – knowing as she did that she loved him with all her loving heart? But, then, his mother! and the sneers of the world, which would have declared that she had set her trap, and caught the foolish young lord! Her pride would not have submitted to that. (Chapter XVI)

This is character in action, the interchange here involving passionate expression and passionate concealment at the same time. The mixed motives which split Lucy are of course unknown to Lord Lufton, and bewildering to Lucy herself. She has lied, certainly, and this brings on the reflex of self-condemnation, but her pride – her refusal to let it be thought or said that she has trapped Lord Lufton (and here Lady Lufton's inevitable conclusion is at the forefront of Lucy's consciousness) – has provoked a situation which is injurious to her and to Lord Lufton. I said that Trollope operates on more than one level, and here we have a scene which is both romantic rejection and realistic revelation, placing character in its private and public world.

More will be said of Lucy later, but first I want to indicate the resonance of Trollope's structure. In the next chapter there is another scene involving lovers, but with what a difference. The public display of the interaction between Lord Dumbello (a superb choice of name) and Griselda Grantly occurs at Mrs Proudie's *conversazione*:

'We were driving to-day, and we thought it rather cold,' said Griselda.

'Deuced cold,' said Lord Dumbello, and then he adjusted his white cravat and touched up his whiskers. Having got so far, he did not proceed to any other immediate conversational efforts; nor did Griselda. But he grouped himself again as became a marquis, and gave very intense satisfaction to Mrs. Proudie.

'This is so kind of you, Lord Dumbello,' said that lady, coming up to him and shaking his hand warmly; 'so very kind of you to come to my poor little tea-party.'

'Uncommonly pleasant, I call it,' said his lordship. 'I like this sort of thing – no trouble, you know.'

'No; that is the charm of it: isn't it? no trouble, or fuss, or parade. That's what I always say. According to my ideas, society consists in giving people facility for an interchange of thoughts – what we call conversation.'

'Aw, yes, exactly.' (Chapter XVII)

Now this passage has many qualities: it is, for example, Trollopian social satire at its best since Mrs Proudie, who can wither a curate with a blink, is here obsequious to an asinine lord who has no thoughts to interchange, and would not interchange them with Mrs Proudie if he had. But here I merely want to consider it in relation to the exchange we have just seen between Lucy and Lord Lufton in order to demonstrate Trollope's acute structural awareness. First, there is an obvious but nonetheless telling contrast. In the first passage the language is everything – it is impassioned with thought and emotion, with direct communication and the poignancy of non-communication. We are aware that Lord Lufton and Lucy are well suited to each other: they speak from the heart even if, in Lucy's case, the lie is from the head. And we note too that Lord Dumbello and Griselda are admirably matched, looking forward to a lifetime of monosyllabic animation if this is anything to go by – and it is. They are society automata, where Lord Lufton and Lucy are positive individuals reacting and interacting with each other. Second, Lucy's fear is Griselda's practice: Lucy is intent upon rejecting any talk which suggests 'she had set her trap, and caught the foolish young lord' while Griselda, if one can credit her with any motivation, has 'caught' Dumbello and certainly will be oblivious of what is said. Griselda is pride personified, Lucy pride introverted. Griselda's languor and calculated indifference compel attention, and romance – and gossip – can invest her with thoughts and feelings, for physical beauty has its own empire, its outward corollary of 'traps': Lucy can compel attention only through sincerity of manner and action, as she demonstrates later with her devoted nursing of Mrs Crawley. Through these characters Trollope's moral commentary embraces appearance and reality. There is no substance to Griselda other than that of appearance; Lucy's substance in action is her reality. Ironically, each of them will marry a nobleman, but again the difference is everything.

Lucy's humanity, her moral motivation, is at the heart of *Framley Parsonage*. I refer to the Crawley household here and Lucy's dedicating herself to Mrs Crawley's recovery at great personal risk, and this despite Mr Crawley's independent assertiveness. On Lucy's part there is subterfuge, then a kind of open defiance and, one feels, a bravado which is sustained by her unremitting activity. Before that we are invited to see Lucy retrospectively in close and loving relationship with her father before his death: her courage and sensitivity afterwards on her translation to Framley are the precursors of those later same qualities in her relations with Mr Crawley and Lady Lufton and, indeed, with Lord Lufton himself. Lucy is no Victorian rose: she gains a sister in Mark's wife Fanny, but loses the safety and security of her old home. She is socially unpretentious (contrast with Griselda again), and this is a considered moral attribute in this novel of social manoeuvring and manipulation. But beneath Lucy's shyness there is much self-will, obstinacy and determination. These last three qualities would apply to Griselda too, but whereas she responds to admiration or negation with the studied acceptance of one who knows her own worth, Lucy responds to and needs sympathy, the warm ambience of personal interest, hence her initial responses to Lord Lufton. This makes her decision to go to the Crawley home all the more praiseworthy. There she has the strength to make her own rules, establishing a regimen which serves the needs of the seriously sick Mrs Crawley.

It is one of the running ironies which constitute the presentation of character in *Framley Parsonage* that we see very little of Mark Robarts, the archdeacon or the bishop as Christians, or of Mrs Proudie either, except in her role of church lawgiver. But Lucy is directly and positively Christian in her practice. And there is nothing cloying in this; to use a commonplace, she gets on with it while others are getting on with their intrigues, whether marital, political or financial. Through Lucy, Crawley himself is brought into the foreground, a poignant contrast to the socially comfortable characters who move easily in and out of the pages of the novel. Crawley is a triumph of characterization here, just as he is in *The Last Chronicle*, not because he is a good but deprived clergyman, but because he is eccentric, bloody-minded, self-suffering, self-defeating and inflicting suffering on those closest to him. His rooted stance and abnormal sensitivity alienate him from normal human behaviour. He has long suffered a sub-cottage economy in the poor living of Hogglestock, made worse by the arrival of children. He has no resources, exerts a petty tyranny over his wife's acceptance of small healing gifts, and is a terrifying study in self-erosion. Yet this mixture of misery and martyrdom is strongly individualized by Trollope. With true fortitude Crawley seeks to help himself (despite the suffering of his family which results) but he rejects the help of others, his reaction to Lucy's arrival exacerbated by the dean (Arabin), once his equal and brother, who castigates him for his false pride:

> 'Call it so if you will; but, Arabin, no preaching of yours can alter it. It is all that is left to me of my manliness. That poor broken reed who is lying there sick, – who has sacrificed all the world to her love for me, – who is the mother of my children, and the partner of my sorrows and the wife of my bosom, – even she cannot change me in this, though she pleads with the eloquence of all her wants. Not even for her can I hold out my hand for a dole.' (Chapter XXXVI)

To condemn Crawley here would be to mistake the Trollopian emphasis: Crawley is mentally unstable, having moments of self-recognition, as here, but showing through the verbal shifts the divisions within himself – like the distance of 'That poor broken reed' and the intimacy of 'the partner of my sorrows and the wife of my bosom'. Even the clichéd language reflects the reduced and broken nature of the man. Trollope traces Crawley's morbid mania with such sure insight that at times the man becomes almost a parody of himself. Biographers have suggested that Crawley and, later, Louis Trevelyan in *He Knew He Was Right* (1869) owe something to the incipient melancholia bordering on madness which characterized Trollope's father. Whatever its sources, this derivation, whether known from life or conjured as imaginative reality, is compulsive reading. We may feel for Crawley or against him, or both, depending on our own sympathetic capacity or bias, but we cannot be indifferent, for Crawley's suffering is our own in those moments when we fear adversity and when that fear, in its intensity, is as real as reality. Crawley is *not* ennobled by suffering, for Trollope leaves us in little doubt that his economic and mental instabilities will continue.

Crawley represents one extreme of Trollope's social and moral analysis. At the other, Griselda triumphant is catechized by her grandfather (as Lucy was, but oh so differently, by Mr Crawley). Mr Harding embodies Trollope's positive moral values:

'You are going to be a great lady, Grizzy,' said he.
'Umph!' said she.
What was she to say when so addressed?
'And I hope you will be happy – and make others happy.'
'I hope I shall,' said she.
'But always think most about the latter, my dear. Think about the happiness of those around you, and your own will come without thinking. You understand that; do you not?'

'Oh yes, I understand,' she said. As they were speaking Mr. Harding still held her hand, but Griselda left it with him unwillingly, and therefore ungraciously, looking as though she were dragging it from him.

'And Grizzy – I believe it is quite as easy for a rich countess to be happy, as for a dairymaid – ' Griselda gave her head a little chuck which was produced by two different operations of her mind. The first was a reflection that her grandpapa was robbing her of her rank. She was to be a rich marchioness. And the second was a feeling of anger at the old man for comparing her lot to that of a dairymaid.

'Quite as easy, I believe,' continued he; 'though others will tell you that it is not so. But with the countess as with the dairymaid, it must depend on the woman herself. Being a countess – that fact alone won't make you happy.'

'Lord Dumbello at present is only a viscount,' said Griselda. 'There is no earl's title in the family.'

'Oh! I did not know,' said Mr Harding, relinquishing his granddaughter's hand; and after that he troubled her with no further advice. (Chapter XL)

The comedy here – and the pathos – hardly require comment. But the exchange sits tellingly beside the loving respect which Mary Gresham (née Thorne) pays to her uncle. Dr Thorne moves towards his new role in life without any acknowledgment of elevation beyond that of having his own quiet affection returned in typically independent kind. There is also both charm and comedy in the unromantic engagement of Miss Dunstable and Dr Thorne. His dignified letter of proposal ensures that his happiness will grow, and her reply ('Then I suppose that I am bound to have him') covers a warm nature and an inward exultation that in this 'arranged' marriage (brought about by the artfulness of Mary Gresham) she is treasured for herself and not for her money:

'Dear Dr. Thorne,

I do and will trust you in everything; and it shall be as you would have it. Mary writes to you; but do not believe a word she says. I never will again, for she has behaved so bad in this matter.

Yours affectionately and very truly,
Martha Dunstable.'

'And so I am going to marry the richest woman in England,' said Dr. Thorne to himself, as he sat down that day to his mutton-chop. (Chapter XXXIX)

Character is always Trollope's main concern, and there is a remarkable consistency in his presentation. Mrs Proudie, for example, moves from the palace reception in *Barchester Towers* to a wider and more prominent position in *Framley Parsonage* without difficulty. There she connives at the marriage of Sowerby to Miss Dunstable, ruins Harold Smith's lecture on the South Sea Islands with her stridently Christian interruption, and hastens to spread rumours about the disintegration of the Griselda-Dumbello engagement. Already we can see that she will undermine her partner, that low church appointee who is always subordinate to his sabbatarian wife. Trollope's ironic verve, which takes in manoeuvring and manipulation, as we have seen, also embraces the fact that professed professional Christians are often guilty of natural human error (witness Mark Robarts) or uncharitable practice (witness Mrs Proudie). Her social expansion reveals her for what she really is – an insensitive, vulgar, loud and domineering woman with an eye to advance. Her war with Mrs Grantly is waged from the position of having a plain daughter who must be married off, while Mrs Grantly (the wife of a mere archdeacon) has the strategic advantage of a beautiful child. What wonder then that Mrs Proudie is forced back upon her domestic power as the one certainty in life after her social forays come to nothing? That certainty itself crumbles in *The Last Chronicle of Barset*. Perhaps one should stress here that the Barchester sequence, unplanned as it was, can nevertheless be seen as one great novel, with each part separately integrated and independent but conducing to our appreciation of the whole.

Within this great novel women play a vital role. No one would call Trollope a feminist, but with such powerful female characters he hardly needs the name. Time and again in his fiction, weak men are supported or governed by powerful women, foolish or headstrong men advised and endured by patient sisters and daughters, long-suffering men dominated by imperious wives. *Framley Parsonage* is especially rich in such characters, from the insupportable Mrs Harold Smith and Mrs Proudie to the admirable Miss Dunstable and Lady Lufton. There is, above all, the heroic Mrs Crawley, who endures her sufferings with the fortitude of heroines in the Greek tragedies which are her husband's consolation in his poverty and madness.

Few things in Trollope's fiction are as extreme as the Crawleys and their predicament. More characteristic of his art is the ability to be bland and subversive at the same time – a peculiar combination which is a major source of his satire. The Duke of Omnium's aristocratic grandeur, for example, is finely undermined by his money-consciousness and his evident parasitism. Sowerby's fine talk barely masks unscrupulous opportunism, while his opponent Supplehouse is an evident hypocrite, and the supposedly Christian Harold Smith a self-seeking politician. Even in the novel's mellower passages, there is usually a sharp critical intelligence at work under the fine romantic sheen. At Gatherum Castle in particular we are invited to appraise the studied insolence of the rich and their hangers-on, beautiful in manners but ugly in morals.

This realistic presentation of character in society is the bench-mark of Trollope's greatness. At such moments we are most aware of his truth and wisdom, seeing in his creatures the twists and turns of personality, the ambiguities and paradoxes of behaviour, the many natural reflexes which constitute their lives in their fictional entity, and which correspond to our miscellaneous reactions in our own lives. Furthermore, it is a register of his own ambivalence that his subversions are not cynical: they are part of his balanced perspective. If we take the parsonage group – and they provide the title and therefore the central focus of the novel – we find that Mark Robarts is weak when it comes to social advancement and in putting his name to a bill, but that he is driven by his conscience to confession, confides (ultimately) in his wife, accepts rebuke from Crawley, and does his limited best to help the Crawley family in their suffering. Fanny Robarts is always aware that her role with Lady Lufton is that of a peacemaker both on the score of her husband's indiscretions and Lucy's developing relationship with Lord Lufton. Yet she displays her own independence together with a convincing integrity, showing a capacity to be obstinate herself, but with a warm and impetuous following reflex which is endearing. Lucy, as I have said earlier, is far from being a simple heroine: she is a complex, resourceful and tremulous girl, alternately brave and anxious and, despite her emotionalism, having a sure sense of moral perspective. These words cannot summarize the sympathetic ambience of Lucy: Hardy is said to have been in love with Tess, and Trollope is certainly so with Lucy, not in an uneasy or possessive way, but conveying his sheer delight in her presentation, sharing the ecstasy and poignancy of it.

Let me finally consider Lady Lufton as epitomizing Trollope's technical and imaginative mastery in *Framley Parsonage*. While Mrs Proudie is occupied in spreading the rumour that Dumbello has deserted Griselda before *their* marriage, Lady Lufton herself proposes to Lucy on her son's behalf. Lady Lufton's change of heart marks another aspect of Trollope's narrative skill, his ability to make possible, even imminent, what the reader has been taught to regard as impossible. Lady Lufton is conscious of her own status, the inheritance of birth and patronage, but she is too honest (and I am inclined to say too Christian) to play the society game. The treaty with Mrs Grantly whereby Lord Lufton and Griselda were to be brought together was never ratified. It was a mother's convenient fantasy. Faced with the reality of losing her son or overcoming her own somewhat narrow ideas of breeding and looks, Lady Lufton descends – or rather, moves sideways – with initial dignity and admirable honesty, and then finds that her emotions are too much for her. The language of conciliation is the index to her heartfelt anxiety:

> 'Well, my dear, all that I said to you then I said to you thinking that it was for the best. You, at any rate, will not be angry with me for loving my own son better than I love any one else.'
>
> 'Oh, no,' said Lucy.
>
> 'He is the best of sons, and the best of men, and I am sure that he will be the best of husbands.'
>
> Lucy had an idea, by instinct, however, rather than by sight, that Lady Lufton's eyes were full of tears as she spoke. As for herself she was altogether blinded, and did not dare to lift her face or to turn her head. As for the utterance of any sound, that was quite out of the question.
>
> 'And I have come here, Lucy, to ask you to be his wife.'
>
> (Chapter XLVI)

There is more to come, but the straight simplicity of this makes it movingly natural. The simplicity cannot hide the distance each character has travelled over the course of the action. Lucy here reduced is the same Lucy who stood up so bravely to Lady Lufton earlier: Lady Lufton is the same person who put Lucy in her place when she previously feared her son's committed interest. Both are the same, yet each is different. Both have come to an increased self-awareness; Lucy feels herself a coward but is in fact responding to the warm magnanimity (and self-acknowledgment) of the other woman. Lady Lufton, with genuine humility, and consequently without loss of face or status, has come to ask what was previously unaskable. These two are one in the shared sympathetic affinity of the moment and, I suggest, in the conscious knowledge that a deep love does not exclude but admits of sharing the beloved, here Lord Lufton. As usual, there is our background awareness which evolves from Trollope's handling of his material: Lady Lufton's sense and sensitivity is being clearly contrasted with Mrs Proudie's lack of it, while Lucy's innate sympathy is being set against Griselda's do-nothing hauteur.

Lady Lufton is convincing in every way throughout the novel. With all her faults, she is compassionate in her social responsibilities, upright in her moral stance, proud and warm in her personal relationships but capable of considered change, of adapting, in short of acknowledging herself to be in error, as we have seen. Trollope's technique of radiating out from the small areas to the wider areas of society shows the profound stability of Lady Lufton and her kind. Society defeats her but she does not feel the loss: her brush with the loathed Duke of Omnium is merely that – she plays no part in the devious activities of Mrs Harold Smith and Mrs Proudie. A knowledge of Tom Towers' power is absent from her waking hours: Ludovic is the centre of her small world, and there is no greater world to corrupt her. She appears autocratic, but is in fact soft-centred: the way she is presented is typical of Trollope's attention to detail in his consideration of human personality: what appears is only part of the whole, what seems may be the cover or index to deeper realities, what is there beneath the words of the dialogue or the silent interaction.

Graham Handley

GRAHAM HANDLEY is Lecturer in English in the Extra-Mural Department, University of London. He has written a study of George Eliot's Midlands and a critical study of *Barchester Towers*, and has edited *Daniel Deronda* (Clarendon Press) and Trollope's *The Three Clerks* (World's Classics).

SELECT BIBLIOGRAPHY

There is a wide-ranging Trollope industry. The following are recommended:

MICHAEL SADLEIR, *Trollope: A Commentary*, Constable, 1927. Virtually the pioneering introduction to the life and works, by a major Trollope scholar and enthusiast.

L.P. and R.P. STEBBINS, *The Trollopes: The Chronicle of a Writing Family*, Secker and Warburg, 1946, is useful in charting the family and showing the influences which helped to mould Trollope.

BRADFORD A. BOOTH, *Anthony Trollope: Aspects of His Life and Work*, Edward Hulton, 1958, did much to foster the revival of interest in Trollope's work, which has risen steadily since.

JAMES POPE HENNESSY, *Anthony Trollope*, Cape, 1971. A good standard biography for the general reader.

R.H. SUPER. *The Chronicler of Barsetshire: A Life of Anthony Trollope*, University of Michigan Press, 1988. This is a fine critical biography despite its modest title. Super is steeped in Trollopian detail and his astute insights integrate the life and the fiction.

RICHARD MULLEN, *Anthony Trollope: A Victorian in His World*, Duckworth, 1990. There is copious research here: particularly impressive on the background and the travel books.

N. JOHN HALL, *Trollope: A Biography*, Oxford, 1991; scholarly, detailed, informative at every turn.

VICTORIA GLENDINNING, *Trollope*, Hutchinson, 1992; dedicated, affectionate, written with narrative verve and stimulating attention to background.

Readers should not neglect Trollope's own *An Autobiography*, Blackwood, 1883, which is readily available (World's Classics, 1980). It is as interesting for its omissions as for what it does say about the making of his fiction and his daily habits of writing, which lowered him in the eyes of late Victorian critics and readers.

N. JOHN HALL, ed., *The Letters of Anthony Trollope*, 2 vols., Stanford University Press, 1983, contain valuable insights into the man as man as well as artist.

Specific criticism is to be found in DONALD SMALLEY, ed., *Trollope: The Critical Heritage*, Routledge, 1969, which has several reviews of *Framley Parsonage*, and finely selected reviews and articles by his contemporaries on the whole range of Trollope's fiction; in DAVID SKILTON's *Anthony Trollope and his Contemporaries*, Longman, 1972, which sets Trollope in his literary context; T. BAREHAM, ed., *The*

Barsetshire Novels: A Selection of Critical Essays, Macmillan, 1983; of particular interest is N. JOHN HALL, *Trollope and His Illustrators*, Macmillan, 1980.

Other book-length studies of value as commentaries on Trollope's fiction or which have some detail on *Framley Parsonage* are: ANTHONY COCKSHUT, *Anthony Trollope: A Critical Study*, Collins, 1955; JAMES R. KINCAID, *The Novels of Anthony Trollope*, Oxford, 1977; P.D. EDWARDS, *Anthony Trollope: His Art and Scope*, Harvester, 1978 (this is particularly recommended for its critical insights); R.C. TERRY, *Anthony Trollope: The Artist in Hiding*, Macmillan, 1977; ANDREW WRIGHT, *Anthony Trollope: Dream and Art*, Macmillan, 1983; MARY HAMER, *Writing by Numbers: Trollope's Serial Fiction*, Cambridge University Press, 1987; STEPHEN WALL, *Trollope and Character*, Faber, 1988.

CHRONOLOGY

Trollope was a prolific writer with over fifty books to his credit. Those which are felt to be important are listed here, together with some events in his life.

DATE	AUTHOR'S LIFE	LITERARY CONTEXT
1811		Thackeray born.
1812		Dickens born.
1813		Jane Austen: *Pride and Prejudice*.
1814		Jane Austen: *Mansfield Park*. Walter Scott: *Waverley*.
1815	Born in Bloomsbury, London, 24 April.	Jane Austen: *Emma*.
1816		Charlotte Brontë born.
1817		Jane Austen dies.
1818		Jane Austen: *Northanger Abbey* and *Persuasion*. Mary Shelley: *Frankenstein*. Walter Scott: *The Heart of Midlothian*.
1819		George Eliot born.
1820		Walter Scott: *Kenilworth*.
1821		Keats dies.
1822	Day boy at Harrow.	Shelley dies. Matthew Arnold born.
1824		Walter Scott: *Redgauntlet*.
1826		Walter Scott: *Woodstock*.
1827	Attends Winchester.	Blake dies.
1828		D. G. Rossetti born.
1829		
1830	Returns to Harrow.	Tennyson: *Poems Chiefly Lyrical*.
1831		
1832		Walter Scott dies.
1833		Carlyle: *Sartor Resartus*. Newman: *Tracts for the Times* (to 1841).
1834	Appointed junior clerk in the General Post Office.	Coleridge dies. Charles Lamb dies.
1836		Dickens: *Pickwick Papers*.
1837		Dickens: *Oliver Twist*. Carlyle: *The French Revolution*.

HISTORICAL EVENTS

Battle of Waterloo.

Spa Fields riot.
Princess Charlotte dies.

Peterloo Massacre. Queen Victoria born.
George III dies. Trial of Queen Caroline. Cato Street conspiracy.

Castlereagh commits suicide. Canning becomes Foreign Secretary.

Canning dies.
Duke of Wellington becomes Prime Minister. Repeal of Test and Corporation Acts.
Catholic Emancipation.
George IV dies. Agitation for reform. Manchester and Liverpool railway. July Revolution in France.
Rejection of First Reform Bill.
Grey passes First Reform Bill.
Factory Act limits children's working hours. Beginning of Oxford Movement. Abolition of slavery in the British Empire.

Transportation of the Tolpuddle Martyrs. The New Poor Law.

Railways begin in London.
Accession of Queen Victoria.

DATE	AUTHOR'S LIFE	LITERARY CONTEXT
1838		Dickens: *Nicholas Nickleby.*
1839		Carlyle: *Chartism.*
1840		Browning: *Sordello.*
1841	Deputy Postal Surveyor in Ireland.	Carlyle: *On Heroes and Hero Worship.* Dickens: *The Old Curiosity Shop.*
1842		Tennyson: *Poems.*
1843		Wordsworth Poet Laureate. Ruskin: *Modern Painters* (to 1860).
1844	Marries Rose Heseltine.	Dickens: *Martin Chuzzlewit.* Disraeli: *Coningsby.*
1845		Disraeli: *Sybil.*
1846	Son, Henry, born.	The Brontës: *Poems.*
1847	*The Macdermots of Ballycloran* published. Second son, Frederic, born.	Charlotte Brontë: *Jane Eyre.* Emily Brontë: *Wuthering Heights.*
1848	*The Kellys and the O'Kellys* published.	Emily Brontë dies. Dickens: *Dombey and Son.* Thackeray: *Vanity Fair.* Charlotte Brontë: *Shirley.*
1850		Wordsworth dies. Tennyson: *In Memoriam.* Dickens: *David Copperfield.* Thackeray: *Pendennis.* Wordsworth: *The Prelude.*
1851	On postal mission in west of England and Wales (to 1852).	
1853	Returns to Ireland as Surveyor of the Northern District (to 1854).	Arnold: *Poems.* Charlotte Brontë: *Villette.* Mrs Gaskell: *Cranford.*
1854		Dickens: *Hard Times.*
1855	*The Warden* published. Works on *The New Zealander* to 1856 (rejected).	Charlotte Brontë dies. Browning: *Men and Women.* Mrs Gaskell: *North and South.* Tennyson: *Maud.* Thackeray: *The Newcomes.*
1856		Elizabeth Barrett Browning: *Aurora Leigh.*
1857	*Barchester Towers.* *The Three Clerks* published.	Dickens: *Little Dorrit.* Mrs Gaskell: *Life of Charlotte Brontë.*

CHRONOLOGY

HISTORICAL EVENTS

Anti-Corn-Law League. Beginning of Chartism.
Chartist riots.
Queen marries Prince Albert. Penny post introduced.
Sir Robert Peel becomes Prime Minister.

Chartist riots. Introduction of income tax. Mines Act – women, and children under ten, were not to be employed underground.

Factory Act – restricted hours of work for women and children.

J. H. Newman joins Catholic Church. Irish potato famine.
Repeal of Corn Laws. Railway expansion.

Communist Manifesto. Chartist Petition presented. Year of revolutions in Europe. Public Health Act.

Great Exhibition in Hyde Park.

Crimean War (Battles of Balaclava and Inkerman).
Palmerston becomes Prime Minister. Sebastopol captured. Florence Nightingale begins work in the Crimea.

Crimean War ends (Treaty of Paris).

Indian Mutiny.

DATE	AUTHOR'S LIFE	LITERARY CONTEXT
1858	Postal mission to Suez. *Dr Thorne* published. Postal mission to the West Indies.	George Eliot: *Scenes of Clerical Life.*
1859	*The Bertrams* published. *The West Indies and the Spanish Main* published. Commissioned to write serial novel for new prestigious magazine, the *Cornhill*, ed. Thackeray. Surveyor of Eastern District of England; moves to Waltham Cross, Hertfordshire.	Dickens: *A Tale of Two Cities.* George Eliot: *Adam Bede.* George Meredith: *The Ordeal of Richard Feverel.* Tennyson: *Idylls of the King* (to 1872).
1860	*Framley Parsonage* begins in *Cornhill* (to April 1861). *Castle Richmond* published. Visits brother in Florence; meets American girl, Kate Field.	Wilkie Collins: *The Woman in White.* George Eliot: *The Mill on the Floss.* *Cornhill* magazine launched.
1861	First number of *Orley Farm* (to October 1862). Leaves in August for the United States.	Elizabeth Barrett Browning dies. Dickens: *Great Expectations.* George Eliot: *Silas Marner.*
1862	Returns in March to England. *North America* published. *The Small House at Allington* begins in *Cornhill* (to April 1864).	
1863	*Rachel Ray* published. Death of mother, Frances Trollope.	Thackeray dies. Mrs Gaskell: *Sylvia's Lovers.*
1864	*Can You Forgive Her?* begins (to August 1865).	
1865	*Miss Mackenzie* published.	Mrs Gaskell dies. Dickens: *Our Mutual Friend.*
1866	*The Last Chronicle of Barset* published (Dec. 1866–July 1867).	George Eliot: *Felix Holt.* Mrs Gaskell: *Wives and Daughters.*
1867	*Phineas Finn* begins as serial (to May 1869). Resigns from Post Office.	
1868	Postal mission to the United States. *He Knew He Was Right* begins in weekly parts. Defeated as Parliamentary Liberal candidate for Beverley.	Browning: *The Ring and the Book.*

CHRONOLOGY

HISTORICAL EVENTS

Jews allowed into Parliament.

Darwin's *On The Origin of Species* published.

Italian unification.

Death of Prince Albert. American Civil War begins.

Lincoln assassinated. American Civil War ends.

Disraeli becomes Prime Minister. Second Reform Bill. Dominion of Canada established.

Gladstone becomes Prime Minister.

DATE	AUTHOR'S LIFE	LITERARY CONTEXT
1869	*The Vicar of Bullhampton* (to May 1870).	Arnold: *Culture and Anarchy*. J. S. Mill: *On the Subjection of Women*.
1870	*Ralph the Heir*.	Dickens dies; *Edwin Drood*.
1871	*The Eustace Diamonds* (to Feb. 1873). Sails for Australia.	Lewis Carroll: *Through the Looking Glass*. Meredith: *Harry Richmond*. Ruskin: *Fors Clavigera*.
1872	Visits New Zealand.	George Eliot: *Middlemarch*. Samuel Butler: *Erewhon*. Hardy: *Under the Greenwood Tree*.
1873	*Australia and New Zealand* published. *Phineas Redux* (to Jan. 1874).	J. S. Mill dies. Arnold: *Literature and Dogma*.
1874	*The Way We Live Now* begins publication in monthly numbers (to Sept. 1875).	Hardy: *Far from the Madding Crowd*.
1875	Leaves London; visits Ceylon on way to Australia, and America on return journey.	Charles Kingsley dies.
1876	Completes *An Autobiography*. *The Prime Minister* published.	George Eliot: *Daniel Deronda*. Meredith: *Beauchamp's Career*. James: *Roderick Hudson*.
1877	*Is He Popenjoy?* (to July 1878). Sails for South Africa.	
1878	*South Africa* published.	Hardy: *The Return of the Native*.
1879	Completes *Dr Wortle's School*. *The Duke's Children* (to July 1880).	
1880	Moves to South Harting, near Petersfield, Sussex.	George Eliot dies.
1881	Goes to Rome with wife and niece.	James: *Portrait of a Lady*.
1882	Suffers a stroke. Dies on 6 December.	Darwin, D. G. Rossetti die.
1883	*An Autobiography* published.	
1884		

CHRONOLOGY

HISTORICAL EVENTS

Franco-Prussian War. Elementary Education Act.
Trades unions become legal.

Secret ballot established.

Annexation of Transvaal.

Congress of Berlin. Irish Land League.

Gladstone becomes Prime Minister. Transvaal becomes an independent republic.
Married Women's Property Act. Irish Land Act.

Phoenix Park murders in Ireland.

Third Reform Bill.

FRAMLEY PARSONAGE

Contents

Contents

FRAMLEY PARSONAGE

CHAPTER I

'Omnes Omnia Bona Dicere'

When young Mark Robarts was leaving college, his father might well declare that all men began to say all good things to him, and to extol his fortune in that he had a son blessed with so excellent a disposition. This father was a physician living at Exeter. He was a gentleman possessed of no private means, but enjoying a lucrative practice, which had enabled him to maintain and educate a family with all the advantages which money can give in this country. Mark was his eldest son and second child; and the first page or two of this narrative must be consumed in giving a catalogue of the good things which chance and conduct together had heaped upon this young man's head.

His first step forward in life had arisen from his having been sent, while still very young, as a private pupil to the house of a clergyman, who was an old friend and intimate friend of his father's. This clergyman had one other, and only one other, pupil – the young Lord Lufton; and between the two boys, there had sprung up a close alliance. While they were both so placed, Lady Lufton had visited her son, and then invited young Robarts to pass his next holidays at Framley Court. This visit was made; and it ended in Mark going back to Exeter with a letter full of praise from the widowed peeress. She had been delighted, she said, in having such a companion for her son, and expressed a hope that the boys might remain together during the course of their education. Dr. Robarts was a man who thought much of the breath of peers and peeresses, and was by no means inclined to throw away any advantage which might arise to his child from such a friendship. When, therefore, the young lord was sent to Harrow, Mark Robarts went there also.

That the lord and his friend often quarrelled, and occasionally fought, – the fact even that for one period of three months they never spoke to each other – by no means interfered with the doctor's hopes. Mark again and again stayed a fortnight at Framley Court, and Lady Lufton always wrote about him in the highest terms. And then the lads went together to Oxford, and here Mark's good fortune followed him, consisting rather in the highly respectable manner in which he lived, than in any wonderful career of collegiate success. His family was proud of him, and the doctor was always ready to talk of him to his patients; not because he was a prizeman, and had gotten medals and scholarships, but on account of the excellence of his general conduct. He lived with the best set – he incurred no debts – he was fond of society, but able to avoid low society – liked his glass of wine, but was never known to be drunk; and above all things, was one of the most popular men in the University. Then came the question of a profession for this young Hyperion, and on this subject Dr. Robarts was invited himself to go over to Framley Court to discuss the matter with Lady Lufton. Dr. Robarts returned with a very strong conception that the Church was the profession best suited to his son.

Lady Lufton had not sent for Dr. Robarts all the way from Exeter for nothing. The living of Framley was in the gift of the Lufton family, and the next presentation would be in Lady Lufton's hands, if it should fall vacant before the young lord was twenty-five years of age, and in the young lord's hands if it should fall afterwards. But the mother and the heir consented to give a joint promise to Dr. Robarts. Now, as the present incumbent was over seventy, and as the living was worth £900 a year, there could be no doubt as to the eligibility of the clerical profession. And I must further say, that the dowager and the doctor were justified in their choice by the life and principles of the young man – as far as any father can be justified in choosing such a profession for his son, and as far as any lay impropriator can be justified in making such a promise. Had Lady Lufton had a second son, that second son would probably have had the living, and no one would have thought it wrong; – certainly not if that second son had been such a one as Mark Robarts.

Lady Lufton herself was a woman who thought much on religious matters, and would by no means have been disposed to place any one in a living, merely because such a one had been her son's friend. Her tendencies were High Church, and she was enabled to perceive that those of young Mark Robarts ran in the same direction. She was very desirous that her son should make an associate of his clergyman, and by this step she would ensure, at any rate, that. She was anxious that the parish vicar should be one with whom she could herself fully co-operate, and was perhaps unconsciously wishful that he might in some measure be subject to her influence. Should she appoint an elder man, this might probably not be the case to the same extent; and should her son have the gift, it might probably not be the case at all. And, therefore, it was resolved that the living should be given to young Robarts.

He took his degree – not with any brilliancy, but quite in the manner that his father desired; he then travelled for eight or ten months with Lord Lufton and a college don, and almost immediately after his return home was ordained.

The living of Framley is in the diocese of Barchester; and, seeing what were Mark's hopes with reference to that diocese, it was by no means difficult to get him a curacy within it. But this curacy he was not allowed long to fill. He had not been in it above a twelvemonth, when poor old Dr. Stopford, the then vicar of Framley, was gathered to his fathers, and the full fruition of his rich hopes fell upon his shoulders.

But even yet more must be told of his good fortune before we can come to the actual incidents of our story. Lady Lufton, who, as I have said, thought much of clerical matters, did not carry her High Church principles so far as to advocate celibacy for the clergy. On the contrary, she had an idea that a man could not be a good parish parson without a wife. So, having given to her favourite a position in the world, and an income sufficient for a gentleman's wants, she set herself to work to find him a partner in those blessings. And here also, as in other matters, he fell in with the views of his patroness – not, however, that they were declared to him in that marked manner in which the affair of the living had been broached. Lady Lufton was much too highly gifted with woman's craft for that. She never told the young vicar that Miss Monsell accompanied her ladyship's married daughter to Framley Court expressly that he, Mark, might fall in love with her; but such was in truth the case.

Lady Lufton had but two children. The eldest, a daughter, had been married some four or five years to Sir George Meredith, and this Miss Monsell was a dear friend of hers. And now looms before me the novelist's great difficulty. Miss Monsell – or, rather, Mrs. Mark Robarts – must be described. As Miss Monsell, our tale will have to take no prolonged note of her. And yet we will call her Fanny Monsell, when we declare that she was one of the pleasantest companions that could be brought near to a man, as the future partner of his home, and owner of his heart. And if high principles without asperity, female gentleness without weakness, a love of laughter without malice, and a true loving heart, can qualify a woman to be a parson's wife, then was Fanny Monsell qualified to fill that station. In person she was somewhat larger than common. Her face would have been beautiful but that her mouth was large. Her hair, which was copious, was of a bright brown; her eyes also were brown, and, being so, were the distinctive feature of her face, for brown eyes are not common. They were liquid, large, and full either of tenderness or of mirth. Mark Robarts still had his accustomed luck, when such a girl as this was brought to Framley for his wooing. And he did woo her – and won her. For Mark himself was a handsome fellow. At this time the vicar was about twenty-five years of age, and the future Mrs. Robarts was two or three years younger. Nor did she come quite empty-handed to the vicarage. It cannot be said that Fanny Monsell was an heiress, but she had been left with a provision of some few thousand pounds. This was so settled, that the interest of his wife's money paid the heavy insurance on his life which young Robarts effected, and there was left to him, over and above, sufficient to furnish his parsonage in the very best style of clerical comfort, and to start him on the road of life rejoicing.

So much did Lady Lufton do for her protégé, and it may well be imagined that the Devonshire physician, sitting meditative over his parlour fire, looking back, as men will look back on the upshot of their life, was well contented with that upshot, as regarded his eldest offshoot, the Rev. Mark Robarts, the vicar of Framley.

But little has as yet been said, personally, as to our hero himself, and perhaps it may not be necessary to say much. Let us hope that by degrees he may come forth upon the canvas, showing to the beholder the nature of the man inwardly and outwardly. Here it may suffice to say that he was no born heaven's cherub, neither was he a born fallen devil's spirit. Such as his training made him, such he was. He had large capabilities for good – and aptitudes also for evil, quite enough: quite enough to make it needful that he should repel temptation as temptation only can be repelled. Much had been done to spoil him, but in the ordinary acceptation of the word he was not spoiled. He had too much tact, too much common sense, to believe himself to be the paragon which his mother thought him. Self-conceit was not, perhaps, his greatest danger. Had he possessed more of it, he might have been a less agreeable man, but his course before him might on that account have been the safer. In person he was manly, tall, and fair-haired, with a square forehead, denoting intelligence rather than thought, with clear white hands, filbert nails, and a power of dressing himself in such a manner that no one should ever observe of him that his clothes were either good or bad, shabby or smart.

Such was Mark Robarts when, at the age of twenty-five, or a little more, he married Fanny Monsell. The marriage was celebrated in his own church, for Miss Monsell had no home of her own, and had been staying for the last three months at Framley Court. She was given away by Sir George Meredith, and Lady Lufton herself saw that the wedding was what it should be, with almost as much care as she bestowed on that of her own daughter. The deed of marrying, the absolute tying of the knot, was performed by the Very Reverend the Dean of Barchester, an esteemed friend of Lady Lufton's. And Mrs. Arabin, the dean's wife, was of the party, though the distance from Barchester to Framley is long, and the roads deep, and no railway lends its assistance. And Lord Lufton was there of course; and people protested that he would surely fall in love with one of the four beautiful bridesmaids, of whom Blanche Robarts, the vicar's second sister, was by common acknowledgement by far the most beautiful. And there was there another and a younger sister of Mark's – who did not officiate at the ceremony, though she was present – and of whom no prediction was made, seeing that she was then only sixteen, but of whom mention is made here, as it will come to pass that my readers will know her hereafter. Her name was Lucy Robarts. And then the vicar and his wife went off on their wedding tour, the old curate taking care of the Framley souls the while. And in due time they returned; and after a further interval, in due course a child was born to them; and then another; and after that came the period at which we will begin our story. But before doing so, may I not assert that all men were right in saying all manner of good things to the Devonshire physician, and in praising his luck in having such a son?

'You were up at the house to-day, I suppose?' said Mark to his wife, as he sat stretching himself in an easy chair in the drawing-room, before the fire, previously to his dressing for dinner. It was a November evening, and he had been out all day, and on such occasions the aptitude for delay in dressing is very powerful. A strong-minded man goes direct from the hall door to his chamber without encountering the temptation of the drawing-room fire.

'No; but Lady Lufton was down here.'

'Full of arguments in favour of Sarah Thompson?'

'Exactly so, Mark.'

'And what did you say about Sarah Thompson?'

'Very little as coming from myself: but I did hint that you thought, or that I thought that you thought, that one of the regular trained schoolmistresses would be better.'

'But her ladyship did not agree?'

'Well, I won't exactly say that; – though I think that perhaps she did not.'

'I am sure she did not. When she has a point to carry, she is very fond of carrying it.'

'But then, Mark, her points are generally so good.'

'But, you see, in this affair of the school she is thinking more of her protégée than she does of the children.'

'Tell her that, and I am sure she will give way.' And then again they were both silent. And the vicar having thoroughly warmed himself, as far as this might be done by facing the fire, turned round and began the operation *à tergo*.

'Come, Mark, it is twenty minutes past six. Will you go and dress?'

'I'll tell you what, Fanny: she must have her way about Sarah Thompson. You can see her to-morrow and tell her so.'

'I am sure, Mark, I would not give way, if I thought it wrong. Nor would she expect it.'

'If I persist this time, I shall certainly have to yield the next; and then the next may probably be more important.'

'But if it's wrong, Mark?'

'I didn't say it was wrong. Besides, if it is wrong, wrong in some infinitesimal degree, one must put up with it. Sarah Thompson is very respectable; the only question is whether she can teach.'

The young wife, though she did not say so, had some idea that her husband was in error. It is true that one must put up with wrong, with a great deal of wrong. But no one need put up with wrong that he can remedy. Why should he, the vicar, consent to receive an incompetent teacher for the parish children, when he was able to procure one that was competent? In such a case – so thought Mrs. Robarts to herself – she would have fought the matter out with Lady Lufton. On the next morning, however, she did as she was bid, and signified to the dowager that all objection to Sarah Thompson would be withdrawn.

'Ah! I was sure he would agree with me,' said her ladyship, 'when he learned what sort of person she is. I know I had only to explain;' – and then she plumed her feathers, and was very gracious; for to tell the truth, Lady Lufton did not like to be opposed in things which concerned the parish nearly.

'And, Fanny,' said Lady Lufton, in her kindest manner, 'you are not going anywhere on Saturday, are you?'

'No, I think not.'

'Then you must come to us. Justinia is to be here, you know' – Lady Meredith was named Justinia – 'and you and Mr. Robarts had better stay with us till Monday. He can have the little book-room all to himself on Sunday.

The Merediths go on Monday; and Justinia won't be happy if you are not with her.' It would be unjust to say that Lady Lufton had determined not to invite the Robartses if she were not allowed to have her own way about Sarah Thompson. But such would have been the result. As it was, however, she was all kindness; and when Mrs. Robarts made some little excuse, saying that she was afraid she must return home in the evening, because of the children, Lady Lufton declared that there was room enough at Framley Court for baby and nurse, and so settled the matter in her own way, with a couple of nods and three taps of her umbrella. This was on a Tuesday morning, and on the same evening, before dinner, the vicar again seated himself in the same chair before the drawing-room fire, as soon as he had seen his horse led into the stable.

'Mark,' said his wife, 'the Merediths are to be at Framley on Saturday and Sunday; and I have promised that we will go up and stay over till Monday.'

'You don't mean it! Goodness gracious, how provoking!'

'Why? I thought you wouldn't mind it. And Justinia would think it unkind if I were not there.'

'You can go, my dear, and of course will go. But as for me, it is impossible.'

'But why, love?'

'Why? Just now, at the school-house, I answered a letter that was brought to me from Chaldicotes. Sowerby insists on my going over there for a week or so; and I have said that I would.'

'Go to Chaldicotes for a week, Mark?'

'I believe I have even consented to ten days.'

'And be away two Sundays?'

'No, Fanny, only one. Don't be so censorious.'

'Don't call me censorious, Mark; you know I am not so. But I am so sorry. It is just what Lady Lufton won't like. Besides, you were away in Scotland two Sundays last month.'

'In September, Fanny. And that is being censorious.'

'Oh, but, Mark, dear Mark; don't say so. You know I don't mean it. But Lady Lufton does not like those Chaldicotes people. You know Lord Lufton was with you the last time you were there; and how annoyed she was!'

'Lord Lufton won't be with me now, for he is still in Scotland. And the reason why I am going is this: Harold Smith and his wife will be there, and I am very anxious to know more of them. I have no doubt that Harold Smith will be in the government some day, and I cannot afford to neglect such a man's acquaintance.'

'But, Mark, what do you want of any government?'

'Well, Fanny, of course I am bound to say that I want nothing; neither in one sense do I; but, nevertheless, I shall go and meet the Harold Smiths.'

'Could you not be back before Sunday?'

'I have promised to preach at Chaldicotes. Harold Smith is going to lecture at Barchester, about the Australasian archipelago, and I am to preach a charity sermon on the same subject. They want to send out more missionaries.'

'A charity sermon at Chaldicotes!'

'And why not? The house will be quite full, you know; and I dare say the Arabins will be there.'

'I think not; Mrs. Arabin may get on with Mrs. Harold Smith, though I doubt that; but I'm sure she's not fond of Mrs. Smith's brother. I don't think she would stay at Chaldicotes.'

'And the bishop will probably be there for a day or two.'

'That is much more likely, Mark. If the pleasure of meeting Mrs. Proudie is taking you to Chaldicotes, I have not a word more to say.'

'I am not a bit more fond of Mrs. Proudie than you are, Fanny,' said the vicar, with something like vexation in the tone of his voice, for he thought that his wife was hard upon him. 'But it is generally thought that a parish clergyman does well to meet his bishop now and then.

And as I was invited there, especially to preach while all these people are staying at the place, I could not well refuse.' And then he got up, and taking his candlestick, escaped to his dressing-room.

'But what am I to say to Lady Lufton?' his wife said to him, in the course of the evening.

'Just write her a note, and tell her that you find I had promised to preach at Chaldicotes next Sunday. You'll go of course?'

'Yes: but I know she'll be annoyed. You were away the last time she had people there.'

'It can't be helped. She must put it down against Sarah Thompson. She ought not to expect to win always.'

'I should not have minded it, if she had lost, as you call it, about Sarah Thompson. That was a case in which you ought to have had your own way.'

'And this other is a case in which I shall have it. It's a pity that there should be such a difference; isn't it?'

Then the wife perceived that, vexed as she was, it would be better that she should say nothing further; and before she went to bed, she wrote the note to Lady Lufton, as her husband recommended.

CHAPTER II

The Framley Set, and The Chaldicotes Set

It will be necessary that I should say a word or two of some of the people named in the few preceding pages, and also of the localities in which they lived. Of Lady Lufton herself enough, perhaps, has been written to introduce her to my readers. The Framley property belonged to her son; but as Lufton Park – an ancient ramshackle place in another county – had heretofore been the family residence of the Lufton family, Framley Court had been apportioned to her for her residence for life. Lord Lufton himself was still unmarried; and as he had no establishment at Lufton Park – which indeed had not been inhabited since his grandfather died – he lived with his mother when it suited him to live anywhere in that neighbourhood. The widow would fain have seen more of him than he allowed her to do. He had a shooting lodge in Scotland, and apartments in London, and a string of horses in Leicestershire – much to the disgust of the county gentry around him, who held that their own hunting was as good as any that England could afford. His lordship, however, paid his subscription to the East Barsetshire pack, and then thought himself at liberty to follow his own pleasure as to his own amusement.

Framley itself was a pleasant country place, having about it nothing of seignorial dignity or grandeur, but possessing everything necessary for the comfort of country life. The house was a low building of two stories, built at different periods, and devoid of all pretensions to any style of architecture; but the rooms, though not lofty, were warm and comfortable, and the gardens were trim and neat beyond all others in the county. Indeed, it was for its gardens only that Framley Court was celebrated. Village there was none, properly speaking. The high road went winding about through the Framley paddocks, shrubberies, and wood-skirted home fields, for a mile and a half, not two hundred yards of which ran in a straight line; and there was a cross-road which passed down through the domain, whereby there came to be a locality called Framley Cross. Here stood the 'Lufton Arms,' and here, at Framley Cross, the hounds occasionally would meet; for the Framley woods were drawn in spite of the young lord's truant disposition; and then, at the Cross also, lived the shoemaker, who kept the post-office.

Framley church was distant from this just a quarter of a mile, and stood immediately opposite to the chief entrance to Framley Court. It was but a mean, ugly building, having been erected about a hundred years since, when all churches then built were made to be mean and ugly;

nor was it large enough for the congregation, some of whom were thus driven to the dissenting chapels, the Sions and Ebenezers, which had got themselves established on each side of the parish, in putting down which Lady Lufton thought that her pet parson was hardly as energetic as he might be. It was, therefore, a matter near to Lady Lufton's heart to see a new church built, and she was urgent in her eloquence both with her son and with the vicar, to have this good work commenced.

Beyond the church, but close to it, were the boys' school and girls' school, two distinct buildings, which owed their erection to Lady Lufton's energy; then came a neat little grocer's shop, the neat grocer being the clerk and sexton, and the neat grocer's wife the pew-opener in the church. Podgens was their name, and they were great favourites with her ladyship, both having been servants up at the house. And here the road took a sudden turn to the left, turning, as it were, away from Framley Court; and just beyond the turn was the vicarage, so that there was a little garden path running from the back of the vicarage grounds into the churchyard, cutting the Podgenses off into an isolated corner of their own; – from whence, to tell the truth, the vicar would have been glad to banish them and their cabbages, could he have had the power to do so. For has not the small vineyard of Naboth been always an eyesore to neighbouring potentates?

The potentate in this case had as little excuse as Ahab, for nothing in the parsonage way could be more perfect than his parsonage. It had all the details requisite for the house of a moderate gentleman with moderate means, and none of those expensive superfluities which immoderate gentlemen demand, or which themselves demand immoderate means. And then the gardens and paddocks were exactly suited to it; and everything was in good order; – not exactly new, so as to be raw and uncovered, and redolent of workmen; but just at that era of their existence in which newness gives way to comfortable homeliness.

Other village at Framley there was none. At the back of the Court, up one of those cross-roads, there was another small shop or two, and there was a very neat cottage residence, in which lived the widow of a former curate, another protégé of Lady Lufton's; and there was a big, staring, brick house, in which the present curate lived; but this was a full mile distant from the church, and farther from Framley Court, standing on that cross-road which runs from Framley Cross in a direction away from the mansion. This gentleman, the Rev. Evan Jones, might, from his age, have been the vicar's father; but he had been for many years curate of Framley; and though he was personally disliked by Lady Lufton, as being Low Church in his principles, and unsightly in his appearance, nevertheless, she would not urge his removal. He had two or three pupils in that large brick house, and, if turned out from these and from his curacy, might find it difficult to establish himself elsewhere. On this account mercy was extended to the Rev. E. Jones, and, in spite of his red face and awkward big feet, he was invited to dine at Framley Court, with his plain daughter, once in every three months.

Over and above these, there was hardly a house in the parish of Framley, outside the bounds of Framley Court, except those of farmers and farm labourers; and yet the parish was of large extent.

Framley is in the eastern division of the county of Barsetshire, which, as all the world knows, is, politically speaking, as true blue a county as any in England. There have been backslidings even here, it is true; but then, in what county have there not been such backslidings? Where, in these pinchbeck days, can we hope to find the old agricultural virtue in all its purity? But, among those backsliders, I regret to say, that men now reckon Lord Lufton. Not that he is a violent Whig, or perhaps that he is a Whig at all. But he jeers and sneers at the old county doings; declares, when solicited on the subject, that, as far as he is concerned, Mr. Bright may sit for the county, if he pleases; and alleges, that being unfortunately a peer, he has no right even to interest himself in the question. All this is deeply regretted, for, in the old days, there was no portion of the county more decidedly true blue than that Framley district; and, indeed, up to the present day, the dowager is able to give an occasional helping hand.

Chaldicotes is the seat of Nathaniel Sowerby, Esq., who, at the moment supposed to be now present, is one of the members for the Western Division of Barsetshire. But this Western Division can boast none of the fine political attributes which grace its twin brother. It is decidedly Whig, and is almost governed in its politics by one or two great Whig families. It has been said that Mark Robarts was about to pay a visit to Chaldicotes, and it has been hinted that his wife would have been as well pleased had this not been the case. Such was certainly the fact; for she, dear, prudent, excellent wife as she was, knew that Mr. Sowerby was not the most eligible friend in the world for a young clergyman, and knew, also, that there was but one other house in the whole county the name of which was so distasteful to Lady Lufton. The reasons for this were, I may say, manifold. In the first place, Mr. Sowerby was a Whig, and was seated in Parliament mainly by the interest of that great Whig autocrat the Duke of Omnium, whose residence was more dangerous even than that of Mr. Sowerby, and whom Lady Lufton regarded as an impersonation of Lucifer upon earth. Mr. Sowerby, too, was unmarried – as indeed, also, was Lord Lufton, much to his mother's grief. Mr. Sowerby, it is true, was fifty, whereas the young lord was as yet only twenty-six, but, nevertheless, her ladyship was becoming anxious on the subject. In her mind every man was bound to marry as soon as he could maintain a wife; and she held an idea – a quite private tenet, of which she was herself but imperfectly conscious – that men in general were inclined to neglect this duty for their own selfish gratifications, that the wicked ones encouraged the more innocent in this neglect, and that many would not marry at all, were not an unseen coercion exercised against them by the other sex. The Duke of Omnium was the very head of all such sinners, and Lady Lufton greatly feared that her son might be made subject to the baneful Omnium influence, by means of Mr. Sowerby and Chaldicotes. And then Mr. Sowerby was known to be a very poor man, with a very large estate. He had wasted, men said, much on electioneering, and more in gambling. A considerable portion of his property had already gone into the hands of the duke, who, as a rule, bought up everything around him that was to be purchased. Indeed it was said of him by his enemies, that so covetous was he of Barsetshire property, that he would lead a young neighbour on to his ruin, in order that he might get his land. What – oh! what if he should come to be possessed in this way of any of the fair acres of Framley Court? What if he should become possessed of them all? It can hardly be wondered at that Lady Lufton should not like Chaldicotes.

The Chaldicotes set, as Lady Lufton called them, were in every way opposed to what a set should be according to her ideas. She liked cheerful, quiet, well-to-do people, who loved their Church, their country, and their Queen, and who were not too anxious to make a noise in the world. She desired that all the farmers round her should be able to pay their rents without trouble, that all the old women should have warm flannel petticoats, that the working men should be saved from rheumatism by healthy food and dry houses, that they should all be obedient to their pastors and masters – temporal as well as spiritual. That was her idea of loving her country. She desired also that the copses should be full of pheasants, the stubble-field of partridges, and the gorse covers of foxes; in that way, also, she loved her country. She had ardently longed, during that Crimean War, that the Russians might be beaten – but not by the French, to the exclusion of the English, as had seemed to her to be too much the case; and hardly by the English under the dictatorship of Lord Palmerston. Indeed, she had had but little faith in that war after Lord Aberdeen had been expelled. If, indeed, Lord Derby could have come in! But now as to this Chaldicotes set. After all, there was nothing so very dangerous about them; for it was in London, not in the country, that Mr. Sowerby indulged, if he did indulge, his bachelor mal-practices. Speaking of them as a set, the chief offender was Mr. Harold Smith, or perhaps his wife. He also was a member of Parliament, and, as many thought, a rising man. His father had been for many years a debater in the House, and had held high office. Harold, in early life, had intended himself for the Cabinet; and if working hard at his trade could ensure success, he ought to obtain it sooner or later. He had already filled more than one subordinate station, had been at the Treasury, and for a month or two at the Admiralty, astonishing official mankind by his diligence. Those last-named few months had been under Lord Aberdeen, with whom he had been forced to retire. He was a younger son, and not possessed of any large fortune. Politics, as a profession, was, therefore, of importance to him. He had in early life married a sister of Mr. Sowerby; and as the lady was some six or seven years older than himself, and had brought with her but a scanty dowry, people thought that in this matter Mr. Harold Smith had not been perspicacious. Mr. Harold Smith was not personally a popular man with any party, though some judged him to be eminently useful. He was laborious, well-informed, and, on the whole, honest; but he was conceited, long-winded, and pompous.

Mrs. Harold Smith was the very opposite of her lord. She was a clever, bright woman, good-looking for her time of life – and she was now over forty – with a keen sense of the value of all worldly things, and a keen relish for all the world's pleasures. She was neither laborious, nor well-informed, nor perhaps altogether honest – what woman ever understood the necessity or recognized the advantage of political honesty? but then she was neither dull nor pompous, and if she was conceited, she did not show it. She was a disappointed woman, as regards her husband; seeing that she had married him on the speculation that he would at once become politically important; and as yet Mr. Smith had not quite fulfilled the prophecies of his early life.

And Lady Lufton, when she spoke of the Chaldicotes set, distinctly included, in her own mind, the Bishop of Barchester, and his wife and daughter. Seeing that Bishop Proudie was, of course, a man much addicted to religion and to religious thinking, and that Mr. Sowerby himself had no peculiar religious sentiments whatever, there would not at first sight appear to be ground for much intercourse, and perhaps there was not much of such intercourse; but Mrs. Proudie and Mrs. Harold Smith were firm friends of four or five years' standing – ever since the Proudies came into the diocese; and therefore the bishop was usually taken to Chaldicotes whenever Mrs. Smith paid her brother a visit. Now Bishop Proudie was by no means a High Church dignitary, and Lady Lufton had never forgiven him for coming into that diocese. She had, instinctively, a high respect for the episcopal office; but of Bishop Proudie himself she hardly thought better than she did of Mr. Sowerby, or of that fabricator of evil, the Duke of Omnium. Whenever Mr. Robarts would plead that in going anywhere he would have the benefit of meeting the bishop, Lady Lufton would slightly curl her upper lip. She could not say in words that Bishop Proudie – bishop as he certainly must be called – was no better than he ought to be; but by that curl of her lip she did explain to those who knew her that such was the inner feeling of her heart.

And then it was understood – Mark Robarts, at least, had so heard, and the information soon reached Framley

Court – that Mr. Supplehouse was to make one of the Chaldicotes party. Now Mr. Supplehouse was a worse companion for a gentlemanlike, young, High Church, conservative county parson than even Harold Smith. He also was in Parliament, and had been extolled during the early days of that Russian War by some portion of the metropolitan daily press, as the only man who could save the country. Let him be in the ministry, the *Jupiter* had said, and there would be some hope of reform, some chance that England's ancient glory would not be allowed in these perilous times to go headlong to oblivion. And upon this the ministry, not anticipating much salvation from Mr. Supplehouse, but willing, as they usually are, to have the *Jupiter* at their back, did send for that gentleman, and gave him some footing among them. But how can a man born to save a nation, and to lead a people, be content to fill the chair of an under-secretary? Supplehouse was not content, and soon gave it to be understood that his place was much higher than any yet tendered to him. The seals of high office, or war to the knife, was the alternative which he offered to a much-belaboured Head of Affairs – nothing doubting that the Head of Affairs would recognize the claimant's value, and would have before his eyes a wholesome fear of the *Jupiter*. But the Head of Affairs, much belaboured as he was, knew that he might pay too high even for Mr. Supplehouse and the *Jupiter*, and the saviour of the nation was told that he might swing his tomahawk. Since that time he had been swinging his tomahawk, but not with so much effect as had been anticipated. He also was very intimate with Mr. Sowerby, and was decidedly one of the Chaldicotes set. And there were many others included in the stigma whose sins were political or religious rather than moral. But they were gall and wormwood to Lady Lufton, who regarded them as children of the Lost One, and who grieved with a mother's grief when she knew that her son was among them, and felt all a patron's anger when she heard that her clerical protégé was about to seek such society. Mrs. Robarts might well say that Lady Lufton would be annoyed.

'You won't call at the house before you go, will you?' the wife asked on the following morning. He was to start after lunch on that day, driving himself in his own gig, so as to reach Chaldicotes, some twenty-four miles distant, before dinner.

'No, I think not. What good should I do?'

'Well, I can't explain; but I think I should call: partly, perhaps, to show her that, as I had determined to go, I was not afraid of telling her so.'

'Afraid! That's nonsense, Fanny. I'm not afraid of her. But I don't see why I should bring down upon myself the disagreeable things she will say. Besides, I have not time. I must walk up and see Jones about the duties; and then, what with getting ready, I shall have enough to do to get off in time.'

He paid his visit to Mr. Jones, the curate, feeling no qualms of conscience there, as he rather boasted of all the members of Parliament he was going to meet, and of the bishop who would be with them. Mr. Evan Jones was only his curate, and in speaking to him on the matter he could talk as though it were quite the proper thing for a vicar to meet his bishop at the house of a county member. And one would be inclined to say that it was proper: only why could he not talk of it in the same tone to Lady Lufton? And then, having kissed his wife and children, he drove off, well pleased with his prospect for the coming ten days, but already anticipating some discomfort on his return.

On the three following days, Mrs. Robarts did not meet her ladyship. She did not exactly take any steps to avoid such a meeting, but she did not purposely go up to the big house. She went to her school as usual, and made one or two calls among the farmers' wives, but put no foot within the Framley Court grounds. She was braver than her husband, but even she did not wish to anticipate the evil day. On the Saturday, just before it began to get dusk, when she was thinking of preparing for the fatal plunge, her friend, Lady Meredith, came to her.

'So, Fanny, we shall again be so unfortunate as to miss Mr. Robarts,' said her ladyship.

'Yes. Did you ever know anything so unlucky? But he had promised Mr. Sowerby before he heard that you were coming. Pray do not think that he would have gone away had he known it.'

'We should have been sorry to keep him from so much more amusing a party.'

'Now, Justinia, you are unfair. You intend to imply that he has gone to Chaldicotes, because he likes it better than Framley Court; but that is not the case. I hope Lady Lufton does not think that it is.'

Lady Meredith laughed as she put her arm round her friend's waist. 'Don't lose your eloquence in defending him to me,' she said. 'You'll want all that for my mother.'

'But is your mother angry?' asked Mrs. Robarts, showing by her countenance how eager she was for true tidings on the subject.

'Well, Fanny, you know her ladyship as well as I do. She thinks so very highly of the vicar of Framley, that she does begrudge him to those politicians at Chaldicotes.'

'But, Justinia, the bishop is to be there, you know.'

'I don't think that that consideration will at all reconcile my mother to the gentleman's absence. He ought to be very proud, I know, to find that he is so much thought of. But come, Fanny, I want you to walk back with me, and you can dress at the house. And now we'll go and look at the children.'

After that, as they walked together to Framley Court, Mrs. Robarts made her friend promise that she would stand by her if any serious attack were made on the absent clergyman.

'Are you going up to your room at once?' said the vicar's wife, as soon as they were inside the porch leading into the hall. Lady Meredith immediately knew what her friend meant, and decided that the evil day should not be postponed. 'We had better go in and have it over,' she said, 'and then we shall be comfortable for the evening.' So the drawing-room door was opened, and there was Lady Lufton alone upon the sofa.

'Now, mamma,' said the daughter, 'you mustn't scold Fanny much about Mr. Robarts. He has gone to preach a charity sermon before the bishop, and, under those circumstances, perhaps, he could not refuse.' This was a stretch on the part of Lady Meredith – put in with much good-nature, no doubt; but still a stretch; for no one had supposed that the bishop would remain at Chaldicotes for the Sunday.

'How do you do, Fanny?' said Lady Lufton, getting up. 'I am not going to scold her; and I don't know how you can talk such nonsense, Justinia. Of course, we are very sorry not to have Mr. Robarts; more especially as he was not here the last Sunday that Sir George was with us. I do like to see Mr. Robarts in his own church, certainly; and I don't like any other clergyman there as well. If Fanny takes that for scolding, why –'

'Oh! no, Lady Lufton; and it's so kind of you to say so. But Mr. Robarts was so sorry that he had accepted this invitation to Chaldicotes, before he heard that Sir George was coming, and –'

'Oh, I know that Chaldicotes has great attractions which we cannot offer,' said Lady Lufton.

'Indeed, it was not that. But he was asked to preach, you know; and Mr. Harold Smith –' Poor Fanny was only making it worse. Had she been worldly wise, she would have accepted the little compliment implied in Lady Lufton's first rebuke, and then have held her peace.

'Oh, yes; the Harold Smiths! They are irresistible, I know. How could any man refuse to join a party, graced both by Mrs. Harold Smith and Mrs. Proudie – even though his duty should require him to stay away?'

'Now, mamma –' said Justinia.

'Well, my dear, what am I to say? You would not wish me to tell a fib. I don't like Mrs. Harold Smith – at least, what I hear of her; for it has not been my fortune to meet her since her marriage. It may be conceited; but to own the truth, I think that Mr. Robarts would be better off with us at Framley than with the Harold Smiths at Chaldicotes – even though Mrs. Proudie be thrown into the bargain.'

It was nearly dark, and therefore the rising colour in the face of Mrs. Robarts could not be seen. She, however, was too good a wife to hear these things said without some anger within her bosom. She could blame her husband in her own mind; but it was intolerable to her that others should blame him in her hearing.

'He would undoubtedly be better off,' she said; 'but then, Lady Lufton, people can't always go exactly where they will be best off. Gentlemen sometimes must –'

'Well – well, my dear, that will do. He has not taken you, at any rate; and so we will forgive him.' And Lady Lufton kissed her. 'As it is,' – and she affected a low whisper between the two young wives – 'as it is, we must e'en put up with poor old Evan Jones. He is to be here to-night, and we must go and dress to receive him.'

And so they went off. Lady Lufton was quite good enough at heart to like Mrs. Robarts all the better for standing up for her absent lord.

CHAPTER III

Chaldicotes

CHALDICOTES is a house of much more pretension than Framley Court. Indeed, if one looks at the ancient marks about it, rather than at those of the present day, it is a place of very considerable pretension. There is an old forest, not altogether belonging to the property, but attached to it, called the Chase of Chaldicotes. A portion of this forest comes up close behind the mansion, and of itself gives a character and celebrity to the place. The Chase of Chaldicotes – the greater part of it, at least – is, as all the world knows, Crown property, and now, in these utilitarian days, is to be disforested. In former times it was a great forest, stretching half across the country, almost as far as Silverbridge; and there are bits of it, here and there, still to be seen at intervals throughout the whole distance; but the larger remaining portion, consisting of aged hollow oaks, centuries old, and wide-spreading withered beeches, stands in the two parishes of Chaldicotes and Uffley. People still come from afar to see the oaks of Chaldicotes, and to hear their feet rustle among the thick autumn leaves. But they will soon come no longer. The giants of past ages are to give way to wheat and turnips; a ruthless Chancellor of the Exchequer, disregarding old associations and rural beauty, requires money returns from the lands; and the Chase of Chaldicotes is to vanish from the earth's surface.

Some part of it, however, is the private property of Mr. Sowerby, who hitherto, through all his pecuniary distresses, has managed to save from the axe and the auction-mart that portion of his paternal heritage. The house of Chaldicotes is a large stone building, probably of the time of Charles the Second. It is approached on both fronts by a heavy double flight of stone steps. In the front of the house a long, solemn, straight avenue through a double row of lime-trees, leads away to lodge-gates, which stand in the centre of the village of Chaldicotes; but to the rear the windows open upon four different vistas, which run down through the forest: four open green rides, which all converge together at a large iron gateway, the barrier which divides the private grounds from the Chase. The Sowerbys, for many generations, have been rangers of the Chase of Chaldicotes, thus having almost as wide an authority over the Crown forest as over their own. But now all this is to cease, for the forest will be disforested.

It was nearly dark as Mark Robarts drove up through the avenue of lime-trees to the hall-door; but it was easy to see that the house, which was dead and silent as the grave through nine months of the year, was now alive in all its parts. There were lights in many of the windows, and a noise of voices came from the stables, and servants were moving about, and dogs barked, and the dark gravel before the front steps was cut up with many a coach-wheel.

'Oh, be that you, sir, Mr. Robarts?' said a groom, taking the parson's horse by the head, and touching his own hat. 'I hope I see your reverence well?'

'Quite well, Bob, thank you. All well at Chaldicotes?'

'Pretty bobbish, Mr. Robarts. Deal of life going on here now, sir. The bishop and his lady came this morning.'

'Oh – ah – yes! I understood they were to be here. Any of the young ladies?'

'One young lady. Miss Olivia, I think they call her, your reverence.'

'And how's Mr. Sowerby?'

'Very well, your reverence. He, and Mr. Harold Smith, and Mr. Fothergill – that's the duke's man of business, you know – is getting off their horses now in the stable-yard there.'

'Home from hunting – eh, Bob?'

'Yes, sir, just home, this minute.' And then Mr. Robarts walked into the house, his portmanteau following on a footboy's shoulder.

It will be seen that our young vicar was very intimate at Chaldicotes; so much so that the groom knew him, and talked to him about the people in the house. Yes; he was intimate there: much more than he had given the Framley people to understand. Not that he had wilfully and overtly deceived any one; not that he had ever spoken a false word about Chaldicotes. But he had never boasted at home that he and Sowerby were near allies. Neither had he told them there how often Mr. Sowerby and Lord Lufton were together in London. Why trouble women with such matters? Why annoy so excellent a woman as Lady Lufton? And then Mr. Sowerby was one whose intimacy few young men would wish to reject. He was fifty, and had lived, perhaps, not the most salutary life; but he dressed young, and usually looked well. He was bald, with a good forehead, and sparkling moist eyes. He was a clever man, and a pleasant companion, and always good-humoured when it so suited him. He was a gentleman, too, of high breeding and good birth, whose ancestors had been known in that country – longer, the farmers around would boast, than those of any other landowner in it, unless it be the Thornes of Ullathorne, or perhaps the Greshams of Greshamsbury – much longer than the De Courcys at Courcy Castle. As for the Duke of Omnium, he, comparatively speaking, was a new man. And then he was a member of Parliament, a friend of some men in power, and of others who might be there; a man who could talk about the world as one knowing the matter of which he talked. And moreover, whatever might be his ways of life at other times, when in the presence of a clergyman he rarely made himself offensive to clerical tastes. He neither swore, nor brought his vices on the carpet, nor sneered at the faith of the Church. If he was no Churchman himself, he at least knew how to live with those who were.

How was it possible that such a one as our vicar should not relish the intimacy of Mr. Sowerby? It might be very well, he would say to himself, for a woman like Lady Lufton to turn up her nose at him – for Lady Lufton, who spent ten months of the year at Framley Court, and who during those ten months, and for the matter of that, during the two months also which she spent in London, saw no one out of her own set. Women did not understand such things, the vicar said to himself; even his own wife – good, and nice, and sensible, and intelligent as she was – even she did not understand that a man in the world must meet all sorts of men; and that in these days it did not do for a clergyman to be a hermit. 'Twas thus that Mark Robarts argued when he found himself called upon to defend himself before the bar of his own conscience for going to Chaldicotes and increasing his intimacy with Mr. Sowerby. He did know that Mr. Sowerby was a dangerous man; he was aware that he was over head and ears in debt, and that he had already entangled young Lord Lufton in some pecuniary embarrassment; his conscience did tell him that it would be well for him, as one of Christ's soldiers, to look out for companions of a different stamp. But nevertheless he went to Chaldicotes, not satisfied with himself indeed, but repeating to himself a great many arguments why he should be so satisfied.

He was shown into the drawing-room at once, and there he found Mrs. Harold Smith, with Mrs. and Miss Proudie, and a lady whom he had never before seen, and whose name he did not at first hear mentioned.

'Is that Mr. Robarts?' said Mrs. Harold Smith, getting up to greet him, and screening her pretended ignorance under the veil of the darkness. 'And have you really driven over four-and-twenty miles of Barsetshire roads on such a day as this to assist us in our little difficulties? Well, we can promise you gratitude at any rate.' And then the vicar shook hands with Mrs. Proudie, in that deferential manner which is due from a vicar to his bishop's wife; and Mrs. Proudie returned the greeting with all that smiling condescension which a bishop's wife should show to a vicar. Miss Proudie was not quite so civil. Had Mr. Robarts been still unmarried, she also could have smiled sweetly; but she had been exercising smiles on clergymen too long to waste them now on a married parish parson.

'And what are the difficulties, Mrs. Smith, in which I am to assist you?'

'We have six or seven gentlemen here, Mr. Robarts, and they always go out hunting before breakfast, and they never come back – I was going to say – till after dinner. I wish it were so, for then we should not have to wait for them.'

'Excepting Mr. Supplehouse, you know,' said the unknown lady, in a loud voice.

'And he is generally shut up in the library, writing articles.'

'He'd be better employed if he were trying to break his neck like the others,' said the unknown lady.

'Only he would never succeed,' said Mrs. Harold Smith. 'But perhaps, Mr. Robarts, you are as bad as the rest; perhaps you, too, will be hunting to-morrow.'

'My dear Mrs. Smith!' said Mrs. Proudie, in a tone denoting slight reproach, and modified horror.

'Oh! I forgot. No, of course, you won't be hunting, Mr. Robarts; you'll only be wishing that you could.'

'Why can't he?' said the lady, with a loud voice.

'My dear Miss Dunstable! a clergyman hunt, while he is staying in the same house with the bishop? Think of the proprieties!'

'Oh – ah! The bishop wouldn't like it – wouldn't he? Now, do tell me, sir, what would the bishop do to you if you did hunt?'

'It would depend upon his mood at the time, madam,' said Mr. Robarts. 'If that were very stern, he might perhaps have me beheaded before the palace gates.'

Mrs. Proudie drew herself up in her chair, showing that she did not like the tone of the conversation; and Miss Proudie fixed her eyes vehemently on her book, showing that Miss Dunstable and her conversation were both beneath her notice.

'If these gentlemen do not mean to break their necks tonight,' said Mrs. Harold Smith, 'I wish they'd let us know it. It's half-past six already.' And then Mr. Robarts gave them to understand that no such catastrophe could be looked for that day, as Mr. Sowerby and the other sportsmen were within the stable-yard when he entered the door.

'Then, ladies, we may as well dress,' said Mrs. Harold Smith. But as she moved towards the door, it opened, and a short gentleman, with a slow, quiet step, entered the room; but was not yet to be distinguished through the dusk by the eyes of Mr. Robarts. 'Oh! bishop, is that you?' said Mrs. Smith. 'Here is one of the luminaries of your diocese.' And then the bishop, feeling through the dark, made his way up to the vicar and shook him cordially by the hand. 'He was delighted to meet Mr. Robarts at Chaldicotes,' he said – 'quite delighted. Was he not going to preach on behalf of the Papuan Mission next Sunday? Ah! so he, the bishop, had heard. It was a good work, an excellent work.' And then Dr. Proudie expressed himself as much grieved that he could not remain at Chaldicotes, and hear the sermon. It was plain that his bishop thought no ill of him on account of his intimacy with Mr. Sowerby. But then he felt in his own heart that he did not much regard his bishop's opinion.

'Ah, Robarts, I'm delighted to see you,' said Mr. Sowerby, when they met on the drawing-room rug before dinner. 'You know Harold Smith? Yes, of course you do. Well, who else is there? Oh! Supplehouse. Mr. Supplehouse, allow me to introduce to you my friend Mr. Robarts. It is he who will extract the five-pound note out of your pocket next Sunday for these poor Papuans whom we are going to Christianize. That is, if Harold Smith does not finish the work out of hand at his Saturday lecture. And, Robarts, you have seen the bishop, of course:' this he said in a whisper. 'A fine thing to be a bishop, isn't it? I wish I had half your chance. But, my dear fellow, I've made such a mistake; I haven't got a bachelor parson for Miss Proudie. You must help me out, and take her in to dinner.' And then the great gong sounded, and off they went in pairs.

At dinner Mark found himself seated between Miss Proudie and the lady whom he had heard named as Miss Dunstable. Of the former he was not very fond, and, in spite of his host's petition, was not inclined to play bachelor parson for her benefit. With the other lady he would willingly have chatted during the dinner, only that everybody else at table seemed to be intent on doing the same thing. She was neither young, nor beautiful, nor peculiarly lady-like; yet she seemed to enjoy a popularity which must have excited the envy of Mr. Supplehouse, and which certainly was not altogether to the taste of Mrs. Proudie – who, however, fêted her as much as did the others. So that our clergyman found himself unable to obtain more than an inconsiderable share of the lady's attention.

'Bishop,' said she, speaking across the table, 'we have missed you so all day! we have had no one on earth to say a word to us.'

'My dear Miss Dunstable, had I known that – But I really was engaged on business of some importance.'

'I don't believe in business of importance; do you, Mrs. Smith?'

'Do I not?' said Mrs. Smith. 'If you were married to Mr. Harold Smith for one week, you'd believe in it.'

'Should I, now? What a pity that I can't have that chance of improving my faith! But you are a man of business, also, Mr. Supplehouse; so they tell me.' And she turned to her neighbour on her right hand.

'I cannot compare myself to Harold Smith,' said he. 'But perhaps I may equal the bishop.'

'What does a man do, now, when he sits himself down to business? How does he set about it? What are his tools? A quire of blotting paper, I suppose, to begin with?'

'That depends, I should say, on his trade. A shoemaker begins by waxing his thread.'

'And Mr. Harold Smith –?'

'By counting up his yesterday's figures, generally, I should say; or else by unrolling a ball of red tape. Well-docketed papers and statistical facts are his forte.'

'And what does a bishop do? Can you tell me that?'

'He sends forth to his clergy either blessings or blowings-up, according to the state of his digestive organs. But Mrs. Proudie can explain all that to you with the greatest accuracy.'

'Can she now? I understand what you mean, but I don't believe a word of it. The bishop manages his own affairs himself, quite as much as you do, or Mr. Harold Smith.'

'I, Miss Dunstable?'

'Yes, you.'

'But I, unluckily, have not a wife to manage them for me.'

'Then you should not laugh at those who have, for you don't know what you may come to yourself, when you're married.'

Mr. Supplehouse began to make a pretty speech, saying that he would be delighted to incur any danger in that respect to which he might be subjected by the companionship of Miss Dunstable. But before he was half through it, she had turned her back upon him, and begun a conversation with Mark Robarts.

'Have you much work in your parish, Mr. Robarts?' she asked. Now, Mark was not aware that she knew his name, or the fact of his having a parish, and was rather surprised by the question. And he had not quite liked the tone in which she had seemed to speak of the bishop and his work. His desire for her further acquaintance was therefore somewhat moderated, and he was not prepared to answer her question with much zeal.

'All parish clergymen have plenty of work, if they choose to do it.'

'Ah, that is it; is it not, Mr. Robarts? If they choose to do it? A great many do – many that I know, do; and see what a result they have. But many neglect it – and see what a result *they* have. I think it ought to be the happiest life that a man can lead, that of a parish clergyman, with a wife and family and a sufficient income.'

'I think it is,' said Mark Robarts, asking himself whether the contentment accruing to him from such blessings had made him satisfied at all points. He had all these things of which Miss Dunstable spoke, and yet he had told his wife, the other day, that he could not afford to neglect the acquaintance of a rising politician like Harold Smith.

'What I find fault with is this,' continued Miss Dunstable, 'that we expect clergymen to do their duty, and don't give them a sufficient income – give them hardly any income at all. Is it not a scandal, that an educated gentleman with a family should be made to work half his life, and perhaps the whole, for a pittance of seventy pounds a year!' Mark said that it was a scandal, and thought of Mr. Evan Jones and his daughter; and thought also of his own worth, and his own house, and his own nine hundred a year.

'And yet you clergymen are so proud – aristocratic would be the genteel word, I know – that you won't take the money of common, ordinary poor people. You must be paid from land and endowments, from tithe and church property. You can't bring yourself to work for what you earn, as lawyers and doctors do. It is better that curates should starve than undergo such ignominy as that.'

'It is a long subject, Miss Dunstable.'

'A very long one; and that means that I am not to say any more about it.'

'I did not mean that exactly.'

'Oh, but you did though, Mr. Robarts. And I can take a hint of that kind when I get it. You clergymen like to keep those long subjects for your sermons, when no one can answer you. Now if I have a longing heart's desire for anything at all in this world, it is to be able to get up into a pulpit, and preach a sermon.'

'You can't conceive how soon that appetite would pall upon you, after its first indulgence.'

'That would depend upon whether I could get people to listen to me. It does not pall upon Mr. Spurgeon, I suppose.' Then her attention was called away by some question from Mr. Sowerby, and Mark Robarts found himself bound to address his conversation to Miss Proudie. Miss Proudie, however, was not thankful, and gave him little but monosyllables for his pains.

'Of course you know Harold Smith is going to give us a lecture about these islanders,' Mr. Sowerby said to him, as they sat round the fire over their wine after dinner. Mark said that he had been so informed, and should be delighted to be one of the listeners.

'You are bound to do that, as he is going to listen to you the day afterwards – or, at any rate, to pretend to do so, which is as much as you will do for him. It'll be a terrible bore – the lecture, I mean, not the sermon.' And he spoke very low into his friend's ear. 'Fancy having to drive ten miles after dusk, and ten miles back, to hear Harold Smith talk for two hours about Borneo! One must do it, you know.'

'I dare say it will be very interesting.'

'My dear fellow, you haven't undergone so many of these things as I have. But he's right to do it. It's his line of life; and when a man begins a thing he ought to go on with it. Where's Lufton all this time?'

'In Scotland, when I last heard from him; but he's probably at Melton now.'

'It's deuced shabby of him, not hunting here in his own county. He escapes all the bore of going to lectures, and giving feeds to the neighbours; that's why he treats us so. He has no idea of his duty, has he?'

'Lady Lufton does all that, you know.'

'I wish I'd a Mrs. Sowerby *mère* to do it for me. But then Lufton has no constituents to look after – lucky dog! By the by, has he spoken to you about selling that outlying bit of land of his in Oxfordshire? It belongs to the Lufton property, and yet it doesn't. In my mind it gives more trouble than it's worth.' Lord Lufton had spoken to Mark about this sale, and had explained to him that such a sacrifice was absolutely necessary, in consequence of certain pecuniary transactions between him, Lord Lufton, and Mr. Sowerby. But it was found impracticable to complete the business without Lady Lufton's knowledge, and her son had commissioned Mr. Robarts not only to inform her ladyship, but to talk her over, and to appease her wrath. This commission he had not yet attempted to execute, and it was probable that this visit to Chaldicotes would not do much to facilitate the business.

'They are the most magnificent islands under the sun,' said Harold Smith to the bishop.

'Are they, indeed!' said the bishop, opening his eyes wide, and assuming a look of intense interest.

'And the most intelligent people.'

'Dear me!' said the bishop.

'All they want is guidance, encouragement, instruction –'

'And Christianity,' suggested the bishop.

'And Christianity, of course,' said Mr. Smith, remembering that he was speaking to a dignitary of the Church. It was well to humour such people, Mr. Smith thought. But the Christianity was to be done in the Sunday sermon, and was not part of his work.

'And how do you intend to begin with them?' asked Mr. Supplehouse, the business of whose life it had been to suggest difficulties.

'Begin with them – oh – why – it's very easy to begin with them. The difficulty is to go on with them, after the money is all spent. We'll begin by explaining to them the benefits of civilization.'

'Capital plan!' said Mr. Supplehouse. 'But how do you set about it, Smith?'

'How do we set about it? How did we set about it with Australia and America? It is very easy to criticize; but in such matters the great thing is to put one's shoulder to the wheel.'

'We sent our felons to Australia,' said Supplehouse, 'and they began the work for us. And as to America, we exterminated the people instead of civilizing them.'

'We did not exterminate the inhabitants of India,' said Harold Smith, angrily.

'Nor have we attempted to Christianize them, as the bishop so properly wished to do with your islanders.'

'Supplehouse, you are not fair,' said Mr. Sowerby, 'neither to Harold Smith nor to us; – you are making him rehearse his lecture, which is bad for him; and making us hear the rehearsal, which is bad for us.'

'Supplehouse belongs to a clique which monopolizes the wisdom of England,' said Harold Smith, 'or, at any rate, thinks that it does. But the worst of them is that they are given to talk leading articles.'

'Better that, than talk articles which are not leading,' said Mr. Supplehouse. 'Some first-class official men do that.'

'Shall I meet you at the duke's next week, Mr. Robarts?' said the bishop to him, soon after they had gone into the drawing-room. Meet him at the duke's! – the established enemy of Barsetshire mankind, as Lady Lufton regarded his grace! No idea of going to the duke's had ever entered our hero's mind; nor had he been aware that the duke was about to entertain any one.

'No, my lord; I think not. Indeed, I have no acquaintance with his grace.'

'Oh – ah! I did not know. Because Mr. Sowerby is going; and so are the Harold Smiths, and, I think, Mr. Supplehouse. An excellent man is the duke; – that is, as regards all the county interests,' added the bishop, remembering that the moral character of his bachelor grace was not the very best in the world. And then his lordship began to ask some questions about the church affairs of Framley, in which a little interest as to Framley Court was also mixed up, when he was interrupted by a rather sharp voice, to which he instantly attended.

'Bishop,' said the rather sharp voice; and the bishop trotted across the room to the back of the sofa, on which his wife was sitting. 'Miss Dunstable thinks that she will be able to come to us for a couple of days, after we leave the duke's.'

'I shall be delighted above all things,' said the bishop, bowing low to the dominant lady of the day. For be it known to all men, that Miss Dunstable was the great heiress of that name.

'Mrs. Proudie is so very kind as to say that she will take me in, with my poodle, parrot, and pet old woman.'

'I tell Miss Dunstable that we shall have quite room for any of her suite,' said Mrs. Proudie. 'And that it will give us no trouble.'

' "The labour we delight in physics pain," ' said the gallant bishop, bowing low, and putting his hand upon his heart. In the meantime Mr. Fothergill had got hold of Mark Robarts. Mr. Fothergill was a gentleman and a magistrate of the county, but he occupied the position of managing man on the Duke of Omnium's estates. He was not exactly his agent; that is to say, he did not receive his rents; but he 'managed' for him, saw people, went about the county, wrote letters, supported the electioneering interest, did popularity when it was too much trouble for the duke to do it himself, and was, in fact, invaluable. People in West Barsetshire would often say that they did not know what *on earth* the duke would do, if it were not for Mr. Fothergill. Indeed, Mr. Fothergill was useful to the duke.

'Mr. Robarts,' he said, 'I am very happy to have the pleasure of meeting you – very happy indeed. I have often heard of you from our friend Sowerby.' Mark bowed, and said that he was delighted to have the honour of making Mr. Fothergill's acquaintance. 'I am commissioned by the Duke of Omnium,' continued Mr. Fothergill, 'to say how glad he will be if you will join his grace's party at Gatherum Castle next week. The bishop will be there, and indeed nearly the whole set who are here now. The duke would have written when he heard that you were to be at Chaldicotes; but things were hardly quite arranged then, so his grace has left it for me to tell you how happy he will be to make your acquaintance in his own house. I have spoken to Sowerby,' continued Mr. Fothergill, 'and he very much hopes that you will be able to join us.'

Mark felt that his face became red when this proposition was made to him. The party in the county to which he properly belonged – he and his wife, and all that made him happy and respectable – looked upon the Duke of Omnium with horror and amazement; and now he had absolutely received an invitation to the duke's house! A proposition was made to him that he should be numbered among the duke's friends!

And though in one sense he was sorry that the proposition was made to him, yet in another he was proud of it. It is not every young man, let his profession be what it may, who can receive overtures of friendship from dukes without some elation. Mark, too, had risen in the world, as far as he had yet risen, by knowing great people; and he certainly had an ambition to rise higher. I will not degrade him by calling him a tuft-hunter; but he undoubtedly had a feeling that the paths most pleasant for a clergyman's feet were those which were trodden by the great ones of the earth. Nevertheless, at the moment he declined the duke's invitation. He was very much flattered, he said, but the duties of his parish would require him to return direct from Chaldicotes to Framley.

'You need not give me an answer to-night, you know,' said Mr. Fothergill. 'Before the week is past, we will talk it over with Sowerby and the bishop. It will be a thousand pities, Mr. Robarts, if you will allow me to say so, that you should neglect such an opportunity of knowing his grace.'

When Mark went to bed, his mind was still set against going to the duke's; but, nevertheless, he did feel that it was a pity that he should not do so. After all, was it necessary that he should obey Lady Lufton in all things?

CHAPTER IV

A Matter of Conscience

IT is no doubt very wrong to long after a naughty thing. But nevertheless we all do so. One may say that hankering after naughty things is the very essence of the evil into which we have been precipitated by Adam's fall. When we confess that we are all sinners, we confess that we all long after naughty things. And ambition is a great vice – as Mark Antony told us a long time ago – a great vice, no doubt, if the ambition of the man be with reference to his own advancement, and not to the advancement of others. But then, how many of us are there who are not ambitious in this vicious manner? And there is nothing viler than the desire to know great people – people of great rank, I should say; nothing worse than the hunting of titles and worshipping of wealth. We all know this, and say it every day of our lives. But presuming that a way into the society of Park Lane was open to us, and a way also into that of Bedford Row, how many of us are there who would prefer Bedford Row because it is so vile to worship wealth and title?

I am led into these rather trite remarks by the necessity of putting forward some sort of excuse for that frame of mind in which the Rev. Mark Robarts awoke on the morning after his arrival at Chaldicotes. And I trust that the fact of his being a clergyman will not be allowed to press against him unfairly. Clergymen are subject to the same passions as other men; and, as far as I can see, give way to them, in one line or in another, almost as frequently. Every clergyman should, by canonical rule, feel a personal disinclination to a bishopric; but yet we do not believe that such personal disinclination is generally very strong. Mark's first thoughts when he woke on that morning flew back to Mr. Fothergill's invitation. The duke had sent a special message to say how peculiarly glad he, the duke, would be to make acquaintance with him, the parson! How much of this message had been of Mr. Fothergill's own manufacture, that Mark Robarts did not consider. He had obtained a living at an age when other young clergymen are beginning to think of a curacy, and he had obtained such a living as middle-aged parsons in their dreams regard as a possible Paradise for their old years. Of course he thought that all these good things had been the results of his own peculiar merits. Of course he felt that he was different from other parsons, – more fitted by nature for intimacy with great persons, more urbane, more polished, and more richly endowed with modern clerical well-to-do aptitudes. He was grateful to Lady Lufton for what she had done for him; but perhaps not so grateful as he should have been.

At any rate he was not Lady Lufton's servant, nor even her dependant. So much he had repeated to himself on many occasions, and had gone so far as to hint the same idea to his wife. In his career as parish priest he must in most things be the judge of his own actions – and in many also it was his duty to be the judge of those of his patroness. The fact of Lady Lufton having placed him in the living, could by no means make her the proper judge of his actions. This he often said to himself; and he said as often that Lady Lufton certainly had a hankering after such a judgement-seat.

Of whom generally did prime ministers and official bigwigs think it expedient to make bishops and deans? Was it not, as a rule, of those clergymen who had shown themselves able to perform their clerical duties efficiently, and able also to take their place with ease in high society? He was very well off certainly at Framley; but he could never hope for anything beyond Framley, if he allowed himself to regard Lady Lufton as a bugbear. Putting Lady Lufton and her prejudices out of the question, was there any reason why he ought not to accept the duke's invitation? He could not see that there was any such reason. If any one could be a better judge on such a subject than himself, it must be his bishop. And it was clear that the bishop wished him to go to Gatherum Castle.

The matter was still left open to him. Mr. Fothergill had especially explained that; and therefore his ultimate decision was as yet within his own power. Such a visit would cost him some money, for he knew that a man does not stay at great houses without expense; and then, in spite of his good income, he was not very flush of money. He had been down this year with Lord Lufton in Scotland. Perhaps it might be more prudent for him to return home. But then an idea came to him that it behoved him as a man and a priest to break through that Framley thraldom under which he felt that he did to a certain extent exist. Was it not the fact that he was about to decline this invitation from fear of Lady Lufton? and if so, was that a motive by which he ought to be actuated? It was incumbent on him to rid himself of that feeling. And in this spirit he got up and dressed.

There was hunting again on that day; and as the hounds were to meet near Chaldicotes, and to draw some coverts lying on the verge of the chase, the ladies were to go in carriages through the drives of the forest, and Mr. Robarts was to escort them on horseback. Indeed it was one of those hunting-days got up rather for the ladies than for the sport. Great nuisances they are to steady, middle-aged hunting men; but the young fellows like them because they have thereby an opportunity of showing off their sporting finery, and of doing a little flirtation on horseback. The bishop, also, had been minded to be of the party: so, at least, he had said on the previous evening; and a place in one of the carriages had been set apart for him: but since that, he and Mrs. Proudie had discussed the matter in private, and at breakfast his lordship declared that he had changed his mind.

Mr. Sowerby was one of those men who are known to be very poor – as poor as debt can make a man – but who, nevertheless, enjoy all the luxuries which money can give. It was believed that he could not live in England out of jail but for his protection as a member of Parliament; and yet it seemed that there was no end to his horses and carriages, his servants and retinue. He had been at this work for a great many years, and practice, they say, makes perfect. Such companions are very dangerous. There is no cholera, no yellow-fever, no smallpox, more contagious than debt. If one lives habitually among embarrassed men, one catches it to a certainty. No one had injured the community in this way more fatally than Mr. Sowerby. But still he carried on the game himself; and now, on this morning, carriages and horses thronged at his gate, as though he were as substantially rich as his friend the Duke of Omnium.

'Robarts, my dear fellow,' said Mr. Sowerby, when they were well under way down one of the glades of the forest, – for the place where the hounds met was some four or five miles from the house of Chaldicotes, – 'ride on with me a moment. I want to speak to you; and if I stay behind we shall never get to the hounds.' So Mark, who had come expressly to escort the ladies, rode on alongside of Mr. Sowerby in his pink coat.

'My dear fellow, Fothergill tells me that you have some hesitation about going to Gatherum Castle.'

'Well, I did decline, certainly. You know I am not a man of pleasure, as you are. I have some duties to attend to.'

'Gammon!' said Mr. Sowerby; and as he said it, he looked with a kind of derisive smile into the clergyman's face.

'It is easy enough to say that, Sowerby; and perhaps I have no right to expect that you should understand me.'

'Ah, but I do understand you; and I say it is gammon. I would be the last man in the world to ridicule your scruples about duty, if this hesitation on your part arose from any such scruple. But answer me honestly, do you not know that such is not the case?'

'I know nothing of the kind.'

'Ah, but I think you do. If you persist in refusing this invitation will it not be because you are afraid of making Lady Lufton angry? I do not know what there can be in that woman that she is able to hold both you and Lufton in leading-strings.' Robarts, of course, denied the charge, and protested that he was not to be taken back to his own parsonage by any fear of Lady Lufton. But though he made such protest with warmth, he knew that he did so ineffectually. Sowerby only smiled, and said that the proof of the pudding was in the eating.

'What is the good of a man keeping a curate if it be not to save him from that sort of drudgery?' he asked.

'Drudgery! If I were a drudge how could I be here today?'

'Well, Robarts, look here. I am speaking now, perhaps, with more of the energy of an old friend than circumstances fully warrant; but I am an older man than you, and as I have a regard for you I do not like to see you throw up a good game when it is in your hands.'

'Oh, as far as that goes, Sowerby, I need hardly tell you that I appreciate your kindness.'

'If you are content,' continued the man of the world, 'to live at Framley all your life, and to warm yourself in the sunshine of the dowager there, why, in such case, it may perhaps be useless for you to extend the circle of your friends; but if you have higher ideas than these, you will be very wrong to omit the present opportunity of going to the duke's. I never knew the duke go so much out of his way to be civil to a clergyman as he has done in this instance.'

'I am sure I am very much obliged to him.'

'The fact is, that you may, if you please, make yourself popular in the county; but you cannot do it by obeying all Lady Lufton's behests. She is a dear old woman, I am sure.'

'She is, Sowerby; and you would say so, if you knew her.'

'I don't doubt it; but it would not do for you or me to live exactly according to her ideas. Now, here, in this case, the bishop of the diocese is to be one of the party, and he has, I believe, already expressed a wish that you should be another.'

'He asked me if I were going.'

'Exactly; and Archdeacon Grantly will be there.'

'Will he?' asked Mark. Now, that would be a great point gained, for Archdeacon Grantly was a close friend of Lady Lufton.

'So I understand from Fothergill. Indeed, it will be very wrong of you not to go, and I tell you so plainly; and what is more, when you talk about your duty – you having a curate as you have – why, it is gammon.' These last words he spoke looking back over his shoulder as he stood up in his stirrups, for he had caught the eye of the huntsman, who was surrounded by his hounds, and was now trotting on to join him. During a great portion of the day, Mark found himself riding by the side of Mrs. Proudie, as that lady leaned back in her carriage. And Mrs. Proudie smiled on him graciously, though her daughter would not do so. Mrs. Proudie was fond of having an attendant clergyman; and as it was evident that Mr. Robarts lived among nice people – titled dowagers, members of Parliament, and people of that sort – she was quite willing to install him as a sort of honorary chaplain *pro tem.*

'I'll tell you what we have settled, Mrs. Harold Smith and I,' said Mrs. Proudie to him. 'This lecture at Barchester will be so late on Saturday evening, that you had all better come and dine with us.' Mark bowed and thanked her, and declared that he should be very happy to make one of such a party. Even Lady Lufton could not object to this, although she was not especially fond of Mrs. Proudie.

'And then they are to sleep at the hotel. It will really be too late for ladies to think of going back so far at this time of the year. I told Mrs. Harold Smith, and Miss Dunstable, too, that we could manage to make room at any rate for them. But they will not leave the other ladies; so they go to the hotel for that night. But, Mr. Robarts, the bishop will never allow you to stay at the inn, so of course you will take a bed at the palace.'

It immediately occurred to Mark that as the lecture was to be given on Saturday evening, the next morning would be Sunday; and, on that Sunday, he would have to preach at Chaldicotes. 'I thought they were all going to return the same night,' said he.

'Well, they did intend it; but you see Mrs. Smith is afraid.'

'I should have to get back here on the Sunday morning, Mrs. Proudie.'

'Ah, yes, that is bad – very bad indeed. No one dislikes any interference with the Sabbath more than I do. Indeed, if I am particular about anything it is about that. But some works are works of necessity, Mr. Robarts; are they not? Now you must necessarily be back at Chaldicotes on Sunday morning!' And so the matter was settled. Mrs. Proudie was very firm in general in the matter of Sabbath-day observances; but when she had to deal with such persons as Mrs. Harold Smith, it was expedient that she should give way a little. 'You can start as soon as it's daylight, you know, if you like it, Mr. Robarts,' said Mrs. Proudie.

There was not much to boast of as to the hunting, but it was a very pleasant day for the ladies. The men rode up and down the grass roads through the chase, sometimes in the greatest possible hurry as though they never could go quick enough; and then the coachmen would drive very fast also, though they did not know why, for a fast pace of movement is another of those contagious diseases. And then again the sportsmen would move at an undertaker's pace, when the fox had traversed and the hounds would be at a loss to know which was the hunt and which was the heel; and then the carriage also would go slowly, and the ladies would stand up and talk. And then the time for lunch came; and altogether the day went by pleasantly enough.

'And so that's hunting, is it?' said Miss Dunstable.

'Yes, that's hunting,' said Mr. Sowerby.

'I did not see any gentleman do anything that I could not do myself, except there was one young man slipped off into the mud; and I shouldn't like that.'

'But there was no breaking of bones, was there, my dear?' said Mrs. Harold Smith.

'And nobody caught any foxes,' said Miss Dunstable. 'The fact is, Mrs. Smith, that I don't think much more of their sport than I do of their business. I shall take to hunting a pack of hounds myself after this.'

'Do, my dear, and I'll be your whipper-in. I wonder whether Mrs. Proudie would join us.'

'I shall be writing to the duke to-night,' said Mr. Fothergill to Mark, as they were all riding up to the stable-yard together. 'You will let me tell his grace that you will accept his invitation – will you not?'

'Upon my word, the duke is very kind,' said Mark.

'He is very anxious to know you, I can assure you,' said Fothergill. What could a young flattered fool of a parson do, but say that he would go? Mark did say that he would go; and in the course of the evening his friend Mr. Sowerby congratulated him, and the bishop joked with him and said that he knew that he would not give up good company so soon; and Miss Dunstable said she would make him her chaplain as soon as Parliament would allow quack doctors to have such articles – an allusion with Mark did not understand, till he learned that

Miss Dunstable was herself the proprietress of the celebrated Oil of Lebanon, invented by her late respected father, and patented by him with such wonderful results in the way of accumulated fortune; and Mrs. Proudie made him quite one of their party, talking to him about all manner of Church subjects; and then at last, even Miss Proudie smiled on him, when she learned that he had been thought worthy of a bed at a duke's castle. And all the world seemed to be open to him.

But he could not make himself happy that evening. On the next morning he must write to his wife; and he could already see the look of painful sorrow which would fall upon his Fanny's brow when she learned that her husband was going to be a guest at the Duke of Omnium's. And he must tell her to send him money, and money was scarce. And then, as to Lady Lufton, should he send her some message, or should he not? In either case he must declare war against her. And then did he not owe everything to Lady Lufton? And thus in spite of all his triumphs he could not get himself to bed in a happy frame of mind.

On the next day, which was Friday, he postponed the disagreeable task of writing. Saturday would do as well; and on Saturday morning, before they all started for Barchester, he did write. And his letter ran as follows: –

'CHALDICOTES, – November, 185–.

'Dearest Love,

'You will be astonished when I tell you how gay we all are here, and what further dissipations are in store for us. The Arabins, as you supposed, are not of our party; but the Proudies are, – as you supposed also. Your suppositions are always right. And what will you think when I tell you that I am to sleep at the palace on Saturday? You know that there is to be a lecture in Barchester on that day. Well; we must all go, of course, as Harold Smith, one of our set here, is to give it. And now it turns out that we cannot get back the same night because there is no moon; and Mrs. Bishop would not allow that my cloth should be contaminated by an hotel; – very kind and considerate, is it not?

'But I have a more astounding piece of news for you than this. There is to be a great party at Gatherum Castle next week, and they have talked me over into accepting an invitation which the duke sent expressly to me. I refused at first; but everybody here said that my doing so would be so strange; and then they all wanted to know my reason. When I came to render it, I did not know what reason I had to give. The bishop is going, and he thought it very odd that I should not go also, seeing that I was asked. I know what my own darling will think, and I know that she will not be pleased, and I must put off my defence till I return to her from this ogreland, – if ever I do get back alive. But joking apart, Fanny, I think that I should have been wrong to stand out, when so much was said about it. I should have been seeming to take upon myself to sit in judgement upon the duke. I doubt if there be a single clergyman in the diocese, under fifty years of age, who would have refused the invitation under such circumstances, – unless it be Crawley, who is so mad on the subject that he thinks it almost wrong to take a walk out of his own parish. I must stay at Gatherum Castle over Sunday week – indeed, we only go there on Friday. I have written to Jones about the duties. I can make it up to him, as I know he wishes to go into Wales at Christmas. My wanderings will all be over then, and he may go for a couple of months if he pleases. I suppose you will take my classes in the school on Sunday, as well as your own; but pray make them have a good fire. If this is too much for you, make Mrs. Podgens take the boys. Indeed I think that will be better.

'Of course you will tell her ladyship of my whereabouts. Tell her from me, that as regards the bishop, as well as regarding another great personage, the colour has been laid on perhaps a little too thickly. Not that Lady Lufton would ever like him. Make her understand that my going to the duke's has almost become a matter of conscience with me. I have not known how to make it appear that it would be right for me to refuse, without absolutely making a party matter of it. I saw that it would be said, that I, coming from Lady Lufton's parish, could not go to the Duke of Omnium's. This I did not choose.

'I find that I shall want a little more money before I leave here, five or ten pounds – say ten pounds. If you cannot spare it, get it from Davis. He owes me more than that, a good deal. And now, God bless and preserve you, my own love. Kiss my darling bairns for papa, and give them my blessing.

'Always and ever your own,
'M. R.'

And then there was written, on an outside scrap which was folded round the full-written sheet of paper, 'Make it as smooth at Framley Court as possible.' However strong, and reasonable, and unanswerable the body of Mark's letter may have been, all his hesitation, weakness, doubt, and fear, were expressed in this short postscript.

CHAPTER V

Amantium Iræ Amoris Integratio

AND now, with my reader's consent, I will follow the postman with that letter to Framley; not by its own circuitous route indeed, or by the same mode of conveyance; for that letter went into Barchester by the Courcy night mail-cart, which, on its road, passes through the villages of Uffley and Chaldicotes, reaching Barchester in time for the up mail train to London. By that train, the letter was sent towards the metropolis as far as the junction of the Barset branch line, but there it was turned in its course, and came down again by the main line as far as Silverbridge; at which place, between six and seven in the morning, it was shouldered by the Framley foot-post messenger, and in due course delivered at the Framley Parsonage exactly as Mrs. Robarts had finished reading prayers to the four servants. Or, I should say rather, that such would in its usual course have been that letter's destiny. As it was, however, it reached Silverbridge on Sunday, and lay there till the Monday, as the Framley people have declined their Sunday post. And then again, when the letter was delivered at the parsonage, on that wet Monday morning, Mrs. Robarts was not at home. As we are all aware, she was staying with her ladyship at Framley Court.

'Oh, but it's mortial wet,' said the shivering postman as he handed in that and the vicar's newspaper. The vicar was a man of the world, and took the *Jupiter*.

'Come in, Robin postman, and warm theeself awhile,' said Jemima the cook, pushing a stool a little to one side, but still well in front of the big kitchen fire.

'Well, I dudna jist know how it'll be. The wery 'edges 'as eyes and tells on me in Silverbridge, if I so much as stops to pick a blackberry.'

'There bain't no hedges here, mon, nor yet no blackberries; so sit thee down and warm theeself. That's better nor blackberries, I'm thinking,' and she handed him a bowl of tea with a slice of buttered toast. Robin postman took the proffered tea, put his dripping hat on the ground, and thanked Jemima cook. 'But I dudna jist know how it'll be,' said he; 'only it do pour so tarnation heavy.' Which among us, O my readers, could have withstood that temptation?

Such was the circuitous course of Mark's letter; but as it left Chaldicotes on Saturday evening, and reached Mrs. Robarts on the following morning, or would have done, but for that intervening Sunday, doing all its peregrinations during the night, it may be held that its course of transport was not inconveniently arranged. We, however, will travel by a much shorter route. Robin, in the course of his daily travels, passed, first the post-office at Framley, then the Framley Court back entrance, and then the vicar's house, so that on this wet morning Jemima cook was not able to make use of his services in transporting this letter back to her mistress; for Robin had got another village before him, expectant of its letters.

'Why didn't thee leave it, mon, with Mr. Applejohn at the Court?' Mr. Applejohn was the butler who took the letter-bag. 'Thee know'st as how missus was there.' And then Robin, mindful of the tea and toast, explained to her courteously how the law made it imperative on him to bring the letter to the very house that was indicated, let the owner of the letter be where she might; and he laid down the law very satisfactorily with sundry long-worded quotations. Not to much effect, however, for the house-maid called him an oaf, and Robin would decidedly have had the worst of it had not the gardener come in and taken his part. 'They women knows nothin', and under-stands nothin',' said the gardener. 'Give us hold of the letter. I'll take it up to the house. It's the master's fist.' And then Robin postman went on one way, and the gardener, he went the other. The gardener never disliked an excuse for going up to the Court gardens, even on so wet a day as this.

Mrs. Robarts was sitting over the drawing-room fire with Lady Meredith, when her husband's letter was brought to her. The Framley Court letter-bag had been discussed at breakfast; but that was now nearly an hour since, and Lady Lufton, as was her wont, was away in her own room writing her own letters, and looking after her own matters: for Lady Lufton was a person who dealt in figures herself, and understood business almost as well as Harold Smith. And on that morning she also had received a letter which had displeased her not a little. Whence arose this displeasure neither Mrs. Robarts nor Lady Meredith knew; but her ladyship's brow had grown black at breakfast time; she had bundled up an ominous-looking epistle into her bag without speaking of it, and had left the room immediately that breakfast was over.

'There's something wrong,' said Sir George.

'Mamma does fret herself so much about Ludovic's money matters,' said Lady Meredith. Ludovic was Lord Lufton, – Ludovic Lufton, Baron Lufton of Lufton, in the county of Oxfordshire.

'And yet I don't think Lufton gets much astray,' said Sir George, as he sauntered out of the room. 'Well, Justy; we'll put off going then till to-morrow; but remember, it must be the first train.' Lady Meredith said she would remember, and then they went into the drawing-room, and there Mrs. Robarts received her letter. Fanny, when she read it, hardly at first realized to herself the idea that her husband, the clergyman of Framley, the family clerical friend of Lady Lufton's establishment, was going to stay with the Duke of Omnium. It was so thoroughly understood at Framley Court that the duke and all belonging to him was noxious and damnable. He was a Whig, he was a bachelor, he was a gambler, he was immoral in every way, he was a man of no Church principle, a corrupter of youth, a sworn foe of young wives, a swallower up of small men's patrimonies; a man whom mothers feared for their sons, and sisters for their brothers; and worse again, whom fathers had cause to fear for their daughters, and brothers for their sisters; – a man who, with his belongings, dwelt, and must dwell, poles asunder from Lady Lufton and her belongings! And it must be remembered that all these evil things were fully believed by Mrs. Robarts. Could it really be that her husband was going to dwell in the halls of Apollyon, to shelter himself beneath the wings of this very Lucifer? A cloud of sorrow settled upon her face, and then she read the letter again very slowly, not omitting the tell-tale postscript.

'Oh, Justinia!' at last she said.

'What, have you got bad news, too?'

'I hardly know how to tell you what has occurred. There; I suppose you had better read it;' and she handed her husband's epistle to Lady Meredith, – keeping back, however, the postscript.

'What on earth will her ladyship say now?' said Lady Meredith, as she folded the paper, and replaced it in the envelope.

'What had I better do, Justinia? how had I better tell her?' And then the two ladies put their heads together, bethinking themselves how they might best deprecate the wrath of Lady Lufton. It had been arranged that Mrs. Robarts should go back to the parsonage after lunch, and she had persisted in her intention after it had been settled that the Merediths were to stay over that evening. Lady Meredith now advised her friend to carry out this determination without saying anything about her husband's terrible iniquities, and then to send the letter up to Lady Lufton as soon as she reached the parsonage. 'Mamma will never know that you received it here,' said Lady Meredith. But Mrs. Robarts would not consent to this. Such a course seemed to her to be cowardly. She knew that her husband was doing wrong; she felt that he knew it himself; but still it was necessary that she should defend him. However terrible might be the storm, it must break upon her own head. So she at once went up and tapped at Lady Lufton's private door; and as she did so Lady Meredith followed her.

'Come in,' said Lady Lufton, and the voice did not sound soft and pleasant. When they entered, they found her sitting at her little writing-table, with her head resting on her arm, and that letter which she had received that morning was lying open on the table before her. Indeed there were two letters now there, one from a London lawyer to herself, and the other from her son to that London lawyer. It needs only be explained that the subject of those letters was the immediate sale of that outlying portion of the Lufton property in Oxfordshire, as to which Mr. Sowerby once spoke. Lord Lufton had told the lawyer that the thing must be done at once, adding that his friend Robarts would have explained the whole affair to his mother. And then the lawyer had written to Lady Lufton, as indeed was necessary; but unfortunately Lady Lufton had not hitherto heard a word of the matter. In her eyes the sale of family property was horrible; the fact that a young man with some fifteen or twenty thousand a year should require subsidiary money was horrible; that her own son should have not written to her himself was horrible; and it was also horrible that her own pet, the clergyman whom she had brought there to be her son's friend, should be mixed up in the matter; should be cognizant of it while she was not cognizant; should be employed in it as a go-between and agent in her son's bad courses. It was all horrible, and Lady Lufton was sitting there with a black brow and an uneasy heart. As regarded our poor parson, we may say that in this matter he was blameless, except that he had hitherto lacked the courage to execute his friend's commission.

'What is it, Fanny?' said Lady Lufton, as soon as the door was opened; 'I should have been down in half an hour, if you wanted me, Justinia.'

'Fanny has received a letter which makes her wish to speak to you at once,' said Lady Meredith.

'What letter, Fanny?' Poor Fanny's heart was in her mouth; she held it in her hand, but had not yet quite made up her mind whether she would show it bodily to Lady Lufton. 'From Mr. Robarts,' she said.

'Well; I suppose he is going to stay another week at Chaldicotes. For my part I should be as well pleased;' and Lady Lufton's voice was not friendly, for she was thinking of that farm in Oxfordshire. The imprudence of the young is very sore to the prudence of their elders. No woman could be less covetous, less grasping than Lady Lufton; but the sale of a portion of the old family property was to her as the loss of her own heart's blood.

'Here is the letter, Lady Lufton; perhaps you had better read it;' and Fanny handed it to her, again keeping back the postcript. She had read and re-read the letter downstairs, but could not make out whether her husband had intended her to show it. From the line of the argument she thought that he must have done so. At any rate he said for himself more than she could say for him, and so, probably, it was best that her ladyship should see it. Lady Lufton took it, and read it, and her face grew blacker and blacker. Her mind was set against the writer before she began it, and every word in it tended to make her feel more estranged from him. 'Oh, he is going to the palace, is he? well; he must choose his own friends. Harold Smith one of his party! It's a pity, my dear, he did not see Miss Proudie before he met you, he might have lived to be the bishop's chaplain. Gatherum Castle! You don't mean to tell me that he is going there? Then I tell you fairly, Fanny, that I have done with him.'

'Oh, Lady Lufton, don't say that,' said Mrs. Robarts, with tears in her eyes.

'Mamma, mamma, don't speak in that way,' said Lady Meredith.

'But, my dear, what am I to say? I must speak in that way. You would not wish me to speak falsehoods, would you? A man must choose for himself, but he can't live with two different sets of people; at least, not if I belong to one and the Duke of Omnium to the other. The bishop going indeed! If there be anything that I hate it is hypocrisy.'

'There is no hypocrisy in that, Lady Lufton.'

'But I say there is, Fanny. Very strange, indeed! "Put off his defence!" Why should a man need any defence to his wife if he acts in a straightforward way? His own language condemns him: "Wrong to stand out!" Now, will either of you tell me that Mr. Robarts would really have thought it wrong to refuse that invitation? I say that that is hypocrisy. There is no other word for it.' By this time the poor wife, who had been in tears, was wiping them away and preparing for action. Lady Lufton's extreme severity gave her courage. She knew that it behoved her to fight for her husband when he was thus attacked. Had Lady Lufton been moderate in her remarks Mrs. Robarts would not have had a word to say.

'My husband may have been ill-judged,' she said, 'but he is no hypocrite.'

'Very well, my dear, I dare say you know better than I; but to me it looks extremely like hypocrisy; eh, Justinia?'

'Oh, mamma, do be moderate.'

'Moderate! That's all very well. How is one to moderate one's feelings when one has been betrayed?'

'You do not mean that Mr. Robarts has betrayed you?' said the wife.

'Oh, no; of course not.' And then she went on reading the letter: ' "Seem to have been standing in judgement upon the duke." Might he not use the same argument as to going into any house in the kingdom, however infamous? We must all stand in judgement one upon another in that sense. "Crawley!" Yes; if he were a little more like Mr. Crawley it would be a good thing for me, and for the parish, and for you too, my dear. God forgive me for bringing him here; that's all.'

'Lady Lufton, I must say that you are very hard upon him – very hard. I did not expect it from such a friend.'

'My dear, you ought to know me well enough to be sure that I shall speak my mind. "Written to Jones" – yes; it is easy enough to write to poor Jones. He had better write to Jones, and bid him do the whole duty. Then he can go and be the duke's domestic chaplain.'

'I believe my husband does as much of his own duty as any clergyman in the whole diocese,' said Mrs. Robarts, now again in tears.

'And you are to take his work in the school; you and Mrs. Podgens. What with his curate and his wife and Mrs. Podgens, I don't see why he should come back at all.'

'Oh, mamma,' said Justinia, 'pray, pray don't be so harsh to her.'

'Let me finish it, my dear; – oh, here I come. "Tell her ladyship my whereabouts." He little thought you'd show me this letter.'

'Didn't he?' said Mrs. Robarts, putting out her hand to get it back, but in vain. 'I thought it was for the best; I did indeed.'

'I had better finish it now, if you please. What is this? How does he dare send his ribald jokes to me in such a matter? No, I do not suppose I ever shall like Dr. Proudie; I have never expected it. A matter of conscience with him! Well – well, well. Had I not read it myself, I could not have believed it of him. I would not positively have believed it. "Coming from my parish he could not go to the Duke of Omnium!" And it is what I would wish to have said. People fit for this parish should not be fit for the Duke of Omnium's house. And I had trusted that he would have this feeling more strongly than any one else in it. I have been deceived – that's all.'

'He has done nothing to deceive you, Lady Lufton.'

'I hope he will not have deceived you, my dear. "More money;" yes, it is probable that he will want more money. There is your letter, Fanny. I am very sorry for it. I can say nothing more.' And she folded up the letter and gave it back to Mrs. Robarts.

'I thought it right to show it to you,' said Mrs. Robarts.

'It did not much matter whether you did or no; of course I must have been told.'

'He especially begs me to tell you.'

'Why, yes; he could not very well have kept me in the dark in such a matter. He could not neglect his own work, and go and live with gamblers and adulterers at the Duke of Omnium's without my knowing it.' And now Fanny Robart's cup was full, full to the overflowing. When she heard these words she forgot all about Lady Lufton, all about Lady Meredith, and remembered only her husband –

that he was her husband, and, in spite of his faults, a good and loving husband; – and that other fact also she remembered, that she was his wife.

'Lady Lufton,' she said, 'you forget yourself in speaking in that way of my husband.'

'What!' said her ladyship; 'you are to show me such a letter as that, and I am not to tell you what I think?'

'Not if you think such hard things as that. Even you are not justified in speaking to me in that way, and I will not hear it.'

'Heighty-tighty!' said her ladyship.

'Whether or no he is right in going to the Duke of Omnium's, I will not pretend to judge. He is the judge of his own actions, and neither you nor I.'

'And when he leaves you with the butcher's bill unpaid and no money to buy shoes for the children, who will be the judge then?'

'Not you, Lady Lufton. If such bad days should ever come – and neither you nor I have a right to expect them – I will not come to you in my troubles; not after this.'

'Very well, my dear. You may go to the Duke of Omnium if that suits you better.'

'Fanny, come away,' said Lady Meredith. 'Why should you try to anger my mother?'

'I don't want to anger her; but I won't hear him abused in that way without speaking up for him. If I don't defend him, who will? Lady Lufton has said terrible things about him; and they are not true.'

'Oh, Fanny!' said Justinia.

'Very well, very well!' said Lady Lufton. 'This is the sort of return that one gets.'

'I don't know what you mean by return, Lady Lufton: but would you wish me to stand by quietly and hear such things said of my husband? He does not live with such people as you have named. He does not neglect his duties. If every clergyman were as much in his parish, it would be well for some of them. And in going to such a house as the Duke of Omnium's it does make a difference that he goes there in company with the bishop. I can't explain why, but I know that it does.'

'Especially when the bishop is coupled up with the devil, as Mr. Robarts has done,' said Lady Lufton; 'he can join the duke with them and then they'll stand for the three Graces, won't they, Justinia?' And Lady Lufton laughed a bitter little laugh at her own wit.

'I suppose I may go now, Lady Lufton.'

'Oh, yes, certainly, my dear.'

'I am sorry if I have made you angry with me; but I will not allow any one to speak against Mr. Robarts without answering them. You have been very unjust to him; and even though I do anger you, I must say so.'

'Come, Fanny; this is too bad,' said Lady Lufton. 'You have been scolding me for the last half-hour because I would not congratulate you on this new friend that your husband has made, and now you are going to begin it all over again. That is more than I can stand. If you have nothing else particular to say, you might as well leave me.' And Lady Lufton's face as she spoke was unbending, severe, and harsh. Mrs. Robarts had never before been so spoken to by her old friend; indeed, she had never been so spoken to by any one, and she hardly knew how to bear herself.

'Very well, Lady Lufton,' she said; 'then I will go. Good-bye.'

'Good-bye,' said Lady Lufton, and turning herself to her table she began to arrange her papers. Fanny had never before left Framley Court to go back to her own parsonage without a warm embrace. Now she was to do so without even having her hand taken. Had it come to this, that there was absolutely to be a quarrel between them – a quarrel for ever?

'Fanny is going, you know, mamma,' said Lady Meredith. 'She will be home before you are down again.'

'I cannot help it, my dear. Fanny must do as she pleases. I am not to be the judge of her actions. She has just told me so.' Mrs. Robarts had said nothing of the kind, but she was far too proud to point this out. So with a gentle step she retreated through the door, and then Lady Meredith, having tried what a conciliatory whisper with her mother would do, followed her. Alas, the conciliatory whisper was altogether ineffectual.

The two ladies said nothing as they descended the stairs, but when they had regained the drawing-room they looked with blank horror into each other's faces. What were they to do now? Of such a tragedy as this they had had no remotest preconception. Was it absolutely the case that Fanny Robarts was to walk out of Lady Lufton's house as a declared enemy – she who, before her marriage as well as since, had been almost treated as an adopted daughter of the family?

'Oh, Fanny, why did you answer my mother in that way?' said Lady Meredith. 'You saw that she was vexed. She had other things to vex her besides this about Mr. Robarts.'

'And would not you answer any one who attacked Sir George?'

'No, not my own mother. I would let her say what she pleased, and leave Sir George to fight his own battles.'

'Ah, but it is different with you. You are her daughter, and Sir George – she would not dare to speak in that way as to Sir George's doings.'

'Indeed she would, if it pleased her. I am sorry I let you go up to her.'

'It is as well that it should be over, Justinia. As those are her thoughts about Mr. Robarts, it is quite as well that we should know them. Even for all that I owe to her, and all the love I bear to you, I will not come to this house if I am to hear my husband abused – not into any house.'

'My dearest Fanny, we all know what happens when two angry people get together.'

'I was not angry when I went up to her; not in the least.'

'It is no good looking back. What are we to do now, Fanny?'

'I suppose I had better go home,' said Mrs. Robarts. 'I will go and put my things up, and then I will send James for them.'

'Wait till after lunch, and then you will be able to kiss my mother before you leave us.'

'No, Justinia; I cannot wait. I must answer Mr. Robarts by this post, and I must think what I have to say to him. I could not write that letter here, and the post goes at four.' And Mrs. Robarts got up from her chair, preparatory to her final departure.

'I shall come to you before dinner,' said Lady Meredith; 'and if I can bring you good tidings, I shall expect you to come back here with me. It is out of the question that I should go away from Framley leaving you and my mother at enmity with each other.' To this Mrs. Robarts made no answer; and in a very few minutes afterwards she was in her own nursery, kissing her children, and teaching the elder one to say something about papa. But, even as she taught him, the tears stood in her eyes, and the little fellow knew that everything was not right. And there she sat till about two, doing little odds and ends of things for the children, and allowing that occupation to stand as an excuse to her for not commencing her letter. But then there remained only two hours to her, and it might be that the letter would be difficult in the writing – would require thought and changes, and must needs be copied, perhaps, more than once. As to the money, that she had in the house – as much, at least, as Mark now wanted, though the sending of it would leave her nearly penniless. She could, however, in case of personal need, resort to Davis as desired by him.

So she got out her desk in the drawing-room and sat down and wrote her letter. It was difficult, though she found that it hardly took so long as she expected. It was difficult, for she felt bound to tell him the truth; and yet she was anxious not to spoil all his pleasure among his friends. She told him, however, that Lady Lufton was very angry, 'unreasonably angry, I must say,' she put in, in order to show that she had not sided against him. 'And, indeed, we have quite quarrelled, and this has made me unhappy, as it will you, dearest; I know that. But we both know how good she is at heart, and Justinia thinks that she had other things to trouble her; and I hope it will all be made up before you come home; only, dearest Mark, pray do not be longer than you said in your last letter.' And then there were three or four paragraphs about the babies, and two about the schools, which I may as well omit. She had just finished her letter, and was carefully folding it for its envelope, with the two whole five-pound notes imprudently placed within it, when she heard a footstep on the gravel path which led up from a small wicket to the front door. The path ran near the drawing-room window, and she was just in time to catch a glimpse of the last fold of a passing cloak. 'It is Justinia,' she said to herself; and her heart became disturbed at the idea of again discussing the morning's adventure. 'What am I to do,' she had said to herself before, 'if she wants me to beg her pardon? I will not own before her that he is in the wrong.'

And then the door opened – for the visitor made her entrance without the aid of any servant – and Lady Lufton herself stood before her. 'Fanny,' she said at once, 'I have come to beg your pardon.'

'Oh, Lady Lufton!'

'I was very much harassed when you came to me just now; – by more things than one, my dear. But, nevertheless, I should not have spoken to you of your husband as I did, and so I have come to beg your pardon.' Mrs. Robarts was past answering by the time that this was said, past answering at least in words; so she jumped up, and with her eyes full of tears, threw herself into her old friend's arms. 'Oh, Lady Lufton!' she sobbed forth again.

'You will forgive me, won't you?' said her ladyship, as she returned her young friend's caress. 'Well, that's right. I have not been at all happy since you left my den this morning, and I don't suppose you have. But, Fanny, dearest, we love each other too well, and know each other too thoroughly, to have a long quarrel, don't we?'

'Oh, yes, Lady Lufton.'

'Of course we do. Friends are not to be picked up on the road-side every day; nor are they to be thrown away lightly. And now sit down, my love, and let us have a little talk. There, I must take my bonnet off. You have pulled the strings so that you have almost choked me.' And Lady Lufton deposited her bonnet on the table, and seated herself comfortably in the corner of the sofa.

'My dear,' she said, 'there is no duty which any woman owes to any other human being at all equal to that which she owes to her husband, and, therefore, you were quite right to stand up for Mr. Robarts this morning.' Upon this Mrs. Robarts said nothing, but she got her hand within that of her ladyship and gave it a slight squeeze.

'And I loved you for what you were doing all the time. I did, my dear; though you were a little fierce, you know. Even Justinia admits that, and she has been at me ever since you went away. And, indeed, I did not know that it was in you to look in that way out of those pretty eyes of yours.'

'Oh, Lady Lufton!'

'But I looked fierce enough too myself, I dare say; so we'll say nothing more about that; will we? But now, about this good man of yours?'

'Dear Lady Lufton, you must forgive him.'

'Well, as you ask me, I will. We'll have nothing more said about the duke, either now or when he comes back; not a word. Let me see – he's to be back; -- when is it?'

'Wednesday week, I think.'

'Ah, Wednesday. Well, tell him to come and dine up at the house on Wednesday. He'll be in time, I suppose, and there shan't be a word said about this horrid duke.'

'I am so much obliged to you, Lady Lufton.'

'But look here, my dear; believe me, he's better off without such friends.'

'Oh, I know he is; much better off.'

'Well, I'm glad you admit that, for I thought you seemed to be in favour of the duke.'

'Oh, no, Lady Lufton.'

'That's right, then. And now, if you'll take my advice, you'll use your influence, as a good, dear sweet wife as you are, to prevent his going there any more. I'm an old woman and he is a young man, and it's very natural that he should think me behind the times. I'm not angry at that. But he'll find that it's better for him, better for him in every way, to stick to his old friends. It will be better for his peace of mind, better for his character as a clergyman, better for his pocket, better for his children and for you, – and better for his eternal welfare. The duke is not such a companion as he should seek; – nor, if he is sought, should he allow himself to be led away.' And then Lady Lufton ceased, and Fanny Robarts kneeling at her feet sobbed, with her face hidden on her friend's knees. She had not a word now to say as to her husband's capability of judging for himself.

'And now I must be going again; but Justinia has made me promise, – promise, mind you, most solemnly, that I would have you back to dinner to-night, – by force if necessary. It was the only way I could make my peace with her; so you must not leave me in the lurch.' Of course, Fanny said that she would go and dine at Framley Court.

'And you must not send that letter, by any means,' said her ladyship at she was leaving the room, poking with her umbrella at the epistle, which lay directed on Mrs. Robarts's desk. 'I can understand very well what it contains. You must alter it altogether, my dear.' And then Lady Lufton went.

Mrs. Robarts instantly rushed to her desk and tore open her letter. She looked at her watch and it was past four. She had hardly begun another when the postman came. 'Oh, Mary,' she said, 'do make him wait. If he'll wait a quarter of an hour I'll give him a shilling.'

'There's no need of that, ma'am. Let him have a glass of beer.'

'Very well, Mary; but don't give him too much, for fear he should drop the letters about. I'll be ready in ten minutes.' And in five minutes she had scrawled a very different sort of letter. But he might want the money immediately, so she would not delay it for a day.

CHAPTER VI

Mr. Harold Smith's Lecture

ON the whole the party at Chaldicotes was very pleasant, and the time passed away quickly enough. Mr. Robarts's chief friend there, independently of Mr. Sowerby, was Miss Dunstable, who seemed to take a great fancy to him, whereas she was not very accessible to the blandishments of Mr. Supplehouse, nor more specially courteous even to her host than good manners required of her. But then Mr. Supplehouse and Mr. Sowerby were both bachelors, while Mark Robarts was a married man. With Mr. Sowerby Robarts had more than one communication respecting Lord Lufton and his affairs, which he would willingly have avoided had it been possible. Sowerby was one of those men who are always mixing up business with pleasure, and who have usually some scheme in their mind which requires forwarding. Men of this class have, as a rule, no daily work, no regular routine of labour; but it may be doubted whether they do not toil much more incessantly than those who have.

'Lufton is so dilatory,' Mr. Sowerby said. 'Why did he not arrange this at once, when he promised it? And then he is so afraid of that old woman at Framley Court. Well, my dear fellow, say what you will; she is an old woman, and she'll never be younger. But do write to Lufton, and tell him that this delay is inconvenient to me; he'll do anything for you, I know.' Mark said that he would write, and, indeed, did do so; but he did not at first like the tone of the conversation into which he was dragged. It was very painful to him to hear Lady Lufton called an old woman, and hardly less so to discuss the propriety of Lord Lufton's parting with his property. This was irksome to him, till habit made it easy. But by degrees his feelings became less acute, and he accustomed himself to his friend Sowerby's mode of talking.

And then on Saturday afternoon they all went over to Barchester. Harold Smith during the last forty-eight hours had become crammed to overflowing with Sarawak, Labuan, New Guinea, and the Salomon Islands. As is the case with all men labouring under temporary specialities, he for the time had faith in nothing else, and was not content that any one near him should have any other faith. They called him Viscount Papua and Baron Borneo; and his wife, who headed the joke against him, insisted on having her title. Miss Dunstable swore that she would wed none but a South Sea islander; and to Mark was offered the income and duties of Bishop of Spices. Nor did the Proudie family set themselves against these little sarcastic quips with any overwhelming severity. It is sweet to unbend oneself at the proper opportunity, and this was the proper opportunity for Mrs. Proudie's unbending. No mortal can be seriously wise at all hours; and in these happy hours did that usually wise mortal, the bishop, lay aside for awhile his serious wisdom.

'We think of dining at five to-morrow, my Lady Papua,' said the facetious bishop; 'will that suit his lordship and the affairs of State? he! he! he!' And the good prelate laughed at the fun. How pleasantly young men and women of fifty or thereabouts can joke and flirt and poke their fun about, laughing and holding their sides, dealing in little innuendoes and rejoicing in nicknames, when they have no Mentors of twenty-five or thirty near them to keep them in order! The vicar of Framley might perhaps have been regarded as such a Mentor, were it not for that capability of adapting himself to the company immediately around him on which he so much piqued himself. He therefore also talked to my Lady Papua, and was jocose about the Baron, – not altogether to the satisfaction of Mr. Harold Smith himself. For Mr. Harold Smith was in earnest, and did not quite relish these jocundities. He had an idea that he could in about three months talk the British world into civilizing New Guinea, and that the world of Barsetshire would be made to go with him by one night's efforts. He did not understand why others should be less serious, and was inclined to resent somewhat stiffly the amenities of our friend Mark.

'We must not keep the Baron waiting,' said Mark, as they were preparing to start for Barchester.

'I don't know what you mean by the Baron, sir,' said Harold Smith. 'But perhaps the joke will be against you, when you are getting up into your pulpit to-morrow, and sending the hat round among the clod-hoppers of Chaldicotes.'

'Those who live in glass houses shouldn't throw stones; eh, Baron?' said Miss Dunstable. 'Mr. Robarts's sermon will be too near akin to your lecture to allow of his laughing.'

'If we can do nothing towards instructing the outer world till it's done by the parsons,' said Harold Smith, 'the outer world will have to wait a long time, I fear.'

'Nobody can do anything of that kind short of a member of Parliament and a would-be minister,' whispered Mrs. Harold. And so they were all very pleasant together, in spite of a little fencing with edge-tools; and at three o'clock the *cortège* of carriages started for Barchester, that of the bishop, of course, leading the way. His lordship, however, was not in it.

'Mrs. Proudie, I'm sure you'll let me go with you,' said Miss Dunstable, at the last moment, as she came down the big stone steps. 'I want to hear the rest of that story about Mr. Slope.' Now this upset everything. The bishop was to have gone with his wife, Mrs. Smith, and Mark Robarts; and Mr. Sowerby had so arranged matters that he could have accompanied Miss Dunstable in his phaeton. But no one ever dreamed of denying Miss Dunstable anything. Of course Mark gave way; but it ended in the bishop declaring that he had no special predilection for his own carriage, which he did in compliance with a glance from his wife's eye. Then other changes of course followed, and, at last, Mr. Sowerby and Harold Smith were the joint occupants of the phaeton. The poor lecturer, as he seated himself, made some remark such as those he had been making for the last two days – for out of a full heart the mouth speaketh. But he spoke to an impatient listener. 'D—the South Sea islanders,' said Mr. Sowerby. 'You'll have it all your own way in a few minutes, like a bull in a china-shop; but for Heaven's sake let us have a little peace till that time comes.' It appeared that Mr. Sowerby's little plan of having Miss Dunstable for his companion was not quite insignificant; and, indeed, it may be said that but few of his little plans were so. At the present moment he flung himself back in the carriage and prepared for sleep. He could further no plan of his by a *tête-à-tête* conversation with his brother-in-law. And then Mrs. Proudie began her story about Mr. Slope, or rather recommenced it. She was very fond of talking about this gentleman, who had once been her pet chaplain, but was now her bitterest foe; and in telling the story, she had sometimes to whisper to Miss Dunstable, for there were one or two fie-fie little anecdotes about a married lady, not altogether fit for young Mr. Robarts's ears. But Mrs. Harold Smith insisted on having them out loud, and Miss Dunstable would gratify that lady in spite of Mrs. Proudie's winks.

'What, kissing her hand, and he a clergyman!' said Miss Dunstable. 'I did not think they ever did such things, Mr. Robarts.'

'Still waters run deepest,' said Mrs. Harold Smith.

'Hush-h-h,' looked, rather than spoke, Mrs. Proudie. 'The grief of spirit which that bad man caused me nearly broke my heart, and all the while, you know, he was courting –' and then Mrs. Proudie whispered a name.

'What, the dean's wife!' shouted Miss Dunstable, in a voice which made the coachman of the next carriage give a chuck to his horses as he overheard her.

'The archdeacon's sister-in-law!' screamed Mrs. Harold Smith.

'What might he not have attempted next?' said Miss Dunstable.

'She wasn't the dean's wife then, you know,' said Mrs. Proudie, explaining.

'Well, you've a gay set in the chapter, I must say,' said Miss Dunstable. 'You ought to make one of them in Barchester, Mr. Robarts.'

'Only perhaps Mrs. Robarts might not like it,' said Mrs. Harold Smith.

'And then the schemes which he tried on with the bishop!' said Mrs. Proudie.

'It's all fair in love and war, you know,' said Miss Dunstable.

'But he little knew whom he had to deal with when he began that,' said Mrs. Proudie.

'The bishop was too many for him,' suggested Mrs. Harold Smith, very maliciously.

'If the bishop was not, somebody else was; and he was obliged to leave Barchester in utter disgrace. He has since married the wife of some tallow-chandler.'

'The wife!' said Miss Dunstable. 'What a man!'

'Widow, I mean; but it's all one to him.'

'The gentleman was clearly born when Venus was in the ascendant,' said Mrs. Smith. 'You clergymen usually are, I believe, Mr. Robarts.' So that Mrs. Proudie's carriage was by no means the dullest as they drove into Barchester that day; and by degrees our friend Mark became accustomed to his companions, and before they reached the palace he acknowledged to himself that Miss Dunstable was very good fun. We cannot linger over the bishop's dinner, though it was very good of its kind; and as Mr. Sowerby contrived to sit next to Miss Dunstable, thereby overturning a little scheme made by Mr. Supplehouse, he again shone forth in unclouded good humour. But Mr. Harold Smith became impatient immediately on the withdrawal of the cloth. The lecture was to begin at seven, and according to his watch that hour had already come. He declared that Sowerby and Supplehouse were endeavouring to delay matters in order that the Barchesterians might become vexed and impatient; and so the bishop was not allowed to exercise his hospitality in true episcopal fashion.

'You forget, Sowerby,' said Supplehouse, 'that the world here for the last fortnight has been looking forward to nothing else.'

'The world shall be gratified at once,' said Mrs. Harold, obeying a little nod from Mrs. Proudie. 'Come, my dear,' and she took hold of Miss Dunstable's arm, 'don't let us keep Barchester waiting. We shall be ready in a quarter of an hour, shall we not, Mrs. Proudie?' and so they sailed off.

'And we shall have time for one glass of claret,' said the bishop.

'There; that's seven by the cathedral,' said Harold Smith, jumping up from his chair as he heard the clock. 'If the people have come it would not be right in me to keep them waiting, and I shall go.'

'Just one glass of claret, Mr. Smith, and we'll be off,' said the bishop.

'Those women will keep me an hour,' said Harold, filling his glass, and drinking it standing. 'They do it on purpose.' He was thinking of his wife, but it seemed to the bishop as though his guest were actually speaking of Mrs. Proudie.

It was rather late when they all found themselves in the big room of the Mechanics' Institute; but I do not know whether this on the whole did them any harm. Most of Mr. Smith's hearers, excepting the party from the palace, were Barchester tradesmen with their wives and families; and they waited, not impatiently, for the big people. And then the lecture was gratis, a fact which is always borne in mind by an Englishman when he comes to reckon up and calculate the way in which he is treated. When he pays his money, then he takes his choice; he may be impatient or not as he likes. His sense of justice teaches him so much, and in accordance with that sense he usually acts. So the people on the benches rose graciously when the palace party entered the room. Seats for them had been kept in the front. There were three armchairs, which were filled, after some little hesitation, by the bishop, Mrs. Proudie, and Miss Dunstable – Mrs. Smith positively declining to take one of them; though, as she admitted, her rank as Lady Papua of the islands did give her some claim. And this remark, as it was made quite out loud, reached Mr. Smith's ears as he stood behind a little table on a small raised dais, holding his white kid gloves; and it annoyed him and rather put him out. He did not like that joke about Lady Papua. And then the others of the party sat upon a front bench covered with red cloth. 'We shall find this very hard and very narrow about the second hour,' said Mr. Sowerby, and Mr. Smith on his dais again overheard the words, and dashed his gloves down to the table. He felt that all the room would hear it.

And there were one or two gentlemen on the second seat who shook hands with some of our party. There was Mr. Thorne, of Ullathorne, a good-natured old bachelor, whose residence was near enough to Barchester to allow of his coming in without much personal inconvenience; and next to him was Mr. Harding, an old clergyman of the chapter, with whom Mrs. Proudie shook hands very graciously, making way for him to seat himself close behind her if he would so please. But Mr. Harding did not so please. Having paid his respects to the bishop he returned quietly to the side of his old friend Mr. Thorne, thereby angering Mrs. Proudie, as might easily be seen by her face. And Mr. Chadwick also was there, the episcopal man of business for the diocese; but he also adhered to the two gentlemen above named. And now that the bishop and the ladies had taken their places, Mr. Harold Smith relifted his gloves and again laid them down, hummed three times distinctly, and then began.

'It was,' he said, 'the most peculiar characteristic of the present era in the British islands that those who were high placed before the world in rank, wealth, and education were willing to come forward and give their time and knowledge without fee or reward, for the advantage and amelioration of those who did not stand so high in the social scale.' And then he paused for a moment, during which Mrs. Smith remarked to Miss Dunstable that that was pretty well for a beginning; and Miss Dunstable replied, 'that as for herself she felt very grateful to rank, wealth, and education.' Mr. Sowerby winked to Mr. Supplehouse, who opened his eyes very wide and shrugged his shoulders. But the Barchesterians took it all in good part and gave the lecturer the applause of their hands and feet. And then, well pleased, he recommenced – 'I do not make these remarks with reference to myself –'

'I hope he's not going to be modest,' said Miss Dunstable.

'It will be quite new if he is,' replied Mrs. Smith.

'– so much as to many noble and talented lords and members of the lower House who have lately from time to time devoted themselves to this good work.' And then he went through a long list of peers and members of Parliament, beginning, of course, with Lord Boanerges, and ending with Mr. Green Walker, a young gentleman who had lately been returned by his uncle's interest for the borough of Crewe Junction, and had immediately made his entrance into public life by giving a lecture on the grammarians of the Latin language as exemplified at Eton School. 'On the present occasion,' Mr. Smith continued, 'our object is to learn something as to those grand and magnificent islands which lie far away, beyond the Indies, in the Southern Ocean; the lands of which produce rich spices and glorious fruits, and whose seas are embedded with pearls and corals, – Papua and the Philippines, Borneo and the Moluccas. My friends, you are familiar with your maps, and you know the track which the equator makes for itself through those distant oceans.' And then many heads were turned down, and there was a rustle of leaves; for not a few of those 'who stood not so high in the social scale' had brought their maps with them, and refreshed their memories as to the whereabouts of these wondrous islands.

And then Mr. Smith also, with a map in his hand, and pointing occasionally to another large map which hung against the wall, went into the geography of the matter. 'We might have found that our from our atlases, I think, without coming all the way to Barchester,' said that unsympathizing helpmate, Mrs. Harold, very cruelly – most illogically too, for there be so many things which we could find out ourselves by search, but which we never do find out unless they be specially told us; and why should not the latitude and longitude of Labuan be one – or rather two of these things? And then, when he had duly marked the path of the line through Borneo, Celebes, and Gilolo, through the Macassar Strait and the Molucca passage, Mr. Harold Smith rose to a higher flight. 'But what,' said he, 'avails all that God can give to man, unless man will open his hand to receive the gift? And what is this opening of the hand but the process of civilization – yes, my friends, the process of civilization? These South Sea islanders have all that a kind Providence can bestow on them; but that all is as nothing without education.

That education and that civilization it is for you to bestow upon them – yes, my friends, for you; for you, citizens of Barchester as you are.' And then he paused again, in order that the feet and hands might go to work. The feet and hands did go to work, during which Mr. Smith took a slight drink of water. He was now quite in his element, and had got into the proper way of punching the table with his fists. A few words dropping from Mr. Sowerby did now and again find their way to his ears, but the sound of his own voice had brought with it the accustomed charm, and he ran on from platitude to truism, and from truism back to platitude, with an eloquence that was charming to himself.

'Civilization,' he exclaimed, lifting up his eyes and hands to the ceiling. 'O Civilization –'

'There will not be a chance for us now for the next hour and a half,' said Mr. Supplehouse, groaning. Harold Smith cast one eye down at him, but it immediately flew back to the ceiling.

'O Civilization! thou that ennoblest mankind and makest him equal to the gods, what is like unto thee?' Here Mrs. Proudie showed evident signs of disapprobation, which no doubt would have been shared by the bishop, had not that worthy prelate been asleep. But Mr. Smith continued unobservant; or at any rate regardless. 'What is like unto thee? Thou art the irrigating stream which makest fertile the barren plain. Till thou comest all is dark and dreary; but at thy advent the noontide sun shines out, the earth gives forth her increase; the deep bowels of the rocks render up their tribute. Forms which were dull and hideous become endowed with grace and beauty, and vegetable existence rises to the scale of celestial life. Then, too, Genius appears clad in a panoply of translucent armour, grasping in his hand the whole terrestrial surface, and making every rood of earth subservient to his purposes; – Genius, the child of Civilization, the mother of the Arts!' The last little bit, taken from the 'Pedigree of Progress,' had a great success, and all Barchester went to work with its hands and feet; – all Barchester, except that ill-natured aristocratic front-row together with the three arm-chairs at the corner of it. The aristocratic front row felt itself to be too intimate with civilization to care much about it; and the three armchairs, or rather that special one which contained Mrs. Proudie, considered that there was a certain heathenness, a pagan sentimentality almost amounting to infidelity, contained in the lecturer's remarks, with which she, a pillar of the Church, could not put up, seated as she was now in public conclave.

'It is to civilization that we must look,' continued Mr. Harold Smith, descending from poetry to prose as a lecturer well knows how, and thereby showing the value of both – 'for any material progress in these islands; and –'

'And to Christianity,' shouted Mrs. Proudie, to the great amazement of the assembled people, and to the thorough wakening of the bishop, who, jumping up in his chair at the sound of the well-known voice, exclaimed, 'Certainly, certainly.'

'Hear, hear, hear,' said those on the benches who particularly belonged to Mrs. Proudie's school of divinity in the city, and among the voices was distinctly heard that of a new verger in whose behalf she had greatly interested herself.

'Oh, yes, Christianity of course,' said Harold Smith, upon whom the interruption did not seem to operate favourably.

'Christianity and Sabbath-day observance,' exclaimed Mrs. Proudie, who, now that she had obtained the ear of the public, seemed well inclined to keep it. 'Let us never forget that these islanders can never prosper unless they keep the Sabbath holy.' Poor Mr. Smith, having been so rudely dragged from his high horse, was never able to mount it again, and completed the lecture in a manner not at all comfortable to himself. He had there, on the table before him, a huge bundle of statistics, with which he had meant to convince the reason of his hearers, after he had taken full possession of their feelings. But they fell very dull and flat. And at the moment when he was interrupted, he was about to explain that that material progress to which he had alluded could not be attained without money; and that it behoved them, the people of Barchester before him, to come forward with their purses like men and brothers. He did also attempt this; but from the moment of that fatal onslaught from the arm-chair, it was clear to him, and to every one else, that Mrs. Proudie was now the hero of the hour. His time had gone by, and the people of Barchester did not care a straw for his appeal. From these causes the lecture was over full twenty minutes earlier than any one had expected, to the great delight of Messrs. Sowerby and Supplehouse, who, on that evening, moved and carried a vote of thanks to Mrs. Proudie. For they had gay doings yet before they went to their beds.

'Robarts, here one moment,' Mr. Sowerby said, as they were standing at the door of the Mechanics' Institute. 'Don't you go off with Mr. and Mrs. Bishop. We are going to have a little supper at the Dragon of Wantly, and, after what we have gone through, upon my word we want it. You can tell one of the palace servants to let you in.' Mark considered the proposal wistfully. He would fain have joined the supper party had he dared; but he, like many others of his cloth, had the fear of Mrs. Proudie before his eyes. And a very merry supper they had; but poor Mr. Harold Smith was not the merriest of the party.

CHAPTER VII

Sunday Morning

IT was, perhaps, quite as well on the whole for Mark Robarts, that he did not go to that supper party. It was eleven o'clock before they sat down and nearly two before the gentlemen were in bed. It must be remembered that he had to preach, on the coming Sunday morning, a charity sermon on behalf of a mission to Mr. Harold Smith's islanders; and, to tell the truth, it was a task for which he had now very little inclination. When first invited to do this, he had regarded the task seriously enough, as he always did regard such work, and he completed his sermon for the occasion before he left Framley; but, since that, an air of ridicule had been thrown over the whole affair, in which he had joined without much thinking of his own sermon, and this made him now heartily wish that he could choose a discourse upon any other subject. He knew well that the very points on which he had most insisted, were those which had drawn most mirth from Miss Dunstable and Mrs. Smith, and had oftenest provoked his own laughter; and how was he now to preach on those matters in a fitting mood, knowing, as he would know, that those two ladies would be looking at him, would endeavour to catch his eye, and would turn him into ridicule as they had already turned the lecturer? In this he did injustice to one of the ladies, unconsciously. Miss Dunstable, with all her aptitude for mirth, and we may almost fairly say for frolic, was in no way inclined to ridicule religion or anything which she thought to appertain to it. It may be presumed that among such things she did not include Mrs. Proudie, as she was willing enough to laugh at that lady; but Mark, had he known her better, might have been sure that she would have sat out his sermon with perfect propriety.

As it was, however, he did feel considerable uneasiness; and in the morning he got up early, with the view of seeing what might be done in the way of emendation. He cut out those parts which referred most specially to the islands, – he rejected altogether those names over which they had all laughed together so heartily, – and he inserted a string of general remarks, very useful, no doubt, which he flattered himself would rob his sermon of all similarity to Harold Smith's lecture. He had, perhaps, hoped, when writing it, to create some little sensation; but now he would be quite satisfied if it passed without remark. But his troubles for that Sunday were destined to be many. It had been arranged that the party at the hotel should breakfast at eight and start at half-past eight punctually, so as to enable them to reach Chaldicotes in ample time to arrange their dresses before they went to church. The church stood in the grounds, close to that long formal avenue of lime trees, but within the front gates. Their walk, therefore, after reaching Mr. Sowerby's house, would not be long.

Mrs. Proudie, who was herself an early body, would not hear of her guest – and he a clergyman – going out to the inn for his breakfast on a Sunday morning. As regarded that Sabbath-day journey to Chaldicotes, to that she had given her assent, no doubt with much uneasiness of mind; but let them have as little desecration as possible. It was therefore an understood thing that he was to return with his friends; but he should not go without the advantage of family prayers and family breakfast. And so Mrs. Proudie on retiring to rest gave the necessary orders, to the great annoyance of her household.

To the great annoyance, at least, of her servants! The bishop himself did not make his appearance till a much later hour. He in all things now supported his wife's rule; in all things, now, I say; for there had been a moment, when in the first flush and pride of his episcopacy, other ideas had filled his mind. Now, however, he gave no opposition to that good woman with whom Providence had blessed him; and in return for such conduct that good woman administered in all things to his little personal comforts. With what surprise did the bishop now look back upon that unholy war which he had once been tempted to wage against the wife of his bosom? Nor did any of the Miss Proudies show themselves at that early hour. They, perhaps, were absent on a different ground. With them Mrs. Proudie had not been so successful as with the bishop. They had wills of their own which became stronger and stronger every day. Of the three with whom Mrs. Proudie was blessed one was already in a position to exercise that will in a legitimate way over a very excellent young clergyman in the diocese, the Rev. Optimus Grey; but the other two, having as yet no such opening for their powers of command, were perhaps a little too much inclined to keep themselves in practice at home. But at half-past seven punctually Mrs. Proudie was there, and so was the domestic chaplain; so was Mr. Robarts, and so were the household servants – all excepting one lazy recreant. 'Where is Thomas?' said she of the Argus eyes, standing up with her book of family prayers in her hand. 'So please you, ma'am, Tummas be bad with the tooth-ache.' 'Tooth-ache!' exclaimed Mrs. Proudie; but her eyes said more terrible things than that. 'Let Thomas come to me before church.' And then they proceeded to prayers. These were read by the chaplain, as it was proper and decent that they should be: but I cannot but think that Mrs. Proudie a little exceeded her office in taking upon herself to pronounce the blessing when the prayers were over. She did it, however, in a clear, sonorous voice, and perhaps with more personal dignity than was within the chaplain's compass.

Mrs. Proudie was rather stern at breakfast, and the vicar of Framley felt an unaccountable desire to get out of the house. In the first place she was not dressed with her usual punctilious attention to the proprieties of her high situation. It was evident that there was to be a further toilet before she sailed up the middle of the cathedral choir. She had on a large loose cap with no other strings than those which were wanted for tying it beneath her chin, a cap with which the household and the chaplain were well acquainted, but which seemed ungracious in the eyes of Mr. Robarts after all the well-dressed holiday doings of the last week. She wore also a large, loose, dark-coloured wrapper, which came well up round her neck, and which was not buoyed out, as were her dresses in general, with an under mechanism of petticoats. It clung to her closely, and added to the inflexibility of her general appearance. And then she had encased her feet in large carpet slippers, which no doubt were comfortable, but which struck her visitor as being strange and unsightly. 'Do you find a difficulty in getting your people together for early morning prayers?' she said, as she commenced her operations with the teapot.

'I can't say that I do,' said Mark. 'But then we are seldom so early as this.'

'Parish clergymen should be early, I think,' said she. 'It sets a good example in the village.'

'I am thinking of having morning prayers in the church,' said Mr. Robarts.

'That's nonsense,' said Mrs. Proudie, 'and usually means worse than nonsense. I know what that comes to. If you have three services on Sunday and domestic prayers at home, you do very well.' And so saying she handed him his cup.

'But I have not three services on Sunday, Mrs. Proudie.'

'Then I think you should have. Where can the poor people be so well off on Sundays as in church? The bishop intends to express a very strong opinion on this subject in his next charge; and then I am sure you will attend to his wishes.' To this Mark made no answer, but devoted himself to his egg.

'I suppose you have not a very large establishment at Framley?' asked Mrs. Proudie.

'What, at the parsonage?'

'Yes; you live at the parsonage, don't you?'

'Certainly – well; not very large, Mrs. Proudie; just enough to do the work, make things comfortable, and look after the children.'

'It is a very fine living,' said she; 'very fine. I don't remember that we have anything so good ourselves, – except it is Plumstead, the archdeacon's place. He has managed to butter his bread pretty well.'

'His father was Bishop of Barchester.'

'Oh, yes, I know all about him. Only for that he would barely have risen to be an archdeacon, I suspect. Let me see; yours is £800, is it not, Mr. Robarts? And you such a young man! I suppose you have insured your life highly.'

'Pretty well, Mrs. Proudie.'

'And then, too, your wife had some little fortune, had she not? We cannot all fall on our feet like that; can we, Mr. White?' and Mrs. Proudie in her playful way appealed to the chaplain. Mrs. Proudie was an imperious woman; but then so also was Lady Lufton; and it may therefore be said that Mr. Robarts ought to have been accustomed to feminine domination; but as he sat there munching his toast he could not but make a comparison between the two. Lady Lufton in her little attempts sometimes angered him; but he certainly thought, comparing the lay lady and the clerical together, that the rule of the former was the lighter and the pleasanter. But then Lady Lufton had given him a living and a wife, and Mrs. Proudie had given him nothing. Immediately after breakfast Mr. Robarts escaped to the Dragon of Wantly, partly because he had had enough of the matutinal Mrs. Proudie, and partly also in order that he might hurry his friends there. He was already becoming fidgety about the time, as Harold Smith had been on the preceding evening, and he did not give Mrs. Smith credit for much punctuality. When he arrived at the inn he asked if they had done breakfast, and was immediately told that not one of them was yet down. It was already half-past eight, and they ought to be now under weigh on the road. He immediately went to Mr. Sowerby's room, and found that gentleman shaving himself. 'Don't be a bit uneasy,' said Mr. Sowerby. 'You and Smith shall have my phaeton, and those horses will take you there in an hour. Not, however, but what we shall all be in time. We'll send round to the whole party and ferret them out.' And then Mr. Sowerby, having evoked manifold aid with various peals of the bell, sent messengers, male and female, flying to all the different rooms.

'I think I'll hire a gig and go over at once,' said Mark. 'It would not do for me to be late, you know.'

'It won't do for any of us to be late; and it's all nonsense about hiring a gig. It would be just throwing a sovereign away, and we should pass you on the road. Go down and see that the tea is made, and all that; and make them have the bill ready; and, Robarts, you may pay it too, if you like it. But I believe we may as well leave that to Baron Borneo – eh?' And then Mark did go down and make the tea, and he did order the bill; and then he walked about the room, looking at his watch, and nervously waiting for the footsteps of his friends. And as he was so employed, he bethought himself whether it was fit that he should be so doing on a Sunday morning; whether it was good that he should be waiting there, in painful anxiety, to gallop over a dozen miles in order that he might not be too late with his sermon; whether his own snug room at home, with Fanny opposite to him, and his bairns crawling on the floor, with his own preparations for his own quiet service, and the warm pressure of Lady Lufton's hands when that service should be over, was not better than all this. He could not afford not to know Harold Smith, and Mr. Sowerby, and the Duke of Omnium, he had said to himself. He had to look to rise in the world, as other men did. But what pleasure had come to him as yet from these intimacies? How much had he hitherto done towards his rising? To speak the truth he was not over well pleased with himself, as he made Mrs. Harold Smith's tea and ordered Mr. Sowerby's mutton-chops on that Sunday morning.

At a little after nine they all assembled; but even then he could not make the ladies understand that there was any cause for hurry; at least Mrs. Smith, who was the leader of the party, would not understand it. When Mark again talked of hiring a gig, Miss Dunstable indeed said that she would join him; and seemed to be so far earnest in the matter that Mr. Sowerby hurried through his second egg in order to prevent such a catastrophe. And then Mark absolutely did order the gig; whereupon Mrs. Smith remarked that in such case she need not hurry herself; but the waiter brought up word that all the horses of the hotel were out, excepting one pair, neither of which could go in single harness. Indeed, half of their stable establishment was already secured by Mr. Sowerby's own party. 'Then let me have the pair,' said Mark, almost frantic with delay.

'Nonsense, Robarts; we are ready now. He won't want them, James. Come, Supplehouse, have you done?'

'Then I am to hurry myself, am I?' said Mrs. Harold Smith. 'What changeable creatures you men are! May I be allowed half a cup more tea, Mr. Robarts?' Mark, who was now really angry, turned away to the window. There was no charity in these people, he said to himself. They knew the nature of his distress, and yet they only laughed at him. He did not, perhaps, reflect that he had assisted in the joke against Harold Smith on the previous evening. 'James,' said he, turning to the waiter. 'let me have that pair of horses immediately, if you please.'

'Yes, sir; round in fifteen minutes, sir: only Ned, sir, the post-boy, sir; I fear he's at his breakfast, sir; but we'll have him there in less than no time, sir!' But before Ned and the pair were there, Mrs. Smith had absolutely got her bonnet on, and at ten they started. Mark did share the phaeton with Harold Smith, but the phaeton did not go any faster than the other carriages. They led the way, indeed, but that was all; and when the vicar's watch told him that it was eleven, they were still a mile from Chaldicotes gate, although the horses were in a lather of steam; and they had only just entered the village when the church bells ceased to be heard.

'Come, you are in time, after all,' said Harold Smith. 'Better time than I was last night.' Robarts could not explain to him that the entry of a clergyman into church, of a clergyman who is going to assist in the service, should not be made at the last minute, that it should be staid and decorous, and not done in scrambling haste, with running feet and scant breath.

'I suppose we'll stop here, sir,' said the postilion, as he pulled up his horses short at the church-door, in the midst of the people who were congregated together ready for the service. But Mark had not anticipated being so late, and said at first that it was necessary that he should go on to the house; then, when the horses had again begun to move, he remembered that he could send for his gown, and as he got out of the carriage he gave his orders accordingly. And now the other two carriages were there, and so there was a noise and confusion at the door – very unseemly, as Mark felt it; and the gentlemen spoke in loud voices, and Mrs. Harold Smith declared that she had no Prayer-Book, and was much too tired to go in at present; she would go home and rest herself, she said. And two other ladies of the party did so also, leaving Miss Dunstable to go alone; – for which, however, she did not care one button. And then one of the party, who had a nasty habit of swearing, cursed at something as he walked in close to Mark's elbow; and so they made their way up the church as the Absolution was being read, and Mark Robarts felt thoroughly ashamed of himself. If his rising in the world brought him in contact with such things as these, would it not be better for him that he should do without rising? His sermon went off without any special notice. Mrs. Harold Smith was not there, much to his satisfaction; and the others who were did not seem to pay any special attention to it. The subject had lost its novelty, except with the ordinary church congregation, the farmers and labourers of the parish; and the 'quality' in the squire's great pew were content to show their sympathy by a moderate subscription. Miss Dunstable, however, gave a ten-pound note, which swelled up the sum total to a respectable amount – for such a place as Chaldicotes.

'And now I hope I may never hear another word about New Guinea,' said Mr. Sowerby, as they all clustered round the drawing-room fire after church. 'That subject may be regarded as having been killed and buried; eh, Harold?'

'Certainly murdered last night,' said Mrs. Harold, 'by that awful woman, Mrs. Proudie.'

'I wonder you did not make a dash at her and pull her out of the arm-chair,' said Miss Dunstable. 'I was expecting it, and thought that I should come to grief in the scrimmage.'

'I never knew a lady do such a brazen-faced thing before,' said Miss Kerrigy, a travelling friend of Miss Dunstable's.

'Nor I – never; in a public place, too,' said Dr. Easyman, a medical gentleman, who also often accompanied her.

'As for brass,' said Mr. Supplehouse, 'she would never stop at anything for want of that. It is well that she has enough, for the poor bishop is but badly provided.'

'I hardly heard what it was she did say,' said Harold Smith; 'so I could not answer her, you know. Something about Sundays, I believe.'

'She hoped you would not put the South Sea islanders up to Sabbath travelling,' said Mr. Sowerby.

'And specially begged that you would establish Lord's day schools,' said Mrs. Smith; and then they all went to work and picked Mrs. Proudie to pieces from the top ribbon of her cap down to the sole of her slipper.

'And then she expects the poor parsons to fall in love with her daughters. That's the hardest thing of all,' said Miss Dunstable. But, on the whole, when our vicar went to bed he did not feel that he had spent a profitable Sunday.

CHAPTER VIII

Gatherum Castle

ON the Tuesday morning Mark did receive his wife's letter, and the ten-pound note, whereby a strong proof was given of the honesty of the post-office people in Barsetshire. That letter, written as it had been in a hurry, while Robin post-boy was drinking a single mug of beer, – well, what of it if it was half filled a second time? – was nevertheless eloquent of his wife's love and of her great triumph. 'I have only half a moment to send you the money,' she said, 'for the postman is here waiting. When I see you I'll explain why I am so hurried. Let me know that you get it safe. It is all right now, and Lady Lufton was here not a minute ago. She did not quite like it; about Gatherum Castle, I mean; but you'll hear *nothing about it*. Only remember that *you must dine* at Framley Court on Wednesday week. *I have promised for you*. You will; won't you, dearest? I shall come and fetch you away if you attempt to stay longer than you have said. But I'm sure you won't. God bless you, my own one! Mr. Jones gave us the same sermon he preached the second Sunday after Easter. Twice in the same year is too often. God bless you! The children *are quite well*. Mark sends a big kiss. – Your own F.'

Robarts, as he read this letter and crumpled the note up into his pocket, felt that it was much more satisfactory than he deserved. He knew that there must have been a fight, and that his wife, fighting loyally on his behalf, had got the best of it; and he knew also that her victory had not been owing to the goodness of her cause. He frequently declared to himself that he would not be afraid of Lady Lufton; but nevertheless these tidings that no reproaches were to be made to him afforded him great relief. On the following Friday they all went to the duke's, and found that the bishop and Mrs. Proudie were there before them; as were also sundry other people, mostly of some note either in the estimation of the world at large or of that of West Barsetshire. Lord Boanerges was there, an old man who would have his own way in everything, and who was regarded by all men – apparently even by the duke himself – as an intellectual king, by no means of the constitutional kind – as an intellectual emperor, rather, who took upon himself to rule all questions of mind without the assistance of any ministers whatever. And Baron Brawl was of the party, one of Her Majesty's puisne Judges, as jovial a guest as ever entered a country house; but given to be rather sharp withal in his jovialities. And there was Mr. Green Walker, a young but rising man, the same who lectured not long since on a popular subject to his constituents at the Crewe Junction. Mr. Green Walker was a nephew of the Marchioness of Hartletop, and the Marchioness of Hartletop was a friend of the Duke of Omnium's. Mr. Mark Robarts was certainly elated when he ascertained who composed the company of which he had been so earnestly pressed to make a portion. Would it have been wise in him to forgo this on account of the prejudices of Lady Lufton?

As the guests were so many and so great, the huge front portals of Gatherum Castle were thrown open, and the vast hall, adorned with trophies – with marble busts from Italy and armour from Wardour Street – was thronged with gentlemen and ladies, and gave forth unwonted echoes to many a footstep. His grace himself, when Mark arrived there with Sowerby and Miss Dunstable – for in this instance Miss Dunstable did travel in the phaeton, while Mark occupied a seat in the dicky – his grace himself was at this moment in the drawing-room, and nothing could exceed his urbanity.

'Oh, Miss Dunstable,' he said, taking that lady by the hand, and leading her up to the fire, 'now I feel for the first time that Gatherum Castle has not been built for nothing.'

'Nobody ever supposed it was, your grace,' said Miss Dunstable. 'I am sure the architect did not think so when his bill was paid.' And Miss Dunstable put her toes up on the fender to warm them with as much self-possession as though her father had been a duke also, instead of a quack doctor.

'We have given the strictest orders about the parrot,' said the duke –'

'Ah! but I have not brought him after all,' said Miss Dunstable.

–'and I have had an aviary built on purpose, – just such as parrots are used to in their own country. Well, Miss Dunstable, I do call that unkind. Is it too late to send for him?'

'He and Dr. Easyman are travelling together. The truth was, I could not rob the doctor of his companion.'

'Why? I have had another aviary built for him. I declare, Miss Dunstable, the honour you are doing me is shorn of half its glory. But the poodle – I still trust in the poodle.'

'And your grace's trust shall not in that respect be in vain. Where is he, I wonder?' And Miss Dunstable looked round as though she expected that somebody would certainly have brought her dog in after her. 'I declare I must go and look for him, – only think if they were to put him among your grace's dogs, – how his morals would be destroyed!'

'Miss Dunstable, is that intended to be personal?' but the lady had turned away from the fire, and the duke was able to welcome his other guests. This he did with much courtesy. 'Sowerby,' he said, 'I am glad to find that you have survived the lecture. I can assure you I had fears for you.'

'I was brought back to life after considerable delay by the administration of tonics at the Dragon of Wantly. Will your grace allow me to present to you Mr. Robarts, who on that occasion was not so fortunate. It was found necessary to carry him off to the palace, where he was obliged to undergo very vigorous treatment.' And then the duke shook hands with Mr. Robarts, assuring him that he was most happy to make his acquaintance. He had often heard of him since he came into the country; and then he asked after Lord Lufton, regretting that he had been unable to induce his lordship to come to Gatherum Castle.

'But you had a diversion at the lecture, I am told,' continued the duke. 'There was a second performer, was there not, who almost eclipsed poor Harold Smith?' And then Mr. Sowerby gave an amusing sketch of the little Proudie episode.

'It has, of course, ruined your brother-in-law for ever as a lecturer,' said the duke, laughing.

'If so, we shall feel ourselves under the deepest obligations to Mrs. Proudie,' said Mr. Sowerby. And then Harold Smith himself came up and received the duke's sincere and hearty congratulations on the success of his enterprise at Barchester. Mark Robarts had now turned away, and his attention was suddenly arrested by the loud voice of Miss Dunstable, who had stumbled across some very dear friends in her passage through the rooms, and who by no means hid from the public her delight upon the occasion.

'Well – well – well!' she exclaimed, and then she seized upon a very quiet-looking, well-dressed, attractive young woman who was walking towards her, in company with a gentleman. The gentleman and lady, as it turned out, were husband and wife. 'Well – well – well! I hardly hoped for this.' And then she took hold of the lady and kissed her enthusiastically, and after that grasped both the gentleman's hands, shaking them stoutly.

'And what a deal I shall have to say to you!' she went on. 'You'll upset all my other plans. But, Mary, my dear, how long are you going to stay here? I go – let me see – I forget when, but it's all put down in a book upstairs. But the next stage is at Mrs. Proudie's. I shan't meet you there, I suppose. And now, Frank, how's the governor?' The gentleman called Frank declared that the governor was all right – 'mad about the hounds, of course, you know.'

'Well, my dear, that's better than the hounds being mad about him, like the poor gentleman they've put into a statue. But talking of hounds, Frank, how badly they manage their foxes at Chaldicotes! I was out hunting all one day –'

'You out hunting!' said the lady called Mary.

'And why shouldn't I go out hunting? I'll tell you what, Mrs. Proudie was out hunting too. But they didn't catch a single fox; and, if you must have the truth, it seemed to me to be rather slow.'

'You were in the wrong division of the county,' said the gentleman called Frank.

'Of course I was. When I really want to practise hunting I'll go to Greshamsbury; not a doubt about that.'

'Or to Boxall Hill,' said the lady; 'you'll find quite as much zeal there as at Greshamsbury.'

'And more discretion, you should add,' said the gentleman.

'Ha! ha! ha!' laughed Miss Dunstable; 'your discretion indeed! But you have not told me a word about Lady Arabella.'

'My mother is quite well,' said the gentleman.

'And the doctor? By the by, my dear, I've had such a letter from the doctor; only two days ago. I'll show it you upstairs to-morrow. But mind, it must be a positive secret. If he goes on in this way he'll get himself into the Tower, or Coventry, or a blue-book, or some dreadful place.'

'Why; what has he said?'

'Never you mind, Master Frank: I don't mean to show you the letter, you may be sure of that. But if your wife will swear three times on a poker and tongs that she won't reveal, I'll show it to her. And so you are quite settled at Boxall Hill, are you?'

'Frank's horses are settled; and the dogs nearly so,' said Frank's wife; 'but I can't boast much of anything else yet.'

'Well, there's a good time coming. I must go and change my things now. But, Mary, mind you get near me this evening; I have such a deal to say to you.' And then Miss Dunstable marched out of the room.

All this had been said in so loud a voice that it was, as a matter of course, overhead by Mark Robarts – that part of the conversation of course I mean which had come from Miss Dunstable. And then Mark learned that this was young Frank Gresham of Boxall Hill, son of old Mr. Gresham of Greshamsbury. Frank had lately married a great heiress; a greater heiress, men said, even than Miss Dunstable; and as the marriage was hardly as yet more than six months old the Barsetshire world was still full of it.

'The two heiresses seem to be very loving, don't they?' said Mr. Supplehouse. 'Birds of a feather flock together, you know. But they did say some little time ago that young Gresham was to have married Miss Dunstable herself.'

'Miss Dunstable! why, she might almost be his mother,' said Mark.

'That makes but little difference. He was obliged to marry money, and I believe there is no doubt that he did at one time propose to Miss Dunstable.'

'I have had a letter from Lufton,' Mr. Sowerby said to him the next morning. 'He declares that the delay was all your fault. You were to have told Lady Lufton before he did anything, and he was waiting to write about it till he heard from you. It seems that you never said a word to her ladyship on the subject.'

'I never did, certainly. My commission from Lufton was to break the matter to her when I found her in a proper humour for receiving it. If you knew Lady Lufton as well as I do, you would know that it is not every day that she would be in a humour for such tidings.'

'And so I was to be kept waiting indefinitely because you two between you were afraid of an old woman! However, I have not a word to say against her, and the matter is settled now.'

'Has the farm been sold?'

'Not a bit of it. The dowager could not bring her mind to suffer such profanation for the Lufton acres, and so she sold five thousand pounds out of the funds and sent the money to Lufton as a present; – sent it to him without saying a word, only hoping that it would suffice for his wants. I wish I had a mother, I know.'

Mark found it impossible at the moment to make any remark upon what had been told him, but he felt a sudden qualm of conscience and a wish that he was at Framley instead of at Gatherum Castle at the present moment. He knew a good deal respecting Lady Lufton's income and the manner in which it was spent. It was very handsome for a single lady, but then she lived in a free and open-handed style; her charities were noble; there was no reason why she should save money, and her annual income was usually spent within the year. Mark knew this, and he knew also that nothing short of an impossibility to maintain them would induce her to lessen her charities. She had now given away a portion of her principal to save the property of her son – her son, who was so much more opulent than herself, – upon whose means, too, the world made fewer effectual claims. And Mark knew, too, something of the purpose for which this money had gone. There had been unsettled gambling claims between Sowerby and Lord Lufton, originating in affairs of the turf. It had now been going on for four years, almost from the period when Lord Lufton had become of age. He had before now spoken to Robarts on the matter with much bitter anger, alleging that Mr. Sowerby was treating him unfairly, nay, dishonestly – that he was claiming money that was not due to him; and then he declared more than once that he would bring the matter before the Jockey Club. But Mark, knowing that Lord Lufton was not clear-sighted in these matters, and believing it to be impossible that Mr. Sowerby should actually endeavour to defraud his friend, had smoothed down the young lord's anger, and recommended him to get the case referred to some private arbiter. All this had afterwards been discussed between Robarts and Mr. Sowerby himself, and hence had originated their intimacy. The matter was so referred,

Mr. Sowerby naming the referee; and Lord Lufton, when the matter was given against him, took it easily. His anger was over by that time. 'I've been clean done among them,' he said to Mark, laughing; 'but it does not signify; a man must pay for his experience. Of course, Sowerby thinks it all right; I am bound to suppose so.' And then there had been some further delay as to the amount, and part of the money had been paid to a third person, and a bill had been given, and Heaven and the Jews only know how much money Lord Lufton had paid in all; and now it was ended by his handing over to some wretched villain of a money-dealer, on behalf of Mr. Sowerby, the enormous sum of five thousand pounds, which had been deducted from the means of his mother, Lady Lufton!

Mark, as he thought of all this, could not but feel a certain animosity against Mr. Sowerby – could not but suspect that he was a bad man. Nay, must he not have known that he was very bad? And yet he continued walking with him through the duke's grounds, still talking about Lord Lufton's affairs, and still listening with interest to what Sowerby told him of his own. 'No man was ever robbed as I have been,' said he. 'But I shall win through yet, in spite of them all. But those Jews, Mark' – he had become very intimate with him in these latter days – 'whatever you do, keep clear of them. Why, I could paper a room with their signatures; and yet I never had a claim upon one of them, though they always have claims on me!'

I have said above that this affair of Lord Lufton's was ended, but it now appeared to Mark that it was not *quite* ended. 'Tell Lufton, you know,' said Sowerby, 'that every bit of paper with his name has been taken up, except what that ruffian Tozer has. Tozer may have one bill, I believe, – something that was not given up when it was renewed. But I'll make my lawyer Gumption get that up. It may cost ten pounds or twenty pounds, not more. You'll remember that when you see Lufton, will you?'

'You'll see Lufton, in all probability, before I shall.'

'Oh, did I not tell you? He's going to Framley Court at once; you'll find him there when you return.'

'Find him at Framley?'

'Yes; this little *cadeau* from his mother has touched his filial heart. He is rushing home to Framley to pay back the dowager's hard moidores in soft caresses. I wish I had a mother; I know that.' And Mark still felt that he feared Mr. Sowerby, but he could not make up his mind to break away from him.

And there was much talk of politics just then at the castle. Not that the duke joined in it with any enthusiasm. He was a Whig – a huge mountain of a colossal Whig – all the world knew that. No opponent would have dreamed of tampering with his Whiggery, nor would any brother Whig have dreamed of doubting it. But he was a Whig who gave very little practical support to any set of men, and very little practical opposition to any other set. He was above troubling himself with such sublunar matters. At election time he supported, and always carried, Whig candidates: and in return he had been appointed lord lieutenant of the county by one Whig minister, and had received the Garter from another. But these things were matters of course to a Duke of Omnium. He was born to be a lord lieutenant and a Knight of the Garter. But not the less on account of his apathy, or rather quiescence, was it thought that Gatherum Castle was a fitting place in which politicians might express to each other their present hopes and future aims, and concoct together little plots in a half-serious and half-mocking way. Indeed it was hinted that Mr. Supplehouse and Harold Smith, with one or two others, were at Gatherum for this express purpose. Mr. Fothergill, too, was a noted politician, and was supposed to know the duke's mind well; and Mr. Green Walker, the nephew of the marchioness, was a young man whom the duke desired to have brought forward. Mr. Sowerby also was the duke's own member, and so the occasion suited well for the interchange of a few ideas.

The then prime minister, angry as many men were with him, had not been altogether unsuccessful. He had brought the Russian war to a close, which, if not glorious, was at any rate much more so than Englishmen at one time had ventured to hope. And he had had wonderful luck in that Indian Mutiny. It is true that many of those even who voted with him would declare that this was in no way attributable to him. Great men had risen in India and done all that. Even his minister there, the Governor whom he had sent out, was not allowed in those days any credit for the success which was achieved under his orders. There was great reason to doubt the man at the helm. But nevertheless he had been lucky. There is no merit in a public man like success! But now, when the evil days were well-nigh over, came the question whether he had not been too successful. When a man has nailed fortune to his chariot-wheels he is apt to travel about in rather a proud fashion. There are servants who think that their masters cannot do without them; and the public also may occasionally have some such servant. What if this too successful minister were one of them! And then a discreet, commonplace, zealous member of the Lower House does not like to be jeered at, when he does his duty by his constituents and asks a few questions. An all-successful minister who cannot keep his triumph to himself, but must needs drive about in a proud fashion, laughing at commonplace zealous members – laughing even occasionally at members who are by no means commonplace, which is outrageous! – may it not be as well to ostracize him for awhile?

'Had we not better throw in our shells against him?' says Mr. Harold Smith.

'Let us throw in our shells, by all means,' says Mr. Supplehouse, mindful as Juno of his despised charms. And when Mr. Supplehouse declares himself an enemy, men know how much it means. They know that that much-belaboured head of affairs must succumb to the terrible blows which are now in store for him. 'Yes, we will throw in our shells.' And Mr. Supplehouse rises from his chair with gleaming eyes. 'Has not Greece as noble sons as him? aye, and much nobler, traitor that he is. We must judge a man by his friends,' says Mr. Supplehouse; and he points away to the East, where our dear allies the French are supposed to live, and where our head of affairs is supposed to have too close an intimacy.

They all understand this, even Mr. Green Walker. 'I don't know that he is any good to any of us at all, now,' says the talented member for the Crewe Junction. 'He's a great deal too uppish to suit my book: and I know a great many people that think so too. There's my uncle –'

'He's the best fellow in the world,' said Mr. Fothergill, who felt, perhaps, that that coming revelation about Mr. Green Walker's uncle might not be of use to them; 'but the fact is one gets tired of the same man always. One does not like partridge every day. As for me, I have nothing to do with it myself; but I would certainly like to change the dish.'

'If we're merely to do as we are bid, and have no voice of our own, I don't see what's the good of going to the shop at all,' said Mr. Sowerby.

'Not the least use,' said Mr. Supplehouse. 'We are false to our constituents in submitting to such a dominion.'

'Let's have a change, then,' said Mr. Sowerby. 'The matter's pretty much in our own hands.'

'Altogether,' said Mr. Green Walker. 'That's what my uncle always says.'

'The Manchester man will only be too happy for the chance,' said Harold Smith.

'And as for the high and dry gentlemen,' said Mr. Sowerby, 'it's not very likely that they will object to pick up the fruit when we shake the tree.'

'As to picking up the fruit, that's as may be,' said Mr. Supplehouse. Was he not the man to save the nation; and if so, why should he not pick up the fruit himself? Had not the greatest power in the country pointed him out as such a saviour? What though the country at the present moment needed no more saving, might there not, nevertheless, be a good time coming? Were there not rumours of other wars still prevalent – if indeed the actual war then going on was being brought to a close without his assistance by some other species of salvation? He thought of that country to which he had pointed, and of that friend of his enemies, and remembered that there might be still work for a mighty saviour. The public mind was now awake, and understood what it was about. When a man gets into his head an idea that the public voice calls for him, it is astonishing how great becomes his trust in the wisdom of the public. *Vox populi, vox Dei.* 'Has it not been so always?' he says to himself, as he gets up and as he goes to bed. And then Mr. Supplehouse felt that he was the master mind there at Gatherum Castle, and that those there were all puppets in his hand. It is such a pleasant thing to feel that one's friends are puppets, and that the strings are in one's own possession. But what if Mr. Supplehouse himself were a puppet? Some months afterwards, when the much-belaboured head of affairs was in very truth made to retire, when unkind shells were thrown in against him in great numbers, when he exclaimed, *'Et tu, Brute!'* till the words were stereotyped upon his lips, all men in all places talked much about the great Gatherum Castle confederation. The Duke of Omnium, the world said, had taken into his high consideration the state of affairs, and seeing with his eagle's eye that the welfare of his countrymen at large required that some great step should be initiated, he had at once summoned to his mansion many members of the Lower House, and some also of the House of Lords, – mention was here especially made of the all-venerable and all-wise Lord Boanerges; and men went on to say that there, in deep conclave, he had made known to them his views. It was thus agreed that the head of affairs, Whig as he was, must fall. The country required it, and the duke did his duty. This was the beginning, the world said, of that celebrated confederation, by which the ministry was overturned, and – as the *Goody Twoshoes* added – the country saved. But the *Jupiter* took all the credit to itself; and the *Jupiter* was not far wrong. All the credit was due to the *Jupiter* – in that, as in everything else.

In the meantime the Duke of Omnium entertained his guests in the quiet princely style, but did not condescend to have much conversation on politics either with Mr. Supplehouse or with Mr. Harold Smith. And as for Lord Boanerges, he spent the morning on which the above-described conversation took place in teaching Miss Dunstable to blow soap-bubbles on scientific principles.

'Dear, dear!' said Miss Dunstable, as sparks of knowledge came flying in upon her mind. 'I always thought that a soap-bubble was a soap-bubble, and I never asked the reason why. One doesn't, you know, my lord.'

'Pardon me, Miss Dunstable,' said the old lord, 'one does; but nine hundred and ninety-nine do not.'

'And the nine hundred and ninety-nine have the best of it,' said Miss Dunstable. 'What pleasure can one have in a ghost after one has seen the phosphorus rubbed on?'

'Quite true, my dear lady. "If ignorance be bliss, 'tis folly to be wise." It all lies in the "if." '

Then Miss Dunstable began to sing:–

' "What tho' I trace each herb and flower
That sips the morning dew –"

– you know the rest, my lord.' Lord Boanerges did know almost everything, but he did not know that; and so Miss Dunstable went on:–

' "Did I not own Jehovah's power
How vain were all I knew." '

'Exactly, exactly, Miss Dunstable,' said his lordship; 'but why not own the power and trace the flower as well?

perhaps one might help the other.' Upon the whole, I am afraid that Lord Boanerges got the best of it. But, then, that is his line. He has been getting the best of it all his life.

It was observed by all that the duke was especially attentive to young Mr. Frank Gresham, the gentleman on whom and on whose wife Miss Dunstable had seized so vehemently. This Mr. Gresham was the richest commoner in the country, and it was rumoured that at the next election he would be one of the members for the East Riding. Now the duke had little or nothing to do with the East Riding, and it was well known that young Gresham would be brought forward as a strong Conservative. But, nevertheless, his acres were so extensive and his money so plentiful that he was worth a duke's notice. Mr. Sowerby, also, was almost more than civil to him, as was natural, seeing that this very young man by a mere scratch of his pen could turn a scrap of paper into a bank-note of almost fabulous value.

'So you have the East Barsetshire hounds at Boxall Hill; have you not?' said the duke.

'The hounds are there,' said Frank. 'But I am not the master.'

'Oh! I understood –'

'My father has them. But he finds Boxall more centrical than Greshamsbury. The dogs and horses have to go shorter distances.'

'Boxall Hill is very centrical.'

'Oh, exactly!'

'And your young gorse coverts are doing well?'

'Pretty well – gorse won't thrive everywhere, I find. I wish it would.'

'That's just what I say to Fothergill; and then where there's much woodland you can't get the vermin to leave it.'

'But we haven't a tree at Boxall Hill,' said Mrs. Gresham.

'Ah, yes; you're new there, certainly; you've enough of it at Greshamsbury in all conscience. There's a larger extent of wood there than we have; isn't there, Fothergill?' Mr. Fothergill said that the Greshamsbury woods were very extensive, but that, perhaps, he thought –

'Oh, ah! I know,' said the duke. 'The Black Forest in its old days was nothing to Gatherum woods, according to Fothergill. And then, again, nothing in East Barsetshire could be equal to anything in West Barsetshire. Isn't that it; eh, Fothergill?' Mr. Fothergill professed that he had been brought up in that faith and intended to die in it.

'Your exotics at Boxall Hill are very fine, magnificent!' said Mr. Sowerby.

'I'd sooner have one full-grown oak standing in its pride alone,' said young Gresham, rather grandiloquently, 'than all the exotics in the world.'

'They'll come in due time,' said the duke.

'But the due time won't be in my days. And so they're going to cut down Chaldicotes Forest, are they, Mr. Sowerby?'

'Well, I can't tell you that. They are going to disforest it. I have been ranger since I was twenty-two, and I don't yet know whether that means cutting down.'

'Not only cutting down, but rooting up,' said Mr. Fothergill.

'It's a murderous shame,' said Frank Gresham; 'and I will say one thing, I don't think any but a Whig government would do it.'

'Ha, ha, ha!' laughed his grace. 'At any rate, I'm sure of this,' he said, 'that if a Conservative government did do so, the Whigs would be just as indignant as you are now.'

'I'll tell you what you ought to do, Mr. Gresham,' said Sowerby: 'put in an offer for the whole of the West Barsetshire Crown property; they will be very glad to sell it.'

'And we should be delighted to welcome you on this side of the border,' said the duke. Young Gresham did feel rather flattered. There were not many men in the county to whom such an offer could be made without an absurdity. It might be doubted whether the duke himself could purchase the Chase of Chaldicotes with ready money; but that he, Gresham, could do so – he and his wife between them – no man did doubt. And then Mr. Gresham thought of a former day when he had once been at Gatherum Castle. He had been poor enough then, and the duke had not treated him in the most courteous manner in the world. How hard it is for a rich man not to lean upon his riches! harder, indeed, than for a camel to go through the eye of a needle.

All Barsetshire knew – at any rate all West Barsetshire – that Miss Dunstable had been brought down in those parts in order that Mr. Sowerby might marry her. It was not surmised that Miss Dunstable herself had had any previous notice of this arrangement, but it was supposed that the thing would turn out as a matter of course. Mr. Sowerby had no money, but then he was witty, clever, good-looking, and a member of Parliament. He lived before the world, represented an old family, and had an old place. How could Miss Dunstable possibly do better? She was not so young now, and it was time that she should look about her. The suggestion, as regarded Mr. Sowerby, was certainly true, and was not the less so as regarded some of Mr. Sowerby's friends. His sister, Mrs. Harold Smith, had devoted herself to the work, and with this view had run up a dear friendship with Miss Dunstable. The bishop had intimated, nodding his head knowingly, that it would be a very good thing. Mrs. Proudie had given in her adherence. Mr. Supplehouse had been made to understand that it must be a case of 'Paws off' with him, as long as he remained in that part of the world; and even the duke himself had desired Fothergill to manage it.

'He owes me an enormous sum of money,' said the duke, who held all Mr. Sowerby's title-deeds, 'and I doubt whether the security will be sufficient.'

'Your grace will find the security quite sufficient,' said Mr. Fothergill; 'but nevertheless it would be a good match.'

'Very good,' said the duke. And then it became Mr. Fothergill's duty to see that Mr. Sowerby and Miss Dunstable became man and wife as speedily as possible. Some of the party, who were more wide awake than others, declared that he had made the offer; others, that he was just going to do so; and one very knowing lady went so far at one time as to say that he was making it at that moment. Bets also were laid as to the lady's answer, as to the terms of the settlement, and as to the period of the marriage – of all which poor Miss Dunstable of course knew nothing. Mr. Sowerby, in spite of the publicity of his proceedings, proceeded in the matter very well. He said little about it to those who joked with him, but carried on the fight with what best knowledge he had in such matters. But so much it is given to us to declare with certainty, that he had not proposed on the evening previous to the morning fixed for the departure of Mark Robarts. During the last two days Mr. Sowerby's intimacy with Mark had grown warmer and warmer. He had talked to the vicar confidentially about the doings of these bigwigs now present at the castle, as though there were no other guest there with whom he could speak in so free a manner. He confided, it seemed, much more in Mark than in his brother-in-law, Harold Smith, or in any of his brother members of Parliament, and had altogether opened his heart to him in this affair of his anticipated marriage. Now Mr. Sowerby was a man of mark in the world, and all this flattered our young clergyman not a little. On that evening before Robarts went away Sowerby asked him to come up into his bedroom when the whole party was breaking up, and there got him into an easy chair, while he, Sowerby, walked up and down the room.

'You can hardly tell, my dear fellow,' said he, 'the state of nervous anxiety in which this puts me.'

'Why don't you ask her and have done with it? She seems to me to be fond of your society.'

'Ah, it is not that only; there are wheels within wheels:' and then he walked once or twice up and down the room, during which Mark thought that he might as well go to bed.

'Not that I mind telling you everything,' said Sowerby. 'I am infernally hard up for a little ready money just at the present moment. It may be, and indeed I think it will be, the case that I shall be ruined in this matter for the want of it.'

'Could not Harold Smith give it you?'

'Ha, ha, ha! you don't know Harold Smith. Did you ever hear of his lending a man a shilling in his life?'

'Or Supplehouse?'

'Lord love you! You see me and Supplehouse together here, and he comes and stays at my house, and all that; but Supplehouse and I are no friends. Look you here, Mark – I would do more for your little finger than for his whole hand, including the pen which he holds in it. Fothergill indeed might – but then I know Fothergill is pressed himself at the present moment. It is deuced hard, isn't it? I must give up the whole game if I can't put my hand upon £400 within the next two days.'

'Ask her for it, herself.'

'What, the woman I wish to marry! No, Mark, I'm not quite come to that. I would sooner lose her than that.' Mark sat silent, gazing at the fire and wishing that he was in his own bedroom. He had an idea that Mr. Sowerby wished him to produce this £400, and he knew also that he had not £400 in the world, and that if he had he would be acting very foolishly to give it to Mr. Sowerby. But nevertheless he felt half fascinated by the man, and half afraid of him.

'Lufton owes it to me to do more than this,' continued Mr. Sowerby, 'but then Lufton is not here.'

'Why, he has just paid five thousand pounds for you.'

'Paid five thousand pounds for me! Indeed he has done no such thing: not a sixpence of it came into my hands. Believe me, Mark, you don't know the whole of that yet. Not that I mean to say a word against Lufton. He is the soul of honour; though so deucedly dilatory in money matters. He thought he was right all through that affair, but no man was ever so confoundedly wrong. Why, don't you remember that that was the very view you took of it yourself?'

'I remember saying that I thought he was mistaken.'

'Of course he was mistaken. And dearly the mistake cost me; I had to make good the money for two or three years. And my property is not like his – I wish it were.'

'Marry Miss Dunstable, and that will set it all right for you.'

'Ah! so I would if I had this money. At any rate I would bring it to the point. Now, I tell you what, Mark, if you'll assist me at this strait I'll never forget it. And the time will come round when I may be able to do something for you.'

'I have not got a hundred, no, not fifty pounds by me in the world.'

'Of course you've not. Men don't walk about the streets with £400 in their pockets. I don't suppose there's a single man here in the house with such a sum at his bankers', unless it be the duke.'

'What is it you want, then?'

'Why, your name, to be sure. Believe me, my dear fellow, I would not ask you really to put your hand into your pocket to such a tune as that. Allow me to draw on you for that amount at three months. Long before that time I shall be flush enough.' And then, before Mark could answer, he had a bill stamp and pen and ink out on the table before him, and was filling in the bill as though his friend had already given his consent.

'Upon my word, Sowerby, I had rather not do that.'

'Why? what are you afraid of?' – Mr. Sowerby asked this very sharply. 'Did you ever hear of my having neglected to take up a bill when it fell due?' Robarts thought that he had heard of such a thing; but in his confusion he was not exactly sure, and so he said nothing.

'No, my boy; I have not come to that. Look here: just you write, "Accepted, Mark Robarts," across that, and then you shall never hear of the transaction again; and you will have obliged me for ever.'

'As a clergyman it would be wrong of me,' said Robarts.

'As a clergyman! Come, Mark! If you don't like to do as much as that for a friend, say so; but don't let us have that sort of humbug. If there be one class of men whose names would be found more frequent on the backs of bills in the provincial banks than another, clergymen are that class. Come, old fellow, you won't throw me over when I am so hard pushed.' Mark Robarts took the pen and signed the bill. It was the first time in his life that he had ever done such an act. Sowerby then shook him cordially by the hand, and he walked off to his own bedroom a wretched man.

CHAPTER IX

The Vicar's Return

THE next morning Mr. Robarts took leave of all his grand friends with a heavy heart. He had lain awake half the night thinking of what he had done and trying to reconcile himself to his position. He had not well left Mr. Sowerby's room before he felt certain that at the end of three months he would again be troubled about that £400. As he went along the passage, all the man's known antecedents crowded upon him much quicker than he could remember them when seated in that arm-chair with the bill stamp before him, and the pen and ink ready to his hand. He remembered what Lord Lufton had told him – how he had complained of having been left in the lurch; he thought of all the stories current through the entire country as to the impossibility of getting money from Chaldicotes; he brought to mind the known character of the man, and then he knew that he must prepare himself to make good a portion at least of that heavy payment. Why had he come to this horrid place? Had he not everything at home at Framley which the heart of man could desire? No; the heart of man can desire deaneries – the heart, that is, of the man vicar; and the heart of the man dean can desire bishoprics; and before the eyes of the man bishop does there not loom the transcendental glory of Lambeth? He had owned to himself that he was ambitious; but he had to own to himself now also that he had hitherto taken but a sorry path towards the object of his ambition. On the next morning at breakfast-time, before his horse and gig arrived for him, no one was so bright as his friend Sowerby. 'So you are off, are you?' said he.

'Yes, I shall go this morning.'

'Say everything that's kind from me to Lufton. I may possibly see him out hunting; otherwise we shan't meet till the spring. As to my going to Framley, that's out of the question. Her ladyship would look for my tail, and swear that she smelt brimstone. By-bye, old fellow!'

The German student when he first made his bargain with the devil felt an indescribable attraction to his new friend; and such was the case now with Robarts. He shook Sowerby's hand very warmly, said that he hoped he should meet him soon somewhere, and professed himself specially anxious to hear how that affair with the lady came off. As he had made his bargain – as he had undertaken to pay nearly half a year's income for his dear friend – ought he not to have as much value as possible for his money? If the dear friendship of this flash member of Parliament did not represent that value, what else did do so? But then he felt, or fancied that he felt, that Mr. Sowerby did not care for him so much this morning as he had done on the previous evening. 'By-bye,' said Mr. Sowerby, but he spoke no word as to such future meetings, nor did he even promise to write. Mr. Sowerby probably had many things on his mind; and it might be that it behoved him, having finished one piece of business, immediately to look to another.

The sum for which Robarts had made himself responsible – which he so much feared that he would be called upon to pay – was very nearly half a year's income; and as yet he had not put by one shilling since he had been married. When he found himself settled in his parsonage, he found also that all the world regarded him as a rich man. He had taken the dictum of all the world as true, and had set himself to work to live comfortably. He had no absolute need of a curate; but he could afford the £70 – as Lady Lufton had said rather injudiciously; and by keeping Jones in the parish he would be acting charitably to a brother clergyman, and would also place himself in a more independent position. Lady Lufton had wished to see her pet clergyman well-to-do and comfortable; but now, as matters had turned out, she much regretted this affair of the curate. Mr. Jones, she said to herself, more than once, must be made to depart from Framley. He had given his wife a pony-carriage, and for himself he had a saddle-horse, and a second horse for his gig. A man in his position, well-to-do as he was, required as much as that. He had a footman also, and a gardener, and a groom. The two latter were absolutely necessary, but about the former there had been a question. His wife had been decidedly hostile to the footman; but in all such matters as that, to doubt is to be lost. When the footman had been discussed for a week it became quite clear to the master that he also was a necessary.

As he drove home that morning he pronounced to himself the doom of that footman, and the doom also of that saddle-horse. They at any rate should go. And then he would spend no more money in trips to Scotland; and above all, he would keep out of the bedrooms of impoverished members of Parliament at the witching hour of midnight. Such resolves did he make to himself as he drove home; and bethought himself wearily how that £400 might be made to be forthcoming. As to any assistance in the matter from Sowerby, – of that he gave himself no promise. But he almost felt himself happy again as his wife came out into the porch to meet him with a silk shawl over her head, and pretending to shiver as she watched him descending from his gig. 'My dear old man,' she said, as she led him into the warm drawing-room with all his wrappings still about him, 'you must be starved.' But Mark during the whole drive had been thinking too much of that transaction in Mr. Sowerby's bedroom to remember that the air was cold. Now he had his arm round his own dear Fanny's waist; but was he to tell her of that transaction? At any rate he would not do it now, while his two boys were in his arms, rubbing the moisture from his whiskers with their kisses. After all, what is there equal to that coming home?

'And so Lufton is here. I say, Frank, gently, old boy,' – Frank was his eldest son – 'you'll have baby into the fender.'

'Let me take baby; it's impossible to hold the two of them, they are so strong,' said the proud mother. 'Oh, yes, he came home early yesterday.'

'Have you seen him?'

'He was here yesterday, with her ladyship; and I lunched there to-day. The letter came, you know, in time to stop the Merediths. They don't go till to-morrow, so you will meet them after all. Sir George is wild about it, but Lady Lufton would have her way. You never saw her in such a state as she is.'

'Good spirits, eh?'

'I should think so. All Lord Lufton's horses are coming, and he's to be here till March.'

'Till March!'

'So her ladyship whispered to me. She could not conceal her triumph at his coming. He's going to give up Leicestershire this year altogether. I wonder what has brought it all about?' Mark knew very well what had brought it about; he had been made acquainted, as the reader has also, with the price at which Lady Lufton had purchased her son's visit. But no one had told Mrs. Robarts that the mother had made her son a present of five thousand pounds.

'She's in a good humour about everything now,' continued Fanny; 'so you need say nothing at all about Gatherum Castle.'

'But she was very angry when she first heard it; was she not?'

'Well, Mark, to tell the truth, she was; and we had quite a scene there up in her own room upstairs – Justinia and I. She had heard something else that she did not like at the same time; and then – but you know her way. She blazed up quite hot.'

'And said all manner of horrid things about me.'

'About the duke she did. You know she never did like the duke; and for the matter of that, neither do I. I tell you that fairly, Master Mark!'

'The duke is not so bad as he's painted.'

'Ah, that's what you say about another great person. However, he won't come here to trouble us, I suppose. And then I left her, not in the best temper in the world; for I blazed up too, you must know.'

'I am sure you did,' said Mark, pressing his arm round her waist.

'And then we were going to have a dreadful war, I thought; and I came home and wrote such a doleful letter to you. But what should happen when I had just closed it, but in came her ladyship – all alone, and –. But I can't tell you what she did or said, only she behaved beautifully; just like herself too; so full of love and truth and honesty. There's nobody like her, Mark; and she's better than all the dukes that ever wore – whatever dukes do wear.'

'Horns and hoofs; that's their usual apparel, according to you and Lady Lufton,' said he, remembering what Mr. Sowerby had said of himself.

'You may say what you like about me, Mark, but you shan't abuse Lady Lufton. And if horns and hoofs mean wickedness and dissipation, I believe it's not far wrong. But get off your big coat and make yourself comfortable.' And that was all the scolding that Mark Robarts got from his wife on the occasion of his great iniquity.

'I will certainly tell her about this bill transaction,' he said to himself; 'but not to-day; not till after I have seen Lufton.' That evening they dined at Framley Court, and there they met the young lord; they found also Lady Lufton still in high good-humour. Lord Lufton himself was a fine, bright-looking young man; not so tall as Mark Robarts, and with perhaps less intelligence marked on his face; but his features were finer, and there was in his countenance a thorough appearance of good-humour and sweet temper. It was, indeed, a pleasant face to look upon, and dearly Lady Lufton loved to gaze at it.

'Well, Mark, so you have been among the Philistines?' that was his lordship's first remark. Robarts laughed as he took his friend's hands, and bethought himself how truly that was the case; that he was, in very truth, already 'himself in bonds under Philistine yoke.' Alas, alas, it is very hard to break asunder the bonds of the latter-day Philistines. When a Samson does now and then pull a temple down about their ears, is he not sure to be engulfed in the ruin with them? There is no horse-leech that sticks so fast as your latter-day Philistine.

'So you have caught Sir George, after all,' said Lady Lufton; and that was nearly all she did say in allusion to his absence. There was afterwards some conversation about the lecture, and from her ladyship's remarks it certainly was apparent that she did not like the people among whom the vicar had been lately staying; but she said no word that was personal to him himself, or that could be taken as a reproach. The little episode of Mrs. Proudie's address in the lecture-room had already reached Framley, and it was only to be expected that Lady Lufton should enjoy the joke. She would affect to believe that the body of the lecture had been given by the bishop's wife; and afterwards, when Mark described her costume at that Sunday morning breakfast table, Lady Lufton would assume that such had been the dress in which she had exercised her faculties in public.

'I would have given a five-pound note to have heard it,' said Sir George.

'So would not I,' said Lady Lufton. 'When one hears of such things described so graphically as Mr. Robarts now tells it, one can hardly help laughing. But it would give me great pain to see the wife of one of our bishops place herself in such a situation. For he is a bishop after all.'

'Well, upon my word, my lady, I agree with Meredith,' said Lord Lufton. 'It must have been good fun. As it did happen, you know, – as the Church was doomed to the disgrace, – I should like to have heard it.'

'I know you would have been shocked, Ludovic.'

'I should have got over that in time, mother. It would have been like a bull-fight, I suppose – horrible to see, no doubt, but extremely interesting. And Harold Smith, Mark; what did he do all the while?'

'It didn't take so very long, you know,' said Robarts.

'And the poor bishop,' said Lady Meredith; 'how did he look? I really do pity him.'

'Well, he was asleep, I think.'

'What, slept through it all?' said Sir George.

'It awakened him; and then he jumped up and said something.'

'What, out loud, too?'

'Only one word, or so.'

'What a disgraceful scene!' said Lady Lufton. 'To those who remember the good old man who was in the diocese before him it is perfectly shocking. He confirmed you, Ludovic, and you ought to remember him. It was over at Barchester, and you went and lunched with him afterwards.'

'I do remember; and especially this, that I never ate such tarts in my life, before or since. The old man particularly called my attention to them, and seemed remarkably pleased that I concurred in his sentiments. There are no such tarts as those going in the palace, now, I'll be bound.'

'Mrs. Proudie will be very happy to do her best for you if you will go and try,' said Sir George.

'I beg that he will do no such thing,' said Lady Lufton; and that was the only severe word she said about any of Mark's visitings. As Sir George Meredith was there, Robarts could say nothing then to Lord Lufton about Mr. Sowerby and Mr. Sowerby's money affairs; but he did make an appointment for a *tête-à-tête* on the next morning.

'You must come down and see my nags, Mark; they came to-day. The Merediths will be off at twelve, and then we can have an hour together.' Mark said he would, and then went home with his wife under his arm.

'Well, now, is not she kind?' said Fanny, as soon as they were out on the gravel together.

'She is kind; kinder than I can tell you just at present. But did you ever know anything so bitter as she is to the poor bishop? And really the bishop is not so bad.'

'Yes; I know something much more bitter: and that is what she thinks of the bishop's wife. And you know, Mark, it was so unladylike, her getting up in that way. What must the people of Barchester think of her?'

'As far as I could see, the people of Barchester liked it.'

'Nonsense, Mark; they could not. But never mind that now. I want you to own that she is good.' And then Mrs. Robarts went on with another long eulogy on the dowager. Since that affair of the pardon-begging at the parsonage, Mrs. Robarts hardly knew how to think well enough of her friend. And the evening had been so pleasant after the dreadful storm and threatenings of hurricanes; her husband had been so well received after his lapse of judgement; the wounds that had looked so sore had been so thoroughly healed, and everything was so pleasant. How all of this would have been changed had she known of that little bill! At twelve the next morning the lord and the vicar were walking through the Framley stables together. Quite a commotion had been made there, for the larger portion of those buildings had of late years seldom been used. But now all was crowding and activity. Seven or eight very precious animals had followed Lord Lufton from Leicestershire, and all of them required dimensions that were thought to be rather excessive by the Framley old-fashioned groom. My lord, however, had a head man of his own who took the matter quite into his own hands. Mark, priest as he was, was quite worldly enough to be fond of a good horse; and for some little time allowed Lord Lufton to descant on the merit of this four-year-old filly, and that magnificent Rattlebones colt, out of a Mouse-trap mare; but he had other things that lay heavy on his mind, and after bestowing half an hour on the stud, he contrived to get his friend away to the shrubbery walks.

'So you have settled with Sowerby,' Robarts began by saying.

'Settled with him; yes, but do you know the price?'

'I believe that you have paid five thousand pounds.'

'Yes, and about three before; and that in a matter in which I did not really owe one shilling. Whatever I do in future, I'll keep out of Sowerby's grip.'

'But you don't think he has been unfair to you.'

'Mark, to tell you the truth I have banished the affair from my mind, and don't wish to take it up again. My mother has paid the money to save the property, and of course I must pay her back. But I think I may promise that I will not have any more money dealings with Sowerby. I will not say that he is dishonest, but at any rate he is sharp.'

'Well, Lufton; what will you say when I tell you that I have put my name to a bill for him, for four hundred pounds?'

'Say; why I should say –; but you're joking; a man in your position would never do such a thing.'

'But I have done it.' Lord Lufton gave a long low whistle.

'He asked me the last night that I was there, making a great favour of it, and declaring that no bill of his had ever yet been dishonoured.'

Lord Lufton whistled again. 'No bill of his dishonoured! Why, the pocket-books of the Jews are stuffed full of his dishonoured papers! And you have really given him your name for four hundred pounds?'

'I have certainly.'

'At what date?'

'Three months.'

'And have you thought where you are to get the money?'

'I know very well that I can't get it, not at least by that time. The bankers must renew it for me, and I must pay it by degrees. That is, if Sowerby really does not take it up.'

'It is just as likely that he will take up the National Debt.' Robarts then told him about the projected marriage with Miss Dunstable, giving it as his opinion that the lady would probably accept the gentleman.

'Not at all improbable,' said his lordship, 'for Sowerby is an agreeable fellow; and if it be so, he will have all that he wants for life. But his creditors will gain nothing. The duke, who has his title-deeds, will doubtless get his money, and the estate will in fact belong to the wife. But the small fry, such as you, will not get a shilling.' Poor Mark! He had had an inkling of this before; but it had hardly presented itself to him in such certain terms. It was, then, a positive fact, that in punishment for his weakness in having signed that bill he would have to pay, not only four hundred pounds, but four hundred pounds with interest, and expenses of renewal, and commission, and bill stamps. Yes; he had certainly got among the Philistines during that visit of his to the duke. It began to appear to him pretty clearly that it would have been better for him to have relinquished altogether the glories of Chaldicotes and Gatherum Castle.

And now, how was he to tell his wife?

CHAPTER X

Lucy Robarts

AND now, how was he to tell his wife? That was the consideration heavy on Mark Robarts's mind when last we left him; and he turned the matter often in his thoughts before he could bring himself to a resolution. At last he did do so, and one may say that it was not altogether a bad one, if only he could carry it out. He would ascertain in what bank that bill of his had been discounted. He would ask Sowerby, and if he could not learn from him, he would go to the three banks in Barchester. That it had been taken to one of them he felt tolerably certain. He would explain to the manager his conviction that he would have to make good the amount, his inability to do so at the end of the three months, and the whole state of his income; and then the banker would explain to him how the matter might be arranged. He thought that he could pay £50 every three months with interest. As soon as this should have been concerted with the banker, he would let his wife know all about it. Were he to tell her at the present moment, while the matter was all unsettled, the intelligence would frighten her into illness. But on the next morning there came to him tidings by the hands of Robin postman, which for a long while upset all his plans. The letter was from Exeter. His father had been taken ill, and had very quickly been pronounced to be in danger. That evening – the evening on which his sister wrote – the old man was much worse, and it was desirable that Mark should go off to Exeter as quickly as possible. Of course he went to Exeter – again leaving the Framley souls at the mercy of the Welsh Low Churchman. Framley is only four miles from Silverbridge, and at Silverbridge he was on the direct road to the West. He was, therefore, at Exeter before nightfall on that day. But, nevertheless, he arrived there too late to see his father again alive. The old man's illness had been sudden and rapid, and he expired without again seeing his eldest son. Mark arrived at the house of mourning just as they were learning to realize the full change in their position.

The doctor's career had been on the whole successful, but nevertheless he did not leave behind him as much money as the world had given him credit for possessing. Who ever does? Dr. Robarts had educated a large family, had always lived with every comfort, and had never possessed a shilling but what he had earned himself. A physician's fees come in, no doubt, with comfortable rapidity as soon as rich old gentlemen and middle-aged ladies begin to put their faith in him; but fees run out almost with equal rapidity when a wife and seven children are treated to everything that the world considers most desirable. Mark, we have seen, had been educated at Harrow and Oxford, and it may be said, therefore, that he had received his patrimony early in life. For Gerald Robarts, the second brother, a commission had been bought in a crack regiment. He also had been lucky, having lived and become a captain in the Crimea; and the purchase-money was lodged for his majority. And John Robarts, the youngest, was a clerk in the Petty Bag Office, and was already assistant private secretary to the Lord Petty Bag himself – a place of considerable trust, if not hitherto of large emolument; and on his education money had been spent freely, for in these days a young man cannot get into the Petty Bag Office without knowing at least three modern languages; and he must be well up in trigonometry too, in Bible theology, or in one dead language – at his option. And the doctor had four daughters. The two elder were married, including that Blanche with whom Lord Lufton was to have fallen in love at the vicar's wedding. A Devonshire squire had done this in the lord's place; but on marrying her it was necessary that he should have a few thousand pounds, two or three perhaps, and the old doctor had imagined that they should be forthcoming. The elder also had not been sent away from the paternal mansion quite empty-handed. There were, therefore, at the time of the doctor's death two children left at home, of whom one only, Lucy, the younger, will come much across us in the course of our story.

Mark stayed for ten days at Exeter, he and the Devonshire squire having been named as executors in the will. In this document it was explained that the doctor trusted that provision had been made for most of his children. As for his dear son Mark, he said, he was aware that he need be under no uneasiness. On hearing this read Mark smiled sweetly, and looked very gracious; but, nevertheless, his heart did sink somewhat within him, for there had been a hope that a small windfall, coming now so opportunely might enable him to rid himself at once of that dreadful Sowerby incubus. And then the will went on to declare that Mary, and Gerald, and Blanche, had also, by God's providence, been placed beyond want. And here, looking into the squire's face, one might have thought that his heart fell a little also; for he had not so full a command of his feelings as his brother-in-law, who had been so much more before the world. To John, the assistant private secretary, was left a legacy of a thousand pounds; and to Jane and Lucy certain sums in certain four per cents which were quite sufficient to add an efficient value to the hands of those young ladies in the eyes of most prudent young would-be Benedicts. Over and beyond this there was nothing but the furniture, which he desired might be sold, and the proceeds divided among them all. It might come to sixty or seventy pounds a piece, and pay the expenses incidental on his death. And then all men and women there and thereabouts said that old Dr. Robarts had done well. His life had been good and prosperous, and his will was just. And Mark, among others, so declared – and was so convinced in spite of his own little disappointment. And on the third morning after the reading of the will Squire Crowdy, of Creamclotted Hall, altogether got over his grief, and said that it was all right. And then it was decided that Jane should go home with him – for there was a brother squire who, it was thought, might have an eye to Jane; – and Lucy, the younger, should be taken to Framley parsonage. In a fortnight from the receipt of that letter Mark arrived at his own house with his sister Lucy under his wing.

All this interfered greatly with Mark's wise resolution as to the Sowerby-bill incubus. In the first place, he could not get to Barchester as soon as he had intended, and then an idea came across him that possibly it might be well that he should borrow the money of his brother John, explaining the circumstances, of course, and paying him due interest. But he had not liked to broach the subject when they were there in Exeter, standing, as it were, over their father's grave, and so the matter was postponed. There was still ample time for arrangement before the bill would come due, and he would not tell Fanny till he had made up his mind what that arrangement would be. It would kill her, he said to himself over and over again, were he to tell her of it without being able to tell her also that the means of liquidating the debt were to be forthcoming.

And now I must say a word about Lucy Robarts. If one might only go on without those descriptions how pleasant it would all be! But Lucy Robarts has to play a forward part in this little drama, and those who care for such matters must be made to understand something of her form and likeness. When last we mentioned her as appearing, though not in any prominent position, at her brother's wedding, she was only sixteen; but now, at the time of her father's death, somewhat over two years having since elapsed, she was nearly nineteen. Laying aside for the sake of clearness that indefinite term of girl – for girls are girls from the age of three up to forty-three, if not previously married – dropping that generic word, we may say that then, at that wedding of her brother, she was a child; and now, at the death of her father, she was a woman. Nothing, perhaps, adds so much to womanhood, turns the child so quickly into a woman, as such death-bed scenes as these. Hitherto but little had fallen to Lucy to do in the way of woman's duties. Of money transactions she had known nothing, beyond a jocose attempt to make her annual allowance of twenty-five pounds cover all her personal wants – an attempt which was made jocose by the loving bounty of her father. Her sister, who was three years her elder – for John came in between them – had managed the house; that is, she had made the tea and talked to the housekeeper about the dinners. But Lucy had sat at her father's elbow, had read to him of evenings when he went to sleep, had brought him his slippers and looked after the comforts of his easy chair. All this she had done as a child; but when she stood at the coffin head, and knelt at the coffin side, then she was a woman.

She was smaller in stature than either of her three sisters, to all of whom had been acceded the praise of being fine women – a eulogy which the people of Exeter, looking back at the elder sisters, and the general remembrance of them which pervaded the city, were not willing to extend to Lucy. 'Dear – dear!' had been said of her; 'poor Lucy is not like a Robarts at all; is she, now, Mrs. Pole?' – for as the daughters had become fine women, so had the sons grown into stalwart men. And then Mrs. Pole had answered: 'Not a bit; is she, now? Only think what Blanche was at her age. But she has fine eyes, for all that; and they do say she is the cleverest of them all.' And that, too, is so true a description of her that I do not know that I can add much to it. She was not like Blanche; for Blanche had a bright complexion, and a fine neck, and a noble bust, *et vera incessu patuit Dea* – a true goddess, that is, as far as the eye went. She had a grand idea, moreover, of an apple-pie, and had not reigned eighteen months at Creamclotted Hall before she knew all the mysteries of pigs and milk, and most of those appertaining to cider and green cheese.

Lucy had no neck at all worth speaking of, – no neck, I mean, that ever produced eloquence; she was brown, too, and had addicted herself in nowise, as she undoubtedly should have done, to larder utility. In regard to the neck and colour, poor girl, she could not help herself; but in that other respect she must be held as having wasted her opportunities. But then what eyes she had! Mrs. Pole was right there. They flashed upon you, not always softly; indeed not often softly if you were a stranger to her; but whether softly or savagely, with a brilliancy that dazzled you as you looked at them. And who shall say of what colour they were? Green, probably, for most eyes are green – green or grey, if green be thought uncomely for an eye-colour. But it was not their colour, but their fire, which struck one with such surprise.

Lucy Robarts was thoroughly a brunette. Sometimes the dark tint of her cheek was exquisitely rich and lovely, and the fringes of her eyes were long and soft, and her small teeth, which one so seldom saw, were white as pearls, and her hair, though short, was beautifully soft – by no means black, but yet of so dark a shade of brown. Blanche, too, was noted for fine teeth. They were white and regular and lofty as a new row of houses in a French city. But then when she laughed she was all teeth; as she was all neck when she sat at the piano. But Lucy's teeth! – it was only now and again, when in some sudden burst of wonder she would sit for a moment with her lips apart, that the fine finished lines and dainty pearl-white colour of that perfect set of ivory could be seen. Mrs. Pole would have said a word of her teeth also, but that to her they had never been made visible. 'But they do say that she is the cleverest of them all,' Mrs. Pole had added, very properly.

The people of Exeter had expressed such an opinion, and had been quite just in doing so. I do not know how it happens, but it always does happen, that everybody in every small town knows which is the brightest-witted in every family. In this respect Mrs. Pole had only expressed public opinion, and public opinion was right. Lucy Robarts was blessed with an intelligence keener than that of her brothers or sisters.

'To tell the truth, Mark, I admire Lucy more than I do Blanche.' This had been said by Mrs. Robarts within a few hours of her having assumed that name. 'She's not a beauty, I know, but yet I do.'

'My dearest Fanny!' Mark had answered in a tone of surprise.

'I do then; of course people won't think so; but I never seem to care about regular beauties. Perhaps I envy them too much.' What Mark said next need not be repeated, but everybody may be sure that it contained some gross flattery for his young bride. He remembered this, however, and had always called Lucy his wife's pet. Neither of the sisters had since that been at Framley; and though Fanny had spent a week at Exeter on the occasion of Blanche's marriage, it could hardly be said that she was very intimate with them. Nevertheless, when it became expedient that one of them should go to Framley, the remembrance of what his wife had said immediately induced Mark to make the offer to Lucy; and Jane, who was of a kindred soul with Blanche, was delighted to go to Creamclotted Hall. The acres of Heavybed House, down in that fat Totnes country, adjoined those of Creamclotted Hall, and Heavybed House still wanted a mistress.

Fanny was delighted when the news reached her. It would of course be proper that one of his sisters should live with Mark under their present circumstances, and she was happy to think that that quiet little bright-eyed creature was to come and nestle with her under the same roof. The children should so love her – only not quite so much as they loved mamma; and the snug little room that looks out over the porch, in which the chimney never smokes, should be made ready for her; and she should be allowed her share of driving the pony – which was a great sacrifice of self on the part of Mrs. Robarts – and Lady Lufton's best good-will should be bespoken. In fact, Lucy was not unfortunate in the destination that was laid out for her. Lady Lufton had of course heard of the doctor's death, and had sent all manner of kind messages to Mark, advising him not to hurry home by any means until everything was settled at Exeter. And then she was told of the new-comer that was expected in the parish. When she heard that it was Lucy, the younger, she also was satisfied; for Blanche's charms, though indisputable, had not been altogether to her taste. If a second Blanche were to arrive there what danger might there not be for young Lord Lufton! 'Quite right,' said her ladyship, 'just what he ought to do. I think I remember the young lady; rather small, is she not, and very retiring?'

'Rather small and very retiring. What a description!' said Lord Lufton.

'Never mind, Ludovic; some young ladies must be small, and some at least ought to be retiring. We shall be delighted to make her acquaintance.'

'I remember your other sister-in-law very well,' said Lord Lufton. 'She was a beautiful woman.'

'I don't think you will consider Lucy a beauty,' said Mrs. Robarts.

'Small, retiring, and –' so far Lord Lufton had gone, when Mrs. Robarts finished by the word, 'plain.' She had liked Lucy's face, but she had thought that others probably did not do so.

'Upon my word,' said Lady Lufton, 'you don't deserve to have a sister-in-law. I remember her very well, and can say that she is not plain. I was very much taken with her manner at your wedding, my dear, and thought more of her than I did of the beauty, I can tell you.'

'I must confess I do not remember her at all,' said his lordship. And so the conversation ended. And then at the end of the fortnight Mark arrived with his sister. They did not reach Framley till long after dark – somewhere between six and seven – and by this time it was December. There was snow on the ground, and frost in the air, and no moon, and cautious men when they went on the roads had their horses' shoes cocked. Such being the state of the weather Mark's gig had been nearly filled with cloaks and shawls when it was sent over to Silverbridge. And a cart was sent for Lucy's luggage, and all manner of preparations had been made. Three times had Fanny gone herself to see that the fire burned brightly in the little room over the porch, and at the moment that the sound of the wheels was heard she was engaged in opening her son's mind as to the nature of an aunt. Hitherto papa and mamma and Lady Lufton were all that he had known, excepting, of course, the satellites of the nursery. And then in three minutes Lucy was standing by the fire. Those three minutes had been taken up in embraces between the husband and the wife. Let who would be brought as a visitor to the house, after a fortnight's absence, she would kiss him before she welcomed any one else. But then she turned to Lucy, and began to assist her with her cloaks.

'Oh, thank you,' said Lucy; 'I'm not cold, – not very at least. Don't trouble yourself: I can do it.' But here she had made a false boast, for her fingers had been so numbed that she could not do nor undo anything. They were all in black, of course; but the sombreness of Lucy's clothes struck Fanny much more than her own. They seemed to have swallowed her up in their blackness, and to have made her almost an emblem of death. She did not look up, but kept her face turned towards the fire, and seemed almost afraid of her position.

'She may say what she likes, Fanny,' said Mark, 'but she is very cold. And so am I, – cold enough. You had better go up with her to her room. We won't do much in the dressing way to-night; eh, Lucy?' In the bedroom Lucy thawed a little, and Fanny, as she kissed her, said to herself that she had been wrong as to that word 'plain.' Lucy, at any rate, was not plain.

'You will be used to us soon,' said Fanny, 'and then I hope we shall make you comfortable.' And she took her sister-in-law's hand and pressed it. Lucy looked up at her, and her eyes then were tender enough. 'I am sure I shall be happy here,' she said, 'with you. But – but – dear papa!' And then they got into each other's arms, and had a great bout of kissing and crying. 'Plain,' said Fanny to herself, as at last she got her guest's hair smoothed and the tears washed from her eyes – 'plain! She has the loveliest countenance that I ever looked at in my life!'

'Your sister is quite beautiful,' she said to Mark, as they talked her over alone before they went to sleep that night.

'No, she's not beautiful; but she's a very good girl, and clever enough too, in her sort of way.'

'I think her perfectly lovely. I never saw such eyes in my life before.'

'I'll leave her in your hands, then; you shall get her a husband.'

'That mayn't be so easy. I don't think she'd marry anybody.'

'Well, I hope not. But she seems to me to be exactly cut out for an old maid; – to be Aunt Lucy for ever and ever to your bairns.'

'And so she shall, with all my heart. But I don't think she will, very long. I have no doubt she will be hard to please; but if I were a man I should fall in love with her at once. Did you ever observe her teeth, Mark?'

'I don't think I ever did.'

'You wouldn't know whether any one had a tooth in their head, I believe.'

'No one except you, my dear; and I know all yours by heart.'

'You are a goose.'

'And a very sleepy one; so, if you please, I'll go to roost.' And thus there was nothing more said about Lucy's beauty on that occasion.

For the first two days Mrs. Robarts did not make much of her sister-in-law. Lucy, indeed, was not demonstrative: and she was, moreover, one of those few persons – for they are very few – who are contented to go on with their existence without making themselves the centre of any special outward circle. To the ordinary run of minds it is impossible not to do this. A man's own dinner is to himself so important that he cannot bring himself to believe that it is a matter utterly indifferent to every one else. A lady's collection of baby-clothes, in early years, and of house linen and curtain-fringes in later life, is so very interesting to her own eyes, that she cannot believe but what other people will rejoice to behold it. I would not, however, be held as regarding this tendency as evil. It leads to conversation of some sort among people, and perhaps to a kind of sympathy. Mrs. Jones will look at Mrs. White's linen chest, hoping that Mrs. White may be induced to look at hers. One can only pour out of a jug that which is in it. For the most of us, if we do not talk of ourselves, or at any rate of the individual circles of which we are the centres, we can talk of nothing. I cannot hold with those who wish to put down the insignificant chatter of the world. As for myself, I am always happy to look at Mrs. Jones's linen, and never omit an opportunity of giving her the details of my own dinners. But Lucy Robarts had not this gift. She had come there as a stranger into her sister-in-law's house, and at first seemed as though she would be contented in simply having her corner in thedrawing-room and her place at the parlour-table. She did not seem to need the comforts of condolence and open-hearted talking. I do not mean to say that she was moody, that she did not answer when she was spoken to, or that she took no notice of the children; but she did not at once throw herself and all her hopes and sorrows into Fanny's heart, as Fanny would have had her do.

Mrs. Robarts herself was what we call demonstrative. When she was angry with Lady Lufton she showed it. And as since that time her love and admiration for Lady Lufton had increased, she showed that also. When she was in any way displeased with her husband, she could not hide it, even though she tried to do so, and fancied herself successful; – no more than she could hide her warm, constant, overflowing woman's love. She could not walk through a room hanging on her husband's arm without seeming to proclaim to every one there that she thought him the best man in it. She was demonstrative, and therefore she was the more disappointed in that Lucy did not rush at once with all her cares into her open heart. 'She is so quiet,' Fanny said to her husband.

'That's her nature,' said Mark. 'She always was quiet as a child. While we were smashing everything, she would never crack a teacup.'

'I wish she would break something now,' said Fanny, 'and then perhaps we should get to talk about it.' But she did not on this account give over loving her sister-in-law. She probably valued her the more, unconsciously, for not having those aptitudes with which she herself was endowed. And then after two days Lady Lufton called: of course it may be supposed that Fanny had said a good deal to her new inmate about Lady Lufton. A neighbour of that kind in the country exercises so large an influence upon the whole tenor of one's life, that to abstain from such talk is out of the question. Mrs. Robarts had been brought up almost under the dowager's wing, and of course she regarded her as being worthy of much talking. Do not let persons on this account suppose that Mrs. Robarts was a tuft-hunter, or a toad-eater. If they do not see the difference they have yet got to study the earliest principles of human nature.

Lady Lufton called, and Lucy was struck dumb. Fanny was particularly anxious that her ladyship's first impression should be favourable, and to effect this, she especially endeavoured to throw the two together during that visit.

But in this she was unwise. Lady Lufton, however, had woman-craft enough not to be led into any egregious error by Lucy's silence. 'And what day will you come and dine with us?' said Lady Lufton, turning expressly to her old friend Fanny.

'Oh, do you name the day. We never have many engagements, you know.'

'Will Thursday do, Miss Robarts? You will meet nobody you know, only my son; so you need not regard it as going out. Fanny here will tell you that stepping over to Framley Court is no more going out, than when you go from one room to another in the parsonage. Is it, Fanny?' Fanny laughed, and said that that stepping over to Framley Court certainly was done so often that perhaps they did not think so much about it as they ought to do.

'We consider ourselves a sort of happy family here, Miss Robarts, and are delighted to have the opportunity of including you in the *ménage.*' Lucy gave her ladyship one of her sweetest smiles, but what she said at that moment was inaudible. It was plain, however, that she could not bring herself even to go as far as Framley Court for her dinner just at present. 'It was very kind of Lady Lufton,' she said to Fanny; 'but it was so very soon, and – and – and if they would only go without her, she would be so happy.' But as the object was to go with her – expressly to take her there – the dinner was adjourned for a short time – *sine die.*

CHAPTER XI

Griselda Grantly

It was nearly a month after this that Lucy was first introduced to Lord Lufton, and then it was brought about only by accident. During that time Lady Lufton had been often at the parsonage, and had in a certain degree learned to know Lucy; but the stranger in the parish had never yet plucked up courage to accept one of the numerous invitations that had reached her. Mr. Robarts and his wife had frequently been at Framley Court, but the dreaded day of Lucy's initiation had not yet arrived. She had seen Lord Lufton in church, but hardly so as to know him, and beyond that she had not seen him at all. One day, however – or rather, one evening, for it was already dusk – he overtook her and Mrs. Robarts on the road walking towards the vicarage. He had his gun on his shoulder, three pointers were at his heels, and a game-keeper followed a little in the rear.

'How are you, Mrs. Robarts?' he said, almost before he had overtaken them. 'I have been chasing you along the road for the last half-mile. I never knew ladies walk so fast.'

'We should be frozen if we were to dawdle about as you gentlemen do,' and then she stopped and shook hands with him. She forgot at the moment that Lucy and he had not met, and therefore she did not introduce them.

'Won't you make me known to your sister-in-law!' said he taking off his hat, and bowing to Lucy. 'I have never yet had the pleasure of meeting her, though we have been neighbours for a month and more.' Fanny made her excuses and introduced them, and then they went on till they came to Framley Gate, Lord Lufton talking to them both, and Fanny answering for the two, and there they stopped for a moment.

'I am surprised to see you alone,' Mrs. Robarts had just said; 'I thought that Captain Culpepper was with you.'

'The captain has left me this one day. If you'll whisper I'll tell you where he has gone. I dare not speak it out loud, even to the woods.'

'To what terrible place can he have taken himself? I'll have no whisperings about such horrors.'

'He has gone to – to – but you'll promise not to tell my mother?'

'Not tell your mother! Well, now you have excited my curiosity! where can he be?'

'Do you promise, then?'

'Oh, yes! I will promise, because I am sure Lady Lufton won't ask me as to Captain Culpepper's whereabouts. We won't tell; will we, Lucy?'

'He has gone to Gatherum Castle for a day's pheasant-shooting. Now, mind, you must not betray us. Her ladyship supposes that he is shut up in his room with a tooth-ache. We did not dare to mention the name to her.' And then it appeared that Mrs. Robarts had some engagement which made it necessary that she should go up and see Lady Lufton, whereas Lucy was intending to walk on to the parsonage alone.

'And I have promised to go to your husband,' said Lord Lufton; 'or rather to your husband's dog, Ponto. And I will do two other good things – I will carry a brace of pheasants with me, and protect Miss Robarts from the evil spirits of Framley roads.' And so Mrs. Robarts turned in at the gate, and Lucy and his lordship walked off together. Lord Lufton, though he had never before spoken to Miss Robarts, had already found out that she was by no means plain. Though he had hardly seen her except at church, he had already made himself certain that the owner of that face must be worth knowing, and was not sorry to have the present opportunity of speaking to her. 'So you have an unknown damsel shut up in your castle,' he had once said to Mrs. Robarts. 'If she be kept a prisoner much longer, I shall find it my duty to come and release her by force of arms.' He had been there twice with the object of seeing her, but on both occasions Lucy had managed to escape. Now we may say she was fairly caught, and Lord Lufton, taking a pair of pheasants from the gamekeeper, and swinging them over his shoulder, walked off with his prey. 'You have been here a long time,' he said, 'without our having had the pleasure of seeing you.'

'Yes, my lord,' said Lucy. Lords had not been frequent among her acquaintance hitherto.

'I tell Mrs. Robarts that she has been confining you illegally, and that we shall release you by force or stratagem.'

'I – I – I have had a great sorrow lately.'

'Yes, Miss Robarts; I know you have; and I am only joking, you know. But I do hope that now you will be able to come amongst us. My mother is so anxious that you should do so.'

'I am sure she is very kind, and you also – my lord.'

'I never knew my own father,' said Lord Lufton, speaking gravely. 'But I can well understand what a loss you have had.' And then, after pausing a moment, he continued, 'I remember Dr. Robarts well.'

'Do you, indeed?' said Lucy, turning sharply towards him, and speaking now with some animation in her voice. Nobody had yet spoken to her about her father since she had been at Framley. It had been as though the subject were a forbidden one. And how frequently is this the case! When those we love are dead, our friends dread to mention them, though to us who are bereaved no subject would be so pleasant as their names. But we rarely understand how to treat our own sorrow or those of others.

There was once a people in some land – and they may be still there for what I know – who thought it sacrilegious to stay the course of a raging fire. If a house were being burned, burn it must, even though there were facilities for saving it. For who would dare to interfere with the course of the god? Our idea of sorrow is much the same. We think it wicked, or at any rate heartless, to put it out. If a man's wife be dead, he should go about lugubrious, with long face, for at least two years, or perhaps with full length for eighteen months, decreasing gradually during the other six. If he be a man who can quench his sorrow – put out his fire as it were – in less time than that, let him at any rate not show his power!

'Yes: I remember him,' continued Lord Lufton. 'He came twice to Framley while I was a boy, consulting with my mother about Mark and myself, – whether the Eton floggings were not more efficacious than those at Harrow. He was very kind to me, foreboding all manner of good things on my behalf.'

'He was very kind to every one,' said Lucy.

'I should think he would have been – a kind, good, genial man – just the man to be adored by his own family.'

'Exactly; and so he was. I do not remember that I ever heard an unkind word from him. There was not a harsh tone in his voice. And he was generous as the day.' Lucy, we have said, was not generally demonstrative, but now, on this subject, and with this absolute stranger, she became almost eloquent.

'I do not wonder that you should feel his loss, Miss Robarts.'

'Oh, I do feel it. Mark is the best of brothers, and, as for Fanny, she is too kind and too good to me. But I had always been specially my father's friend. For the last year or two we had lived so much together!'

'He was an old man when he died, was he not?'

'Just seventy, my lord.'

'Ah, then he was old. My mother is only fifty, and we sometimes call her the old woman. Do you think she looks older than that? We all say that she makes herself out to be so much more ancient than she need do.'

'Lady Lufton does not dress young.'

'That is it. She never has, in my memory. She always used to wear black when I first recollect her. She has given that up now; but she is still very sombre; is she not?'

'I do not like ladies to dress very young, that is, ladies of – of –'

'Ladies of fifty, we will say?'

'Very well; ladies of fifty, if you like it.'

'Then I am sure you will like my mother.'

They had now turned up through the parsonage wicket, a little gate that opened into the garden at a point on the road nearer than the chief entrance. 'I suppose I shall find Mark up at the house?' said he.

'I dare say you will, my lord.'

'Well, I'll go round this way, for my business is partly in the stable. You see I am quite at home here, though you never have seen me before. But, Miss Robarts, now that the ice is broken, I hope that we may be friends.' He then put out his hand, and when she gave him hers he pressed it almost as an old friend might have done. And, indeed, Lucy had talked to him almost as though he were an old friend. For a minute or two she had forgotten that he was a lord and a stranger – had forgotten also to be stiff and guarded as was her wont. Lord Lufton had spoken to her as though he had really cared to know her; and she, unconsciously, had been taken by the compliment. Lord Lufton, indeed, had not thought much about it – excepting as thus, that he liked the glance of a pair of bright eyes, as most other young men do like it. But, on this occasion, the evening had been so dark, that he had hardly seen Lucy's eyes at all.

'Well, Lucy, I hope you liked your companion,' Mrs. Robarts said, as the three of them clustered round the drawing-room fire before dinner.

'Oh, yes; pretty well,' said Lucy.

'That is not at all complimentary to his lordship.'

'I did not mean to be complimentary, Fanny.'

'Lucy is a great deal too matter-of-fact for compliments,' said Mark.

'What I meant was, that I had no great opportunity for judging, seeing that I was only with Lord Lufton for about ten minutes.'

'Ah! but there are girls here who would give their eyes for ten minutes of Lord Lufton to themselves. You do not know how he's valued. He has the character of being always able to make himself agreeable to ladies at half a minute's warning.'

'Perhaps he had not the half-minute's warning in this case,' said Lucy, – hypocrite that she was.

'Poor Lucy,' said her brother; 'he was coming up to see Ponto's shoulder, and I am afraid he was thinking more about the dog than you.'

'Very likely,' said Lucy; and then they went in to dinner. Lucy had been a hypocrite, for she had confessed to herself, while dressing, that Lord Lufton had been very pleasant; but then it is allowed to young ladies to be hypocrites when the subject under discussion is the character of a young gentleman.

Soon after that Lucy did dine at Framley Court. Captain Culpepper, in spite of his enormity with reference to Gatherum Castle, was still staying there, as was also a clergyman from the neighbourhood of Barchester with his wife and daughter. This was Archdeacon Grantly, a gentleman whom we have mentioned before, and who was as well known in the diocese as the bishop himself – and more thought about by many clergymen than even that illustrious prelate. Miss Grantly was a young lady not much older than Lucy Robarts, and she also was quiet, and not given to much talking in open company. She was decidedly a beauty, but somewhat statuesque in her loveliness. Her forehead was high and white, but perhaps too like marble to gratify the taste of those who are fond of flesh and blood. Her eyes were large and exquisitely formed, but they seldom showed much emotion. She, indeed, was impassive herself, and betrayed but little of her feelings. Her nose was nearly Grecian, not coming absolutely in a straight line from her forehead, but doing so nearly enough to entitle it to be considered as classical. Her mouth, too, was very fine – artists, at least, said so, and connoisseurs in beauty; but to me she always seemed as though she wanted fullness of lip. But the exquisite symmetry of her cheek and chin and lower face no man could deny. Her hair was light, and being always dressed with considerable care, did not detract from her appearance; but it lacked that richness which gives such luxuriance to feminine loveliness. She was tall and slight, and very graceful in her movements; but there were those who thought that she wanted the ease and *abandon* of youth. They said that she was too composed and stiff for her age, and that she gave but little to society beyond the beauty of her form and face. There can be no doubt, however, that she was considered by most men and women to be the beauty of Barsetshire, and that gentlemen from neighbouring counties would come many miles through dirty roads on the mere hope of being able to dance with her. Whatever attractions she may have lacked, she had at any rate created for herself a great reputation. She had spent two months of the last spring in London, and even there she had made a sensation; and people had said that Lord Dumbello, Lady Hartletop's eldest son, had been peculiarly struck with her.

It may be imagined that the archdeacon was proud of her, and so, indeed, was Mrs. Grantly – more proud, perhaps, of her daughter's beauty, than so excellent a woman should have allowed herself to be of such an attribute. Griselda – that was her name – was now an only daughter. One sister she had had, but that sister had died. There were two brothers also left, one in the Church, and the other in the Army. That was the extent of the archdeacon's family, and as the archdeacon was a very rich man – he was the only child of his father, who had been Bishop of Barchester for a great many years; and in those years it had been worth a man's while to be Bishop of Barchester – it was supposed that Miss Grantly would have a large fortune. Mrs. Grantly, however, had been heard to say, that she was in no hurry to see her daughter established in the world; – ordinary young ladies are merely married, but those of real importance are established: – and this, if anything, added to the value of the prize. Mothers sometimes depreciate their wares by an undue solicitude to dispose of them. But to tell the truth openly and at once – a virtue for which a novelist does not receive very much commendation – Griselda Grantly was, to a certain extent, already given away. Not that she, Griselda, knew anything about it, or that the thrice happy gentleman had been made aware of his good fortune: nor even had the archdeacon been told. But Mrs. Grantly and Lady Lufton had been closeted together more than once, and terms had been signed and sealed between them. Not signed on parchment, and sealed with wax, as is the case with treaties made by kings and diplomats – to be broken by the same; but signed with little words, and sealed with certain pressings of the hand – a treaty which between two such contracting parties would be binding enough. And by the terms of this treaty Griselda Grantly was to become Lady Lufton. Lady Lufton had hitherto been fortunate in her matrimonial speculations. She had selected Sir George for her daughter, and Sir George, with the utmost good-nature, had fallen in with her views. She had selected Fanny Monsell for Mr. Robarts, and Fanny Monsell had not rebelled against her for a moment. There was a prestige of success about her doings, and she felt almost confident that her dear son Ludovic must fall in love with Griselda. As to the lady herself, nothing, Lady Lufton thought, could be much better than such a match for her son. Lady Lufton, I have said, was a good Churchwoman, and the archdeacon was the very type of that branch of the Church which she venerated. The Grantlys, too, were of a good family – not noble, indeed; but in such matters Lady Lufton did not want everything. She was one of those persons who, in placing their hopes at a moderate pitch, may fairly trust to see them realized. She would fain that her son's wife should be handsome; this she wished for his sake, that he might be proud of his wife, and because men love to look on beauty. But she was afraid of vivacious beauty, of those soft, sparkling feminine charms which are spread out as lures for all the world, soft dimples, laughing eyes, luscious lips, conscious smiles, and easy whispers. What if her son should bring her home a rattling, rapid-spoken, painted piece of Eve's flesh such as this? Would not the glory and joy of her life be over, even though such child of their first mother should have come forth to the present day ennobled by the blood of two dozen successive British peers?

And then, too, Griselda's money would not be useless. Lady Lufton, with all her high-flown ideas, was not an imprudent woman. She knew that her son had been extravagant, though she did not believe that he had been reckless; and she was well content to think that some balsam from the old bishop's coffers should be made to cure the slight wounds which his early imprudence might have inflicted on the carcass of the family property. And thus, in this way, and for these reasons, Griselda Grantly had been chosen out from all the world to be the future Lady Lufton. Lord Lufton had met Griselda more than once already; had met her before these high contracting parties had come to any terms whatsoever, and had evidently admired her. Lord Dumbello had remained silent one whole evening in London with ineffable disgust, because Lord Lufton had been rather particular in his attentions; but then Lord Dumbello's muteness was his most eloquent mode of expression. Both Lady Hartletop and Mrs. Grantly, when they saw him, knew very well what he meant. But that match would not exactly have suited Mrs. Grantly's views. The Hartletop people were not in her line. They belonged altogether to another set, being connected, as we have heard before, with the Omnium interest – 'those *horrid* Gatherum people,' as Lady Lufton would say to her, raising her hands and eyebrows, and shaking her head. Lady Lufton probably thought that they ate babies in pies during their midnight orgies at Gatherum Castle; and that widows were kept in cells, and occasionally put on racks for the amusement of the duke's guests.

When the Robarts's party entered the drawing-room the Grantlys were already there, and the archdeacon's voice sounded loud and imposing in Lucy's ears, as she heard him speaking while she was yet on the threshold of the door. 'My dear Lady Lufton, I would believe anything on earth about her – anything. There is nothing too outrageous for her. Had she insisted on going there with the bishop's apron on, I should not have been surprised.' And then they all knew that the archdeacon was talking about Mrs. Proudie, for Mrs. Proudie was his bugbear.

Lady Lufton after receiving her guests introduced Lucy to Griselda Grantly. Miss Grantly smiled graciously, bowed slightly, and then remarked in the lowest voice possible that it was exceedingly cold. A low voice, we know, is an excellent thing in woman. Lucy, who thought that she was bound to speak, said that it was cold, but that she did not mind it when she was walking. And then Griselda smiled again, somewhat less graciously than before, and so the conversation ended. Miss Grantly was the elder of the two, and having seen most of the world, should have been the best able to talk, but perhaps she was not very anxious for a conversation with Miss Robarts.

'So, Robarts, I hear that you have been preaching at Chaldicotes,' said the archdeacon, still rather loudly. 'I saw Sowerby the other day, and he told me that you gave them the fag end of Mrs. Proudie's lecture.'

'It was ill-natured of Sowerby to say the fag end,' said Robarts. 'We divided the matter into thirds. Harold Smith took the first part, I the last –'

'And the lady the intervening portion. You have electrified the county between you; but I am told that she had the best of it.'

'I was so sorry that Mr. Robarts went there,' said Lady Lufton, as she walked into the dining-room leaning on the archdeacon's arm.

'I am inclined to think he could not very well have helped himself,' said the archdeacon, who was never willing to lean heavily on a brother parson, unless on one who had utterly and irrevocably gone away from his side of the Church.

'Do you think not, archdeacon?'

'Why, no: Sowerby is a friend of Lufton's –'

'Not particularly,' said poor Lady Lufton, in a deprecating tone.

'Well, they have been intimate; and Robarts, when he was asked to preach at Chaldicotes, could not well refuse.'

'But then he went afterwards to Gatherum Castle. Not that I am vexed with him at all now, you understand. But it is such a dangerous house, you know.'

'So it is. – But the very fact of the duke's wishing to have a clergyman there, should always be taken as a sign of grace, Lady Lufton. The air was impure, no doubt; but it was less impure with Robarts there than it would have been without him. But, gracious heavens! what blasphemy have I been saying about impure air? Why, the bishop was there!'

'Yes, the bishop was there,' said Lady Lufton, and they both understood each other thoroughly.

Lord Lufton took out Mrs. Grantly to dinner, and matters were so managed that Miss Grantly sat on his other side. There was no management apparent in this to anybody; but there she was, while Lucy was placed between her brother and Captain Culpepper. Captain Culpepper was a man with an enormous moustache, and a great aptitude for slaughtering game; but as he had no other strong characteristics it was not probable that he would make himself very agreeable to poor Lucy. She had seen Lord Lufton once, for two minutes, since the day of that walk, and then he had addressed her quite like an old friend. It had been in the parsonage drawing-room, and Fanny had been there. Fanny now was so well accustomed to his lordship, that she thought but little of this, but to Lucy it had been very pleasant. He was not forward or familiar, but kind, and gentle, and pleasant; and Lucy did feel that she liked him. Now, on this evening, he had hitherto hardly spoken to her; but then she knew that there were other people in the company to whom he was bound to speak. She was not exactly humble-minded in the usual sense of the word; but she did recognize the fact that her position was less important than that of other people there, and that therefore it was probable that to a certain extent she would be overlooked. But not the less would she have liked to occupy the seat to which Miss Grantly had found her way. She did not want to flirt with Lord Lufton; she was not such a fool as that; but she would have liked to have heard the sound of his voice close to her ear, instead of that of Captain Culpepper's knife and fork. This was the first occasion on which she had endeavoured to dress herself with care since her father had died; and now, sombre though she was in her deep mourning, she did look very well.

'There is an expression about her forehead that is full of poetry,' Fanny had said to her husband.

'Don't you turn her head, Fanny, and make her believe that she is a beauty,' Mark had answered.

'I doubt it is not so easy to turn her head, Mark. There is more in Lucy than you imagine, and so you will find out before long.' It was thus that Mrs. Robarts prophesied about her sister-in-law. Had she been asked she might perhaps have said that Lucy's presence would be dangerous to the Grantly interest at Framley Court.

Lord Lufton's voice was audible enough as he went on talking to Miss Grantly – his voice, but not his words. He talked in such a way that there was no appearance of whispering, and yet the person to whom he spoke, and she only, could hear what he said. Mrs. Grantly the while conversed constantly with Lucy's brother, who sat at Lucy's left hand. She never lacked for subjects on which to speak to a country clergyman of the right sort, and thus Griselda was left quite uninterrupted. But Lucy could not but observe that Griselda herself seemed to have very little to say – or at any rate to say very little. Every now and then she did open her mouth, and some word or brace of words would fall from it. But for the most part she seemed to be content in the fact that Lord Lufton was paying her attention. She showed no animation, but sat there still and graceful, composed and classical, as she always was. Lucy, who could not keep her ears from listening or her eyes from looking, thought that had she been there she would have endeavoured to take a more prominent part in the conversation. But then Griselda Grantly probably knew much better than Lucy did how to comport herself in such a situation. Perhaps it might be that young men, such as Lord Lufton, liked to hear the sound of their own voices.

'Immense deal of game about here,' Captain Culpepper said to her towards the end of the dinner. It was the second attempt he had made; on the former he had asked her whether she knew any of the fellows of the 9th.

'Is there?' said Lucy. 'Oh! I saw Lord Lufton the other day with a great armful of pheasants.'

'An armful! Why we had seven cartloads the other day at Gatherum.'

'Seven carts full of pheasants!' said Lucy, amazed.

'That's not so much. We had eight guns, you know. Eight guns will do a deal of work when the game has been well got together. They manage all that capitally at Gatherum. Been at the duke's, eh?' Lucy had heard the Framley report as to Gatherum Castle, and said with a sort of shudder that she had never been at that place. After this, Captain Culpepper troubled her no further.

When the ladies had taken themselves to the drawing-room Lucy found herself hardly better off than she had been at the dinner-table. Lady Lufton and Mrs. Grantly got themselves on to a sofa together, and there chatted confidentially into each other's ears. Her ladyship had introduced Lucy and Miss Grantly, and then she naturally thought that the young people might do very well together. Mrs. Robarts did attempt to bring about a joint conversation, which should include the three, and for ten minutes or so she worked hard at it. But it did not thrive. Miss

Grantly was monosyllabic, smiling, however, at every monosyllable; and Lucy found that nothing would occur to her at that moment worthy of being spoken. There she sat, still and motionless, afraid to take up a book, and thinking in her heart how much happier she would have been at home at the parsonage. She was not made for society; she felt sure of that; and another time she would let Mark and Fanny come to Framley Court by themselves. And then the gentlemen came in, and there was another stir in the room. Lady Lufton got up and bustled about; she poked the fire and shifted the candles, spoke a few words to Dr. Grantly, whispered something to her son, patted Lucy on the cheek, told Fanny, who was a musician, that they would have a little music, and ended by putting her two hands on Griselda's shoulders and telling her that the fit of her frock was perfect. For Lady Lufton, though she did dress old herself, as Lucy had said, delighted to see those around her neat and pretty, jaunty and graceful.

'Dear Lady Lufton!' said Griselda, putting up her hand so as to press the end of her ladyship's fingers. It was the first piece of animation she had shown, and Lucy Robarts watched it all. And then there was music. Lucy neither played nor sang; Fanny did both, and for an amateur did both well. Griselda did not sing, but she played; and did so in a manner that showed that neither her own labour nor her father's money had been spared in her instruction. Lord Lufton sang also, a little, and Captain Culpepper a very little; so that they got up a concert among them. In the meantime the doctor and Mark stood talking together on the rug before the fire; the two mothers sat contented, watching the billings and the cooings of their offspring – and Lucy sat alone, turning over the leaves of a book of pictures. She made up her mind fully, then and there, that she was quite unfitted by disposition for such work as this. She cared for no one, and no one cared for her. Well, she must go through with it now; but another time she would know better. With her own book and a fireside she never felt herself to be miserable as she was now. She had turned her back to the music for she was sick of seeing Lord Lufton watch the artistic motion of Miss Grantly's fingers, and was sitting at a small table as far away from the piano as a long room would permit, when she was suddenly roused from a reverie of self-reproach by a voice close behind her: 'Miss Robarts,' said the voice, 'why have you cut us all?' and Lucy felt that, though she heard the words plainly, nobody else did. Lord Lufton was now speaking to her as he had before spoken to Miss Grantly.

'I don't play, my lord,' said Lucy, 'nor yet sing.'

'That would have made your company so much more valuable to us, for we are terribly badly off for listeners. Perhaps you don't like music?'

'I do like it, – sometimes very much.'

'And when are the sometimes? But we shall find it all out in time. We shall have unravelled all your mysteries, and read all your riddles by – when shall I say? – by the end of the winter. Shall we not?'

'I do not know that I have got any mysteries.'

'Oh, but you have! It is very mysterious in you to come and sit here – with your back to us all –'

'Oh, Lord Lufton; if I have done wrong –!' and poor Lucy almost started from her chair, and a deep flush came across her dark cheek.

'No – no; you have done no wrong. I was only joking. It is we who have done wrong in leaving you to yourself – you who are the greatest stranger among us.'

'I have been very well, thank you. I don't care about being left alone. I have always been used to it.'

'Ah! but we must break you of the habit. We won't allow you to make a hermit of yourself. But the truth is, Miss Robarts, you don't know us yet, and therefore you are not quite happy among us.'

'Oh! yes, I am; you are all very good to me.'

'You must let us be good to you. At any rate, you must let me be so. You know, don't you, that Mark and I have been dear friends since we were seven years old. His wife has been my sister's dearest friend almost as long; and now that you are with them, you must be a dear friend too. You won't refuse the offer, will you?'

'Oh, no,' she said, quite in a whisper; and, indeed, she could hardly raise her voice above a whisper, fearing that tears would fall from her tell-tale eyes.

'Dr. and Mrs. Grantly will have gone in a couple of days, and then we must get you down here. Miss Grantly is to remain for Christmas, and you two must become bosom friends.' Lucy smiled, and tried to look pleased, but she felt that she and Griselda Grantly could never be bosom friends – could never have anything in common between them. She felt sure that Griselda despised her, little, brown, plain, and unimportant as she was. She herself could not despise Griselda in turn; indeed she could not but admire Miss Grantly's great beauty and dignity of demeanour; but she knew that she could never love her. It is hardly possible that the proud-hearted should love those who despise them; and Lucy Robarts was very proud-hearted.

'Don't you think she is very handsome?' said Lord Lufton.

'Oh, very,' said Lucy. 'Nobody can doubt that.'

'Ludovic,' said Lady Lufton – not quite approving of her son's remaining so long at the back of Lucy's chair – 'won't you give us another song? Mrs. Robarts and Miss Grantly are still at the piano.'

'I have sung away all that I knew, mother. There's Culpepper has not had a chance yet. He has got to give us his dream – how he "dreamt that he dwelt in marble halls!" '

'I sang that an hour ago,' said the captain, not over-pleased.

'But you certainly have not told us how "your little lovers came!" ' The captain, however, would not sing any more. And then the party was broken up, and the Robartses went home to their parsonage.

CHAPTER XII

The Little Bill

LUCY, during those last fifteen minutes of her sojourn journ in the Framley Court drawing-room, somewhat modified the very strong opinion she had before formed as to her unfitness for such society. It was very pleasant sitting there in that easy chair, while Lord Lufton stood at the back of it saying nice, soft, good-natured words to her. She was sure that in a little time she could feel a true friendship for him, and that she could do so without any risk of falling in love with him. But then she had a glimmering of an idea that such a friendship would be open to all manner of remarks, and would hardly be compatible with the world's ordinary ways. At any rate it would be pleasant to be at Framley Court, if he would come and occasionally notice her. But she did not admit to herself that such a visit would be intolerable if his whole time were devoted to Griselda Grantly. She neither admitted it, nor thought it; but nevertheless, in a strange unconscious way, such a feeling did find entrance in her bosom. And then the Christmas holidays passed away. How much of this enjoyment fell to her share, and how much of this suffering she endured, we will not attempt accurately to describe. Miss Grantly remained at Framley Court up to Twelfth Night, and the Robartses also spent most of the season at the house. Lady Lufton, no doubt, had hoped that everything might have been arranged on this occasion in accordance with her wishes, but such had not been the case. Lord Lufton had evidently admired Miss Grantly very much: indeed, he had said so to his mother half a dozen times; but it may almost be questioned whether the pleasure Lady Lufton derived from this was not more than neutralized by an opinion he once put forward that Griselda Grantly wanted some of the fire of Lucy Robarts.

'Surely, Ludovic, you would never compare the two girls,' said Lady Lufton.

'Of course not. They are the very antipodes to each other. Miss Grantly would probably be more to my taste; but then I am wise enough to know that it is so because my taste is a bad taste.'

'I know no man with a more accurate or refined taste in such matters,' said Lady Lufton. Beyond this she did not dare to go. She knew very well that her strategy would be vain should her son once learn that she had a strategy. To tell the truth, Lady Lufton was becoming somewhat indifferent to Lucy Robarts. She had been very kind to the little girl; but the little girl seemed hardly to appreciate the kindness as she should do – and then Lord Lufton would talk to Lucy, 'which was so unnecessary, you know;' and Lucy had got into a way of talking quite freely with Lord Lufton, having completely dropped that short, spasmodic, ugly exclamation of 'my lord.' And so the Christmas festivities were at an end, and January wore itself away. During the greater part of this month Lord Lufton did not remain at Framley, but was nevertheless in the county, hunting with the hounds of both divisions, and staying at various houses. Two or three nights he spent at Chaldicotes; and one – let it only be told in an under voice – at Gatherum Castle! Of this he said nothing to Lady Lufton. 'Why make her unhappy?' as he said to Mark. But Lady Lufton knew it, though she said not a word to him – knew it, and was unhappy. 'If he would only marry Griselda, there would be an end of that danger,' she said to herself.

But now we must go back for a while to the vicar and his little bill. It will be remembered, that his first idea with reference to that trouble, after the reading of his father's will, was to borrow the money from his brother John. John was down at Exeter at the time, and was to stay one night at the parsonage on his way to London. Mark would broach the matter to him on the journey, painful though it would be to him to tell the story of his own folly to a brother so much younger than himself, and who had always looked up to him, clergyman and full-blown vicar as he was, with a deference greater than that which such difference in age required. The story was told, however; but was told all in vain, as Mark found out before he reached Framley. His brother John immediately declared that he would lend him the money, of course – eight hundred, if his brother wanted it. He, John, confessed that, as regarded the remaining two, he should like to feel the pleasure of immediate possession. As for interest, he would not take any – take interest from a brother! of course not. Well, if Mark made such a fuss about it, he supposed he must take it; but would rather not. Mark should have his own way, and do just what he liked.

This was all very well, and Mark had fully made up his mind that his brother should not be kept long out of his money. But then arose the question, how was that money to be reached? He, Mark, was executor, or one of the executors under his father's will, and, therefore, no doubt, could put his hand upon it; but his brother wanted five months of being of age, and could not therefore as yet be put legally in possession of the legacy. 'That's a bore,' said the assistant private secretary to the Lord Petty Bag, thinking, perhaps, as much of his own immediate wish for ready cash as he did of his brother's necessities. Mark felt that it was a bore, but there was nothing more to be done in that direction. He must now find out how far the bankers could assist him.

Some week or two after his return to Framley he went over to Barchester, and called there on a certain Mr. Forrest, the manager of one of the banks, with whom he was acquainted; and with many injunctions as to secrecy told this manager the whole of his story. At first he concealed the name of his friend Sowerby, but it soon appeared that no such concealment was of any avail. 'That Sowerby, of course,' said Mr. Forrest. 'I know you are intimate with him; and all his friends go through that, sooner or later.' It seemed to Mark as though Mr. Forrest made very light of the whole transaction.

'I cannot possibly pay the bill when it falls due,' said Mark.

'Oh, no, of course not,' said Mr. Forrest. 'It's never very convenient to hand out four hundred pounds at a blow. Nobody will expect you to pay it!'

'But I suppose I shall have to do it sooner or later?'

'Well, that's as may be. It will depend partly on how you manage with Sowerby, and partly on the hands it gets into. As the bill has your name on it, they'll have patience as long as the interest is paid, and the commissions on renewal. But no doubt it will have to be met some day by somebody.' Mr. Forrest said that he was sure that the bill was not in Barchester; Mr. Sowerby would not, he thought, have brought it to a Barchester bank. The bill was probably in London, but doubtless would be sent to Barchester for collection. 'If it comes in my way,' said Mr. Forrest, 'I will give you plenty of time, so that you may manage about the renewal with Sowerby. I suppose he'll pay the expense of doing that.'

Mark's heart was somewhat lighter as he left the bank. Mr. Forrest had made so little of the whole transaction that he felt himself justified in making little of it also. 'It may be as well,' said he to himself, as he drove home, 'not to tell Fanny anything about it till the three months have run round. I must make some arrangement then.' And in this way his mind was easier during the last of those three months than it had been during the two former. That feeling of over-due bills, of bills coming due, of accounts over-drawn, of tradesmen unpaid, of general money cares, is very dreadful at first; but it is astonishing how soon men get used to it. A load which would crush a man at first becomes, by habit, not only endurable, but easy and comfortable to the bearer. The habitual debtor goes along jaunty and with elastic step, almost enjoying the excitement of his embarrassments. There was Mr. Sowerby himself; who ever saw a cloud on his brow? It made one almost in love with ruin to be in his company. And even now, already, Mark Robarts was thinking to himself quite comfortably about this bill; – how very pleasantly those bankers managed these things. Pay it! No; no one will be so unreasonable as to expect you to do that! And then Mr. Sowerby certainly was a pleasant fellow, and gave a man something in return for his money. It was still a question with Mark whether Lord Lufton had not been too hard on Sowerby. Had that gentleman fallen across his clerical friend at the present moment, he might no doubt have gotten from him an acceptance for another four hundred pounds.

One is almost inclined to believe that there is something pleasurable in the excitement of such embarrassments, as there is also in the excitement of drink. But then, at last, the time does come when the excitement is over, and when nothing but the misery is left. If there be an existence of wretchedness on earth it must be that of the elderly, worn out roué, who has run this race of debt and bills of accommodation and acceptances – of what, if we were not in these days somewhat afraid of good broad English, we might call lying and swindling, falsehood and fraud – and who, having ruined all whom he should have loved, having burnt up every one who would trust him much, and scorched all who would trust him a little, is at last left to finish his life with such bread and water as these men get, without one honest thought to strengthen his sinking heart, or one honest friend to hold his shivering hand! If a man could only think of that, as he puts his name to the first little bill, as to which he is so good-naturedly assured that it can easily be renewed!

When the three months had nearly run out, it so happened that Robarts met his friend Sowerby. Mark had once or twice ridden with Lord Lufton as far as the meet of the hounds, and may, perhaps, have gone a field or two farther on some occasions. The reader must not think that he had taken to hunting, as some parsons do; and it is singular enough that whenever they do so they always show a special aptitude for the pursuit, as though hunting were an employment peculiarly congenial with a cure of souls in the country. Such a thought would do our vicar injustice. But when Lord Lufton would ask him what on earth could be the harm of riding along the roads to look at the hounds, he hardly knew what sensible answer to give his lordship. It would be absurd to say that his time would be better employed at home in clerical matters, for it was notorious that he had not clerical pursuits for the employment of half his time. In this way, therefore, he had got into a habit of looking at the hounds, and keeping up his acquaintance in the county, meeting Lord Dumbello, Mr. Green Walker, Harold Smith, and other such like sinners; and on one such occasion, as the three months were nearly closing, he did meet Mr. Sowerby. 'Look here, Sowerby; I want to speak to you for half a moment. What are you doing about that bill?'

'Bill – bill! what bill? – which bill? The whole bill, and nothing but the bill. That seems to be the conversation nowadays of all men, morning, noon, and night.'

'Don't you know the bill I signed for you for four hundred pounds?'

'Did you, though? Was not that rather green of you?' This did seem strange to Mark. Could it really be the fact that Mr. Sowerby had so many bills flying about that he had absolutely forgotten that occurrence in the Gatherum Castle bedroom? And then to be called green by the very man whom he had obliged!

'Perhaps I was,' said Mark, in a tone that showed that he was somewhat piqued. 'But all the same I should be glad to know how it will be taken up.'

'Oh, Mark, what a ruffian you are to spoil my day's sport in this way. Any man but a parson would be too good a Christian for such intense cruelty. But let me see – four hundred pounds? Oh, yes – Tozer has it.'

'And what will Tozer do with it?'

'Make money of it; whatever way he may go to work he will do that.'

'But will Tozer bring it to me on the 20th?'

'Oh, Lord, no! Upon my word, Mark, you are deliciously green. A cat would as soon think of killing a mouse directly she had got it into her claws. But, joking apart, you need not trouble yourself. Maybe you will hear no more about it; or, perhaps, which no doubt is more probable, I may have to send it to you to be renewed. But you need do nothing till you hear from me or somebody else.'

'Only do not let any one come down upon me for the money.'

'There is not the slightest fear of that. Tally-ho, old fellow! He's away. Tally-ho! right over by Gossetts' barn. Come along, and never mind Tozer – "Sufficient for the day is the evil thereof." ' And away they both went together, parson and member of Parliament. And then again on that occasion Mark went home with a sort of feeling that the bill did not matter. Tozer would manage it somehow; and it was quite clear that it would not do to tell his wife of it just at present.

On the 21st of that month of February, however, he did receive a reminder that the bill and all concerning it had not merely been a farce. This was a letter from Mr. Sowerby, dated from Chaldicotes, though not bearing the Barchester post-mark, in which that gentleman suggested a renewal – not exactly of the old bill, but of a new one. It seemed to Mark that the letter had been posted in London. If I give it entire, I shall, perhaps, most quickly explain its purport:

'CHALDICOTES, – 20th February, 185–.

'My dear Mark,

' "Lend not thy name to the money-dealers, for the same is a destruction and a snare." If that be not in the Proverbs, it ought to be. Tozer has given me certain signs of his being alive and strong this cold weather. As we can neither of us take up that bill for £400 at the moment, we must renew it, and pay him his commission and interest, with all the rest of his perquisites, and pickings, and stealings – from all which, I can assure you, Tozer does not keep his hands as he should do. To cover this and some other little outstanding trifles, I have filled in the new bill for £500, making it due 23rd of May next. Before that time, a certain accident will, I trust, have occurred to your impoverished friend. By the by, I never told you how she went off from Gatherum Castle, the morning after you left us, with the Greshams. Cart-ropes would not hold her, even though the duke held them; which he did, with all the strength of his ducal hands. She would go to meet some doctor of theirs, and so I was put off for that time; but I think that the matter stands in a good train.

'Do not lose a post in sending back the bill accepted, as Tozer may annoy you – nay, undoubtedly will, if the matter be not in his hand, duly signed by both of us, the day after to-morrow. He is an ungrateful brute; he has lived on me for these eight years, and would not let me off a single squeeze now to save my life. But I am specially anxious to save you from the annoyance and cost of lawyers' letters; and if delayed, it might get into the papers. Put it under cover to me, at No. 7, Duke Street, St. James's. I shall be in town by that time.

'Good-bye, old fellow. That was a decent brush we had the other day from Cobbold's Ashes. I wish I could get that brown horse from you. I would not mind going to a hundred and thirty.

'Yours ever,
'N. Sowerby.'

When Mark had read it through he looked down on his table to see whether the old bill had fallen from the letter; but no, there was no enclosure, and had been no enclosure but the new bill. And then he read the letter through again, and found that there was no word about the old bill – not a syllable, at least, as to its whereabouts. Sowerby did not even say that it would remain in his own hands. Mark did not in truth know much about such things. It might be that the very fact of his signing this second document would render that first document null and void; and from Sowerby's silence on the subject, it might be argued that this was so well known to be the case, that he had not thought of explaining it. But yet Mark could not see how this should be so. But what was he to do? That threat of cost and lawyers, and specially of the newspapers, did have its effect upon him – as no doubt it was intended to do. And then he was utterly dumbfounded by Sowerby's impudence in drawing on him for £500 instead of £400, 'covering,' as Sowerby so good-humouredly said, 'sundry little outstanding trifles.'

But at last he did sign the bill, and sent it off, as Sowerby had directed. What else was he to do? Fool that he was. A man always can do right, even though he has done wrong before. But that previous wrong adds so much difficulty to the path – a difficulty which increases in tremendous ratio, till a man at last is choked in his struggling, and is drowned beneath the waters. And then he put away Sowerby's letter carefully, locking it up from his wife's sight. It was a letter that no parish clergyman should have received. So much he acknowledged to himself. But nevertheless it was necessary that he should keep it. And now again for a few hours this affair made him very miserable.

CHAPTER XIII

Delicate Hints

LADY LUFTON had been greatly rejoiced at that good deed which her son did in giving up his Leicestershire hunting, and coming to reside for the winter at Framley. It was proper, and becoming, and comfortable in the extreme. An English nobleman ought to hunt in the county where he himself owns the fields over which he rides; he ought to receive the respect and honour due to him from his own tenants; he ought to sleep under a roof of his own, and he ought also – so Lady Lufton thought – to fall in love with a young embryo bride of his own mother's choosing. And then it was so pleasant to have him there in the house. Lady Lufton was not a woman who allowed her life to be what people in common parlance call dull. She had too many duties, and thought too much of them, to allow of her suffering from tedium and ennui. But nevertheless the house was more joyous to her when he was there. There was a reason for some little gaiety, which would never have been attracted thither by herself, but which, nevertheless, she did enjoy when it was brought about by his presence. She was younger and brighter when he was there, thinking more of the future and less of the past. She could look at him, and that alone was happiness to her. And then he was pleasant-mannered with her; joking with her on her little old-world prejudices in a tone that was musical to her ear as coming from him; smiling on her, reminding her of those smiles which she had loved so dearly when as yet he was all her own, Lying there in his little bed beside her chair. He was kind and gracious to her, behaving like a good son, at any rate while he was there in her presence. When we add to this, her fears that he might not be so perfect in his conduct when absent, we may well imagine that Lady Lufton was pleased to have him there at Framley Court.

She had hardly said a word to him as to that five thousand pounds. Many a night, as she lay thinking on her pillow, she said to herself that no money had ever been better expended, since it had brought him back to his own house. He had thanked her for it in his own open way, declaring that he would pay it back to her during the coming year, and comforting her heart by his rejoicing that the property had not been sold. 'I don't like the idea of parting with an acre of it,' he had said.

'Of course not, Ludovic. Never let the estate decrease in your hands. It is only by such resolutions as that that English noblemen and English gentlemen can preserve their country. I cannot bear to see property changing hands.'

'Well, I suppose it's a good thing to have land in the market sometimes, so that the millionaires may know what to do with their money.'

'God forbid that yours should be there!' And the widow made a little mental prayer that her son's acres might be protected from the millionaires and other Philistines.

'Why, yes: I don't exactly want to see a Jew tailor investing his earnings at Lufton,' said the lord.

'Heaven forbid!' said the widow. All this, as I have said, was very nice. It was manifest to her ladyship, from his lordship's way of talking, that no vital injury had as yet been done: he had no cares on his mind, and spoke freely about the property: but nevertheless there were clouds even now, at this period of bliss, which somewhat obscured the brilliancy of Lady Lufton's sky. Why was Ludovic so slow in that affair of Griselda Grantly? why so often in these latter winter days did he saunter over to the parsonage? And then that terrible visit to Gatherum Castle! What actually did happen at Gatherum Castle, she never knew. We, however, are more intrusive, less delicate in our inquiries, and we can say. He had a very bad day's sport with the West Barsetshire. The county is altogether short of foxes, and some one who understands the matter must take that point up before they can do any good. And after that he had had rather a dull dinner with the duke. Sowerby had been there, and in the evening he and Sowerby had played billiards. Sowerby had won a pound or two, and that had been the extent of the damage done. But those saunterings over to the parsonage might be more dangerous. Not that it ever occurred to Lady Lufton as possible that her son should fall in love with Lucy Robarts. Lucy's personal attractions were not of a nature to give ground for such a fear as that. But he might turn the girl's head with his chatter; she might be fool enough to fancy any folly; and, moreover, people would talk. Why should he go to the parsonage now more frequently than he had ever done before Lucy came there?

And then her ladyship, in reference to the same trouble, hardly knew how to manage her invitations to the parsonage. These hitherto had been very frequent, and she had been in the habit of thinking that they could hardly be too much so; but now she was almost afraid to continue the custom. She could not ask the parson and his wife without Lucy; and when Lucy was there, her son would pass the greater part of the evening in talking to her, or playing chess with her. Now this did disturb Lady Lufton not a little. And then Lucy took it all so quietly. On her first arrival at Framley she had been so shy, so silent, and so much awestruck by the grandeur of Framley Court, that Lady Lufton had sympathized with her and encouraged her. She had endeavoured to moderate the blaze of her own splendour, in order that Lucy's unaccustomed eyes might not be dazzled. But all this was changed now. Lucy could listen to the young lord's voice by the hour together – without being dazzled in the least. Under these circumstances two things occurred to her. She would speak either to her son or to Fanny Robarts, and by a little diplomacy have this evil remedied. And then she had to determine on which step she would take. 'Nothing could be more reasonable than Ludovic.' So at least she said to herself over and over again. But then Ludovic understood nothing about such matters; and had, moreover, a habit, inherited from his father, of taking the bit between his teeth whenever he suspected interference. Drive him gently without pulling his mouth about, and you might take him anywhere, almost at any pace; but a smart touch, let it be ever so slight, would bring him on his haunches, and then it might be a question whether you could get him another mile that day. So that on the whole Lady Lufton thought that the other plan would be the best. I have no doubt that Lady Lufton was right.

She got Fanny up into her own den one afternoon, and seated her discreetly in an easy arm-chair, making her guest take off her bonnet, and showing by various signs that the visit was regarded as one of great moment. 'Fanny,' she said, 'I want to speak to you about something that is important and necessary to mention, and yet it is a very delicate affair to speak of.' Fanny opened her eyes, and said that she hoped that nothing was wrong. 'No, my dear, I think nothing is wrong: I hope so, and I think I may say I'm sure of it; but then it's always well to be on one's guard.'

'Yes, it is,' said Fanny, who knew that something unpleasant was coming – something as to which she might probably be called upon to differ from her ladyship. Mrs. Robarts's own fears, however, were running entirely in the direction of her husband; – and, indeed, Lady Lufton had a word or two to say on that subject also, only not exactly now. A hunting parson was not at all to her taste; but that matter might be allowed to remain in abeyance for a few days.

'Now, Fanny, you know that we have all liked your sister-in-law, Lucy, very much.' And then Mrs. Robarts's mind was immediately opened, and she knew the rest as well as though it had all been spoken. 'I need hardly tell you that, for I am sure we have shown it.'

'You have, indeed, as you always do.'

'And you must not think that I am going to complain,' continued Lady Lufton.

'I hope there is nothing to complain of,' said Fanny, speaking by no means in a defiant tone, but humbly as it were, and deprecating her ladyship's wrath. Fanny had gained one signal victory over Lady Lufton, and on that account, with a prudence equal to her generosity, felt that she could afford to be submissive. It might, perhaps, not be long before she would be equally anxious to conquer again.

'Well, no; I don't think there is,' said Lady Lufton. 'Nothing to complain of; but a little chat between you and me may, perhaps, set matters right, which, otherwise, might become troublesome.'

'Is it about Lucy?'

'Yes, my dear – about Lucy. She is very nice, good girl, and a credit to her father –'

'And a great comfort to us,' said Fanny.

'I am sure she is: she must be a very pleasant companion to you, and so useful about the children; but –' And then Lady Lufton paused for a moment; for she, eloquent and discreet as she always was, felt herself rather at a loss for words to express her exact meaning.

'I don't know what I should do without her,' said Fanny, speaking with the object of assisting her ladyship in her embarrassment.

'But the truth is this: she and Lord Lufton are getting into the way of being too much together – of talking to each other too exclusively. I am sure you must have noticed it, Fanny. It is not that I suspect any evil. I don't think that I am suspicious by nature.'

'Oh! no,' said Fanny.

'But they will each of them get wrong ideas about the other, and about themselves. Lucy will, perhaps, think that Ludovic means more than he does, and Ludovic will –' But it was not quite so easy to say what Ludovic might do or think; but Lady Lufton went on:

'I am sure that you understand me, Fanny, with your excellent sense and tact. Lucy is clever, and amusing, and all that; and Ludovic, like all young men, is perhaps ignorant that his attentions may be taken to mean more than he intends –'

'You don't think that Lucy is in love with him?'

'Oh dear, no – nothing of the kind. If I thought it had come to that, I should recommend that she should be sent away altogether. I am sure she is not so foolish as that.'

'I don't think there is anything in it at all, Lady Lufton.'

'I don't think there is, my dear, and therefore I would not for worlds make any suggestion about it to Lord Lufton. I would not let him suppose that I suspected Lucy of being so imprudent. But still, it may be well that you should just say a word to her. A little management now and then, in such matters, is so useful.'

'But what shall I say to her?'

'Just explain to her that any young lady who talks so much to the same young gentleman will certainly be observed – that people will accuse her of setting her cap at Lord Lufton. Not that I suspect her – I give her credit for too much proper feeling: I know her education has been good, and her principles are upright. But people will talk of her. You must understand that, Fanny, as well as I do.' Fanny could not help meditating whether proper feeling, education, and upright principles did forbid Lucy Robarts to fall in love with Lord Lufton; but her doubts on this subject, if she held any, were not communicated to her ladyship. It had never entered into her mind that a match was possible between Lord Lufton and Lucy Robarts, nor had she the slightest wish to encourage it now that the idea was suggested to her. On such a matter she could sympathize with Lady Lufton, though she did not completely agree with her as to the expediency of any interference. Nevertheless, she at once offered to speak to Lucy. 'I don't think that Lucy has any idea in her head upon the subject,' said Mrs. Robarts.

'I dare say not – I don't suppose she has. But young ladies sometimes allow themselves to fall in love, and then to think themselves very ill-used, just because they have had no idea in their head.'

'I will put her on her guard if you wish it, Lady Lufton.'

'Exactly, my dear; that is just it. Put her on her guard – that is all that is necessary. She is a dear, good, clever girl, and it would be very sad if anything were to interrupt our comfortable way of getting on with her.' Mrs. Robarts knew to a nicety the exact meaning of this threat. If Lucy would persist in securing to herself so much of Lord Lufton's time and attention, her visits to Framley Court must become less frequent. Lady Lufton would do much, very much, indeed, for her friends at the parsonage; but not even for them could she permit her son's prospects in life to be endangered. There was nothing more said between them, and Mrs. Robarts got up to take her leave, having promised to speak to Lucy.

'You manage everything so perfectly,' said Lady Lufton, as she pressed Mrs. Robarts's hand, 'that I am quite at ease now that I find you will agree with me.' Mrs. Robarts did not exactly agree with her ladyship, but she hardly thought it worth her while to say so. Mrs. Robarts immediately started off on her walk to her own home, and when she had got out of the grounds into the road, where it makes a turn towards the parsonage, nearly opposite to Podgens' shop, she saw Lord Lufton on horseback, and Lucy standing beside him. It was already nearly five o'clock, and it was getting dusk; but as she approached, or rather as she came suddenly within sight of them, she could see that they were in close conversation. Lord Lufton's face was towards her, and his horse was standing still; he was leaning over towards his companion, and the whip, which he held in his right hand, hung almost over her arm and down her back, as though his hand had touched and perhaps rested on her shoulder. She was standing by his side, looking up into his face, with one gloved hand resting on the horse's neck. Mrs. Robarts, as she saw them, could not but own that there might be cause for Lady Lufton's fears. But then Lucy's manner, as Mrs. Robarts approached, was calculated to dissipate any such fears, and to prove that there was no ground for them. She did not move from her position, or allow her hand to drop, or show that she was in any way either confused or conscious. She stood her ground, and when her sister-in-law came up was smiling and at her ease. 'Lord Lufton wants me to learn to ride,' said she.

'To learn to ride!' said Fanny, not knowing what answer to make to such a proposition.

'Yes,' said he. 'This horse would carry her beautifully: he is as quiet as a lamb, and I made Gregory go out with him yesterday with a sheet hanging over him like a lady's habit, and the man got up into a lady's saddle.'

'I think Gregory would make a better hand of it than Lucy.'

'The horse cantered with him as though he had carried a lady all his life, and his mouth is like velvet; indeed, that is his fault – he is too soft-mouthed.'

'I suppose that's the same sort of thing as a man being soft-hearted,' said Lucy.

'Exactly: you ought to ride them both with a very light hand. They are difficult cattle to manage, but very pleasant when you know how to do it.'

'But you see I don't know how to do it,' said Lucy.

'As regards the horse, you will learn in two days, and I do hope you will try. Don't you think it will be an excellent thing for her, Mrs. Robarts?'

'Lucy has got no habit,' said Mrs. Robarts, making use of the excuse common on all such occasions.

'There is one of Justinia's in the house, I know. She always leaves one here, in order that she may be able to ride when she comes.'

'She would not think of taking such a liberty with Lady Meredith's things,' said Fanny, almost frightened at the proposal.

'Of course it is out of the question, Fanny,' said Lucy, now speaking rather seriously. 'In the first place, I would not take Lord Lufton's horse; in the second place, I would not take Lady Meredith's habit; in the third place, I should be a great deal too much frightened; and, lastly, it is quite out of the question for a great many other very good reasons.'

'Nonsense,' said Lord Lufton.

'A great deal of nonsense,' said Lucy, laughing, 'but all of it of Lord Lufton's talking. But we are getting cold – are we not, Fanny? – so we will wish you good-night.' And then the two ladies shook hands with him, and walked on towards the parsonage. That which astonished Mrs. Robarts the most in all this was the perfectly collected manner in which Lucy spoke and conducted herself. This, connected, as she could not but connect it, with the air of chagrin with which Lord Lufton received Lucy's decision, made it manifest to Mrs. Robarts that Lord Lufton was annoyed because Lucy would not consent to learn to ride; whereas she, Lucy herself, had given her refusal in a firm and decided tone, as though resolved that nothing more should be said about it. They walked on in silence for a minute or two, till they reached the parsonage gate, and then Lucy said, laughing, 'Can't you fancy me sitting on that great big horse? I wonder what Lady Lufton would say if she saw me there, and his lordship giving me my first lesson?'

'I don't think she would like it,' said Fanny.

'I'm sure she would not. But I will not try her temper in that respect. Sometimes I fancy that she does not even like seeing Lord Lufton talking to me.'

'She does not like it, Lucy, when she sees him flirting with you.' This Mrs. Robarts said rather gravely, whereas Lucy had been speaking in a half-bantering tone. As soon as even the word flirting was out of Fanny's mouth, she was conscious that she had been guilty of an injustice in using it. She had wished to say something which would convey to her sister-in-law an idea of what Lady Lufton would dislike; but in doing so, she had unintentionally brought against her an accusation.

'Flirting, Fanny!' said Lucy, standing still in the path, and looking up into her companion's face with all her eyes. 'Do you mean to say that I have been flirting with Lord Lufton?'

'I did not say that.'

'Or that I have allowed him to flirt with me?'

'I did not mean to shock you, Lucy.'

'What did you mean, Fanny?'

'Why, just this: that Lady Lufton would not be pleased if he paid you marked attentions, and if you received them; just like that affair of the riding; it was better to decline it.'

'Of course I declined it; of course I never dreamt of accepting such an offer. Go riding about the country on his horses! What have I done, Fanny, that you should suppose such a thing?'

'You have done nothing, dearest.'

'Then why did you speak as you did just now?'

'Because I wished to put you on your guard. You know, Lucy, that I do not intend to find fault with you; but you may be sure, as a rule, that intimate friendships between young gentlemen and young ladies are dangerous things.' They then walked up to the hall-door in silence. When they had reached it, Lucy stood in the doorway instead of entering it, and said, 'Fanny, let us take another turn together, if you are not tired.'

'No, I'm not tired.'

'It will be better that I should understand you at once,' – and then they again moved away from the house. 'Tell me truly now, do you think that Lord Lufton and I have been flirting?'

'I do think that he is a little inclined to flirt with you.'

'And Lady Lufton has been asking you to lecture me about it?' Poor Mrs. Robarts hardly knew what to say. She thought well of all the persons concerned, and was very anxious to behave well by all of them; – was particularly anxious to create no ill feeling, and wished that everybody should be comfortable, and on good terms with everybody else. But yet the truth was forced out of her when this question was asked so suddenly. 'Not to lecture you, Lucy,' she said at last.

'Well, to preach to me, or to talk to me, or to give me a lesson; to say something that shall drive me to put my back up against Lord Lufton?'

'To caution you, dearest. Had you heard what she said, you would hardly have felt angry with Lady Lufton.'

'Well, to caution me. It is such a pleasant thing for a girl to be cautioned against falling in love with a gentleman, especially when the gentleman is very rich, and a lord, and all that sort of thing!'

'Nobody for a moment attributes anything wrong to you, Lucy.'

'Anything wrong – no. I don't know whether it would be anything wrong, even if I were to fall in love with him. I wonder whether they cautioned Griselda Grantly when she was here? I suppose when young lords go about, all the girls are cautioned as a matter of course. Why do they not label him "dangerous"?' And then again they were silent for a moment, as Mrs. Robarts did not feel that she had anything further to say on the matter.

' "Poison" should be the word with any one so fatal as Lord Lufton; and he ought to be made up of some particular colour, for fear he should be swallowed in mistake.'

'You will be safe, you see,' said Fanny, laughing, 'as you have been specially cautioned as to this individual bottle.'

'Ah! but what's the use of that after I have had so many doses? It is no good telling me about it now; when the mischief is done, – after I have been taking it for I don't know how long. Dear! dear! dear! and I regarded it as a mere commonplace powder, good for the complexion. I wonder whether it's too late, or whether there's any antidote?' Mrs. Robarts did not always quite understand her sister-in-law, and now she was a little at a loss. 'I don't think there's much harm done yet on either side,' she said, cheerily.

'Ah! you don't know, Fanny. But I do think that if I die – as I shall – I feel I shall; – and if so, I do think it ought to go very hard with Lady Lufton. Why didn't she label him "dangerous" in time?' And then they went into the house and up to their own rooms. It was difficult for any one to understand Lucy's state of mind at present, and it can hardly be said that she understood it herself. She felt that she had received a severe blow in having been thus made the subject of remark with reference to Lord Lufton. She knew that her pleasant evenings at Framley Court were now over, and that she could not again talk to him in an unrestrained tone and without embarrassment. She had felt the air of the whole place to be very cold before her intimacy with him, and now it must be cold again. Two homes had been open to her; Framley Court and the parsonage; and now, as far as comfort was concerned, she must confine herself to the latter. She could not again be comfortable in Lady Lufton's drawing-room. But then she could not help asking herself whether Lady Lufton was not right. She had had courage enough, and presence of mind, to joke about the matter when her sister-in-law spoke to her, and yet she was quite aware that it was no joking matter. Lord Lufton had not absolutely made love to her, but he had latterly spoken to her in a manner which she knew was not compatible with that ordinary comfortable masculine friendship with the idea of which she had once satisfied herself. Was not Fanny right when she said that intimate friendships of that nature were dangerous things?

Yes, Lucy, very dangerous. Lucy, before she went to bed that night, had owned to herself that they were so; and lying there with sleepless eyes and a moist pillow, she was driven to confess that the label would in truth be now too late, that the caution had come to her after the poison had been swallowed. Was there any antidote? That was all that was left for her to consider. But, nevertheless, on the following morning she could appear quite at her ease. And when Mark had left the house after breakfast, she could still joke with Fanny as to Lady Lufton's poisoned cupboard.

CHAPTER XIV

Mr. Crawley of Hogglestock

AND then there was that other trouble in Lady Lufton's mind, the sins, namely, of her selected parson. She had selected him, and she was by no means inclined to give him up, even though his sins against parsondom were grievous. Indeed she was a woman not prone to give up anything, and of all things not prone to give up a protégé. The very fact that she herself had selected him was the strongest argument in his favour. But his sins against parsondom were becoming very grievous in her eyes, and she was at a loss to know what steps to take. She hardly dared to take him to task, him himself. Were she to do so, and should he then tell her to mind her own business – as he probably might do, though not in those words – there would be a schism in the parish; and almost anything would be better than that. The whole work of her life would be upset, all the outlets of her energy would be impeded if not absolutely closed, if a state of things were to come to pass in which she and the parson of her parish should not be on good terms.

But what was to be done? Early in the winter he had gone to Chaldicotes and to Gatherum Castle, consorting with gamblers, Whigs, atheists, men of loose pleasure, and Proudieites. That she had condoned; and now he was turning out a hunting parson on her hands. It was all very well for Fanny to say that he merely looked at the hounds as he rode about his parish. Fanny might be deceived. Being his wife, it might be her duty not to see her husband's iniquities. But Lady Lufton could not be deceived. She knew very well in what part of the country Cobbold's Ashes lay. It was not in Framley parish, nor in the next parish to it. It was half-way across to Chaldicotes – in the western division; and she had heard of that run in which two horses had been killed, and in which Parson Robarts had won such immortal glory among West Barsetshire sportsmen. It was not easy to keep Lady Lufton in the dark as to matters occurring in her own county.

All these things she knew, but as yet had not noticed, grieving over them in her own heart the more on that account. Spoken grief relieves itself; and when one can give counsel, one always hopes at least that the counsel will be effective. To her son she had said, more than once, that it was a pity that Mr. Robarts should follow the hounds. – 'The world has agreed that it is unbecoming in a clergyman,' she would urge, in her deprecatory tone. But her son would by no means give her any comfort. 'He doesn't hunt, you know – not as I do,' he would say. 'And if he did, I really don't see the harm of it. A man must have some amusement, even if he be an archbishop.' 'He has amusement at home,' Lady Lufton would answer. 'What does his wife do – and his sister?' This allusion to Lucy, however, was very soon dropped.

Lord Lufton would in no wise help her. He would not even passively discourage the vicar, or refrain from offering to give him a seat in going to the meets. Mark and Lord Lufton had been boys together, and his lordship knew that Mark in his heart would enjoy a brush across the country quite as well as he himself; and then what was the harm of it? Lady Lufton's best aid had been in Mark's own conscience. He had taken himself to task more than once, and had promised himself that he would not become a sporting parson. Indeed, where would be his hopes of ulterior promotion, if he allowed himself to degenerate so far as that? It had been his intention, in reviewing what he considered to be the necessary proprieties of clerical life, in laying out his own future mode of living, to assume no peculiar sacerdotal strictness; he would not be known as a denouncer of dancing or of card-tables, of theatres or of novel-reading; he would take the world around him as he found it, endeavouring by precept and practice to lend a hand to the gradual amelioration which Christianity is producing; but he would attempt no sudden or majestic reforms. Cake and ale would still be popular, and ginger be hot in the mouth, let him preach ever so – let him be never so solemn a hermit; but a bright face, a true trusting heart, a strong arm, and an humble mind, might do much in teaching those around him that men may be gay and yet not profligate, that women may be devout and yet not dead to the world.

Such had been his ideas as to his own future life; and though many would think that, as a clergyman, he should have gone about his work with more serious devotion of thought, nevertheless there was some wisdom in them; – some folly also, undoubtedly, as appeared by the troubles into which they led him. 'I will not affect to think that to be bad,' he said to himself, 'which in my heart of hearts does not seem to be bad.' And thus he resolved that he might live without contamination among hunting squires. And then, being a man only too prone by nature to do as others did around him, he found by degrees that that could hardly be wrong for him which he admitted to be right for others.

But still his conscience upbraided him, and he declared to himself more than once that after this year he would hunt no more. And then his own Fanny would look at him on his return home on those days in a manner that cut him to the heart. She would say nothing to him. She never inquired in a sneering tone, and with angry eyes, whether he had enjoyed his day's sport: but when he spoke of it, she could not answer him with enthusiasm; and in other matters which concerned him she was always enthusiastic. After a while, too, he made matters worse, for about the end of March he did another very foolish thing. He almost consented to buy an expensive horse from Sowerby – an animal which he by no means wanted, and which, if once possessed, would certainly lead him into further trouble. A gentleman, when he has a good horse in his stable, does not like to leave him there eating his head off. If he be a gig-horse, the owner of him will be keen to drive a gig; if a hunter, the happy possessor will wish to be with a pack of hounds.

'Mark,' said Sowerby to him one day, when they were out together, 'this brute of mine is so fresh, I can hardly ride him; you are young and strong; change with me for an hour or so.' And then they did change, and the horse on which Robarts found himself mounted went away with him beautifully.

'He's a splendid animal,' said Mark, when they again met.

'Yes, for a man of your weight. He's thrown away upon me; – too much of a horse for my purposes. I don't get along now quite as well as I used to do. He is a nice sort of hunter; just rising six, you know.' How it came to pass that the price of the splendid animal was mentioned between them, I need not describe with exactness. But it did come to pass that Mr. Sowerby told the parson that the horse should be his for £130. 'And I really wish you'd take him,' said Sowerby. 'It would be the means of partially relieving my mind of a great weight.' Mark looked up into his friend's face with an air of surprise, for he did not at the moment understand how this should be the case.

'I am afraid, you know, that you will have to put your hand into your pocket sooner or later about that accursed bill' – Mark shrank as the profane words struck his ears – 'and I should be glad to think that you had got something in hand in the way of value.'

'Do you mean that I shall have to pay the whole sum of £500?'

'Oh! dear, no; nothing of the kind. But something I dare say you will have to pay: if you like to take Dandy for a hundred and thirty, you can be prepared for that amount when Tozer comes to you. The horse is dog cheap, and you will have a long day for your money.' Mark at first declared, in a quiet, determined tone, that he did not want the horse; but it afterwards appeared to him that if it were so fated that he must pay a portion of Mr. Sowerby's debts he might as well repay himself to any extent within his power. It would be as well perhaps that he should take the horse and sell him. It did not occur to him that by so doing he would put it in Mr. Sowerby's power to say that some valuable consideration had passed between them with reference to this bill, and that he would be aiding that gentleman in preparing an inextricable confusion of money-matters between them. Mr. Sowerby well knew the value of this. It would enable him to make a plausible story, as he had done in that other case of Lord Lufton. 'Are you going to have Dandy?' Sowerby said to him again.

'I can't say that I will just at present,' said the parson. 'What should I want of him now the season's over?'

'Exactly, my dear fellow; and what do I want of him now the season's over? If it were the beginning of October instead of the end of March, Dandy would be up at two hundred and thirty instead of one: in six months' time that horse will be worth anything you like to ask for him. Look at his bone.' The vicar did look at his bones, examining the brute in a very knowing and unclerical manner. He lifted the animal's four feet, one after another, handling the frogs, and measuring with his eye the proportion of the parts; he passed his hand up and down the legs, spanning the bones of the lower joint; he peered into his eyes, took into consideration the width of his chest, the dip of his back, the form of his ribs, the curve of his haunches, and his capabilities for breathing when pressed by work. And then he stood away a little, eyeing him from the side, and taking in a general idea of the form and make of the whole. 'He seems to stand over a little, I think,' said the parson.

'It's the lie of the ground. Move him about, Bob. There now, let him stand there.'

'He's not perfect,' said Mark. 'I don't quite like his heels; but no doubt he's a niceish cut of a horse.'

'I rather think he is. If he were perfect, as you say, he would not be going into your stables for a hundred and thirty. Do you ever remember to have seen a perfect horse?'

'Your mare Mrs. Gamp was as nearly perfect as possible.'

'Even Mrs. Gamp had her faults. In the first place she was a bad feeder. But one certainly doesn't often come across anything much better than Mrs. Gamp.' And thus the matter was talked over between them with much stable conversation, all of which tended to make Sowerby more and more oblivious of his friend's sacred profession, and perhaps to make the vicar himself too frequently oblivious of it also. But no: he was not oblivious of it. He was even mindful of it; but mindful of it in such a manner that his thoughts on the subject were nowadays always painful.

There is a parish called Hogglestock lying away quite in the northern extremity of the eastern division of the county – lying also on the borders of the western division. I almost fear that it will become necessary, before this history be completed, to provide a map of Barsetshire for the due explanation of all these localities. Framley is also in the northern portion of the county, but just to the south of the grand trunk line of railway from which the branch to Barchester strikes off at a point some thirty miles nearer to London. The station for Framley Court is Silverbridge, which is, however, in the western division of the county. Hogglestock is to the north of the railway, the line of which, however, runs through a portion of the parish, and it adjoins Framley, though the churches are as much as seven miles apart. Barsetshire, taken altogether, is a pleasant green tree-becrowded county, with large bosky hedges, pretty damp deep lanes, and roads with broad grass margins running along them. Such is the general nature of the county; but just up in its northern extremity this nature alters. There it is bleak and ugly, with low artificial hedges and without wood; not uncultivated, as it is all portioned out into new-looking large fields, bearing turnips, and wheat, and mangel, all in due course of agricultural rotation; but it has none of the special beauties of English cultivation. There is not a gentleman's house in the parish of Hogglestock besides that of the clergyman; and this, though it is certainly the house of a gentleman, can hardly be said to be fit to be so. It is ugly, and straight, and small. There is a garden attached to the house, half in front of it and half behind; but this garden, like the rest of the parish, is by no means ornamental, though sufficiently useful. It produces cabbages, but no trees: potatoes of, I believe, an excellent description, but hardly any flowers, and nothing worthy of the name of a shrub. Indeed the whole parish of Hogglestock should have been in the adjoining county, which is by no means so attractive as Barsetshire; – a fact well known to those few of my readers who are well acquainted with their own country.

Mr. Crawley, whose name has been mentioned in these pages, was the incumbent of Hogglestock. On what principle the remuneration of our parish clergymen was settled when the original settlement was made, no deepest, keenest lover of middle-aged ecclesiastical black-letter learning can, I take it, now say. That the priests were to be paid from tithes of the parish produce, out of which tithes certain other good things were to be bought and paid for, such as church repairs and education, of so much the most of us have an inkling. That a rector, being a big sort of parson, owned the tithes of his parish in full, – or at any rate that part of them intended for the clergyman, – and that a vicar was somebody's deputy, and therefore entitled only to little tithes, as being a little body: of so much we that are simple in such matters have a general idea. But one cannot conceive that even in this way any approximation could have been made, even in those old mediaeval days, towards a fair proportioning of the pay to the work. At any rate, it is clear enough that there is no such approximation now. And what a screech would there not be among the clergy of the Church, even in these reforming days, if any over-bold reformer were to suggest that such an approximation should be attempted? Let those who know clergymen, and like them, and have lived with them, only fancy it! Clergymen to be paid, not according to the temporalities of any living which they may have acquired, either by merit or favour, but in accordance with the work to be done! O Doddington! and O Stanhope, think of this, if an idea so sacrilegious can find entrance into your warm ecclesiastical bosoms! Ecclesiastical work to be bought and paid for according to its quantity and quality!

But, nevertheless, one may prophesy that we Englishmen must come to this, disagreeable as the idea undoubtedly is. Most pleasant-minded Churchmen feel, I think, on this subject pretty much in the same way. Our present arrangement of parochial incomes is beloved as being time-honoured, gentlemanlike, English, and picturesque. We would fain adhere to it closely as long as we can, but we know that we do so by the force of our prejudices, and not by that of our judgement. A time-honoured, gentlemanlike, English, picturesque arrangement is so far very delightful. But are there not other attributes very desirable – nay, absolutely necessary – in respect to which this time-honoured, picturesque arrangement is so very deficient?

How pleasant it was, too, that one bishop should be getting fifteen thousand a year, and another with an equal cure of parsons only four! That a certain prelate could get twenty thousand one year and his successor in the same diocese only five the next! There was something in it pleasant, and picturesque; it was an arrangement endowed with feudal charms, and the change which they have made was distasteful to many of us. A bishop with a regular salary, and no appanage of land and land-bailiffs, is only half a bishop. Let any man prove to me the contrary ever so thoroughly – let me prove it to my own self ever so often – my heart in this matter is not thereby a whit altered. One liked to know that there was a dean or two who got his three thousand a year, and that old Dr. Purple held four stalls, one of which was golden, and the other three silver-gilt! Such knowledge was always pleasant to me! A golden stall! How sweet is the sound thereof to church-loving ears! But bishops have been shorn of their beauty, and deans are in their decadence. A utilitarian age requires the fatness of the ecclesiastical land, in order that it may be divided out into small portions of provender, on which necessary working clergymen may live, – into portions so infinitesimally small that working clergymen can hardly live. And the full-blown rectors and vicars, with full-blown tithes – with tithes when too full-blown for strict utilitarian principles – will necessarily follow. Stanhope and Doddington must bow their heads, with such compensation for temporal rights as may be extracted, – but probably without such compensation as may be desired. In other trades, professions, and lines of life, men are paid according to their work. Let it be so in the Church. Such will sooner or later be the edict of a utilitarian, reforming, matter-of-fact House of Parliament.

I have a scheme of my own on the subject, which I will not introduce here, seeing that neither men nor women would read it. And with reference to this matter, I will only here further explain that all these words have been brought about by the fact, necessary to be here stated, that Mr. Crawley only received one hundred and thirty pounds a year for performing the whole parochial duty of the parish of Hogglestock. And Hogglestock is a large parish. It includes two populous villages, abounding in brickmakers, a race of men very troublesome to a zealous parson who won't let men go rollicking to the devil without interference. Hogglestock has full work for two men; and yet all the funds therein applicable to parson's work is this miserable stipend of one hundred and thirty pounds a year. It is a stipend neither picturesque, nor time-honoured, nor feudal, for Hogglestock takes rank only as a perpetual curacy.

Mr. Crawley has been mentioned before as a clergyman of whom Mr. Robarts said, that he almost thought it wrong to take a walk out of his own parish. In so saying Mark Robarts of course burlesqued his brother parson; but there can be no doubt that Mr. Crawley was a strict man, – a strict, stern, unpleasant man, and one who feared God and his own conscience. We must say a word or two of Mr. Crawley and his concerns. He was now some forty years of age, but of these he had not been in possession even of his present benefice for more than four or five. The first ten years of his life as a clergyman had been passed in performing the duties and struggling through the life of a curate in a bleak, ugly, cold parish on the northern coast of Cornwall. It had been a weary life and a fearful struggle, made up of duties ill requited and not always satisfactorily performed, of love and poverty, of increasing cares, of sickness, debt, and death. For Mr. Crawley had married almost as soon as he was ordained, and children had been born to him in that chill, comfortless Cornish cottage. He had married a lady well educated and softly nurtured, but not dowered with worldly wealth. They two had gone forth determined to fight bravely together; to disregard the world and the world's ways, looking only to God and to each other for their comfort. They would give up ideas of gentle living, of soft raiment, and delicate feeding. Others, – those that work with their hands, even the bettermost of such workers – could live in decency and health upon even such provision as he could earn as a clergyman. In such manner would they live, so poorly and so decently, working out their work, not with their hands but with their hearts.

And so they had established themselves, beginning the world with one bare-footed little girl of fourteen to aid them in their small household matters; and for a while they had both kept heart, loving each other dearly, and prospering somewhat in their work. But a man who has once walked the world as a gentleman knows not what it is to change his postion, and place himself lower down in the social rank. Much less can he know what it is so to put down the woman whom he loves. There are a thousand things, mean and trifling in themselves, which a man despises when he thinks of them in his philosophy, but to dispense with which puts his philosophy to so stern a proof. Let any plainest man who reads this think of his usual mode of getting himself into his matutinal garments, and confess how much such a struggle would cost him. And then children had come. The wife of the labouring man does rear her children, and often rears them in health, without even so many appliances of comfort as found their way into Mrs. Crawley's cottage; but the task to her was almost more than she could accomplish. Not that she ever fainted or gave way: she was made of the sterner metal of the two, and could last on while he was prostrate.

And sometimes he was prostrate – prostrate in soul and spirit. Then would he complain with bitter voice, crying out that the world was too hard for him, that his back was broken with his burden, that his God had deserted him. For days and days, in such moods, he would stay within his cottage, never darkening the door or seeing other face than those of his own inmates. Those days were terrible both to him and her. He would sit there unwashed, with his unshorn face resting on his hand, with an old dressing-gown hanging loose about him, hardly tasting food, seldom speaking, striving to pray, but striving so frequently in vain. And then he would rise from his chair, and, with a burst of frenzy, call upon his Creator to remove him from this misery. In these moments she never deserted him. At one period they had had four children, and though the whole weight of this young brood rested on her arms, on her muscles, on her strength of mind and body, she never ceased in her efforts to comfort him. Then at length, falling utterly upon the ground, he would pour forth piteous prayers for mercy, and after a night of sleep would once more go forth to his work.

But she never yielded to despair: the struggle was never beyond her powers of endurance. She had possessed her share of woman's loveliness, but that was now all gone. Her colour quickly faded, and the fresh, soft tints soon deserted her face and forehead. She became thin, and rough, and almost haggard: thin till her cheek-bones were nearly pressing through her skin, till her elbows were sharp, and her finger-bones as those of a skeleton. Her eye did not lose its lustre, but it became unnaturally bright, prominent, and too large for her wan face. The soft brown locks which she had once loved to brush back, scorning, as she would boast to herself, to care that they should be seen, were now sparse enough and all untidy and unclean. It was matter of little thought now whether they were seen or no. Whether he could be made fit to go into his pulpit – whether they might be fed – those four innocents – and their backs kept from the cold wind – that was now the matter of her thought. And then two of them died, and she went forth herself to see them laid under the frost-bound sod, lest he should faint in his work over their graves. For he would ask aid from no man – such at least was his boast through all. Two of them died, but their illness had been long; and then debts came upon them. Debt, indeed, had been creeping on them with slow but sure feet during the last five years. Who can see his children hungry, and not take bread if it be offered? Who can see his wife lying in sharpest want, and not seek a remedy if there be a remedy within reach? So debt had come upon them, and rude men pressed for small sums of money – for sums small to the world, but impossibly large to them. And he would hide himself within there, in that cranny of an inner chamber – hide himself with deep shame from the world, with shame, and a sinking heart, and a broken spirit.

But had such a man no friend? it will be said. Such men, I take it, do not make many friends. But this man was not utterly friendless. Almost every year one visit was paid to him in his Cornish curacy by a brother clergyman, an old college friend, who, as far as might in him lie, did give aid to the curate and his wife. This gentleman would take up his abode for a week at a farmer's, in the neighbourhood, and though he found Mr. Crawley in despair, he would leave him with some drops of comfort in his soul. Nor were the benefits in this respect all on one side. Mr. Crawley, though at some periods weak enough for himself, could be strong for others; and, more than once, was strong for the great advantage of this man whom he loved. And then, too, pecuniary assistance was forthcoming – in those earlier years not in great amount, for this friend was not then among the rich ones of the earth – but in amount sufficient for that moderate hearth, if only its acceptance would have been managed. But in that matter there were difficulties without end. Of absolute money tenders Mr. Crawley would accept none. But a bill here and there was paid, the wife assisting; and shoes came for Kate – till Kate was placed beyond the need of shoes; and cloth for Harry and Frank found its way surreptitiously in beneath the cover of that wife's solitary trunk – cloth with which those lean fingers worked garments for the two boys, to be worn – such was God's will – only by the one.

Such were Mr. and Mrs. Crawley in their Cornish curacy, and during their severest struggles. To one who thinks that a fair day's work is worth a fair day's wages, it seems hard enough that a man should work so hard and receive so little. There will be those who think that the fault was all his own in marrying so young. But still there remains that question, Is not a fair day's work worth a fair day's wages? This man did work hard – at a task perhaps the hardest of any that a man may do; and for ten years he earned some seventy pounds a year. Will any one say that he received fair wages for his fair work, let him be married or single? And yet there are so many who would fain pay their clergy, if they only knew how to apply their money! But that is a long subject, as Mr. Robarts had told Miss Dunstable. Such was Mr. Crawley in his Cornish curacy.

CHAPTER XV

Lady Lufton's Ambassador

AND then, in the days which followed, that friend of Mr. Crawley's, whose name, by the by, is yet to be mentioned, received quick and great promotion. Mr. Arabin by name he was then; Dr. Arabin afterwards, when that quick and great promotion reached its climax. He had been simply a Fellow of Lazarus in those former years. Then he became vicar of St. Ewold's, in East Barsetshire, and had not yet got himself settled there when he married the Widow Bold, a widow with belongings in land and funded money, and with but one small baby as an encumbrance. Nor had he even yet married her, had only engaged himself so to do, when they made him Dean of Barchester – all which may be read in the diocesan and county chronicles. And now that he was wealthy, the new dean did contrive to pay the debts of his poor friend, some lawyer of Camelford assisting him. It was but a paltry schedule after all, amounting in the total to something not much above a hundred pounds. And then, in the course of eighteen months, this poor piece of preferment fell in the dean's way, this incumbency of Hogglestock with its stipend reaching one hundred and thirty pounds a year. Even that was worth double the Cornish curacy, and there was, moreover, a house attached to it. Poor Mrs. Crawley, when she heard of it, thought that their struggles of poverty were now wellnigh over. What might not be done with a hundred and thirty pounds by people who had lived for ten years on seventy?

And so they moved away out of that cold, bleak country, carrying with them their humble household gods, and settled themselves in another country, cold and bleak also, but less terribly so than the former. They settled themselves, and again began their struggles against man's hardness and the devil's zeal. I have said that Mr. Crawley was a stern, unpleasant man; and it certainly was so. The man must be made of very sterling stuff, whom continued and undeserved misfortune does not make unpleasant. This man had so far succumbed to grief, that it had left upon him its marks, palpable and not to be effaced. He cared little for society, judging men to be doing evil who did care for it. He knew as a fact, and believed with all his heart, that these sorrows had come to him from the hand of God, and that they would work for his weal in the long run; but not the less did they make him morose, silent and dogged. He had always at his heart a feeling that he and his had been ill-used, and too often solaced himself, at the devil's bidding, with the conviction that eternity would make equal that which life in this world had made so unequal; the last bait that with which the devil angles after those who are struggling to elude his rod and line.

The Framley property did not run into the parish of Hogglestock; but nevertheless Lady Lufton did what she could in the way of kindness to these new-comers. Providence had not supplied Hogglestock with a Lady Lufton, or with any substitute in the shape of lord or lady, squire or squires. The Hogglestock farmers, male and female, were a rude, rough set, not bordering in their social rank on the farmer gentle; and Lady Lufton, knowing this, and hearing something of these Crawleys from Mrs. Arabin the dean's wife, trimmed her lamps, so that they should shed a wider light, and pour forth some of their influence on that forlorn household. And as regards Mrs. Crawley,

Lady Lufton by no means found that her work and goodwill were thrown away. Mrs. Crawley accepted her kindness with thankfulness, and returned to some of the softnesses of life under her hand. As for dining at Framley Court, that was out of the question. Mr. Crawley, she knew, would not hear of it, even if other things were fitting and appliances were at command. Indeed Mrs. Crawley at once said that she felt herself unfit to go through such a ceremony with anything like comfort. The dean, she said, would talk of their going to stay at the deanery; but she thought it quite impossible that either of them should endure even that. But, all the same, Lady Lufton was a comfort to her; and the poor woman felt that it was well to have a lady near her in case of need.

The task was much harder with Mr. Crawley, but even with him it was not altogether unsuccessful. Lady Lufton talked to him of his parish and of her own; made Mark Robarts go to him, and by degrees did something towards civilizing him. Between him and Robarts too there grew up an intimacy rather than a friendship. Robarts would submit to his opinion on matters of ecclesiastical and even theological law, would listen to him with patience, would agree with him where he could, and differ from him mildly when he could not. For Robarts was a man who made himself pleasant to all men. And thus, under Lady Lufton's wing, there grew up a connexion between Framley and Hogglestock, in which Mrs. Robarts also assisted. And now that Lady Lufton was looking about her, to see how she might best bring proper clerical influence to bear upon her own recreant fox-hunting parson, it occurred to her that she might use Mr. Crawley in the matter. Mr. Crawley would certainly be on her side as far as opinion went, and would have no fear as to expressing his opinion to his brother clergyman. So she sent for Mr. Crawley. In appearance he was the very opposite to Mark Robarts. He was a lean, slim, meagre man, with shoulders slightly curved, and pale, lank, long locks of ragged hair;

his forehead was high, but his face was narrow; his small grey eyes were deeply sunken in his head, his nose was well-formed, his lips thin, and his mouth expressive. Nobody could look at him without seeing that there was a purpose and a meaning in his countenance. He always wore, in summer and winter, a long dusky grey coat, which buttoned close up to his neck and descended almost to his heels. He was full six feet high, but being so slight in build, he looked as though he were taller. He came at once at Lady Lufton's bidding, putting himself into the gig beside the servant, to whom he spoke no single word during the journey. And the man, looking into his face, was struck with taciturnity. Now Mark Robarts would have talked with him the whole way from Hogglestock to Framley Court; discoursing partly as to horses and land, but partly also as to higher things. And then Lady Lufton opened her mind and told her griefs to Mr. Crawley, urging, however, through the whole length of her narrative, that Mr. Robarts was an excellent parish clergyman, – 'just such a clergyman in his church as I would wish him to be,' she explained, with the view of saving herself from an expression of any of Mr. Crawley's special ideas as to church teaching, and of confining him to the one subject-matter in hand; 'but he got this living so young, Mr. Crawley, that he is hardly quite as steady as I could wish him to be. It has been as much my fault as his own in placing him in such a position so early in life.'

'I think it has,' said Mr. Crawley, who might perhaps be a little sore on such a subject.

'Quite so, quite so,' continued her ladyship, swallowing down with a gulp a certain sense of anger. 'But that is done now, and is past cure. That Mr. Robarts will become a credit to his profession, I do not doubt, for his heart is in the right place and his sentiments are good; but I fear that at present he is succumbing to temptation.'

'I am told that he hunts two or three times a week. Everybody round us is talking about it.'

'No, Mr. Crawley; not two or three times a week; very seldom above once, I think. And then I do believe he does it more with the view of being with Lord Lufton than anything else.'

'I cannot see that that would make the matter better,' said Mr. Crawley.

'It would show that he was not strongly imbued with a taste which I cannot but regard as vicious in a clergyman.'

'It must be vicious in all men,' said Mr. Crawley. 'It is in itself cruel, and leads to idleness and profligacy.' Again Lady Lufton made a gulp. She had called Mr. Crawley thither to her aid, and felt that it would be inexpedient to quarrel with him. But she did not like to be told that her son's amusement was idle and profligate. She had always regarded hunting as a proper pursuit for a country gentleman. It was, indeed, in her eyes one of the peculiar institutions of country life in England, and it may be almost said that she looked upon the Barsetshire Hunt as something sacred. She could not endure to hear that a fox was trapped, and allowed her turkeys to be purloined without a groan. Such being the case, she did not like being told that it was vicious, and had by no means wished to consult Mr. Crawley on that matter. But nevertheless she swallowed down her wrath.

'It is at any rate unbecoming in a clergyman,' she said; 'and as I know that Mr. Robarts places a high value on your opinion, perhaps you will not object to advise him to discontinue it. He might possibly feel aggrieved were I to interfere personally on such a question.'

'I have no doubt he would,' said Mr. Crawley. 'It is not within a woman's province to give counsel to a clergyman on such a subject, unless she be very near and very dear to him – his wife, or mother, or sister.'

'As living in the same parish, you know, and being, perhaps –' the leading person in it, and the one who naturally rules the others. Those would have been the fitting words for the expression of her ladyship's ideas; but she remembered herself, and did not use them. She had made up her mind that, great as her influence ought to be, she was not the proper person to speak to Mr. Robarts as to his pernicious, unclerical habits, and she would not now depart from her resolve by attempting to prove that she was the proper person.

'Yes,' said Mr. Crawley, 'just so. All that would entitle him to offer you his counsel if he thought that your mode of life was such as to require it, but could by no means justify you in addressing yourself to him.' This was very hard upon Lady Lufton. She was endeavouring with all her woman's strength to do her best, and endeavouring so to do it that the feelings of the sinner might be spared; and yet the ghostly comforter whom she had evoked to her aid, treated her as though she were arrogant and overbearing. She acknowledged the weakness of her own position with reference to her parish clergyman by calling in the aid of Mr. Crawley; and, under such circumstances, he might, at any rate, have abstained from throwing that weakness in her teeth.

'Well, sir; I hope my mode of life may not require it; but that is not exactly to the point: what I wish to know is, whether you will speak to Mr. Robarts?'

'Certainly I will,' said he.

'Then I shall be much obliged to you. But, Mr. Crawley, pray – pray, remember this: I would not on any account wish that you should be harsh with him. He is an excellent young man, and –'

'Lady Lufton, if I do this, I can only do it in my own way, as best I may, using such words as God may give me at the time. I hope that I am harsh to no man; but it is worse than useless, in all cases, to speak anything but the truth.'

'Of course – of course.'

'If the ears be too delicate to hear the truth, the mind will be too perverse to profit by it.' And then Mr. Crawley got up to take his leave. But Lady Lufton insisted that he should go with her to luncheon. He hummed and ha'd and would fain have refused, but on this subject she was peremptory. It might be that she was unfit to advise a clergyman as to his duties, but in a matter of hospitality she did know what she was about. Mr. Crawley should not leave the house without refreshment. As to this, she carried her point; and Mr. Crawley – when the matter before him was cold roast-beef and hot potatoes, instead of the relative position of a parish priest and his parishioner – became humble, submissive, and almost timid. Lady Lufton recommended Madeira instead of sherry, and Mr. Crawley obeyed at once, and was, indeed, perfectly unconscious of the difference. Then there was a basket of seakale in the gig for Mrs. Crawley; that he would have left behind had he dared, but he did not dare. Not a word was said to him as to the marmalade for the children which was hidden under the seakale, Lady Lufton feeling well aware that that would find its way to its proper destination without any necessity for his co-operation. And then Mr. Crawley returned home in the Framley Court gig.

Three or four days after this he walked over to Framley parsonage. This he did on a Saturday, having learned that the hounds never hunted on that day; and he started early, so that he might be sure to catch Mr. Robarts before he went out on his parish business. He was quite early enough to attain this object, for when he reached the parsonage door at about half-past nine, the vicar, with his wife and sister, were just sitting down to breakfast. 'Oh, Crawley,' said Robarts, before the other had well spoken, 'you are a capital fellow;' and then he got him into a chair, and Mrs. Robarts had poured him out tea, and Lucy had surrendered to him a knife and plate, before he knew under what guise to excuse his coming among them.

'I hope you will excuse this intrusion,' at last he muttered; 'but I have a few words of business to which I will request your attention presently.'

'Certainly,' said Robarts, conveying a broiled kidney on to the plate before Mr. Crawley; 'but there is no preparation for business like a good breakfast. Lucy, hand Mr. Crawley the buttered toast. Eggs, Fanny; where are the eggs?' And then John, in livery, brought in the fresh eggs. 'Now we shall do. I always eat my eggs while they're hot, Crawley, and I advise you to do the same.' To all this Mr. Crawley said very little, and he was not at all at home under the circumstances. Perhaps a thought did pass across his brain, as to the difference between the meal which he had left on his own table, and that which he now saw before him; and as to any cause which might exist for such difference. But, if so, it was a very fleeting thought, for he had far other matter now fully occupying his mind. And then the breakfast was over, and in a few minutes the two clergymen found themselves together in the parsonage study.

'Mr. Robarts,' began the senior, when he had seated himself uncomfortably on one of the ordinary chairs at the farther side of the well-stored library table, while Mark was sitting at his ease in his own arm-chair by the fire, 'I have called upon you on an unpleasant business.' Mark's mind immediately flew off to Mr. Sowerby's bill, but he could not think it possible that Mr. Crawley could have had anything to do with that.

'But as a brother clergyman, and as one who esteems you much and wishes you well, I have thought myself bound to take this matter in hand.'

'What matter is it, Crawley?'

'Mr. Robarts, men say that your present mode of life is one that is not befitting a soldier in Christ's army.'

'Men say so! what men?'

'The men around you, of your own neighbourhood; those who watch your life, and know all your doings; those who look to see you walking as a lamp to guide their feet, but find you consorting with horse-jockeys and hunters, galloping after hounds, and taking your place among the vainest of worldly pleasure-seekers. Those who have a right to expect an example of good living, and who think that they do not see it.' Mr. Crawley had gone at once to the root of the matter, and in doing so had certainly made his own task so much the easier. There is nothing like going to the root of the matter at once when one has on hand an unpleasant piece of business.

'And have such men deputed you to come here?'

'No one has or could depute me. I have come to speak my own mind, not that of any other. But I refer to what those around you think and say, because it is to them that your duties are due. You owe it to those around you to live a godly, cleanly life; – as you owe it also, in a much higher way, to your Father who is in heaven. I now make bold to ask you whether you are doing your best to lead such a life as that?' And then he remained silent, waiting for an answer. He was a singular man; so humble and meek, so unutterably inefficient and awkward in the ordinary intercourse of life, but so bold and enterprising, almost eloquent, on the one subject which was the work of his mind! As he sat there, he looked into his companion's face from out his sunken grey eyes with a gaze which made his victim quail. And then repeated his words: 'I now make bold to ask you, Mr. Robarts, whether you are doing your best to lead such a life as may become a parish clergyman among his parishioners?' And again he paused for an answer.

'There are but few of us,' said Mark, in a low tone, 'who could safely answer that question in the affirmative.'

'But are there many, think you, among us who would find the question so unanswerable as yourself? And even were there many, would you, young, enterprising, and talented as you are, be content to be numbered among them? Are you satisfied to be a castaway after you have taken upon yourself Christ's armour? If you will say so, I am mistaken in you, and will go my way.' There was again a pause, and then he went on. 'Speak to me, my brother, and open your heart, if it be possible.' And rising from his chair, he walked across the room, and laid his hand tenderly on Mark's shoulder. Mark had been sitting lounging in his chair, and had at first, for a moment only, thought to brazen it out. But all idea of brazening had now left him. He had raised himself from his comfortable ease, and was leaning forward with his elbow on the table; but now, when he heard these words, he allowed his head to sink upon his arms, and he buried his face between his hands.

'It is a terrible falling off,' continued Crawley: 'terrible in the fall, but doubly terrible through that difficulty of returning. But it cannot be that it should content you to place yourself as one among those thoughtless sinners, for the crushing of whose sin you have been placed here among them. You become a hunting parson, and ride with a happy mind among blasphemers and mocking devils – you, whose aspirations were so high, who have spoken so often and so well of the duties of a minister of Christ; you, who can argue in your pride as to the petty details of your Church, as though the broad teachings of its great and simple lessons were not enough for your energies! It cannot be that I have had a hypocrite beside me in all those eager controversies!'

'Not a hypocrite – not a hypocrite,' said Mark, in a tone which was almost reduced to sobbing.

'But a castaway! Is it so that I must call you? No, Mr. Robarts, not a castaway; neither a hypocrite, nor a castaway; but one who in walking has stumbled in the dark and bruised his feet among the stones. Henceforth let him take a lantern in his hand, and look warily to his path, and walk cautiously among the thorns and rocks – cautiously, but yet boldly, with manly courage, but Christian meekness, as all men should walk on their pilgrimage through this vale of tears.' And then, without giving his companion time to stop him he hurried out of the room, and from the house, and without again seeing any others of the family, stalked back on his road to Hogglestock, thus tramping fourteen miles through the deep mud in performance of the mission on which he had been sent.

It was some hours before Mr. Robarts left his room. As soon as he found that Crawley was really gone, and that he should see him no more, he turned the lock of his door, and sat himself down to think over his present life. At about eleven his wife knocked, not knowing whether that other strange clergyman were there or no, for none had seen his departure. But Mark, answering cheerily, desired that he might be left to his studies. Let us hope that his thoughts and mental resolves were then of service to him.

CHAPTER XVI

Mrs. Podgens' Baby

THE hunting season had now nearly passed away, and the great ones of the Barsetshire world were thinking of the glories of London. Of these glories Lady Lufton always thought with much inquietude of mind. She would fain have remained throughout the whole year at Framley Court, did not certain grave considerations render such a course on her part improper in her own estimation. All the Lady Luftons of whom she had heard, dowager and ante-dowager, had always had their seasons in London, till old age had incapacitated them for such doings – sometimes for clearly long after the arrival of such period. And then she had an idea, perhaps not altogether erroneous, that she annually imported back with her into the country some what of the passing civilization of the times: – may we not say an idea that certainly was not erroneous? for how otherwise is it that the forms of new caps and remodelled shapes for women's waists find their way down into agricultural parts, and that the rural eye learns to appreciate grace and beauty? There are those who think that remodelled waists and new caps had better be kept to the towns; but such people, if they would follow out their own argument, would wish to see plough-boys painted with ruddle and milkmaids covered with skins. For these and other reasons Lady Lufton always went to London in April and stayed there till the beginning of June. But for her this was usually a period of penance. In London she was no very great personage. She had never laid herself out for greatness of that sort, and did not shine as a lady-patroness or state secretary in the female cabinet of fashion. She was dull and listless, and without congenial pursuits in London, and spent her happiest moments in reading accounts of what was being done at Framley, and in writing orders for further local information of the same kind. But on this occasion there was a matter of vital import to give an interest of its own to her visit to town. She was to entertain Griselda Grantly, and, as far as might be possible, to induce her son to remain in Griselda's society. The plan of the campaign was to be as follows: – Mrs. Grantly and the archdeacon were in the first place to go up to London for a month, taking Griselda with them; and then, when they returned to Plumstead, Griselda was to go to Lady Lufton. This arrangement was not at all points agreeable to Lady Lufton, for she knew that Mrs. Grantly did not turn her back on the Hartletop people quite as cordially as she should do, considering the terms of the Lufton-Grantly family treaty. But then Mrs. Grantly might have alleged in excuse the slow manner in which Lord Lufton proceeded in the making and declaring of his love, and the absolute necessity which there is for two strings to one's bow, when one string may be in any way doubtful. Could it be possible that Mrs. Grantly had heard anything of that unfortunate Platonic friendship with Lucy Robarts?

There came a letter from Mrs. Grantly just about the end of March, which added much to Lady Lufton's uneasiness, and made her more than ever anxious to be herself on the scene of action, and to have Griselda in her own hands. After some communications of mere ordinary importance with reference to the London world in general and the Lufton-Grantly world in particular, Mrs. Grantly wrote confidentially about her daughter: – 'It would be useless to deny,' she said, with a mother's pride and a mother's humility, 'that she is very much admired. She is asked out a great deal more than I can take her, and to houses to which I myself by no means wish to go. I could not refuse her as to Lady Hartletop's first ball, for there will be nothing else this year like them; and of course when with you, dear Lady Lufton, that house will be out of the question. So indeed would it be with me, were I myself only concerned. The duke was there, of course, and I really wonder Lady Hartletop should not be more discreet in her own drawing-room when all the world is there. It is clear to me that Lord Dumbello admires Griselda much more than I could wish. She, dear girl, has such excellent sense that I do not think it likely that her head should be turned by it; but with how many girls would not the admiration of such a man be irresistible? The marquis, you know, is very feeble, and I am told that since this rage for building has come on, the Lancashire property is over two hundred thousand a year! ! I do not think that Lord Dumbello has said much to her. Indeed it seems to me that he never does say much to any one. But he always stands up to dance with her, and I see that he is uneasy and fidgety when she stands up with any other partner whom he could care about. It was really embarrassing to see him the other night at Miss Dunstable's, when Griselda was dancing with a certain friend of ours. But she did look very well that evening, and I have seldom seen her more animated!'

All this, and a great deal more of the same sort in the same letter, tended to make Lady Lufton anxious to be in London. It was quite certain – there was no doubt of that, at any rate – that Griselda would see no more of

Lady Hartletop's meretricious grandeur when she had been transferred to Lady Lufton's guardianship. And she, Lady Lufton, did wonder that Mrs. Grantly should have taken her daughter to such a house. All about Lady Hartletop was known to all the world. It was known that it was almost the only house in London at which the Duke of Omnium was constantly to be met. Lady Lufton herself would almost as soon think of taking a young girl to Gatherum Castle; and on these accounts she did feel rather angry with her friend Mrs. Grantly. But then perhaps she did not sufficiently calculate that Mrs. Grantly's letter had been written purposely to produce such feelings – with the express view of awakening her ladyship to the necessity of action. Indeed, in such a matter as this, Mrs. Grantly was a more able woman than Lady Lufton – more able to see her way and to follow it out. The Lufton-Grantly alliance was in her mind the best, seeing that she did not regard money as everything. But failing that, the Hartletop-Grantly alliance was not bad. Regarding it as a second string to her bow, she thought that it was not at all bad. Lady Lufton's reply was very affectionate. She declared how happy she was to know that Griselda was enjoying herself; she insinuated that Lord Dumbello was known to the world as a fool, and his mother as—being not a bit better than she ought to be; and then she added that circumstances would bring herself up to town four days sooner than she had expected, and that she hoped her dear Griselda would come to her at once. Lord Lufton, she said, though he would not sleep in Bruton Street – Lady Lufton lived in Bruton Street – had promised to pass there as much of his time as his parliamentary duties would permit.

O Lady Lufton! Lady Lufton! did it not occur to you when you wrote those last words, intending that they should have so strong an effect on the mind of your correspondent, that you were telling a—tarradiddle? Was it not the case that you had said to your son, in your own dear, kind, motherly way: 'Ludovic, we shall see something of you in Bruton Street this year, shall we not? Griselda Grantly will be with me, and we must not let her be dull – must we?' And then had he not answered, 'Oh, of course, mother,' and sauntered out of the room, not altogether graciously? Had he, or you, said a word about his parliamentary duties? Not a word! O Lady Lufton! have you not now written a tarradiddle to your friend? In these days we are becoming very strict about truth with our children; terribly strict occasionally, when we consider the natural weakness of the moral courage at the ages of ten, twelve, and fourteen. But I do not know that we are at all increasing the measure of strictness with which we, grown-up people, regulate our own truth and falsehood. Heaven forbid that I should be thought to advocate falsehood in children; but an untruth is more pardonable in them than in their parents. Lady Lufton's tarradiddle was of a nature that is usually considered excusable – at least with grown people; but, nevertheless, she would have been nearer to perfection could she have confined herself to the truth. Let us suppose that a boy were to write home from school, saying that another boy had promised to come and stay with him, that other having given no such promise – what a very naughty boy would that first boy be in the eyes of his pastors and masters!

That little conversation between Lord Lufton and his mother – in which nothing was said about his lordship's parliamentary duties – took place on the evening before he started for London. On that occasion he certainly was not in his best humour, nor did he behave to his mother in his kindest manner. He had then left the room when she began to talk about Miss Grantly; and once again in the course of the evening, when his mother, not very judiciously, said a word or two about Griselda's beauty, he had remarked that she was no conjurer, and would hardly set the Thames on fire. 'If she were a conjurer,' said Lady Lufton, rather piqued, 'I should not now be going to take her out in London. I know many of those sort of girls whom you call conjurers; they can talk for ever, and always talk either loudly or in a whisper. I don't like them, and I am sure that you do not in your heart.'

'Oh, as to liking them in my heart – that is being very particular.'

'Griselda Grantly is a lady, and as such I shall be happy to have her with me in town. She is just the girl that Justinia will like to have with her.'

'Exactly,' said Lord Lufton. 'She will do exceedingly well for Justinia.' Now this was not good-natured on the part of Lord Lufton; and his mother felt it the more strongly, inasmuch as it seemed to signify that he was setting his back up against the Lufton-Grantly alliance. She had been pretty sure that he would do so in the event of his suspecting that a plot was being laid to catch him; and now it almost appeared that he did suspect such a plot. Why else that sarcasm as to Griselda doing very well for his sister?

And now we must go back and describe a little scene at Framley, which will account for his Lordship's ill-humour and suspicions, and explain how it came to pass that he so snubbed his mother. This scene took place about ten days after the evening on which Mrs. Robarts and Lucy were walking together in the parsonage garden, and during those ten days Lucy had not once allowed herself to be entrapped into any special conversation with the young peer. She had dined at Framley Court during that interval, and had spent a second evening there; Lord Lufton had also been up at the parsonage on three or four occasions, and had looked for her in her usual walks; but, nevertheless, they had never come together in their old familiar way, since the day on which Lady Lufton had hinted her fears to Mrs. Robarts.

Lord Lufton had very much missed her. At first he had not attributed this change to a purposed scheme of action on the part of any one; nor, indeed, had he much thought about it, although he had felt himself to be annoyed. But as the period fixed for his departure grew near, it did occur to him as very odd that he should never hear Lucy's voice unless when she said a few words to his mother, or to her sister-in-law. And then he made up his mind that he would speak to her before he went, and that the mystery should be explained to him. And he carried out his purpose, calling at the parsonage on one special afternoon; and it was on the evening of the same day that his mother sang the praises of Griselda Grantly so inopportunely. Robarts, he knew, was then absent from home, and Mrs. Robarts was with his mother down at the house, preparing lists of the poor people to be specially attended to in Lady Lufton's approaching absence. Taking advantage of this, he walked boldly in through the parsonage garden; asked the gardener, with an indifferent voice, whether either of the ladies were at home, and then caught poor Lucy exactly on the doorstep of the house.

'Were you going in or out, Miss Robarts?'

'Well, I was going out,' said Lucy; and she began to consider how best she might get quit of any prolonged encounter.

'Oh, going out, were you? I don't know whether I may offer to –'

'Well, Lord Lufton, not exactly, seeing that I am about to pay a visit to our dear neighbour, Mrs. Podgens. Perhaps, you have no particular call towards Mrs. Podgens' just at present, or to her new baby?'

'And have you any very particular call that way?'

'Yes, and especially to Baby Podgens. Baby Podgens is a real little duck – only just two days old.' And Lucy, as she spoke, progressed a step or two, as though she were determined not to remain there talking on the doorstep. A slight cloud came across his brow as he saw this, and made him resolve that she should not gain her purpose. He was not going to be foiled in that way by such a girl as Lucy Robarts. He had come there to speak to her, and speak to her he would. There had been enough of intimacy between them to justify him in demanding, at any rate, as much as that.

'Miss Robarts,' he said, 'I am starting for London tomorrow, and if I do not say good-bye to you now, I shall not be able to do so at all.'

'Good-bye, Lord Lufton,' she said, giving him her hand, and smiling on him with her old genial, good-humoured, racy smile. 'And mind you bring into Parliament that law which you promised me for defending my young chickens.'

He shook her hand, but that was not all he wanted. 'Surely Mrs. Podgens and her baby can wait ten minutes. I shall not see you again for months to come, and yet you seem to begrudge me two words.'

'Not two hundred if they can be of any service to you,' said she, walking cheerily back into the drawing-room: 'only I did not think it worth while to waste your time, as Fanny is not here.' She was infinitely more collected, more master of herself than he was. Inwardly, she did tremble at the idea of what was coming, but outwardly she showed no agitation – none as yet; if only she could so possess herself as to refrain from doing so, when she heard what he might have to say to her.

He hardly knew what it was for the saying of which he had so resolutely come thither. He had by no means made up his mind that he loved Lucy Robarts; nor had he made up his mind that, loving her, he would, or that, loving her, he would not, make her his wife. He had never used his mind in the matter in any way, either for good or evil. He had learned to like her and to think that she was very pretty. He had found out that it was very pleasant to talk to her; whereas, talking to Griselda Grantly, and, indeed, to some other young ladies of his acquaintance, was often hard work. The half-hours which he had spent with Lucy had always been satisfactory to him. He had found himself to be more bright with her than with other people, and more apt to discuss subjects worth discussing; and thus it had come about that he thoroughly liked Lucy Robarts. As to whether his affection was Platonic or anti-Platonic he had never asked himself; but he had spoken words to her, shortly before that sudden cessation of their intimacy, which might have been taken as anti-Platonic by any girl so disposed to regard them. He had not thrown himself at her feet, and declared himself to be devoured by a consuming passion; but he had touched her hand as lovers touch those of women whom they love; he had had his confidences with her, talking to her of his own mother, of his sister, and of his friends; and he had called her his own dear friend Lucy. All this had been very sweet to her, but very poisonous also. She had declared to herself very frequently that her liking for this young nobleman was as purely a feeling of mere friendship as was that of her brother; and she had professed to herself that she would give the lie to the world's cold sarcasms on such subjects. But she had now acknowledged that the sarcasms of the world on that matter, cold though they may be, are not the less true; and having so acknowledged, she had resolved that all close alliance between herself and Lord Lufton must be at an end. She had come to a conclusion, but he had come to none; and in this frame of mind he was now there with the object of reopening that dangerous friendship which she had had the sense to close.

'And so you are going to-morrow?' she said, as soon as they were both within the drawing-room.

'Yes: I'm off by the early train to-morrow morning, and Heaven knows when we may meet again.'

'Next winter, shall we not?'

'Yes, for a day or two, I suppose. I do not know whether I shall pass another winter here. Indeed, one can never say where one will be.'

'No, one can't; such as you, at least, cannot. I am not of a migratory tribe myself.'

'I wish you were.'

'I'm not a bit obliged to you. Your nomad life does not agree with young ladies.'

'I think they are taking to it pretty freely, then. We have unprotected young women all about the world.'

'And great bores you find them, I suppose?'

'No; I like it. The more we can get out of old-fashioned grooves the better I am pleased. I should be a Radical to-morrow – a regular man of the people – only I should break my mother's heart.'

'Whatever you do, Lord Lufton, do not do that.'

'That is why I have liked you so much,' he continued, 'because you get out of the grooves.'

'Do I?'

'Yes; and go along by yourself, guiding your own footsteps; not carried hither and thither, just as your grandmother's old tramway may chance to take you.'

'Do you know I have a strong idea that my grandmother's old tramway will be the safest and the best after all? I have not left it very far, and I certainly mean to go back to it.'

'That's impossible! An army of old women, with coils of ropes made out of time-honoured prejudices, could not draw you back.'

'No, Lord Lufton, that is true. But one –' and then she stopped herself. She could not tell him that one loving mother, anxious for her only son, had sufficed to do it. She could not explain to him that this departure from the established tramway had already broken her own rest, and turned her peaceful happy life into a grievous battle.

'I know that you are trying to go back,' he said. 'Do you think that I have eyes and cannot see? Come, Lucy, you and I have been friends, and we must not part in this way. My mother is a paragon among women. I say it in earnest; – a paragon among women: and her love for me is the perfection of motherly love.'

'It is, it is; and I am so glad that you acknowledge it.'

'I should be worse than a brute did I not do so; but, nevertheless, I cannot allow her to lead me in all things. Were I to do so, I should cease to be a man.'

'Where can you find any one who will counsel you so truly?'

'But, nevertheless, I must rule myself. I do not know whether my suspicions may be perfectly just, but I fancy that she has created this estrangement between you and me. Has it not been so?'

'Certainly not by speaking to me,' said Lucy, blushing ruby-red through every vein of her deep-tinted face. But though she could not command her blood, her voice was still under her control – her voice and her manner.

'But has she not done so? You, I know, will tell me nothing but the truth.'

'I will tell you nothing on this matter, Lord Lufton, whether true or false. It is a subject on which it does not concern me to speak.'

'Ah! I understand,' he said; and rising from his chair, he stood against the chimney-piece with his back to the fire. 'She cannot leave me alone to choose for myself, my friends, and my own –;' but he did not fill up the void.

'But why tell me this, Lord Lufton?'

'No! I am not to choose my own friends, though they be amongst the best and purest of God's creatures. Lucy, I cannot think that you have ceased to have a regard for me. That you had a regard for me, I am sure.' She felt that it was almost unmanly of him thus to seek her out, and hunt her down, and then throw upon her the whole weight of the explanation that his coming thither made necessary. But, nevertheless, the truth must be told, and with God's help she would find strength for the telling of it.

'Yes, Lord Lufton, I had a regard for you – and have. By that word you mean something more than the customary feeling of acquaintance which may ordinarily prevail between a gentleman and lady of different families, who have known each other so short a time as we have done.'

'Yes, something much more,' said he with energy.

'Well, I will not define the much – something closer than that?'

'Yes, and warmer, and dearer, and more worthy of two human creatures who value each other's minds and hearts.'

'Some such closer regard I have felt for you – very foolishly. Stop! You have made me speak, and do not interrupt me now. Does not your conscience tell you that in doing so I have unwisely deserted those wise old grandmother's tramways of which you spoke just now? It has been pleasant to me to do so. I have liked the feeling of independence with which I have thought that I might indulge in an open friendship with such as you are. And your rank, so different from my own, has doubtless made this more attractive.'

'Nonsense!'

'Ah! but it has. I know it now. But what will the world say of me as to such an alliance?'

'The world!'

'Yes, the world! I am not such a philosopher as to disregard it, though you may afford to do so. The world will say that I, the parson's sister, set my cap at the young lord, and that the young lord had made a fool of me.'

'The world shall say no such thing!' said Lord Lufton, very imperiously.

'Ah! but it will. You can no more stop it, than King Canute could the waters. Your mother has interfered wisely to spare me from this; and the only favour that I can ask you is, that you will spare me also.' And then she got up, as though she intended at once to walk forth to her visit to Mrs. Podgens' baby.

'Stop, Lucy!' he said, putting himself between her and the door.

'It must not be Lucy any longer, Lord Lufton; I was madly foolish when I first allowed it.'

'By heavens! but it shall be Lucy – Lucy before all the world. My Lucy, my own Lucy – my heart's best friend, and chosen love. Lucy, there is my hand. How long you may have had my heart it matters not to say now.' The game was at her feet now, and no doubt she felt her triumph. Her ready wit and speaking lip, not her beauty, had brought him to her side; and now he was forced to acknowledge that her power over him had been supreme. Sooner than leave her he would risk all. She did feel her triumph; but there was nothing in her face to tell him that she did so. As to what she would now do she did not for a moment doubt. He had been precipitated into the declaration he had made not by his love, but by his embarrassment. She had thrown in his teeth the injury which he had done her, and he had then been moved by his generosity to repair that injury by the noblest sacrifice which he could make. But Lucy Robarts was not the girl to accept a sacrifice. He had stepped forward as though he were going to clasp her round the waist, but she receded, and got beyond the reach of his hand. 'Lord Lufton!' she said, 'when you are more cool you will know that this is wrong. The best thing for both of us now is to part.'

'Not the best thing, but the very worst, till we perfectly understand each other.'

'Then perfectly understand me, that I cannot be your wife.'

'Lucy! do you mean that you cannot learn to love me?'

'I mean that I shall not try. Do not persevere in this, or you will have to hate yourself for your own folly.'

'But I will persevere till you accept my love, or say with your hand on your heart that you cannot and will not love me.'

'Then I must beg you to let me go,' and having so said, she paused while he walked once or twice hurriedly up and down the room. 'And Lord Lufton,' she continued, 'if you will leave me now, the words that you have spoken shall be as though they had never been uttered.'

'I care not who knows they have been uttered. The sooner that they are known to all the world the better I shall be pleased, unless indeed –'

'Think of your mother, Lord Lufton.'

'What can I do better than give her as a daughter the best and sweetest girl I have ever met? When my mother really knows you, she will love you as I do. Lucy, say one word to me of comfort.'

'I will say no word to you that shall injure your future comfort. It is impossible that I should be your wife.'

'Do you mean that you cannot love me?'

'You have no right to press me any further,' she said; and sat down upon the sofa, with an angry frown upon her forehead.

'By heavens,' he said, 'I will take no such answer from you till you put your hand upon your heart, and say that you cannot love me.'

'Oh, why should you press me so, Lord Lufton?'

'Why, because my happiness depends upon it; because it behoves me to know the very truth. It has come to this, that I love you with my whole heart, and I must know how your heart stands towards me.' She had now again risen from the sofa, and was looking steadily in his face.

'Lord Lufton,' she said, 'I cannot love you,' and as she spoke she did put her hand, as he had desired, upon her heart.

'Then God help me! for I am wretched. Good-bye, Lucy,' and he stretched out his hand to her.

'Good-bye, my lord. Do not be angry with me.'

'No, no, no!' and without further speech he left the room and the house and hurried home. It was hardly surprising that he should that evening tell his mother that Griselda Grantly would be a companion sufficiently good for his sister. He wanted no such companion.

And when he was well gone – absolutely out of sight from the window – Lucy walked steadily up to her room, locked the door, and then threw herself on the bed. Why

– oh! why had she told such a falsehood? Could anything justify her in a lie? was it not a lie – knowing as she did that she loved him with all her loving heart? But, then, his mother! and the sneers of the world, which would have declared that she had set her trap, and caught the foolish young lord! Her pride would not have submitted to that. Strong as her love was, yet her pride was, perhaps, stronger – stronger at any rate during that interview. But how was she to forgive herself the falsehood she had told?

CHAPTER XVII

Mrs. Proudie's Conversazione

IT was grievous to think of the mischief and danger into which Griselda Grantly was brought by the worldliness of her mother in those few weeks previous to Lady Lufton's arrival in town – very grievous, at least, to her ladyship, as from time to time she heard of what was done in London. Lady Hartletop's was not the only objectionable house at which Griselda was allowed to reap fresh fashionable laurels. It had been stated openly in the *Morning Post* that that young lady had been the most admired among the beautiful at one of Miss Dunstable's celebrated soirées and then she was heard of as gracing the drawing-room at Mrs. Proudie's conversazione.

Of Miss Dunstable herself Lady Lufton was not able openly to allege any evil. She was acquainted, Lady Lufton knew, with very many people of the right sort, and was the dear friend of Lady Lufton's highly conservative and not very distant neighbours, the Greshams. But then she was also acquainted with so many people of the bad sort. Indeed, she was intimate with everybody, from the Duke of Omnium to old Dowager Lady Goodygaffer, who had represented all the cardinal virtues for the last quarter of a century. She smiled with equal sweetness on treacle and on brimstone; was quite at home at Exeter Hall, having been consulted – so the world said, probably not with exact truth – as to the selection of more than one disagreeably Low Church bishop; and was not less frequent in her attendance at the ecclesiastical doings of a certain terrible prelate in the Midland counties, who was supposed to favour stoles and vespers, and to have no proper Protestant hatred for auricular confession and fish on Fridays. Lady Lufton, who was very staunch, did not like this, and would say of Miss Dunstable that it was impossible to serve both God and Mammon. But Mrs. Proudie was much more objectionable to her. Seeing how sharp was the feud between the Proudies and the Grantlys down in Barsetshire, how absolutely unable they had always been to carry a decent face towards each other in Church matters, how they headed two parties in the diocese, which were, when brought together, as oil and vinegar, in which battles the whole Lufton influence had always been brought to bear on the Grantly side; – seeing all this, I say, Lady Lufton was surprised to hear that Griselda had been taken to Mrs. Proudie's evening exhibition. 'Had the archdeacon been consulted about it,' she said to herself, 'this would never have happened.' But there she was wrong, for in matters concerning his daughter's introduction to the world the archdeacon never interfered.

On the whole, I am inclined to think that Mrs. Grantly understood the world better than did Lady Lufton. In her heart of hearts Mrs. Grantly hated Mrs. Proudie – that is, with that sort of hatred one Christian lady allows herself to feel towards another. Of course Mrs. Grantly forgave Mrs. Proudie all her offences, and wished her well, and was at peace with her, in the Christian sense of the word, as with all other women. But under this forbearance and meekness, and perhaps, we may say, wholly unconnected with it, there was certainly a current of antagonistic feeling which, in the ordinary unconsidered language of every day, men and women do call hatred. This raged and was strong throughout the whole year in Barsetshire, before the eyes of all mankind. But, nevertheless, Mrs. Grantly took Griselda to Mrs. Proudie's evening parties in London. In these days Mrs. Proudie considered herself to be by no means the least among bishops' wives. She had opened the season this year in a new house in Gloucester Place, at which the reception rooms, at any rate, were all that a lady bishop could desire. Here she had a front drawing-room of very noble dimensions, a second drawing-room rather noble also, though it had lost one of its back corners awkwardly enough, apparently in a jostle with the neighbouring house; and then there was a third – shall we say drawing-room, or closet? – in which Mrs. Proudie delighted to be seen sitting, in order that the world might know that there was a third room; altogether a noble suite, as Mrs. Proudie herself said in confidence to more than one clergyman's wife from Barsetshire. 'A noble suite, indeed, Mrs. Proudie!' the clergymen's wives from Barsetshire would usually answer.

For some time Mrs. Proudie was much at a loss to know by what sort of party or entertainment she would make herself famous. Balls and suppers were of course out of the question. She did not object to her daughters dancing all night at other houses – at least, of late she had not objected, for the fashionable world required it, and the young ladies had perhaps a will of their own – but dancing at her house – absolutely under the shade of the bishop's apron – would be a sin and a scandal. And then as to suppers – of all modes in which one may extend one's hospitality to a large acquaintance, they are the most costly. 'It is horrid to think that we should go out among our friends for the mere sake of eating and drinking,' Mrs. Proudie would say to the clergymen's wives from Barsetshire. 'It shows such a sensual propensity.'

'Indeed it does, Mrs. Proudie; and is so vulgar too!' those ladies would reply. But the elder among them would remember with regret, the unsparing, open-handed hospitality of Barchester Palace in the good old days of Bishop Grantly – God rest his soul! One old vicar's wife there was whose answer had not been so courteous –

'When we are hungry, Mrs. Proudie,' she had said, 'we do all have sensual propensities.'

'It would be much better, Mrs. Athill, if the world would provide for all that at home,' Mrs. Proudie had rapidly replied; with which opinion I must here profess that I cannot by any means bring myself to coincide. But a conversazione would give play to no sensual propensity, nor occasion that intolerable expense which the gratification of sensual propensities too often produces. Mrs. Proudie felt that the word was not all that she could have desired. It was a little faded by old use and present oblivion, and seemed to address itself to that portion of the London world that is considered blue, rather than fashionable. But, nevertheless, there was a spirituality about it which suited her, and one may also say an economy. And then as regarded fashion, it might perhaps not be beyond the power of a Mrs. Proudie to regild the word with a newly burnished gilding. Some leading person must produce fashion at first hand, and why not Mrs. Proudie?

Her plan was to set the people by the ears talking, if talk they would, or to induce them to show themselves there inert if no more could be got from them. To accommodate with chairs and sofas as many as the furniture of her noble suite of rooms would allow, especially with the two chairs and padded bench against the wall in the back closet – the small inner drawing-room, as she would call it to the clergymen's wives from Barsetshire – and to let the others stand about upright, or 'group themselves,' as she described it. Then four times during the two hours' period of her conversazione tea and cake were to be handed round on salvers. It is astonishing how far a very little cake will go in this way, particularly if administered tolerably early after dinner. The men can't eat it, and the women, having no plates and no table, are obliged to abstain. Mrs. Jones knows that she cannot hold a piece of crumbly cake in her hand till it be consumed without doing serious injury to her best dress. When Mrs. Proudie, with her weekly books before her, looked into the financial upshot of her conversazione, her conscience told her that she had done the right thing. Going out to tea is not a bad thing, if one can contrive to dine early and then be allowed to sit round a big table with a tea urn in the middle. I would, however, suggest that breakfast cups should always be provided for the gentlemen. And then with pleasant neighbours, – or more especially with a pleasant neighbour, – the affair is not, according to my taste, by any means the worst phase of society. But I do dislike that handing round, unless it be of a subsidiary thimbleful when the business of the social intercourse has been dinner.

And indeed this handing round has become a vulgar and an intolerable nuisance among us second-class gentry with our eight hundred a year – there or thereabouts; – doubly intolerable as being destructive of our natural comforts, and a wretchedly vulgar aping of men with large incomes. The Duke of Omnium and Lady Hartletop are undoubtedly wise to have everything handed round. Friends of mine who occasionally dine at such houses tell me that they get their wine quite as quickly as they can drink it, that their mutton is brought to them without delay, and that the potato bearer follows quick upon the heels of carnifer. Nothing can be more comfortable, and we may no doubt acknowledge that these first-class grandees do understand their material comforts. But we of the eight hundred can no more come up to them in this than we can in their opera-boxes and equipages. May I not say that the usual tether of this class, in the way of carnifers, cup-bearers, and the rest, does not reach beyond neat-handed Phyllis and the greengrocer? and that Phyllis, neat-handed as she probably is, and the greengrocer, though he be ever so active, cannot administer a dinner to twelve people who are prohibited by a Medo-Persian law from all self-administration whatever? And may I not further say that the lamentable consequence to us eight hundreders dining out among each other is this, that we too often get no dinner at all. Phyllis, with the potatoes, cannot reach us till our mutton is devoured, or in a lukewarm state past our power of managing; and Ganymede, the greengrocer, though we admire the skill of his necktie and the whiteness of his unexceptionable gloves, fails to keep us going in sherry. Seeing a lady the other day in this strait, left without a small modicum of stimulus which was no doubt necessary for her good digestion, I ventured to ask her to drink wine with me. But when I bowed my head at her, she looked at me with all her eyes, struck with amazement. Had I suggested that she should join me in a wild Indian war-dance, with nothing on but my paint, her face could not have shown greater astonishment. And yet I should have thought she might have remembered the days when Christian men and women used to drink wine with each other. God be with the good old days when I could hob-nob with my friend over the table as often as I was inclined to lift my glass to my lips, and make a long arm for a hot potato whenever the exigencies of my plate required it.

I think it may be laid down as a rule in affairs of hospitality, that whatever extra luxury or grandeur we introduce at our tables when guests are with us, should be introduced for the advantage of the guest and not for our own. If, for instance, our dinner be served in a manner different from that usual to us, it should be so served in order that our friends may with more satisfaction eat our repast than our everyday practice would produce on them. But the change should by no means be made to their material detriment in order that our fashion may be acknowledged. Again, if I decorate my sideboard and table, wishing that the eyes of my visitors may rest on that which is elegant and pleasant to the sight, I act in that matter with a becoming sense of hospitality; but if my object be to kill Mrs. Jones with envy at the sight of all my silver trinkets, I am a very mean-spirited fellow. This, in a broad way, will be acknowledged; but if we would bear in mind the same idea at all times, – on occasions when the way perhaps may not be so broad, when more thinking may be required to ascertain what is true hospitality, – I think we of the eight hundred would make a greater advance towards really entertaining our own friends than by any rearrangement of the actual meats and dishes which we set before them.

Knowing as we do, that the terms of the Lufton-Grantly alliance had been so solemnly ratified between the two mothers, it is perhaps hardly open to us to suppose that Mrs. Grantly was induced to take her daughter to Mrs. Proudie's by any knowledge which she may have acquired that Lord Dumbello had promised to grace the bishop's assembly. It is certainly the fact that high contracting parties do sometimes allow themselves a latitude which would be considered dishonest by contractors of a lower sort; and it may be possible that the archdeacon's wife did think of that second string with which her bow was furnished. Be that as it may, Lord Dumbello was at Mrs. Proudie's, and it did so come to pass that Griselda was seated at a corner of a sofa close to which was a vacant space in which his lordship could – 'group himself.' They had not been long there before Lord Dumbello did group himself. 'Fine day,' he said, coming up and occupying the vacant position by Miss Grantly's elbow.

'We were driving to-day, and we thought it rather cold,' said Griselda.

'Deuced cold,' said Lord Dumbello, and then he adjusted his white cravat and touched up his whiskers. Having got so far, he did not proceed to any other immediate conversational efforts; nor did Griselda. But he grouped himself again as became a marquis, and gave very intense satisfaction to Mrs. Proudie.

'This is so kind of you, Lord Dumbello,' said that lady, coming up to him and shaking his hand warmly; 'so very kind of you to come to my poor little tea-party.'

'Uncommonly pleasant, I call it,' said his lordship. 'I like this sort of thing – no trouble, you know.'

'No; that is the charm of it: isn't it? no trouble, or fuss, or parade. That's what I always say. According to my ideas, society consists in giving people facility for an interchange of thoughts – what we call conversation.'

'Aw, yes, exactly.'

'Not in eating and drinking together – eh, Lord Dumbello? And yet the practice of our lives would seem to show that the indulgence of those animal propensities can alone suffice to bring people together. The world in this has surely made a great mistake.'

'I like a good dinner all the same,' said Lord Dumbello.

'Oh, yes, of course – of course. I am by no means one of those who would pretend to preach that our tastes have not been given to us for our enjoyment. Why should things be nice if we are not to like them?'

'A man who can really give a good dinner has learned a great deal,' said Lord Dumbello, with unusual animation.

'An immense deal. It is quite an art in itself: and one which I, at any rate, by no means despise. But we cannot always be eating – can we?'

'No,' said Lord Dumbello, 'not always.' And he looked as though he lamented that his powers should be so circumscribed. And then Mrs. Proudie passed on to Mrs. Grantly. The two ladies were quite friendly in London; though down in their own neighbourhood they waged a war so internecine in its nature. But nevertheless Mrs. Proudie's manner might have showed to a very close observer that she knew the difference between a bishop and an archdeacon. 'I am so delighted to see you,' said she. 'No, don't mind moving; I won't sit down just at present. But why didn't the archdeacon come?'

'It was quite impossible; it was indeed,' said Mrs. Grantly. 'The archdeacon never has a moment in London that he can call his own.'

'You don't stay up very long, I believe.'

'A good deal longer than we either of us like, I can assure you. London life is a perfect nuisance to me.'

'But people in a certain position must go through with it, you know,' said Mrs. Proudie. 'The bishop, for instance, must attend the House.'

'Must he?' asked Mrs. Grantly; as though she were not at all well informed with reference to this branch of a bishop's business. 'I am very glad that archdeacons are under no such liability.'

'Oh, no; there's nothing of that sort,' said Mrs. Proudie, very seriously. 'But how uncommonly well Miss Grantly is looking! I do hear that she has quite been admired.' This phrase certainly was a little hard for the mother to bear. All the world had acknowledged, so Mrs. Grantly had taught herself to believe, that Griselda was undoubtedly the beauty of the season. Marquises and lords were already contending for her smiles, and paragraphs had been written in newspapers as to her profile. It was too hard to be told, after that, that her daughter had been 'quite admired.' Such a phrase might suit a pretty little red-cheeked milk-maid of a girl.

'She cannot, of course, come near your girls in that respect,' said Mrs. Grantly, very quietly. Now the Miss Proudies had not elicited from the fashionable world any very loud encomiums on their beauty. Their mother felt the taunt in its fullest force, but she would not essay to do battle on the present arena. She jotted down the item in her mind, and kept it over for Barchester and the chapter. Such debts as those she usually paid on some day, if the means of doing so were at all within her power. 'But there is Miss Dunstable, I declare,' she said, seeing that that lady had entered the room; and away went Mrs. Proudie to welcome her distinguished guest.

'And so this is a conversazione, is it?' said that lady, speaking, as usual, not in a suppressed voice. 'Well, I declare, it's very nice. It means conversation, don't it, Mrs. Proudie?'

'Ha, ha, ha! Miss Dunstable, there is nobody like you, I declare.'

'Well, but don't it? and tea and cake? and then, when we're tired of talking, we go away, isn't that it?'

'But you must not be tired for these three hours yet.'

'Oh, I am never tired of talking; all the world knows that. How do, bishop? A very nice sort of thing this conversazione, isn't it now?' The bishop rubbed his hands together and smiled, and said that he thought it was rather nice.

'Mrs. Proudie is so fortunate in all her little arrangements,' said Miss Dunstable.

'Yes, yes,' said the bishop. 'I think she is happy in these matters. I do flatter myself that she is so. Of course, Miss Dunstable, you are accustomed to things on a much grander scale.'

'I! Lord bless you, no! Nobody hates grandeur so much as I do. Of course I must do as I am told. I must live in a big house, and have three footmen six feet high. I must have a coachman with a top-heavy wig, and horses so big that they frighten me. If I did not, I should be made out a lunatic and declared unable to manage my own affairs. But as for grandeur, I hate it. I certainly think that I shall have some of these conversaziones. I wonder whether Mrs. Proudie will come and put me up to a wrinkle or two.' The bishop again rubbed his hands, and said that he was sure she would. He never felt quite at his ease with Miss Dunstable, as he rarely could ascertain whether or no she was earnest in what she was saying. So he trotted off, muttering some excuse as he went, and Miss Dunstable chuckled with an inward chuckle at his too evident bewilderment. Miss Dunstable was by nature kind, generous, and open-hearted; but she was living now very much with people on whom kindness, generosity, and open-heartedness were thrown away. She was clever also, and could be sarcastic; and she found that those qualities told better in the world around her than generosity and an open heart. And so she went on from month to month, and year to year, not progressing in a good spirit as she might have done, but still carrying within her bosom a warm affection for those she could really love. And she knew that she was hardly living as she should live, – that the wealth which she affected to despise was eating into the soundness of her character, not by its splendour, but by the style of life which it had seemed to produce as a necessity. She knew that she was gradually becoming irreverent, scornful, and prone to ridicule; but yet, knowing this, and hating it, she hardly knew how to break from it. She had seen so much of the blacker side of human nature that blackness no longer startled her as it should do. She had been the prize at which so many ruined spendthrifts had aimed; so many pirates had endeavoured to run her down while sailing in the open waters of life, that she had ceased to regard such attempts on her money-bags as unmanly or over-covetous. She was content to fight her own battle with her own weapons, feeling secure in her own strength of purpose and strength of wit.

Some few friends she had whom she really loved, – among whom her inner self could come out and speak boldly what it had to say with its own true voice. And the woman who thus so spoke was very different from that Miss Dunstable whom Mrs. Proudie courted, and the Duke of Omnium fêted, and Mrs. Harold Smith claimed as her bosom friend. If only she could find among such one special companion on whom her heart might rest, who would help her to bear the heavy burdens of her world! But where was she to find such a friend? – she with her keen wit, her untold money, and loud laughing voice. Everything about her was calculated to attract those whom she could not value, and to scare from her the sort of friend to whom she would fain have linked her lot. And then she met Mrs. Harold Smith, who had taken Mrs. Proudie's noble suite of rooms in her tour for the evening, and was devoting to them a period of twenty minutes. 'And so I may congratulate you,' Miss Dunstable said eagerly to her friend.

'No, in mercy's name, do no such thing, or you may too probably have to uncongratulate me again; and that will be so unpleasant.'

'But they told me that Lord Brock had sent for him yesterday.' Now at this period Lord Brock was Prime Minister.

'So he did, and Harold was with him backwards and forwards all the day. But he can't shut his eyes and open his mouth, and see what God will send him, as a wise and prudent man should do. He is always for bargaining, and no Prime Minister likes that.'

'I would not be in his shoes if, after all, he has to come home and say that the bargain is off.'

'Ha, ha, ha! Well, I should not take it very quietly. But what can we poor women do, you know? When it is settled, my dear, I'll send you a line at once.' And then Mrs. Harold Smith finished her course round the rooms, and regained her carriage within the twenty minutes.

'Beautiful profile, has she not?' said Miss Dunstable, somehat later in the evening, to Mrs. Proudie. Of course, the profile spoken of belonged to Miss Grantly.

'Yes, it is beautiful, certainly,' said Mrs. Proudie. 'The pity is that it means nothing.'

'The gentlemen seem to think that it means a good deal.'

'I am not sure of that. She has no conversation, you see; not a word. She has been sitting there with Lord Dumbello at her elbow for the last hour, and yet she has hardly opened her mouth three times.'

'But, my dear Mrs. Proudie, who on earth could talk to Lord Dumbello?' Mrs. Proudie thought that her own daughter Olivia would undoubtedly be able to do so, if only she could get the opportunity. But, then, Olivia had so much conversation. And while the two ladies were yet looking at the youthful pair, Lord Dumbello did speak again. 'I think I have had enough of this now,' said he, addressing himself to Griselda.

'I suppose you have other engagements,' said she.

'Oh, yes; and I believe I shall go to Lady Clantelbrocks.' And then he took his departure. No other word was spoken that evening between him and Miss Grantly beyond those given in this chronicle, and yet the world declared that he and that young lady had passed the evening in so close a flirtation as to make the matter more than ordinarily particular; and Mrs. Grantly, as she was driven home to her lodgings, began to have doubts in her mind whether it would be wise to discountenance so great an alliance as that which the head of the great Hartletop family now seemed so desirous to establish. The prudent mother had not yet spoken a word to her daughter on these subjects, but it might soon become necessary to do so. It was all very well for Lady Lufton to hurry up to town, but of what service would that be, if Lord Lufton were not to be found in Bruton Street?

CHAPTER XVIII

The New Minister's Patronage

At that time, just as Lady Lufton was about to leave Framley for London, Mark Robarts received a pressing letter, inviting him also to go up to the metropolis for a day or two – not for pleasure, but on business. The letter was from his indefatigable friend Sowerby. 'My dear Robarts,' the letter ran: – 'I have just heard that poor little Burslem, the Barsetshire prebendary, is dead. We must all die some day, you know, – as you have told your parishioners from the Framley pulpit more than once, no doubt. The stall must be filled up, and why should not you have it as well as another? It is six hundred a year and a house. Little Burslem had nine, but the good old times are gone. Whether the house is letable or not under the present ecclesiastical régime, I do not know. It used to be so, for I remember Mrs. Wiggins, the tallow-chandler's widow, living in old Stanhope's house.

'Harold Smith has just joined the Government as Lord Petty Bag, and could, I think, at the present moment, get this for asking. He cannot well refuse me, and, if you will say the word, I will speak to him. You had better come up yourself; but say the word "Yes," or "No," by the wires.

'If you say "Yes," as of course you will, do not fail to come up. You will find me at the "Travellers," or at the House. The stall will just suit you, – will give you no trouble, improve your position, and give some little assistance towards bed and board and rack and manger. – Yours ever faithfully, N. Sowerby.

'Singularly enough, I hear that your brother is private secretary to the new Lord Petty Bag. I am told that his chief duty will consist in desiring the servants to call my sister's carriage. I have only seen Harold once since he accepted office; but my Lady Petty Bag says that he has certainly grown an inch since that occurrence.'

This was certainly very good-natured on the part of Mr. Sowerby, and showed that he had a feeling within his bosom that he owed something to his friend the parson for the injury he had done him. And such was in truth the case. A more reckless being than the member for West Barsetshire could not exist. He was reckless for himself, and reckless for all others with whom he might be concerned. He could ruin his friends with as little remorse as he had ruined himself. All was fair game that came in the way of his net. But, nevertheless, he was good-natured, and willing to move heaven and earth to do a friend a good turn, if it came in his way to do so.

He did really love Mark Robarts as much as it was given him to love any among his acquaintance. He knew that he had already done him an almost irreparable injury, and might very probably injure him still deeper before he had done with him. That he would undoubtedly do so, if it came in his way, was very certain. But then, if it also came in his way to repay his friend by any side blow, he would also undoubtedly do that. Such an occasion had now come, and he had desired his sister to give the new Lord Petty Bag no rest till he should have promised to use all his influence in getting the vacant prebend for Mark Robarts.

This letter of Sowerby's Mark immediately showed to his wife. How lucky, thought he to himself, that not a word was said in it about those accursed money transactions! Had he understood Sowerby better he would have known that that gentleman never said anything about money transactions until it became absolutely necessary. 'I know you don't like Mr. Sowerby,' he said; 'but you must own that this is very good-natured.'

'It is the character I hear of him that I don't like,' said Mrs. Robarts.

'But what shall I do now, Fanny? As he says, why should not I have the stall as well as another?'

'I suppose it would not interfere with your parish?' she asked.

'Not in the least, at the distance at which we are. I did think of giving up old Jones; but if I take this, of course I must keep a curate.' His wife could not find it in her heart to dissuade him from accepting promotion when it came in his way – what vicar's wife would have so persuaded her husband? But yet she did not altogether like it. She feared that Greek from Chaldicotes, even when he came with the present of a prebendal stall in his hands. And then what would Lady Lufton say?

'And do you think that you must go up to London, Mark?'

'Oh, certainly; that is, if I intend to accept Harold Smith's kind offices in the matter.'

'I suppose it will be better to accept them,' said Fanny, feeling perhaps that it would be useless in her to hope that they should not be accepted.

'Prebendal stalls, Fanny, don't generally go begging long among parish clergymen. How could I reconcile it to the duty I owe to my children to refuse such an increase to my income?' And so it was settled that he should at once drive to Silverbridge and send off a message by telegraph, and that he should himself proceed to London on the following day. 'But you must see Lady Lufton first, of course,' said Fanny, as soon as all this was settled. Mark would have avoided this if he could have decently done so, but he felt that it would be impolitic, as well as indecent. And why should he be afraid to tell Lady Lufton that he hoped to receive this piece of promotion from the present Government? There was nothing disgraceful in a clergyman becoming a prebendary of Barchester. Lady Lufton herself had always been very civil to the prebendaries, and especially to little Dr. Burslem, the meagre little man who had just now paid the debt of nature. She had always been very fond of the chapter, and her original dislike to Bishop Proudie had been chiefly founded on his interference with the cathedral clergy, – on his interference, or on that of his wife or chaplain. Considering these things Mark Robarts tried to make himself believe that Lady Lufton would be delighted at his good fortune. But yet he did not believe it. She at any rate would revolt from the gift of the Greek of Chaldicotes. 'Oh, indeed,' she said, when the vicar had with some difficulty explained to her all the circumstances of the case. 'Well, I congratulate you, Mr. Robarts, on your powerful new patron.'

'You will probably feel with me, Lady Lufton, that the benefice is one which I can hold without any detriment to me in my position here at Framley,' said he, prudently resolving to let the slur upon his friends pass by unheeded.

'Well, I hope so. Of course, you are a very young man, Mr. Robarts, and these things have generally been given to clergymen more advanced in life.'

'But you do not mean to say that you think I ought to refuse it?'

'What my advice to you might be if you really came to me for advice, I am hardly prepared to say at so very short a notice. You seem to have made up your mind, and therefore I need not consider it. As it is, I wish you joy, and hope that it may turn out to your advantage in every way.'

'You understand, Lady Lufton, that I have by no means got it as yet.'

'Oh, I thought it had been offered to you: I thought you spoke of this new minister as having all that in his own hand.'

'Oh dear, no. What may be the amount of his influence in that respect I do not at all know. But my correspondent assures me –'

'Mr. Sowerby, you mean. Why don't you call him by his name?'

'Mr. Sowerby assures me that Mr. Smith will ask for it; and thinks it most probable that his request will be successful.'

'Oh, of course. Mr. Sowerby and Mr. Harold Smith together would no doubt be successful in anything. They are the sort of men who are successful nowadays. Well, Mr. Robarts, I wish you joy.' And she gave him her hand in token of her sincerity. Mark took her hand, resolving to say nothing further on that occasion. That Lady Lufton was not now cordial with him, as she used to be, he was well aware; and sooner or later he was determined to have the matter out with her. He would ask her why she now so constantly met him with a taunt, and so seldom greeted him with that kind old affectionate smile which he knew and appreciated so well. That she was honest and true he was quite sure. If he asked her the question plainly, she would answer him openly. And if he could induce her to say that she would return to her old ways, return to them she would in a hearty manner. But he could not do this just at present. It was but a day or two since Mr. Crawley had been with him; and was it not probable that Mr. Crawley had been sent thither by Lady Lufton? His own hands were not clean enough for a remonstrance at the present moment. He would cleanse them, and then he would remonstrate. 'Would you like to live part of the year in Barchester?' he said to his wife and sister that evening.

'I think that two houses are only a trouble,' said his wife. 'And we have been very happy here.'

'I have always liked a cathedral town,' said Lucy; 'and I am particularly fond of the close.'

'And Barchester Close is the closest of all closes,' said Mark. 'There is not a single house within the gateways that does not belong to the chapter.'

'But if we are to keep up two houses, the additional income will soon be wasted,' said Fanny, prudently.

'The thing would be to let the house furnished every summer,' said Lucy.

'But I must take my residence as the terms come,' said the vicar; 'and I certainly should not like to be away from Framley all the winter; I should never see anything of Lufton.' And perhaps he thought of his hunting, and then thought again of that cleansing of his hands.

'I should not a bit mind being away during the winter,' said Lucy, thinking of what the last winter had done for her.

'But where on earth should we find money to furnish one of those large, old-fashioned houses? Pray, Mark, do not do anything rash.' And the wife laid her hand affectionately on her husband's arm. In this manner the question of the prebend was discussed between them on the evening before he started for London. Success had at last crowned the earnest effort with which Harold Smith had carried on the political battle of his life for the last ten years. The late Lord Petty Bag had resigned in disgust, having been unable to digest the Prime Minister's ideas on Indian Reform, and Mr. Harold Smith, after sundry hitches in the business, was installed in his place. It was said that Harold Smith was not exactly the man whom the Premier would himself have chosen for that high office; but the Premier's hands were a good deal tied by circumstances. The last great appointment he had made had been terribly unpopular, – so much so as to subject him, popular as he undoubtedly was himself, to a screech from the whole nation. The *Jupiter*, with withering scorn, had asked whether vice of every kind was to be considered, in these days of Queen Victoria, as a passport to the Cabinet. Adverse members of both Houses had arrayed themselves in a pure panoply of morality, and thundered forth their sarcasms with the indignant virtue and keen discontent of political Juvenals; and even his own friends had held up their hands in dismay. Under these circumstances he had thought himself obliged in the present instance to select a man who would not be especially objectionable to any party. Now Harold Smith lived with his wife, and his circumstances were not more than ordinarily embarrassed. He kept no racehorses; and, as Lord Brock now heard for the first time, gave lectures in provincial towns on popular subjects. He had a seat which was tolerably secure, and could talk to the House by the yard if required to do so. Moreover, Lord Brock had a great idea that the whole machinery of his own ministry would break to pieces very speedily. His own reputation was not bad, but it was insufficient for himself and that lately selected friend of his. Under all these circumstances combined, he chose Harold Smith to fill the vacant office of Lord Petty Bag. And very proud the Lord Petty Bag was. For the last three or four months, he and Mr. Supplehouse had been agreeing to consign the ministry to speedy perdition. 'This sort of dictatorship will never do,'

Harold Smith had himself said, justifying that future vote of his as to want of confidence in the Queen's Government. And Mr. Supplehouse in this matter had fully agreed with him. He was a Juno whose form that wicked old Paris had utterly despised, and he, too, had quite made up his mind as to the lobby in which he would be found when that day of vengeance should arrive. But now things were much altered in Harold Smith's views. The Premier had shown his wisdom in seeking for new strength where strength ought to be sought, and introducing new blood into the body of his ministry. The people would now feel fresh confidence, and probably the House also. As to Mr. Supplehouse – he would use all his influence on Supplehouse. But, after all, Mr. Supplehouse was not everything.

On the morning after our vicar's arrival in London he attended at the Petty Bag Office. It was situated in the close neighbourhood of Downing Street and the higher governmental gods; and though the building itself was not much, seeing that it was shored up on one side, that it bulged out in the front, was foul with smoke, dingy with dirt, and was devoid of any single architectural grace or modern scientific improvement, nevertheless its position gave it a status in the world which made the clerks in the Lord Petty Bag's office quite respectable in their walk in life. Mark had seen his friend Sowerby on the previous evening, and had then made an appointment with him for the following morning at the new minister's office. And now he was there a little before his time, in order that he might have a few moments' chat with his brother. When Mark found himself in the private secretary's room he was quite astonished to see the change in his brother's appearance which the change in his official rank had produced. Jack Robarts had been a well-built, straight-legged, lissom young fellow, pleasant to the eye because of his natural advantages, but rather given to a harum-scarum style of gait, and occasionally careless, not to say slovenly, in his dress. But now he was the very pink of perfection. His jaunty frock-coat fitted him to perfection; not a hair of his head was out of place; his waistcoat and trousers were glossy and new, and his umbrella, which stood in the umbrella-stand in the corner, was tight, and neat, and small, and natty. 'Well, John, you've become quite a great man,' said his brother.

'I don't know much about that,' said John; 'but I find that I have an enormous deal of fagging to go through.'

'Do you mean work? I thought you had about the easiest berth in the whole Civil Service.'

'Ah! that's just the mistake that people make. Because we don't cover whole reams of foolscap paper at the rate of fifteen lines to a page, and five words to a line, people think that we private secretaries have got nothing to do. Look here,' and he tossed over scornfully a dozen or so of little notes. 'I tell you what, Mark; it is no easy matter to manage the patronage of a Cabinet minister. Now I am bound to write to every one of these fellows a letter that will please him; and yet I shall refuse to every one of them the request which he asks.'

'That must be difficult.'

'Difficult is no word for it. But, after all, it consists chiefly in the knack of the thing. One must have the wit "from such a sharp and waspish word as No to pluck the sting." I do it every day, and I really think that the people like it.'

'Perhaps your refusals are better than other people's acquiescences.'

'I don't mean that at all. We private secretaries have all to do the same thing. Now, would you believe it? I have used up three lifts of notepaper already in telling people that there is no vacancy for a lobby messenger in the Petty Bag Office. Seven peeresses have asked for it for their favourite footmen. But there – there's the Lord Petty Bag!' A bell rang and the private secretary, jumping up from his notepaper, tripped away quickly to the great man's room. 'He'll see you at once,' said he, returning. 'Buggins, show the Reverend Mr. Robarts to the Lord Petty Bag.' Buggins was the messenger for whose not vacant place all the peeresses were striving with so much animation. And then Mark, following Buggins for two steps, was ushered into the next room.

If a man be altered by becoming a private secretary, he is much more altered by being made a Cabinet minister. Robarts, as he entered the room, could hardly believe that this was the same Harold Smith whom Mrs. Proudie bothered so cruelly in the lecture-room at Barchester. Then he was cross, and touchy, and uneasy, and insignificant. Now, as he stood smiling on the hearth-rug of his official fireplace, it was quite pleasant to see the kind, patronizing smile which lighted up his features. He delighted to stand there, with his hands in his trousers' pocket, the great man of the place, conscious of his lordship, and feeling himself every inch a minister. Sowerby had come with him, and was standing a little in the background, from which position he winked occasionally at the parson over the minister's shoulder. 'Ah, Robarts, delighted to see you. How odd, by the by, that your brother should be my private secretary!' Mark said that it was a singular coincidence.

'A very smart young fellow, and, if he minds himself, he'll do well.'

'I'm quite sure he'll do well,' said Mark.

'Ah! well, yes; I think he will. And now, what can I do for you, Robarts?' Hereupon Mr. Sowerby struck in, making it apparent by his explanation that Mr. Robarts himself by no means intended to ask for anything; but that, as his friends had thought that this stall at Barchester might be put into his hands with more fitness than in those of any other clergyman of the day, he was willing to accept the piece of preferment from a man whom he respected so much as he did the new Lord Petty Bag. The minister did not quite like this, as it restricted him from much of his condescension, and robbed him of the incense of a petition which he had expected Mark Robarts would make to him. But, nevertheless, he was very gracious. 'He could not take upon himself to declare,' he said, 'what might be Lord Brock's pleasure with reference to the preferment at Barchester which was vacant. He had certainly already spoken to his lordship on the subject, and had perhaps some reason to believe that his own wishes would be consulted. No distinct promise had been made, but he might perhaps go so far as to say that he expected such result. If so, it would give him the greatest pleasure in the world to congratulate Mr. Robarts on the possession of the stall – a stall which he was sure Mr. Robarts would fill with dignity, piety, and brotherly love.' And then, when he had finished, Mr. Sowerby gave a final wink, and said that he regarded the matter as settled.

'No, not settled, Nathaniel,' said the cautious minister.

'It's the same thing,' rejoined Sowerby. 'We all know what all that flummery means. Men in office, Mark, never do make a distinct promise, – not even to themselves of the leg of mutton which is roasting before their kitchen fires. It is so necessary in these days to be safe; is it not, Harold?'

'Most expedient,' said Harold Smith, shaking his head wisely. 'Well, Robarts, who is it now?' This he said to his private secretary, who came to notice the arrival of some bigwig. 'Well, yes. I will say good morning, with your leave, for I am a little hurried. And remember, Mr. Robarts, I will do what I can for you; but you must distinctly understand that there is no promise.'

'Oh, no promise at all,' said Sowerby – 'of course not.' And then, as he sauntered up Whitehall towards Charing Cross, with Robarts on his arm, he again pressed upon him the sale of that invaluable hunter, who was eating his head off his shoulders in the stable at Chaldicotes.

CHAPTER XIX

Money Dealings

Mr. Sowerby, in his resolution to obtain this good gift for the vicar of Framley, did not depend quite alone on the influence of his near connexion with the Lord Petty Bag. He felt the occasion to be one on which he might endeavour to move even higher powers than that, and therefore he had opened the matter to the duke – not by direct application, but through Mr. Fothergill. No man who understood matters ever thought of going direct to the duke in such an affair as that. If one wanted to speak about a woman or a horse or a picture the duke could, on occasions, be affable enough. But through Mr. Fothergill the duke was approached. It was represented, with some cunning, that this buying over of the Framley clergyman from the Lufton side would be a praiseworthy spoiling of the Amalekites. The doing so would give the Omnium interest a hold even in the cathedral close. And then it was known to all men that Mr. Robarts had considerable influence over Lord Lufton himself. So guided, the Duke of Omnium did say two words to the Prime Minister, and two words from the duke went a great way, even with Lord Brock. The upshot of all this was, that Mark Robarts did get the stall; but he did not hear the tidings of his success till some days after his return to Framley.

Mr. Sowerby did not forget to tell him of the great effort – the unusual effort, as he of Chaldicotes called it – which the duke had made on the subject. 'I don't know when he has done such a thing before,' said Sowerby; 'and you may be quite sure of this, he would not have done it now, had you not gone to Gatherum Castle when he asked you: indeed, Fothergill would have known that it was vain to attempt it. And I'll tell you what, Mark – it does not do for me to make little of my own nest, but

I truly believe the duke's word will be more efficacious than the Lord Petty Bag's solemn adjuration.' Mark, of course, expressed his gratitude in proper terms, and did buy the horse for a hundred and thirty pounds. 'He's as well worth it,' said Sowerby, 'as any animal that ever stood on four legs; and my only reason for pressing him on you is, that when Tozer's day does come round, I know you will have to stand to us to something about that tune.' It did not occur to Mark to ask him why the horse should not be sold to some one else, and the money forthcoming in the regular way. But this would not have suited Mr. Sowerby.

Mark knew that the beast was good, and as he walked to his lodgings was half proud of his new possession. But then, how would he justify it to his wife, or how introduce the animal into his stables without attempting any justification in the matter? And yet, looking to the absolute amount of his income, surely he might feel himself entitled to buy a new horse when it suited him. He wondered what Mr. Crawley would say when he heard of the new purchase. He had lately fallen into a state of much wondering as to what his friends and neighbours would say about him. He had now been two days in town, and was to go down after breakfast on the following morning so that he might reach home by Friday afternoon. But on that evening, just as he was going to bed, he was surprised by Lord Lufton coming into the coffee-room at his hotel. He walked in with a hurried step, his face was red, and it was clear that he was very angry. 'Robarts,' said he, walking up to his friend and taking the hand that was extended to him, 'do you know anything about this man Tozer?'

'Tozer – what Tozer? I have heard Sowerby speak of such a man.'

'Of course you have. If I do not mistake you have written to me about him yourself.'

'Very probably. I remember Sowerby mentioning the man with reference to your affairs. But why do you ask me?'

'This man has not only written to me, but has absolutely forced his way into my rooms when I was dressing for dinner; and absolutely had the impudence to tell me that if I did not honour some bill which he holds for eight hundred pounds he would proceed against me.'

'But you settled all that matter with Sowerby?'

'I did settle it at a very great cost to me. Sooner than have a fuss, I paid him through the nose – like a fool that I was – everything that he claimed. This is an absolute swindle, and if it goes on I will expose it as such.' Robarts looked round the room, but luckily there was not a soul in it but themselves. 'You do not mean to say that Sowerby is swindling you?' said the clergyman.

'It looks very like it,' said Lord Lufton; 'and I tell you fairly that I am not in a humour to endure any more of this sort of thing. Some years ago I made an ass of myself through that man's fault. But four thousand pounds should have covered the whole of what I really lost. I have now paid more than three times that sum; and, by heavens! I will not pay more without exposing the whole affair.'

'But, Lufton, I do not understand. What is this bill? – has it your name to it?'

'Yes, it has: I'll not deny my name, and if there be absolute need I will pay it; but, if I do so, my lawyer shall sift it, and it shall go before a jury.'

'But I thought all those bills were paid?'

'I left it to Sowerby to get up the old bills when they were renewed, and now one of them that has in truth been already honoured is brought against me.' Mark could not but think of the two documents which he himself had signed, and both of which were now undoubtedly in the hands of Tozer, or of some other gentleman of the same profession; – which both might be brought against him, the second as soon as he should have satisfied the first. And then he remembered that Sowerby had said something to him about an outstanding bill, for the filling up of which some trifle must be paid, and of this he reminded Lord Lufton.

'And do you call eight hundred pounds a trifle? If so, I do not.'

'They will probably make no such demand as that.'

'But I tell you they do make such a demand, and have made it. The man whom I saw, and who told me that he was Tozer's friend, but who was probably Tozer himself, positively swore to me that he would be obliged to take legal proceedings if the money were not forthcoming within a week or ten days. When I explained to him that it was an old bill that had been renewed, he declared that his friend had given full value for it.'

'Sowerby said that you would probably have to pay ten pounds to redeem it. I should offer the man some such sum as that.'

'My intention is to offer the man nothing, but to leave the affair in the hands of my lawyer with instructions to him to spare none; neither myself nor any one else. I am not going to allow such a man as Sowerby to squeeze me like an orange.'

'But, Lufton, you seem as though you were angry with me.'

'No, I am not. But I think it is as well to caution you about this man; my transactions with him lately have chiefly been through you, and therefore –'

'But they have only been so through his and your wish: because I have been anxious to oblige you both. I hope you don't mean to say that I am concerned in these bills.

'I know that you are concerned in bills with him.'

'Why, Lufton, am I to understand, then, that you are accusing me of having any interest in these transactions which you have called swindling?'

'As far as I am concerned there has been swindling, and there is swindling going on now.'

'But you do not answer my question. Do you bring any accusation against me? If so, I agree with you that you had better go to your lawyer.'

'I think that is what I shall do.'

'Very well. But, upon the whole, I never heard of a more unreasonable man, or of one whose thoughts are more unjust than yours. Solely with the view of assisting you, and solely at your request, I spoke to Sowerby about these money transactions of yours. Then, at his request, which originated out of your request, he using me as his ambassador to you, as you had used me as yours to him, I wrote and spoke to you. And now this is the upshot.'

'I bring no accusation against you, Robarts; but I know you have dealings with this man. You have told me so yourself.'

'Yes, at his request to accommodate him. I have put my name to a bill.'

'Only to one?'

'Only to one; and then to that same renewed, or not exactly to that same, but to one which stands for it. The first was for four hundred pounds; the last for five hundred.'

'All which you will have to make good, and the world will of course tell you that you have paid that price for this stall at Barchester.' This was terrible to be borne. He had heard much lately which had frightened and scared him, but nothing so terrible as this; nothing which so stunned him, or conveyed to his mind so frightful a reality of misery and ruin. He made no immediate answer, but standing on the hearth-rug with his back to the fire, looked up the whole length of the room. Hitherto his eyes had been fixed upon Lord Lufton's face, but now it seemed to him as though he had but little more to do with Lord Lufton. Lord Lufton and Lord Lufton's mother were neither now to be counted among those who wished him well. Upon whom indeed could he now count, except that wife of his bosom upon whom he was bringing all this wretchedness? In that moment of agony ideas ran quickly through his brain. He would immediately abandon this preferment at Barchester, of which it might be said with so much colour that he had bought it. He would go to Harold Smith, and say positively that he declined it. Then he would return home and tell his wife all that had occurred; – tell the whole also to Lady Lufton, if that might still be of any service. He would make arrangement for the payment of both those bills as they might be presented, asking no questions as to the justice of the claim, making no complaint to any one, not even to Sowerby. He would put half his income, if half were necessary, into the hands of Forrest the banker, till all was paid. He would sell every horse he had. He would part with his footman and groom, and at any rate strive like a man to get again a firm footing on good ground. Then, at that moment, he loathed with his whole soul the position in which he found himself placed, and his own folly which had placed him there. How could he reconcile it to his conscience that he was there in London with Sowerby and Harold Smith, petitioning for Church preferment to a man who should have been altogether powerless in such a matter, buying horses, and arranging about past due bills? He did not reconcile it to his conscience. Mr. Crawley had been right when he told him that he was a castaway.

Lord Lufton, whose anger during the whole interview had been extreme, and who had become more angry the more he talked, had now walked once or twice up and down the room; and as he so walked the idea did occur to him that he had been unjust. He had come there with the intention of exclaiming against Sowerby, and of inducing Robarts to convey to that gentleman, that if he, Lord Lufton, were made to undergo any further annoyance about this bill, the whole affair should be thrown into the lawyer's hands; but instead of doing this, he had brought an accusation against Robarts. That Robarts had latterly become Sowerby's friend rather than his own in all these horrid money dealings, had galled him; and now he had expressed himself in terms much stronger than he had intended to use. 'As to you personally, Mark,' he said, coming back to the spot on which Robarts was standing, 'I do not wish to say anything that shall annoy you.'

'You have said quite enough, Lord Lufton.'

'You cannot be surprised that I should be angry and indignant at the treatment I have received.'

'You might, I think, have separated in your mind those who have wronged you, if there has been such wrong, from those who have only endeavoured to do your will and pleasure for you. That I, as a clergyman, have been very wrong in taking any part whatsoever in these matters, I am well aware. That as a man I have been outrageously foolish in lending my name to Mr. Sowerby, I also know well enough: it is, perhaps, as well that I should be told of this somewhat rudely; but I certainly did not expect the lesson to come from you.'

'Well, there has been mischief enough. The question is, what we had better now both do?'

'You have said what you mean to do. You will put the affair into the hands of your lawyer.'

'Not with any object of exposing you.'

'Exposing me, Lord Lufton! Why, one would think that I had the handling of your money.'

'You will misunderstand me. I think no such thing. But do you not know yourself that if legal steps be taken in this wretched affair, your arrangements with Sowerby will be brought to light?'

'My arrangements with Sowerby will consist in paying or having to pay, on his account, a large sum of money, for which I have never had and shall never have any consideration whatever.'

'And what will be said about this stall at Barchester?'

'After the charge which you brought against me just now, I shall decline to accept it.' At this moment three or four other gentlemen entered the room, and the conversation between our two friends was stopped. They still remained standing near the fire, but for a few minutes neither of them said anything. Robarts was waiting till Lord Lufton should go away, and Lord Lufton had not yet said that which he had come to say. At last he spoke again, almost in a whisper: 'I think it will be best to ask

Sowerby to come to my rooms to-morrow, and I think also that you should meet him there.'

'I do not see any necessity for my presence,' said Robarts. 'It seems probable that I shall suffer enough for meddling with your affairs, and I will do so no more.'

'Of course, I cannot make you come; but I think it will be only just to Sowerby, and it will be a favour to me.' Robarts again walked up and down the room for half a dozen times, trying to resolve what it would most become him to do in the present emergency. If his name were dragged before the courts, – if he should be shown up in the public papers as having been engaged in accommodation bills, that would certainly be ruinous to him. He had already learned from Lord Lufton's innuendoes what he might expect to hear as the public version of his share in these transactions! And then his wife, – how would she bear such exposure? 'I will meet Mr. Sowerby at your rooms to-morrow, on one condition,' he at last said.

'And what is that?'

'That I receive your positive assurance that I am not suspected by you of having had any pecuniary interest whatever in any money matters with Mr. Sowerby, either as concerns your affairs or those of anybody else.'

'I have never suspected you of any such thing. But I have thought that you were compromised with him.'

'And so I am – I am liable for these bills. But you ought to have known, and do know, that I have never received a shilling on account of such liability. I have endeavoured to oblige a man whom I regarded first as your friend, and then as my own; and this has been the result.' Lord Lufton did at last give him the assurance that he desired, as they sat with their heads together over one of the coffee-room tables; and then Robarts promised that he would postpone his return to Framley till the Saturday, so that he might meet Sowerby at Lord Lufton's chambers in the Albany on the following afternoon. As soon as this was arranged, Lord Lufton took his leave and went his way.

After that poor Mark had a very uneasy night of it. It was clear enough that Lord Lufton had thought, if he did not still think, that the stall at Barchester was to be given as pecuniary recompense in return for certain money accommodation to be afforded by the nominee to the dispenser of this patronage. Nothing on earth could be worse than this. In the first place it would be simony; and then it would be simony beyond all description mean and simoniacal. The very thought of it filled Mark's soul with horror and dismay. It might be that Lord Lufton's suspicions were now at rest; but others would think the same thing, and their suspicions it would be impossible to allay; those others would consist of the outer world, which is always so eager to gloat over the detected vice of a clergyman. And then that wretched horse which he had purchased, and the purchase of which should have prohibited him from saying that nothing of value had accrued to him in these transactions with Mr. Sowerby! what was he to do about that? And then of late he had been spending, and had continued to spend, more money than he could well afford. This very journey of his up to London would be most imprudent, if it should become necessary for him to give up all hope of holding the prebend. As to that he had made up his mind; but then again he unmade it, as men always do in such troubles. That line of conduct which he had laid down for himself in the first moments of his indignation against Lord Lufton, by adopting which he would have to encounter poverty, and ridicule, and discomfort, the annihilation of his high hopes, and the ruin of his ambition – that, he said to himself over and over again, would now be the best for him. But it is so hard for us to give up our high hopes, and willingly encounter poverty, ridicule, and discomfort!

On the following morning, however, he boldly walked down to the Petty Bag Office, determined to let Harold Smith know that he was no longer desirous of the Barchester stall. He found his brother there, still writing artistic notes to anxious peeresses on the subject of Buggins's non-vacant situation; but the great man of the place, the Lord Petty Bag himself, was not there. He might probably look in when the House was beginning to sit, perhaps at four or a little after; but he certainly would not be at the office in the morning. The functions of the Lord Petty Bag he was no doubt performing elsewhere. Perhaps he had carried his work home with him – a practice which the world should know is not uncommon with civil servants of exceeding zeal. Mark did think of opening his heart to his brother, and of leaving his message with him. But his courage failed him, or perhaps it might be more correct to say that his prudence prevented him. It would be better for him, he thought, to tell his wife before he told any one else. So he merely chatted with his brother for half an hour and then left him. The day was very tedious till the hour came at which he was to attend at Lord Lufton's rooms; but at last it did come, and just as the clock struck he turned out of Piccadilly into the Albany. As he was going across the court before he entered the building, he was greeted by a voice just behind him. 'As punctual as the big clock on Barchester tower,' said Mr. Sowerby. 'See what it is to have a summons from a great man, Mr. Prebendary.' He turned round and extended his hand mechanically to Mr. Sowerby, and as he looked at him he thought he had never before seen him so pleasant in appearance, so free from care, and so joyous in demeanour.

'You have heard from Lord Lufton,' said Mark, in a voice that was certainly very lugubrious.

'Heard from him! oh, yes, of course I have heard from him. I'll tell you what it is, Mark,' and he now spoke almost in a whisper as they walked together along the Albany passage, 'Lufton is a child in money matters – a perfect child. The dearest, finest fellow in the world, you know; but a very baby in money matters.' And then they entered his lordship's rooms. Lord Lufton's countenance also was lugubrious enough, but this did not in the least abash Sowerby, who walked quickly up to the young lord with his gait perfectly self-possessed and his face radiant with satisfaction.

'Well, Lufton, how are you?' said he. 'It seems that my worthy friend Tozer has been giving you some trouble?' Then Lord Lufton with a face by no means radiant with satisfaction again began the story of Tozer's fraudulent demand upon him. Sowerby did not interrupt him, but listened patiently to the end; – quite patiently, although Lord Lufton, as he made himself more and more angry by the history of his own wrongs, did not hesitate to pronounce certain threats against Mr. Sowerby, as he had pronounced them before against Mark Robarts. He would not, he said, pay a shilling, except through his lawyer; and he would instruct his lawyer, that before he paid anything, the whole matter should be exposed openly in court. He did not care, he said, what might be the effect on himself or any one else. He was determined that the whole case should go to a jury. 'To grand jury, and special jury, and common jury, and Old Jewry, if you like,' said Sowerby. 'The truth is, Lufton, you lost some money, and as there was some delay in paying it, you have been harassed.'

'I have paid more than I lost three times over,' said Lord Lufton, stamping his foot.

'I will not go into that question now. It was settled, as I thought, some time ago by persons to whom you yourself referred it. But will you tell me this: Why on earth should Robarts be troubled in this matter? What has he done?'

'Well, I don't know. He arranged the matter with you.'

'No such thing. He was kind enough to carry a message from you to me, and to convey back a return message from me to you. That has been his part in it.'

'You don't suppose that I want to implicate him: do you?'

'I don't think you want to implicate any one, but you are hot-headed and difficult to deal with, and very irrational into the bargain. And, what is worse, I must say you are a little suspicious. In all this matter I have harassed myself greatly to oblige you, and in return I have got more kicks than halfpence.'

'Did not you give this bill to Tozer – the bill which he now holds?'

'In the first place he does not hold it; and in the next place I did not give it to him. These things pass through scores of hands before they reach the man who makes the application for payment.'

'And who came to me the other day?'

'That, I take it, was Tom Tozer, a brother of our Tozer's.'

'Then he holds the bill, for I saw it with him.'

'Wait a moment; that is very likely. I sent you word that you would have to pay for taking it up. Of course they don't abandon those sort of things without some consideration.'

'Ten pounds, you said,' observed Mark.

'Ten or twenty; some such sum as that. But you were hardly so soft as to suppose that the man would ask for such a sum. Of course he would demand the full payment. There is the bill, Lord Lufton,' and Sowerby, producing a document, handed it across the table to his lordship. 'I gave five-and-twenty pounds for it this morning.' Lord Lufton took the paper and looked at it. 'Yes,' said he, 'that's the bill. What am I to do with it now?'

'Put it with the family archives,' said Sowerby, – 'or behind the fire, just which you please.'

'And is this the last of them? Can no other be brought up?'

'You know better than I do what paper you may have put your hand to. I know of no other. At the last renewal that was the only outstanding bill of which I was aware.'

'And you have paid five-and-twenty pounds for it?'

'I have. Only that you have been in such a tantrum about it, and would have made such a noise this afternoon if I had not brought it, I might have had it for fifteen or twenty. In three or four days they would have taken fifteen.'

'The odd ten pounds does not signify, and I'll pay you the twenty-five, of course,' said Lord Lufton, who now began to feel a little ashamed of himself.

'You may do as you please about that.'

'Oh! it's my affair, as a matter of course. Any amount of that kind I don't mind,' and he sat down to fill in a cheque for the money.

'Well, now, Lufton, let me say a few words to you,' said Sowerby, standing with his back against the fireplace, and playing with a small cane which he held in his hand. 'For heaven's sake try and be a little more charitable to those around you. When you become fidgety about anything, you indulge in language which the world won't stand, though men who know you as well as Robarts and I may consent to put up with it. You have accused me, since I have been here, of all manner of iniquity –'

'Now, Sowerby –'

'My dear fellow, let me have my say out. You have accused me, I say, and I believe that you have accused him. But it has never occurred to you, I dare say, to accuse yourself.'

'Indeed it has.'

'Of course you have been wrong in having to do with such men as Tozer. I have also been very wrong. It wants no great moral authority to tell us that. Pattern gentlemen don't have dealings with Tozer, and very much the better they are for not having them. But a man should have back enough to bear the weight which he himself puts on it. Keep away from Tozer, if you can, for the future; but if you do deal with him, for heaven's sake keep your temper.'

'That's all very fine, Sowerby; but you know as well as I do –'

'I know this,' said the devil, quoting Scripture, as he folded up the check for twenty-five pounds, and put it in his pocket, 'that when a man sows tares, he won't reap wheat, and it's no use to expect it. I am tough in these matters, and can bear a great deal – that is, if I be not pushed too far,' and he looked full into Lord Lufton's face as he spoke; 'but I think you have been very hard upon Robarts.'

'Never mind me, Sowerby; Lord Lufton and I are very old friends.'

'And may therefore take a liberty with each other. Very well. And now I've done my sermon. My dear dignitary, allow me to congratulate you. I hear from Fothergill that that little affair of yours has been definitely settled.' Mark's face again became clouded. 'I rather think,' said he, 'that I shall decline the presentation.'

'Decline it!' said Sowerby, who, having used his utmost efforts to obtain it, would have been more absolutely offended by such vacillation on the vicar's part than by any personal abuse which either he or Lord Lufton could heap upon him.

'I think I shall,' said Mark.

'And why?' Mark looked up at Lord Lufton, and then remained silent for a moment.

'There can be no occasion for such a sacrifice under the present circumstances,' said his lordship.

'And under what circumstances could there be occasion for it?' asked Sowerby. 'The Duke of Omnium has used some little influence to get the place for you as a parish clergyman belonging to his county, and I should think it monstrous if you were now to reject it.' And then Robarts openly stated the whole of his reasons, explaining exactly what Lord Lufton had said with reference to the bill transactions, and to the allegation which would be made as to the stall having been given in payment for the accommodation.

'Upon my word that's too bad,' said Sowerby.

'Now, Sowerby, I won't be lectured,' said Lord Lufton.

'I have done my lecture,' said he, aware, perhaps, that it would not do for him to push his friend too far, 'and I shall not give a second. But, Robarts, let me tell you this: as far as I know, Harold Smith has had little or nothing to do with the appointment. The duke has told the Prime Minister that he was very anxious that a parish clergyman from the county should go into the chapter, and then, at Lord Brock's request, he named you. If under those circumstances you talk of giving it up, I shall believe you to be insane. As for the bill which you accepted for me, you need have no uneasiness about it. The money will be ready; but of course, when that time comes, you will let me have the hundred and thirty for –' And then Mr. Sowerby took his leave, having certainly made himself master of the occasion. If a man of fifty have his wits about him, and be not too prosy, he can generally make himself master of the occasion, when his companions are under thirty. Robarts did not stay at the Albany long after him, but took his leave, having received some assurances of Lord Lufton's regret for what had passed and many promises of his friendship for the future. Indeed Lord Lufton was a little ashamed of himself. 'And as for the prebend, after what has passed, of course you must accept it.' Nevertheless his lordship had not omitted to notice Mr. Sowerby's hint about the horse and the hundred and thirty pounds.

Robarts, as he walked back to his hotel, thought that he certainly would accept the Barchester promotion, and was very glad that he had said nothing on the subject to his brother. On the whole his spirits were much raised. That assurance of Sowerby's about the bill was very comforting to him; and, strange to say, he absolutely believed it. In truth, Sowerby had been so completely the winning horse at the late meeting, that both Lord Lufton and Robarts were inclined to believe almost anything he said; – which was not always the case with either of them.

CHAPTER XX

Harold Smith in The Cabinet

FOR a few days the whole Harold Smith party held their heads very high. It was not only that their man had been made a Cabinet minister; but a rumour had got abroad that Lord Brock, in selecting him, had amazingly strengthened his party, and done much to cure the wounds which his own arrogance and lack of judgement had inflicted on the body politic of his Government. So said the Harold Smithians, much elated. And when we consider what Harold had himself achieved, we need not be surprised that he himself was somewhat elated also. It must be a proud day for any man when he first walks into a Cabinet. But when a humble-minded man thinks of such a phase of life, his mind becomes lost in wondering what a Cabinet is. Are they gods that attend there or men? Do they sit on chairs, or hang about on clouds? When they speak, is the music of the spheres audible in their Olympian mansion, making heaven drowsy with its harmony? In what way do they congregate? In what order do they address each other? Are the voices of all the deities free and equal? Is plodding Themis from the Home Department, or Ceres from the Colonies, heard with as rapt attention as powerful Pallas of the Foreign Office, the goddess that is never seen without her lance and helmet? Does our Whitehall Mars make eyes there at bright young Venus of the Privy Seal, disgusting that quaint tinkering Vulcan, who is blowing his bellows at our Exchequer, not altogether unsuccessfully? Old Saturn of the Woolsack sits there mute, we will say, a relic of other days, as seated in this divan. The hall in which he rules is now elsewhere. Is our Mercury of the Post Office ever ready to fly nimbly from globe to globe, as great Jove may order him, while Neptune, unaccustomed to the waves, offers needful assistance to the Apollo of the India Board? How Juno sits apart, glum and huffy, uncared for, Council President though she be, great in name, but despised among gods – that we can guess. if Bacchus and Cupid share Trade and the Board of Works between them, the fitness of things will have been as fully consulted as is usual. And modest Diana of the Petty Bag, latest summoned to these banquets of ambrosia, – does she not cling retiring near the doors, hardly able as yet to make her low voice heard among her brother deities? But Jove, great Jove – old Jove, the King of Olympus, hero among gods and men, how does he carry himself in these councils summoned by his voice? Does he lie there at his ease, with his purple cloak cut from the firmament around his shoulders? Is his thunderbolt ever at his hand to reduce a recreant god to order? Can he proclaim silence in that immortal hall? Is it not there, as elsewhere, in all places, and among all nations, that a king of gods and a king of men is and will be king, rules and will rule, over those who are smaller than himself?

Harold Smith, when he was summoned to the august hall of divine councils, did feel himself to be a proud man; but we may perhaps conclude that at the first meeting or two he did not attempt to take a very leading part. Some of my readers may have sat at vestries, and will remember how mild, and, for the most part, mute is a new-comer at their board. He agrees generally, with abated enthusiasm; but should he differ, he apologizes for the liberty. But anon, when the voices of his colleagues have become habitual in his ears – when the strangeness of the room is gone, and the table before him is known and trusted – he throws off his awe and dismay, and electrifies his brotherhood by the vehemence of his declamation and the violence of his thumping. So let us suppose it will be with Harold Smith, perhaps in the second or third season of his Cabinet practice. Alas! alas! that such pleasures should be so fleeting! And then, too, there came upon him a blow which somewhat modified his triumph – a cruel, dastard blow, from a hand which should have been friendly to him, from one to whom he had fondly looked to buoy him up in the great course that was before him. It had been said by his friends that in obtaining Harold Smith's services the Prime Minister had infused new young healthy blood into his body. Harold himself had liked the phrase, and had seen at a glance how it might have been made to tell by some friendly Supplehouse or the like. But why should a Supplehouse out of Elysium be friendly to a Harold Smith within it? Men lapped in Elysium, steeped to the neck in bliss, must expect to see their friends fall off from them. Human nature cannot stand it. If I want to get anything from my old friend Jones, I like to see him shoved up into a high place. But if Jones, even in his high place, can do nothing for me, then his exaltation above my head is an insult and an injury. Who ever believes his own dear intimate companion to be fit for the highest promotion? Mr. Supplehouse had known Mr. Smith too closely to think much of his young blood.

Consequently, there appeared an article in the *Jupiter*, which was by no means complimentary to the ministry in general. It harped a good deal on the young-blood view of the question, and seemed to insinuate that Harold Smith was not much better than diluted water. 'The Prime Minister,' the article said, 'having lately recruited his impaired vigour by a new infusion of aristocratic influence of the highest moral tone, had again added to himself another tower of strength chosen from among the people. What might he not hope, now that he possessed the services of Lord Brittleback and Mr. Harold Smith! Renovated in a Medea's cauldron of such potency, all his effete limbs – and it must be acknowledged that some of them had become very effete – would come forth young and round and robust. A new energy would diffuse itself through every department; India would be saved and quieted; the ambition of France would be tamed; even-handed reform would remodel our courts of law and parliamentary elections; and Utopia would be realized. Such, it seems, is the result expected in the ministry from Mr. Harold Smith's young blood!'

This was cruel enough, but even this was hardly so cruel as the words with which the article ended. By that time irony had been dropped, and the writer spoke out earnestly his opinion upon the matter. 'We beg to assure

Lord Brock,' said the article, 'that such alliances as these will not save him from the speedy fall with which his arrogance and want of judgement threaten to overwhelm it. As regards himself we shall be sorry to hear of his resignation. He is in many respects the best statesman that we possess for the emergencies of the present period. But if he be so ill-judged as to rest on such men as Mr. Harold Smith and Lord Brittleback for his assistants in the work which is before him, he must not expect that the country will support him. Mr. Harold Smith is not made of the stuff from which Cabinet ministers should be formed.' Mr. Harold Smith, as he read this, seated at his breakfast-table recognized, or said that he recognized, the hand of Mr. Supplehouse in every touch. That phrase about the effete limbs was Supplehouse all over, as was also the realization of Utopia. 'When he wants to be witty, he always talks about Utopia,' said Mr. Harold Smith – to himself; for Mrs. Harold was not usually present in the flesh at these matutinal meals. And then he went down to his office, and saw in the glance of every man that he met an announcement that that article in the *Jupiter* had been read. His private secretary tittered in evident allusion to the article, and the way in which Buggins took his coat made it clear that it was well known in the messengers' lobby. 'He won't have to fill up my vacancy when I go,' Buggins was saying to himself. And then in the course of the morning came the Cabinet council, the second that he had attended, and he read in the countenance of every god and goddess there assembled that their chief was thought to have made another mistake. If Mr. Supplehouse could have been induced to write in another strain, then indeed that new blood might have been felt to have been efficacious.

All this was a great drawback to his happiness, but still it could not rob him of the fact of his position. Lord Brock could not ask him to resign because the *Jupiter* had written against him; nor was Lord Brock the man to desert a new colleague for such a reason. So Harold Smith girded his loins, and went about the duties of the Petty Bag with new zeal. 'Upon my word, the *Jupiter* is right,' said young Robarts to himself, as he finished his fourth dozen of private notes explanatory of everything in and about the Petty Bag Office. Harold Smith required that his private secretary's notes should be so terribly precise. But nevertheless, in spite of his drawbacks, Harold Smith was happy in his new honours, and Mrs. Harold Smith enjoyed them also. She certainly, among her acquaintance, did quiz the new Cabinet minister not a little, and it may be a question whether she was not as hard upon him as the writer in the *Jupiter*. She whispered a great deal to Miss Dunstable about new blood, and talked of going down to Westminster Bridge to see whether the Thames were really on fire. But though she laughed, she triumphed, and though she flattered herself that she bore her honours without any outward sign, the world knew that she was triumphing, and ridiculed her elation.

About this time she also gave a party – not a pure-minded conversazione like Mrs. Proudie, but a downright wicked worldly dance, at which there were fiddles, ices, and champagne sufficient to run away with the first quarter's salary accruing to Harold from the Petty Bag Office. To us this ball is chiefly memorable from the fact that Lady Lufton was among the guests. Immediately on her arrival in town she received cards from Mrs. H. Smith for herself and Griselda, and was about to send back a reply at once declining the honour. What had she to do at the house of Mr. Sowerby's sister? But it so happened that at that moment her son was with her, and as he expressed a wish that she should go, she yielded. Had there been nothing in his tone of persuasion more than ordinary, – had it merely had reference to herself, – she would have smiled on him for his kind solicitude, have made out some occasion for kissing his forehead as she thanked him, and would still have declined. But he had reminded her both of himself and Griselda. 'You might as well go, mother, for the sake of meeting me,' he said; 'Mrs. Harold caught me the other day, and would not liberate me till I had given her a promise.'

'That is an attraction certainly,' said Lady Lufton. 'I do like going to a house when I know that you will be there.'

'And now that Miss Grantly is with you – you owe it to her to do the best you can for her.'

'I certainly do, Ludovic; and I have to thank you for reminding me of my duty so gallantly.' And so she said that she would go to Mrs. Harold Smith's. Poor lady! She gave much more weight to those few words about Miss Grantly than they deserved. It rejoiced her heart to think that her son was anxious to meet Griselda – that he should perpetrate this little *ruse* in order to gain his wish. But he had spoken out of the mere emptiness of his mind, without thought of what he was saying, excepting that he wished to please his mother. But nevertheless he went to Mrs. Harold Smith's, and when there he did dance more than once with Griselda Grantly – to the manifest discomfiture of Lord Dumbello. He came in late, and at the moment Lord Dumbello was moving slowly up the room, with Griselda on his arm, while Lady Lufton was sitting near looking on with unhappy eyes. And then Griselda sat down, and Lord Dumbello stood mute at her elbow.

'Ludovic,' whispered his mother, 'Griselda is absolutely bored by that man, who follows her like a ghost. Do go and rescue her.' He did go and rescue her, and afterwards danced with her for the best part of an hour consecutively. He knew that the world gave Lord Dumbello the credit of admiring the young lady, and was quite alive to the pleasure of filling his brother nobleman's heart with jealousy and anger. Moreover, Griselda was in his eyes very beautiful, and had she been one whit more animated, or had his mother's tactics been but a thought better concealed, Griselda might have been asked that night to share the vacant throne at Lufton, in spite of all that had been said and sworn in the drawing-room of Framley parsonage. It must be remembered that our gallant, gay Lothario had passed some considerable number of days with Miss Grantly in his mother's house, and the danger of such contiguity must be remembered also. Lord Lufton was by no means a man capable of seeing beauty unmoved or of spending hours with a young lady without some approach to tenderness. Had there been no such approach, it is probable that Lady Lufton would not have pursued the matter. But, according to her ideas on such subjects, her son Ludovic had on some occasions shown quite sufficient partiality for Miss Grantly to justify her in her hopes, and to lead her to think that nothing but opportunity was wanted. Now, at this ball of Mrs. Smith's, he did, for a while, seem to be taking advantage of such opportunity, and his mother's heart was glad. If things should turn out well on this evening she would forgive Mrs. Harold Smith all her sins. And for a while it looked as though things would turn out well. Not that it must be supposed that Lord Lufton had come there with any intention of making love to Griselda, or that he ever had any fixed thought that he was doing so. Young men in such matters are so often without any fixed thoughts! They are such absolute moths. They amuse themselves with the light of the beautiful candle, fluttering about, on and off, in and out of the flame with dazzled eyes, till in a rash moment they rush in too near the wick, and then fall with singed wings and crippled legs, burnt up and reduced to tinder by the consuming fire of matrimony. Happy marriages, men say, are made in heaven, and I believe it. Most marriages are fairly happy, in spite of Sir Cresswell Cresswell; and yet how little care is taken on earth towards such a result! – 'I hope my mother is using you well?' said Lord Lufton to Griselda, as they were standing together in a doorway between the dances.

'Oh, yes: she is very kind.'

'You have been rash to trust yourself in the hands of so very staid and demure a person. And, indeed, you owe your presence here at Mrs. Harold Smith's first Cabinet ball altogether to me. I don't know whether you are aware of that.'

'Oh, yes: Lady Lufton told me.'

'And are you grateful or otherwise? Have I done you an injury or a benefit? Which do you find best, sitting with a novel in the corner of a sofa in Bruton Street, or pretending to dance polkas here with Lord Dumbello?'

'I don't know what you mean. I haven't stood up with Lord Dumbello all the evening. We were going to dance a quadrille, but we didn't.'

'Exactly; just what I say; – pretending to do it. Even that's a good deal for Lord Dumbello; isn't it?' And then Lord Lufton, not being a pretender himself, put his arm round her waist, and away they went up and down the room, and across and about, with an energy which showed that what Griselda lacked in her tongue she made up with her feet. Lord Dumbello, in the meantime, stood by, observant, thinking to himself that Lord Lufton was a glib-tongued, empty-headed ass, and reflecting that if his rival were to break the tendons of his leg in one of those rapid evolutions, or suddenly come by any other dreadful misfortune, such as the loss of all his property, absolute blindness, or chronic lumbago, it would only serve him right. And in that frame of mind he went to bed, in spite of the prayer which no doubt he said as to his forgiveness of other people's trespasses. And then, when they were again standing, Lord Lufton, in the little intervals between his violent gasps for fresh breath, asked Griselda if she liked London. 'Pretty well,' said Griselda, gasping also a little herself.

'I am afraid – you were very dull – down at Framley.'

'Oh, no; – I liked it particularly.'

'It was a great bore when you went – away, I know. There wasn't a soul – about the house worth speaking to.' And they remained silent for a minute till their lungs had become quiescent.

'Not a soul,' he continued – not of falsehood prepense, for he was not in fact thinking of what he was saying. It did not occur to him at the moment that he had truly found Griselda's going a great relief, and that he had been able to do more in the way of conversation with Lucy Robarts in one hour than with Miss Grantly during a month of intercourse in the same house. But, nevertheless, we should not be hard upon him. All is fair in love and war; and if this was not love, it was the usual thing that stands as a counterpart for it.

'Not a soul,' said Lord Lufton. 'I was very nearly hanging myself in the Park next morning – only it rained.'

'What nonsense! You had your mother to talk to.'

'Oh, my mother, – yes; and you may tell me too, if you please, that Captain Culpepper was there. I do love my mother dearly; but do you think that she could make up for your absence?' And his voice was very tender, and so were his eyes.

'And Miss Robarts; I thought you admired her very much?'

'What, Lucy Robarts?' said Lord Lufton, feeling that Lucy's name was more than he at present knew how to manage. Indeed that name destroyed all the life there was in that little flirtation. 'I do like Lucy Robarts, certainly. She is very clever; but it so happened that I saw little or nothing of her after you were gone.' To this Griselda made no answer, but drew herself up, and looked as cold as Diana when she froze Orion in the cave. Nor could she be got to give more than monosyllabic answers to the three or four succeeding attempts at conversation which Lord Lufton made. And then they danced again, but Griselda's steps were by no means so lively as before. What took place between them on that occasion was very little more than what has been here related. There may have been an ice or a glass of lemonade into the bargain, and perhaps the faintest possible attempt at hand-pressing. But if so, it was all on one side. To such overtures as that

Griselda Grantly was as cold as any Diana. But little as all this was, it was sufficient to fill Lady Lufton's mind and heart. No mother with six daughters was ever more anxious to get them off her hands, than Lady Lufton was to see her son married, – married, that is, to some girl of the right sort. And now it really did seem as though he were actually going to comply with her wishes. She had watched him during the whole evening, painfully endeavouring not to be observed in doing so. She had seen Lord Dumbello's failure and wrath, and she had seen her son's victory and pride. Could it be the case that he had already said something, which was still allowed to be indecisive only through Griselda's coldness? Might it not be the case, that by some judicious aid on her part, that indecision might be turned into certainty, and that coldness into warmth? But then any such interference requires so delicate a touch, – as Lady Lufton was well aware. – 'Have you had a pleasant evening?' Lady Lufton said, when she and Griselda were seated together with their feet on the fender of her ladyship's dressing-room. Lady Lufton had especially invited her guest into this, her most private sanctum, to which as a rule none had admittance but her daughter, and sometimes Fanny Robarts. But to what sanctum might not such a daughter-in-law as Griselda have admittance? 'Oh, yes – very,' said Griselda.

'It seemed to me that you bestowed most of your smiles upon Ludovic.' And Lady Lufton put on a look of good pleasure that such should have been the case.

'Oh! I don't know,' said Griselda; 'I did dance with him two or three times.'

'Not once too often to please me, my dear. I like to see Ludovic dancing with my friends.'

'I am sure I am very much obliged to you, Lady Lufton.'

'Not at all, my dear. I don't know where he could get so nice a partner.' And then she paused a moment, not feeling how far she might go. In the meantime Griselda sat still, staring at the hot coals. 'Indeed, I know that he admires you very much,' continued Lady Lufton. – 'Oh! no, I am sure he doesn't,' said Griselda; and then there was another pause.

'I can only say this,' said Lady Lufton, 'that if he does do so – and I believe he does – it would give me very great pleasure. For you know, my dear, that I am very fond of you myself.'

'Oh! thank you,' said Griselda, and stared at the coals more perseveringly than before.

'He is a young man of a most excellent disposition – though he is my own son, I will say that – and if there should be anything between you and him –'

'There isn't, indeed, Lady Lufton.'

'But if there ever should be, I should be delighted to think that Ludovic had made so good a choice.'

'But there will never be anything of the sort, I'm sure, Lady Lufton. He is not thinking of such a thing in the least.'

'Well, perhaps he may, some day. And now, good night, my dear.'

'Good night, Lady Lufton.' And Griselda kissed her with the utmost composure, and betook herself to her own bedroom. Before she retired to sleep she looked carefully to her different articles of dress, discovering what amount of damage the evening's wear and tear might have inflicted.

CHAPTER XXI

Why Puck, The Pony, Was Beaten

MARK ROBARTS returned home the day after the scene at the Albany, considerably relieved in spirit. He now felt that he might accept the stall without discredit to himself as a clergyman in doing so. Indeed, after what Mr. Sowerby had said, and after Lord Lufton's assent to it, it would have been madness, he considered, to decline it. And then, too, Mr. Sowerby's promise about the bills was very comfortable to him.

After all, might it not be possible that he might get rid of all these troubles with no other drawback than that of having to pay £130 for a horse that was well worth the money?

On the day after his return he received proper authentic tidings of his presentation to the prebend. He was, in fact, already prebendary, or would be as soon as the dean and chapter had gone through the form of instituting him in his stall. The income was already his own; and the house also would be given up to him in a week's time – a part of the arrangement with which he would most willingly have dispensed had it been at all possible to do so. His wife congratulated him nicely, with open affection, and apparent satisfaction at the arrangement. The enjoyment of one's own happiness at such windfalls depends so much on the free and freely expressed enjoyment of others! Lady Lufton's congratulations had nearly made him throw up the whole thing; but his wife's smiles re-encouraged him; and Lucy's warm and eager joy made him feel quite delighted with Mr. Sowerby and the Duke of Omnium. And then that splendid animal, Dandy, came home to the parsonage stables, much to the delight of the groom and gardener, and of the assistant stable boy who had been allowed to creep into the establishment, unawares, as it were, since 'master' had taken so keenly to hunting. But this satisfaction was not shared in the drawing-room. The horse was seen on his first journey round to the stable gate, and questions were immediately asked. It was a horse, Mark said, 'which he had bought from Mr. Sowerby some little time since, with the object of obliging him. He, Mark, intended to sell him again, as soon as he could do so judiciously.' This, as I have said above, was not satisfactory. Neither of the two ladies at Framley parsonage knew much about horses, or of the manner in which one gentleman might think it proper to oblige another by purchasing the superfluities of his stable; but they did both feel that there were horses enough in the parsonage stable without Dandy, and that the purchasing of a hunter with a view of immediately selling him again, was, to say the least of it, an operation hardly congenial with the usual tastes and pursuits of a clergyman. 'I hope you did not give very much money for him, Mark,' said Fanny.

'Not more than I shall get again,' said Mark; and Fanny saw from the form of his countenance that she had better not pursue the subject any further at that moment.

'I suppose I shall have to go into residence almost immediately,' said Mark, recurring to the more agreeable subject of the stall.

'And shall we all have to go and live at Barchester at once?' asked Lucy.

'The house will not be furnished, will it, Mark!' said his wife. 'I don't know how we shall get on.'

'Don't frighten yourselves. I shall take lodgings in Barchester.'

'And we shall not see you all the time,' said Mrs. Robarts with dismay. But the prebendary explained that he would be backwards and forwards at Framley every week, and that in all probability he would only sleep at Barchester on the Saturdays, and Sundays – and, perhaps, not always then.

'It does not seem very hard work, that of a prebendary,' said Lucy.

'But it is very dignified,' said Fanny. 'Prebendaries are dignitaries of the Church – are they not, Mark?'

'Decidedly,' said he; 'and their wives also, by special canon law. The worst of it is that both of them are obliged to wear wigs.'

'Shall you have a hat, Mark, with curly things at the side, and strings through to hold them up?' asked Lucy.

'I fear that does not come within my perquisites.'

'Nor a rosette? Then I shall never believe that you are a dignitary. Do you mean to say that you will wear a hat like a common parson – like Mr. Crawley, for instance?'

'Well – I believe I may give a twist to the leaf; but I am by no means sure till I shall have consulted the dean in chapter.'

And thus at the parsonage they talked over the good things that were coming to them, and endeavoured to forget the new horse, and the hunting boots that had been used so often during the last winter, and Lady Lufton's altered countenance. It might be that the evils would vanish away, and the good things alone remain to them. It was now the month of April, and the fields were beginning to look green, and the wind had got itself out of the east and was soft and genial, and the early spring flowers were showing their bright colours in the parsonage garden, and all things were sweet and pleasant. This was a period of the year that was usually dear to Mrs. Robarts. Her husband was always a better parson when the warm months came than he had been during the winter. The distant county friends whom she did not know and of whom she did not approve, went away when the spring came, leaving their houses innocent, and empty. The parish duty was better attended to, and perhaps domestic duties also. At such period he was a pattern parson and a pattern husband, atoning to his own conscience for past shortcomings by present zeal. And then, though she had never acknowledged it to herself, the absence of her dear friend Lady Lufton was perhaps in itself not disagreeable. Mrs. Robarts did love Lady Lufton heartily; but it must be acknowledged of her ladyship, that with all her good qualities, she was inclined to be masterful. She liked to rule, and she made people feel that she liked it. Mrs. Robarts would never have confessed that she laboured under a sense of thraldom; but perhaps she was mouse enough to enjoy the temporary absence of her kind-hearted cat. When Lady Lufton was away Mrs. Robarts herself had more play in the parish. And Mark also was not unhappy, though he did not find it practicable immediately to turn Dandy into money. Indeed, just at this moment, when he was a good deal over at Barchester, going throught those deep mysteries and rigid ecclesiastical examinations which are necessary before a clergyman can become one of a chapter, Dandy was rather a thorn in his side. Those wretched bills were to come due early in May, and before the end of April Sowerby wrote to him saying that he was doing his utmost to provide for the evil day; but that if the price of Dandy could be remitted to him *at once*, it would greatly facilitate his object. Nothing could be more different than Mr. Sowerby's tone about money at different times. When he wanted to raise the wind, everything was so important; haste and superhuman efforts, and men running to and fro with blank acceptances in their hands, could alone stave off the crack of doom; but at other times, when retaliatory applications were made to him, he could prove with the easiest voice and most jaunty manner that everything was quite serene. Now, at this period, he was in that mood of superhuman efforts, and he called loudly for the hundred and thirty pounds for Dandy. After what had passed, Mark could not bring himself to say that he would pay nothing till the bills were safe; and therefore with the assistance of Mr. Forrest of the Bank, he did remit the price of Dandy to his friend Sowerby in London.

And Lucy Robarts – we must now say a word of her. We have seen how, on that occasion, when the world was at her feet, she had sent her noble suitor away, not only dismissed, but so dismissed that he might be taught never again to offer to her the sweet incense of his vows. She had declared to him plainly that she did not love him and could not love him, and had thus thrown away not only riches and honour and high station, but more than that – much worse than that – she had flung away from her the lover to whose love her warm heart clung. That her love did cling to him, she knew even then, and owned more thoroughly as soon as he was gone. So much her pride had done for her, and that strong resolve that Lady Lufton should not scowl on her and tell her that she had entrapped her son.

I know it will be said of Lord Lufton himself that, putting aside his peerage and broad acres, and handsome, sonsy face, he was not worth a girl's care and love. That will be said because people think that heroes in books should be so much better than heroes got up for the world's common wear and tear. I may as well confess that of absolute, true heroism there was only a moderate admixture in Lord Lufton's composition; but what would the world come to if none but absolute true heroes were to be thought worthy of women's love? What would the men do? and what – oh! what would become of the women? Lucy Robarts in her heart did not give her dismissed lover credit for much more heroism than did truly appertain to him; – did not, perhaps, give him full credit for a certain amount of heroism which did really appertain to him; but, nevertheless, she would have been very glad to take him could she have done so without wounding her pride.

That girls should not marry for money we are all agreed. A lady who can sell herself for a title or an estate, for an income or a set of family diamonds, treats herself as a farmer treats his sheep and oxen – makes hardly more of herself, of her own inner self, in which are comprised a mind and soul, than the poor wretch of her own sex who earns her bread in the lowest stage of degradation. But a title, and an estate, and an income, are matters which will weigh in the balance with all Eve's daughters – as they do with all Adam's sons. Pride of place, and the power of living well in front of the world's eye, are dear to us all; – are, doubtless, intended to be dear. Only in acknowledging so much, let us remember that there are prices at which these good things may be too costly. Therefore, being desirous, too, of telling the truth in this matter, I must confess that Lucy did speculate with some regret on what it would have been to be Lady Lufton. To have been the wife of such a man, the owner of such a heart, the mistress of such a destiny – what more or what better could the world have done for her? And now she had thrown all that aside because she would not endure that Lady Lufton should call her a scheming, artful girl! Actuated by that fear she had repulsed him with a falsehood, though the matter was one on which it was so terribly expedient that she should tell the truth. And yet she was cheerful with her brother and sister-in-law. It was when she was quite alone, at night in her own room, or in her solitary walks, that a single silent tear would gather in the corner of her eye and gradually moisten her eyelids. 'She never told her love,' nor did she allow concealment to 'feed on her damask cheek.' In all her employments, in her ways about the house, and her accustomed quiet mirth, she was the same as ever. In this she showed the peculiar strength which God had given her. But not the less did she in truth mourn for her lost love and spoiled ambition. 'We are going to drive over to Hogglestock this morning,' Fanny said one day at breakfast. 'I suppose, Mark, you won't go with us?'

'Well, no; I think not. The pony carriage is wretched for three.'

'Oh, as for that, I should have thought the new horse might have been able to carry you as far as that. I heard you say you wanted to see Mr. Crawley.'

'So I do; and the new horse, as you call him, shall carry me there to-morrow. Will you say that I'll be over about twelve o'clock?'

'You had better say earlier, as he is always out about the parish.'

'Very well, say eleven. It is parish business about which I am going, so it need not irk his conscience to stay in for me.'

'Well, Lucy, we must drive ourselves, that's all. You shall be charioteer going, and then we'll change coming back.' To all which Lucy agreed, and as soon as their work in the school was over they started. Not a word had been spoken between them about Lord Lufton since that evening, now more than a month ago, on which they had been walking together in the garden. Lucy had so demeaned herself on that occasion as to make her sister-in-law quite sure that there had been no love passages up to that time; and nothing had since occurred which had created any suspicion in Mrs. Robarts's mind. She had seen at once that all the close intimacy between them was over, and thought that everything was as it should be.

'Do you know, I have an idea,' she said in the pony carriage that day, 'that Lord Lufton will marry Griselda Grantly.' Lucy could not refrain from giving a little check at the reins which she was holding, and she felt that the blood rushed quickly to her heart. But she did not betray herself. 'Perhaps he may,' she said, and then gave the pony a little touch with her whip.

'Oh, Lucy, I won't have Puck beaten. He was going very nicely.'

'I beg Puck's pardon. But you see when one is trusted with a whip one feels such a longing to use it.'

'Oh, but you should keep it still. I feel almost certain that Lady Lufton would like such a match.'

'I dare say she might. Miss Grantly will have a large fortune, I believe.'

'It is not that altogether: but she is the sort of young lady that Lady Lufton likes. She is ladylike and very beautiful –'

'Come, Fanny!'

'I really think she is; not what I should call lovely, you know, but very beautiful. And then she is quiet and reserved; she does not require excitement, and I am sure is conscientious in the performance of her duties.'

'Very conscientious, I have no doubt,' said Lucy, with something like a sneer in her tone. 'But the question, I suppose, is, whether Lord Lufton likes her.'

'I think he does, – in a sort of way. He did not talk to her so much as he did to you—'

'Ah! that was all Lady Lufton's fault, because she didn't have him properly labelled.'

'There does not seem to have been much harm done?'

'Oh! by God's mercy, very little. As for me, I shall get over it in three or four years I don't doubt – that's if I can get ass's milk and change of air.'

'We'll take you to Barchester for that. But as I was saying, I really do think Lord Lufton likes Griselda Grantly.'

'Then I really do think that he has uncommon bad taste,' said Lucy, with a reality in her voice differing much from the tone of banter she had hitherto used.

'What, Lucy!' said her sister-in-law, looking at her. 'Then I fear we shall really want the ass's milk.'

'Perhaps, considering my position, I ought to know nothing of Lord Lufton, for you say that it is very dangerous for young ladies to know young gentlemen. But I do know enough of him to understand that he ought not to like such a girl as Griselda Grantly. He ought to know that she is a mere automaton, cold, lifeless, spiritless, and even vapid. There is, I believe, nothing in her mentally, whatever may be her moral excellences. To me she is more absolutely like a statue than any other human being I ever saw. To sit still and be admired is all that she desires; and if she cannot get that, to sit still and not be admired would almost suffice for her. I do not worship Lady Lufton as you do; but I think quite well enough of her to wonder that she should choose such a girl as that for her son's wife. That she does wish it I do not doubt. But I shall indeed be surprised if he wishes it also.' And then as she finished her speech, Lucy again flogged the pony. This she did in vexation, because she felt that the tell-tale blood had suffused her face.

'Why, Lucy, if he were your brother you could not be more eager about it.'

'No, I could not. He is the only man friend with whom I was ever intimate, and I cannot bear to think that he should throw himself away. It's horridly improper to care about such a thing, I have no doubt.'

'I think we might acknowledge that if he and his mother are both satisfied, we may be satisfied also.'

'I shall not be satisfied. It's no use your looking at me, Fanny. You will make me talk of it, and I won't tell a lie on the subject. I do like Lord Lufton very much; and I do dislike Griselda Grantly almost as much. Therefore I shall not be satisfied if they become man and wife. However, I do not suppose that either of them will ask my consent; nor is it probable that Lady Lufton will do so.' And then they went on for perhaps a quarter of a mile without speaking.

'Poor Puck!' at last Lucy said. 'He shan't be whipped any more, shall he, because Miss Grantly looks like a statue? And, Fanny, don't tell Mark to put me into a lunatic asylum. I also know a hawk from a heron, and that's why I don't like to see such a very unfitting marriage.' There was then nothing more said on the subject, and in two minutes they arrived at the house of the Hogglestock clergyman. Mrs. Crawley had brought two children with her when she came from the Cornish curacy to Hogglestock, and two other babies had been added to her cares since then. One of these was now ill with croup, and it was with the object of offering to the mother some comfort and solace, that the present visit was made. The two ladies got down from their carriage, having obtained the services of a boy to hold Puck, and soon found themselves in Mrs. Crawley's single sitting-room. She was sitting there with her foot on the board of a child's cradle, rocking it, while an infant about three months old was lying in her lap. For the elder one, who was the sufferer, had in her illness usurped the baby's place. Two other children, considerably older, were also in the room. The eldest was a girl, perhaps nine years of age, and the other a boy three years her junior. These were standing at their father's elbow, who was studiously endeavouring to initiate them in the early mysteries of grammar. To tell the truth Mrs. Robarts would much have preferred that Mr. Crawley had not been there, for she had with her and about her certain contraband articles, presents for the children, as they were to be called, but in truth relief for that poor, much-tasked mother, which they knew it would be impossible to introduce in Mr. Crawley's presence. She, as we have said, was not quite so gaunt, not altogether so haggard as in the latter of those dreadful Cornish days. Lady Lufton and Mrs. Arabin between them, and the scanty comfort of their improved, though still wretched, income, had done something towards bringing her back to the world in which she had lived in the soft days of her childhood. But even the liberal stipend of a hundred and thirty pounds a year – liberal according to the scale by which the incomes of clergymen in some of our new districts are now apportioned – would not admit of a gentleman with his wife and four children living with the ordinary comforts of an artisan's family. As regards the mere eating and drinking, the amounts of butcher's meat and tea and butter, they of course were used in quantities which any artisan would have regarded as compatible only with demi-starvation. Better clothing for her children was necessary, and better clothing for him. As for her own raiment, the wives of few artisans would have been content to put up with Mrs. Crawley's best gown. The stuff of which it was made had been paid for by her mother when she with much difficulty bestowed upon her daughter her modest wedding trousseau.

Lucy had never seen Mrs. Crawley. These visits to Hogglestock were not frequent, and had generally been made by Lady Lufton and Mrs. Robarts together. It was known that they were distasteful to Mr. Crawley, who felt a savage satisfaction in being left to himself. It may almost be said of him that he felt angry with those who relieved him, and he had certainly never as yet forgiven the Dean of Barchester for paying his debts. The dean had also given him his present living; and consequently his old friend was not now so dear to him as when in old days he would come down to that farm-house, almost as penniless as the curate himself. Then they would walk together for hours along the rock-bound shore, listening to the waves, discussing deep polemical mysteries, sometimes with hot fury, then again with tender, loving charity, but always with a mutual acknowledgement of each other's truth. Now they lived comparatively near together, but no opportunities arose for such discussions. At any rate once a quarter Mr. Crawley was pressed by his old friend, to visit him at the deanery, and Dr. Arabin had promised that no one else should be in the house if Mr. Crawley objected to society. But this was not what he wanted. The finery and grandeur of the deanery, and the comfort of that warm, snug library, would silence him at once. Why did not Dr. Arabin come out there to Hogglestock, and tramp with him through the dirty lanes as they used to tramp? Then he could have enjoyed himself; then he could have talked; then old days would have come back to them. But now! – 'Arabin always rides on a sleek, fine horse, nowadays,' he once said to his wife with a sneer. His poverty had been so terrible to himself that it was not in his heart to love a rich friend.

CHAPTER XXII

Hogglestock Parsonage

AT the end of the last chapter, we left Lucy Robarts waiting for an introduction to Mrs. Crawley, who was sitting with one baby in her lap while she was rocking another who lay in a cradle at her feet. Mr. Crawley, in the meanwhile, had risen from his seat with his finger between the leaves of an old grammar out of which he had been teaching his two elder children. The whole Crawley family was thus before them when Mrs. Robarts and Lucy entered the sitting-room. 'This is my sister-in-law, Lucy,' said Mrs. Robarts. 'Pray don't move now, Mrs. Crawley; or if you do, let me take baby.' And she put out her arms and took the infant into them, making him quite at home there; for she had work of this kind of her own, which she by no means neglected, though the attendance of nurses was more plentiful with her than at Hogglestock. Mrs. Crawley did get up, and told Lucy that she was glad to see her, and Mr. Crawley came forward, grammar in hand, looking humble and meek. Could we have looked into the innermost spirit of him and and his life's partner, we should have seen that mixed with the pride of his poverty there was some feeling of disgrace that he was poor, but that with her, regarding this matter, there was neither pride nor shame. The realities of life had become so stern to her that the outward aspects of them were as nothing. She would have liked a new gown because it would have been useful; but it would have been nothing to her if all the county knew that the one in which she went to church had been turned three times. It galled him, however, to think that he and his were so poorly dressed. 'I am afraid you can hardly find a chair, Miss Robarts,' said Mr. Crawley.

'Oh, yes, there is nothing here but this young gentleman's library,' said Lucy, moving a pile of ragged, coverless books on to the table. 'I hope he'll forgive me for moving them.'

'They are not Bob's – at least, not the most of them, – but mine,' said the girl.

'But some of them are mine,' said the boy; 'ain't they, Grace?'

'And are you a great scholar?' asked Lucy, drawing the child to her.

'I don't know,' said Grace, with a sheepish face. 'I am in Greek Delectus and the irregular verbs.'

'Greek Delectus and the irregular verbs!' And Lucy put up her hands with astonishment.

'And she knows an ode of Horace all by heart,' said Bob.

'An ode of Horace!' said Lucy, still holding the young shamefaced female prodigy close to her knees.

'It is all that I can give them,' said Mr. Crawley, apologetically. 'A little scholarship is the only fortune that has come in my way, and I endeavour to share that with my children.'

'I believe men say that it is the best fortune any of us can have,' said Lucy, thinking, however, in her own mind, that Horace and the irregular Greek verbs savoured too much of precocious forcing in a young lady of nine years old. But, nevertheless, Grace was a pretty, simple-looking girl, and clung to her ally closely, and seemed to like being fondled. So that Lucy anxiously wished that Mr. Crawley could be got rid of and the presents produced.

'I hope you have left Mr. Robarts quite well,' said Mr. Crawley, with a stiff, ceremonial voice, differing very much from that in which he had so energetically addressed his brother clergyman when they were alone together in the study at Framley. 'He is quite well, thank you. I suppose you have heard of his good fortune?'

'Yes; I have heard of it,' said Mr. Crawley, gravely. 'I hope that his promotion may tend in every way to his advantage here and hereafter.' It seemed, however, to be manifest from the manner in which he expressed his kind wishes, that his hopes and expectations did not go hand-in-hand together.

'By the by, he desired us to say that he will call here tomorrow; at about eleven, didn't he say, Fanny?'

'Yes; he wishes to see you about some parish business, I think,' said Mrs. Robarts, looking up for a moment from the anxious discussion in which she was already engaged with Mrs. Crawley on nursery matters.

'Pray tell him,' said Mr. Crawley, 'that I shall be happy to see him; though, perhaps, now that new duties have been thrown upon him, it will be better that I should visit him at Framley.'

'His new duties do not disturb him much as yet,' said Lucy. 'And his riding over here will be no trouble to him.'

'Yes; there he has the advantage over me. I unfortunately have no horse.' And then Lucy began petting the little boy, and by degrees slipped a small bag of gingerbread-nuts out of her muff into his hands. She had not the patience necessary for waiting, as had her sister-in-law. The boy took the bag, peeped into it, and then looked up into her face.

'What is that, Bob?' said Mr. Crawley.

'Gingerbread,' faltered Bobby, feeling that a sin had been committed, though, probably, feeling also that he himself could hardly as yet be accounted as deeply guilty.

'Miss Robarts,' said the father, 'we are very much obliged to you; but our children are hardly used to such things.'

'I am a lady with a weak mind, Mr. Crawley, and always carry things of this sort about with me when I go to visit children; so you must forgive me, and allow your little boy to accept them.'

'Oh, certainly. Bob, my child, give the bag to your mamma, and she will let you and Grace have them, one at a time.' And then the bag in a solemn manner was carried over to their mother, who, taking it from her son's hands, laid it high on a bookshelf.

'And not one now?' said Lucy Robarts, very piteously. 'Don't be so hard, Mr. Crawley, – not upon them, but upon me. May I not learn whether they are good of their kind?'

'I am sure they are very good; but I think their mamma will prefer their being put by for the present.' This was very discouraging to Lucy. If one small bag of gingerbread-nuts created so great a difficulty, how was she to dispose of the pot of guava jelly and box of bonbons, which were still in her muff; or how distribute the packet of oranges with which the pony carriage was laden? And there was jelly for the sick child, and chicken broth, which was, indeed, another jelly; and, to tell the truth openly, there was also a joint of fresh pork and a basket of eggs from the Framley parsonage farmyard, which Mrs. Robarts was to introduce, should she find herself capable of doing so; but which would certainly be cast out with utter scorn by Mr. Crawley, if tendered in his immediate presence. There had also been a suggestion as to adding two or three bottles of port: but the courage of the ladies had failed them on that head, and the wine was not now added to their difficulties. Lucy found it very difficult to keep up a conversation with Mr. Crawley – the more so, as Mrs. Robarts and Mrs.Crawley presently withdrew into a bedroom, taking the two younger children with them. 'How unlucky,' thought Lucy, 'that she has not got my muff with her!' But the muff lay in her lap, ponderous with its rich enclosures.

'I suppose you will live in Barchester for a portion of the year now,' said Mr. Crawley.

'I really do not know as yet; Mark talks of taking lodgings for his first month's residence.'

'But he will have the house, will he not?'

'Oh, yes; I suppose so.'

'I fear he will find it interfere with his own parish – with his general utility there: the schools, for instance.'

'Mark thinks that, as he is so near, he need not be much absent from Framley, even during his residence. And then Lady Lufton is so good about the schools.'

'Ah! yes: but Lady Lufton is not a clergyman, Miss Robarts.' It was on Lucy's tongue to say that her ladyship was pretty nearly as bad, but she stopped herself. At this moment Providence sent great relief to Miss Robarts in the shape of Mrs. Crawley's red-armed maid-of-all-work, who, walking up to her master, whispered into his ear that he was wanted. It was the time of day at which his attendance was always required in his parish school; and that attendance being so punctually given, those who wanted him looked for him there at this hour, and if he were absent, did not scruple to send for him. 'Miss Robarts, I am afraid you must excuse me,' said he, getting up and taking his hat and stick. Lucy begged that she might not be at all in the way, and already began to speculate how she might best unload her treasures. 'Will you make my compliments to Mrs. Robarts, and say that I am sorry to miss the pleasure of wishing her good-bye? But I shall probably see her as she passes the school-house.' And then, stick in hand, he walked forth, and Lucy fancied that Bobby's eyes immediately rested on the bag of gingerbread-nuts.

'Bob,' said she, almost in a whisper, 'do you like sugar-plums?'

'Very much, indeed,' said Bob, with exceeding gravity, and with his eye upon the window to see whether his father had passed.

'Then come here,' said Lucy. But as she spoke the door again opened, and Mr. Crawley reappeared. 'I have left a book behind me,' he said; and coming back through the room, he took up the well-worn Prayer Book which accompanied him in all his wanderings through the parish. Bobby, when he saw his father, had retreated a few steps back, as also did Grace, who, to confess the truth, had been attracted by the sound of sugar-plums, in spite of the irregular verbs. And Lucy withdrew her hand from her muff, and looked guilty. Was she not deceiving the good man – nay, teaching his own children to deceive him? But there are men made of such stuff that an angel could hardly live with them without some deceit. 'Papa's gone now,' whispered Bobby; 'I saw him turn round the corner.' He, at any rate, had learned his lesson – as it was natural that he should do. Some one else, also, had learned that papa was gone; for while Bob and Grace were still counting the big lumps of sugar-candy, each employed the while for inward solace with an inch of barley-sugar, the front-door opened, and a big basket, and a bundle done up in a kitchen-cloth, made surreptitious entrance into the house, and were quickly unpacked by Mrs. Robarts herself on the table in Mrs. Crawley's bedroom.

'I did venture to bring them,' said Fanny, with a look of shame, 'for I know how a sick child occupies the whole house.'

'Ah! my friend,' said Mrs. Crawley, taking hold of Mrs. Robarts's arm and looking into her face, 'that sort of shame is over with me. God has tried us with want, and for my children's sake I am glad of such relief.'

'But will he be angry?'

'I will manage it. Dear Mrs. Robarts, you must not be surprised at him. His lot is sometimes very hard to bear; such things are so much worse for a man than for a woman.' Fanny was not quite prepared to admit this in her own heart, but she made no reply on that head. 'I am sure I hope we may be able to be of use to you,' she said, 'if you will only look upon me as an old friend, and write to me if you want me. I hesitate to come frequently for fear that I should offend him.' And then, by degrees, there was confidence between them, and the poverty-stricken helpmate of the perpetual curate was able to speak of the weight of her burden to the well-to-do young wife of the Barchester prebendary. 'It was hard,' the former said, 'to feel herself so different from the wives of other clergymen around her – to know that they lived softly, while she, with all the work of her hands, and unceasing struggle of her energies, could hardly manage to place wholesome food before her husband and children. It was a terrible thing – a grievous thing to think of, that all the work of her mind should be given up to such subjects as these. But, nevertheless, she could bear it,' she said, 'as long as he would carry himself like a man, and face his lot boldly before the world.' And then she told how he had been better there at Hogglestock than in their former residence down in Cornwall, and in warm language she expressed her thanks to the friend who had done so much for them. 'Mrs. Arabin told me that she was so anxious you should go to them,' said Mrs. Robarts.

'Ah, yes; but that, I fear, is impossible. The children, you know, Mrs. Robarts.'

'I would take care of two of them for you.'

'Oh, no; I could not punish you for your goodness in that way. But he would not go. He could go and leave me at home. Sometimes I have thought that it might be so, and I have done all in my power to persuade him. I have told him that if he could mix once more with the world, with the clerical world, you know, that he would be better fitted for the performance of his own duties. But he answers me angrily, that it is impossible – that his coat is not fit for the dean's table,' and Mrs. Crawley almost blushed as she spoke of such a reason.

'What! with an old friend like Dr. Arabin? Surely that must be nonsense.'

'I know that it is. The dean would be glad to see him with any coat. But the fact is that he cannot bear to enter the house of a rich man unless his duty calls him there.'

'But surely that is a mistake?'

'It is a mistake. But what can I do? I fear that he regards the rich as his enemies. He is pining for the solace of some friend to whom he could talk – for some equal, with a mind educated like his own, to whose thoughts he could listen, and to whom he could speak his own thoughts. But such a friend must be equal, not only in mind, but in purse; and where can he ever find such a man as that?'

'But you may get better preferment.'

'Ah, no; and if he did, we are hardly fit for it now. If I could think that I could educate my children; if I could only do something for my poor Grace –' In answer to this Mrs. Robarts said a word or two, but not much. She resolved, however, that if she could get her husband's leave, something should be done for Grace. Would it not be a good work? and was it not incumbent on her to make some kindly use of all the goods with which Providence had blessed herself? And then they went back to the sitting-room, each again with a young child in her arms, Mrs. Crawley having stowed away in the kitchen the chicken broth and the leg of pork and the supply of eggs. Lucy had been engaged the while with the children, and when the two married ladies entered, they found that a shop had been opened at which all manner of luxuries were being readily sold and purchased at marvellously easy prices; the guava jelly was there, and the oranges, and the sugarplums, red and yellow and striped; and, moreover, the gingerbread had been taken down in the audacity of their commercial speculations, and the nuts were spread out upon a board, behind which Lucy stood as shop-girl, disposing of them for kisses. 'Mamma, mamma,' said Bobby, running up to his mother, 'you must buy something of her,' and he pointed with his fingers at the shop-girl. 'You must give her two kisses for that heap of barley-sugar.' Looking at Bobby's mouth at the time, one would have said that his kisses might be dispensed with.

When they were again in the pony carriage behind the impatient Puck, and were well away from the door, Fanny was the first to speak. 'How very different those two are,' she said; 'different in their minds and in their spirit!'

'But how much higher toned is her mind than his! How weak he is in many things, and how strong she is in everything! How false is his pride, and how false his shame!'

'But we must remember what he has to bear. It is not every one that can endure such a life as his without false pride and false shame.'

'But she has neither,' said Lucy.

'Because you have one hero in a family, does that give you a right to expect another?' said Mrs. Robarts. 'Of all my own acquaintance, Mrs. Crawley, I think, comes nearest to heroism.' And then they passed by the Hogglestock school, and Mr. Crawley, when he heard the noise of the wheels, came out. 'You have been very kind,' said he, 'to remain so long with my poor wife.'

'We had a great many things to talk about, after you went.'

'It is very kind of you, for she does not often see a friend, nowadays. Will you have the goodness to tell Mr. Robarts that I shall be here at the school, at eleven o'clock tomorrow?' And then he bowed, taking off his hat to them, and they drove on.

'If he really does care about her comfort, I shall not think so badly of him,' said Lucy.

CHAPTER XXIII

The Triumph of The Giants

AND now about the end of April news arrived almost simultaneously in all quarters of the habitable globe that was terrible in its import to one of the chief persons of our history; – some may think to the chief person in it. All high parliamentary people will doubtless so think, and the wives and daughters of such. The Titans warring against the gods had been for awhile successful. Typhœus and Mimas, Porphyrion and Rhœcus, the giant brood of old, steeped in ignorance and wedded to corruption, had scaled the heights of Olympus, assisted by that audacious flinger of deadly ponderous missiles, who stands ever ready armed with his terrific sling – Supplehouse, the Enceladus of the press. And in this universal cataclasm of the starry councils, what could a poor Diana do, Diana of the Petty Bag, but abandon her pride of place to some rude Orion? In other words, the ministry had been compelled to resign, and with them Mr. Harold Smith. 'And so poor Harold is out, before he has well tasted the sweets of office,' said Sowerby, writing to his friend the parson; 'and as far as I know, the only piece of Church patronage which has fallen in the way of the ministry since he joined it, has made its way down to Framley – to my great joy and contentment.' But it hardly tended to Mark's joy and contentment on the same subject that he should be so often reminded of the benefit conferred upon him.

Terrible was this break-down of the ministry, and especially to Harold Smith, who to the last had had confidence in that theory of new blood. He could hardly believe that a large majority of the House should vote against a Government which he had only just joined. 'If we are to go on in this way,' he said to his young friend Green Walker, 'the Queen's Government cannot be carried on.' That alleged difficulty as to carrying on the Queen's Government has been frequently mooted in late years since a certain great man first introduced the idea. Nevertheless, the Queen's Government is carried on, and the propensity and aptitude of men for this work seems to be not at all on the decrease. If we have but few young statesmen, it is because the old stagers are so fond of the rattle of their harness.

'I really do not see how the Queen's Government is to be carried on,' said Harold Smith to Green Walker, standing in a corner of one of the lobbies of the House of Commons on the first of those days of awful interest, in which the Queen was sending for one crack statesman after another; and some anxious men were beginning to doubt whether or no we should, in truth, be able to obtain the blessing of another Cabinet. The gods had all vanished from their places. Would the giants be good enough to do anything for us or no? There were men who seemed to think that the giants would refuse to do anything for us. 'The House will now be adjourned over till Monday, and I would not be in Her Majesty's shoes for something,' said Mr. Harold Smith.

'By Jove! no,' said Green Walker, who in these days was a staunch Harold Smithian, having felt a pride in joining himself on as a substantial support to a Cabinet minister. Had he contented himself with being merely a Brockite, he would have counted as nobody. 'By Jove! no,' and Green Walker opened his eyes and shook his head, as he thought of the perilous condition in which Her Majesty must be placed. 'I happen to know that Lord — won't join them unless he has the Foreign Office,' and he mentioned some hundred-handed Gyas supposed to be of the utmost importance to the counsels of the Titans.

'And that, of course, is impossible. I don't see what on earth they are to do. There's Sidonia; they do say that he's making some difficulty now.' Now Sidonia was another giant, supposed to be very powerful.

'We all know that the Queen won't see him,' said Green Walker, who, being a member of Parliament for the Crewe Junction, and nephew to Lady Hartletop, of course had perfectly correct means of ascertaining what the Queen would do, and what she would not.

'The fact is,' said Harold Smith, recurring again to his own situation as an ejected god, 'that the House does not in the least understand what it is about; – doesn't know what it wants. The question I should like to ask them is this: do they intend that the Queen shall have a Government, or do they not? Are they prepared to support such men as Sidonia and Lord De Terrier? If so, I am their obedient humble servant; but I shall be very much surprised, that's all.' Lord De Terrier was at this time recognized by all men as the leader of the giants.

'And so shall I, deucedly surprised. They can't do it, you know. There are the Manchester men. I ought to know something about them down in my country; and I say they can't support Lord De Terrier. It wouldn't be natural.'

'Natural! Human nature has come to an end, I think,' said Harold Smith, who could hardly understand that the world should conspire to throw over a Government which he had joined, and that, too, before the world had waited to see how much he would do for it; 'the fact is this, Walker, we have no longer among us any strong feeling of party.'

'No, not a d—,' said Green Walker, who was very energetic in his present political aspirations.

'And till we can recover that, we shall never be able to have a Government firm-seated and sure-handed. Nobody can count on men from one week to another. The very members who in one month place a minister in power, are the very first to vote against him in the next.'

'We must put a stop to that sort of thing, otherwise we shall never do any good.'

'I don't mean to deny that Brock was wrong with reference to Lord Brittleback. I think that he was wrong, and I said so all through. But, heavens on earth –!' and instead of completing his speech Harold Smith turned away his head, and struck his hands together in token of his astonishment at the fatuity of the age. What he probably meant to express was this: that if such a good deed as that late appointment made at the Petty Bag Office were not held sufficient to atone for that other evil deed to which he had alluded, there would be an end of all justice in sublunary matters. Was no offence to be forgiven, even when so great virtue had been displayed? 'I attribute it all to Supplehouse,' said Green Walker, trying to console his friend.

'Yes,' said Harold Smith, now verging on the bounds of parliamentary eloquence, although he still spoke with bated breath, and to one solitary hearer. 'Yes; we are becoming the slaves of a mercenary and irresponsible press – of one single newspaper. There is a man endowed with no great talent, enjoying no public confidence, untrusted as a politician, and unheard of even as a writer by the world at large, and yet, because he is on the staff of the *Jupiter*, he is able to overturn the Government and throw the whole country into dismay. It is astonishing to me that a man like Lord Brock should allow himself to be so timid.' And nevertheless it was not yet a month since Harold Smith had been counselling with Supplehouse how a series of strong articles in the *Jupiter*, together with the expected support of the Manchester men, might probably be effective in hurling the minister from his seat. But at that time the minister had not revigorated himself with young blood. 'How the Queen's Government is to be carried on, that is the question now,' Harold Smith repeated. A difficulty which had not caused him much dismay at that period, about a month since, to which we have alluded.

At this moment Sowerby and Supplehouse together joined them, having come out of the House, in which some unimportant business had been completed after the minister's notice of adjournment.

'Well, Harold,' said Sowerby, 'what do you say to your governor's statement?'

'I have nothing to say to it,' said Harold Smith, looking up very solemnly from under the penthouse of his hat, and, perhaps, rather savagely. Sowerby had supported the Government at the late crisis; but why was he now seen herding with such a one as Supplehouse?

'He did it pretty well, I think,' said Sowerby.

'Very well, indeed,' said Supplehouse; 'as he always does those sort of things. No man makes so good an explanation of circumstances, or comes out with so telling a personal statement. He ought to keep himself in reserve for those sort of things.'

'And who in the meantime is to carry on the Queen's Government?' said Harold Smith, looking very stern.

'That should be left to men of lesser mark,' said he of the *Jupiter*. 'The points as to which one really listens to a minister, the subjects about which men really care, are always personal. How many of us are truly interested as to the best mode of governing India? But in a question touching the character of a prime minister we all muster together like bees round a sounding cymbal.'

'That arises from envy, malice, and all uncharitableness,' said Harold Smith.

'Yes; and from picking and stealing, evil speaking, lying, and slandering,' said Mr. Sowerby.

'We are so prone to desire and covet other men's places,' said Supplehouse.

'Some men are so,' said Sowerby; 'but it is the evil speaking, lying, and slandering, which does the mischief. Is it not, Harold?'

'And in the meantime how is the Queen's Government to be carried on?' said Mr. Green Walker. On the following morning it was known that Lord De Terrier was with the Queen at Buckingham Palace, and at about twelve a list of the new ministry was published, which must have been in the highest degree satisfactory to the whole brood of giants. Every son of Tellus was included in it, as were also very many of the daughters. But then, late in the afternoon, Lord Brock was again summoned to the palace, and it was thought in the West End among the clubs that the gods had again a chance. 'If only,' said the *Purist*, an evening paper which was supposed to be very much in the interest of Mr. Harold Smith, 'if only Lord Brock can have the wisdom to place the right men in the right places. It was only the other day that he introduced Mr. Smith into his Government. That this was a step in the right direction every one has acknowledged, though unfortunately it was made too late to prevent the disturbance which has since occurred. It now appears probable that his lordship will again have an opportunity of selecting a list of statesmen with the view of carrying on the Queen's Government; and it is to be hoped that such men as Mr. Smith may be placed in situations in which their talents, industry, and acknowledged official aptitudes, may be of permanent service to the country.' Supplehouse, when he read this at the club with Mr. Sowerby at his elbow, declared that the style was too well marked to leave any doubt as to the author; but we ourselves are not inclined to think that Mr. Harold Smith wrote the article himself, although it may be probable that he saw it in type. But the *Jupiter* the next morning settled the whole question, and made it known to the world that, in spite of all the sendings and resendings, Lord Brock and the gods were permanently out, and Lord De Terrier and the giants permanently in. That fractious giant who would only go to the Foreign Office, had, in fact, gone to some sphere of much less important duty, and Sidonia, in spite of the whispered dislike of an illustrious personage, opened the campaign with all the full appanages of a giant of the highest standing. 'We hope,' said the *Jupiter*, 'that Lord Brock may not yet be too old to take a lesson. If so, the present decision of the House of Commons, and we may say of the country also, may teach him not to put his trust in such princes as Lord Brittleback, or such broken reeds as Mr. Harold Smith.' Now this parting blow we always thought to be exceedingly unkind, and altogether unnecessary, on the part of Mr. Supplehouse.

'My dear,' said Mrs. Harold, when she first met Miss Dunstable after the catastrophe was known, 'how am I possibly to endure this degradation?' And she put her deeply laced handkerchief up to her eyes.

'Christian resignation,' suggested Miss Dunstable.

'Fiddlestick!' said Mrs. Harold Smith. 'You millionaires always talk of Christian resignation, because you never are called on to resign anything. If I had any Christian resignation, I shouldn't have cared for such pomps and vanities. Think of it, my dear; a Cabinet minister's wife for only three weeks!'

'How does poor Mr. Smith endure it?'

'What? Harold? He only lives on the hope of vengeance. When he has put an end to Mr. Supplehouse, he will be content to die.' And then there were further explanations in both Houses of Parliament, which were altogether satisfactory. The high-bred, courteous giants assured the gods that they had piled Pelion on Ossa and thus climbed up into power, very much in opposition to their own goodwills; for they, the giants themselves, preferred the sweets of dignified retirement. But the voice of the people had been too strong for them; the effort had been made, not by themselves, but by others, who were determined that the giants should be at the head of affairs. Indeed, the spirit of the times was so clearly in favour of giants that there had been no alternative. So said Briareus to the Lords, and Orion to the Commons. And then the gods were absolutely happy in ceding their places; and so far were they from any uncelestial envy or malice which might not be divine, that they promised to give the giants all the assistance in their power in carrying on the work of government; upon which the giants declared how deeply indebted they would be for such valuable counsel and friendly assistance. All this was delightful in the extreme; but not the less did ordinary men seem to expect that the usual battle would go on in the old customary way. It is easy to love one's enemy when one is making fine speeches; but so difficult to do so in the actual everyday work of life. But there was and always has been this peculiar good point about the giants, that they are never too proud to follow in the footsteps of the gods. If the gods, deliberating painfully together, have elaborated any skilful project, the giants are always willing to adopt it as their own, not treating the bantling as a foster child, but praising it and pushing it so that men should regard it as the undoubted offspring of their own brains. Now just at this time there had been a plan much thought of for increasing the number of the bishops. Good active bishops were very desirable, and there was a strong feeling among certain excellent Churchmen that there could hardly be too many of them. Lord Brock had his measure cut and dry. There should be a Bishop of Westminster to share the Herculean toils of the metropolitan prelate, and another up in the North to Christianize the mining interests and wash white the blackamoors of Newcastle: Bishop of Beverley he should be called. But, in opposition to this, the giants, it was known, had intended to put forth the whole measure of their brute force. More curates, they said, were wanting, and district incumbents; not more bishops rolling in carriages. That bishops should roll in carriages was very good; but of such blessings the English world for the present had enough. And therefore Lord Brock and the gods had had much fear as to their little project. But now, immediately on the accession of the giants, it was known that the bishop bill was to be gone on with immediately. Some small changes would be effected so that the bill should be gigantic rather than divine; but the result would be altogether the same. It must, however, be admitted that bishops appointed by ourselves may be very good things, whereas those appointed by our adversaries will be anything but good. And, no doubt, this feeling went a long way with the giants. Be that as it may, the new bishop bill was to be their first work of government, and it was to be brought forward and carried, and the new prelates selected and put into their chairs all at once, – before the grouse should begin to crow and put an end to the doings of gods as well as giants. Among other minor effects arising from this decision was the following, that Archdeacon and Mrs. Grantly returned to London, and again took the lodgings in which they had before been staying. On various occasions also during the first week of this second sojourn, Dr. Grantly might be seen entering the official chambers of the First Lord of the Treasury. Much counsel was necessary among High-Churchmen of great repute before any fixed resolution could wisely be made in such a matter as this; and few Churchmen stood in higher repute than the Archdeacon of Barchester. And then it began to be rumoured in the world that the minister had disposed at any rate of the see of Westminster. This present time was a very nervous one for Mrs. Grantly. What might be the aspirations of the archdeacon himself, we will not stop to inquire. It may be that time and experience had taught him the futility of earthly honours, and made him content with the comfortable opulence of his Barsetshire rectory. But there is no theory of Church discipline which makes it necessary that a clergyman's wife should have an objection to a bishopric. The archdeacon probably was only anxious to give a disinterested aid to the minister, but Mrs. Grantly did long to sit in high places, and be at any rate equal to Mrs. Proudie. It was for her children, she said to herself, that she was thus anxious – that they should have a good position before the world, and the means of making the best of themselves. 'One is able to do nothing, you know, shut up there, down at Plumstead,' she had remarked to Lady Lufton on the occasion of her first visit to London, and yet the time was not long past when she had thought that rectory house at Plumstead to be by no means insufficient or contemptible. And then there came a question whether or no Griselda should go back to her mother; but this idea was very strongly opposed by Lady Lufton, and ultimately with success. 'I really think the dear girl is very happy with me,' said Lady Lufton, 'and if ever she is to belong to me more closely, it will be so well that we should know and love one another.'

To tell the truth, Lady Lufton had been trying hard to know and love Griselda, but hitherto she had scarcely succeeded to the full extent of her wishes. That she loved Griselda was certain, – with that sort of love which springs from a person's volition and not from the judgement. She had said all along to herself and others that she did love Griselda Grantly. She had admired the young lady's face, liked her manner, approved of her fortune and family, and had selected her for a daughter-in-law in a somewhat impetuous manner. Therefore she loved her. But it was by no means clear to Lady Lufton that she did as yet know her young friend. The match was a plan of her own, and therefore she stuck to it as warmly as ever, but she began to have some misgivings whether or no the dear girl would be to her herself all that she had dreamed of in a daughter-in-law. 'But, dear Lady Lufton,' said Mrs. Grantly, 'is it not possible that we may put her affections to too severe a test? What, if she should learn to regard him, and then –'

'Ah! if she did, I should have no fear of the result. If she showed anything like love for Ludovic, he would be at her feet in a moment. He is impulsive, but she is not.'

'Exactly, Lady Lufton. It is his privilege to be impulsive and to sue for her affection, and hers to have her love sought for without making any demonstration. It is perhaps the fault of young ladies of the present day that they are too impulsive. They assume privileges which are not their own, and thus lose those which are.'

'Quite true! I quite agree with you. It is probably that very feeling that has made me think so highly of Griselda. But then –' But then a young lady, though she need not jump down a gentleman's throat, or throw herself into his face, may give some signs that she is made of flesh and blood; especially when her papa and mamma and all belonging to her are so anxious to make the path of her love run smooth. That was what was passing through Lady Lufton's mind; but she did not say it all; she merely looked it.

'I don't think she will ever allow herself to indulge in an unauthorized passion,' said Mrs. Grantly.

'I am sure she will not,' said Lady Lufton, with ready agreement, fearing perhaps in her heart that Griselda would never indulge in any passion, authorized or unauthorized.

'I don't know whether Lord Lufton sees much of her now,' said Mrs. Grantly, thinking perhaps of that promise of Lady Lufton's with reference to his lordship's spare time.

'Just lately, during these changes, you know, everybody has been so much engaged. Ludovic has been constantly at the House, and then men find it so necessary to be at their clubs just now.'

'Yes, yes, of course,' said Mrs. Grantly, who was not at all disposed to think little of the importance of the present crisis, or to wonder that men should congregate together when such deeds were to be done as those which now occupied the breasts of the Queen's advisers. At last, however, the two mothers perfectly understood each other. Griselda was still to remain with Lady Lufton; and was to accept her ladyship's son, if he could only be induced to exercise his privilege of asking her; but in the meantime, as this seemed to be doubtful, Griselda was not to be debarred from her privilege of making what use she could of any other string which she might have to her bow.

'But, mamma,' said Griselda, in a moment of unwatched intercourse between the mother and daughter, 'is it really true that they are going to make papa a bishop?'

'We can tell nothing as yet, my dear. People in the world are talking about it. Your papa has been a good deal with Lord De Terrier.'

'And isn't he Prime Minister?'

'Oh, yes; I am happy to say that he is.'

'I thought the Prime Minister could make any one a bishop that he chooses, – any clergyman, that is.'

'But there is no see vacant,' said Mrs. Grantly.

'Then there isn't any chance,' said Griselda, looking very glum.

'They are going to have an Act of Parliament for making two more bishops. That's what they are talking about at least. And if they do –'

'Papa will be Bishop of Westminster – won't he? And we shall live in London?'

'But you must not talk about it, my dear.'

'No, I won't. But, mamma, a Bishop of Westminster will be higher than a Bishop of Barchester; won't he? I shall so like to be able to snub those Miss Proudies.' It will therefore be seen that there were matters on which even Griselda Grantly could be animated. Like the rest of her family she was devoted to the Church. Late on that afternoon the archdeacon returned home to dine in Mount Street, having spent the whole of the day between the Treasury chambers, a meeting of Convocation, and his club. And when he did get home it was soon manifest to his wife that he was not laden with good news. 'It is almost incredible,' he said, standing with his back to the drawing-room fire.

'What is incredible?' said his wife, sharing her husband's anxiety to the full.

'If I had not learned it as fact, I would not have believed it, even of Lord Brock,' said the archdeacon.

'Learned what?' said the anxious wife.

'After all, they are going to oppose the bill.'

'Impossible!' said Mrs. Grantly.

'But they are.'

'The bill for the two new bishops, archdeacon? oppose their own bill!'

'Yes – oppose their own bill. It is almost incredible; but so it is. Some changes have been forced upon us; little things which they had forgotten – quite minor matters; and they now say that they will be obliged to divide against us on these twopenny-halfpenny, hair-splitting points. It is Lord Brock's own doing too, after all that he said about abstaining from factious opposition to the Government.'

'I believe there is nothing too bad or too false for that man,' said Mrs. Grantly.

'After all they said, too, when they were in power themselves, as to the present Government opposing the cause of religion! They declare now that Lord De Terrier cannot be very anxious about it, as he had so many good reasons against it a few weeks ago. Is it not dreadful that there should be such double-dealing in men in such positions?'

'It is sickening,' said Mrs. Grantly. And then there was a pause between them as each thought of the injury that was done to them.

'But, archdeacon –'

'Well?'

'Could you not give up those small points and shame them into compliance?'

'Nothing would shame them.'

'But would it not be well to try?' The game was so good a one, and the stake so important, that Mrs. Grantly felt that it would be worth playing for to the last.

'It is no good.'

'But I certainly would suggest it to Lord De Terrier. I am sure the country would go along with him; at any rate the Church would.'

'It is impossible,' said the archdeacon. 'To tell the truth, it did occur to me. But some of them down there seemed to think that it would not do.' Mrs. Grantly sat awhile on the sofa, still meditating in her mind whether there might not yet be some escape from so terrible a downfall.

'But, archdeacon –'

'I'll go upstairs and dress,' said he, in despondency.

'But, archdeacon, surely the present ministry may have a majority on such a subject as that; I thought they were sure of a majority now.'

'No; not sure.'

'But at any rate the chances are in their favour? I do hope they'll do their duty, and exert themselves to keep their members together.' And then the archdeacon told out the whole of the truth.

'Lord De Terrier says that under the present circumstances he will not bring the matter forward this session at all. So we had better go back to Plumstead.' Mrs. Grantly then felt that there was nothing further to be said, and it will be proper that the historian should drop a veil over their sufferings.

CHAPTER XXIV

Magna Est Veritas

IT was made known to the reader that in the early part of the winter Mr. Sowerby had a scheme for retrieving his lost fortunes, and setting himself right in the world, by marrying that rich heiress, Miss Dunstable. I fear my friend Sowerby does not, at present, stand high in the estimation of those who have come on with me thus far in this narrative. He has been described as a spendthrift and gambler, and as one scarcely honest in his extravagance and gambling. But nevertheless there are worse men than Mr. Sowerby, and I am not prepared to say that, should he be successful with Miss Dunstable, that lady would choose by any means the worst of the suitors who are continually throwing themselves at her feet. Reckless as this man always appeared to be, reckless as he absolutely was, there was still within his heart a desire for better things, and in his mind an understanding that he had hitherto missed the career of an honest English gentleman. He was proud of his position as a member for his county, though hitherto he had done so little to grace it; he was proud of his domain at Chaldicotes, though the possession of it had so nearly passed out of his own hands; he was proud of the old blood that flowed in his veins; and he was proud also of that easy, comfortable, gay manner, which went so far in the world's judgement to atone for his extravagance and evil practices. If only he could get another chance, as he now said to himself, things should go very differently with him. He would utterly forswear the whole company of Tozers. He would cease to deal in bills, and to pay Heaven only knows how many hundred per cent for his moneys. He would no longer prey upon his friends, and would redeem his title-deeds from the clutches of the Duke of Omnium. If only he could get another chance! Miss Dunstable's fortune would do all this and ever so much more, and then, moreover, Miss Dunstable was a woman whom he really liked. She was not soft, feminine, or pretty, nor was she very young; but she was clever, self-possessed, and quite able to hold her own in any class; and as to age, Mr. Sowerby was not very young himself. In making such a match he would have no cause of shame. He could speak of it before his friends without fear of their grimaces, and ask them to his house, with the full assurance that the head of his table would not disgrace him. And then as the scheme grew clearer and clearer to him, he declared to himself that if he should not be successful, he would use her well, and not rob her of her money – beyond what was absolutely necessary. He had intended to have laid his fortunes at her feet at Chaldicotes; but the lady had been coy. Then the deed was to have been done at Gatherum Castle, but the lady ran away from

Gatherum Castle just at the time on which he had fixed. And since that, one circumstance after another had postponed the affair in London, till now at last he was resolved that he would know his fate, let it be what it might. If he could not contrive that things should speedily be arranged, it might come to pass that he would be altogether debarred from presenting himself to the lady as Mr. Sowerby of Chaldicotes. Tidings had reached him, through Mr. Fothergill, that the duke would be glad to have matters arranged; and Mr. Sowerby well knew the meaning of that message.

Mr. Sowerby was not fighting this campaign alone, without the aid of an ally. Indeed, no man ever had a more trusty ally in any campaign than he had in this. And it was this ally, the only faithful comrade that clung to him through good and ill during his whole life, who first put it into his head that Miss Dunstable was a woman and might be married. 'A hundred needy adventurers have attempted it, and failed already,' Mr. Sowerby had said, when the plan was first proposed to him.

'But, nevertheless, she will some day marry some one; and why not you as well as another?' his sister had answered. For Mrs. Harold Smith was the ally of whom I have spoken. Mrs. Harold Smith, whatever may have been her faults, could boast of this virtue – that she loved her brother. He was probably the only human being that she did love. Children she had none; and as for her husband, it had never occurred to her to love him. She had married him for a position; and being a clever woman, with a good digestion and command of her temper, had managed to get through the world without much of that unhappiness which usually follows ill-assorted marriages. At home she managed to keep the upper hand, but she did so in an easy, good-humoured way that made her rule bearable; and away from home she assisted her lord's political standing, though she laughed more keenly than any one else at his foibles. But the lord of her heart was her brother; and in all his scrapes, all his extravagances, and all his recklessness, she had ever been willing to assist him. With the view of doing this she had sought the intimacy of Miss Dunstable, and for the last year past had indulged every caprice of that lady. Or rather, she had had the wit to learn that Miss Dunstable was to be won, not by the indulgence of caprices, but by free and easy intercourse, with a dash of fun, and, at any rate, a semblance of honesty. Mrs. Harold Smith was not, perhaps, herself very honest by disposition; but in these latter days she had taken up a theory of honesty for the sake of Miss Dunstable – not altogether in vain, for Miss Dunstable and Mrs. Harold Smith were certainly very intimate.

'If I am to do it at all, I must not wait any longer,' said Mr. Sowerby to his sister a day or two after the final breakdown of the gods. The affection of the sister for the brother may be imagined from the fact that at such a time she could give up her mind to such a subject. But, in truth, her husband's position as a Cabinet minister was as nothing to her compared with her brother's position as a county gentleman. 'One time is as good as another,' said Mrs. Harold Smith.

'You mean that you would advise me to ask her at once.'

'Certainly. But you must remember, Nat, that you will have no easy task. It will not do for you to kneel down and swear that you love her.'

'If I do it at all, I shall certainly do it without kneeling – you may be sure of that, Harriet.'

'Yes, and without swearing that you love her. There is only one way in which you can be successful with Miss Dunstable – you must tell her the truth.'

'What! Tell her that I am ruined, horse, foot, and dragoons, and then bid her help me out of the mire?'

'Exactly: that will be your only chance, strange as it may appear.'

'This is very different from what you used to say, down at Chaldicotes.'

'So it is; but I know her much better than I did when we were there. Since then I have done but little else than study the freaks of her character. If she really likes you – and I think she does – she could forgive you any other crime but that of swearing that you loved her.'

'I should hardly know how to propose without saying something about it.'

'But you must say nothing – not a word; you must tell her that you are a gentleman of good blood and high station, but sadly out at elbows.'

'She knows that already.'

'Of course she does; but she must know it as coming directly from your own mouth. And then tell her that you propose to set yourself right by marrying her – by marrying her for the sake of her money.'

'That will hardly win her, I should say.'

'If it does not, no other way, that I know of, will do so. As I told you before, it will be no easy task. Of course you must make her understand that her happiness shall be cared for; but that must not be put prominently forward as your object. Your first object is her money, and your only chance for success is in telling the truth.'

'It is very seldom that a man finds himself in such a position as that,' said Sowerby, walking up and down his sister's room; 'and, upon my word, I don't think I am up to the task. I should certainly break down. I don't believe there's a man in London could go to a woman with such a story as that, and then ask her to marry him.'

'If you cannot, you may as well give it up,' said Mrs. Harold Smith. 'But if you can do it – if you can go through with it in that manner – my own opinion is that your chance of success would not be bad. The fact is,' added the sister after awhile, during which her brother was continuing his walk and meditating on the difficulties of his position – 'the fact is, you men never understand a woman; you give her credit neither for her strength, nor for her weakness. You are too bold, and too timid: you think she is a fool and tell her so, and yet never can trust her to do a kind action. Why should she not marry you with the intention of doing you a good turn? After all, she would lose very little: there is the estate, and if she redeemed it, it would belong to her as well as to you.'

'It would be a good turn, indeed. I fear I should be too modest to put it to her in that way.'

'Her position would be much better as your wife than it is at present. You are good-humoured and good-tempered, you would intend to treat her well, and, on the whole, she would be much happier as Mrs. Sowerby, of Chaldicotes, than she can be in her present position.'

'If she cared about being married, I suppose she could be a peer's wife to-morrow.'

'But I don't think she cares about being a peer's wife. A needy peer might perhaps win her in the way that I propose to you; but then a needy peer would not know how to set about it. Needy peers have tried – half a dozen I have no doubt – and have failed, because they have pretended that they were in love with her. It may be difficult, but your only chance is to tell her the truth.'

'And where shall I do it?'

'Here if you choose; but her own house will be better.'

'But I never can see her there – at least, not alone. I believe that she never is alone. She always keeps a lot of people round her in order to stave off her lovers. Upon my word, Harriet, I think I'll give it up. It is impossible that I should make such a declaration to her as that you propose.'

'Faint heart, Nat – you know the rest.'

'But the poet never alluded to such wooing as that you have suggested. I suppose I had better begin with a schedule of my debts, and make reference, if she doubts me, to Fothergill, the sheriff's officers, and the Tozer family.'

'She will not doubt you, on that head; nor will she be a bit surprised.' Then there was again a pause, during which Mr. Sowerby still walked up and down the room, thinking whether or no he might possibly have any chance of success in so hazardous an enterprise.

'I tell you what, Harriet,' at last he said; 'I wish you'd do it for me.'

'Well,' said she, 'if you really mean it, I will make the attempt.'

'I am sure of this, that I shall never make it myself. I positively should not have the courage to tell her in so many words, that I wanted to marry her for her money.'

'Well, Nat, I will attempt it. At any rate, I am not afraid of her. She and I are excellent friends, and, to tell the truth, I think I like her better than any other woman that I know; but I never should have been intimate with her, had it not been for your sake.'

'And now you will have to quarrel with her, also for my sake?'

'Not at all. You'll find that whether she accedes to my proposition or not, we shall continue friends. I do not think that she would die for me – nor I for her. But as the world goes we suit each other. Such a little trifle as this will not break our loves.' And so it was settled. On the following day Mrs. Harold Smith was to find an opportunity of explaining the whole matter to Miss Dunstable, and was to ask that lady to share her fortune – some incredible number of thousands of pounds – with the bankrupt member for West Barsetshire, who in return was to bestow on her – himself and his debts. Mrs. Harold Smith had spoken no more than the truth in saying that she and Miss Dunstable suited one another. And she had not improperly described their friendship. They were not prepared to die, one for the sake of the other. They had said nothing to each other of mutual love and affection. They never kissed, or cried, or made speeches, when they met or when they parted. There was no great benefit for which either had to be grateful to the other; no terrible injury which either had forgiven. But they suited each other; and this, I take it, is the secret of most of our pleasantest intercourse in the world. And it was almost grievous that they should suit each other, for Miss Dunstable was much the worthier of the two, had she but known it herself. It was almost to be lamented that she should have found herself able to live with Mrs. Harold Smith on terms that were perfectly satisfactory to herself. Mrs. Harold Smith was worldly, heartless – to all the world but her brother – and, as has been above hinted, almost dishonest. Miss Dunstable was not worldly, though it was possible that her present style of life might make her so; she was affectionate, fond of truth, and prone to honesty, if those around would but allow her to exercise it. But she was fond of ease and humour, sometimes of wit that might almost be called broad, and she had a thorough love of ridiculing the world's humbugs. In all these propensities Mrs. Harold Smith indulged her.

Under these circumstances they were now together almost every day. It had become quite a habit with Mrs. Harold Smith to have herself driven early in the forenoon to Miss Dunstable's house; and that lady, though she could never be found alone by Mr. Sowerby, was habitually so found by his sister. And after that they would go out together, or each separately, as fancy or the business of the day might direct them. Each was easy to the other in this alliance, and they so managed that they never trod on each other's corns. On the day following the agreement made between Mr. Sowerby and Mrs. Harold Smith, that lady as usual called on Miss Dunstable, and soon found herself alone with her friend in a small room which the heiress kept solely for her own purposes. On special occasions persons of various sorts were there admitted; occasionally a parson who had a church to build, or a dowager laden with the last morsel of town slander, or a poor author who could not get due payment for the efforts of his brain, or a poor governess on whose feeble stamina the weight of the world had borne too hardly. But men who by possibility could be lovers did not make their way thither, nor women who could be bores. In these latter days, that is, during the present London season, the doors of it had been oftener opened to Mrs. Harold Smith than to any other person. And now the effort was to be made with the object of which all this intimacy had been effected. As she came thither in her carriage, Mrs. Harold Smith herself was not altogether devoid of that sinking of the heart which is so frequently the forerunner of any difficult and hazardous undertaking. She had declared that she would feel no fear in making the little proposition. But she did feel something very like it: and when she made her entrance into the little room she certainly wished that the work was done and over.

'How is poor Mr. Smith to-day?' asked Miss Dunstable, with an air of mock condolence, as her friend seated herself in her accustomed easy chair. The downfall of the gods was as yet a history hardly three days old, and it might well be supposed that the late lord of the Petty Bag had hardly recovered from his misfortune. 'Well, he is better, I think, this morning; at least I should judge so from the manner in which he confronted his eggs. But still I don't like the way he handles the carving-knife. I am sure he is always thinking of Mr. Supplehouse at those moments.'

'Poor man! I mean Supplehouse. After all, why shouldn't he follow his trade as well as another? Live and let live, that's what I say.'

'Aye, but it's kill and let kill with him. That is what Horace says. However, I am tired of all that now, and I came here to-day to talk about something else.'

'I rather like Mr. Supplehouse myself,' exclaimed Miss Dunstable. 'He never makes any bones about the matter. He has a certain work to do, and a certain cause to serve – namely, his own; and in order to do that work, and serve that cause, he uses such weapons as God has placed in his hands.'

'That's what the wild beasts do.'

'And where will you find men honester than they? The tiger tears you up because he is hungry and wants to eat you. That's what Supplehouse does. But there are so many among us tearing up one another without any excuse of hunger. The mere pleasure of destroying is reason enough.'

'Well, my dear, my mission to you to-day is certainly not one of destruction, as you will admit when you hear it. It is one, rather, very absolutely of salvation. I have come to make love to you.'

'Then the salvation, I suppose, is not for myself,' said Miss Dunstable. It was quite clear to Mrs. Harold Smith that Miss Dunstable had immediately understood the whole purport of this visit, and that she was not in any great measure surprised. It did not seem from the tone of the heiress's voice, or from the serious look which at once settled on her face, that she would be prepared to give a very ready compliance. But then great objects can only be won with great efforts.

'That's as may be,' said Mrs. Harold Smith. 'For you and another also, I hope. But I trust, at any rate, that I may not offend you?'

'Oh, laws, no; nothing of that kind ever offends me now.'

'Well, I suppose you're used to it.'

'Like the eels, my dear. I don't mind it the least in the world – only sometimes, you know, it is a little tedious.'

'I'll endeavour to avoid that, so I may as well break the ice at once. You know enough of Nathaniel's affairs to be aware that he is not a very rich man.'

'Since you do ask me about it, I suppose there's no harm in saying that I believe him to be a very poor man.'

'Not the least harm in the world, but just the reverse. Whatever may come of this, my wish is that the truth should be told scrupulously on all sides; the truth, the whole truth, and nothing but the truth.'

'*Magna est veritas*,' said Miss Dunstable. 'The Bishop of Barchester taught me as much Latin as that at Chaldicotes; and he did add some more, but there was a long word, and I forgot it.'

'The bishop was quite right, my dear, I'm sure. But if you go to your Latin, I'm lost. As we were just now saying, my brother's pecuniary affairs are in a very bad state. He has a beautiful property of his own, which has been in the family for I can't say how many centuries – long before the Conquest, I know.'

'I wonder what my ancestors were then?'

'It does not much signify to any of us,' said Mrs. Harold Smith, with a moral shake of her head, 'what our ancestors were; but it's a sad thing to see an old property go to ruin.'

'Yes, indeed; we none of us like to see our property going to ruin, whether it be old or new. I have some of that sort of feeling already, although mine was only made the other day out of an apothecary's shop.'

'God forbid that I should ever help you to ruin it,' said Mrs. Harold Smith. 'I should be sorry to be the means of your losing a ten-pound note.'

'*Magna est veritas*, as the dear bishop said,' exclaimed Miss Dunstable. 'Let us have the truth, the whole truth, and nothing but the truth, as we agreed just now.' Mrs. Harold Smith did begin to find that the task before her was difficult. There was a hardness about Miss Dunstable when matters of business were concerned on which it seemed almost impossible to make any impression. It was not that she had evinced any determination to refuse the tender of Mr. Sowerby's hand; but she was so painfully resolute not to have dust thrown in her eyes! Mrs. Harold Smith had commenced with a mind fixed upon avoiding what she called humbug; but this sort of humbug had become so prominent a part of her usual rhetoric, that she found it very hard to abandon it. 'And that's what I wish,' said she. 'Of course my chief object is to secure my brother's happiness.'

'That's very unkind to poor Mr. Harold Smith.'

'Well, well, well – you know what I mean.'

'Yes, I think I do know what you mean. Your brother is a gentleman of good family, but of no means.'

'Not quite so bad as that.'

'Of embarrassed means, then, or anything that you will; whereas I am a lady of no family, but of sufficient wealth. You think that if you brought us together and made a match of it, it would be a very good thing for – for whom?' said Miss Dunstable.

'Yes, exactly,' said Mrs. Harold Smith.

'For which of us? Remember the bishop now and his nice little bit of Latin.'

'For Nathaniel then,' said Mrs. Harold Smith, boldly. 'It would be a very good thing for him.' And a slight smile came across her face as she said it. 'Now that's honest, or the mischief is in it.'

'Yes, that's honest enough. And did he send you here to tell me this?'

'Well, he did that, and something else.'

'And now let's have the something else. The really important part, I have no doubt, has been spoken.'

'No, by no means, by no means all of it. But you are so hard on one, my dear, with your running after honesty, that one is not able to tell the real facts as they are. You make one speak in such a bald, naked way.'

'Ah, you think that anything naked must be indecent; even truth.'

'I think it is more proper-looking, and better suited, too, for the world's work, when it goes about with some sort of a garment on it. We are so used to a leaven of falsehood in all we hear and say, nowadays, that nothing is more likely to deceive us than the absolute truth. If a shopkeeper told me that his wares were simply middling, of course, I should think that they were not worth a farthing. But all that has nothing to do with my poor brother. Well, what was I saying?'

'You were going to tell me how well he would use me, no doubt.'

'Something of that kind.'

'That he wouldn't beat me; or spend all my money if I managed to have it tied up out of his power; or look down on me with contempt because my father was an apothecary! Was not that what you were going to say?'

'I was going to tell you that you might be more happy as Mrs. Sowerby of Chaldicotes than you can be as Miss Dunstable –'

'Of Mount Lebanon. And had Mr. Sowerby no other message to send? – nothing about love, or anything of that sort? I should like, you know, to understand what his feelings are before I take such a leap.'

'I do believe he has as true a regard for you as any man of his age ever does have –'

'For any woman of mine. That is not putting it in a very devoted way certainly; but I am glad to see that you remember the bishop's maxim.'

'What would you have me say? If I told you that he was dying for love, you would say, I was trying to cheat you; and now because I don't tell you so, you say that he is wanting in devotion. I must say you are hard to please.'

'Perhaps I am, and very unreasonable into the bargain. I ought to ask no questions of the kind when your brother proposes to do me so much honour. As for my expecting the love of a man who condescends to wish to be my husband, that, of course, would be monstrous. What right can I have to think that any man should love me? It ought to be enough for me to know that as I am rich, I can get a husband. What business can such as I have to inquire whether the gentleman who would so honour me really would like my company, or would only deign to put up with my presence in his household?'

'Now, my dear Miss Dunstable –'

'Of course I am not such an ass as to expect that any gentleman should love me; and I feel that I ought to be obliged to your brother for sparing me the string of complimentary declarations which are usual on such occasions. He, at any rate, is not tedious – or rather you on his behalf; for no doubt his own time is so occupied with his parliamentary duties that he cannot attend to this little matter himself. I do feel grateful to him; and perhaps nothing more will be necessary than to give him a schedule of the property, and name an early day for putting him in possession.' Mrs. Smith did feel that she was rather badly used. This Miss Dunstable, in their mutual confidences, had so often ridiculed the love-making grimaces of her mercenary suitors – had spoken so fiercely against those who had persecuted her, not because they had desired her money, but on account of their ill-judgement in thinking her to be a fool – that Mrs. Smith had a right to expect that the method she had adopted for opening the negotiation would be taken in a better spirit. Could it be possible, after all, thought Mrs. Smith to herself, that Miss Dunstable was like other women, and that she did like to have men kneeling at her feet? Could it be the case that she had advised her brother badly, and that it would have been better for him to have gone about his work in the old-fashioned way? 'They are very hard to manage,' said Mrs. Harold Smith to herself, thinking of her own sex.

'He was coming here himself,' said she, 'but I advised him not to do so.'

'That was so kind of you.'

'I thought that I could explain to you more openly and more freely, what his intentions really are.'

'Oh! I have no doubt that they are honourable,' said Miss Dunstable. 'He does not want to deceive me in that way, I am quite sure.' It was impossible to help laughing, and Mrs. Harold Smith did laugh. 'Upon my word you would provoke a saint,' said she.

'I am not likely to get into any such company by the alliance that you are now suggesting to me. There are not many saints usually at Chaldicotes, I believe; – always excepting my dear bishop and his wife.'

'But, my dear, what am I to say to Nathaniel?'

'Tell him, of course, how much obliged to him I am.'

'Do listen to me one moment. I dare say that I have done wrong to speak to you in such a bold, unromantic way.'

'Not at all. The truth, the whole truth, and nothing but the truth. That's what we agreed upon. But one's first efforts in any line are always apt to be a little uncouth.'

'I will send Nathaniel to you himself.'

'No, do not do so. Why torment either him or me? I do like your brother; in a certain way I like him much. But no earthly consideration would induce me to marry him. Is it not so glaringly plain that he would marry me for my money only, that you have not even dared to suggest any other reason?'

'Of course it would have been nonsense to say that he had no regard whatever towards your money.'

'Of course it would – absolute nonsense. He is a poor man with a good position, and he wants to marry me because I have got that which he wants. But, my dear, I do not want that which he has got, and therefore the bargain would not be a fair one.'

'But he would do his very best to make you happy.'

'I am so much obliged to him; but you see, I am very happy as I am. What should I gain?'

'A companion whom you confess that you like.'

'Ah! but I don't know that I should like too much even of such a companion as your brother. No, my dear – it won't do. Believe me when I tell you, once for all, that it won't do.'

'Do you mean, then, Miss Dunstable, that you'll never marry?'

'To-morrow – if I met any one that I fancied, and he would have me. But I rather think that any that I may fancy won't have me. In the first place, if I marry any one, the man must be quite indifferent to money.'

'Then you'll not find him in this world, my dear.'

'Very possibly not,' said Miss Dunstable. All that was further said upon the subject need not be here repeated. Mrs. Harold Smith did not give up her cause quite at once, although Miss Dunstable had spoken so plainly. She tried to explain how eligible would be her friend's situation as mistress of Chaldicotes, when Chaldicotes should owe no penny to any man; and went so far as to hint that the master of Chaldicotes, if relieved of his embarrassments and known as a rich man, might in all probability be found worthy of a peerage when the goods should return to Olympus. Mr. Harold Smith, as a Cabinet minister, would, of course, do his best. But it was all of no use. 'It's not my destiny,' said Miss Dunstable, 'and therefore do not press it any longer.'

'But we shall not quarrel,' said Mrs. Harold Smith, almost tenderly.

'Oh, no – why should we quarrel?'

'And you won't look glum at my brother?'

'Why should I look glum at him? But, Mrs. Smith, I'll do more than not looking glum at him. I do like you, and I do like your brother, and if I can in any moderate way assist him in his difficulties, let him tell me so.' Soon after this, Mrs. Harold Smith went her way. Of course, she declared in a very strong manner that her brother could not think of accepting from Miss Dunstable any such pecuniary assistance as that offered – and, to give her her due, such was the feeling of her mind at the moment; but as she went to meet her brother and gave him an account of this interview, it did occur to her that possibly Miss Dunstable might be a better creditor than the Duke of Omnium for the Chaldicotes property.

CHAPTER XXV

Non-Impulsive

IT cannot be held as astonishing, that that last decision on the part of the giants in the matter of the two bishoprics should have disgusted Archdeacon Grantly. He was a politician, but not a politician as they were. As is the case with all exoteric men, his political eyes saw a short way only, and his political aspirations were as limited. When his friends came into office, that bishop bill, which as the original product of his enemies had been regarded by him as being so pernicious – for was it not about to be made law in order that other Proudies and such like might be hoisted up into high places and large incomes, to the terrible detriment of the Church? – that bishop bill, I say, in the hands of his friends, had appeared to him to be a means of almost national salvation. And then, how great had been the good fortune of the giants in this matter! Had they been the originators of such a measure they would not have had a chance of success; but now – now that the two bishops were falling into their mouths out of the weak hands of the gods, was not their success ensured? So Dr. Grantly had girded up his loins and marched up to the fight, almost regretting that the triumph would be so easy. The subsequent failure was very trying to his temper as a party man. It always strikes me that the supporters of the Titans are in this respect much to be pitied. The giants themselves, those who are actually handling Pelion and breaking their shins over the lower rocks of Ossa, are always advancing in some sort towards the councils of Olympus. Their highest policy is to snatch some ray from heaven. Why else put Pelion on Ossa, unless it be that a furtive hand, making its way through Jove's windows, may pluck forth a thunderbolt or two, or some article less destructive, but of manufacture equally divine? And in this consists the wisdom of the higher giants – that, in spite of their mundane antecedents, theories, and predilections, they can see that articles of divine manufacture are necessary. But then they never carry their supporters with them. The whole army is an army of martyrs. 'For twenty years I have stuck to them, and see how they have treated me!' Is not that always the plaint of an old giant-slave? 'I have been true to my party all my life, and where am I now?' he says. Where, indeed, my friend? Looking about you, you begin to learn that you cannot describe your whereabouts. I do not marvel at that. No one finds himself planted at last in so terribly foul a morass, as he would fain stand still for ever on dry land.

Dr. Grantly was disgusted; and although he was himself too true and thorough in all his feelings, to be able to say aloud that any giant was wrong, still he had a sad feeling within his heart that the world was sinking from under him. He was still sufficiently exoteric to think that a good stand-up fight in a good cause was a good thing. No doubt he did wish to be Bishop of Westminster, and was anxious to compass that preferment by any means that might appear to him to be fair. And why not? But this was not the end of his aspirations. He wished that the giants might prevail in everything, in bishoprics as in all other matters; and he could not understand that they should give way on the very first appearance of a skirmish. In his open talk he was loud against many a god; but in his heart of hearts he was bitter enough against both Porphyrion and Orion.

'My dear doctor, it would not do; – not in this session; it would not indeed.' So had spoken to him a half-fledged but especially esoteric young monster-cub at the Treasury, who considered himself as up to all the dodges of his party, and regarded the army of martyrs who supported it as a rather heavy, but very useful collection of fogies. Dr. Grantly had not cared to discuss the matter with the half-fledged monster-cub. The best licked of all the monsters, the giant most like a god of them all, had said a word or two to him; and he also had said a word or two to that giant. Porphyrion had told him that the bishop bill would not do; and he, in return, speaking with warm face, and blood in his cheeks, had told Porphyrion that he saw no reason why the bill should not do. The courteous giant had smiled as he shook his ponderous head, and then the archdeacon had left him, unconsciously shaking some dust from his shoes, as he paced the passages of the Treasury chambers for the last time. As he walked back to his lodgings in Mount Street, many thoughts, not altogether bad in their nature, passed through his mind. Why should he trouble himself about a bishopric? Was he not well as he was, in his rectory down at Plumstead? Might it not be ill for him at his age to transplant himself into new soil, to engage in new duties, and live among new people? Was he not useful at Barchester, and respected also; and might it not be possible, that up there at Westminster, he might be regarded merely as a tool with which other men could work? He had not quite liked the tone of that specially esoteric young monster-cub, who had clearly regarded him as a distinguished fogy from the army of martyrs. He would take his wife back to Barsetshire, and there live contented with the good things which Providence had given him.

Those high political grapes had become sour, my sneering friends will say. Well? Is it not a good thing that grapes should become sour which hang out of reach? Is he not wise who can regard all grapes as sour which are manifestly too high for his hand? Those grapes of the Treasury bench, for which gods and giants fight, suffering so much when they are forced to abstain from eating, and so much more when they do eat, – those grapes are very sour to me. I am sure that they are indigestible, and that those who eat them undergo all the ills which the Revallenta Arabica is prepared to cure. And so it was now with the archdeacon. He thought of the strain which would have been put on his conscience had he come up there to sit in London as Bishop of Westminster; and in this frame of mind he walked home to his wife. During the first few moments of his interview with her all his regrets had come back upon him. Indeed, it would have hardly suited for him then to have preached this new doctrine of rural contentment. The wife of his bosom, who he so fully trusted – had so fully loved – wished for grapes that hung high upon the wall, and he knew that it was past his power to teach her at the moment to drop her ambition. Any teaching that he might effect in that way, must come by degrees. But before many minutes were over he had told her of her fate and of his own decision. 'So we had better go back to Plumstead,' he said; and she had not dissented.

'I am sorry for poor Griselda's sake,' Mrs. Grantly had remarked later in the evening, when they were again together.

'But I thought she was to remain with Lady Lufton?'

'Well; so she will, for a little time. There is no one with whom I would so soon trust her out of my own care as with Lady Lufton. She is all that one can desire.'

'Exactly; and as far as Griselda is concerned, I cannot say that I think she is to be pitied.'

'Not to be pitied, perhaps,' said Mrs. Grantly. 'But, you see, archdeacon, Lady Lufton, of course, has her own views.'

'Her own views?'

'It is hardly any secret that she is very anxious to make a match between Lord Lufton and Griselda. And though that might be a very proper arrangement if it were fixed –'

'Lord Lufton marry Griselda!' said the archdeacon, speaking quick and raising his eyebrows. His mind had as yet been troubled by but few thoughts respecting his child's future establishment. 'I had never dreamt of such a thing.'

'But other people have done more than dream of it, archdeacon. As regards the match itself, it would, I think, be unobjectionable. Lord Lufton will not be a very rich man, but his property is respectable, and as far as I can learn his character is on the whole good. If they like each other, I should be contented with such a marriage. But, I must own, I am not quite satisfied at the idea of leaving her all alone with Lady Lufton. People will look on it as a settled thing, when it is not settled – and very probably may not be settled; and that will do the poor girl harm. She is very much admired; there can be no doubt of that; and Lord Dumbello –'

The archdeacon opened his eyes still wider. He had had no idea that such a choice of sons-in-law was being prepared for him; and, to tell the truth, was almost bewildered by the height of his wife's ambition. Lord Lufton, with his barony and twenty thousand a year, might be accepted as just good enough; but failing him there was an embryo marquis, whose fortune would be more than ten times as great, all ready to accept his child! And then he thought, as husbands sometimes will think, of Susan Harding as she was when he had gone a-courting to her under the elms before the house in the warden's garden at Barchester, and of dear old Mr. Harding, his wife's father, who still lived in humble lodgings in that city; and as he thought, he wondered at and admired the greatness of that lady's mind. 'I never can forgive Lord De Terrier,' said the lady, connecting various points together in her own mind.

'That's nonsense,' said the archdeacon. 'You must forgive him.'

'And I must confess that it annoys me to leave London at present.'

'It can't be helped,' said the archdeacon, somewhat gruffly; for he was a man who, on certain points, chose to have his own way – and had it.

'Oh, no: I know it can't be helped,' said Mrs. Grantly, in a tone which implied a deep injury. 'I know it can't be helped. Poor Griselda!' And then they went to bed. On the next morning Griselda came to her, and in an interview that was strictly private, her mother said more to her than she had ever yet spoken, as to the prospects of her future life. Hitherto, on this subject, Mrs. Grantly had said little or nothing. She would have been well pleased that her daughter should have received the incense of Lord Lufton's vows – or, perhaps, as well pleased had it been the incense of Lord Dumbello's vows – without any interference on her part. In such case her child, she knew, would have told her with quite sufficient eagerness, and the matter in either case would have been arranged as a very pretty love match. She had no fear of any impropriety or of any rashness on Griselda's part. She had thoroughly known her daughter when she boasted that Griselda would never indulge in an unauthorized passion. But as matters now stood, with those two strings to her bow, and with that Lufton-Grantly alliance treaty in existence – of which she, Griselda herself, knew nothing – might it not be possible that the poor child should stumble through want of adequate direction? Guided by these thoughts, Mrs. Grantly had resolved to say a few words before she left London. So she wrote a line to her daughter, and Griselda reached Mount Street at two o'clock in Lady Lufton's carriage, which, during the interview, waited for her at the beer-shop round the corner.

'And papa won't be Bishop of Westminster?' said the young lady, when the doings of the giants had been sufficiently explained to make her understand that all those hopes were over.

'No, my dear; at any rate not now.'

'What a shame! I thought it was all settled. What's the good, mamma, of Lord De Terrier being Prime Minister, if he can't make whom he likes a bishop?'

'I don't think that Lord De Terrier has behaved at all well to your father. However, that's a long question, and we can't go into it now.'

'How glad those Proudies will be!' Griselda would have talked by the hour on this subject had her mother allowed her, but it was necessary that Mrs. Grantly should go to other matters. She began about Lady Lufton, saying what a dear woman her ladyship was; and then went on to say that Griselda was to remain in London as long as it suited her friend and hostess to stay there with her; but added, that this might probably not be very long, as it was notorious that Lady Lufton, when in London, was always in a hurry to get back to Framley.

'But I don't think she is in such a hurry this year, mamma,' said Griselda, who in the month of May preferred

Bruton Street to Plumstead, and had no objection whatever to the coronet on the panels of Lady Lufton's coach. And then Mrs. Grantly commenced her explanation – very cautiously. 'No, my dear, I dare say she is not in such a hurry this year, – that is, as long as you remain with her.'

'I am sure she is very kind.'

'She is very kind, and you ought to love her very much. I know I do. I have no friend in the world for whom I have a greater regard than for Lady Lufton. It is that which makes me so happy to leave you with her.'

'All the same, I wish that you and papa had remained up; that is, if they had made papa a bishop.'

'It's no good thinking of that now, my dear. What I particularly wanted to say to you was this: I think you should know what are the ideas which Lady Lufton entertains.'

'Her ideas!' said Griselda, who had never troubled herself much in thinking about other people's thoughts.

'Yes, Griselda. While you were staying down at Framley Court, and also, I suppose, since you have been up here in Bruton Street, you must have seen a good deal of – Lord Lufton.'

'He doesn't come very often to Bruton Street, – that is to say, not *very* often.'

'H-m,' ejaculated Mrs. Grantly, very gently. She would willingly have repressed the sound altogether, but it had been too much for her. If she found reason to think that Lady Lufton was playing her false, she would immediately take her daughter away, break up the treaty, and prepare for the Hartletop alliance. Such were the thoughts that ran through her mind. But she knew all the while that Lady Lufton was not false. The fault was not with Lady Lufton; nor, perhaps, altogether with Lord Lufton. Mrs. Grantly had understood the full force of the complaint which Lady Lufton had made against her daughter; and though she had of course defended her child, and on the whole had defended her successfully, yet she confessed to herself that Griselda's chance of a first-rate establishment would be better if she were a little more impulsive. A man does not wish to marry a statue, let the statue be ever so statuesque. She could not teach her daughter to be impulsive, any more than she could teach her to be six feet high; but might it not be possible to teach her to seem so? The task was a very delicate one, even for a mother's hand. 'Of course he cannot be at home now as much as he was down in the country, when he was living in the same house,' said Mrs. Grantly, whose business it was to take Lord Lufton's part at the present moment. 'He must be at his club, and at the House of Lords, and in twenty places.'

'He is very fond of going to parties, and he dances beautifully.'

'I am sure he does. I have seen as much as that myself, and I think I know some one with whom he likes to dance.' And the mother gave the daughter a loving little squeeze.

'Do you mean me, mamma?'

'Yes, I do mean you, my dear. And is it not true? Lady Lufton says that he likes dancing with you better than with any one else in London.'

'I don't know,' said Griselda, looking down upon the ground. Mrs. Grantly thought that this upon the whole was rather a good opening. It might have been better. Some point of interest more serious in its nature than that of a waltz might have been found on which to connect her daughter's sympathies with those of her future husband. But any point of interest was better than none; and it is so difficult to find points of interest in persons who by their nature are not impulsive.

'Lady Lufton says so, at any rate,' continued Mrs. Grantly, ever so cautiously. 'She thinks that Lord Lufton likes no partner better. What do you think yourself, Griselda?'

'I don't know, mamma.'

'But young ladies must think of such things, must they not?'

'Must they, mamma?'

'I suppose they do, don't they? The truth is, Griselda, that Lady Lufton thinks that if – Can you guess what it is she thinks?'

'No, mamma.' But that was a fib on Griselda's part.

'She thinks that my Griselda would make the best possible wife in the world for her son: and I think so too. I think that her son will be a very fortunate man if he can get such a wife. And now what do you think, Griselda?'

'I don't think anything, mamma.' But that would not do. It was absolutely necessary that she should think, and absolutely necessary that her mother should tell her so. Such a degree of unimpulsiveness as this would lead to – Heaven knows what results? Lufton-Grantly treaties and Hartletop interests would be all thrown away upon a young lady who would not think anything of a noble suitor sighing for her smiles. Besides, it was not natural. Griselda, as her mother knew, had never been a girl of headlong feeling; but still she had had her likes and her dislikes. In that matter of the bishopric she was keen enough; and no one could evince a deeper interest in the subject of a well-made new dress than Griselda Grantly. It was not possible that she should be indifferent as to her future prospects, and she must know that those prospects depended mainly on her marriage. Her mother was almost angry with her, but nevertheless she went on very gently:

'You don't think anything! But, my darling, you must think. You must make up your mind what would be your answer if Lord Lufton were to propose to you. That is what Lady Lufton wishes him to do.'

'But he never will, mamma.'

'And if he did?'

'But I'm sure he never will. He doesn't think of such a thing at all – and – and –'

'And what, my dear?'

'I don't know, mamma.'

'Surely you can speak out to me, dearest! All I care about is your happiness. Both Lady Lufton and I think that it would be a happy marriage if you both cared for each other enough. She thinks that he is fond of you. But if he were ten times Lord Lufton I would not tease you about it if I thought that you could not learn to care about him. What was it you were going to say, my dear?'

'Lord Lufton thinks a great deal more of Lucy Robarts than he does of – of – of any one else, I believe,' said Griselda, showing now some little animation by her manner, 'dumpy little black thing that she is.'

'Lucy Robarts!' said Mrs. Grantly, taken by surprise at finding that her daughter was moved by such a passion as jealousy, and feeling also perfectly assured that there could not be any possible ground for jealousy in such a direction as that. 'Lucy Robarts, my dear! I don't suppose Lord Lufton ever thought of speaking to her, except in the way of civility.'

'Yes, he did, mamma! Don't you remember at Framley?' Mrs. Grantly began to look back in her mind, and she thought she did remember having once observed Lord Lufton talking in rather a confidential manner with the parson's sister. But she was sure that there was nothing in it. If that was the reason why Griselda was so cold to her proposed lover, it would be a thousand pities that it should not be removed. 'Now you mention her, I do remember the young lady,' said Mrs. Grantly, 'a dark girl, very low, and without much figure. She seemed to me to keep very much in the background.'

'I don't know much about that, mamma.'

'As far as I saw her, she did. But, my dear Griselda, you should not allow yourself to think of such a thing. Lord Lufton, of course, is bound to be civil to any young lady in his mother's house, and I am quite sure that he has no other idea whatever with regard to Miss Robarts. I certainly cannot speak as to her intellect, for I do not think she opened her mouth in my presence; but –'

'Oh! she has plenty to say for herself, when she pleases. She's a sly little thing.'

'But, at any rate, my dear, she has no personal attractions whatever, and I do not at all think that Lord Lufton is a man to be taken by – by – by anything that Miss Robarts might do or say.' As those words 'personal attractions' were uttered, Griselda managed so to turn her neck as to catch a side view of herself in one of the mirrors on the wall, and then she bridled herself up, and made a little play with her eyes, and looked, as her mother thought, very well. 'It is all nothing to me, mamma, of course,' she said.

'Well, my dear, perhaps not. I don't say that it is. I do not wish to put the slightest constraint upon your feelings. If I did not have the most thorough dependence on your good sense and high principles, I should not speak to you in this way. But as I have, I thought it best to tell you that both Lady Lufton and I should be well pleased if we thought that you and Lord Lufton were fond of each other.'

'I am sure he never thinks of such a thing, mamma.'

'And as for Lucy Robarts, pray get that idea out of your head; if not for your sake, then for his. You should give him credit for better taste.' But it was not so easy to take anything out of Griselda's head that she had once taken into it. 'As for tastes, mamma, there is no accounting for them,' she said; and then the colloquy on that subject was over. The result of it on Mrs. Grantly's mind was a feeling amounting almost to a conviction in favour of the Dumbello interest.

CHAPTER XXVI

Impulsive

I TRUST my readers will all remember how Puck the pony was beaten during that drive to Hogglestock. It may be presumed that Puck himself on that occasion did not suffer much. His skin was not so soft as Mrs.

Robarts's heart. The little beast was full of oats and all the good things of this world, and therefore, when the whip touched him, he would dance about and shake his little ears, and run on at a tremendous pace for twenty yards, making his mistress think that he had endured terrible things. But, in truth, during those whippings Puck was not the chief sufferer. Lucy had been forced to declare – forced by the strength of her own feelings, and by the impossibility of assenting to the propriety of a marriage between Lord Lufton and Miss Grantly –, she had been forced to declare that she did care about Lord Lufton as much as though he were her brother. She had said all this to herself – nay, much more than this – very often. But now she had said it out loud to her sister-in-law; and she knew that what she had said was remembered, considered, and had, to a certain extent, become the cause of altered conduct. Fanny alluded very seldom to the Luftons in casual conversation, and never spoke about Lord Lufton, unless when her husband made it impossible that she should not speak of him. Lucy had attempted on more than one occasion to remedy this, by talking about the young lord in a laughing and, perhaps, half-jeering way; she had been sarcastic as to his hunting and shooting, and had boldly attempted to say a word in joke about his love for Griselda. But she felt that she had failed; that she had failed altogether as regarded Fanny; and that as to her brother, she would more probably be the means of opening his eyes, than have any effect in keeping them closed. So she gave up her efforts and spoke no further word about Lord Lufton. Her secret had been told, and she knew that it had been told. At this time the two ladies were left a great deal alone together in the drawing-room at the parsonage; more, perhaps, than had ever yet been the case since Lucy had been there. Lady Lufton was away, and therefore the almost daily visit to Framley Court was not made; and Mark in these days was a great deal at Barchester, having, no doubt, very onerous duties to perform before he could be admitted as one of that chapter. He went into, what he was pleased to call residence, almost at once. That is, he took his month of preaching, aiding also, in some slight and very dignified way, in the general Sunday morning services. He did not exactly live at Barchester, because the house was not ready. That at least was the assumed reason. The chattels of Dr. Stanhope, the late prebendary, had not been as yet removed, and there was likely to be some little delay, creditors asserting their right to them. This might have been very inconvenient to a gentleman anxiously expecting the excellent house which the liberality of past ages had provided for his use; but it was not so felt by Mr. Robarts. If Dr. Stanhope's family or creditors would keep the house for the next twelve months, he would be well pleased. And by this arrangement he was enabled to get through his first month of absence from the church of Framley without any notice from Lady Lufton, seeing that Lady Lufton was in London all the time. This also was convenient, and taught our young prebendary to look on his new preferment more favourably than he had hitherto done.

Fanny and Lucy were thus left much alone: and as out of the full head the mouth speaks, so is the full heart more prone to speak at such periods of confidence as these. Lucy, when she first thought of her own state, determined to endow herself with a powerful gift of reticence. She would never tell her love, certainly; but neither would she let concealment feed on her damask cheek, nor would she ever be found for a moment sitting like Patience on a monument. She would fight her own fight bravely within her own bosom, and conquer her enemy altogether. She would either preach, or starve, or weary her love into subjection, and no one should be a bit the wiser. She would teach herself to shake hands with Lord Lufton without a quiver, and would be prepared to like his wife amazingly – unless indeed that wife should be Griselda Grantly. Such were her resolutions; but at the end of the first week they were broken into shivers and scattered to the winds. They had been sitting in the house together the whole of one wet day; and as Mark was to dine in Barchester with the dean, they had had dinner early, eating with the children almost in their laps. It is so that ladies do, when their husbands leave them to themselves. It was getting dusk towards evening, and they were still sitting in the drawing-room, the children now having retired, when Mrs. Robarts for the fifth time since her visit to Hogglestock began to express her wish that she could do some good to the Crawleys, – to Grace Crawley in particular, who, standing up there at her father's elbow, learning Greek irregular verbs, had appeared to Mrs. Robarts to be an especial object of pity.

'I don't know how to set about it,' said Mrs. Robarts. Now any allusion to that visit to Hogglestock always drove Lucy's mind back to the consideration of the subject which had most occupied it at the time. She at such moments remembered how she had beaten Puck, and how in her half-bantering but still too serious manner she had apologized for doing so, and had explained the reason. And therefore she did not interest herself about Grace Crawley as vividly as she should have done. 'No; one never does,' she said.

'I was thinking about it all that day as I drove home,' said Fanny. 'The difficulty is this: What can we do with her?'

'Exactly,' said Lucy, remembering the very point of the road at which she had declared that she did like Lord Lufton very much.

'If we could have her here for a month or so and then send her to school; – but I know Mr. Crawley would not allow us to pay for her schooling.'

'I don't think he would,' said Lucy, with her thoughts far removed from Mr. Crawley and his daughter Grace.

'And then we should not know what to do with her; should we?'

'No; you would not.'

'It would never do to have the poor girl about the house here, with no one to teach her anything. Mark would not teach her Greek verbs, you know.'

'I suppose not.'

'Lucy, you are not attending to a word I say to you, and I don't think you have for the last hour. I don't believe you know what I am talking about.'

'Oh, yes I do – Grace Crawley; I'll try and teach her if you like, only I don't know anything myself.'

'That's not what I mean at all, and you know I would not ask you to take such a task as that on yourself. But I do think you might talk it over with me.'

'Might I? very well; I will. What is it? Oh, Grace Crawley – you want to know who is to teach her the irregular Greek verbs. Oh, dear, Fanny, my head does ache so: pray don't be angry with me.' And then Lucy, throwing herself back on the sofa, put one hand up painfully to her forehead, and altogether gave up the battle. Mrs. Robarts was by her side in a moment.

'Dearest Lucy, what is it makes your head ache so often now? you used not to have those headaches.'

'It's because I'm growing stupid: never mind. We will go on about poor Grace. It would not do to have a governess, would it?'

'I can see that you are not well, Lucy,' said Mrs. Robarts, with a look of deep concern. 'What is it, dearest? I can see that something is the matter.'

'Something the matter! No, there's not; nothing worth talking of. Sometimes I think I'll go back to Devonshire and live there. I could stay with Blanche for a time, and then get a lodging in Exeter.'

'Go back to Devonshire!' and Mrs. Robarts looked as though she thought that her sister-in-law was going mad. 'Why do you want to go away from us? This is to be your own, own home, always now.'

'Is it? Then I am in a bad way. Oh dear, oh dear, what a fool I am! What an idiot I've been! Fanny, I don't think

I can stay here; and I do so wish I'd never come. I do – I do – I do, though you look at me so horribly,' and jumping up she threw herself into her sister-in-law's arms and began kissing her violently. 'Don't pretend to be wounded, for you know that I love you. You know that I could live with you all my life, and think you were perfect – as you are; but –'

'Has Mark said anything?'

'Not a word, – not a ghost of a syllable. It is not Mark; oh, Fanny!'

'I am afraid I know what you mean,' said Mrs. Robarts in a low tremulous voice, and with deep sorrow painted on her face.

'Of course you do; of course you know; you have known it all along; since that day in the pony carriage. I knew that you knew it. You do not dare to mention his name; would not that tell me that you know it? And I, I am hypocrite enough for Mark; but my hypocrisy won't pass muster before you. And, now, had I not better go to Devonshire?'

'Dearest, dearest Lucy.'

'Was I not right about that labelling? O heavens! what idiots we girls are! That a dozen soft words should have bowled me over like a ninepin, and left me without an inch of ground to call my own. And I was so proud of my own strength; so sure that I should never be missish, and spoony, and sentimental! I was so determined to like him as Mark does, or you –'

'I shall not like him at all if he has spoken words to you that he should not have spoken.'

'But he has not.' And then she stopped a moment to consider. 'No, he has not. He never said a word to me that would make you angry with him if you knew of it. Except, perhaps, that he called me Lucy; and that was my fault, not his.'

'Because you talked of soft words.'

'Fanny, you have no idea what an absolute fool I am, what an unutterable ass. The soft words of which I tell you were of the kind which he speaks to you when he asks you how the cow gets on which he sent you from Ireland, or to Mark about Ponto's shoulder. He told me that he knew papa, and that he was at school with Mark, and that as he was such good friends with you here at the parsonage, he must be good friends with me too. No; it has not been his fault. The soft words which did the mischief were such as those. But how well his mother understood the world! In order to have been safe, I should not have dared to look at him.'

'But, dearest Lucy –'

'I know what you are going to say, and I admit it all. He is no hero. There is nothing on earth wonderful about him. I never heard him say a single word of wisdom, or utter a thought that was akin to poetry. He devotes all his energies to riding after a fox or killing poor birds, and I never heard of his doing a single great action in my life. And yet –' Fanny was so astounded by the way her sister-in-law went on, that she hardly knew how to speak. 'He is an excellent son, I believe,' at last she said.

'Except when he goes to Gatherum Castle. I'll tell you what he has: he has fine straight legs, and a smooth forehead, and a good-humoured eye, and white teeth. Was it possible to see such a catalogue of perfections, and not fall down, stricken to the very bone? But it was not that that did it all, Fanny. I could have stood against that. I think I could at least. It was his title that killed me. I had never spoken to a lord before. Oh, me! what a fool, what a beast I have been!' And then she burst out into tears. Mrs. Robarts, to tell the truth, could hardly understand poor Lucy's ailment. It was evident enough that her misery was real; but yet she spoke of herself and her sufferings with so much irony, with so near an approach to joking, that it was very hard to tell how far she was in earnest. Lucy, too, was so much given to a species of badinage which Mrs. Robarts did not always quite understand, that the latter was afraid sometimes to speak out what came uppermost to her tongue. But now that Lucy was absolutely in tears, and was almost breathless with excitement, she could not remain silent any longer. 'Dearest Lucy, pray do not speak in that way; it will all come right. Things always do come right when no one has acted wrongly.'

'Yes, when nobody has done wrongly. That's what papa used to call begging the question. But I'll tell you what, Fanny; I will not be beaten. I will either kill myself or get through it. I am so heartily self-ashamed that I owe it to myself to fight the battle out.'

'To fight what battle, dearest?'

'This battle. Here, now, at the present moment I could not meet Lord Lufton. I should have to run like a scared fowl if he were to show himself within the gate; and I should not dare to go of the house, if I knew that he was in the parish.'

'I don't see that, for I am sure you have not betrayed yourself.'

'Well, no; as for myself, I believe I have done the lying and the hypocrisy pretty well. But, dearest Fanny, you don't know half; and you cannot and must not know.'

'But I thought you said there had been nothing whatever between you.'

'Did I? Well, to you I have not said a word that was not true. I said that he had spoken nothing that it was wrong for him to say. It could not be wrong – But never mind. I'll tell you what I mean to do. I have been thinking of it for the last week – only I shall have to tell Mark.'

'If I were you I would tell him all.'

'What, Mark! If you do, Fanny, I'll never, never, never speak to you again. Would you – when I have given you all my heart in true sisterly love?' Mrs. Robarts had to explain that she had not proposed to tell anything to Mark herself, and was persuaded, moreover, to give a solemn promise that she would not tell anything to him unless specially authorized to do so.

'I'll go into a home, I think,' continued Lucy. 'You know what these homes are?' Mrs. Robarts assured her that she knew very well, and then Lucy went on: 'A year ago I should have said that I was the last girl in England to think of such a life, but I do believe now that it would be the best thing for me. And then I'll starve myself, and flog myself, and in that way I'll get back my own mind and my own soul.'

'Your own soul, Lucy!' said Mrs. Robarts, in a tone of horror.

'Well, my own heart, if you like it better; but I hate to hear myself talking about hearts. I don't care for my heart. I'd let it go – with this young popinjay lord or any one else, so that I could read, and talk, and walk, and sleep, and eat, without always feeling that I was wrong here – here – here –' and she pressed her hand vehemently against her side. 'What is it that I feel, Fanny? Why am I so weak in body that I cannot take exercise? Why cannot I keep my mind on a book for one moment? Why can I not write two sentences together? Why should every mouthful that I eat stick in my throat? Oh, Fanny, is it his legs, think you, or is it his title?' Through all her sorrow – and she was very sorrowful – Mrs. Robarts could not help smiling. And, indeed, there was every now and then something even in Lucy's look that was almost comic. She acted the irony so well with which she strove to throw ridicule on herself! 'Do laugh at me,' she said. 'Nothing on earth will do me so much good as that; nothing, unless it be starvation and a whip. If you would only tell me that I must be a sneak and an idiot to care for a man because he is good-looking and a lord!'

'But that has not been the reason. There is a great deal more in Lord Lufton than that; and since I must speak, dear Lucy, I cannot but say that I should not wonder at your being in love with him, only – only that –'

'Only what? Come, out with it. Do not mince matters, or think that I shall be angry with you because you scold me.'

'Only that I should have thought that you would have been too guarded to have – have cared for any gentleman till – till he had shown that he cared for you.'

'Guarded! Yes, that's it; that's just the word. But it's he that should have been guarded. He should have had a fire-guard hung before him, or a love-guard, if you will. Guarded! Was I not guarded, till you all would drag me out? Did I want to go there? And when I was there, did I not make a fool of myself, sitting in a corner, and thinking how much better placed I should have been down in the servants' hall. Lady Lufton – she dragged me out, and then cautioned me, and then, then – Why is Lady Lufton to have it all her own way? Why am I to be sacrificed for her? I did not want to know Lady Lufton, or any one belonging to her.'

'I cannot think that you have any cause to blame Lady Lufton, nor, perhaps, to blame anybody very much.'

'Well, no, it has been all my own fault; though, for the life of me, Fanny, going back and back, I cannot see where I took the first false step. I do not know where I went wrong. One wrong thing I did, and it is the only thing that I do not regret.'

'What was that, Lucy?'

'I told him a lie.'

Mrs. Robarts was altogether in the dark, and feeling that she was so, she knew that she could not give counsel as a friend or a sister. Lucy had begun by declaring – so Mrs. Robarts thought – that nothing had passed between her and Lord Lufton but words of most trivial import, and yet she now accused herself of falsehood, and declared that that falsehood was the only thing which she did not regret!

'I hope not,' said Mrs. Robarts. 'If you did, you were very unlike yourself.'

'But I did, and were he here again, speaking to me in the same way, I should repeat it. I know I should. If I did not, I should have all the world on me. You would frown on me, and be cold. My darling Fanny, how would you look if I really displeasured you?'

'I don't think you will do that, Lucy?'

'But if I told him the truth I should, should I not? Speak now. But no, Fanny, you need not speak. It was not the fear of you; no, nor even of her: though Heaven knows that her terrible glumness would be quite unendurable.'

'I cannot understand you, Lucy. What truth or what untruth can you have told him, if, as you say, there has been nothing between you but ordinary conversation?'

Lucy then got up from the sofa, and walked twice the length of the room before she spoke. Mrs. Robarts had all the ordinary curiosity – I was going to say, of a woman, but I mean to say, of humanity; and she had, moreover, all the love of a sister. She was both curious and anxious, and remained sitting where she was, silent, and with her eyes fixed on her companion. 'Did I say so?' Lucy said at last. 'No, Fanny, you have mistaken me – I did not say that. Ah, yes, about the cow and the dog. All that was true. I was telling you of what his soft words had been while I was becoming such a fool. Since that he has said more.'

'What more has he said, Lucy?'

'I yearn to tell you, if only I can trust you;' and Lucy knelt down at the feet of Mrs. Robarts, looking up into her face and smiling through the remaining drops of her tears. 'I would fain tell you, but I do not know you yet – whether you are quite true. I could be true – true against all the world, if my friend told me. I will tell you, Fanny, if you say that you can be true. But if you doubt yourself, if you must whisper all to Mark – then let us be silent.'

There was something almost awful in this to Mrs. Robarts. Hitherto, since their marriage, hardly a thought had passed through her mind which she had not shared with her husband. But now all this had came upon her so suddenly, that she was unable to think whether it would be well that she should become the depositary of such a secret – not to be mentioned to Lucy's brother, not to be mentioned to her own husband. But who ever yet was offered a secret and declined it? Who at least ever declined a love secret? What sister could do so? Mrs. Robarts, therefore, gave the promise, smoothing Lucy's hair as she did so, and kissing her forehead and looking into her eyes, which, like a rainbow, were the brighter for her tears. 'And what has he said to you, Lucy?'

'What? Only this, that he asked me to be his wife.'

'Lord Lufton proposed to you?'

'Yes; proposed to me. It is not credible, is it? You cannot bring yourself to believe that such a thing happened, can you?' And Lucy rose again to her feet, as the idea of the scorn with which she felt that others would treat her – with which she herself treated herself – made the blood rise to her cheek. 'And yet it is not a dream – I think that it is not a dream. I think that he really did.'

'Think, Lucy!'

'Well, I may say that I am sure.'

'A gentleman would not make you a formal proposal, and leave you in doubt as to what he meant.'

'Oh dear, no. There was no doubt at all of that kind – none in the least. Mr. Smith, in asking Miss Jones to do him the honour of becoming Mrs. Smith, never spoke more plainly. I was alluding to the possibility of having dreamt it all.'

'Lucy!'

'Well, it was not a dream. Here, standing here, on this very spot – on that flower of the carpet – he begged me a dozen times to be his wife. I wonder whether you and Mark would let me cut it out and keep it.'

'And what answer did you make to him?'

'I lied to him, and told him that I did not love him.'

'You refused him?'

'Yes; I refused a live lord. There is some satisfaction in having that to think of, is there not? Fanny, was I wicked to tell that falsehood?'

'And why did you refuse him?'

'Why? Can you ask? Think what it would have been to go down to Framley Court, and to tell her ladyship, in the course of conversation, that I was engaged to her son.

Think of Lady Lufton. But yet it was not that, Fanny. Had I thought that it was good for him, that he would not have repented, I would have braved anything – for his sake. Even your frown, for you would have frowned. You would have thought it sacrilege for me to marry Lord Lufton! You know you would.'

Mrs. Robarts hardly knew how to say what she thought, or indeed what she ought to think. It was a matter on which much meditation would be required before she could give advice, and there was Lucy expecting counsel from her at that very moment. If Lord Lufton really loved Lucy Robarts, and was loved by Lucy Robarts, why should not they two become man and wife? And yet she did feel that it would be – perhaps not sacrilege, as Lucy had said, but something almost as troublesome. What would Lady Lufton say, or think, or feel? What would she say, and think, and feel as to that parsonage from which so deadly a blow would fall upon her? Would she not accuse the vicar and the vicar's wife of the blackest ingratitude? Would life be endurable at Framley under such circumstances as those?

'What you tell me so surprises me, that I hardly as yet know how to speak about it,' said Mrs. Robarts.

'It was amazing, was it not? He must have been insane at the time; there can be no other excuse made for him. I wonder whether there is anything of that sort in the family?'

'What; madness?' said Mrs. Robarts, quite in earnest.

'Well, don't you think he must have been mad when such an idea as that came into his head? But you don't believe it; I can see that. And yet it is as true as heaven. Standing exactly here, on this spot, he said that he would persevere till I accepted his love. I wonder what made me specially observe that both his feet were within the lines of that division.'

'And you would not accept his love?'

'No; I would have nothing to say to it. Look you, I stood here, and putting my hand upon my heart – for he bade me to do that – I said that I could not love him.'

'And what then?'

'He went away – with a look as though he were heart-broken. He crept away slowly, saying that he was the most wretched soul alive. For a minute I believed him, and could almost have called him back; but no, Fanny, do not think that I am over proud, or conceited about my conquest. He had not reached the gate before he was thanking God for his escape.'

'That I do not believe.'

'But I do; and I thought of Lady Lufton too. How could I bear that she should scorn me, and accuse me of stealing her son's heart? I know that it is better as it is; but tell me – is a falsehood always wrong, or can it be possible that the end should justify the means? Ought I to have told him the truth, and to have let him know that I could almost kiss the ground on which he stood?'

This was a question for the doctors which Mrs. Robarts would not take upon herself to answer. She would not make that falsehood matter of accusation, but neither would she pronounce for it any absolution. In that matter Lucy must regulate her own conscience.

'And what shall I do next?' said Lucy, still speaking in a tone that was half tragic and half jeering.

'Do?' said Mrs. Robarts.

'Yes, something must be done. If I were a man I should go to Switzerland, of course; or, as the case is a bad one, perhaps as far as Hungary. What is it that girls do? they don't die nowadays, I believe.'

'Lucy, I do not believe that you care for him one jot. If you were in love you would not speak of it like that.'

'There, there. That's my only hope. If I could laugh at myself till it had become incredible to you, I also, by degrees, should cease to believe that I had cared for him. But, Fanny, it is very hard. If I were to starve, and rise before daybreak, and pinch myself, or do some nasty work, – clean the pots and pans and the candlesticks; that I think would do the most good. I have got a piece of sack-cloth, and I mean to wear that, when I have made it up.'

'You are joking now, Lucy, I know.'

'No, by my word; not in the spirit of what I am saying. How shall I act upon my heart, if I do not do it through the blood and the flesh?'

'Do you not pray that God will give you strength to bear these troubles?'

'But how is one to word one's prayer, or how even to word one's wishes? I do not know what is the wrong that I have done. I say it boldly; in this matter I cannot see my own fault. I have simply found that I have been a fool.'

It was now quite dark in the room, or would have been so to any one entering it afresh. They had remained there talking till their eyes had become accustomed to the gloom, and would still have remained, had they not suddenly been disturbed by the sound of a horse's feet.

'There is Mark,' said Fanny, jumping up and running to the bell, that lights might be ready when he should enter.

'I thought he remained in Barchester to-night.'

'And so did I; but he said it might be doubtful. What shall we do if he has not dined?' That, I believe, is always the first thought in the mind of a good wife when her husband returns home. Has he had his dinner? What can I give him for dinner? Will he like his dinner? Oh dear, oh dear! there is nothing in the house but cold mutton. But on this occasion the lord of the mansion had dined, and came home radiant with good-humour, and owing, perhaps, a little of his radiance to the dean's claret. 'I have told them,' said he, 'that they may keep possession of the house for the next two months, and they have agreed to that arrangement.'

'That is very pleasant,' said Mrs. Robarts.

'And I don't think we shall have so much trouble about the dilapidations after all.'

'I am very glad of that,' said Mrs. Robarts. But nevertheless she was thinking much more of Lucy than of the house in Barchester Close.

'You won't betray me,' said Lucy, as she gave her sister-in-law a parting kiss at night.

'No; not unless you give me permission.'

'Ah; I shall never do that.'

CHAPTER XXVII

South Audley Street

THE Duke of Omnium had notified to Mr. Fothergill his wish that some arrangement should be made about the Chaldicotes mortgages, and Mr. Fothergill had understood what the duke meant as well as though his instructions had been written down with all a lawyer's verbosity. The duke's meaning was this, that Chaldicotes was to be swept up and garnered, and made part and parcel of the Gatherum property. It had seemed to the duke that that affair between his friend and Miss Dunstable was hanging fire, and, therefore, it would be well that Chaldicotes should be swept up and garnered. And, moreover, tidings had come into the western division of the county that young Frank Gresham of Boxall Hill was in treaty with the Government for the purchase of all that Crown property called the Chace of Chaldicotes. It had been offered to the duke, but the duke had given no definite answer. Had he got his money back from Mr. Sowerby he could have forestalled Mr. Gresham; but now that did not seem to be probable, and his grace was resolved that either the one property or the other should be duly garnered. Therefore Mr. Fothergill went up to town, and therefore Mr. Sowerby was, most unwillingly, compelled to have a business interview with Mr. Fothergill. In the meantime, since last we saw him, Mr. Sowerby had learned from his sister the answer which Miss Dunstable had given to his proposition, and knew that he had no further hope in that direction. There was no further hope thence of absolute deliverance, but there had been a tender of money services. To give Mr. Sowerby his due, he had at once declared that it would be quite out of the question that he should now receive any assistance of that sort from Miss Dunstable; but his sister had explained to him that it would be a mere business transaction; that Miss Dunstable would receive her interest; and that, if she would be content with four per cent., whereas the duke received five, and other creditors six, seven, eight, ten, and Heaven only knows how much more, it might be well for all parties. He, himself, understood, as well as Fothergill had done, what was the meaning of the duke's message. Chaldicotes was to be gathered up and garnered, as had been done with so many another fair property lying in those regions. It was to be swallowed whole, and the master was to walk out from his old family hall, to leave the old woods that he loved, to give up utterly to another the parks and paddocks and pleasant places which he had known from his earliest infancy, and owned from his earliest manhood.

There can be nothing more bitter to a man than such a surrender. What, compared to this, can be the loss of wealth to one who has himself made it, and brought it together, but has never actually seen it with his bodily eyes? Such wealth has come by one chance, and goes by another: the loss of it is part of the game which the man is playing; and if he cannot lose as well as win, he is a poor, weak, cowardly creature. Such men, as a rule, do know how to bear a mind fairly equal to adversity. But to have squandered the acres which have descended from generation to generation; to be the member of one's family that has ruined that family; to have swallowed up in one's own maw all that should have graced one's children, and one's grandchildren! It seems to me that the misfortunes of this world can hardly go beyond that! Mr. Sowerby, in spite of his recklessness and that dare-devil gaiety which he knew so well how to wear and use, felt all this as keenly as any man could feel it. It had been absolutely his own fault. The acres had come to him all his own, and now, before his death, every one of them would have gone bodily into that greedy maw. The duke had bought up nearly all the debts which had been secured upon the property, and now could make a clean sweep of it. Sowerby, when he received that message from Mr. Fothergill, knew well that this was intended; and he knew well also, that when once he should cease to be Mr. Sowerby of Chaldicotes, he need never again hope to be returned as member for West Barsetshire. This world would for him be all over. And what must such a man feel when he reflects that this world is for him all over? On the morning in question he went to his appointment, still bearing a cheerful countenance. Mr. Fothergill, when in town on such business as this, always had a room at his service in the house of Messrs. Gumption & Gagebee, the duke's London law agents, and it was thither that Mr. Sowerby had been summoned. The house of business of Messrs. Gumption & Gagebee was in South Audley Street; and it may be said that there was no spot on the whole earth which Mr. Sowerby so hated as he did the gloomy, dingy back sitting-room upstairs in that house. He had been there very often, but had never been there without annoyance. It was a horrid torture-chamber, kept for such dread purposes as these, and no doubt had been furnished, and papered, and curtained with the express object of finally breaking down the spirits of such poor country gentlemen as chanced to be involved. Everything was of a brown crimson, – of a crimson that had become brown. Sunlight, real genial light of the sun, never made its way there, and no amount of candles could illumine the gloom of that brownness. The windows were never washed; the ceiling was of a dark brown; the old Turkey carpet was thick with dust, and brown withal. The ungainly office-table, in the middle of the room, had been covered with black leather, but that was now brown. There was a bookcase full of dingy brown law books in a recess on one side of the fireplace, but no one had touched them for years, and over the chimney-piece hung some old legal pedigree table, black with soot. Such was the room which Mr. Fothergill always used in the business house of Messrs. Gumption & Gagebee, in South Audley Street, near to Park Lane.

I once heard this room spoken of by an old friend of mine, one Mr. Gresham of Greshamsbury, the father of Frank Gresham, who was now about to purchase that part of the Chace of Chaldicotes which belonged to the Crown. He also had had evil days, though now happily they were past and gone; and he, too, had sat in that room, and listened to the voice of men who were powerful over his property, and intended to use that power. The idea which he left on my mind was much the same as that which I had entertained, when a boy, of a certain room in the castle of Udolpho. There was a chair in that Udolpho room in which those who sat were dragged out limb by limb, the head one way and the legs another; the fingers were dragged off from the hands, and the teeth out from the jaws, and the hair off the head, and the flesh from the bones, and the joints from their sockets, till there was nothing left but a lifeless trunk seated in the chair. Mr. Gresham, as he told me, always sat in the same seat, and the tortures he suffered when so seated, the dislocations of his property which he was forced to discuss, the operations on his very self which he was forced to witness, made me regard that room as worse than the chamber of Udolpho. He, luckily – a rare instance of good fortune – had lived to see all his bones and joints put together again, and flourishing soundly; but he never could speak of the room without horror. 'No consideration on earth,' he once said to me, very solemnly, – 'I say none, should make me again enter that room.' And indeed this feeling was so strong with him, that from the day when his affairs took a turn he would never even walk down South Audley Street. On the morning in question into this torture-chamber Mr. Sowerby went, and there, after some two or three minutes, he was joined by Mr. Fothergill.

Mr. Fothergill was, in one respect, like to his friend Sowerby. He enacted two altogether different persons on occasions which were altogether different. Generally speaking, with the world at large, he was a jolly, rollicking, popular man, fond of eating and drinking, known to be devoted to the duke's interests, and supposed to be somewhat unscrupulous, or at any rate hard, when they were concerned; but in other respects a good-natured fellow: and there was a report about that he had once lent somebody money, without charging him interest or taking security. On the present occasion Sowerby saw at a glance that he had come thither with all the aptitudes and appurtenances of his business about him. He walked into the room with a short, quick step; there was no smile on his face as he shook hands with his old friend; he brought with him a box laden with papers and parchments, and he had not been a minute in the room before he was seated in one of the old dingy chairs. 'How long have you been in town, Fothergill?' said Sowerby, still standing with his back against the chimney. He had resolved on only one thing – that nothing should induce him to touch, look at, or listen to any of those papers. He knew well enough that no good would come of that. He also had his own lawyer, to see that he was pilfered according to rule.

'How long? Since the day before yesterday. I never was so busy in my life. The duke, as usual, wants to have everything done at once.'

'If he wants to have all that I owe him paid at once, he is like to be out in his reckoning.'

'Ah, well; I'm glad you are ready to come quickly to business, because it's always best. Won't you come and sit down here?'

'No, thank you; I'll stand.'

'But we shall have to go through these figures, you know.'

'Not a figure, Fothergill. What good would it do? None to me, and none to you either, as I take it. If there is anything wrong, Potter's fellows will find it out. What is it the duke wants?'

'Well; to tell the truth, he wants his money.'

'In one sense, and that the main sense, he has got it. He gets his interest regularly, does not he?'

'Pretty well for that, seeing how times are. But, Sowerby, that's nonsense. You understand the duke as well as I do, and you know very well what he wants. He has given you time, and if you had taken any steps towards getting the money, you might have saved the property.'

'A hundred and eighty thousand pounds! What steps could I take to get that? Fly a bill, and let Tozer have it to get cash on it in the City!'

'We hoped you were going to marry.'

'That's all off.'

'Then I don't think you can blame the duke for looking for his own. It does not suit him to have so large a sum standing out any longer. You see, he wants land, and will have it. Had you paid off what you owed him, he would have purchased the Crown property; and now, it seems young Gresham has bid against him, and is to have it. This has riled him, and I may as well tell you fairly, that he is determined to have either money or marbles.'

'You mean that I am to be dispossessed.'

'Well, yes; if you choose to call it so. My instructions are to foreclose at once.'

'Then I must say the duke is treating me most uncommonly ill.'

'Well, Sowerby, I can't see it.'

'I can, though. He has his money like clock-work; and he has bought up these debts from persons who would have never disturbed me as long as they got their interest.'

'Haven't you had the seat?'

'The seat! and is it expected that I am to pay for that?'

'I don't see that any one is asking you to pay for it. You are like a great many other people that I know. You want to eat your cake and have it. You have been eating it for the last twenty years, and now you think yourself very ill-used because the duke wants to have his turn.'

'I shall think myself very ill-used if he sells me out – worse than ill-used. I do not want to use strong language, but it will be more than ill-usage. I can hardly believe that he really means to treat me in that way.'

'It is very hard that he should want his own money!'

'It is not his money that he wants. It is my property.'

'And has he not paid for it? Have you not had the price of your property? Now, Sowerby, it is of no use for you to be angry; you have known for the last three years what was coming on you as well as I did. Why should the duke lend you money without an object? Of course he has his own views. But I do say this; he has not hurried you; and had you been able to do anything to save the place you might have done it. You have had time enough to look about you.' Sowerby still stood in the place in which he had first fixed himself, and now for awhile he remained silent. His face was very stern, and there was in his countenance none of those winning looks which often told so powerfully with his young friends, – which had caught Lord Lufton and had charmed Mark Robarts. The world was going against him, and things around him were coming to an end. He was beginning to perceive that he had in truth eaten his cake, and that there was now little left for him to do, – unless he chose to blow out his brains. He had said to Lord Lufton that a man's back should be broad enough for any burden with which he himself might load it. Could he now boast that his back was broad enough and strong enough for this burden? But he had even then, at that bitter moment, a strong remembrance that it behoved him still to be a man. His final ruin was coming on him, and he would soon be swept away out of the knowledge and memory of those with whom he had lived.

But, nevertheless, he would bear himself well to the last. It was true that he had made his own bed, and he understood the justice which required him to lie upon it.

During all this time Fothergill occupied himself with the papers. He continued to turn over one sheet after another, as though he were deeply engaged in money considerations and calculations. But, in truth, during all that time he did not read a word. There was nothing there for him to read. The reading and the writing, and the arithmetic in such matters, are done by underlings – not by such big men as Mr. Fothergill. His business was to tell Sowerby that he was to go. All those records there were of very little use. The duke had the power; Sowerby knew that the duke had the power; and Fothergill's business was to explain that the duke meant to exercise his power. He was used to the work, and went on turning over the papers and pretending to read them, as though his doing so were of the greatest moment. 'I shall see the duke myself,' Mr. Sowerby said at last, and there was something almost dreadful in the sound of his voice.

'You know that the duke won't see you on a matter of this kind. He never speaks to any one about money; you know that as well as I do.'

'By –, but he shall speak to me. Never speak to any one about money! Why is he ashamed to speak of it when he loves it so dearly? He shall see me.'

'I have nothing further to say, Sowerby. Of course I shan't ask his grace to see you; and if you force your way in on him you know what will happen. It won't be my doing if he is set against you. Nothing that you say to me in that way, – nothing that anybody ever says, – goes beyond myself.'

'I shall manage the matter through my own lawyer,' said Sowerby; and then he took his hat, and, without uttering another word, left the room.

We know not what may be the nature of that eternal punishment to which those will be doomed who shall be judged to have been evil at the last; but methinks that no more terrible torment can be devised than the memory of self-imposed ruin. What wretchedness can exceed that of remembering from day to day that the race has been all run, and has been altogether lost; that the last chance has gone, and has gone in vain; that the end has come, and with it disgrace, contempt, and self-scorn – disgrace that never can be redeemed, contempt that never can be removed, and self-scorn that will eat into one's vitals for ever? Mr. Sowerby was now fifty; he had enjoyed his chances in life; and as he walked back, up South Audley Street, he could not but think of the uses he had made of them. He had fallen into the possession of a fine property on the attainment of his manhood; he had been endowed with more than average gifts of intellect; never-failing health had been given to him, and a vision fairly clear in discerning good from evil; and now to what a pass had he brought himself! And that man Fothergill had put all this before him in so terribly clear a light! Now that the day of his final demolishment had arrived, the necessity that he should be demolished – finished away at once, out of sight and out of mind – had not been softened, or, as it were, half hidden, by any ambiguous phrase. 'You have had your cake, and eaten it – eaten it greedily. Is not that sufficient for you? Would you eat your cake twice? Would you have a succession of cakes? No, my friend; there is no succession of these cakes for those who eat them greedily. Your proposition is not a fair one, and we who have the whip-hand of you will not listen to it. Be good enough to vanish. Permit yourself to be swept quietly into the dunghill. All that there was about you of value has departed from you; and allow me to say that you are now – rubbish.' And then the ruthless besom comes with irresistible rush, and the rubbish is swept into the pit, there to be hidden for ever from the sight. And the pity of it is this – that a man, if he will only restrain his greed, may eat his cake and yet have it;

aye, and in so doing will have twice more the flavour of the cake than he who with gormandizing maw will devour his dainty all at once. Cakes in this world will grow by being fed on, if only the feeder be not too insatiate. On all which wisdom Mr. Sowerby pondered with sad heart and very melancholy mind as he walked away from the premises of Messrs. Gumption & Gagebee. His intention had been to go down to the House after leaving Mr. Fothergill, but the prospect of immediate ruin had been too much for him, and he knew that he was not fit to be seen at once among the haunts of men. And he had intended also to go down to Barchester early on the following morning – only for a few hours, that he might make further arrangements respecting that bill which Robarts had accepted for him. That bill – the second one – had now become due, and Mr. Tozer had been with him.

'Now it ain't no use in life, Mr. Sowerby,' Tozer had said. 'I ain't got the paper myself, nor didn't 'old it, not two hours. It went away through Tom Tozer; you knows that, Mr. Sowerby, as well as I do.' Now, whenever Tozer, Mr. Sowerby's Tozer, spoke of Tom Tozer, Mr. Sowerby knew that seven devils were being evoked, each worse than the first devil. Mr. Sowerby did feel something like sincere regard, or rather love, for that poor parson whom he had inveigled into mischief, and would fain save him, if it were possible, from the Tozer fang. Mr. Forrest, of the Barchester bank, would probably take up that last five hundred pound bill, on behalf of Mr. Robarts, – only it would be needful that he, Sowerby, should run down and see that this was properly done. As to the other bill – the former and lesser one – as to that, Mr. Tozer would probably be quiet for a while. Such had been Sowerby's programme for these two days; but now – what further possibility was there now that he should care for Robarts, or any other human being; he that was to be swept at once into the dung-heap? In this frame of mind he walked up South Audley Street, and crossed one side of Grosvenor Square, and went almost mechanically into Green Street. At the farther end of Green Street, near to Park Lane, lived Mr. and Mrs. Harold Smith.

CHAPTER XXVIII

Dr. Thorne

WHEN Miss Dunstable met her friends the Greshams – young Frank Gresham and his wife – at Gatherum Castle, she immediately asked after one Dr. Thorne, who was Mrs. Gresham's uncle. Dr. Thorne was an old bachelor, in whom both as a man and a doctor Miss Dunstable was inclined to place much confidence. Not that she had ever entrusted the cure of her bodily ailments to Dr. Thorne – for she kept a doctor of her own, Dr. Easyman, for this purpose – and it may moreover be said that she rarely had bodily ailments requiring the care of any doctor. But she always spoke of Dr. Thorne among her friends as a man of wonderful erudition and judgement; and had once or twice asked and acted on his advice in matters of much moment. Dr. Thorne was not a man accustomed to the London world; he kept no house there, and seldom even visited the metropolis; but Miss Dunstable had known him at Greshamsbury, where he lived, and there had for some months past grown up a considerable intimacy between them. He was now staying at the house of his niece, Mrs. Gresham; but the chief reason of his coming up had been a desire expressed by Miss Dunstable, that he should do so. She had wished for his advice; and at the instigation of his niece he had visited London and given it. The special piece of business as to which Dr. Thorne had thus been summoned from the bedsides of his country patients, and especially from the bedside of Lady Arabella Gresham, to whose son his niece was married, related to certain large money interests, as to which one might have imagined that Dr. Thorne's advice would not be peculiarly valuable. He had never been much versed in such matters on his own account, and was knowing neither in the ways of the share market, nor in the prices of land. But Miss Dunstable was a lady accustomed to have her own way, and to be indulged in her own wishes without being called on to give adequate reasons for them. 'My dear,' she had said to young Mrs. Gresham, 'if your uncle don't come up to London now, when I make such a point of it, I shall think that he is a bear and a savage; and I certainly will never speak to him again, – or to Frank – or to you; so you had better see to it.' Mrs. Gresham had not probably taken her friend's threat as meaning quite all that it threatened. Miss Dunstable habitually used strong language; and those who knew her well, generally understood when she was to be taken as expressing her thoughts by figures of speech. In this instance she had not meant it all; but, nevertheless, Mrs. Gresham had used violent influence in bringing the poor doctor up to London. 'Besides,' said Miss Dunstable, 'I have resolved on having the doctor at my conversazione, and if he won't come of himself, I shall go down and fetch him. I have set my heart on trumping my dear friend Mrs. Proudie's best card; so I mean to get everybody!'

The upshot of all this was, that the doctor did come up to town, and remained the best part of a week at his niece's house in Portman Square – to the great disgust of the Lady Arabella, who conceived that she must die if neglected for three days. As to the matter of business, I have no doubt but that he was of great use. He was possessed of common sense and an honest purpose; and I am inclined to think that they are often a sufficient counterpoise to a considerable amount of worldly experience. If one could have the worldly experience also –! True! but then it is so difficult to get everything. But with that special matter of business we need not have any further concern. We will presume it to have been discussed and completed, and will now dress ourselves for Miss Dunstable's conversazione. But it must not be supposed that she was so poor in genius as to call her party openly by a name borrowed for the nonce from Mrs. Proudie. It was only among her specially intimate friends, Mrs. Harold Smith and some few dozen others, that she indulged in this little joke. There had been nothing in the least pretentious about the card with which she summoned her friends to her house on this occasion. She had merely signified in some ordinary way, that she would be glad to see them as soon after nine o'clock on Thursday evening, the – instant, as might be convenient. But all the world understood that all the world was to be gathered together at Miss Dunstable's house on the night in question – that an effort was to be made to bring together people of all classes, gods and giants, saints and sinners, those rabid through the strength of their morality, such as our dear friend Lady Lufton, and those who were rabid in the opposite direction, such as Lady Hartletop, the Duke of Omnium, and Mr. Sowerby. An orthodox martyr had been caught from the East, and an oily latter-day St. Paul, from the other side of the water – to the horror and amazement of Archdeacon Grantly, who had come up all the way from Plumstead to be present on the occasion. Mrs. Grantly also had hankered to be there; but when she heard of the presence of the latter-day St. Paul, she triumphed loudly over her husband, who had made no offer to take her. That Lords Brock and De Terrier were to be at the gathering was nothing. The pleasant king of the gods and the courtly chief of the giants could shake hands with each other in any house with the greatest pleasure; but men were to meet who, in reference to each other, could shake nothing but their heads or their fists. Supplehouse was to be there, and Harold Smith, who now hated his enemy with a hatred surpassing that of women – or even of politicians. The minor gods, it was thought, would congregate together in one room, very bitter in their present state of banishment; and the minor giants in another, terribly loud in their triumph. That is the fault of the giants, who, otherwise, are not bad fellows; they are unable to endure the weight of any temporary success. When attempting Olympus – and this work of attempting is doubtless their natural condition – they scratch and scramble, diligently using both toes and fingers, with a mixture of good-humoured virulence and self-satisfied industry that is gratifying to all parties. But whenever their efforts are unexpectedly, and for themselves unfortunately successful, they are so taken aback that they lose the power of behaving themselves with even gigantesque propriety.

Such, so great and so various, was to be the intended gathering at Miss Dunstable's house. She herself laughed, and quizzed herself – speaking of the affair to Mrs. Harold Smith as though it were an excellent joke, and to Mrs. Proudie as though she were simply emulous of rivalling those world-famous assemblies in Gloucester Place; but the town at large knew that an effort was being made, and it was supposed that even Miss Dunstable was somewhat nervous. In spite of her excellent joking it was presumed that she would be unhappy if she failed. To Mrs. Frank Gresham she did speak with some little seriousness. 'But why on earth should you give yourself all this trouble?' that lady had said, when Miss Dunstable owned that she was doubtful, and unhappy in her doubts, as to the coming of one of the great colleagues of Mr. Supplehouse. 'When such hundreds are coming, big wigs and little wigs of all shades, what can it matter whether Mr. Towers be there or not?' But Miss Dunstable had answered almost with a screech, –

'My dear, it will be nothing without him. You don't understand; but the fact is that Tom Towers is everybody and everything at present.' And then, by no means for the first time, Mrs. Gresham began to lecture her friend as to her vanity; in answer to which lecture Miss Dunstable mysteriously hinted, that if she were only allowed her full swing on this occasion, – if all the world would now indulge her, she would – She did not quite say what she would do, but the inference drawn by Mrs. Gresham was this: that if the incense now offered on the altar of Fashion were accepted, Miss Dunstable would at once abandon the pomps and vanities of this wicked world, and all the sinful lusts of the flesh.

'But the doctor will stay, my dear? I hope I may look on that as fixed.' Miss Dunstable, in making this demand on the doctor's time, showed an energy quite equal to that with which she invoked the gods that Tom Towers might not be absent. Now, to tell the truth, Dr. Thorne had at first thought it very unreasonable that he should be asked to remain up in London in order that he might be present at an evening party, and had for a while pertinaciously refused; but when he learned that three or four prime ministers were expected, and that it was possible that even Tom Towers might be there in the flesh, his philosophy also had become weak, and he had written to Lady Arabella to say that his prolonged absence for two days further must be endured, and that the mild tonics, morning and evening, might be continued. But why should Miss Dunstable be so anxious that Dr. Thorne should be present on this grand occasion? Why, indeed, should she be so frequently inclined to summon him away from his country practice, his compounding board, and his useful ministrations to rural ailments? The doctor was connected with her by no ties of blood. Their friendship, intimate as it was, had as yet been but of short date. She was a very rich woman, capable of purchasing all manner of advice and good counsel, whereas he was so far from being rich, that any continued disturbance to his practice might be inconvenient to him. Nevertheless, Miss Dunstable seemed to have no more compunction in making calls upon his time than she might have felt had he been her brother. No ideas on this matter suggested themselves to the doctor himself. He was a simple-minded man, taking things as they came, and especially so taking things that came pleasantly. He liked Miss Dunstable, and was gratified by her friendship, and did not think of asking himself whether she had a right to put him to trouble and inconvenience. But such ideas did occur to Mrs. Gresham, the doctor's niece. Had Miss Dunstable any object, and if so, what object? Was it simply veneration for the doctor, or was it caprice? Was it eccentricity – or could it possibly be love? In speaking of the ages of these two friends it may be said in round terms that the lady was well past forty, and that the gentleman was well past fifty. Under such circumstances could it be love? The lady, too, was one who had had offers almost by the dozen, – offers from men of rank, from men of fashion, and from men of power; from men endowed with personal attractions, with pleasant manners, with cultivated tastes, and with eloquent tongues. Not only had she loved none such, but by none such had she been cajoled into an idea that it was possible that she could love them. That Dr. Thorne's tastes were cultivated, and his manners pleasant, might probably be admitted by three or four old friends in the country who valued him; but the world in London, that world to which Miss Dunstable was accustomed, and which was apparently becoming dearer to her day by day, would not have regarded the doctor as a man likely to become the object of a lady's passion. But nevertheless the idea did occur to Mrs. Gresham. She had been brought up at the elbow of this country practitioner; she had lived with him as though she had been his daughter; she had been for years the ministering angel of his household; and, till her heart had opened to the natural love of womanhood, all her closest sympathies had been with him. In her eyes the doctor was all but perfect; and it did not seem to her to be out of the question that Miss Dunstable should have fallen in love with her uncle.

Miss Dunstable once said to Mrs. Harold Smith that it was possible that she might marry, the only condition then expressed being this, that the man elected should be one who was quite indifferent as to money. Mrs. Harold Smith, who, by her friends, was presumed to know the world with tolerable accuracy, had replied that such a man Miss Dunstable would never find in this world. All this had passed in that half-comic vein of banter which Miss Dunstable so commonly used when conversing with such friends as Mrs. Harold Smith; but she had spoken words of the same import more than once to Mrs. Gresham; and Mrs. Gresham, putting two and two together as women do, had made four of the little sum; and as the final result of the calculation, determined that Miss Dunstable would marry Dr. Thorne if Dr. Thorne would ask her. And then Mrs. Gresham began to bethink herself of two other questions. Would it be well that her uncle should marry Miss Dunstable? and if so, would it be possible to induce him to make such a proposition? After the consideration of many pros and cons, and the balancing of very various arguments, Mrs. Gresham thought that the arrangement on the whole might not be a bad one. For Miss Dunstable she herself had a sincere affection, which was shared by her husband. She had often grieved at the sacrifices Miss Dunstable made to the world, thinking that her friend was falling into vanity, indifference, and an ill mode of life; but such a marriage as this would probably cure all that. And then as to Dr. Thorne himself, to whose benefit were of course applied Mrs. Gresham's most earnest thoughts in this matter, she could not but think that he would be happier married than he was single. In point of temper, no woman could stand higher than Miss Dunstable; no one had ever heard of her being in an ill-humour; and then though Mrs. Gresham was gifted with a mind which was far removed from being mercenary, it was impossible not to feel that some benefit must accrue from the bride's wealth. Mary Thorne, the present Mrs.

Frank Gresham, had herself been a great heiress. Circumstances had weighted her hand with enormous possessions, and hitherto she had not realized the truth of that lesson which would teach us to believe that happiness and riches are incompatible. Therefore she resolved that it might be well if the doctor and Miss Dunstable were brought together. But could the doctor be induced to make such an offer? Mrs. Gresham acknowledged a terrible difficulty in looking at the matter from that point of view. Her uncle was fond of Miss Dunstable; but she was sure that an idea of such a marriage had never entered his head; that it would be very difficult – almost impossible – to create such an idea; and that if the idea were there, the doctor could hardly be instigated to make the proposition. Looking at the matter as a whole, she feared that the match was not practicable.

On the day of Miss Dunstable's party, Mrs. Gresham and her uncle dined together alone in Portman Square. Mr. Gresham was not yet in Parliament, but an almost immediate vacancy was expected in his division of the county, and it was known that no one could stand against him with any chance of success. This threw him much among the politicians of his party – those giants, namely, whom it would be his business to support – and on this account he was a good deal away from his own house at the present moment. 'Politics make a terrible demand on a man's time,' he said to his wife; and then went down to dine at his club in Pall Mall, with sundry other young philogeants. On men of that class politics do make a great demand – at the hour of dinner and thereabouts.

'What do you think of Miss Dunstable?' said Mrs. Gresham to her uncle, as they sat together over their coffee. She added nothing to the question, but asked it in all its baldness.

'Think about her!' said the doctor; 'well, Mary, what do you think about her? I dare say we think the same.'

'But that's not the question. What do you think about her? Do you think she's honest?'

'Honest? Oh, yes, certainly – very honest, I should say.'

'And good-tempered?'

'Uncommonly good-tempered.'

'And affectionate?'

'Well, yes; and affectionate. I should certainly say that she is affectionate.'

'I'm sure she's clever.'

'Yes, I think she's clever.'

'And, and—and womanly in her feelings.' Mrs. Gresham felt that she could not quite say lady-like, though she would fain have done so had she dared.

'Oh, certainly,' said the doctor. 'But, Mary, why are you dissecting Miss Dunstable's character with so much ingenuity?'

'Well, uncle, I will tell you why; because –' and Mrs. Gresham, while she was speaking, got up from her chair, and going round the table to her uncle's side, put her arm round his neck till her face was close to his, and then continued speaking as she stood behind him out of his sight – 'because – I think that Miss Dunstable is – is very fond of you; and that it would make her happy if you would – ask her to be your wife.'

'Mary!' said the doctor, turning round with an endeavour to look his niece in the face.

'I am quite in earnest, uncle – quite in earnest. From little things that she has said, and little things that I have seen, I do believe what I now tell you.'

'And you want me to –'

'Dear uncle; my own one darling uncle, I want you only to do that which will make you – make you happy. What is Miss Dunstable to me compared to you?' And then she stooped down and kissed him. The doctor was apparently too much astounded by the intimation given him to make any further immediate reply. His niece, seeing this, left him that she might go and dress; and when they met again in the drawing-room Frank Gresham was with them.

CHAPTER XXIX

Miss Dunstable at Home

MISS DUNSTABLE did not look like a love-lorn maiden, as she stood in a small ante-chamber at the top of her drawing-room stairs, receiving her guests. Her house was one of those abnormal mansions, which are to be seen here and there in London, built in compliance rather with the rules of rural architecture, than with those which usually govern the erection of city streets and town terraces. It stood back from its brethren, and alone, so that its owner could walk round it. It was approached by a short carriage-way; the chief door was in the back of the building; and the front of the house looked on to one of the parks. Miss Dunstable in procuring it had had her usual luck. It had been built by an eccentric millionaire at an enormous cost; and the eccentric millionaire, after living in it for twelve months, had declared that it did not possess a single comfort, and that it was deficient in most of those details which, in point of house accommodation, are necessary to the very existence of man. Consequently the mansion was sold, and Miss Dunstable was the purchaser. Cranbourn House it had been named, and its present owner had made no change in this respect; but the world at large very generally called it Ointment Hall, and Miss Dunstable herself as frequently used that name for it as any other. It was impossible to quiz Miss Dunstable with any success, because she always joined in the joke herself. Not a word further had passed between Mrs. Gresham and Dr. Thorne on the subject of their last conversation; but the doctor as he entered the lady's portals amongst a tribe of servants and in a glare of light, and saw the crowd before him and the crowd behind him, felt that it was quite impossible that he should ever be at home there. It might be all right that a Miss Dunstable should live in this way, but it could not be right that the wife of Dr. Thorne should so live. But all this was a matter of the merest speculation, for he was well aware – as he said to himself a dozen times – that his niece had blundered strangely in her reading of Miss Dunstable's character.

When the Gresham party entered the ante-room into which the staircase opened, they found Miss Dunstable standing there surrounded by a few of her most intimate allies. Mrs. Harold Smith was sitting quite close to her; Dr. Easyman was reclining on a sofa against the wall, and the lady who habitually lived with Miss Dunstable was by his side. One or two others were there also, so that a little running conversation was kept up in order to relieve Miss Dunstable of the tedium which might otherwise be engendered by the work she had in hand. As Mrs. Gresham, leaning on her husband's arm, entered the room, she saw the back of Mrs. Proudie, as that lady made her way through the opposite door, leaning on the arm of the bishop. Mrs. Harold Smith had apparently recovered from the annoyance which she must no doubt have felt when Miss Dunstable so utterly rejected her suit on behalf of her brother. If any feeling had existed, even for a day, calculated to put a stop to the intimacy between the two ladies, that feeling had altogether died away, for Mrs. Harold Smith was conversing with her friend, quite in the old way. She made some remark on each of the guests as they passed by, and apparently did so in a manner satisfactory to the owner of the house, for Miss Dunstable answered with her kindest smiles, and in that genial, happy tone of voice which gave its peculiar character to her good humour: 'She is quite convinced that you are a mere plagiarist in what you are doing,' said Mrs. Harold Smith, speaking of Mrs. Proudie.

'And so I am. I don't suppose there can be anything very original nowadays about an evening party.'

'But she thinks you are copying her.'

'And why not? I copy everybody that I see, more or less. You did not at first begin to wear big petticoats out of your own head? If Mrs. Proudie has any such pride as that, pray don't rob her of it. Here's the doctor and the Greshams. Mary, my darling, how are you?' and in spite of all her grandeur of apparel, Miss Dunstable took hold of Mrs. Gresham and kissed her – to the disgust of the dozen and a half of the distinguished fashionable world who were passing up the stairs behind. The doctor was somewhat repressed in his mode of address by the communication which had so lately been made to him. Miss Dunstable was now standing on the very top of the pinnacle of wealth, and seemed to him to be not only so much above his reach, but also so far removed from his track in life, that he could not in any way put himself on a level with her. He could neither aspire so high nor descend so low; and thinking of this he spoke to Miss Dunstable as though there were some great distance between them, – as though there had been no hours of intimate friendship down at Greshamsbury. There had been such hours, during which Miss Dunstable and Dr. Thorne had lived as though they belonged to the same world: and this at any rate may be said of Miss Dunstable, that she had no idea of forgetting them.

Dr. Thorne merely gave her his hand, and then prepared to pass on.

'Don't go, doctor,' she said; 'for heaven's sake, don't go yet. I don't know when I may catch you if you get in there. I shan't be able to follow you for the next two hours. Lady Meredith, I am so much obliged to you for coming – your mother will be here, I hope. Oh, I am so glad! From her you know that is quite a favour. You, Sir George, are half a sinner yourself, so I don't think so much about it.'

'Oh, quite so,' said Sir George; 'perhaps rather the largest half.'

'The men divide the world into gods and giants,' said Miss Dunstable. 'We women have our divisions also. We are saints or sinners according to our party. The worst of it is, that we rat almost as often as you do.' Whereupon Sir George laughed and passed on.

'I know, doctor, you don't like this kind of thing,' she continued, 'but there is no reason why you should indulge yourself altogether in your own way, more than another – is there, Frank?'

'I am not so sure but he does like it,' said Mr. Gresham. 'There are some of your reputed friends whom he owns that he is anxious to see.'

'Are there? Then there is some hope of his ratting too. But he'll never make a good staunch sinner; will he, Mary? You're too old to learn new tricks; eh, doctor?'

'I am afraid I am,' said the doctor, with a faint laugh.

'Does Doctor Thorne rank himself among the army of saints?' asked Mrs. Harold Smith.

'Decidedly,' said Miss Dunstable. 'But you must always remember that there are saints of different orders; are there not, Mary? and nobody supposes that the Franciscans and the Dominicans agree very well together. Dr. Thorne does not belong to the school of St. Proudie, of Barchester; he would prefer the priestess whom I see coming round the corner of the staircase, with a very famous young novice at her elbow.'

'From all that I can hear, you will have to reckon Miss Grantly among the sinners,' said Mrs. Harold Smith – seeing that Lady Lufton with her young friend was approaching – 'unless, indeed, you can make a saint of Lady Hartletop.' And then Lady Lufton entered the room, and Miss Dunstable came forward to meet her with more quiet respect in her manner than she had as yet shown to many of her guests. 'I am much obliged to you for coming, Lady Lufton,' she said, 'and the more so, for bringing Miss Grantly with you.' Lady Lufton uttered some pretty little speech, during which Dr. Thorne came up and shook hands with her; as did also Frank Gresham and his wife. There was a county acquaintance between the Framley people and the Greshamsbury people, and therefore there was a little general conversation before Lady Lufton passed out of the small room into what Mrs. Proudie would have called the noble suite of apartments. 'Papa will be here,' said Miss Grantly; 'at least so I understand. I have not seen him yet myself.'

'Oh, yes, he has promised me,' said Miss Dunstable; 'and the archdeacon, I know, will keep his word. I should by no means have the proper ecclesiastical balance without him.'

'Papa always does keep his word,' said Miss Grantly, in a tone that was almost severe. She had not at all understood poor Miss Dunstable's little joke, or at any rate she was too dignified to respond to it.

'I understand that old Sir John is to accept the Chiltern Hundreds at once,' said Lady Lufton, in a half whisper to Frank Gresham.

Lady Lufton had always taken a keen interest in the politics of East Barsetshire, and was now desirous of expressing her satisfaction that a Gresham should again sit for the county. The Greshams had been old county members in Barsetshire, time out of mind.

'Oh, yes; I believe so,' said Frank, blushing. He was still young enough to feel almost ashamed of putting himself forward for such high honours.

'There will be no contest, of course,' said Lady Lufton, confidentially. 'There seldom is in East Barsetshire, I am happy to say. But if there were, every tenant at Framley would vote on the right side; I can assure you of that. Lord Lufton was saying so to me only this morning.' Frank Gresham made a pretty little speech in reply, such as young sucking politicians are expected to make; and this, with sundry other small courteous murmurings, detained the Lufton party for a minute or two in the ante-chamber. In the meantime the world was pressing on and passing through to the four or five large reception-rooms – the noble suite which was already piercing poor Mrs. Proudie's heart with envy to the very core. 'These are the sort of rooms,' she said to herself unconsciously, 'which ought to be provided by the country for the use of its bishops.'

'But the people are not brought enough together,' she said to her lord.

'No, no; I don't think they are,' said the bishop.

'And that is so essential for a conversazione,' continued Mrs. Proudie. 'Now in Gloucester Place –' But we will not record all her adverse criticisms, as Lady Lufton is waiting for us in the ante-room. And now another arrival of moment had taken place; – an arrival indeed of very great moment. To tell the truth, Miss Dunstable's heart had been set upon having two special persons; and though no stone had been left unturned, – no stone which could be turned with discretion, – she was still left in doubt as to both these two wondrous potentates. At the very moment of which we are now speaking, light and airy as she appeared to be – for it was her character to be light and airy – her mind was torn with doubts. If the wished-for two would come, her evening would be thoroughly successful; but if not, all her trouble would have been thrown away, and the thing would have been a failure; and there were circumstances connected with the present assembly which made Miss Dunstable very anxious that she should not fail. That the two great ones of the earth were Tom Towers of the *Jupiter*, and the Duke of Omnium, need hardly be expressed in words. And now, at this very moment, as Lady Lufton was making her civil speeches to young Gresham, apparently in no hurry to move on, and while Miss Dunstable was endeavouring to whisper something into the doctor's ear, which would make him feel himself at home in this new world, a sound was heard which made that lady know that half her wish had at any rate been granted to her. A sound was heard – but only by her own and one other attentive pair of ears. Mrs. Harold Smith had also caught the name, and knew that the duke was approaching. There was great glory and triumph in this; but why had his grace come at so unchancy a moment? Miss Dunstable had been fully aware of the impropriety of bringing Lady Lufton and the Duke of Omnium into the same house at the same time; but when she had asked Lady Lufton, she had been led to believe that there was no hope of obtaining the duke; and then, when that hope had dawned upon her, she had comforted herself with the reflection that the two suns, though they might for some few minutes be in the same hemisphere, could hardly be expected to clash, or come across each other's orbits. Her rooms were large and would be crowded; the duke would probably do little more than walk through them once, and Lady Lufton would certainly be surrounded by persons of her own class. Thus Miss Dunstable had comforted herself. But now all things were going wrong, and Lady Lufton would find herself in close contiguity to the nearest representative of Satanic agency, which, according to her ideas, was allowed to walk this nether English world of ours. Would she scream? or indignantly retreat out of the house? – or would she proudly raise her head, and with outstretched hand and audible voice, boldly defy the devil and all his works? In thinking of these things as the duke approached Miss Dunstable almost lost her presence of mind. But Mrs. Harold Smith did not lose hers. 'So here at last is the duke,' she said, in a tone intended to catch the express attention of Lady Lufton.

Mrs. Smith had calculated that there might still be time for her ladyship to pass on and avoid the interview. But Lady Lufton, if she heard the words, did not completely understand them. At any rate they did not convey to her mind at the moment the meaning they were intended to convey. She paused to whisper a last little speech to Frank Gresham, and then looking round, found that the gentleman who was pressing against her dress was – the Duke of Omnium! On this great occasion, when the misfortune could no longer be avoided, Miss Dunstable was by no means beneath herself or her character. She deplored the calamity, but she now saw that it was only left to her to make the best of it. The duke had honoured her by coming to her house, and she was bound to welcome him, though in doing so she should bring Lady Lufton to her last gasp. 'Duke,' she said, 'I am greatly honoured by this kindness on the part of your grace. I hardly expected that you would be so good to me.'

'The goodness is all on the other side,' said the duke, bowing over her hand. And then in the usual course of things this would have been all. The duke would have walked on and shown himself, would have said a word or two to Lady Hartletop, to the bishop, to Mr. Gresham, and such like, and would then have left the rooms by another way, and quietly escaped. This was the duty expected from him, and this he would have done, and the value of the party would have been increased thirty per cent. by such doing; but now, as it was, the newsmongers of the West End were likely to get much more out of him.

Circumstances had so turned out that he had absolutely been pressed close against Lady Lufton, and she, when she heard the voice, and was made positively acquainted with the fact of the great man's presence by Miss Dunstable's words, turned round quickly, but still with much feminine dignity, removing her dress from the contact. In doing this she was brought absolutely face to face with the duke, so that each could not but look full at the other. 'I beg your pardon,' said the duke. They were the only words that had ever passed between them, nor have they spoken to each other since; but simple as they were, accompanied by the little by-play of the speakers, they gave rise to a considerable amount of ferment in the fashionable world. Lady Lufton, as she retreated back on to Dr. Easyman, curtsied low; she curtsied low and slowly, and with a haughty arrangement of her drapery that was all her own; but the curtsy, though it was eloquent, did not say half so much, – did not reprobate the habitual iniquities of the duke with a voice nearly as potent, as that which was expressed in the gradual fall of her eye and the gradual pressure of her lips. When she commenced her curtsy she was looking full in her foe's face. By the time that she had completed it her eyes were turned upon the ground, but there was an ineffable amount of scorn expressed in the lines of her mouth. She spoke no word, and retreated, as modest virtue and feminine weakness must ever retreat, before barefaced vice and virile power; but nevertheless she was held by all the world to have had the best of the encounter. The duke, as he begged her pardon, wore in his countenance that expression of modified sorrow which is common to any gentleman who is supposed by himself to have incommoded a lady. But over and above this, – or rather under it, – there was a slight smile of derision, as though it were impossible for him to look upon the bearing of Lady Lufton without some amount of ridicule. All this was legible to eyes so keen as those of Miss Dunstable and Mrs. Harold Smith, and the duke was known to be a master of this silent inward sarcasm; but even by them, – by Miss Dunstable and Mrs. Harold Smith, – it was admitted that Lady Lufton had conquered. When her ladyship again looked up, the duke had passed on; she then resumed the care of Miss Grantly's hand, and followed in among the company.

'That is what I call unfortunate,' said Miss Dunstable, as soon as both belligerents had departed from the field of battle. 'The Fates sometimes will be against one.'

'But they have not been at all against you here,' said Mrs. Harold Smith. 'If you could arrive at her ladyship's private thoughts to-morrow morning, you would find her to be quite happy in having met the duke. It will be years before she has done boasting of her triumph, and it will be talked of by the young ladies of Framley for the next three generations.'

The Gresham party, including Dr. Thorne, had remained in the ante-chamber during the battle. The whole combat did not occupy above two minutes, and the three of them were hemmed off from escape by Lady Lufton's retreat into Dr. Easyman's lap; but now they, too, essayed to pass on.

'What, you will desert me,' said Miss Dunstable. 'Very well; but I shall find you out by and by. Frank, there is to be some dancing in one of the rooms, – just to distinguish the affair from Mrs. Proudie's conversazione. It would be stupid, you know, if all conversaziones were alike; wouldn't it? So I hope you will go and dance.'

'There will, I presume, be another variation at feeding time,' said Mrs. Harold Smith.

'Oh yes, certainly; I am the most vulgar of all wretches in that respect. I do love to set people eating and drinking. – Mr. Supplehouse, I am delighted to see you; but do tell me –' and then she whispered with great energy into the ear of Mr. Supplehouse, and Mr. Supplehouse again whispered into her ear. 'You think he will, then?' said Miss Dunstable. Mr. Supplehouse assented; he did think so; but he had no warrant for stating the circumstance as a fact. And then he passed on, hardly looking at Mrs. Harold Smith as he passed.

'What a hang-dog countenance he has,' said that lady.

'Ah, you're prejudiced, my dear, and no wonder; as for myself I always like Supplehouse. He means mischief; but then mischief is his trade, and he does not conceal it. If I were a politician I should as soon think of being angry with Mr. Supplehouse for turning against me as I am now with a pin for pricking me. It's my own awkwardness, and I ought to have known how to use the pin more craftily.'

'But you must detest a man who professes to stand by his party, and then does his best to ruin it.'

'So many have done that, my dear; and with much more success than Mr. Supplehouse! All is fair in love and war, – why not add politics to the list? If we could only agree to do that, it would save us from such a deal of heartburning, and would make none of us a bit the worse.'

Miss Dunstable's rooms, large as they were – 'a noble suite of rooms certainly, though perhaps a little too – too – too scattered, we will say, eh, bishop?' – were now nearly full, and would have been inconveniently crowded, were it not that many who came only remained for half an hour or so. Space, however, had been kept for the dancers – much to Mrs. Proudie's consternation. Not that she disapproved of dancing in London, as a rule; but she was indignant that the laws of a conversazione, as re-established by herself in the fashionable world, should be so violently infringed.

'Conversaziones will come to mean nothing,' she said to the bishop, putting great stress on the latter word, 'nothing at all, if they are to be treated in this way.'

'No, they won't, nothing in the least,' said the bishop.

'Dancing may be very well in its place,' said Mrs. Proudie.

'I have never objected to it myself; that is, for the laity,' said the bishop.

'But when people profess to assemble for higher objects,' said Mrs. Proudie, 'they ought to act up to their professions.'

'Otherwise they are no better than hypocrites,' said the bishop.

'A spade should be called a spade,' said Mrs. Proudie.

'Decidedly,' said the bishop, assenting.

'And when I undertook the trouble and expense of introducing conversaziones,' continued Mrs. Proudie, with an evident feeling that she had been ill-used, 'I had no idea of seeing the word so – so – so misinterpreted;' and then observing certain desirable acquaintances at the other side of the room, she went across, leaving the bishop to fend for himself.

Lady Lufton, having achieved her success, passed on to the dancing, whither it was not probable that her enemy would follow her, and she had not been there very long before she was joined by her son. Her heart at the present moment was not quite satisfied at the state of affairs with reference to Griselda. She had gone so far as to tell her young friend what were her own wishes; she had declared her desire that Griselda should become her daughter-in-law; but in answer to this Griselda herself had declared nothing. It was, to be sure, no more than natural that a young lady so well brought up as Miss Grantly should show no signs of a passion till she was warranted in showing them by the proceedings of the gentleman; but not-withstanding this, fully aware as she was of the propriety of such reticence – Lady Lufton did think that to her Griselda might have spoken some word evincing that the alliance would be satisfactory to her. Griselda, however, had spoken no such word, nor had she uttered a syllable to show that she would accept Lord Lufton if he did offer. Then again she had uttered no syllable to show that she would not accept him; but, nevertheless, although she knew that the world had been talking about her and Lord Dumbello, she stood up to dance with the future marquess on every possible occasion. All this did give annoyance to Lady Lufton, who began to bethink herself that if she could not quickly bring her little plan to a favourable issue, it might be well for her to wash her hands of it. She was still anxious for the match on her son's account. Griselda would, she did not doubt, make a good wife; but Lady Lufton was not so sure as she once had been that she herself would be able to keep up so strong a feeling for her daughter-in-law as she had hitherto hoped to do. 'Ludovic, have you been here long?' she said, smiling as she always did smile when her eyes fell upon her son's face.

'This instant arrived; and I hurried on after you, as Miss Dunstable told me that you were here. What a crowd she has! Did you see Lord Brock?'

'I did not observe him.'

'Or Lord De Terrier? I saw them both in the centre room.'

'Lord De Terrier did me the honour of shaking hands with me as I passed through.'

'I never saw such a mixture of people. There is Mrs. Proudie going out of her mind because you are all going to dance.'

'The Miss Proudies dance,' said Griselda Grantly.

'But not at conversaziones. You don't see the difference. And I saw Spermoil there, looking as pleased as Punch. He had quite a circle of his own round him, and was chattering away as though he were quite accustomed to the wickedness of the world.'

'There certainly are people here whom one would not have wished to meet, had one thought of it,' said Lady Lufton, mindful of her late engagement.

'But it must be all right, for I walked up the stairs with the archdeacon. That is an absolute proof, is it not, Miss Grantly?'

'I have no fears. When I am with your mother I know I must be safe.'

'I am not so sure of that,' said Lord Lufton, laughing. 'Mother, you hardly know the worst of it yet. Who is here, do you think?'

'I know whom you mean; I have seen him,' said Lady Lufton, very quietly.

'We came across him just at the top of the stairs,' said Griselda, with more animation in her face than ever Lord Lufton had seen there before.

'What; the duke?'

'Yes, the duke,' said Lady Lufton. 'I certainly should not have come had I expected to be brought in contact with that man. But it was an accident, and on such an occasion as this it could not be helped.' Lord Lufton at once perceived, by the tone of his mother's voice and by the shades of her countenance that she had absolutely endured some personal encounter with the duke, and also that she was by no means so indignant at the occurrence as might have been expected. There she was, still in Miss Dunstable's house, and expressing no anger as to Miss Dunstable's conduct. Lord Lufton could hardly have been more surprised had he seen the duke handing his mother down to supper; he said, however, nothing further on the subject.

'Are you going to dance, Ludovic?' said Lady Lufton.

'Well, I am not sure that I do not agree with Mrs. Proudie in thinking that dancing would contaminate a conversazione. What are your ideas, Miss Grantly?' Griselda was never very good at a joke, and imagined that Lord Lufton wanted to escape the trouble of dancing with her. This angered her. For the only species of love-making, or flirtation, or sociability between herself as a young lady, and any other self as a young gentleman, which recommended itself to her taste, was to be found in the amusement of dancing. She was altogether at variance with Mrs. Proudie on this matter, and gave Miss Dunstable great credit for her innovation. In society Griselda's toes were more serviceable to her than her tongue, and she was to be won by a rapid twirl much more probably than by a soft word. The offer of which she would approve would be conveyed by two all but breathless words during a spasmodic pause in a waltz; and then as she lifted up her arm to receive the accustomed support at her back, she might just find power enough to say, 'You – must ask – papa.' After that she would not care to have the affair mentioned till everything was properly settled.

'I have not thought about it,' said Griselda, turning her face away from Lord Lufton.

It must not, however, be supposed that Miss Grantly had not thought about Lord Lufton, or that she had not considered how great might be the advantage of having

Lady Lufton on her side if she made up her mind that she did wish to become Lord Lufton's wife. She knew well that now was her time for a triumph, now in this very first season of her acknowledged beauty; and she knew also that young, good-looking bachelor lords do not grow on hedges like blackberries. Had Lord Lufton offered to her, she would have accepted him at once without any remorse as to the greater glories which might appertain to a future Marchioness of Hartletop. In that direction she was not without sufficient wisdom. But then Lord Lufton had not offered to her, nor given any signs that he intended to do so; and to give Griselda Grantly her due, she was not a girl to make a first overture. Neither had Lord Dumbello offered; but he had given signs, – dumb signs, such as birds give to each other, quite as intelligible as verbal signs to a girl who preferred the use of her toes to that of her tongue. 'I have not thought about it,' said Griselda, very coldly, and at that moment a gentleman stood before her and asked her hand for the next dance. It was Lord Dumbello; and Griselda, making no reply except by a slight bow, got up and put her hand within her partner's arm.

'Shall I find you here, Lady Lufton, when we have done?' she said; and then started off among the dancers. When the work before one is dancing the proper thing for a gentleman to do is, at any rate, to ask a lady; this proper thing Lord Lufton had omitted, and now the prize was taken away from under his very nose.

There was clearly an air of triumph about Lord Dumbello as he walked away with the beauty. The world had been saying that Lord Lufton was to marry her, and the world had also been saying that Lord Dumbello admired her. Now this had angered Lord Dumbello, and made him feel as though he walked about, a mark of scorn, as a disappointed suitor. Had it not been for Lord Lufton, perhaps he would not have cared so much for Griselda Grantly; but circumstances had so turned out that he did care for her, and felt it to be encumbent upon him, as the heir to a marquisate, to obtain what he wanted, let who would have a hankering after the same article. It is in this way that pictures are so well sold at auctions; and Lord Dumbello regarded Miss Grantly as being now subject to the auctioneer's hammer, and conceived that Lord Lufton was bidding against him. There was, therefore, an air of triumph about him as he put his arm round Griselda's waist and whirled her up and down the room in obedience to the music. Lady Lufton and her son were left together looking at each other. Of course, he had intended to ask Griselda to dance, but it cannot be said that he very much regretted his disappointment. Of course also Lady Lufton had expected that her son and Griselda would stand up together, and she was a little inclined to be angry with her protégée. 'I think she might have waited a minute,' said Lady Lufton.

'But why, mother? There are certain things for which no one ever waits: to give a friend, for instance, the first passage through a gate out hunting, and such like. Miss Grantly was quite right to take the first that offered.' Lady Lufton had determined to learn what was to be the end of this scheme of hers. She could not have Griselda always with her, and if anything were to be arranged it must be arranged now, while both of them were in London. At the close of the season Griselda would return to Plumstead, and Lord Lufton would go – nobody as yet knew where. It would be useless to look forward to further opportunities. If they did not contrive to love each other now, they would never do so. Lady Lufton was beginning to fear that her plan would not work, but she made up her mind that she would learn the truth then and there – at least as far as her son was concerned.

'Oh, yes; quite so; – if it is equal to her with which she dances,' said Lady Lufton.

'Quite equal, I should think – unless it be that Dumbello is longer-winded than I am.'

'I am sorry to hear you speak of her in that way, Ludovic.'

'Why sorry, mother?'

'Because I had hoped – that you and she would have liked each other.' This she said in a serious tone of voice, tender and sad, looking up into his face with a plaintive gaze, as though she knew that she were asking of him some great favour.

'Yes, mother, I have known that you have wished that.'

'You have known it, Ludovic!'

'Oh, dear, yes; you are not at all sharp at keeping your secrets from me. And, mother, at one time, for a day or so, I thought that I could oblige you. You have been so good to me, that I would almost do anything for you.'

'Oh, no, no, no,' she said, deprecating his praise, and the sacrifice which he seemed to offer of his own hopes and aspirations. 'I would not for worlds have you do so for my sake. No mother ever had a better son, and my only ambition is for your happiness.'

'But, mother, she would not make me happy. I was mad enough for a moment to think that she could do so – for a moment I did think so. There was one occasion on which I would have asked her to take me, but –'

'But what, Ludovic?'

'Never mind; it passed away; and now I shall never ask her. Indeed I do not think she would have me. She is ambitious, and flying at higher game than I am. And I must say this for her, that she knows well what she is doing, and plays her cards as though she had been born with them in her hand.'

'You will never ask her?'

'No; mother; had I done so, it would have been for love of you – only for love of you.'

'I would not for worlds that you should do that.'

'Let her have Dumbello; she will make an excellent wife for him, just the wife that he will want. And you, you will have been so good to her in assisting her to such a matter.'

'But, Ludovic, I am so anxious to see you settled.'

'All in good time, mother!'

'Ah, but the good time is passing away. Years run so very quickly. I hope you think about marrying, Ludovic.'

'But, mother, what if I brought you a wife that you did not approve?'

'I will approve of anyone that you love; that is –'

'That is, if you love her also; eh, mother?'

'But I rely with such confidence on your taste. I know that you can like no one that is not ladylike and good.'

'Ladylike and good; will that suffice?' said he, thinking of Lucy Robarts.

'Yes; it will suffice, if you love her. I don't want you to care for money. Griselda will have a fortune that would have been convenient; but I do not wish you to care for that.' And thus, as they stood together in Miss Dunstable's crowded room, the mother and son settled between themselves that the Lufton-Grantly alliance treaty was not to be ratified. 'I suppose I must let Mrs. Grantly know,' said Lady Lufton to herself, as Griselda returned to her side. There had not been above a dozen words spoken between Lord Dumbello and his partner, but that young lady also had now fully made up her mind that the treaty above mentioned should never be brought into operation.

We must go back to our hostess, whom we should not have left for so long a time, seeing that this chapter is written to show how well she could conduct herself in great emergencies. She had declared that after awhile she would be able to leave her position near the entrance door, and find out her own peculiar friends among the crowd; but the opportunity for doing so did not come till very late in the evening. There was a continuation of arrivals; she was wearied to death with making little speeches, and had more than once declared that she must depute Mrs. Harold Smith to take her place. That Lady stuck to her through all her labours with admirable constancy, and made the work bearable. Without some such constancy on a friend's part, it would have been unbearable; and it must be acknowledged that this was much to the credit of Mrs. Harold Smith. Her own hopes with reference to the great heiress had all been shattered, and her answer had been given to her in very plain language. But, nevertheless, she was true to her friendship, and was almost as willing to endure fatigue on the occasion as though she had a sister-in-law's right in the house. At about one o'clock her brother came. He had not yet seen Miss Dunstable since the offer had been made, and had now with difficulty been persuaded by his sister to show himself.

'What can be the use?' said he. 'The game is up with me now;' – meaning, poor ruined ne'er-do-well, not only that that game with Miss Dunstable was up, but that the great game of his whole life was being brought to an uncomfortable termination.

'Nonsense,' said his sister; 'do you mean to despair because a man like the Duke of Omnium wants his money? What has been good security for him will be good security for another;' and then Mrs. Harold Smith made herself more agreeable than ever to Miss Dunstable.

When Miss Dunstable was nearly worn out, but was still endeavouring to buoy herself up by a hope of the still-expected great arrival – for she knew that the hero would show himself only at a very late hour if it were to be her good fortune that he showed himself at all – Mr. Sowerby walked up the stairs. He had schooled himself to go through this ordeal with all the cool effrontery which was at his command; but it was clearly to be seen that all his effrontery did not stand him in sufficient stead, and that the interview would have been embarrassing had it not been for the genuine good-humour of the lady. 'Here is my brother,' said Mrs. Harold Smith, showing by the tremulousness of the whisper that she looked forward to the meeting with some amount of apprehension.

'How do you do, Mr. Sowerby?' said Miss Dunstable, walking almost into the doorway to welcome him. 'Better late than never.'

'I have only just got away from the House,' said he, as he gave her his hand.

'Oh, I know well that you are *sans reproche* among senators – as Mr. Harold Smith is *sans peur*, – eh, my dear?'

'I must confess that you have contrived to be uncommonly severe upon them both,' said Mrs. Harold, laughing; 'and as regards poor Harold, most undeservedly so: Nathaniel is here, and may defend himself.'

'And no one is better able to do so on all occasions. But, my dear Mr. Sowerby, I am dying of despair. Do you think he'll come?'

'He? who?'

'You stupid man – as if there were more than one he! There were two, but the other has been.'

'Upon my word, I don't understand,' said Mr. Sowerby, now again at his ease. 'But can I do anything? shall I go and fetch anyone? Oh, Tom Towers; I fear I can't help you. But here he is at the foot of the stairs!' And then Mr. Sowerby stood back with his sister to make way for the great representative man of the age.

'Angels and ministers of grace assist me!' said Miss Dunstable. 'How on earth am I to behave myself? Mr. Sowerby, do you think that I ought to kneel down? My dear, will he have a reporter at his back in the royal livery?' And then Miss Dunstable advanced two or three steps – not into the doorway, as she had done for Mr. Sowerby – put out her hand, and smiled her sweetest on Mr. Towers, of the *Jupiter*.

'Mr. Towers,' she said, 'I am delighted to have this opportunity of seeing you in my own house.'

'Miss Dunstable, I am immensely honoured by the privilege of being here,' said he.

'The honour done is all conferred on me,' and she bowed and curtsied with very stately grace. Each thoroughly understood the badinage of the other; and then, in a few moments, they were engaged in very easy conversation.

'By the by, Sowerby, what do you think of this threatened dissolution?' said Tom Towers.

'We are all in the hands of Providence,' said Mr. Sowerby, striving to take the matter without any outward show of emotion. But the question was one of terrible import to him, and up to this time he had heard of no such threat. Nor had Mrs. Harold Smith, nor Miss Dunstable, nor had a hundred others who now either listened to the vaticinations of Mr. Towers, or to the immediate report made of them. But it is given to some men to originate such tidings, and the performance of the prophecy is often brought about by the authority of the prophet. On the following morning the rumour that there would be a dissolution was current in all high circles. 'They have no conscience in such matters; no conscience whatever,' said a small god, speaking of the giants – a small god, whose constituency was expensive. Mr. Towers stood there chatting for about twenty minutes, and then took his departure without making his way into the room. He had answered the purpose for which he had been invited, and left Miss Dunstable in a happy frame of mind.

'I am very glad that he came,' said Mrs. Harold Smith, with an air of triumph.

'Yes, I am glad,' said Miss Dunstable, 'though I am thoroughly ashamed that I should be so. After all, what good has he done to me or to anyone?' And having uttered this moral reflection she made her way into the rooms, and soon discovered Dr. Thorne standing by himself against the wall.

'Well, doctor,' she said, 'where are Mary and Frank? You do not look at all comfortable, standing here by yourself.'

'I am quite as comfortable as I expected, thank you,' said he. 'They are in the room somewhere, and, as I believe, equally happy.'

'That's spiteful in you, doctor, to speak in that way. What would you say if you were called on to endure all that I have gone through this evening?'

'There is no accounting for tastes, but I presume you like it.'

'I am not so sure of that. Give me your arm and let me get some supper. One always likes the idea of having done hard work, and one always likes to have been successful.'

'We all know that virtue is its own reward,' said the doctor.

'Well, that is something hard upon me,' said Miss Dunstable, as she sat down to table. 'And you really think that no good of any sort can come from my giving such a party as this?'

'Oh, yes; some people, no doubt, have been amused.'

'It is all vanity in your estimation,' said Miss Dunstable; 'vanity and vexation of spirit. Well; there is a good deal of the latter, certainly. Sherry, if you please. I would give anything for a glass of beer, but that is out of the question. Vanity and vexation of spirit! And yet I meant to do good.'

'Pray, do not suppose that I am condemning you, Miss Dunstable.'

'Ah, but I do suppose it. Not only you, but another also, whose judgement I care for, perhaps, more than yours; and that, let me tell you, is saying a great deal. You do condemn me, Dr. Thorne, and I also condemn myself. It is not that I have done wrong, but the game is not worth the candle.'

'Ah; that's the question.'

'The game is not worth the candle. And yet it was a triumph to have both the duke and Tom Towers. You must confess that I have not managed badly.' Soon after that the Greshams went away, and in an hour's time or so, Miss Dunstable was allowed to drag herself to her own bed.

That is the great question to be asked on all such occasions, 'Is the game worth the candle?'

CHAPTER XXX

The Grantly Triumph

IT has been mentioned cursorily – the reader, no doubt, will have forgotten it – that Mrs. Grantly was not specially invited by her husband to go up to town with a view of being present at Miss Dunstable's party. Mrs. Grantly said nothing on the subject, but she was somewhat chagrined; not on account of the loss she sustained with reference to that celebrated assembly, but because she felt that her daughter's affairs required the supervision of a mother's eye. She also doubted the final ratification of that Lufton-Grantly treaty, and, doubting it, she did not feel quite satisfied that her daughter should be left in Lady Lufton's hands. She had said a word or two to the archdeacon before he went up, but only a word or two, for she hesitated to trust him in so delicate a matter. She was, therefore, not a little surprised at receiving, on the second morning after her husband's departure, a letter from him desiring her immediate presence in London. She was surprised; but her heart was filled rather with hope than dismay, for she had full confidence in her daughter's discretion. On the morning after the party, Lady Lufton and Griselda had breakfasted together as usual, but each felt that the manner of the other was altered. Lady Lufton thought that her young friend was somewhat less attentive, and perhaps less meek in her demeanour than usual; and Griselda felt that Lady Lufton was less affectionate. Very little, however, was said between them, and Lady Lufton expressed no surprise when Griselda begged to be left alone at home, instead of accompanying her ladyship when the carriage came to the door. Nobody called in Bruton Street that afternoon – no one, at least, was let in – except the archdeacon. He came there late in the day, and remained with his daughter till Lady Lufton returned. Then he took his leave, with more abruptness than was usual with him, and without saying anything special to account for the duration of his visit. Neither did Griselda say anything special; and so the evening wore away, each feeling in some unconscious manner that she was on less intimate terms with the other than had previously been the case.

On the next day also Griselda would not go out, but at four o'clock a servant brought a letter to her from Mount Street. Her mother had arrived in London and wished to see her at once. Mrs. Grantly sent her love to Lady Lufton, and would call at half-past five, or at any later hour at which it might be convenient for Lady Lufton to see her. Griselda was to stay and dine in Mount Street; so said the letter. Lady Lufton declared that she would be very happy to see Mrs. Grantly at the hour named; and then, armed with this message, Griselda started for her mother's lodgings. 'I'll send the carriage for you,' said Lady Lufton. 'I suppose about ten will do.'

'Thank you,' said Griselda, 'that will do very nicely;' and then she went. Exactly at half-past five Mrs. Grantly was shown into Lady Lufton's drawing-room. Her daughter did not come with her, and Lady Lufton could see by the expression of her friend's face that business was to be discussed. Indeed, it was necessary that she herself should discuss business, for Mrs. Grantly must now be told that the family treaty could not be ratified. The gentleman declined the alliance, and poor Lady Lufton was uneasy in her mind at the nature of the task before her.

'Your coming up has been rather unexpected,' said Lady Lufton, as soon as her friend was seated on the sofa.

'Yes, indeed; I got a letter from the archdeacon only this morning, which made it absolutely necessary that I should come.'

'No bad news, I hope?' said Lady Lufton.

'No; I can't call it bad news. But, dear Lady Lufton, things won't always turn out exactly as one would have them.'

'No, indeed,' said her ladyship, remembering that it was incumbent on her to explain to Mrs. Grantly now at this present interview the tidings with which her mind was fraught. She would, however, let Mrs. Grantly first tell her own story, feeling, perhaps, that the one might possibly bear upon the other.

'Poor dear Griselda!' said Mrs. Grantly, almost with a sigh. 'I need not tell you, Lady Lufton, what my hopes were regarding her.'

'Has she told you anything – anything that –'

'She would have spoken to you at once – and it was due to you that she should have done so – but she was timid; and not unnaturally so. And then it was right that she should see her father and me before she quite made up her own mind. But I may say that it is settled now.'

'What is settled?' asked Lady Lufton.

'Of course it is impossible for anyone to tell beforehand how these things will turn out,' continued Mrs. Grantly, beating about the bush rather more than was necessary. 'The dearest wish of my heart was to see her married to Lord Lufton. I should so much have wished to have her in the same county with me, and such a match as that would have fully satisfied my ambition.' 'Well, I should rather think it might!' Lady Lufton did not say this out loud, but she thought it. Mrs. Grantly was absolutely speaking of a match between her daughter and Lord Lufton as though she would have displayed some amount of Christian moderation in putting up with it! Griselda Grantly might be a very nice girl; but even she – so thought Lady Lufton at the moment – might possibly be priced too highly.

'Dear Mrs. Grantly,' she said, 'I have foreseen for the last few days that our mutual hopes in this respect would not be gratified. Lord Lufton, I think; – but perhaps it is not necessary to explain – Had you not come up to town

I should have written to you, – probably to-day. Whatever may be dear Griselda's fate in life, I sincerely hope that she may be happy.'

'I think she will,' said Mrs. Grantly, in a tone that expressed much satisfaction.

'Has – has anything –'

'Lord Dumbello proposed to Griselda the other night, at Miss Dunstable's party,' said Mrs. Grantly, with her eyes fixed upon the floor, and assuming on the sudden much meekness in her manner; 'and his lordship was with the archdeacon yesterday, and again this morning, I fancy he is in Mount Street at the present moment.'

'Oh, indeed!' said Lady Lufton. She would have given worlds to have possessed at the moment sufficient self-command to have enabled her to express in her tone and manner unqualified satisfaction at the tidings. But she had not such self-command, and was painfully aware of her own deficiency.

'Yes,' said Mrs. Grantly. 'And as it is all so far settled, and as I know you are so kindly anxious about dear Griselda, I thought it right to let you know at once. Nothing can be more upright, honourable, and generous, than Lord Dumbello's conduct; and, on the whole, the match is one with which I and the archdeacon cannot but be contented.'

'It is certainly a great match,' said Lady Lufton. 'Have you seen Lady Hartletop yet?'

Now Lady Hartletop could not be regarded as an agreeable connexion, but this was the only word which escaped from Lady Lufton that could be considered in any way disparaging, and, on the whole, I think that she behaved well.

'Lord Dumbello is so completely his own master that that has not been necessary,' said Mrs. Grantly. 'The marquess has been told, and the archdeacon will see him either tomorrow or the day after.' There was nothing left for Lady Lufton but to congratulate her friend, and this she did in words perhaps not very sincere, but which, on the whole, were not badly chosen.

'I am sure I hope she will be very happy,' said Lady Lufton, 'and I trust that the alliance' – the word was very agreeable to Mrs. Grantly's ear – 'will give unalloyed gratification to you and to her father. The position which she is called to fill is a very splendid one, but I do not think that it is above her merits.' This was very generous, and so Mrs. Grantly felt it. She had expected that her news would be received with the coldest shade of civility, and she was quite prepared to do battle if there were occasion. But she had no wish for war, and was almost grateful to Lady Lufton for her cordiality.

'Dear Lady Lufton,' she said, 'it is so kind of you to say so. I have told no one else, and of course would tell no one till you knew it. No one has known her and understood her so well as you have done. And I can assure you of this, that there is no one to whose friendship she looks forward in her new sphere of life with half so much pleasure as she does to yours.' Lady Lufton did not say much further. She could not declare that she expected much gratification from an intimacy with the future Marchioness of Hartletop. The Hartletops and Luftons must, at any rate for her generation, live in a world apart, and she had now said all that her old friendship with Mrs. Grantly required. Mrs. Grantly understood all this quite as well as did Lady Lufton; but then Mrs. Grantly was much the better woman of the world. It was arranged that Griselda should come back to Bruton Street for the night, and that her visit should then be brought to a close.

'The archdeacon thinks that for the present I had better remain up in town,' said Mrs. Grantly, 'and under the very peculiar circumstances Griselda will be – perhaps more comfortable with me.' To this Lady Lufton entirely agreed; and so they parted, excellent friends, embracing each other in a most affectionate manner. That evening Griselda did return to Bruton Street, and Lady Lufton had to go through the further task of congratulating her. This was the more disagreeable of the two, especially so as it had to be thought over beforehand. But the young lady's excellent good sense and sterling qualities made the task comparatively an easy one. She neither cried, nor was impassioned, nor went into hysterics, nor showed any emotion. She did not even talk of her noble Dumbello, – her generous Dumbello. She took Lady Lufton's kisses almost in silence, thanked her gently for her kindness, and made no allusion to her own future grandeur.

'I think I should like to go to bed early,' she said, 'as I must see to my packing up.'

'Richards will do all that for you, my dear.'

'Oh, yes, thank you, nothing can be kinder than Richards. But I'll just see to my own dresses.' And so she went to bed early.

Lady Lufton did not see her son for the next two days, but when she did, of course she said a word or two about Griselda. 'You have heard the news, Ludovic?' she asked.

'Oh, yes; it's at all the clubs. I have been overwhelmed with presents of willow branches.'

'You, at any rate, have got nothing to regret,' she said.

'Nor you either, mother. I am sure that you do not think you have. Say that you do not regret it. Dearest mother, say so for my sake. Do you not know in your heart of hearts that she was not suited to be happy as my wife, – or to make me happy?'

'Perhaps not,' said Lady Lufton, sighing. And then she kissed her son, and declared to herself that no girl in England could be good enough for him.

CHAPTER XXXI

Salmon Fishing in Norway

LORD DUMBELLO'S engagement with Griselda Grantly was the talk of the town for the next ten days. It formed, at least, one of two subjects which monopolized attention, the other being that dreadful rumour, first put in motion by Tom Towers at Miss Dunstable's party, as to a threatened dissolution of Parliament. 'Perhaps, after all, it will be the best thing for us,' said Mr. Green Walker, who felt himself to be tolerably safe at Crewe Junction.

'I regard it as a most wicked attempt,' said Harold Smith, who was not equally secure in his own borough, and to whom the expense of an election was disagreeable. 'It is done in order that they may get time to tide over the autumn. They won't gain ten votes by a dissolution, and less than forty would hardly give them a majority. But they have no sense of public duty – none whatever. Indeed, I don't know who has.'

'No, by Jove; that's just it. That's what my aunt Lady Hartletop says; there is no sense of duty left in the world. By the by, what an uncommon fool Dumbello is making himself!' And then the conversation went off to that other topic.

Lord Lufton's joke against himself about the willow branches was all very well, and nobody dreamed that his heart was sore in that matter. The world was laughing at Lord Dumbello for what it chose to call a foolish match, and Lord Lufton's friends talked to him about it as though they had never suspected that he could have made an ass of himself in the same direction; but, nevertheless, he was not altogether contented. He by no means wished to marry Griselda; he had declared to himself a dozen times since he had first suspected his mother's manoeuvres that no consideration on earth should induce him to do so; he had pronounced her to be cold, insipid, and unattractive in spite of her beauty: and yet he felt almost angry that Lord Dumbello should have been successful. And this, too, was the more inexcusable, seeing that he had never forgotten Lucy Robarts, had never ceased to love her, and that, in holding those various conversations within his own bosom, he was as loud in Lucy's favour as he was in dispraise of Griselda.

'Your hero, then,' I hear some well-balanced critic say, 'is not worth very much.' In the first place Lord Lufton is not my hero; and in the next place, a man may be very imperfect and yet worth a great deal. A man may be as imperfect as Lord Lufton, and yet worthy of a good mother and a good wife. If not, how many of us are unworthy of the mothers and wives we have! It is my belief that few young men settle themselves down to the work of the world, to the begetting of children, and carving and paying and struggling and fretting for the same, without having first been in love with four or five possible mothers for them, and probably with two or three at the same time. And yet these men are, as a rule, worthy of the excellent wives that ultimately fall to their lot. In this way Lord Lufton had, to a certain extent, been in love with Griselda. There had been one moment in his life in which he would have offered her his hand, had not her discretion been so excellent; and though that moment never returned, still he suffered from some feeling akin to disappointment when he learned that Griselda had been won and was to be worn. He was, then, a dog in the manger, you will say. Well; and are we not all dogs in the manger more or less actively? Is not that manger-doggishness one of the most common phases of the human heart? But not the less was Lord Lufton truly in love with Lucy Robarts. Had he fancied that any Dumbello was carrying on a siege before that fortress, his vexation would have manifested itself in a very different manner. He could joke about Griselda Grantly with a frank face and a happy tone of voice; but had he heard of any tidings of a similar import with reference to Lucy, he would have been past all joking, and I much doubt whether it would not even have affected his appetite. 'Mother,' he said to Lady Lufton, a day or two after the declaration of Griselda's engagement, 'I am going to Norway to fish.'

'To Norway, – to fish!'

'Yes. We've got rather a nice party. Clontarf is going, and Culpepper –'

'What – that horrid man!'

'He's an excellent hand at fishing; and Haddington Peebles, and – and – there'll be six of us altogether; and we start this day week.'

'That's rather sudden, Ludovic.'

'Yes, it is sudden; but we're sick of London. I should not care to go so soon myself, but Clontarf and Culpepper say that the season is early this year. I must go down to Framley before I start – about my horses; and therefore I came to tell you that I shall be there to-morrow.'

'At Framley to-morrow! If you could put it off for three days I should be going myself.' But Lord Lufton could not put it off for three days. It may be that on this occasion he did not wish for his mother's presence at Framley while he was there; that he conceived that he should be more at his ease in giving orders about his stable if he were alone while so employed. At any rate he declined her company, and on the following morning did go down to Framley by himself.

'Mark,' said Mrs. Robarts, hurrying into her husband's book-room about the middle of the day, 'Lord Lufton is at home. Have you heard it?'

'What! here at Framley?'

'He is over at Framley Court; so the servants say. Carson saw him in the paddock with some of the horses. Won't you go and see him?'

'Of course I will,' said Mark, shutting up his papers. 'Lady Lufton can't be here, and if he is alone he will probably come and dine.'

'I don't know about that,' said Mrs. Robarts, thinking of poor Lucy.

'He is not in the least particular. What does for us will do for him. I shall ask him, at any rate.' And without further parley the clergyman took up his hat and went off in search of his friend. Lucy Robarts had been present when the gardener brought in tidings of Lord Lufton's arrival at Framley, and was aware that Fanny had gone to tell her husband.

'He won't come here, will he?' she said, as soon as Mrs. Robarts returned.

'I can't say,' said Fanny. 'I hope not. He ought not to do so, and I don't think he will. But Mark says that he will ask him to dinner.'

'Then, Fanny, I must be taken ill. There is nothing else for it.'

'I don't think he will come. I don't think he can be so cruel. Indeed, I feel sure that he won't; but I thought it right to tell you.' Lucy also conceived that it was improbable that Lord Lufton should come to the parsonage under the present circumstances; and she declared to herself that it would not be possible that she should appear at table if he did do so; but, nevertheless, the idea of his being at Framley was, perhaps, not altogether painful to her. She did not recognize any pleasure as coming to her from his arrival, but still there was something in his presence which was, unconsciously to herself, soothing to her feelings. But that terrible question remained; – How was she to act if it should turn out that he was coming to dinner?

'If he does come, Fanny,' she said, solemnly, after a pause, 'I must keep to my own room, and leave Mark to think what he pleases. It will be better for me to make a fool of myself there, than in his presence in the drawing-room.'

Mark Robarts took his hat and stick and went over at once to the home paddock, in which he knew that Lord Lufton was engaged with the horses and grooms. He also was in no supremely happy frame of mind, for his correspondence with Mr. Tozer was on the increase. He had received notice from that indefatigable gentleman that certain 'overdue bills' were now lying at the bank in Barchester, and were very desirous of his, Mr. Robarts's, notice. A concatenation of certain peculiarly unfortunate circumstances made it indispensably necessary that Mr. Tozer should be repaid, without further loss of time, the various sums of money which he had advanced on the credit of Mr. Robarts's name, &c. &c. &c. No absolute threat was put forth, and, singular to say, no actual amount was named. Mr. Robarts, however, could not but observe, with a most painfully accurate attention, that mention was made, not of an overdue bill, but of overdue bills. What if Mr. Tozer were to demand from him the instant repayment of nine hundred pounds? Hitherto he had merely written to Mr. Sowerby, and he might have had an answer from that gentleman this morning, but no such answer had as yet reached him. Consequently he was not, at the present moment, in a very happy frame of mind.

He soon found himself with Lord Lufton and the horses. Four or five of them were being walked slowly about the paddock in the care of as many men or boys, and the sheets were being taken off them – off one after another, so that their master might look at them with the more accuracy and satisfaction. But though Lord Lufton was thus doing his duty, and going through his work, he was not doing it with his whole heart, – as the head groom perceived very well. He was fretful about the nags, and seemed anxious to get them out of his sight as soon as he had made a decent pretext of looking at them. 'How are you, Lufton?' said Robarts, coming forward. 'They told me that you were down, and so I came across at once.'

'Yes; I only got here this morning, and should have been over with you directly. I am going to Norway for six weeks or so, and it seems that the fish are so early this year that we must start at once. I have a matter on which I want to speak to you before I leave; and, indeed, it was that which brought me down more than anything else.' There was something hurried and not altogether easy about his manner as he spoke, which struck Robarts, and made him think that this promised matter to be spoken of would not be agreeable in discussion. He did not know whether Lord Lufton might not again be mixed up with Tozer and the bills.

'You will dine with us to-day,' he said, 'if, as I suppose, you are all alone.'

'Yes, I am all alone.'

'Then you'll come?'

'Well, I don't quite know. No, I don't think I can go over to dinner. Don't look so disgusted. I'll explain it all to you just now.' What could there be in the wind; and how was it possible that Tozer's bill should make it inexpedient for Lord Lufton to dine at the parsonage? Robarts, however, said nothing further about it at the moment, but turned off to look at the horses.

'They are an uncommonly nice set of animals,' said he.

'Well, yes; I don't know. When a man has four or five horses to look at, somehow or other he never has one fit to go. That chestnut mare is a picture, now that nobody wants her; but she wasn't able to carry me well to hounds a single day last winter. Take them in, Pounce; that'll do.'

'Won't your lordship run your eye over the old black 'oss?' said Pounce, the head groom, in a melancholy tone; 'he's as fine, sir – as fine as a stag.'

'To tell you the truth, I think they're too fine; but that'll do; take them in. And now, Mark, if you're at leisure, we'll take a turn round the place.' Mark, of course, was at leisure, and so they started on their walk.

'You're too difficult to please about your stable,' Robarts began.

'Never mind the stable now,' said Lord Lufton. 'The truth is, I am not thinking about it. Mark,' he then said, very abruptly, 'I want you to be frank with me. Has your sister ever spoken to you about me?'

'My sister; Lucy?'

'Yes; your sister Lucy.'

'No, never; at least nothing especial; nothing that I can remember at this moment.'

'Nor your wife?'

'Spoken about you! – Fanny? Of course she has, in an ordinary way. It would be impossible that she should not. But what do you mean?'

'Have either of them told you that I made an offer to your sister?'

'That you made an offer to Lucy?'

'Yes, that I made an offer to Lucy.'

'No; nobody has told me so. I have never dreamed of such a thing; nor, as far as I believe, have they. If anybody has spread such a report, or said that either of them have hinted at such a thing, it is a base lie. Good heavens! Lufton, for what do you take them?'

'But I did,' said his lordship.

'Did what?' said the parson.

'I did make your sister an offer.'

'You made Lucy an offer of marriage!'

'Yes, I did; – in as plain language as a gentleman could use to a lady.'

'And what answer did she make?'

'She refused me. And now, Mark, I have come down here with the express purpose of making that offer again. Nothing could be more decided than your sister's answer. It struck me as being almost uncourteously decided. But still it is possible that circumstances may have weighed with her which ought not to weigh with her. If her love be not given to anyone else, I may still have a chance of it. It's the old story of faint heart, you know: at any rate, I mean to try my luck again; and thinking over it with deliberate purpose, I have come to the conclusion that I ought to tell you before I see her.'

Lord Lufton in love with Lucy! As these words repeated themselves over and over again within Mark Robarts's mind, his mind added to them notes of surprise without end. How had it possibly come about, – and why? In his estimation his sister Lucy was a very simple girl – not plain indeed, but by no means beautiful; certainly not stupid, but by no means brilliant. And then, he would have said, that of all men whom he knew, Lord Lufton would have been the last to fall in love with such a girl as his sister. And now, what was he to say or do? What views was he bound to hold? In what direction should he act? There was Lady Lufton on the one side, to whom he owed everything. How would life be possible to him in that parsonage – within a few yards of her elbow – if he consented to receive Lord Lufton as the acknowledged suitor of his sister? It would be a great match for Lucy, doubtless; but – Indeed, he could not bring himself to believe that Lucy could in truth become the absolute reigning queen of Framley Court.

'Do you think that Fanny knows anything of all this?' he said after a moment or two.

'I cannot possibly tell. If she does it is not with my knowledge. I should have thought that you could best answer that.'

'I cannot answer it at all,' said Mark. 'I, at least, have had no remotest idea of such a thing.'

'Your ideas of it now need not be at all remote,' said Lord Lufton, with a faint smile; 'and you may know it as a fact. I did make her an offer of marriage; I was refused; I am going to repeat it; and I am now taking you into my confidence, in order that, as her brother, and as my friend, you may give me such assistance as you can.' They then walked on in silence for some yards, after which Lord Lufton added: 'And now I'll dine with you to-day if you wish it.' Mr. Robarts did not know what to say; he could not bethink himself what answer duty required of him. He had no right to interfere between his sister and such a marriage, if she herself should wish it; but still there was something terrible in the thought of it! He had a vague conception that it must come to evil; that the project was a dangerous one; and that it could not finally result happily for any of them. What would Lady Lufton say? That undoubtedly was the chief source of his dismay.

'Have you spoken to your mother about this?' he said.

'My mother? no; why speak to her till I know my fate? A man does not like to speak much of such matters if there be a probability of his being rejected. I tell you because I do not like to make my way into your house under a false pretence.'

'But what would Lady Lufton say?'

'I think it probable that she would be displeased on the first hearing it; that in four-and-twenty hours she would be reconciled; and that after a week or so Lucy would be her dearest favourite and the Prime Minister of all her machinations. You don't know my mother as well as I do. She would give her head off her shoulders to do me a pleasure.'

'And for that reason,' said Mark Robarts, 'you ought, if possible, to do her pleasure.'

'I cannot absolutely marry a wife of her choosing, if you mean that,' said Lord Lufton. They went on walking about the garden for an hour, but they hardly got any farther than the point to which we have now brought them. Mark Robarts could not make up his mind on the spur of the moment; nor, as he said more than once to Lord Lufton, could he be at all sure that Lucy would in any way be guided by him. It was, therefore, at last settled between them that Lord Lufton should come to the parsonage immediately after breakfast on the following morning. It was agreed also that the dinner had better not come off, and Robarts promised that he would, if possible, have determined by the morning as to what advice he would give his sister. He went direct home to the parsonage from Framley Court, feeling that he was altogether in the dark till he should have consulted his wife. How would he feel if Lucy were to become Lady Lufton? and how would he look Lady Lufton in the face in telling her that such was to be his sister's destiny? On returning home he immediately found his wife, and had not been closeted with her five minutes before he knew, at any rate, all that she knew. 'And you mean to say that she does love him?' said Mark.

'Indeed she does; and is it not natural that she should? When I saw them so much together I feared that she would. But I never thought that he would care for her.' Even Fanny did not as yet give Lucy credit for half her attractiveness. After an hour's talking the interview between the husband and wife ended in a message to Lucy, begging her to join them both in the book-room.

'Aunt Lucy,' said a chubby little darling, who was taken up into his aunt's arms as he spoke, 'papa and mamma 'ant 'oo in the tuddy, and I mustn't go wis 'oo.' Lucy, as she kissed the boy and pressed his face against her own, felt that her blood was running quick to her heart.

'Musn't oo' go wis me, my own one?' she said as she put her playfellow down; but she played with the child only because she did not wish to betray, even to him, that she was hardly mistress of herself. She knew that Lord Lufton was at Framley; she knew that her brother had been to him; she knew that a proposal had been made that he should come there that day to dinner. Must it not, therefore, be the case that this call to a meeting in the study had arisen out of Lord Lufton's arrival at Framley? and yet, how could it have done so? Had Fanny betrayed her in order to prevent the dinner invitation? It could not be possible that Lord Lufton himself should have spoken on the subject! And then she again stooped to kiss the child, rubbed her hands across her forehead to smooth her hair, and erase, if that might be possible, the look of care which she wore, and then descended slowly to her brother's sitting-room. Her hand paused for a second on the door ere she opened it, but she had resolved that, come what might, she would be brave. She pushed it open and walked in with a bold front, with eyes wide open, and a slow step. 'Frank says that you want me,' she said. Mr. Robarts and Fanny were both standing up by the fireplace, and each waited a second for the other to speak, when Lucy entered the room, and then Fanny began, –

'Lord Lufton is here, Lucy.'

'Here! Where? At the parsonage?'

'No, not at the parsonage; but over at Framley Court,' said Mark.

'And he promises to call here after breakfast to-morrow,' said Fanny. And then again there was a pause. Mrs. Robarts hardly dared to look Lucy in the face. She had not betrayed her trust, seeing that the secret had been told to Mark, not by her, but by Lord Lufton; but she could not but feel that Lucy would think that she had betrayed it.

'Very well,' said Lucy, trying to smile; 'I have no objection in life.'

'But, Lucy, dear,' – and now Mrs. Robarts put her arm round her sister-in-law's waist – 'he is coming here especially to see you.'

'Oh; that makes a difference. I am afraid that I shall be—engaged.'

'He has told everything to Mark,' said Mrs. Robarts. Lucy now felt that her bravery was almost deserting her. She hardly knew which way to look or how to stand. Had Fanny told everything also? There was so much that Fanny knew that Lord Lufton could not have known. But, in truth, Fanny had told all – the whole story of Lucy's love, and had described the reasons which had induced her to reject her suitor; and had done so in words which, had Lord Lufton heard them, would have made him twice as passionate in his love. And then it certainly did occur to Lucy to think why Lord Lufton should have come to Framley and told all this history to her brother. She attempted for a moment to make herself believe that she was angry with him for doing so. But she was not angry. She had not time to argue much about it, but there came upon her a gratified sensation of having been remembered, and thought of, and – loved. Must it not be so?

Could it be possible that he himself would have told this tale to her brother, if he did not still love her? Fifty times she had said to herself that his offer had been an affair of the moment, and fifty times she had been unhappy in so saying. But this new coming of his could not be an affair of the moment. She had been the dupe, she had thought, of an absurd passion on her own part; but now – how was it now? She did not bring herself to think that she should ever be Lady Lufton. She had still, in some perversely obstinate manner, made up her mind against that result. But yet, nevertheless, it did in some unaccountable manner satisfy her to feel that Lord Lufton had himself come down to Framley and himself told this story. 'He has told everything to Mark,' said Mrs. Robarts; and then again there was a pause for a moment, during which these thoughts passed through Lucy's mind.

'Yes,' said Mark, 'he has told me all, and he is coming here to-morrow morning that he may receive an answer from yourself.'

'What answer?' said Lucy, trembling.

'Nay, dearest; who can say that but yourself?' and her sister-in-law, as she spoke, pressed close against her. 'You must say that yourself.' Mrs. Robarts, in her long conversation with her husband, had pleaded strongly on Lucy's behalf, taking as it were a part against Lady Lufton. She had said that if Lord Lufton persevered in his suit, they at the parsonage would not be justified in robbing Lucy of all that she had won for herself, in order to do Lady Lufton's pleasure.

'But she will think,' said Mark, 'that we have plotted and intrigued for this. She will call us ungrateful, and will make Lucy's life wretched.' To which the wife had answered, that all that must be left in God's hands. They had not plotted or intrigued. Lucy, though loving the man in her heart of hearts, had already once refused him, because she would not be thought to have snatched at so great a prize. But if Lord Lufton loved her so warmly that he had come down there in this manner, on purpose, as he himself had put it, that he might learn his fate, then – so argued Mrs. Robarts – they two, let their loyalty to Lady Lufton be ever so strong, could not justify it to their consciences to stand between Lucy and her lover. Mark had still somewhat demurred to this, suggesting how terrible would be their plight if they should now encourage Lord Lufton, and if he, after such encouragement, when they should have quarrelled with Lady Lufton, should allow himself to be led away from his engagement by his mother. To which Fanny had answered that justice was justice, and that right was right. Everything must be told to Lucy, and she must judge for herself.

'But I do not know what Lord Lufton wants,' said Lucy, with her eyes fixed upon the ground, and now trembling more than ever. 'He did come to me, and I did give him an answer.'

'And is that answer to be final?' said Mark – somewhat cruelly, for Lucy had not yet been told that her lover had made any repetition of his proposal. Fanny, however, determined that no injustice should be done, and therefore she at last continued the story.

'We know that you did give him an answer, dearest; but gentlemen sometimes will not put up with one answer on such a subject. Lord Lufton has declared to Mark that he means to ask again. He has come down here on purpose to do so.'

'And Lady Lufton –' said Lucy, speaking hardly above a whisper, and still hiding her face as she leaned against her sister's shoulder.

'Lord Lufton has not spoken to his mother about it,' said Mark; and it immediately became clear to Lucy, from the tone of her brother's voice, that he, at least, would not be pleased, should she accept her lover's vow.

'You must decide out of your own heart, dear,' said Fanny, generously. 'Mark and I know how well you have behaved, for I have told him everything.' Lucy shuddered and leaned closer against her sister as this was said to her. 'I had no alternative, dearest, but to tell him. It was best so; was it not? But nothing has been told to Lord Lufton. Mark would not let him come here to-day, because it would have flurried you, and he wished to give you time to think. But you can see him tomorrow morning – can you not? and then answer him.'

Lucy now stood perfectly silent, feeling that she dearly loved her sister-in-law for her sisterly kindness – for that sisterly wish to promote a sister's love; but still there was in her mind a strong resolve not to allow Lord Lufton to come there under the idea that he would be received as a favoured lover. Her love was powerful, but so also was her pride, and she could not bring herself to bear the scorn which would lay in Lady Lufton's eyes. 'His mother will despise me, and then he will despise me too,' she said to herself; and with a strong gulp of disappointed love and ambition she determined to persist. 'Shall we leave you now, dear; and speak of it again to-morrow morning before he comes?' said Fanny.

'That will be the best,' said Mark. 'Turn it in your mind every way to-night. Think of it when you have said your prayers – and, Lucy, come here to me;' – then, taking her in his arms, he kissed her with a tenderness that was not customary with him towards her. 'It is fair,' said he, 'that I should tell you this: that I have perfect confidence in your judgement and feeling; and that I will stand by you as your brother in whatever decision you may come to. Fanny and I both think that you have behaved excellently, and are both of us sure that you will do what is best. Whatever you do I will stick to you; – and so will Fanny.'

'Dearest, dearest Mark!'

'And now we will say nothing more about it till to-morrow morning,' said Fanny. But Lucy felt that this saying nothing more about it till to-morrow morning would be tantamount to an acceptance on her part of Lord

Lufton's offer. Mrs. Robarts knew, and Mr. Robarts also now knew, the secret of her heart; and if, such being the case, she allowed Lord Lufton to come there with the acknowledged purpose of pleading his own suit, it would be impossible for her not to yield. If she were resolved that she would not yield, now was the time for her to stand her ground and make her fight. 'Do not go, Fanny; at least not quite yet,' she said.

'Well, dear?'

'I want you to stay while I tell Mark. He must not let Lord Lufton come here to-morrow.'

'Not let him!' said Mrs. Robarts. Mr. Robarts said nothing, but he felt that his sister was rising in his esteem from minute to minute.

'No; Mark must bid him not come. He will not wish to pain me when it can do no good. Look here, Mark;' and she walked over to her brother, and put both her hands upon his arm. 'I do love Lord Lufton. I had not such meaning or thought when I first knew him. But I do love him – I love him dearly; – almost as well as Fanny loves you, I suppose. You may tell him so if you think proper – nay, you must tell him so, or he will not understand me. But tell him this, as coming from me: that I will never marry him, unless his mother asks me.'

'She will not do that, I fear,' said Mark, sorrowfully.

'No; I suppose not,' said Lucy, now regaining all her courage. 'If I thought it probable that she should wish me to be her daughter-in-law, it would not be necessary that I should make such a stipulation. It is because she will not wish it; because she would regard me as unfit to – to – to mate with her son. She would hate me, and scorn me; and then he would begin to scorn me, and perhaps would cease to love me. I could not bear her eye upon me, if she thought that I had injured her son. Mark, you will go to him now; will you not? and explain this to him; – as much of it as is necessary. Tell him, that if his mother asks me I will – consent. But that as I know that she never will, he is to look upon all that he has said as forgotten. With me it shall be the same as though it were forgotten.' Such was her verdict, and so confident were they both of her firmness – of her obstinacy Mark would have called it on any other occasion, – that they neither of them sought to make her alter it.

'You will go to him now – this afternoon; will you not?' she said; and Mark promised that he would. He could not but feel that he himself was greatly relieved. Lady Lufton might, probably, hear that her son had been fool enough to fall in love with the parson's sister; but under existing circumstances she could not consider herself aggrieved either by the parson or by his sister. Lucy was behaving well, and Mark was proud of her. Lucy was behaving with fierce spirit, and Fanny was grieving for her.

'I'd rather be by myself till dinner-time,' said Lucy, as Mrs. Robarts prepared to go with her out of the room. 'Dear Fanny, don't look unhappy; there's nothing to make us unhappy. I told you I should want goat's milk, and that will be all.' Robarts, after sitting for an hour with his wife, did return again to Framley Court; and, after a considerable search, found Lord Lufton returning home to a late dinner.

'Unless my mother asks her,' said he, when the story had been told him. 'That is nonsense. Surely you told her that such is not the way of the world.' Robarts endeavoured to explain to him that Lucy could not endure to think that her husband's mother should look on her with disfavour.

'Does she think that my mother dislikes her; her specially?' asked Lord Lufton. No; Robarts could not suppose that that was the case; but Lady Lufton might probably think that a marriage with a clergyman's sister would be a mésalliance.

'That is out of the question,' said Lord Lufton; 'as she has especially wanted me to marry a clergyman's daughter for some time past. But, Mark, it is absurd talking about my mother. A man in these days is not to marry as his mother bids him.' Mark could only assure him, in answer to all this, that Lucy was very firm in what she was doing, that she had quite made up her mind, and that she altogether absolved Lord Lufton from any necessity to speak to his mother, if he did not think well of doing so. But all this was to very little purpose. 'She does love me then?' said Lord Lufton.

'Well,' said Mark, 'I will not say whether she does or does not. I can only repeat her own message. She cannot accept you, unless she does so at your mother's request.' And having said that again, he took his leave, and went back to the parsonage. Poor Lucy, having finished her interview with so much dignity, having fully satisfied her brother, and declined any immediate consolation from her sister-in-law, betook herself to her own bedroom. She had to think over what she had said and done, and it was necessary that she should be alone to do so. It might be that, when she came to reconsider the matter, she would not be quite so well satisfied as was her brother. Her grandeur of demeanour and slow propriety of carriage lasted her till she was well into her own room. There are animals who, when they are ailing in any way, contrive to hide themselves, ashamed, as it were, that the weakness of their suffering should be witnessed. Indded, I am not sure whether all dumb animals do not do so more or less; and in this respect Lucy was like a dumb animal. Even in her confidences with Fanny she made a joke of her own misfortunes, and spoke of her heart ailments with self-ridicule. But now, having walked up the staircase with no hurried step, and having deliberately locked the door, she turned herself round to suffer in silence and solitude – as do the beasts and birds. She sat herself down on a low chair, which stood at the foot of her bed, and, throwing back her head, held her handkerchief across her eyes and forehead, holding it tight in both her hands; and then she began to think. She began to think and also to cry, for the tears came running down from beneath the handkerchief; and low sobs were to be heard – only that the animal had taken itself off, to suffer in solitude. Had she not thrown from her all her chances of happiness? Was it possible that he should come to her yet again – a third time? No; it was not possible. The very mode and pride of this, her second rejection of him, made it impossible. In coming to her determination, and making her avowal, she had been actuated by the knowledge that Lady Lufton would regard such a marriage with abhorrence. Lady Lufton would not and could not ask her to condescend to be her son's bride. Her chance of happiness, of glory, of ambition, of love, was all gone. She had sacrificed everything, not to virtue, but to pride; and she had sacrificed not only herself, but him. When first he came there – when she had meditated over his first visit – she had hardly given him credit for deep love; but now – there could be no doubt that he loved her now. After his season in London, his days and nights passed with all that was beautiful, he had returned there, to that little country parsonage, that he might again throw himself at her feet. And she – she had refused to see him, though she loved him with all her heart, she had refused to see him because she was so vile a coward that she could not bear the sour looks of an old woman! 'I will come down directly,' she said, when Fanny at last knocked at the door, begging to be admitted. 'I won't open it, love, but I will be with you in ten minutes; I will, indeed.' And so she was; not, perhaps, without traces of tears, discernible by the experienced eye of Mrs. Robarts, but yet with a smooth brow, and voice under her own command.

'I wonder whether she really loves him,' Mark said to his wife that night.

'Love him!' his wife had answered: 'indeed she does; and, Mark, do not be led away by the stern quiet of her demeanour. To my thinking she is a girl who might almost die for love.'

On the next day Lord Lufton left Framley; and started, according to his arrangements, for the Norway salmon fishing.

CHAPTER XXXII

The Goat and Compasses

HAROLD SMITH had been made unhappy by that rumour of a dissolution; but the misfortune to him would be as nothing compared to the severity with which it would fall on Mr. Sowerby. Harold Smith might or might not lose his borough, but Mr. Sowerby would undoubtedly lose his county; and, in losing that, he would lose everything. He felt very certain now that the duke would not support him again, let who would be master of Chaldicotes; and as he reflected on these things he found it very hard to keep up his spirits. Tom Towers, it seems, had known all about it, as he always does. The little remark which had dropped from him at Miss Dunstable's, made, no doubt, after mature deliberation, and with profound political motives, was the forerunner, only by twelve hours, of a very general report that the giants were going to the country. It was manifest that the giants had not a majority in Parliament, generous as had been the promises of support disinterestedly made to them by the gods. This indeed was manifest, and therefore they were going to the country, although they had been deliberately warned by a very prominent scion of Olympus that if they did so that disinterested support must be withdrawn. This threat did not seem to weigh much, and by two o'clock on the day following Miss Dunstable's party, the fiat was presumed to have gone forth. The rumour had begun with Tom Towers, but by that time it had reached Buggins at the Petty Bag Office. 'It won't make no difference to hus, sir; will it, Mr. Robarts?' said Buggins, as he leaned respectfully against the wall near the door, in the room of the private secretary at that establishment.

A good deal of conversation, miscellaneous, special, and political, went on between young Robarts and Buggins in the course of the day; as was natural, seeing that they were thrown in these evil times very much upon each other. The Lord Petty Bag of the present ministry was not such a one as Harold Smith. He was a giant indifferent to his private notes, and careless as to the duties even of patronage; he rarely visited the office, and as there were no other clerks in the establishment – owing to a root and branch reform carried out in the short reign of Harold Smith – to whom could young Robarts talk, if not to Buggins? 'No; I suppose not,' said Robarts, as he completed on his blotting-paper an elaborate picture of a Turk seated on his divan.

' 'Cause, you see, sir, we're in the Upper 'Ouse, now – as I always thinks we hought to be. I don't think it ain't constitutional for the Petty Bag to be in the Commons, Mr. Robarts. Hany ways, it never usen't.'

'They're changing all those sort of things nowadays, Buggins,' said Robarts, giving the final touch to the Turk's smoke.

'Well; I'll tell you what it is, Mr. Robarts: I think I'll go. I can't stand all these changes. I'm turned of sixty now, and don't want any 'stifflicates. I think I'll take my pension and walk. The hoffice ain't the same place at all since it come down among the Commons.' And then Buggins retired sighing, to console himself with a pot of porter behind a large open office ledger, set up on end on a small table in the little lobby outside the private secretary's room. Buggins sighed again as he saw that the date made visible in the open book was almost as old as his own appointment; for such a book as this lasted long in the Petty Bag Office. A peer of high degree had been Lord Petty Bag in those days; one whom a messenger's heart could respect with infinite veneration, as he made his unaccustomed visits to the office with much solemnity – perhaps four times during the season. The Lord Petty Bag then was highly regarded by his staff, and his coming among them was talked about for some hours previously and for some days afterwards; but Harold Smith had bustled in and out like the managing clerk in a Manchester house. 'The service is going to the dogs,' said Buggins to himself, as he put down the porter pot, and looked up over the book at a gentleman who presented himself at the door. 'Mr. Robarts in his room?' said Buggins, repeating the gentleman's words. 'Yes, Mr. Sowerby; you'll find him there – first door to the left.' And then, remembering that the visitor was a county member – a position which Buggins regarded as next to that of a peer – he got up, and, opening the private secretary's door, ushered in the visitor.

Young Robarts and Mr. Sowerby had, of course, become acquainted in the days of Harold Smith's reign. During that short time the member for East Barset had on most days dropped in at the Petty Bag Office for a minute or two, finding out what the energetic Cabinet minister was doing, chatting on semi-official subjects, and teaching the private secretary to laugh at his master. There was nothing, therefore, in his present visit which need appear to be singular, or which required any immediate special explanation. He sat himself down in his ordinary way, and began to speak of the subject of the day. 'We're all to go,' said Sowerby.

'So I hear,' said the private secretary. 'It will give me no trouble, for, as the respectable Buggins says, we're in the Upper House now.'

'What a delightful time those lucky dogs of lords do have!' said Sowerby. 'No constituents, no turning out, no fighting, no necessity for political opinions; and, as a rule, no such opinions at all!'

'I suppose you're tolerably safe in East Barsetshire?' said Robarts. 'The duke has it pretty much his own way there.'

'Yes; the duke does have it pretty much his own way. By the by, where is your brother?'

'At home,' said Robarts; 'at least I presume so.'

'At Framley or at Barchester? I believe he was in residence at Barchester not long since.'

'He's at Framley now, I know. I got a letter only yesterday from his wife, with a commission. He was there, and Lord Lufton had just left.'

'Yes; Lufton was down. He started for Norway this morning. I want to see your brother. You have not heard from him yourself, have you?'

'No; not lately. Mark is a bad correspondent. He would not do at all for a private secretary.'

'At any rate, not to Harold Smith. But you are sure I should not catch him at Barchester?'

'Send down by telegraph, and he would meet you.'

'I don't want to do that. A telegraph message makes such a fuss in the country, frightening people's wives, and setting all the horses about the place galloping.'

'What is it about?'

'Nothing of any great consequence. I didn't know whether he might have told you. I'll write down by tonight's post, and then he can meet me at Barchester tomorrow. Or do you write. There's nothing I hate so much as letter-writing; just tell him that I called, and that I shall be much obliged if he can meet me at the Dragon of Wantly – say at two to-morrow. I will go down by the express.'

Mark Robarts, in talking over this coming money trouble with Sowerby, had once mentioned that if it were necessary to take up the bill for a short time he might be able to borrow the money from his brother. So much of the father's legacy still remained in the hands of the private secretary as would enable him to produce the amount of the latter bill, and there could be no doubt that he would lend it if asked. Mr. Sowerby's visit to the Petty Bag Office had been caused by a desire to learn whether any such request had been made – and also by a half-formed resolution to make the request himself if he should find that the clergyman had not done so. It seemed to him to be a pity that such a sum should be lying about, as it were, within reach, and that he should not stoop to put his hands upon it. Such abstinence would be so contrary to all the practice of his life that it was as difficult to him as it is for a sportsman to let pass a cock-pheasant. But yet something like remorse touched his heart as he sat there balancing himself on his chair in the private secretary's room, and looking at the young man's open face.

'Yes; I'll write to him,' said John Robarts; 'but he hasn't said anything to me about anything particular.'

'Hasn't he? It does not much signify. I only mentioned it because I thought I understood him to say that he would.' And then Mr. Sowerby went on swinging himself. How was it that he felt so averse to mention that little sum of £500 to a young man like John Robarts, a fellow without wife or children or calls on him of any sort, who would not even be injured by the loss of the money, seeing that he had an ample salary on which to live? He wondered at his own weakness. The want of the money was urgent on him in the extreme. He had reasons for supposing that Mark would find it very difficult to renew the bills, but he, Sowerby, could stop their presentation if he could get this money at once into his own hands.

'Can I do anything for you?' said the innocent lamb, offering his throat to the butcher. But some unwonted feeling numbed the butcher's fingers, and blunted his knife. He sat still for half a minute after the question, and then jumping from his seat, declined the offer. 'No, no; nothing, thank you. Only write to Mark, and say that I shall be there to-morrow,' and then, taking his hat, he hurried out of the office. 'What an ass I am,' he said to himself as he went: 'as if it were of any use now to be particular!'

He then got into a cab and had himself driven half-way up Portman Street towards the New Road, and walking from thence a few hundred yards down a cross-street he came to a public-house. It was called the 'Goat and Compasses,' – a very meaningless name, one would say; but the house boasted of being a place of public entertainment very long established on that site, having been a tavern out in the country in the days of Cromwell. At that time the pious landlord, putting up a pious legend for the benefit of his pious customers, had declared that – 'God encompasseth us.' The 'Goat and Compasses' in these days does quite as well; and, considering the present character of the house, was perhaps less unsuitable than the old legend. 'Is Mr. Austen here?' asked Mr. Sowerby of the man at the bar.

'Which on 'em? Not Mr. John; he ain't here. Mr. Tom is in – the little room on the left-hand side.' The man whom Mr. Sowerby would have preferred to see was the elder brother, John; but as he was not to be found, he did go into the little room. In that room he found – Mr. Austen, junior, according to one arrangement of nomenclature, and Mr. Tom Tozer according to another. To gentlemen of the legal profession he generally chose to introduce himself as belonging to the respectable family of the Austens; but among his intimates he had always been – Tozer. Mr. Sowerby, though he was intimate with the family, did not love the Tozers: but he especially hated Tom Tozer. Tom Tozer was a bull-necked, beetle-browed fellow, the expression of whose face was eloquent with acknowledged roguery. 'I am a rogue,' it seemed to say. 'I know it; all the world knows it: but you're another. All the world don't know that, but I do. Men are all rogues, pretty nigh. Some are soft rogues, and some are 'cute rogues. I am a 'cute one; so mind your eye.' It was with such words that Tom Tozer's face spoke out; and though a thorough liar in his heart, he was not a liar in his face. 'Well, Tozer,' said Mr. Sowerby, absolutely shaking hands with the dirty miscreant, 'I wanted to see your brother.'

'John ain't here, and ain't like; but it's all as one.'

'Yes, yes; I suppose it is. I know you two hunt in couples.'

'I don't know what you mean about hunting, Mr. Sowerby. You gents 'as all the hunting, and we poor folk 'as all the work. I hope you're going to make up this trifle of money we're out of so long.'

'It's about that I've called. I don't know what you call long, Tozer; but the last bill was only dated in February.'

'It's overdue; ain't it?'

'Oh, yes; it's overdue. There's no doubt about that.'

'Well; when a bit of paper is come round, the next thing is to take it up. Them's my ideas. And to tell you the truth, Mr. Sowerby, we don't think as 'ow you've been treating us just on the square lately. In that matter of Lord Lufton's you was down on us uncommon.'

'You know I couldn't help myself.'

'Well; and we can't help ourselves now. That's where it is, Mr. Sowerby. Lord love you; we know what's what, we do. And so, the fact is we're uncommon low as to the ready just at present, and we must have them few hundred pounds. We must have them at once, or we must sell up that clerical gent. I'm dashed if it ain't as hard to get money from a parson as it is to take a bone from a dog. 'E's 'ad 'is account, no doubt, and why don't 'e pay?'

Mr. Sowerby had called with the intention of explaining that he was about to proceed to Barchester on the following day with the express view of 'making arrangements' about this bill; and had he seen John Tozer, John would have been compelled to accord to him some little extension of time. Both Tom and John knew this; and, therefore, John – the soft-hearted one – kept out of the way. There was no danger that Tom would be weak; and, after some half-hour of parley, he was again left by Mr. Sowerby, without having evinced any symptom of weakness.

'It's the dibs as we want, Mr. Sowerby; that's all,' were the last words which he spoke as the member of Parliament left the room. Mr. Sowerby then got into another cab, and had himself driven to his sister's house. It is a remarkable thing with reference to men who are distressed for money – distressed as was now the case with Mr. Sowerby – that they never seem at a loss for small sums, or deny themselves those luxuries which small sums purchase. Cabs, dinners, wine, theatres, and new gloves are always at the command of men who are drowned in pecuniary embarrassments, whereas those who don't owe a shilling are so frequently obliged to go without them! It would seem that there is no gratification so costly as that of keeping out of debt. But then it is only fair that, if a man has a hobby, he should pay for it. Any one else would have saved his shilling, as Mrs. Harold Smith's house was only just across Oxford Street, in the neighbourhood of Hanover Square; but Mr. Sowerby never thought of this. He had never saved a shilling in his life, and it did not occur to him to begin now. He had sent word to her to remain at home for him, and he now found her waiting. 'Harriet,' said he, throwing himself back into an easy chair, 'the game is pretty well up at last.'

'Nonsense,' said she. 'The game is not up at all if you have the spirit to carry it on.'

'I can only say that I got a formal notice this morning from the duke's lawyer, saying that he meant to foreclose at once; – not from Fothergill, but from those people in South Audley Street.'

'You expected that,' said his sister.

'I don't see how that makes it any better; besides, I am not quite sure that I did expect it; at any rate I did not feel certain. There is no doubt now.'

'It is better that there should be no doubt. It is much better that you should know on what ground you have to stand.'

'I shall soon have no ground to stand on, none at least of my own – not an acre,' said the unhappy man, with great bitterness in his tone.

'You can't in reality be poorer now than you were last year. You have not spent anything to speak of. There can be no doubt that Chaldicotes will be ample to pay all you owe the duke.'

'It's as much as it will; and what am I to do then? I almost think more of the seat than I do of Chaldicotes.'

'You know what I advise,' said Mrs. Smith. 'Ask Miss Dunstable to advance the money on the same security which the duke holds. She will be as safe then as he is now. And if you can arrange that, stand for the county against him; perhaps you may be beaten.'

'I shouldn't have a chance.'

'But it would show that you are not a creature in the duke's hands. That's my advice,' said Mrs. Smith, with much spirit; 'and if you wish, I'll broach it to Miss Dunstable, and ask her to get her lawyer to look into it.'

'If I had done this before I had run my head into that other absurdity!'

'Don't fret yourself about that; she will lose nothing by such an investment, and therefore you are not asking any favour of her. Besides, did she not make the offer? and she is just the woman to do this for you now, because she refused to do that other thing for you yesterday. You understand most things, Nathaniel; but I am not sure that you understand women; not, at any rate, such a woman as her.' It went against the grain with Mr. Sowerby, this seeking of pecuniary assistance from the very woman whose hand he had attempted to gain about a fortnight since; but he allowed his sister to prevail. What could any man do in such straits that would not go against the grain? At the present moment he felt in his mind an infinite hatred against the duke, Mr. Fothergill, Gumption & Gagebee, and all the tribes of Gatherum Castle and South Audley Street; they wanted to rob him of that which had belonged to the Sowerbys before the name of Omnium had been heard of in the county, or in England! The great leviathan of the deep was anxious to swallow him up as a prey! He was to be swallowed up, and made away with, and put out of sight, without a pang of remorse. Any measure which could now present itself as the means of staving off so evil a day would be acceptable; and therefore he gave his sister the commission of making this second proposal to Miss Dunstable. In cursing the duke – for he did curse the duke lustily – it hardly occurred to him to think that, after all, the duke only asked for his own. As for Mrs. Harold Smith, whatever may be the view taken of her general character as a wife and a member of society, it must be admitted that as a sister she had virtues.

CHAPTER XXXIII

Consolation

On the next day at two o'clock punctually, Mark Robarts was at the 'Dragon of Wantly', walking up and down the very room in which the party had breakfasted after Harold Smith's lecture, and waiting for the arrival of Mr. Sowerby. He had been very well able to divine what was the business on which his friend wished to see him, and he had been rather glad than otherwise to receive the summons. Judging of his friend's character by what he had hitherto seen, he thought that Mr. Sowerby would have kept out of the way, unless he had it in his power to make some provision for these terrible bills. So he walked up and down the dingy room, impatient for the expected arrival, and thought himself wickedly ill-used in that Mr. Sowerby was not there when the clock struck a quarter to three. But when the clock struck three, Mr. Sowerby was there, and Mark Robarts's hopes were nearly at an end.

'Do you mean that they will demand nine hundred pounds?' said Robarts, standing up and glaring angrily at the member of Parliament.

'I fear that they will,' said Sowerby. 'I think it is best to tell you the worst, in order that we may see what can be done.'

'I can do nothing, and will do nothing,' said Robarts. 'They may do what they choose – what the law allows them.' And then he thought of Fanny and his nursery, and Lucy refusing in her pride Lord Lufton's offer, and he turned away his face that the hard man of the world before him might not see the tear gathering in his eye.

'But, Mark, my dear fellow –' said Sowerby, trying to have recourse to the power of his cajoling voice. Robarts, however, would not listen.

'Mr. Sowerby,' said he, with an attempt at calmness which betrayed itself at every syllable, 'it seems to me that you have robbed me. That I have been a fool, and worse than a fool, I know well; but – but – but I thought that your position in the world would guarantee me from such treatment as this.' Mr. Sowerby was by no means without feeling, and the words which he now heard cut him very deeply – the more so because it was impossible that he should answer them with an attempt at indignation. He had robbed his friend, and, with all his wit, knew no words at the present moment sufficiently witty to make it seem that he had not done so. 'Robarts,' said he, 'you may say what you like to me now; I shall not resent it.'

'Who would care for your resentment?' said the clergyman, turning on him with ferocity. 'The resentment of a gentleman is terrible to a gentleman; and the resentment of one just man is terrible to another. Your resentment!' – and then he walked twice the length of the room, leaving Sowerby dumb in his seat. 'I wonder whether you ever thought of my wife and children when you were plotting this ruin for me!' And then again he walked the room.

'I suppose you will be calm enough presently to speak of this with some attempt to make a settlement?'

'No; I will make no such attempt. These friends of yours, you tell me, have a claim on me for nine hundred pounds, of which they demand immediate payment. You shall be asked in a court of law how much of that money I have handled. You know that I have never touched – have never wanted to touch – one shilling. I will make no attempt at any settlement. My person is here, and there is my house. Let them do their worst.'

'But, Mark –'

'Call me by my name, sir, and drop that affection of regard. What an ass I have been to be so cozened by a sharper!' Sowerby had by no means expected this. He had always known that Robarts possessed what he, Sowerby, would have called the spirit of a gentleman. He had regarded him as a bold, open, generous fellow, able to take his own part when called on to do so, and by no means disinclined to speak his own mind; but he had not expected from him such a torrent of indignation, or thought that he was capable of such a depth of anger. 'If you use such language as that, Robarts, I can only leave you.'

'You are welcome. Go. You tell me that you are the messenger of these men who intend to work nine hundred pounds out of me. You have done your part in the plot, and have now brought their message. It seems to me that you had better go back to them. As for me, I want my time to prepare my wife for the destiny before her.'

'Robarts, you will be sorry some day for the cruelty of your words.'

'I wonder whether you will ever be sorry for the cruelty of your doings, or whether these things are really a joke to you.'

'I am at this moment a ruined man,' said Sowerby. 'Everything is going from me, – my place in the world, the estate of my family, my father's house, my seat in Parliament, the power of living among my countrymen, or, indeed, of living anywhere; – but all this does not oppress me now so much as the misery which I have brought upon you.' And then Sowerby also turned away his face, and wiped from his eyes tears which were not artificial. Robarts was still walking up and down the room, but it was not possible for him to continue his reproaches after this. This is always the case. Let a man endure to heap contumely on his own head, and he will silence the contumely of others – for the moment. Sowerby, without meditating on the matter, had had some inkling of this, and immediately saw that there was at last an opening for conversation. 'You are unjust to me,' said he, 'in supposing that I have now no wish to save you. It is solely in the hope of doing so that I have come here.'

'And what is your hope? That I should accept another brace of bills, I suppose.'

'Not a brace; but one renewed bill for –'

'Look here, Mr. Sowerby. On no earthly consideration that can be put before me will I again sign my name to any bill in the guise of an acceptance. I have been very weak, and am ashamed of my weakness; but so much strength as that, I hope, is left to me. I have been very wicked, and am ashamed of my wickedness; but so much right principle as that, I hope, remains. I will put my name to no other bill; not for you, not even for myself.'

'But, Robarts, under your present circumstances that will be madness.'

'Then I will be mad.'

'Have you seen Forrest? If you will speak to him I think you will find that everything can be accommodated.'

'I already owe Mr. Forrest a hundred and fifty pounds, which I obtained from him when you pressed me for the price of that horse, and I will not increase the debt. What a fool I was again there! Perhaps you do not remember that, when I agreed to buy the horse, the price was to be my contribution to the liquidation of these bills.'

'I do remember it; but I will tell you how that was.'

'It does not signify. It has been all of a piece.'

'But listen to me. I think you would feel for me if you knew all that I have gone through. I pledge you my solemn word that I had no intention of asking you for the money when you took the horse; – indeed I had not. But you remember that affair of Lufton's, when he came to you at your hotel in London and was so angry about an outstanding bill.'

'I know that he was very unreasonable as far as I was concerned.'

'He was so; but that makes no difference. He was resolved, in his rage, to expose the whole affair; and I saw that, if he did so, it would be most injurious to you, seeing that you had just accepted your stall at Barchester.' Here the poor prebendary winced terribly. 'I moved heaven and earth to get up that bill. Those vultures stuck to their prey when they found the value which I attached to it, and I was forced to raise above a hundred pounds at the moment to obtain possession of it, although every shilling absolutely due on it had long since been paid. Never in my life did I wish to get money as I did to raise that hundred and twenty pounds: and as I hope for mercy in my last moments, I did that for your sake. Lufton could not have injured me in that matter.'

'But you told him that you got it for twenty-five pounds.'

'Yes, I told him so. I was obliged to tell him that, or I should have apparently condemned myself by showing how anxious I was to get it. And you know I could not have explained all this before him and you. You would have thrown up the stall in disgust.' Would that he had! That was Mark's wish now, – his futile wish. In what a slough of despond had he come to wallow in consequence of his folly on that night at Gatherum Castle! He had then done a silly thing, and was he now to rue it by almost total ruin? He was sickened also with all these lies. His very soul was dismayed by the dirt through which he was forced to wade. He had become unconsciously connected with the lowest dregs of mankind, and would have to see his name mingled with theirs in the daily newspapers. And for what had he done this? Why had he thus filed his mind and made himself a disgrace to his cloth? In order that he might befriend such a one as Mr. Sowerby!

'Well,' continued Sowerby,' I did get the money, but you would hardly believe the rigour of the pledge which was exacted from me for repayment. I got it from Harold Smith, and never, in my worst straits, will I again look to him for assistance. I borrowed it only for a fortnight; and in order that I might repay it, I was obliged to ask you for the price of the horse. Mark, it was on your behalf that I did all this, – indeed it was.'

'And now I am to repay you for your kindness by the loss of all that I have in the world.'

'If you will put the affair into the hands of Mr. Forrest, nothing need be touched, – not a hair of a horse's back; no, not though you should be obliged to pay the whole amount yourself gradually out of your income. You must execute a series of bills, falling due quarterly, and then –'

'I will execute no bill, I will put my name to no paper in the matter; as to that my mind is fully made up. They may come and do their worst.' Mr. Sowerby persevered for a long time, but he was quite unable to move the parson from this position. He would no nothing towards making what Mr. Sowerby called an arrangement, but persisted that he would remain at home at Framley, and that any one who had a claim upon him might take legal steps. 'I shall do nothing myself,' he said; 'but if proceedings against me be taken, I shall prove that I have never had a shilling of the money.' And in this resolution he quitted the Dragon of Wantly. Mr. Sowerby at one time said a word as to the expediency of borrowing that sum of money from John Robarts; but as to this Mark would say nothing. Mr. Sowerby was not the friend with whom he now intended to hold consultation in such matters. 'I am not at present prepared,' he said, 'to declare what I may do; I must first see what steps others take.' And then he took his hat and went off; and mounting his horse in the yard of the Dragon of Wantly – that horse which he now had so many reasons to dislike – he slowly rode back home.

Many thoughts passed through his mind during that ride, but only one resolution obtained for itself a fixture there. He must now tell his wife everything. He would not be so cruel as to let it remain untold until a bailiff were at the door, ready to walk him off to the county jail, or until the bed on which they slept was to be sold from under them. Yes, he would tell her everything, – immediately, before his resolution could again have faded away. He got off his horse in the yard, and seeing his wife's maid at the kitchen door, desired her to beg her mistress to come to him in the book-room. He would not allow one half-hour to pass towards the waning of his purpose. If it be ordained that a man shall drown, had he not better drown and have done with it? Mrs. Robarts came to him in his room, reaching him in time to touch his arm as he entered it. 'Mary says you want me. I have been gardening, and she caught me just as I came in.'

'Yes, Fanny, I do want you. Sit down for a moment.' And walking across the room, he placed his whip in its proper place.

'Oh, Mark, is there anything the matter?'

'Yes, dearest; yes. Sit down, Fanny: I can talk to you better if you will sit.' But she, poor lady, did not wish to sit. He had hinted at some misfortune, and therefore she felt a longing to stand by him and cling to him.

'Well, there; I will if I must; but, Mark, do not frighten me. Why is your face so very wretched?'

'Fanny, I have done very wrong,' he said. 'I have been very foolish. I fear that I have brought upon you great sorrow and trouble.' And then he leaned his head upon his hand and turned his face away from her.

'Oh, Mark, dearest Mark, my own Mark! what is it?' and she was quickly up from her chair, and went down on her knees before him. 'Do not turn from me. Tell me, Mark! tell me, that we may share it.'

'Yes, Fanny, I must tell you now; but I hardly know what you will think of me when you have heard it.'

'I will think that you are my own husband, Mark; I will think that – that chiefly, whatever it may be.' And then she caressed his knees, and looked up in his face, and, getting hold of one of his hands, pressed it between her own. 'Even if you have been foolish, who should forgive you if I cannot?' And then he told it her all, beginning from that evening when Mr. Sowerby had got him into his bedroom, and going on gradually, now about the bills, and now about the horses, till his poor wife was utterly lost in the complexity of the accounts. She could by no means follow him in the details of his story; nor could she quite sympathize with him in his indignation against Mr. Sowerby, seeing that she did not comprehend at all the nature of the renewing of a bill. The only part to her of importance in the matter was the amount of money which her husband would be called upon to pay; that, and her strong hope, which was already a conviction, that he would never again incur such debts.

'And how much is it, dearest, altogether?'

'These men claim nine hundred pounds of me.'

'Oh, dear! that is a terrible sum.'

'And then there is the hundred and fifty which I have borrowed from the bank – the price of the horse, you know; and there are some other debts, – not a great deal, I think; but people will now look for every shilling that is due to them. If I have to pay it all, it will be twelve or thirteen hundred pounds.'

'That will be as much as a year's income, Mark; even with the stall.' That was the only word of reproach she said – if it could be called a reproach.

'Yes,' he said; 'and it is claimed by men who will have no pity in exacting it at any sacrifice, if they have the power. And to think that I should have incurred all this debt without having received anything for it. Oh, Fanny, what will you think of me!' But she swore to him that she would think nothing of it – that she would never bear it in her mind against him – that it could have no effect in lessening her trust in him. Was he not her husband? She was so glad she knew it, that she might comfort him. And she did comfort him, making the weight seem lighter and lighter on his shoulders as he talked of it. And such weights do thus become lighter. A burden that will crush a single pair of shoulders will, when equally divided – when shared by two, each of whom is willing to take the heavier part – become light as a feather. Is not that sharing of the mind's burdens one of the chief purposes for which a man wants a wife? For there is no folly so great as keeping one's sorrows hidden. And this wife cheerfully, gladly, thankfully took her share. To endure with her lord all her lord's troubles was easy to her; it was the work to which she had pledged herself. But to have thought that her lord had troubles not communicated to her, – that would have been to her the one thing not to be borne. And then they discussed their plans; what mode of escape they might have out of this terrible money difficulty. Like a true woman, Mrs. Robarts proposed at once to abandon all superfluities. They would sell all their horses; they would not sell their cows, but would sell the butter that came from them; they would sell the pony-carriage, and get rid of the groom. That the footman must go was so much a matter of course, that it was hardly mentioned. But then, as to that house at Barchester, the dignified prebendal mansion in the close – might they not be allowed to leave it unoccupied for one year longer – perhaps to let it? The world of course must know of their misfortune; but if that misfortune was faced bravely, the world would be less bitter in its condemnation. And then, above all things, everything must be told to Lady Lufton.

'You may, at any rate, believe this, Fanny,' said he, 'that for no consideration which can be offered to me will I ever put my name to another bill.' The kiss with which she thanked him for this was as warm and generous as though he had brought to her that day news of the brightest; and when he sat, as he did that evening, discussing it all, not only with his wife, but with Lucy, he wondered how it was that his troubles were now so light. Whether or no a man should have his own private pleasures, I will not now say; but it never can be worth his while to keep his sorrows private.

CHAPTER XXXIV

Lady Lufton is Taken by Surprise

LORD LUFTON, as he returned to town, found some difficulty in resolving what step he would next take. Sometimes, for a minute or two, he was half inclined to think – or rather to say to himself – that Lucy was perhaps not worth the trouble which she threw in his way. He loved her very dearly, and would willingly make her his wife, he thought or said at such moment; but – Such moments, however, were only moments. A man in love seldom loves less because his love becomes difficult. And thus, when those moments were over, he would determine to tell his mother at once, and urge her to signify her consent to Miss Robarts. That she would not be quite pleased he knew; but if he were firm enough to show that he had a will of his own in this matter, she would probably not gainsay him. He would not ask this humbly, as a favour, but request her ladyship to go through the ceremony as though it were one of those motherly duties which she as a good mother could not hesitate to perform on behalf of her son. Such was the final resolve with which he reached his chambers in the Albany. On the next day he did not see his mother. It would be well, he thought, to have his interview with her immediately before he started for Norway, so that there might be no repetition of it; and it was on the day before he did start that he made his communication, having invited himself to breakfast in Brook Street on the occasion.

'Mother,' he said, quite abruptly, throwing himself into one of the dining-room arm-chairs, 'I have a thing to tell you.' His mother at once knew that the thing was important, and with her own peculiar motherly instinct imagined that the question to be discussed had reference to matrimony. Had her son desired to speak to her about money, his tone and look would have been different; as would also have been the case – in a different way – had he entertained any thought of a pilgrimage to Pekin, or a prolonged fishing expedition to the Hudson Bay Territories.

'A thing, Ludovic! well, I am quite at liberty.'

'I want to know what you think of Lucy Robarts?' Lady Lufton became pale and frightened, and the blood ran cold to her heart. She had feared more than rejoiced in conceiving that her son was about to talk of love, but she had feared nothing so bad as this.

'What do I think of Lucy Robarts?' she said, repeating her son's words in a tone of evident dismay.

'Yes, mother; you have said once or twice lately that you thought I ought to marry, and I am beginning to think so too. You selected one clergyman's daughter for me, but that lady is going to do much better with herself –'

'Indeed she is not,' said Lady Lufton sharply.

'And therefore I rather think I shall select for myself another clergyman's sister. You don't dislike Miss Robarts, I hope?'

'Oh, Ludovic!' It was all that Lady Lufton could say at the spur of the moment.

'Is there any harm in her? Have you any objection to her? Is there anything about her that makes her unfit to be my wife?'

For a moment or two Lady Lufton sat silent, collecting her thoughts. She thought that there was very great objection to Lucy Robarts, regarding her as the possible future Lady Lufton. She could hardly have stated all her reasons, but they were very cogent. Lucy Robarts had, in her eyes, neither beauty, nor style, nor manner, nor even the education which was desirable. Lady Lufton was not herself a worldly woman. She was almost as far removed from being so as a woman could be in her position. But, nevertheless, there were certain worldly attributes which she regarded as essential to the character of any young lady who might be considered fit to take the place which she herself had so long filled. It was her desire in looking for a wife for her son to combine these with certain moral excellences which she regarded as equally essential. Lucy Robarts might have the moral excellences, or she might not; but as to the other attributes Lady Lufton regarded her as altogether deficient. She could never look like a Lady Lufton, or carry herself in the county as a Lady Lufton should do. She had not that quiet personal demeanour – that dignity of repose – which Lady Lufton loved to look upon in a young married woman of rank. Lucy, she would have said, could be nobody in a room except by dint of her tongue, whereas Griselda Grantly would have held her peace for a whole evening, and yet would have impressed everybody by the majesty of her presence. Then again Lucy had no money – and, again, Lucy was only the sister of her own parish clergyman. People are rarely prophets in their own country, and Lucy was no prophet at Framley; she was none, at least, in the eyes of Lady Lufton. Once before, as may be remembered, she had had fears on this subject – fears, not so much for her son, whom she could hardly bring herself to suspect of such a folly, but for Lucy, who might be foolish enough to fancy that the lord was in love with her. Alas! alas! her son's question fell upon the poor woman at the present moment with the weight of a terrible blow. 'Is there anything about her which makes her unfit to be my wife?' Those were her son's last words.

'Dearest Ludovic, dearest Ludovic!' and she got up and came over to him, 'I do think so; I do, indeed.'

'Think what?' said he, in a tone that was almost angry.

'I do think that she is unfit to be your wife. She is not of that class from which I would wish to see you choose.'

'She is of the same class as Griselda Grantly.'

'No, dearest. I think you are in error there. The Grantlys have moved in a different sphere of life. I think you must feel that they are –'

'Upon my word, mother, I don't. One man is Rector of Plumstead, and the other is Vicar of Framley. But it is no good arguing that. I want you to take to Lucy Robarts. I have come to you on purpose to ask it of you as a favour.'

'Do you mean as your wife, Ludovic?'

'Yes; as my wife.'

'Am I to understand that you are – are engaged to her?'

'Well, I cannot say that I am – not actually engaged to her. But you may take this for granted, that, as far as it lies in my power, I intend to become so. My mind is made up, and I certainly shall not alter it.'

'And the young lady knows all this?'

'Certainly.'

'Horrid, sly, detestable, underhand girl,' Lady Lufton said to herself, not being by any means brave enough to speak out such language before her son. What hope could there be if Lord Lufton had already committed himself by a positive offer? 'And her brother, and Mrs. Robarts; are they aware of it?'

'Yes; both of them.'

'And both approve of it?'

'Well, I cannot say that. I have not seen Mrs. Robarts, and do not know what may be her opinion. To speak my mind honestly about Mark, I do not think he does cordially approve. He is afraid of you, and would be desirous of knowing what you think.'

'I am glad, at any rate, to hear that,' said Lady Lufton, gravely. 'Had he done anything to encourage this, it would have been very base.' And then there was another short period of silence. Lord Lufton had determined not to explain to his mother the whole state of the case. He would not tell her that everything depended on her word – that Lucy was ready to marry him only on condition that she, Lady Lufton, would desire her to do so. He would not let her know that everything depended on her – according to Lucy's present verdict. He had a strong disinclination to ask his mother's permission to get married; and he would have to ask it were he to tell her the whole truth. His object was to make her think well of Lucy, and to induce her to be kind, and generous, and affectionate down at Framley. Then things would all turn out comfortably when he again visited that place, as he intended to do on his return from Norway. So much he thought it possible he might effect, relying on his mother's probable calculation that it would be useless for her to oppose a measure which she had no power of stopping by authority. But were he to tell her that she was to be the final judge, that everything was to depend on her will, then, so thought Lord Lufton, that permission would in all probability be refused.

'Well, mother, what answer do you intend to give me?' he said. 'My mind is positively made up. I should not have come to you had not that been the case. You will now be going down home, and I would wish you to treat Lucy as you yourself would wish to treat any girl to whom you knew that I was engaged.'

'But you say that you are not engaged.'

'No, I am not; but I have made my offer to her, and I have not been rejected. She has confessed that she – loves me, – not to myself, but to her brother. Under these circumstances, may I count upon your obliging me?' There was something in his manner which almost frightened his mother, and made her think that there was more behind than was told to her. Generally speaking, his manner was open, gentle, and unguarded; but now he spoke as though he had prepared his words, and was resolved on being harsh as well as obstinate.

'I am so much taken by surprise, Ludovic, that I can hardly give you an answer. If you ask me whether I approve of such a marriage, I must say that I do not; I think that you would be throwing yourself away in marrying Miss Robarts.'

'That is because you do not know her.'

'May it not be possible that I know her better than you do, dear Ludovic? You have been flirting with her –'

'I hate that word; it always sounds to me to be vulgar.'

'I will say making love to her, if you like it better; and gentlemen under these circumstances will sometimes become infatuated.'

'You would not have a man marry a girl without making love to her. The fact is, mother, that your tastes and mine are not exactly the same; you like silent beauty, whereas I like talking beauty, and then –'

'Do you call Miss Robarts beautiful?'

'Yes, I do; very beautiful; she has the beauty that I admire. Good-bye now, mother; I shall not see you again before I start. It will be no use writing, as I shall be away so short a time, and I don't quite know where we shall be. I shall come down to Framley immediately I return, and shall learn from you how the land lies. I have told you my wishes, and you will consider how far you think it right to fall in with them.' He then kissed her, and without waiting for her reply he took his leave. Poor Lady Lufton, when she was left to herself, felt that her head was going round and round. Was this to be the end of all her ambition, – of all her love for her son? and was this to be the result of all her kindness to the Robarts's? She almost hated Mark Robarts as she reflected that she had been the means of bringing him and his sister to Framley. She thought over all his sins, his absences from the parish, his visit to Gatherum Castle, his dealings with reference to that farm which was to have been sold, his hunting, and then his acceptance of that stall, given, as she had been told, through the Omnium interest. How could she love him at such a moment as this? And then she thought of his wife. Could it be possible that Fanny Robarts, her own friend Fanny, would be so untrue to her as to lend any assistance to such a marriage as this; as not to use all her power in preventing it? She had spoken to Fanny on this very subject – not fearing for her son, but with a general idea of the impropriety of intimacies between such girls as Lucy and such men as Lord Lufton, and then Fanny had agreed with her. Could it be possible that even she must be regarded as an enemy? And then by degrees Lady Lufton began to reflect what steps she had better take. In the first place, should she give in at once, and consent to the marriage? The only thing quite certain to her was this, that life would not be worth having if she were forced into a permanent quarrel with her son. Such an event would probably kill her. When she read of quarrels in other noble families – and the accounts of such quarrels will sometimes, unfortunately, force themselves upon the attention of unwilling readers – she would hug herself, with a spirit that was almost pharisaical, reflecting that her destiny was not like that of others. Such quarrels and hatreds between fathers and daughters, and mothers and sons, were in her eyes disreputable to all the persons concerned. She had lived happily with her husband, comfortably with her neighbours, respectably with the world, and, above all things, affectionately with her children. She spoke everywhere of Lord Lufton as though he were nearly perfect, – and in so speaking, she had not belied her convictions. Under these circumstances, would not any marriage be better than a quarrel? But, then, again, how much of the pride of her daily life would be destroyed by such a match as that! And might it not be within her power to prevent it without any quarrel? That her son would be sick of such a chit as Lucy before he had been married to her six months – of that Lady Lufton entertained no doubt, and therefore her conscience would not be disquieted in disturbing the consummation of an arrangement so pernicious. It was evident that the matter was not considered as settled even by her son; and also evident that he regarded the matter as being in some way dependent on his mother's consent. On the whole, might it not be better for her – better for them all – that she should think wholly of her duty, and not of the disagreeable results to which that duty might possibly lead? It could not be her duty to accede to such an alliance? and therefore she would do her best to prevent it. Such, at least, should be her attempt in the first instance.

Having so decided, she next resolved on her course of action. Immediately on her arrival at Framley, she would send for Lucy Robarts, and use all her eloquence – and perhaps also a little of that stern dignity for which she was so remarkable – in explaining to that young lady how very wicked it was on her part to think of forcing herself into such a family as that of the Luftons. She would explain to Lucy that no happiness could come of it, that people placed by misfortune above their sphere are always miserable; and, in short, make use of all those excellent moral lessons which are so customary on such occasions. The morality might perhaps be thrown away; but Lady Lufton depended much on her dignified sternness. And then, having so resolved, she prepared for her journey home. Very little had been said at Framley parsonage about Lord Lufton's offer after the departure of that gentleman; very little, at least, in Lucy's presence. That the parson and his wife should talk about it between themselves was a matter of course; but very few words were spoken on the matter either by or to Lucy. She was left to her own thoughts, and possibly to her own hopes. And then other matters came up at Framley which turned the current of interest into other tracks. In the first place there was the visit made by Mr. Sowerby to the Dragon of Wantly, and the consequent revelation made by Mark Robarts to his wife. And while that latter subject was yet new, before Fanny and Lucy had as yet made up their minds as to all the little economies which might be practised in the household without serious detriment to the master's comfort, news reached them that Mrs. Crawley of Hogglestock had been stricken with fever. Nothing of the kind could well be more dreadful than this. To those who knew the family it seemed impossible that their most ordinary wants could be supplied if that courageous head were even for a day laid low; and then the poverty of poor Mr. Crawley was such that the sad necessities of a sick bed could hardly be supplied without assistance. 'I will go over at once,' said Fanny.

'My dear!' said her husband, 'it is typhus, and you must first think of the children. I will go.'

'What on earth could you do, Mark?' said his wife. 'Men on such occasions are almost worse than useless; and then they are so much more liable to infection.'

'I have no children, nor am I a man,' said Lucy, smiling; 'for both of which exemptions I am thankful. I will go, and when I come back I will keep clear of the bairns.'

So it was settled, and Lucy started in the pony-carriage, carrying with her such things from the parsonage storehouse as were thought to be suitable to the wants of the sick lady at Hogglestock. When she arrived there, she made her way into the house, finding the door open, and not being able to obtain the assistance of the servant girl in ushering her in. In the parlour she found Grace Crawley, the eldest child, sitting demurely in her mother's chair nursing an infant. She, Grace herself, was still a young child, but not the less, on this occasion of well-understood sorrow, did she go through her task, not only with zeal but almost with solemnity. Her brother, a boy of six years old, was with her, and he had the care of another baby. There they sat in a cluster, quiet, grave, and silent, attending on themselves, because it had been willed by fate that no one else should attend on them. 'How is your mamma, dear Grace?' said Lucy, walking up to her, and holding out her hand.

'Poor mamma is very ill, indeed,' said Grace.

'And papa is very unhappy,' said Bobby, the boy.

'I can't get up because of baby,' said Grace; 'but Bobby can go and call papa out.'

'I will knock at the door,' said Lucy; and so saying she walked up to the bedroom door, and tapped against it lightly. She repeated this for the third time before she was summoned in by a low hoarse voice, and then on entering she saw Mr. Crawley standing by the bedside with a book in his hand. He looked at her uncomfortably, in a manner which seemed to show that he was annoyed by this intrusion, and Lucy was aware that she had disturbed him while at prayers by the bedside of his wife. He came across the room, however, and shook hands with her, and answered her inquiries in his ordinary grave and solemn voice. 'Mrs. Crawley is very ill,' he said – 'very ill. God has stricken us heavily, but His will be done. But you had better not go to her, Miss Robarts. It is typhus.'

The caution, however, was too late; for Lucy was already by the bedside, and had taken the hand of the sick woman, which had been extended on the coverlet to greet her. 'Dear Miss Robarts,' said a weak voice; 'this is very good of you; but it makes me unhappy to see you here.' Lucy lost no time in taking sundry matters into her own hands, and ascertaining what was most wanted in that wretched household. For it was wretched enough. Their only servant, a girl of sixteen, had been taken away by her mother as soon as it became known that Mrs. Crawley was ill with fever. The poor mother, to give her her due, had promised to come down morning and evening herself, to do such work as might be done in an hour or so; but she could not, she said, leave her child to catch the fever. And now, at the period of Lucy's visit, no step had been taken to procure a nurse, Mr. Crawley having resolved to take upon himself the duties of that position.

In his absolute ignorance of all sanatory measures, he had thrown himself on his knees to pray; and if prayers – true prayers – might succour his poor wife, of such succour she might be confident. Lucy, however, thought that other aid also was wanting to her. 'If you can do anything for us,' said Mrs. Crawley, 'let it be for the poor children.'

'I will have them all moved from this till you are better,' said Lucy, boldly.

'Moved!' said Mr. Crawley, who even now – even in his present strait – felt a repugnance to the idea that any one should relieve him of any portion of his burden.

'Yes,' said Lucy; 'I am sure it will be better that you should lose them for a week or two, till Mrs. Crawley may be able to leave her room.'

'But where are they to go?' said he, very gloomily. As to this Lucy was not as yet able to say anything. Indeed when she left Framley parsonage there had been no time for discussion. She would go back and talk it all over with Fanny, and find out in what way the children might be best put out of danger. Why should they not all be harboured at the parsonage, as soon as assurance could be felt that they were not tainted with the poison of the fever? An English lady of the right sort will do all things but one for a sick neighbour; but for no neighbour will she wittingly admit contagious sickness within the precincts of her own nursery. Lucy unloaded her jellies and her febrifuges, Mr. Crawley frowning at her bitterly the while. It had come to this with him, that food had been brought into his house, as an act of charity, in his very presence, and in his heart of hearts he disliked Lucy Robarts in that she had brought it. He could not cause the jars and the pots to be replaced in the pony-carriage, as he would have done had the position of his wife been different. In her state it would have been barbarous to refuse them, and barbarous also to have created the *fracas* of a refusal; but each parcel that was introduced was an additional weight laid on the sore withers of his pride, till the total burden became almost intolerable. All this his wife saw and recognized even in her illness, and did make some slight ineffectual efforts to give him ease; but Lucy in her new power was ruthless, and the chicken to make the chicken-broth was taken out of the basket under his very nose. But Lucy did not remain long. She had made up her mind what it behoved her to do herself, and she was soon ready to return to Framley. 'I shall be back again, Mr. Crawley,' she said, 'probably this evening, and I shall stay with her till she is better.' 'Nurses don't want rooms,' she went on to say, when Mr. Crawley muttered something as to there being no bed-chamber. 'I shall make up some kind of a litter near her; you'll see that I shall be very snug.' And then she got into the pony-chaise, and drove herself home.

CHAPTER XXXV

The Story of King Cophetua

LUCY as she drove herself home had much as to which it was necessary that she should arouse her thoughts. That she would go back and nurse Mrs. Crawley through her fever she was resolved. She was free agent enough to take so much on herself, and to feel sure that she could carry it through. But how was she to redeem her promise about the children? Twenty plans ran through her mind, as to farm-houses in which they might be placed, or cottages which might be hired for them; but all these entailed the want of money; and at the present moment, were not all the inhabitants of the parsonage pledged to a dire economy? This use of the pony-carriage would have been illicit under any circumstances less pressing than the present, for it had been decided that the carriage, and even poor Puck himself, should be sold. She had, however, given her promise about the children, and though her own stock of money was very low, that promise should be redeemed.

When she reached the parsonage she was of course full of her schemes, but she found that another subject of interest had come up in her absence, which prevented her from obtaining the undivided attention of her sister-in-law to her present plans. Lady Lufton had returned that day, and immediately on her return had sent up a note addressed to Miss Lucy Robarts, which note was in Fanny's hands when Lucy stepped out of the pony-carriage. The servant who brought it had asked for an answer, and a verbal answer had been sent, saying that Miss Robarts was away from home, and would herself send a reply when she returned. It cannot be denied that the colour came to Lucy's face, and that her hand trembled when she took the note from Fanny in the drawing-room. Everything in the world to her might depend on what that note contained; and yet she did not open it at once, but stood with it in her hand, and when Fanny pressed her on the subject, still endeavoured to bring back the conversation to the subject of Mrs. Crawley. But yet her mind was intent on the letter, and she had already augured ill from the handwriting and even from the words of the address. Had Lady Lufton intended to be propitious, she would have directed her letter to Miss Robarts, without the Christian name; so at least argued Lucy – quite unconsciously, as one does argue in such matters. One forms half the conclusions of one's life without any distinct knowledge that the premises have even passed through one's mind. They were now alone together, as Mark was out. 'Won't you open her letter?' said Mrs. Robarts.

'Yes, immediately; but, Fanny, I must speak to you about Mrs. Crawley first. I must go back there this evening, and stay there; I have promised to do so, and shall certainly keep my promise. I have promised also that the children shall be taken away, and we must arrange about that. It is dreadful, the state she is in. There is no one to see to her but Mr. Crawley, and the children are altogether left to themselves.'

'Do you mean that you are going back to stay?'

'Yes, certainly; I have made a distinct promise that I would do so. And about the children; could not you manage for the children, Fanny – not perhaps in the house; at least not at first, perhaps?' And yet during all the time that she was thus speaking and pleading for the Crawleys, she was endeavouring to imagine what might be the contents of that letter which she held between her fingers.

'And is she so very ill?' asked Mrs. Robarts.

'I cannot say how ill she may be, except this, that she certainly has typhus fever. They have had some doctor or doctor's assistant from Silverbridge; but it seems to me that they are greatly in want of better advice.'

'But, Lucy, will you not read your letter? It is astonishing to me that you should be so indifferent about it.' Lucy was anything but indifferent, and now did proceed to tear the envelope. The note was very short, and ran in these words —

'My dear Miss Robarts,

'I am particularly anxious to see you, and shall feel much obliged to you if you can step over to me here, at Framley Court. I must apologize for taking this liberty with you, but you will probably feel that an interview here would suit us both better than one at the parsonage.

'Truly yours,
'M. Lufton.'

'There: I am in for it now,' said Lucy, handing the note over to Mrs. Robarts. 'I shall have to be talked to as never poor girl was talked to before: and when one thinks of what I have done, it is hard.'

'Yes; and of what you have not done.'

'Exactly; and of what I have not done. But I suppose I must go,' and she proceeded to re-tie the strings of her bonnet, which she had loosened.

'Do you mean that you are going over at once?'

'Yes; immediately. Why not? it will be better to have it over, and then I can go to the Crawleys. But, Fanny, the pity of it is that I know it all as well as though it had been already spoken; and what good can there be in my having to endure it? Can't you fancy the tone in which she will explain to me the conventional inconveniences which arose when King Cophetua would marry the beggar's daughter? how she will explain what Griselda went through; – not the archdeacon's daughter, but the other Griselda?'

'But it all came right with her.'

'Yes; but then I am not Griselda, and she will explain how it would certainly all go wrong with me. But what's the good when I know it all beforehand? Have I not desired King Cophetua to take himself and sceptre elsewhere?' And then she started, having first said another word or two about the Crawley children, and obtained a promise of Puck and the pony-carriage for the afternoon. It was also almost agreed that Puck on his return to Framley should bring back the four children with him; but on this subject it was necessary that Mark should be consulted. The present scheme was to prepare for them a room outside the house, once the dairy, at present occupied by the groom and his wife; and to bring them into the house as soon as it was manifest that there was no danger from infection. But all this was to be matter for deliberation. Fanny wanted her to send over a note, in reply to Lady Lufton's, as harbinger of her coming; but Lucy marched off, hardly answering this proposition.

'What's the use of such a deal of ceremony?' she said. 'I know she's at home; and if she is not, I shall only lose ten minutes in going.' And so she went, and on reaching the door of Framley Court house found that her ladyship was at home. Her heart almost came to her mouth as she was told so, and then, in two minutes' time, she found herself in the little room upstairs. In that little room we found ourselves once before – you and I, O my reader;

– but Lucy had never before visited that hallowed precinct. There was something in its air calculated to inspire awe in those who first saw Lady Lufton sitting bolt upright in the cane-bottomed arm-chair, which she always occupied when at work at her books and papers; and this she knew when she determined to receive Lucy in that apartment. But there was there another arm-chair, an easy, cosy chair, which stood by the fireside; and for those who had caught Lady Lufton napping in that chair of an afternoon, some of this awe had perhaps been dissipated. 'Miss Robarts,' she said, not rising from her chair, but holding out her hand to her visitor, 'I am much obliged to you for having come over to me here. You, no doubt, are aware of the subject on which I wish to speak to you, and will agree with me that it is better that we should meet here than over at the parsonage.' In answer to which Lucy merely bowed her head, and took her seat on the chair which had been prepared for her. 'My son,' continued her ladyship, 'has spoken to me on the subject of —I think I understand, Miss Robarts, that there has been no encouragement between you and him?'

'None whatever,' said Lucy. 'He made me an offer and I refused him.' This she said very sharply; – more so undoubtedly than the circumstances required; and with a brusqueness that was injudicious as well as uncourteous. But at the moment, she was thinking of her own position with reference to Lady Lufton – not to Lord Lufton; and of her feelings with reference to the lady – not to the gentleman.

'Oh,' said Lady Lufton, a little startled by the manner of the communication. 'Then I am to understand that there is nothing now going on between you and my son; that the whole affair is over?'

'That depends entirely upon you.'

'On me; does it?'

'I do not know what your son may have told you, Lady Lufton. For myself, I do not care to have any secrets from you in this matter; and as he has spoken to you about it, I suppose that such is his wish also. Am I right in presuming that he has spoken to you on the subject?'

'Yes, he has; and it is for that reason that I have taken the liberty of sending for you.'

'And may I ask what he has told you? I mean, of course, as regards myself,' said Lucy. Lady Lufton, before she answered this question, began to reflect that the young lady was taking too much of the initiative in this conversation, and was, in fact, playing the game in her own fashion, which was not at all in accordance with those motives which had induced Lady Lufton to send for her. 'He has told me that he made you an offer of marriage,' replied Lady Lufton: 'a matter which, of course, is very serious to me, as his mother; and I have thought, therefore, that I had better see you, and appeal to your own good sense and judgement and high feeling. Of course you are aware –'

Now was coming the lecture to be illustrated by King Cophetua and Griselda, as Lucy had suggested to Mrs. Robarts; but she succeeded in stopping it for awhile. 'And did Lord Lufton tell you what was my answer?'

'Not in words. But you yourself now say that you refused him; and I must express my admiration for your good –'

'Wait half a moment, Lady Lufton. Your son did make me an offer. He made it to me in person, up at the parsonage, and I then refused him; – foolishly, as I now believe, for I dearly love him. But I did so from a mixture of feelings which I need not, perhaps, explain; that most prominent, no doubt, was a fear of your displeasure. And then he came again, not to me, but to my brother, and urged his suit to him. Nothing can have been kinder to me, more noble, more loving, more generous, than his conduct. At first I thought, when he was speaking to myself, that he was led on thoughtlessly to say all that he did say. I did not trust his love, though I saw that he did trust it himself. But I could not but trust it when he came again – to my brother, and made his proposal to him. I don't know whether you will understand me, Lady Lufton; but a girl placed as I am feels ten times more assurance in such a tender of affection as that, than in one made to herself, at the spur of the moment, perhaps. And then you must remember that I – I myself – I loved him from the first. I was foolish enough to think that I could know him and not love him.'

'I saw all that going on,' said Lady Lufton, with a certain assumption of wisdom about her; 'and took steps which I hoped would have put a stop to it in time.'

'Everybody saw it. It was a matter of course,' said Lucy, destroying her ladyship's wisdom at a blow. 'Well; I did learn to love him, not meaning to do so; and I do love him with all my heart. It is no use my striving to think that I do not; and I could stand with him at the altar to-morrow and give him my hand, feeling that I was doing my duty by him, as a woman should do. And now he has told you of his love, and I believe in that as I do in my own –' And then for a moment she paused.

'But, my dear Miss Robarts –' began Lady Lufton. Lucy, however, had now worked herself up into a condition of power, and would not allow her ladyship to interrupt her in her speech. 'I beg your pardon, Lady Lufton; I shall have done directly, and then I will hear you. And so my brother came to me, not urging this suit, expressing no wish for such a marriage, but allowing me to judge for myself, and proposing that I should see your son again on the following morning. Had I done so, I could not but have accepted him. Think of it, Lady Lufton. How could I have done other than accept him, seeing that in my heart I had accepted his love already?'

'Well?' said Lady Lufton, not wishing now to put in any speech of her own.

'I did not see him – I refused to do so – because I was a coward. I could not endure to come into this house as your son's wife, and be coldly looked on by your son's mother. Much as I loved him, much as I do love him, dearly as I prize the generous offer which he came down here to repeat to me, I could not live with him to be made the object of your scorn. I sent him word, therefore, that I would have him when you would ask me, and not before.' And, then, having thus pleaded her cause – and pleaded, as she believed, the cause of her lover also – she ceased from speaking, and prepared herself to listen to the story of King Cophetua. But Lady Lufton felt considerable difficulty in commencing her speech. In the first place she was by no means a hard-hearted or a selfish woman; and were it not that her own son was concerned, and all the glory which was reflected upon her from her son, her sympathies would have been given to Lucy Robarts. As it was, she did sympathize with her, and admire her, and to a certain extent like her. She began also to understand what it was that had brought about her son's love, and to feel that but for certain unfortunate concomitant circumstances the girl before her might have made a fitting Lady Lufton. Lucy had grown bigger in her eyes while sitting there and talking, and had lost much of that missish want of importance – that lack of social weight – which Lady Lufton in her own opinion had always imputed to her. A girl that could thus speak up and explain her own position now, would be able to speak up and explain her own, and perhaps some other positions at any future time. But not for all or any of these reasons did Lady Lufton think of giving way. The power of making or marring this marriage was placed in her hands, as was very fitting, and that power it behoved her to use, as best she might use it, to her son's advantage. Much as she might admire Lucy, she could not sacrifice her son to that admiration. The unfortunate concomitant circumstances still remained, and were of sufficient force, as she thought, to make such a marriage inexpedient. Lucy was the sister of a gentleman who by his peculiar position as parish clergyman of Framley was unfitted to be the brother-in-law of the owner of Framley. Nobody liked clergymen better than Lady Lufton or was more willing to live with them on terms of affectionate intimacy, but she could not get over the feeling that the clergyman of her own parish, – or of her son's, – was a part of her own establishment, of her own appanage, – or of his, – and that it could not be well that Lord Lufton should marry among his own dependants. Lady Lufton would not have used the word, but she did think it. And then, too, Lucy's education had been so deficient. She had had no one about her in early life accustomed to the ways of, —of what shall I say without making Lady Lufton appear more worldly than she was? Lucy's wants in this respect, not to be defined in words, had been exemplified by the very way in which she had just now stated her case. She had shown talent, good temper, and sound judgement; but there had been no quiet, no repose about her. The species of power in young ladies which Lady Lufton most admired was the *vis inertiæ* belonging to beautiful and dignified reticence; of this poor Lucy had none. Then, too, she had no fortune, which, though a minor evil, was an evil; and she had no birth, in the high-life sense of the word, which was a greater evil. And then, though her eyes had sparkled when she confessed her love, Lady Lufton was not prepared to admit that she was possessed of positive beauty. Such were the unfortunate concomitant circumstances which still induced Lady Lufton to resolve that the match must be marred.

But the performance of her part in this play was much more difficult than she had imagined, and she found herself obliged to sit silent for a minute or two, during which, however, Miss Robarts made no attempt at further speech. 'I am greatly struck,' Lady Lufton said at last, 'by the excellent sense you have displayed in the whole of this affair; and you must allow me to say, Miss Robarts, that I now regard you with very different feelings from those which I entertained when I left London.' Upon this Lucy bowed her head, slightly but very stiffly; acknowledging rather the former censure implied than the present eulogium expressed.

'But my feelings,' continued Lady Lufton, 'my strongest feelings in this matter, must be those of a mother. What might be my conduct if such a marriage did take place, I need not now consider. But I must confess that I should think such a marriage very – very ill-judged. A better-hearted young man than Lord Lufton does not exist, nor one with better principles, or a deeper regard for his word; but he is exactly the man to be mistaken in any hurried outlook as to his future life. Were you and he to become man and wife, such a marriage would tend to the happiness neither of him nor of you.' It was clear that the whole lecture was now coming; and as Lucy had openly declared her own weakness, and thrown all the power of decision into the hands of Lady Lufton, she did not see why she should endure this.

'We need not argue about that, Lady Lufton,' she said. 'I have told you the only circumstances under which I would marry your son; and you, at any rate, are safe.'

'No; I was not wishing to argue,' answered Lady Lufton, almost humbly; 'but I was desirous of excusing myself to you, so that you should not think me cruel in withholding my consent. I wished to make you believe that I was doing the best for my son.'

'I am sure that you think you are, and therefore no excuse is necessary.'

'No, exactly; of course it is a matter of opinion, and I do think so. I cannot believe that this marriage would make either of you happy, and therefore I should be very wrong to express my consent.'

'Then, Lady Lufton,' said Lucy, rising from her chair, 'I suppose we have both now said what is necessary, and I will therefore wish you good-bye.'

'Good-bye, Miss Robarts. I wish I could make you understand how very highly I regard your conduct in this matter. It has been above all praise, and so I shall not hesitate to say when speaking of it to your relatives.' This was disagreeable enough to Lucy, who cared but little for any praise which Lady Lufton might express to her relatives in this matter. 'And pray,' continued Lady Lufton, 'give my best love to Mrs. Robarts, and tell her that I shall hope to see her over here very soon, and Mr. Robarts also. I would name a day for you all to dine; but perhaps it will be better that I should have a little talk with Fanny first.'

Lucy muttered something, which was intended to signify that any such dinner party had better not be made up with the intention of including her, and then took her leave. She had decidedly had the best of the interview, and there was a consciousness of this in her heart as she allowed Lady Lufton to shake hands with her. She had stopped her antagonist short on each occasion on which an attempt had been made to produce the homily which had been prepared, and during the interview had spoken probably three words for every one which her ladyship had been able to utter. But, nevertheless, there was a bitter feeling of disappointment about her heart as she walked back home; and a feeling, also, that she herself had caused her own unhappiness. Why should she have been so romantic and chivalrous and self-sacrificing, seeing that her romance and chivalry had all been to his detriment as well as to hers, – seeing that she sacrificed him as well as herself? Why should she have been so anxious to play into Lady Lufton's hands? It was not because she thought it right, as a general social rule, that a lady should refuse a gentleman's hand, unless the gentleman's mother were a consenting party to the marriage. She would have held any such doctrine as absurd. The lady, she would have said, would have had to look to her own family and no further. It was not virtue but cowardice which had influenced her, and she had none of that solace which may come to us in misfortune from a consciousness that our own conduct has been blameless. Lady Lufton had inspired her with awe, and any such feeling on her part was mean, ignoble, and unbecoming the spirit with which she wished to think that she was endowed. That was the accusation which she brought against herself, and it forbade her to feel any triumph as to the result of her interview. When she reached the parsonage, Mark was there, and they were of course expecting her. 'Well,' said she, in her short, hurried manner, 'is Puck ready again? I have no time to lose, and I must go and pack up a few things. Have you settled about the children, Fanny?'

'Yes; I will tell you directly; but you have seen Lady Lufton?'

'Seen her! Oh, yes, of course I have seen her. Did she not send for me? and in that case it was not on the cards that I should disobey her.'

'And what did she say?'

'How green you are, Mark; and not only green, but impolite also, to make me repeat the story of my own disgrace. Of course she told me that she did not intend that I should marry my lord, her son; and of course I said that under those circumstances I should not think of doing such a thing.'

'Lucy, I cannot understand you,' said Fanny, very gravely. 'I am sometimes inclined to doubt whether you have any deep feeling in the matter or not. If you have, how can you bring yourself to joke about it?'

'Well, it is singular; and sometimes I doubt myself whether I have. I ought to be pale, ought I not? and very thin, and to go mad by degrees? I have not the least intention of doing anything of the kind, and, therefore, the matter is not worth any further notice.'

'But was she civil to you, Lucy?' asked Mark: 'civil in her manner, you know?'

'Oh, uncommonly so. You will hardly believe it, but she actually asked me to dine. She always does, you know, when she wants to show her good humour. If you'd broken your leg, and she wished to commiserate you, she'd ask you to dinner.'

'I suppose she meant to be kind,' said Fanny, who was not disposed to give up her old friend, though she was quite ready to fight Lucy's battle, if there were any occasion for a battle to be fought.

'Lucy is so perverse,' said Mark, 'that it is impossible to learn from her what really has taken place.'

'Upon my word, then, you know it all as well as I can tell you. She asked me if Lord Lufton had made me an offer. I said, yes. She asked next, if I meant to accept it. Not without her approval, I said. And then she asked us all to dinner. That is exactly what took place, and I cannot see that I have been perverse at all.' After that she threw herself into a chair, and Mark and Fanny stood looking at each other.

'Mark,' she said, after a while, 'don't be unkind to me. I make as little of it as I can, for all our sakes. It is better so, Fanny, than that I should go about moaning, like a sick cow;' and then they looked at her, and saw that the tears were already brimming over from her eyes.

'Dearest, dearest Lucy,' said Fanny, immediately going down on her knees before her, 'I won't be unkind to you again.' And then they had a great cry together.

CHAPTER XXXVI

Kidnapping at Hogglestock

THE great cry, however, did not take long, and Lucy was soon in the pony-carriage again. On this occasion her brother volunteered to drive her, and it was now understood that he was to bring back with him all the Crawley children. The whole thing had been arranged; the groom and his wife were to be taken into the house, and the big bedroom across the yard, usually occupied by them, was to be converted into a quarantine hospital until such time as it might be safe to pull down the yellow flag. They were about half-way on their road to Hogglestock when they were overtaken by a man on horseback, whom, when he came up beside them, Mr. Robarts recognized as Dr. Arabin, Dean of Barchester, and head of the chapter to which he himself belonged. It immediately appeared that the dean also was going to Hogglestock, having heard of the misfortune that had befallen his friends there; he had, he said, started as soon as the news reached him, in order that he might ascertain how best he might render assistance. To effect this he had undertaken a ride of nearly forty miles, and explained that he did not expect to reach home again much before midnight. 'You pass by Framley?' said Robarts.

'Yes, I do,' said the dean.

'Then of course you will dine with us as you go home; you and your horse also, which will be quite as important.' This having been duly settled, and the proper ceremony of introduction having taken place between the dean and Lucy, they proceeded to discuss the character of Mr. Crawley.

'I have known him all my life,' said the dean, 'having been at school and college with him, and for years since that I was on terms of the closest intimacy with him; but in spite of that, I do not know how to help him in his need. A prouder-hearted man I never met, or one less willing to share his sorrows with his friends.'

'I have often heard him speak of you,' said Mark.

'One of the bitterest feelings I have is that a man so dear to me should live so near to me, and that I should see so little of him. But what can I do? He will not come to my house; and when I go to his he is angry with me because I wear a shovel hat and ride on horseback.'

'I should leave my hat and my horse at the borders of the last parish,' said Lucy, timidly.

'Well; yes, certainly; one ought not to give offence even in such matters as that; but my coat and waistcoat would then be equally objectionable. I have changed, – in outward matters I mean, – and he has not. That irritates him, and unless I could be what I was in the old days, he will not look at me with the same eyes'; and then he rode on, in order, as he said, that the first pang of the interview might be over before Robarts and his sister came upon the scene. Mr. Crawley was standing before his door, leaning over the little wooden railing, when the dean trotted up on his horse. He had come out after hours of close watching to get a few mouthfuls of the sweet summer air, and as he stood there he held the youngest of his children in his arms. The poor little baby sat there, quiet indeed, but hardly happy. This father, though he loved his offspring with an affection as intense as that which human nature can supply, was not gifted with the knack of making children fond of him; for it is hardly more than a knack, that aptitude which some men have of gaining the good graces of the young. Such men are not always the best fathers or the safest guardians; but they carry about with them a certain *duc ad me* which children recognize, and which in three minutes upsets all the barriers between five and five-and-forty. But Mr. Crawley was a stern man, thinking ever of the souls and minds of his bairns – as a father should do; and thinking also that every season was fitted for operating on these souls and minds – as, perhaps, he should not have done either as a father or as a teacher. And consequently his children avoided him when the choice was given them, thereby adding fresh wounds to his torn heart, but by no means quenching any of the great love with which he regarded them.

He was standing there thus with a placid little baby in his arms – a baby placid enough, but one that would not kiss him eagerly, and stroke his face with her soft little hands, as he would have had her do – when he saw the dean coming towards him. He was sharp-sighted as a lynx out in the open air, though now obliged to pore over his well-fingered books with spectacles on his nose; and thus he knew his friend from a long distance, and had time to meditate the mode of his greeting. He too doubtless had come, if not with jelly and chicken, then with money and advice; – with money and advice such as a thriving dean might offer to a poor brother clergyman; and Mr. Crawley, though no husband could possibly be more anxious for a wife's safety than he was, immediately put his back up and began to bethink himself how these tenders might be rejected.

'How is she?' were the first words which the dean spoke as he pulled up his horse close to the little gate, and put out his hand to take that of his friend.

'How are you, Arabin?' said he. 'It is very kind of you to come so far, seeing how much there is to keep you at Barchester. I cannot say that she is any better, but I do not know that she is worse. Sometimes I fancy that she is delirious, though I hardly know. At any rate her mind wanders, and then after that she sleeps.'

'But is the fever less?'

'Sometimes less and sometimes more, I imagine.'

'And the children?'

'Poor things; they are well as yet.'

'They must be taken from this, Crawley, as a matter of course.'

Mr. Crawley fancied that there was a tone of authority in the dean's advice, and immediately put himself into opposition.

'I do not know how that may be; I have not yet made up my mind.'

'But, my dear Crawley –'

'Providence does not admit of such removals in all cases,' said he. 'Among the poorer classes the children must endure such perils.'

'In many cases it is so,' said the dean, by no means inclined to make an argument of it at the present moment; 'but in this case they need not. You must allow me to make arrangements for sending for them, as of course your time is occupied here.' Miss Robarts, though she had mentioned her intention of staying with Mrs. Crawley, had said nothing of the Framley plan with reference to the children.

'What you mean is that you intend to take the burden off my shoulders – in fact, to pay for them. I cannot allow that, Arabin. They must take the lot of their father and their mother, as it is proper that they should do.' Again the dean had no inclination for arguing, and thought it might be well to let the question of the children drop for a little while.

'And is there no nurse with her?' said he.

'No, no; I am seeing to her myself at the present moment. A woman will be here just now.'

'What woman?'

'Well; her name is Mrs. Stubbs; she lives in the parish. She will put the younger children to bed, and – and—but it's no use troubling you with all that. There was a young lady talked of coming, but no doubt she has found it too inconvenient. It will be better as it is.'

'You mean Miss Robarts; she will be here directly; I passed her as I came here;' and as Dr. Arabin was yet speaking, the noise of the carriage wheels was heard upon the road.

'I will go in now,' said Mr. Crawley, 'and see if she still sleeps;' and then he entered the house, leaving the dean at the door still seated upon his horse. 'He will be afraid of the infection, and I will not ask him to come in,' said Mr. Crawley to himself.

'I shall seem to be prying into his poverty, if I enter unasked,' said the dean to himself. And so he remained there till Puck, now acquainted with the locality, stopped at the door.

'Have you not been in?' said Robarts.

'No; Crawley has been at the door talking to me; he will be here directly, I suppose;' and then Mark Robarts also prepared himself to wait till the master of the house should reappear. But Lucy had no such punctilious misgivings; she did not much care now whether she offended

Mr. Crawley or no. Her idea was to place herself by the sick woman's bedside, and to send the four children away; – with their father's consent if it might be; but certainly without it if that consent were withheld. So she got down from the carriage, and taking certain packages in her hand made her way direct into the house.

'There's a big bundle under the seat, Mark,' she said; 'I'll come and fetch it directly if you'll drag it out.' For some five minutes the two dignitaries of the Church remained at the door, one on his cob and the other in his low carriage, saying a few words to each other and waiting till some one should again appear from the house. 'It is all arranged, indeed it is,' were the first words which reached their ears, and these came from Lucy. 'There will be no trouble at all, and no expense, and they shall all come back as soon as Mrs. Crawley is able to get out of bed.'

'But, Miss Robarts, I can assure –' That was Mr. Crawley's voice, heard from him as he followed Miss Robarts to the door; but one of the elder children had then called him into the sick room, and Lucy was left to do her worst.

'Are you going to take the children back with you?' said the dean.

'Yes; Mrs. Robarts has prepared for them.'

'You can take greater liberties with my friend here than I can.'

'It is all my sister's doing,' said Robarts. 'Women are always bolder in such matters than men.' And then Lucy reappeared, bringing Bobby with her, and one of the younger children.

'Do not mind what he says,' said she, 'but drive away when you have got them all. Tell Fanny I have put into the basket what things I could find, but they are very few. She must borrow things for Grace from Mrs. Granger's little girl' – (Mrs. Granger was the wife of a Framley farmer); – 'and, Mark, turn Puck's head round, so that you may be off in a moment. I'll have Grace and the other one here directly.' And then, leaving her brother to pack Bobby and his little sister on the back part of the vehicle, she returned to her business in the house. She had just looked in at Mrs. Crawley's bed, and finding her awake, had smiled on her, and deposited her bundle in token of her intended stay, and then, without speaking a word, had gone on her errand about the children. She had called to Grace to show her where she might find such things as were to be taken to Framley, and having explained to the bairns, as well as she might, the destiny which immediately awaited them, prepared them for their departure without saying a word to Mr. Crawley on the subject. Bobby and the elder of the two infants were stowed away safely in the back part of the carriage, where they allowed themselves to be placed without saying a word. They opened their eyes and stared at the dean, who sat by on his horse, and assented to such orders as Mr. Robarts gave them, – no doubt with much surprise, but nevertheless in absolute silence.

'Now, Grace, be quick, there's a dear,' said Lucy, returning with the infant in her arms. 'And, Grace, mind you are very careful about baby; and bring the basket; I'll give it you when you are in.' Grace and the other child were then packed on to the other seat, and a basket with children's clothes put in on the top of them. 'That'll do, Mark; good-bye; tell Fanny to be sure and send the day after tomorrow, and not to forget –' and then she whispered into her brother's ear an injunction about certain dairy comforts which might not be spoken of in the hearing of Mr. Crawley. 'Good-bye, dears; mind you are good children; you shall hear about mamma the day after tomorrow,' said Lucy; and Puck, admonished by a sound from his master's voice, began to move just as Mr. Crawley reappeared at the house door.

'Oh, oh, stop!' he said. 'Miss Robarts, you really had better not –'

'Go on, Mark,' said Lucy, in a whisper, which, whether audible or not by Mr. Crawley, was heard very plainly by the dean. And Mark, who had slightly arrested Puck by the reins on the appearance of Mr. Crawley, now touched the impatient little beast with his whip; and the vehicle with its freight darted off rapidly, Puck shaking his head and going away with a tremendously quick short trot, which soon separated Mr. Crawley from his family.

'Miss Robarts,' he began, 'this step has been taken altogether without –'

'Yes,' said she, interrupting him. 'My brother was obliged to return at once. The children, you know, will remain all together at the parsonage; and that, I think, is what Mrs. Crawley will best like. In a day or two they will be under Mrs. Robarts's own charge.'

'But, my dear Miss Robarts, I had no intention whatever of putting the burden of my family on the shoulders of another person. They must return to their own home immediately – that is, as soon as they can be brought back.'

'I really think Miss Robarts has managed very well,' said the dean. 'Mrs. Crawley must be so much more comfortable to think that they are out of danger.'

'And they will be quite comfortable at the parsonage,' said Lucy.

'I do not at all doubt that,' said Mr. Crawley; 'but too much of such comforts will unfit them for their home; and – and I could have wished that I had been consulted more at leisure before the proceeding had been taken.'

'It was arranged, Mr. Crawley, when I was here before, that the children had better go away,' pleaded Lucy.

'I do not remember agreeing to such a measure, Miss Robarts; however – I suppose they cannot be had back tonight?'

'No, not to-night,' said Lucy. 'And now I will go in to your wife.' And then she returned to the house, leaving the two gentlemen at the door. At this moment a labourer's boy came sauntering by, and the dean, obtaining possession of his services for the custody of his horse, was able to dismount and put himself on a more equal footing for conversation with his friend.

'Crawley,' said he, putting his hand affectionately on his friend's shoulder, as they both stood leaning on the little rail before the door; 'that is a good girl – a very good girl.'

'Yes,' said he slowly; 'she means well.'

'Nay, but she does well; she does excellently. What can be better than her conduct now? While I was meditating how I might possibly assist your wife in this strait –'

'I want no assistance; none, at least, from man,' said Crawley, bitterly.

'Oh, my friend, think of what you are saying! Think of the wickedness which must accompany such a state of mind! Have you ever known any man able to walk alone, without assistance from his brother men?' Mr. Crawley did not make any immediate answer, but putting his arms behind his back and closing his hands, as was his wont when he walked alone thinking of the general bitterness of his lot in life, began to move slowly along the road in front of his house. He did not invite the other to walk with him, but neither was there anything in his manner which seemed to indicate that he had intended to be left to himself. It was a beautiful summer afternoon, at that delicious period of the year when summer has just burst forth from the growth of spring; when the summer is yet but three days old, and all the various shades of green which nature can put forth are still in their unsoiled purity of freshness. The apple blossoms were on the trees, and the hedges were sweet with May. The cuckoo at five o'clock was still sounding his soft summer call with unabated energy, and even the common grasses of the hedgerows were sweet with the fragrance of their new growth. The foliage of the oaks was complete, so that every bough and twig was clothed; but the leaves did not yet hang heavy in masses, and the bend of every bough and the tapering curve of every twig were visible through their light green covering. There is no time of the year equal in beauty to the first week in summer: and no colour which nature gives, not even the gorgeous hues of autumn, which can equal the verdure produced by the first warm suns of May.

Hogglestock, as has been explained, has little to offer in the way of landskip beauty, and the clergyman's house at Hogglestock was not placed on a green slopy bank of land, retired from the road, with its windows opening on to a lawn, surrounded by shrubs, with a view of the small church tower seen through them; it had none of that beauty which is so common to the cosy houses of our spiritual pastors in the agricultural parts of England. Hogglestock parsonage stood bleak beside the road, with no pretty paling lined inside by hollies and laburnum, Portugal laurels and rose-trees. But, nevertheless, even Hogglestock was pretty now. There were apple-trees there covered with blossom, and the hedgerows were in full flower. There were thrushes singing, and here and there an oak-tree stood in the roadside, perfect in its solitary beauty.

'Let us walk on a little,' said the dean. 'Miss Robarts is with her now, and you will be better for leaving the room for a few minutes.'

'No,' said he; 'I must go back; I cannot leave that young lady to do my work.'

'Stop, Crawley!' And the dean, putting his hand upon him, stayed him in the road. 'She is doing her own work, and if you were speaking of her with reference to any other household than your own, you would say so. Is it not a comfort to you to know that your wife has a woman near her at such a time as this; and a woman, too, who can speak to her as one lady does to another?'

'These are comforts which we have no right to expect. I could not have done much for poor Mary; but what a man could have done should not have been wanting.'

'I am sure of it; I know it well. What any man could do by himself you would do – excepting one thing.' And the dean as he spoke looked full into the other's face.

'And what is there I would not do?' said Crawley.

'Sacrifice your own pride.'

'My pride?'

'Yes; your own pride.'

'I have had but little pride this many a day. Arabin, you do not know what my life has been. How is a man to be proud who –' And then he stopped himself, not wishing to go through the catalogue of those grievances, which, as he thought, had killed the very germs of pride within him, or to insist by spoken words on his poverty, his wants, and the injustice of his position. 'No; I wish I could be proud; but the world has been too heavy to me, and I have forgotten all that.'

'How long have I known you, Crawley?'

'How long? Ah dear! a lifetime nearly, now.'

'And we were like brothers once.'

'Yes; we were equal as brothers then – in our fortunes, our tastes, and our modes of life.'

'And yet you would begrudge me the pleasure of putting my hand in my pocket, and relieving the inconveniences which have been thrown on you, and those you love better than yourself, by the chances of your fate in life.'

'I will live on no man's charity,' said Crawley, with an abruptness which amounted almost to an expression of anger.

'And is not that pride?'

'No – yes; – it is a species of pride, but not that pride of which you spoke. A man cannot be honest if he have not some pride. You yourself; would you not rather starve than become a beggar?'

'I would rather beg than see my wife starve,' said Arabin.

Crawley when he heard these words turned sharply round, and stood with his back to the dean, with his hands still behind him, and with his eyes fixed upon the ground.

'But in this case there is no question of begging,' continued the dean. 'I, out of those superfluities which it has pleased God to put at my disposal, am anxious to assist the needs of those whom I love.'

'She is not starving,' said Crawley, in a voice very bitter, but still intended to be exculpatory of himself.

'No, my dear friend; I know she is not, and do not you be angry with me because I have endeavoured to put the matter to you in the strongest language I could use.'

'You look at it, Arabin, from one side only; I can only look at it from the other. It is very sweet to give; I do not doubt that. But the taking of what is given is very bitter. Gift bread chokes in a man's throat and poisons his blood, and sits like lead upon the heart. You have never tried it.'

'But that is the very fault for which I blame you. That is the pride which I say you ought to sacrifice.'

'And why should I be called on to do so? Is not the labourer worthy of his hire? Am I not able to work, and willing? Have I not always had my shoulder to the collar, and is it right that I should now be contented with the scraps from a rich man's kitchen? Arabin, you and I were equal once and we were then friends, understanding each other's thoughts and sympathizing with each other's sorrows. But it cannot be so now.'

'If there be such inability, it is all with you.'

'It is all with me, – because in our connexion the pain would all be on my side. It would not hurt you to see me at your table with worn shoes and a ragged shirt. I do not think so meanly of you as that. You would give me your feast to eat though I were not clad a tithe as well as the menial behind your chair. But it would hurt me to know that there were those looking at me who thought me unfit to sit in your rooms.'

'That is the pride of which I speak; – false pride.'

'Call it so if you will; but, Arabin, no preaching of yours can alter it. It is all that is left to me of my manliness. That poor broken reed who is lying there sick, – who has sacrificed all the world to her love for me, – who is the mother of my children, and the partner of my sorrows and the wife of my bosom, – even she cannot change me in this, though she pleads with the eloquence of all her wants. Not even for her can I hold out my hand for a dole.' They had now come back to the door of the house, and Mr. Crawley, hardly conscious of what he was doing, was preparing to enter.

'Will Mrs. Crawley be able to see me if I come in?' said the dean.

'Oh, stop; no; you had better not do so,' said Mr. Crawley. 'You, no doubt, might be subject to infection, and then Mrs. Arabin would be frightened.'

'I do not care about it in the least,' said the dean.

'But it is of no use; you had better not. Her room, I fear, is quite unfit for you to see; and the whole house, you know, may be infected.' Dr. Arabin by this time was in the sitting-room; but seeing that his friend was really anxious that he should not go farther, he did not persist.

'It will be a comfort to us, at any rate, to know that Miss Robarts is with her.'

'The young lady is very good – very good indeed,' said Crawley; 'but I trust she will return to her home to-morrow. It is impossible that she should remain in so poor a house as mine. There will be nothing here of all the things that she will want.' The dean thought that Lucy Robarts's wants during her present occupation of nursing would not be so numerous as to make her continued sojourn in Mrs. Crawley's sick room impossible, and therefore took his leave with a satisfied conviction that the poor lady would not be left wholly to the somewhat unskilful nursing of her husband.

CHAPTER XXXVII

Mr. Sowerby Without Company

AND now there were going to be wondrous doings in West Barsetshire, and men's minds were much disturbed. The fiat had gone forth from the high places, and the Queen had dissolved her faithful Commons.

The giants, finding that they could effect little or nothing with the old House, had resolved to try what a new venture would do for them, and the hubbub of a general election was to pervade the country. This produced no inconsiderable irritation and annoyance, for the House was not as yet quite three years old; and members of Parliament, though they naturally feel a constitutional pleasure in meeting their friends and in pressing the hands of their constituents, are, nevertheless, so far akin to the lower order of humanity that they appreciate the danger of losing their seats; and the certainty of a considerable outlay in their endeavours to retain them is not agreeable to the legislative mind. Never did the old family fury between the gods and giants rage higher than at the present moment. The giants declared that every turn which they attempted to take in their country's service had been thwarted by faction, in spite of those benign promises of assistance made to them only a few weeks since by their opponents; and the gods answered by asserting that they were driven to this opposition by the Bœotian fatuity of the giants. They had no doubt promised their aid, and were ready to give it to measures that were decently prudent; but not to a bill enabling Government at its will to pension aged bishops! No; there must be some limit to their tolerance, and when such attempts as these were made that limit had been clearly passed. All this had taken place openly only a day or two after that casual whisper dropped by Tom Towers at Miss Dunstable's party – by Tom Towers, that most pleasant of all pleasant fellows. And how should he have known it, – he who flutters from one sweetest flower of the garden to another,

> 'Adding sugar to the pink, and honey to the rose,
> So loved for what he gives, but taking nothing as he goes'?

But the whisper had grown into a rumour, and the rumour into a fact, and the political world was in a ferment. The giants, furious about their bishops' pension bill, threatened the House – most injudiciously; and then it was beautiful to see how indignant members got up, glowing with honesty, and declared that it was base to conceive that any gentleman in that House could be actuated in his vote by any hopes or fears with reference to his seat. And so matters grew from bad to worse, and these contending parties never hit at each other with such envenomed wrath as they did now; – having entered the ring together so lately with such manifold promises of good-will, respect, and forbearance!

But going from the general to the particular, we may say that nowhere was a deeper consternation spread than in the electoral division of West Barsetshire. No sooner had the tidings of the dissolution reached the county than it was known that the duke intended to change his nominee. Mr. Sowerby had now sat for the division since the Reform Bill! He had become one of the county institutions, and by the dint of custom and long establishment had been borne with and even liked by the county gentlemen, in spite of his well-known pecuniary irregularities. Now all this was to be changed. No reason had as yet been publicly given, but it was understood that Lord Dumbello was to be returned, although he did not own an acre of land in the county. It is true that rumour went on to say that Lord Dumbello was about to form close connexions with Barsetshire. He was on the eve of marrying a young lady, from the other division indeed, and was now engaged, so it was said, in completing arrangements with the Government for the purchase of that noble Crown property usually known as the Chace of Chaldicotes. It was also stated – this statement, however, had hitherto been only announced in confidential whispers – that Chaldicotes House itself would soon become the residence of the marquis. The duke was claiming it as his own – would very shortly have completed his claims and taken possession: – and then, by some arrangement between them, it was to be made over to Lord Dumbello. But very contrary rumours to these got abroad also. Men said – such as dared to oppose the duke, and some few also who did not dare to oppose him when the day of battle came – that it was beyond his grace's power to turn Lord Dumbello into a Barsetshire magnate. The Crown property – such men said – was to fall into the hands of young Mr. Gresham, of Boxall Hill, in the other division, and that the terms of purchase had been already settled. And as to Mr. Sowerby's property and the house of Chaldicotes – these opponents of the Omnium interest went on to explain – it was by no means as yet so certain that the duke would be able to enter it and take possession. The place was not to be given up to him quietly. A great fight would be made, and it was beginning to be believed that the enormous mortgages would be paid off by a lady of immense wealth. And then a dash of romance was not wanting to make these stories palatable. This lady of immense wealth had been courted by Mr. Sowerby, had acknowledged her love, – but had refused to marry him on account of his character. In testimony of her love, however, she was about to pay all his debts.

It was soon put beyond a rumour, and became manifest enough, that Mr. Sowerby did not intend to retire from the county in obedience to the duke's behests. A placard was posted through the whole division in which no allusion was made by name to the duke, but in which Mr. Sowerby warned his friends not to be led away by any report that he intended to retire from the representation of West Barsetshire. 'He had sat,' the placard said, 'for the same county during the full period of a quarter of a century, and he would not lightly give up an honour that had been extended to him so often and which he prized so dearly. There were but few men now in the House whose connexion with the same body of constituents had remained unbroken so long as had that which bound him to West Barsetshire; and he confidently hoped that that connexion might be continued through another period of coming years till he might find himself in the glorious position of being the father of the county members of the House of Commons.' The placard said much more than this, and hinted at sundry and various questions, all of great interest to the county; but it did not say one word of the Duke of Omnium, though every one knew what the duke was supposed to be doing in the matter. He was, as it were, a great Llama, shut up in a holy of holies, inscrutable, invisible, inexorable, – not to be seen by men's eyes or heard by their ears, hardly to be mentioned by ordinary men at such periods as these without an inward quaking. But, nevertheless, it was he who was supposed to rule them. Euphemism required that his name should be mentioned at no public meetings in connexion with the coming election; but, nevertheless, most men in the county believed that he could send his dog up to the House of Commons as member for West Barsetshire if it so pleased him.

It was supposed, therefore, that our friend Sowerby would have no chance; but he was lucky in finding assistance in a quarter from which he certainly had not deserved it. He had been a staunch friend of the gods during the whole of his political life, – as, indeed, was to be expected, seeing that he had been the duke's nominee; but, nevertheless, on the present occasion, all the giants connected with the county came forward to his rescue. They did not do this with the acknowledged purpose of opposing the duke; they declared that they were actuated by a generous disinclination to see an old county member put from his seat; but the world knew that the battle was to be waged against the great Llama. It was to be a contest between the powers of aristocracy and the powers of oligarchy, as those powers existed in West Barsetshire, – and, it may be added, that democracy would have very little to say to it, on one side or on the other. The lower order of voters, the small farmers and tradesmen, would no doubt range themselves on the side of the duke, and would endeavour to flatter themselves that they were thereby furthering the views of the Liberal side; but they would in fact be led to the poll by an old-fashioned, time-honoured adherence to the will of their great Llama; and by an apprehension of evil if that Llama should arise and shake himself in his wrath. What might not come to the county if the Llama were to walk himself off, he with his satellites and armies and courtiers? There he was, a great Llama; and though he came among them but seldom, and was scarcely seen when he did come, nevertheless – and not the less but rather the more – was obedience to him considered as salutary and opposition regarded as dangerous. A great rural Llama is still sufficiently mighty in rural England. But the priest of the temple, Mr. Fothergill, was frequent enough in men's eyes, and it was beautiful to hear with how varied a voice he alluded to the things around him and to the changes which were coming. To the small farmers, not only on the Gatherum property, but on others also, he spoke of the duke as a beneficent influence shedding prosperity on all around him, keeping up prices by his presence, and forbidding the poor rates to rise above one and four-pence in the pound by the general employment which he occasioned. Men must be mad, he thought, who would willingly fly in the duke's face. To the squires from a distance he declared that no one had a right to charge the duke with any interference; as far, at least, as he knew the duke's mind. People would talk of things of which they understood nothing. Could any one say that he had traced a single request for a vote home to the duke? All this did not alter the settled conviction on men's minds; but it had its effect, and tended to increase the mystery in which the duke's doings were enveloped. But to his own familiars, to the gentry immediately around him, Mr. Fothergill merely winked his eye. They knew what was what, and so did he. The duke had never been bit yet in such matters, and Mr. Fothergill did not think that he would now submit himself to any such operation.

I never heard in what manner and at what rate Mr. Fothergill received remuneration for the various services performed by him with reference to the duke's property in Barsetshire; but I am very sure that, whatever might be the amount, he earned it thoroughly. Never was there a more faithful partisan, or one who, in his partisanship, was more discreet. In this matter of the coming election he declared that he himself – personally, on his own hook – did intend to bestir himself actively on behalf of Lord Dumbello. Mr. Sowerby was an old friend of his, and a very good fellow. That was true. But all the world must admit that Sowerby was not in the position which a county member ought to occupy. He was a ruined man, and it would not be for his own advantage that he should be maintained in a position which was fit only for a man of property. He knew – he, Fothergill – that Mr. Sowerby must abandon all right and claim to Chaldicotes; and if so, what would be more absurd than to acknowledge that he had a right and claim to the seat in Parliament? As to Lord Dumbello, it was probable that he would soon become one of the largest landowners in the county; and, as such, who could be more fit for the representation? Beyond this, Mr. Fothergill was not ashamed to confess – so he said – that he hoped to hold Lord Dumbello's agency. It would be compatible with his other duties, and therefore, as a matter of course, he intended to support Lord Dumbello; he himself, that is. As to the duke's mind in the matter –! But I have already explained how Mr. Fothergill disposed of that.

In these days, Mr. Sowerby came down to his own house – for ostensibly it was still his own house – but he came very quietly, and his arrival was hardly known in his own village. Though his placard was stuck up so widely, he himself took no electioneering steps; none, at least, as yet. The protection against arrest which he derived from Parliament would soon be over, and those who were most bitter against the duke averred that steps would be taken to arrest him, should he give sufficient opportunity to the myrmidons of the law. That he would, in such case, be arrested was very likely; but it was not likely that this would be done in any way at the duke's instance. Mr. Fothergill declared indignantly that this insinuation made him very angry; but he was too prudent a man to be very angry at anything, and he knew how to make capital on his own side of charges such as these which overshot their own mark. Mr. Sowerby came down very quietly to Chaldicotes, and there he remained for a couple of days, quite alone. The place bore a very different aspect now to that which we noticed when Mark Robarts drove up to it, in the early pages of this little narrative. There were no lights in the windows now, and no voices came from the stables; no dogs barked, and all was dead and silent as the grave. During the greater portion of those two days he sat alone within the house, almost unoccupied. He did not even open his letters, which lay piled on a crowded table in the small breakfast parlour in which he sat; for the letters of such men come in piles, and there are few of them which are pleasant in the reading. There he sat, troubled with thoughts which were sad enough, now and then moving to and fro the house, but for the most part occupied in thinking over the position to which he had brought himself. What would he be in the world's eye, if he ceased to be the owner of Chaldicotes, and ceased also to be the member for his county? He had lived ever before the world, and, though always harassed by encumbrances, had been sustained and comforted by the excitement of a prominent position. His debts and difficulties had hitherto been bearable, and he had borne them with ease so long that he had almost taught himself to think that they would never be unendurable. But now –

The order for foreclosing had gone forth, and the harpies of the law, by their present speed in sticking their claws into the carcass of his property, were atoning to themselves for the delay with which they had hitherto been compelled to approach their prey. And the order as to his seat had gone forth also. That placard had been drawn up by the combined efforts of his sister, Miss Dunstable, and a certain well-known electioneering agent, named Closerstill, presumed to be in the interest of the giants. But poor Sowerby had but little confidence in the placard. No one knew better than he how great was the duke's power. He was hopeless, therefore, as he walked about through those empty rooms, thinking of his past life and of that life which was to come. Would it not be well for him that he were dead, now that he was dying to all that had made the world pleasant? We see and hear of such men as Mr. Sowerby, and are apt to think that they enjoy all that the world can give, and that they enjoy that all without payment either in care or labour; but I doubt that, with even the most callous of them, their periods of wretchedness must be frequent, and that wretchedness very intense. Salmon and lamb in February, and green pease and new potatoes in March, can hardly make a man happy, even though nobody pays for them; and the feeling that one is an *antecedentem scelestum* after whom a sure, though lame, Nemesis is hobbling, must sometimes disturb one's slumbers. On the present occasion Scelestus felt that his Nemesis had overtaken him. Lame as she had been, and swift as he had run, she had mouthed him at last, and there was nothing left for him but to listen to the 'whoop' set up at the sight of his own death-throes.

It was a melancholy, dreary place now, that big house of Chaldicotes; and though the woods were all green with their early leaves, and the garden thick with flowers, they also were melancholy and dreary. The lawns were untrimmed and weeds were growing through the gravel, and here and there a cracked Dryad, tumbled from her pedestal and sprawling in the grass, gave a look of disorder to the whole place. The wooden trellis-work was shattered here and bending there, the standard rose-trees were stooping to the ground, and the leaves of the winter still encumbered the borders. Late in the evening of the second day Mr. Sowerby strolled out, and went through the gardens into the wood. Of all the inanimate things of the world this wood of Chaldicotes was the dearest to him. He was not a man to whom his companions gave much credit for feelings or thoughts akin to poetry, but here, out in the Chace, his mind would be almost poetical. While wandering among the forest trees, he became susceptible of the tenderness of human nature: he would listen to the birds singing, and pick here and there a wild flower on his path. He would watch the decay of the old trees and the progress of the young, and make pictures in his eyes of every turn in the wood. He would mark the colour of a bit of road as it dipped into a dell, and then, passing through a water-course, rose brown, rough, irregular, and beautiful against the bank on the other side. And then he would sit and think of his old family: how they had roamed there time out of mind in those Chaldicotes woods, father and son and grandson in regular succession, each giving them over, without blemish or decrease, to his successor. So he would sit; and so he did sit even now, and, thinking of these things, wished that he had never been born.

It was dark night when he returned to the house, and as he did so he resolved that he would quit the place altogether, and give up the battle as lost. The duke should take it and do as he pleased with it; and as for the seat in Parliament, Lord Dumbello, or any other equally gifted young patrician, might hold it for him. He would vanish from the scene and betake himself to some land from whence he would be neither heard nor seen, and there – starve. Such were now his future outlooks into the world; and yet, as regards health and all physical capacities, he knew that he was still in the prime of his life. Yes; in the prime of his life! But what could he do with what remained to him of such prime? How could he turn either his mind or his strength to such account as might now be serviceable? How could he, in his sore need, earn for himself even the barest bread? Would it not be better for him that he should die? Let not any one covet the lot of a spendthrift, even though the days of his early pease and champagne seem to be unnumbered; for that lame Nemesis will surely be up before the game has been all played out. When Mr. Sowerby reached his house he found that a message by telegraph had arrived for him in his absence. It was from his sister, and it informed him that she would be with him that night. She was coming down by the mail train, had telegraphed to Barchester for post-horses, and would be at Chaldicotes about two hours after midnight. It was therefore manifest enough that her business was of importance. Exactly at two the Barchester post-chaise did arrive, and Mrs. Harold Smith, before she retired to her bed, was closeted for about an hour with her brother. 'Well,' she said, the following morning, as they sat together at the breakfast table, 'what do you say to it now? If you accept her offer you should be with her lawyer this afternoon.'

'I suppose I must accept it,' said he.

'Certainly, I think so. No doubt it will take the property out of your own hands as completely as though the duke had it, but it will leave you the house, at any rate, for your life.'

'What good will the house be, when I can't keep it up?'

'But I am not so sure of that. She will not want more than her fair interest; and as it will be thoroughly well managed, I should think that there would be something over – something enough to keep up the house. And then, you know, we must have some place in the country.'

'I tell you fairly, Harriet, that I will have nothing further to do with Harold in the way of money.'

'Ah! that was because you would go to him. Why did you not come to me? And then, Nathaniel, it is the only way in which you can have a chance of keeping the seat. She is the queerest woman I ever met, but she seems resolved on beating the duke.'

'I do not quite understand it, but I have not the slightest objection.'

'She thinks that he is interfering with young Gresham about the Crown property. I had no idea that she had so much business at her fingers' ends. When I first proposed the matter she took it up quite as a lawyer might, and seemed to have forgotten altogether what occurred about that other matter.'

'I wish I could forget it also,' said Mr. Sowerby.

'I really think that she does. When I was obliged to make some allusion to it – at least I felt myself obliged, and was very sorry afterwards that I did – she merely laughed – a great loud laugh as she always does, and then went on about the business. However, she was clear about this, that all the expenses of the election should be added to the sum to be advanced by her, and that the house should be left to you without any rent. If you choose to take the land round the house you must pay for it, by the acre, as the tenants do. She was as clear about it all as though she had passed her life in a lawyer's office.'

My readers will now pretty well understand what last step that excellent sister, Mrs. Harold Smith, had taken on her brother's behalf, nor will they be surprised to learn that in the course of the day Mr. Sowerby hurried back to town and put himself into communication with Miss Dunstable's lawyer.

CHAPTER XXXVIII

Is There Cause or Just Impediment?

I NOW purpose to visit another country house in Barsetshire, but on this occasion our sojourn shall be in the eastern division, in which, as in every other county in England, electioneering matters are paramount at the present moment. It has been mentioned that Mr. Gresham, junior, young Frank Gresham as he was always called, lived at a place called Boxall Hill. This property had come to his wife by will, and he was now settled there, – seeing that his father still held the family seat of the Greshams at Greshamsbury. At the present moment Miss Dunstable was staying at Boxall Hill with Mrs. Frank Gresham. They had left London, as, indeed, all the world had done, to the terrible dismay of the London tradesmen. This dissolution of Parliament was ruining everybody except the country publicans, and had of course destroyed the London season among other things.

Mrs. Harold Smith had only just managed to catch Miss Dunstable before she left London; but she did do so, and the great heiress had at once seen her lawyers, and instructed them how to act with reference to the mortgages on the Chaldicotes property. Miss Dunstable was in the habit of speaking of herself and her own pecuniary concerns as though she herself were rarely allowed to meddle in their management; but this was one of those small jokes which she ordinarily perpetrated; for in truth few ladies, and perhaps not many gentlemen, have a more thorough knowledge of their own concerns or a more potent voice in their own affairs, than was possessed by Miss Dunstable. Circumstances had lately brought her much into Barsetshire, and she had there contracted very intimate friendships. She was now disposed to become, if possible, a Barsetshire proprietor, and with this view had lately agreed with young Mr. Gresham that she would become the purchaser of the Crown property. As, however, the purchase had been commenced in his name, it was so to be continued; but now, as we are aware, it was rumoured that, after all, the duke, or, if not the duke, then the Marquis of Dumbello, was to be the future owner of the Chace. Miss Dunstable, however, was not a person to give up her object if she could attain it, nor, under the circumstances, was she at all displeased at finding herself endowed with the power of rescuing the Sowerby portion of the Chaldicotes property from the duke's clutches.

Why had the duke meddled with her or with her friend, as to the other property? Therefore it was arranged also that the full amount due to the duke on mortgage should be ready for immediate payment; but it was arranged also that the security as held by Miss Dunstable should be very valid.

Miss Dunstable, at Boxall Hill or at Greshamsbury, was a very different person from Miss Dunstable in London; and it was this difference which so vexed Mrs. Gresham; not that her friend omitted to bring with her into the country her London wit and aptitude for fun, but that she did not take with her up to town the genuine goodness and love of honesty which made her lovable in the country. She was, as it were, two persons, and Mrs. Gresham could not understand that any lady should permit herself to be more worldly at one time of the year than at another – or in one place than in any other. 'Well, my dear, I am heartily glad we've done with that,' Miss Dunstable said to her, as she sat herself down to her desk in the drawing-room on the first morning after her arrival at Boxall Hill.

'What does "that" mean?' said Mrs. Gresham.

'Why, London and smoke and late hours, and standing on one's legs for four hours at a stretch on the top of one's own staircase, to be bowed at by any one who chooses to come. That's all done – for one year, at any rate.'

'You know you like it.'

'No, Mary; that's just what I don't know. I don't know whether I like it or not. Sometimes, when the spirit of that dearest of all women, Mrs. Harold Smith, is upon me, I think that I do like it; but then, again, when other spirits are on me, I think that I don't.'

'And who are the owners of the other spirits?'

'Oh, you are one, of course. But you are a weak little thing, by no means able to contend with such a Samson as Mrs. Harold. And then you are a little given to wickedness yourself, you know. You've learned to like London well enough since you sat down to the table of Dives.

Your uncle – he's the real, impracticable, unapproachable Lazarus who declares that he can't come down because of the big gulf. I wonder how he'd behave, if somebody left him ten thousand a year?'

'Uncommonly well, I am sure.'

'Oh, yes; he is a Lazarus now, so of course we are bound to speak well of him; but I should like to see him tried. I don't doubt but what he'd have a house in Belgrave Square, and become noted for his little dinners before the first year of his trial was over.'

'Well, and why not? You would not wish him to be an anchorite?'

'I am told that he is going to try his luck – not with ten thousand a year, but with one or two.'

'What do you mean?'

'Jane tells me that they all say at Greshamsbury that he is going to marry Lady Scatcherd.' Now Lady Scatcherd was a widow living in those parts; an excellent woman, but one not formed by nature to grace society of the highest order.

'What!' exclaimed Mrs. Gresham, rising up from her chair, while her eyes flashed with anger at such a rumour.

'Well, my dear, don't eat me. I don't say it is so; I only say that Jane said so.'

'Then you ought to send Jane out of the house.'

'You may be sure of this, my dear: Jane would not have told me if somebody had not told her.'

'And you believed it?'

'I have said nothing about that.'

'But you look as if you had believed it.'

'Do I? Let us see what sort of a look it is, this look of faith.' And Miss Dunstable got up and went to the glass over the fireplace. 'But, Mary, my dear, ain't you old enough to know that you should not credit people's looks? You should believe nothing nowadays; and I did not believe the story about poor Lady Scatcherd. I know the doctor well enough to be sure that he is not a marrying man.'

'What a nasty, hackneyed, false phrase that is – that of a marrying man! It sounds as though some men were in the habit of getting married three or four times a month.'

'It means a great deal all the same. One can tell very soon whether a man is likely to marry or no.'

'And can one tell the same of a woman?'

'The thing is so different. All unmarried women are necessarily in the market; but if they behave themselves properly they make no signs. Now there was Griselda Grantly; of course she intended to get herself a husband, and a very grand one she has got: but she always looked as though butter would not melt in her mouth. It would have been very wrong to call her a marrying girl.'

'Oh, of course she was,' says Mrs. Gresham, with that sort of acrimony which one pretty young woman so frequently expresses with reference to another. 'But if one could always tell of a woman, as you say you can of a man, I should be able to tell of you. Now, I wonder whether you are a marrying woman? I have never been able to make up my mind yet.'

Miss Dunstable remained silent for a few moments, as though she were at first minded to take the question as being, in some sort, one made in earnest; but then she attempted to laugh it off. 'Well, I wonder at that,' said she, 'as it was only the other day I told you how many offers I had refused.'

'Yes; but you did not tell me whether any had been made that you meant to accept.'

'None such was ever made to me. Talking of that, I shall never forget your cousin, the Honourable George.'

'He is not my cousin.'

'Well, your husband's. It would not be fair to show a man's letters; but I should like to show you his.'

'You are determined, then, to remain single?'

'I didn't say that. But why do you cross-question me so?'

'Because I think so much about you. I am afraid that you will become so afraid of men's motives as to doubt that any one can be honest. And yet sometimes I think you would be a happier woman and a better woman, if you were married.'

'To such an one as the Honourable George, for instance?'

'No, not to such an one as him; you have probably picked out the worst.'

'Or to Mr. Sowerby?'

'Well, no; not to Mr. Sowerby, either. I would not have you marry any man that looked to you for your money principally.'

'And how is it possible that I should expect any one to look to me principally for anything else? You don't see my difficulty, my dear? If I had only five hundred a year, I might come across some decent middle-aged personage, like myself, who would like me, myself, pretty well, and would like my little income – pretty well also. He would not tell me any violent lie, and perhaps no lie at all. I should take to him in the same sort of way, and we might do very well. But, as it is, how is it possible that any disinterested person should learn to like me? How could such a man set about it? If a sheep have two heads, is not the fact of the two heads the first and, indeed, only thing which the world regards in that sheep? Must it not be so as a matter of course? I am a sheep with two heads. All this money which my father put together, and which has been growing since like grass under May showers, has turned me into an abortion. I am not the giantess eight feet high, or the dwarf that stands in the man's hand –'

'Or the two-headed sheep –'

'But I am the unmarried woman with – half a dozen millions of money – as I believe some people think. Under such circumstances have I a fair chance of getting my own sweet bit of grass to nibble, like any ordinary animal with one head? I never was very beautiful, and I am not more so now than I was fifteen years ago.'

'I am quite sure it is not that which hinders it. You would not call yourself plain; and even plain women are married every day, and are loved too, as well as pretty women.'

'Are they? Well, we won't say more about that; but I don't expect a great many lovers on account of my beauty. If ever you hear of such an one, mind you tell me.' It was almost on Mrs. Gresham's tongue to say that she did know of one such – meaning her uncle. But in truth, she did not know any such thing; nor could she boast to herself that she had good grounds for feeling that it was so – certainly none sufficient to justify her in speaking of it. Her uncle had said no word to her on the matter, and had been confused and embarrassed when the idea of such a marriage was hinted to him. But, nevertheless, Mrs. Gresham did think that each of these two was well inclined to love the other, and that they would be happier together than they would be single. The difficulty, however, was very great, for the doctor would be terribly afraid of being thought covetous in regard to Miss Dunstable's money; and it would hardly be expected that she should be induced to make the first overture to the doctor.

'My uncle would be the only man that I can think of that would be at all fit for you,' said Mrs. Gresham, boldly.

'What, and rob poor Lady Scatcherd!' said Miss Dunstable.

'Oh, very well. If you choose to make a joke of his name in that way I have done.'

'Why, God bless the girl, what does she want me to say? And as for joking, surely that is innocent enough. You're as tender about the doctor as though he were a girl of seventeen.'

'It's not about him; but it's such a shame to laugh at poor dear Lady Scatcherd. If she were to hear it she'd lose all comfort in having my uncle near her.'

'And I'm to marry him, so that she may be safe with her friend!'

'Very well; I have done.' And Mrs. Gresham, who had already got up from her seat, employed herself very sedulously in arranging flowers which had been brought in for the drawing-room tables. Thus they remained silent for a minute or two, during which she began to reflect that, after all, it might probably be thought that she also was endeavouring to catch the great heiress for her uncle.

'And now you are angry with me,' said Miss Dunstable.

'No, I am not.'

'Oh, but you are. Do you think I'm such a fool as not to see when a person's vexed? You wouldn't have twitched that geranium's head off if you'd been in a proper frame of mind.'

'I don't like that joke about Lady Scatcherd.'

'And is that all, Mary? Now do try and be true, if you can. You remember the bishop? *Magna est veritas.*'

'The fact is you've got into such a way of being sharp, and saying sharp things among your friends up in London, that you can hardly answer a person without it.'

'Can't I! Dear, dear, what a Mentor you are, Mary! No poor lad that ever ran up from Oxford for a spree in town got so lectured for his dissipation and iniquities as I do. Well, I beg Dr. Thorne's pardon, and Lady Scatcherd's, and I won't be sharp any more; and I will – let me see, what was it I was to do? Marry him myself, I believe; was not that it?'

'No; you're not half good enough for him.'

'I know that. I'm quite sure of that. Though I am so sharp, I'm very humble. You can't accuse me of putting any very great value on myself.'

'Perhaps not as much as you ought to do – on yourself.'

'Now what do you mean, Mary? I won't be bullied and teased, and have innuendoes thrown out at me, because you've got something on your mind, and don't quite dare to speak it out. If you have got anything to say, say it.' But Mrs. Gresham did not choose to say it at that moment. She held her peace, and went on arranging her flowers – now with a more satisfied air, and without destruction to the geraniums. And when she had grouped her bunches properly she carried the jar from one part of the room to another, backwards and forwards, trying the effect of the colours, as though her mind was quite intent upon her flowers, and was for the moment wholly unoccupied with any other subject. But Miss Dunstable was not the woman to put up with this. She sat silent in her place, while her friend made one or two turns about the room; and then she got up from her seat also. 'Mary,' she said, 'give over those wretched bits of green branches, and leave the jars where they are. You're trying to fidget me into a passion.'

'Am I?' said Mrs. Gresham, standing opposite to a big bowl, and putting her head a little on one side, as though she could better look at her handiwork in that position.

'You know you are; and it's all because you lack courage to speak out. You didn't begin at me in this way for nothing.'

'I do lack courage. That's just it,' said Mrs. Gresham, still giving a twist here and a set there to some of the small sprigs which constituted the background of her bouquet. 'I do lack courage – to have ill motives imputed to me. I was thinking of saying something, and I am afraid, and therefore I will not say it. And now, if you like, I will be ready to take you out in ten minutes.' But Miss Dunstable was not going to be put off in this way. And to tell the truth, I must admit that her friend Mrs. Gresham was not using her altogether well. She should either have held her peace on the matter altogether – which would probably have been her wiser course – or she should have declared her own ideas boldly, feeling secure in her own conscience as to her own motives. 'I shall not stir from this room,' said Miss Dunstable, 'till I have had this matter out with you. And as for imputations – my imputing bad motives to you – I don't know how far you may be joking, and saying what you call sharp things to me; but you have no right to think that I should think evil of you. If you really do think so, it is treason to the love I have for you. If I thought that you thought so, I could not remain in the house with you. What, you are not able to know the difference which one makes between one's real friends and one's mock friends! I don't believe it of you, and I know you are only striving to bully me.' And Miss Dunstable now took her turn of walking up and down the room.

'Well, she shan't be bullied,' said Mrs. Gresham, leaving her flowers, and putting her arm round her friend's waist; – 'at least, not here, in this house, although she is sometimes such a bully herself.'

'Mary, you have gone too far about this to go back. Tell me what it was that was on your mind, and as far as it concerns me, I will answer you honestly.' Mrs. Gresham now began to repent that she had made her little attempt. That uttering of hints in a half-joking way was all very well, and might possibly bring about the desired results, without the necessity of any formal suggestion on her part; but now she was so brought to book that she must say something formal. She must commit herself to the expression of her own wishes, and to an expression also of an opinion as to what had been the wishes of her friend; and this she must do without being able to say anything as to the wishes of that third person. 'Well,' she said, 'I suppose you know what I meant.'

'I suppose I did,' said Miss Dunstable; 'but it is not at all the less necessary that you should say it out. I am not to commit myself by my interpretation of your thoughts, while you remain perfectly secure in having only hinted your own. I hate hints, as I do – the mischief. I go in for the bishop's doctrine. *Magna est veritas.*'

'Well, I don't know,' said Mrs. Gresham.

'Ah! but I do,' said Miss Dunstable. 'And therefore go on, or for ever hold your peace.'

'That's just it,' said Mrs. Gresham.

'What's just it?' said Miss Dunstable.

'The quotation out of the Prayer Book which you finished just now. "If any of you know cause or just impediment why these two persons should not be joined together in holy matrimony, ye are to declare it. This is the first time of asking." Do you know any cause, Miss Dunstable?'

'Do you know any, Mrs. Gresham?'

'None, on my honour!' said the younger lady, putting her hand upon her breast.

'Ah! but do you not?' and Miss Dunstable caught hold of her arm, and spoke almost abruptly in her energy.

'No, certainly not. What impediment? If I did, I should not have broached the subject. I declare I think you would both be very happy together. Of course, there is one impediment; we all know that. That must be your look out.'

'What do you mean? What impediment?'

'Your own money.'

'Psha! Did you find that an impediment in marrying Frank Gresham?'

'Ah! the matter was so different there. He had much more to give than I had, when all was counted. And I had no money when we – when we were first engaged.' And the tears came into her eyes as she thought of the circumstances of her early love; – all of which have been narrated in the county chronicles of Barsetshire, and may now be read by men and women interested therein.

'Yes; yours was a love match. I declare, Mary, I often think that you are the happiest woman of whom I ever heard; to have it all to give, when you were so sure that you were loved while you yet had nothing.'

'Yes; I was sure,' and she wiped the sweet tears from her eyes, as she remembered a certain day when a certain youth had come to her, claiming all kinds of privileges in a very determined manner. She had been no heiress then.

'Yes; I was sure. But now with you, dear, you can't make yourself poor again. If you can trust no one –'

'I can. I can trust him. As regards that I do trust him altogether. But how can I tell that he would care for me?'

'Do you not know that he likes you?'

'Ah, yes; and so he does Lady Scatcherd.'

'Miss Dunstable!'

'And why not Lady Scatcherd, as well as me? We are of the same kind – come from the same class.'

'Not quite that, I think.'

'Yes, from the same class; only I have managed to poke myself up among dukes and duchesses, whereas she has been content to remain where God placed her. Where I beat her in art, she beats me in nature.'

'You know you are talking nonsense.'

'I think that we are both doing that – absolute nonsense; such as schoolgirls of eighteen talk to each other. But there is a relief in it; is there not? It would be a terrible curse to have to talk sense always. Well, that's done; and now let us go out.' Mrs. Gresham was sure after this that Miss Dunstable would be a consenting party to the little arrangement which she contemplated. But of that she had felt but little doubt for some considerable time past. The difficulty lay on the other side, and all that she had as yet done was to convince herself that she would be safe in assuring her uncle of success if he could be induced to take the enterprise in hand. He was to come to Boxall Hill that evening, and to remain there for a day or two. If anything could be done in the matter, now would be the time for doing it. So at least thought Mrs. Gresham.

The doctor did come, and did remain for the allotted time at Boxall Hill; but when he left, Mrs. Gresham had not been successful. Indeed, he did not seem to enjoy his visit as was usual with him; and there was very little of that pleasant friendly intercourse which for some time past had been customary between him and Miss Dunstable.

There were no passages of arms between them; no abuse from the doctor against the lady's London gaiety; no raillery from the lady as to the doctor's country habits. They were very courteous to each other, and, as Mrs. Gresham thought, too civil by half; nor, as far as she could see, did they ever remain alone in each other's company for five minutes at a time during the whole period of the doctor's visit. What, thought Mrs. Gresham to herself, – what if she had set these two friends at variance with each other, instead of binding them together in the closest and most durable friendship! But still she had an idea that, as she had begun to play this game, she must play it out. She felt conscious that what she had done must do evil, unless she could so carry it on as to make it result in good. Indeed, unless she could so manage, she would have done a manifest injury to Miss Dunstable in forcing her to declare her thoughts and feelings. She had already spoken to her uncle in London, and though he had said nothing to show that he approved of her plan, neither had he said anything to show that he disapproved it. Therefore she had hoped through the whole of those three days that he would make some sign, – at any rate to her; that he would in some way declare what were his own thoughts on this matter. But the morning of his departure came, and he had declared nothing. 'Uncle,' she said, in the last five minutes of his sojourn there, after he had already taken leave of Miss Dunstable and shaken hands with Mrs. Gresham, 'have you ever thought of what I said to you up in London?'

'Yes, Mary; of course I have thought about it. Such an idea as that, when put into a man's head, will make itself thought about.'

'Well; and what next? Do talk to me about it. Do not be so hard and unlike yourself.'

'I have very little to say about it.'

'I can tell you this for certain, you may if you like.'

'Mary! Mary!'

'I would not say so if I were not sure that I should not lead you into trouble.'

'You are foolish in wishing this, my dear; foolish in trying to tempt an old man into a folly.'

'Not foolish if I know that it will make you both happier.' He made her no further reply, but stooping down that she might kiss him, as was his wont, went his way, leaving her almost miserable in the thought that she had troubled all these waters to no purpose. What would Miss Dunstable think of her? But on that afternoon Miss Dunstable seemed to be as happy and even-tempered as ever.

CHAPTER XXXIX

How to Write a Love Letter

DR. THORNE, in the few words which he spoke to his niece before he left Boxall Hill, had called himself an old man; but he was as yet on the right side of sixty by five good years, and bore about with him less of the marks of age than most men of fifty-five do bear. One would have said, in looking at him, that there was no reason why he should not marry if he found that such a step seemed good to him; and, looking at the age of the proposed bride, there was nothing unsuitable in that respect. But nevertheless he felt almost ashamed of himself, in that he allowed himself even to think of the proposition which his niece had made. He mounted his horse that day at Boxall Hill – for he made all his journeys about the county on horseback – and rode slowly home to Greshamsbury, thinking not so much of the suggested marriage as of his own folly in thinking of it. How could he be such an ass at his time of life as to allow the even course of his way to be disturbed by any such idea? Of course he could not propose to himself such a wife as Miss Dunstable without having some thoughts as to her wealth; and it had been the pride of his life so to live that the world might know that he was indifferent about money. His profession was all in all to him; the air which he breathed as well as the bread which he ate; and how could he follow his profession if he made such a marriage as this? She would expect him to go to London with her; and what would he become, dangling at her heels there, known only to the world as the husband of the richest woman in the town? The kind of life was one which would be unsuitable to him; and yet, as he rode home, he could not resolve to rid himself of the idea. He went on thinking of it, though he still continued to condemn himself for keeping it in his thoughts. That night at home he would make up his mind, so he declared to himself; and would then write to his niece begging her to drop the subject. Having so far come to a resolution he went on meditating what course of life it might be well for him to pursue if he and Miss Dunstable should after all become man and wife.

There were two ladies whom it behoved him to see on the day of his arrival – whom, indeed, he generally saw every day except when absent from Greshamsbury. The first of these – first in the general consideration of the people of the place – was the wife of the squire, Lady Arabella Gresham, a very old patient of the doctor's. Her it was his custom to visit early in the afternoon; and then, if he were able to escape the squire's daily invitation to dinner, he customarily went to the other, Lady Scatcherd, when the rapid meal in his own house was over. Such, at least, was his summer practice. 'Well, doctor, how are they at Boxall Hill?' said the squire, waylaying him on the gravel sweep before the door. The squire was very hard set for occupation in these summer months.

'Quite well, I believe.'

'I don't know what's come to Frank. I think he hates this place now. He's full of the election, I suppose.'

'Oh, yes; he told me to say he should be over here soon. Of course there'll be no contest, so he need not trouble himself.'

'Happy dog, isn't he, doctor? to have it all before him instead of behind him. Well, well; he's as good a lad as ever lived – as ever lived. And let me see; Mary's time –' And then there were a few very important words spoken on that subject.

'I'll just step up to Lady Arabella now,' said the doctor.

'She's as fretful as possible,' said the squire. 'I've just left her.'

'Nothing special the matter, I hope?'

'No, I think not; nothing in your way, that is; only specially cross, which always comes in my way. You'll stop and dine to-day, of course?'

'Not to-day, squire.'

'Nonsense; you will. I have been quite counting on you. I have a particular reason for wanting to have you to-day – a most particular reason.' But the squire always had his particular reasons.

'I'm very sorry, but it is impossible to-day. I shall have a letter to write that I must sit down to seriously. Shall I see you when I come down from her ladyship?' The squire turned away sulkily, almost without answering him, for he now had no prospect of any alleviation to the tedium of the evening; and the doctor went upstairs to his patient. For Lady Arabella, though it cannot be said that she was ill, was always a patient. It must not be supposed that she kept her bed and swallowed daily doses, or was prevented from taking her share in such prosy gaieties as came from time to time in the way of her prosy life; but it suited her turn of mind to be an invalid and to have a doctor; and as the doctor whom her good fates had placed at her elbow thoroughly understood her case, no great harm was done.

'It frets me dreadfully that I cannot get to see Mary,' Lady Arabella said, as soon as the first ordinary question as to her ailments had been asked and answered.

'She's quite well, and will be over to see you before long.'

'Now I beg that she won't. She never thinks of coming when there can be no possible objection, and travelling, at the present moment, would be –' Whereupon the Lady Arabella shook her head very gravely. 'Only think of the importance of it, doctor,' she said. 'Remember the enormous stake there is to be considered.'

'It would not do her a ha'porth of harm if the stake were twice as large.'

'Nonsense, doctor, don't tell me; as if I didn't know myself. I was very much against her going to London this spring, but of course what I said was overruled. It always is. I do believe Mr. Gresham went over to Boxall Hill, on purpose to induce her to go. But what does he care? He's fond of Frank; but he never thinks of looking beyond the present day. He never did, as you know well enough, doctor.'

'The trip did her all the good in the world,' said Dr. Thorne, preferring anything to a conversation respecting the squire's sins.

'I very well remember that when I was in that way it wasn't thought that such trips would do me any good. But, perhaps, things are altered since then.'

'Yes, they are,' said the doctor. 'We don't interfere so much nowadays.'

'I know I never asked for such amusements when so much depended on quietness. I remember before Frank was born – and, indeed, when all of them were born – But, as you say, things were different then; and I can easily believe that Mary is a person quite determined to have her own way.'

'Why, Lady Arabella, she would have stayed at home without wishing to stir if Frank had done so much as hold up his little finger.'

'So did I always. If Mr. Gresham made the slightest hint I gave way. But I really don't see what one gets in return for such implicit obedience. Now this year, doctor, of course I should have liked to have been up in London for a week or two. You seemed to think yourself that I might as well see Sir Omicron.'

'There could be no possible objection, I said.'

'Well; no; exactly; and as Mr. Gresham knew I wished it, I think he might as well have offered it. I suppose there can be no reason now about money.'

'But I understand that Mary specially asked you and Augusta?'

'Yes; Mary was very good. She did ask me. But I know very well that Mary wants all the room she has got in London. The house is not at all too large for herself. And, for the matter of that, my sister, the countess, was very anxious that I should be with her. But one does like to be independent if one can, and for one fortnight I do think that Mr. Gresham might have managed it. When I knew that he was so dreadfully out at elbows I never troubled him about it, – though, goodness knows, all that was never my fault.'

'The squire hates London. A fortnight there in warm weather would nearly be the death of him.'

'He might at any rate have paid me the compliment of asking me. The chances are ten to one I should not have gone. It is that indifference that cuts me so. He was here just now, and would you believe it? –'

But the doctor was determined to avoid further complaint for the present day. 'I wonder what you would feel, Lady Arabella, if the squire were to take it into his head to go away and amuse himself, leaving you at home. There are worse men than Mr. Gresham, if you will believe me.' All this was an allusion to Earl de Courcy, her ladyship's brother, as Lady Arabella very well understood; and the argument was one which was very often used to silence her.

'Upon my word, then, I should like it better than his hanging about here doing nothing but attend to those nasty dogs. I really sometimes think that he has no spirit left.'

'You are mistaken there, Lady Arabella,' said the doctor, rising with his hat in his hand, and making his escape without further parley. As he went home he could not but think that that phase of married life was not a very pleasant one. Mr. Gresham and his wife were supposed by the world to live on the best of terms. They always inhabited the same house, went out together when they did go out, always sat in their respective corners in the family pew, and in their wildest dreams after the happiness of novelty never thought of Sir Cresswell Cresswell. In some respects – with regard, for instance, to the continued duration of their joint domesticity at the family mansion of Greshamsbury – they might have been taken for a pattern couple. But yet, as far as the doctor could see, they did not seem to add much to the happiness of each other. They loved each other, doubtless, and had either of them been in real danger, that danger would have made the other miserable; but yet it might well be a question whether either would not be more comfortable without the other.

The doctor, as was his custom, dined at five, and at seven he went up to the cottage of his old friend Lady Scatcherd. Lady Scatcherd was not a refined woman, having in her early days been a labourer's daughter, and having then married a labourer. But her husband had risen in the world – as has been told in those chronicles before mentioned, – and his widow was now Lady Scatcherd with a pretty cottage and a good jointure. She was in all things the very opposite to Lady Arabella Gresham; nevertheless, under the doctor's auspices, the two ladies were in some measure acquainted with each other. Of her married life, also, Dr. Thorne had seen something, and it may be questioned whether the memory of that was more alluring than the reality now existing at Greshamsbury. Of the two women Dr. Thorne much preferred his humbler friend, and to her he made his visits not in the guise of a doctor, but as a neighbour. 'Well, my lady,' he said, as he sat down by her on a broad garden seat – all the world called Lady Scatcherd 'my lady,' – 'and how do these long summer days agree with you? Your roses are twice better out than any I see up at the big house.'

'You may well call them long, doctor. They're long enough surely.'

'But not too long. Come, now, I won't have you complaining. You don't mean to tell me that you have anything to make you wretched? You had better not, for I won't believe you.'

'Eh; well; wretched! I don't know as I'm wretched. It'd be wicked to say that, and I with such comforts about me.'

'I think it would, almost.' The doctor did not say this harshly, but in a soft, friendly tone, and pressing her hand gently as he spoke.

'And I didn't mean to be wicked. I'm very thankful for everything – leastways, I always try to be. But, doctor, it is so lonely like.'

'Lonely! not more lonely than I am.'

'Oh, yes; you're different. You can go everywheres. But what can a lone woman do? I'll tell you what, doctor; I'd give it all up to have Roger back with his apron on and his pick in his hand. How well I mind his look when he'd come home o' nights!'

'And yet it was a hard life you had then, eh, old woman? It would be better for you to be thankful for what you've got.'

'I am thankful. Didn't I tell you so before?' said she, somewhat crossly. 'But it's a sad life, this living alone. I declares I envy Hannah, 'cause she's got Jemima to sit in the kitchen with her. I want her to sit with me sometimes, but she won't.'

'Ah! but you shouldn't ask her. It's letting yourself down.'

'What do I care about down or up? It makes no difference, as he's gone. If he had lived one might have cared about being up, as you call it. Eh, deary; I'll be going after him before long, and it will be no matter then.'

'We shall all be going after him, sooner or later; that's sure enough.'

'Eh, dear, that's true surely. It's only a span long, as Parson Oriel tells us, when he gets romantic in his sermons. But it's a hard thing, doctor, when two is married, as they can't have their span, as he calls it, out together. Well I must only put up with it, I suppose, as others does. Now, you're not going, doctor? You'll stop and have a dish of tea with me. You never see such cream as Hannah has from the Alderney cow. Do'ey now, doctor.' But the doctor had his letter to write, and would not allow himself to be tempted even by the promise of Hannah's cream. So he went his way, angering Lady Scatcherd by his departure as he had before angered the squire, and thinking as he went which was most unreasonable in her wretchedness, his friend Lady Arabella or his friend Lady Scatcherd. The former was always complaining of an existing husband who never refused her any moderate request; and the other passed her days in murmuring at the loss of a dead husband, who in his life had ever been to her imperious and harsh, and had sometimes been cruel and unjust.

The doctor had his letter to write, but even yet he had not quite made up his mind what he would put into it; indeed, he had not hitherto resolved to whom it should be written. Looking at the matter as he had endeavoured to look at it, his niece, Mrs. Gresham, would be his correspondent; but if he brought himself to take this jump in the dark, in that case he would address himself direct to Miss Dunstable. He walked home, not by the straightest road, but taking a considerable curve, round by narrow lanes, and through thick flower-laden hedges, – very thoughtful. He was told that she wished to marry him; and was he to think only of himself? And as to that pride of his about money, was it in truth a hearty, manly feeling; or was it a false pride, of which it behoved him to be ashamed as it did of many cognate feelings? If he acted rightly in this matter, why should he be afraid of the thoughts of any one? A life of solitude was bitter enough, as poor Lady Scatcherd had complained. But then, looking at Lady Scatcherd, and looking also at his other near neighbour, his friend the squire, there was little thereabouts to lead him on to matrimony. So he walked home slowly through the lanes, very meditative, with his hands behind his back. Nor when he got home was he much more inclined to any resolute line of action. He might have drunk his tea with Lady Scatcherd, as well as have sat there in his own drawing-room, drinking it alone; for he got no pen and paper, and he dawdled over his teacup with the utmost dilatoriness, putting off, at it were, the evil day. To only one thing was he fixed – to this, namely, that that letter should be written before he went to bed.

Having finished his tea, which did not take place till near eleven, he went downstairs to an untidy little room which lay behind his dépôt of medicines, and in which he was wont to do his writing; and herein he did at last set himself down to his work. Even at that moment he was in doubt. But he would write his letter to Miss Dunstable and see how it looked. He was almost determined not to send it; so, at least, he said to himself: but he could do no harm by writing it. So he did write it, as follows: – 'Greshamsbury, June, 185–. My dear Miss Dunstable –' When he had got so far, he leaned back in his chair and looked at the paper. How on earth was he to find words to say that which he now wished to have said? He had never written such a letter in his life, or anything approaching to it, and now found himself overwhelmed with a difficulty of which he had not previously thought. He spent another half-hour in looking at the paper, and was at last nearly deterred by this new difficulty. He would use the simplest, plainest language, he said to himself over and over again; but it is not always easy to use simple, plain language, – by no means so easy as to mount on stilts, and to march along with sesquipedalian words, with pathos, spasms, and notes of interjection. But the letter did at last get itself written, and there was not a note of interjection in it.

'My Dear Miss Dunstable,

'I think it right to confess that I should not now be writing this letter to you, had I not been led to believe by other judgement than my own that the proposition which I am going to make would be regarded by you with favour. Without such other judgement I should, I own, have feared that the great disparity between you and me in regard to money would have given to such a proposition an appearance of being false and mercenary. All I ask of you now, with confidence, is to acquit me of such fault as that.

'When you have read so far you will understand what I mean. We have known each other now somewhat intimately, though indeed not very long, and I have sometimes fancied that you were almost as well pleased to be with me as I have been to be with you. If I have been wrong in this, tell me so simply, and I will endeavour to let our friendship run on as though this letter had not been written. But if I have been right, and if it be possible that you can think that a union between us will make us both happier than we are single, I will plight you my word and troth with good faith, and will do what an old man may do to make the burden of the world lie light on your shoulders. Looking at my age I can hardly keep myself from thinking that I am an old fool; but I try to reconcile myself to that by remembering that you yourself are no longer a girl. You see that I pay you no compliments, and that you need expect none from me.

'I do not know that I could add anything to the truth of this, if I were to write three times as much. All that is necessary is, that you should know what I mean. If you do not believe me to be true and honest already, nothing that I can write will make you believe it.

'God bless you. I know you will not keep me long in suspense for an answer.

'Affectionately your friend,

'Thomas Thorne.'

When he had finished he meditated again for another half-hour whether it would not be right that he should add something about her money. Would it not be well for him to tell her – it might be said in a postcript – that with regard to all her wealth she would be free to do what she chose? At any rate he owed no debts for her to pay, and would still have his own income, sufficient for his own purposes. But about one o'clock he came to the conclusion that it would be better to leave the matter alone. If she cared for him, and could trust him, and was worthy also that he should trust her, no omission of such a statement would deter her from coming to him: and if there were no such trust, it would not be created by any such assurance on his part. So he read the letter over twice, sealed it, and took it up, together with his bed candle, into his bedroom. Now that the letter was written it seemed to be a thing fixed by fate that it must go. He had written it that he might see how it looked when written; but now that it was written, there remained no doubt that it must be sent. So he went to bed, with the letter on the toilette-table beside him; and early in the morning – so early as to make it seem that the importance of the letter had disturbed his rest – he sent it off by a special messenger to Boxall Hill. 'I'se wait for an answer?' said the boy.

'No,' said the doctor: 'leave the letter, and come away.'

The breakfast hour was not very early at Boxall Hill in these summer months. Frank Gresham, no doubt, went round his farm before he came in for prayers, and his wife was probably looking to the butter in the dairy. At any rate, they did not meet till near ten, and therefore, though the ride from Greshamsbury to Boxall Hill was nearly two hours' work, Miss Dunstable had her letter in her own room before she came down. She read it in silence as she was dressing, while the maid was with her in the room; but she made no sign which could induce her Abigail to think that the epistle was more than ordinarily important. She read it, and then quietly refolding it and placing it in the envelope, she put it down on the table at which she was sitting. It was full fifteen minutes afterwards that she begged her servant to see if Mrs. Gresham were still in her own room. 'Because I want to see her for five minutes, alone, before breakfast,' said Miss Dunstable.

'You traitor; you false, black traitor!' were the first words which Miss Dunstable spoke when she found herself alone with her friend.

'Why, what's the matter?'

'I did not think there was so much mischief in you, nor so keen and commonplace a desire for match-making. Look here. Read the first four lines; not more, if you please; the rest is private. Whose is the other judgement of whom your uncle speaks in his letter?'

'Oh, Miss Dunstable! I must read it all.'

'Indeed you'll do no such thing. You think it's a love-letter, I dare say; but indeed there's not a word about love in it.'

'I know he has offered. I shall be so glad, for I know you like him.'

'He tells me that I am an old woman, and insinuates that I may probably be an old fool.'

'I am sure he does not say that.'

'Ah! but I'm sure that he does. The former is true enough, and I never complain of the truth. But as to the latter, I am by no means so certain that it is true – not in the sense that he means it.'

'Dear, dearest woman, don't go on in that way now. Do speak out to me, and speak without jesting.'

'Whose was the other judgement to whom he trusts so implicitly? Tell me that.'

'Mine, mine of course. No one else can have spoken to him about it. Of course I talked to him.'

'And what did you tell him?'

'I told him –'

'Well, out with it. Let me have the real facts. Mind, I tell you fairly that you had no right to tell him anything. What passed between us, passed in confidence. But let us hear what you did say.'

'I told him that you would have him if he offered.' And Mrs. Gresham, as she spoke, looked into her friend's face doubtingly, not knowing whether in very truth Miss Dunstable were pleased with her or displeased. If she were displeased, then how had her uncle been deceived!

'You told him that as a fact?'

'I told him that I thought so.'

'Then I suppose I am bound to have him,' said Miss Dunstable, dropping the letter on to the floor in mock despair.

'My dear, dear, dearest woman!' said Mrs. Gresham, bursting into tears, and throwing herself on to her friend's neck.

'Mind you are a dutiful niece,' said Miss Dunstable. 'And now let me go and finish dressing.'

In the course of the afternoon, an answer was sent back to Greshamsbury, in these words:-

'Dear Dr. Thorne,

'I do and will trust you in everything; and it shall be as you would have it. Mary writes to you; but do not believe a word she says. I never will again, for she has behaved so bad in this matter.

'Yours affectionately and very truly,
'Martha Dunstable.'

'And so I am going to marry the richest woman in England,' said Dr. Thorne to himself, as he sat down that day to his mutton-chop.

CHAPTER XL

Internecine

IT must be conceived that there was some feeling of triumph at Plumstead Episcopi, when the wife of the rector returned home with her daughter, the bride elect of the Lord Dumbello. The heir of the Marquess of Hartletop was, in wealth, the most considerable unmarried young nobleman of the day; he was noted, too, as a man difficult to be pleased, as one who was very fine and who gave himself airs; and to have been selected as the wife of such a man as this was a great thing for the daughter of a parish clergyman. We have seen in what manner the happy girl's mother communicated the fact to Lady Lufton, hiding, as it were, her pride under a veil; and we have seen also how meekly the happy girl bore her own great fortune, applying herself humbly to the packing of her clothes, as though she ignored her own glory. But nevertheless there was triumph at Plumstead Episcopi. The mother, when she returned home, began to feel that she had been thoroughly successful in the great object of her life. While she was yet in London she had hardly realized her satisfaction, and there were doubts then whether the cup might not be dashed from her lips before it was tasted. It might be that even the son of the Marquess of Hartletop was subject to parental authority, and that barriers should spring up between Griselda and her coronet; but there had been nothing of the kind. The archdeacon had been closeted with the marquess, and Mrs. Grantly had been closeted with the marchioness; and though neither of those noble persons had expressed themselves gratified by their son's proposed marriage, so also neither of them had made any attempt to prevent it. Lord Dumbello was a man who had a will of his own – as the Grantlys boasted amongst themselves. Poor Griselda! the day may perhaps come when this fact of her lord's masterful will may not to her be matter of much boasting. But in London, as I was saying, there had been no time for an appreciation of the family joy. The work to be done was nervous in its nature, and self-glorification might have been fatal; but now, when they were safe at Plumstead, the great truth burst upon them in all its splendour.

Mrs. Grantly had but one daughter, and the formation of that child's character and her establishment in the world had been the one main object of the mother's life. Of Griselda's great beauty the Plumstead household had long been conscious; of her discretion also, of her conduct, and of her demeanour there had been no doubt. But the father had sometimes hinted to the mother that he did not think that Grizzy was quite so clever as her brothers. 'I don't agree with you at all,' Mrs. Grantly had answered. 'Besides, what you call cleverness is not at all necessary in a girl; she is perfectly lady-like; even you won't deny that.' The archdeacon had never wished to deny it, and was now fain to admit that what he had called cleverness was not necessary in a young lady. At this period of the family glory the archdeacon himself was kept a little in abeyance, and was hardly allowed free intercourse with his own magnificent child. Indeed, to give him his due, it must be said of him that he would not consent to walk in the triumphal procession which moved with stately step, to and fro, through the Barchester regions. He kissed his daughter and blessed her, and bade her love her husband and be a good wife; but such injunctions as these, seeing how splendidly she had done her duty in securing to herself a marquess, seemed out of place and almost vulgar. Girls about to marry curates or sucking barristers should be told to do their duty in that station of life to which God might be calling them; but it seemed to be almost an impertinence in a father to give such an injunction to a future marchioness.

'I do not think that you have any ground for fear on her behalf,' said Mrs. Grantly, 'seeing in what way she has hitherto conducted herself.'

'She has been a good girl,' said the archdeacon, 'but she is about to be placed in a position of great temptation.'

'She has a strength of mind suited for any position,' replied Mrs. Grantly, vaingloriously. But nevertheless even the archdeacon moved about through the close at Barchester with a somewhat prouder step since the tidings of this alliance had become known there. The time had been – in the latter days of his father's lifetime – when he was the greatest man of the close. The dean had been old and infirm, and Dr. Grantly had wielded the bishop's authority. But since that things had altered. A new bishop had come there, absolutely hostile to him. A new dean had also come, who was not only his friend, but the brother-in-law of his wife; but even this advent had lessened the authority of the archdeacon. The vicars choral did not hang upon his words as they had been wont to do, and the minor canons smiled in return to his smile less obsequiously when they met him in the clerical circles of Barchester. But now it seemed that his old supremacy was restored to him. In the minds of many men an archdeacon, who was the father-in-law of a marquess, was himself as good as any bishop. He did not say much of his new connexion to others beside the dean, but he was conscious of the fact, and conscious also of the reflected glory which shone around his own head.

But as regards Mrs. Grantly it may be said that she moved in an unending procession of stately ovation. It must not be supposed that she continually talked to her friends and neighbours of Lord Dumbello and the marchioness. She was by far too wise for such folly as that. The coming alliance having been once announced, the name of Hartletop was hardly mentioned by her out of her own domestic circle. But she assumed, with an ease that was surprising even to herself, the airs and graces of a mighty woman. She went through her work of morning calls as though it were her business to be affable to the country gentry. She astonished her sister, the dean's wife, by the simplicity of her grandeur; and condescended to Mrs. Proudie in a manner which nearly broke that lady's heart. 'I shall be even with her yet,' said Mrs. Proudie to herself, who had contrived to learn various very deleterious circumstances respecting the Hartletop family since the news about Lord Dumbello and Griselda had become known to her. Griselda herself was carried about in the procession, taking but little part in it of her own, like an Eastern god. She suffered her mother's caresses and smiled in her mother's face as she listened to her own praises, but her triumph was apparently within. To no one did she say much on the subject, and greatly disgusted the old family housekeeper by declining altogether to discuss the future Dumbello *ménage*. To her aunt, Mrs. Arabin, who strove hard to lead her into some open-hearted speech as to her future aspirations, she was perfectly impassive. 'Oh, yes, aunt, of course,' and 'I'll think about it, Aunt Eleanor,' or 'Of course I shall do that if Lord Dumbello wishes it.' Nothing beyond this could be got from her; and so, after half a dozen ineffectual attempts, Mrs. Arabin abandoned the matter.

But then there arose the subject of clothes – of the wedding trousseau! Sarcastic people are wont to say that the tailor makes the man. Were I such a one, I might certainly assert that the milliner makes the bride. As regarding her bridehood, in distinction either to her girlhood or her wifehood – as being a line of plain demarcation between those two periods of a woman's life – the milliner does do much to make her. She would be hardly a bride if the trousseau were not there. A girl married without some such appendage would seem to pass into the condition of a wife without any such line of demarcation. In that moment in which she finds herself in the first fruition of her marriage finery she becomes a bride; and in that other moment when she begins to act upon the finest of these things as clothes to be packed up, she becomes a wife. When this subject was discussed Griselda displayed no lack of a becoming interest. She went to work steadily, slowly, and almost with solemnity, as though the business in hand were one which it would be wicked to treat with impatience. She even struck her mother with awe by the grandeur of her ideas and the depth of her theories. Nor let it be supposed that she rushed away at once to the consideration of the great fabric which was to be the ultimate sign and mark of her status, the quintessence of her briding, the outer veil, as it were, of the tabernacle – namely, her wedding-dress. As a great poet works himself up by degrees to that inspiration which is necessary for the grand turning-point of his epic, so did she slowly approach the hallowed ground on which she would sit, with her ministers around her, when about to discuss the nature, the extent, the design, the colouring, the structure, and the ornamentation of that momentous piece of apparel. No; there was much indeed to be done before she came to this; and as the poet, to whom I have already alluded, first invokes his muse, and then brings his smaller events gradually out upon his stage, so did Miss Grantly with sacred fervour ask her mother's aid, and then prepare her list of all those articles of underclothing which must be the substratum for the visible magnificence of her trousseau. Money was no object. We all know what that means; and frequently understand, when the words are used, that a blaze of splendour is to be attained at the cheapest possible price. But, in this instance, money was no object; – such an amount of money, at least, as could by any possibility by spent on a lady's clothes, independently of her jewels. With reference to diamonds and such like, the archdeacon at once declared his intention of taking the matter into his own hands – except in so far as Lord Dumbello, or the Hartletop interest, might be pleased to participate in the selection. Nor was Mrs. Grantly sorry for such a decision. She was not an imprudent woman, and would have dreaded the responsibility of trusting herself on such an occasion among the dangerous temptations of a jeweller's shop. But as far as silks and satins went – in the matter of French bonnets, muslins, velvets, hats, riding-habits, artificial flowers, head-gilding, curious nettings, enamelled buckles, golden tagged bobbins, and mechanical petticoats – as regarded shoes, and gloves, and corsets, and stockings, and linen, and flannel, and calico – money, I may conscientiously assert, was no object. And, under these circumstances, Griselda Grantly went to work with a solemn industry and a steady perseverance that was beyond all praise. 'I hope she will be happy,' Mrs. Arabin said to her sister, as the two were sitting together in the dean's drawing-room.

'Oh, yes; I think she will. Why should she not?' said the mother.

'Oh, no; I know of no reason. But she is going up into a station so much above her own in the eyes of the world that one cannot but feel anxious for her.'

'I should feel much more anxious if she were going to marry a poor man,' said Mrs. Grantly. 'It has always seemed to me that Griselda was fitted for a high position; that nature intended her for rank and state. You see that she is not a bit elated. She takes it all as if it were her own by right. I do not think that there is any danger that her head will be turned, if you mean that.'

'I was thinking rather of her heart,' said Mrs. Arabin.

'She never would have taken Lord Dumbello without loving him,' said Mrs. Grantly, speaking rather quickly.

'That is not quite what I mean either, Susan. I am sure she would not have accepted him had she not loved him. But it is so hard to keep the heart fresh among all the grandeurs of high rank; and it is harder for a girl to do so who has not been born to it, than for one who has enjoyed it as her birthright.'

'I don't quite understand about fresh hearts,' said Mrs. Grantly, pettishly. 'If she does her duty, and loves her husband, and fills the position in which God has placed her with propriety, I don't know that we need look for anything more. I don't at all approve of the plan of frightening a young girl when she is making her first outset into the world.'

'No; I would not frighten her. I think it would be almost difficult to frighten Griselda.'

'I hope it would. The great matter with a girl is whether she has been brought up with proper notions as to a woman's duty. Of course it is not for me to boast on this subject. Such as she is, I, of course, am responsible. But I must own that I do not see occasion to wish for any change.' And then the subject was allowed to drop.

Among those of her relations who wondered much at the girl's fortune, but allowed themselves to say but little, was her grandfather, Mr. Harding. He was an old clergyman, plain and simple in his manners, and not occupying a very prominent position, seeing that he was only precentor to the chapter. He was loved by his daughter, Mrs. Grantly, and was treated by the archdeacon, if not invariably with the highest respect, at least always with consideration and regard. But, old and plain as he was, the young people at Plumstead did not hold him in any great reverence. He was poorer than their other relatives, and made no attempt to hold his head high in Barsetshire circles. Moreover, in these latter days, the home of his heart had been at the deanery. He had, indeed, a lodging of his own in the city, but was gradually allowing himself to be weaned away from it. He had his own bedroom in the dean's house, his own arm-chair in the dean's library, and his own corner on a sofa in Mrs. Dean's drawing-room. It was not, therefore, necessary that he should interfere greatly in this coming marriage; but still it became his duty to say a word of congratulation to his granddaughter – and perhaps to say a word of advice.

'Grizzy, my dear,' he said to her – he always called her Grizzy, but the endearment of the appellation had never been appreciated by the young lady – 'come and kiss me, and let me congratulate you on your great promotion. I do so very heartily.'

'Thank you, grandpapa,' she said, touching his forehead with her lips, thus being, as it were, very sparing with her kiss. But those lips now were august and reserved for nobler foreheads than that of an old cathedral hack. For Mr. Harding still chanted the Litany from Sunday to Sunday, unceasingly, standing at that well-known desk in the cathedral choir; and Griselda had a thought in her mind that when the Hartletop people should hear of the practice they would not be delighted. Dean and archdeacon might be very well, and if her grandfather had even been a prebendary, she might have put up with him; but he had, she thought, almost disgraced his family in being, at his age, one of the working menial clergy of the cathedral. She kissed him, therefore, sparingly, and resolved that her words with him should be few.

'You are going to be a great lady, Grizzy,' said he.

'Umph!' said she.

What was she to say when so addressed?

'And I hope you will be happy – and make others happy.'

'I hope I shall,' said she.

'But always think most about the latter, my dear. Think about the happiness of those around you, and your own will come without thinking. You understand that; do you not?'

'Oh, yes, I understand,' she said. As they were speaking Mr. Harding still held her hand, but Griselda left it with him unwillingly, and therefore ungraciously, looking as though she were dragging it from him.

'And Grizzy – I believe it is quite as easy for a rich countess to be happy, as for a dairymaid –' Griselda gave her head a little chuck which was produced by two different operations of her mind. The first was a reflection that her grandpapa was robbing her of her rank. She was to be a rich marchioness. And the second was a feeling of anger at the old man for comparing her lot to that of a dairymaid.

'Quite as easy, I believe,' continued he; 'though others will tell you that it is not so. But with the countess as with the dairymaid, it must depend on the woman herself. Being a countess – that fact alone won't make you happy.'

'Lord Dumbello at present is only a viscount,' said Griselda. 'There is no earl's title in the family.'

'Oh! I did not know,' said Mr. Harding, relinquishing his granddaughter's hand; and, after that, he troubled her with no further advice. Both Mrs. Proudie and the bishop had called at Plumstead since Mrs. Grantly had come back from London, and the ladies from Plumstead, of course, returned the visit. It was natural that the Grantlys and Proudies should hate each other. They were essentially Church people, and their views on all Church matters were antagonistic. They had been compelled to fight for supremacy in the diocese, and neither family had so conquered the other as to have become capable of magnanimity and good-humour. They did hate each other, and this hatred had, at one time, almost produced an absolute disseverance of even the courtesies which are so necessary between a bishop and his clergy. But the bitterness of this rancour had been overcome, and the ladies of the families had continued on visiting terms. But now this match was almost more than Mrs. Proudie could bear. The great disappointment which, as she well knew, the Grantlys had encountered in that matter of the proposed new bishopric had for the moment mollified her. She had been able to talk of poor dear Mrs. Grantly! 'She is heartbroken, you know, in this matter, and the repetition of such misfortunes is hard to bear,' she had been heard to say, with a complacency which had been quite becoming to her. But now that complacency was at an end. Olivia

Proudie had just accepted a widowed preacher at a district church in Bethnal Green – a man with three children, who was dependent on pew-rents; and Griselda Grantly was engaged to the eldest son of the Marquess of Hartletop! When women are enjoined to forgive their enemies it cannot be intended that such wrongs as these should be included. But Mrs. Proudie's courage was nothing daunted. It may be boasted of her that nothing could daunt her courage. Soon after her return to Barchester, she and Olivia – Olivia being very unwilling – had driven over to Plumstead, and, not finding the Grantlys at home, had left their cards; and now, at a proper interval, Mrs. Grantly and Griselda returned the visit. It was the first time that Miss Grantly had been seen by the Proudie ladies since the fact of her engagement had become known.

The first bevy of compliments that passed might be likened to a crowd of flowers on a hedge rose-bush. They were beautiful to the eye, but were so closely environed by thorns that they could not be plucked without great danger. As long as the compliments were allowed to remain on the hedge – while no attempt was made to garner them and realize their fruits for enjoyment – they did no mischief; but the first finger that was put forth for such a purpose was soon drawn back, marked with spots of blood. 'Of course it is a great match for Griselda,' said Mrs. Grantly, in a whisper the meekness of which would have disarmed an enemy whose weapons were less firmly clutched than those of Mrs. Proudie; 'but, independently of that, the connexion is one which is gratifying in many ways.'

'Oh, no doubt,' said Mrs. Proudie.

'Lord Dumbello is so completely his own master,' continued Mrs. Grantly, and a slight, unintended semi-tone of triumph mingled itself with the meekness of that whisper.

'And is likely to remain so, from all I hear,' said Mrs. Proudie, and the scratched hand was at once drawn back.

'Of course the estab –,' and then Mrs. Proudie, who was blandly continuing her list of congratulation, whispered her sentence close into the ear of Mrs. Grantly, so that not a word of what she said might be audible by the young people.

'I never heard a word of it,' said Mrs. Grantly, gathering herself up, 'and I don't believe it.'

'Oh, I may be wrong; and I'm sure I hope so. But young men will be young men, you know; – and children will take after their parents. I suppose you will see a great deal of the Duke of Omnium now.' But Mrs. Grantly was not a woman to be knocked down and trampled on without resistance; and though she had been lacerated by the rose-bush she was not as yet placed altogether *hors de combat.* She said some word about the Duke of Omnium very tranquilly, speaking of him merely as a Barsetshire proprietor, and then, smiling with her sweetest smile, expressed a hope that she might soon have the pleasure of becoming acquainted with Mr. Tickler; and as she spoke she made a pretty little bow towards Olivia Proudie. Now Mr. Tickler was the worthy clergyman attached to the district church at Bethnal Green.

'He'll be down here in August,' said Olivia, boldly, determined not to be shamefaced about her love affairs.

'You'll be starring it about the Continent by that time, my dear,' said Mrs. Proudie to Griselda. 'Lord Dumbello is well known at Homburg and Ems, and places of that sort; so you will find yourself quite at home.'

'We are going to Rome,' said Griselda, majestically.

'I suppose Mr. Tickler will come into the diocese soon,' said Mrs. Grantly. 'I remember hearing him very favourably spoken of by Mr. Slope, who was a friend of his.' Nothing short of a fixed resolve on the part of Mrs. Grantly that the time had now come in which she must throw away her shield and stand behind her sword, declare war to the knife, and neither give nor take quarter, could have justified such a speech as this. Any allusion to Mr. Slope acted on Mrs. Proudie as a red cloth is supposed to act on a bull; but when that allusion connected the name of Mr. Slope in a friendly bracket with that of Mrs. Proudie's future son-in-law it might be certain that the effect would be terrific. And there was more than this: for that very Mr. Slope had once entertained audacious hopes – hopes not thought to be audacious by the young lady herself – with reference to Miss Olivia Proudie. All this Mrs. Grantly knew, and, knowing it, still dared to mention his name.

The countenance of Mrs. Proudie became darkened with black anger, and the polished smile of her company manners gave place before the outraged feelings of her nature. 'The man you speak of, Mrs. Grantly,' said she, 'was never known as a friend by Mr. Tickler.'

'Oh, indeed,' said Mrs. Grantly. 'Perhaps I have made a mistake. I am sure I have heard Mr. Slope mention him.'

'When Mr. Slope was running after your sister, Mrs. Grantly, and was encouraged by her as he was, you perhaps saw more of him than I did.'

'Mrs. Proudie, that was never the case.'

'I have reason to know that the archdeacon conceived it to be so, and that he was very unhappy about it.' Now this, unfortunately, was a fact which Mrs. Grantly could not deny.

'The archdeacon may have been mistaken about Mr. Slope,' she said, 'as were some other people at Barchester. But it was you, I think, Mrs. Proudie, who were responsible for bringing him here.' Mrs. Grantly, at this period of the engagement, might have inflicted a fatal wound by referring to poor Olivia's former love affairs, but she was not destitute of generosity. Even in the extremest heat of the battle she knew how to spare the young and tender.

'When I came here, Mrs. Grantly, I little dreamed what a depth of wickedness might be found in the very close of a cathedral city,' said Mrs. Proudie.

'Then, for dear Olivia's sake, pray do not bring poor Mr. Tickler to Barchester.'

'Mr. Tickler, Mrs. Grantly, is a man of assured morals and of a highly religious tone of thinking. I wish every one could be so safe as regards their daughters' future prospects as I am.'

'Yes, I know he has the advantage of being a family man,' said Mrs. Grantly, getting up. 'Good morning, Mrs. Proudie; good day, Olivia.'

'A great deal better that than –' But the blow fell upon the empty air; for Mrs. Grantly had already escaped on to the staircase while Olivia was ringing the bell for the servant to attend the front-door.

Mrs. Grantly, as she got into her carriage, smiled slightly, thinking of the battle, and as she sat down she gently pressed her daughter's hand. But Mrs. Proudie's face was still dark as Acheron when her enemy withdrew, and with angry tone she sent her daughter to her work. 'Mr. Tickler will have great reason to complain if, in your position, you indulge such habits of idleness,' she said. Therefore I conceive that I am justified in saying that in that encounter Mrs. Grantly was the conqueror.

CHAPTER XLI

Don Quixote

ON the day on which Lucy had her interview with Lady Lufton the dean dined at Framley parsonage. He and Robarts had known each other since the latter had been in the diocese, and now, owing to Mark's preferment in the chapter, had become almost intimate. The dean was greatly pleased with the manner in which poor Mr. Crawley's children had been conveyed away from Hogglestock, and was inclined to open his heart to the whole Framley household. As he still had to ride home he could only allow himself to remain half an hour after dinner, but in that half-hour he said a great deal about Crawley, complimented Robarts on the manner in which he was playing the part of the Good Samaritan, and then by degrees informed him that it had come to his, the dean's, ears, before he left Barchester, that a writ was in the hands of certain persons in the city, enabling them to seize – he did not know whether it was the person or the property of the vicar of Framley.

The fact was that these tidings had been conveyed to the dean with the express intent that he might put Robarts on his guard; but the task of speaking on such a subject to a brother clergyman had been so unpleasant to him that he had been unable to introduce it till the last five minutes before his departure. 'I hope you will not put it down as an impertinent interference,' said the dean, apologizing.

'No,' said Mark; 'no, I do not think that.' He was so sad at heart that he hardly knew how to speak of it.

'I do not understand much about such matters,' said the dean; 'but I think, if I were you, I should go to a lawyer. I should imagine that anything so terribly disagreeable as an arrest might be avoided.'

'It is a hard case,' said Mark, pleading his own cause. 'Though these men have this claim against me I have never received a shilling either in money or money's worth.'

'And yet your name is to the bills!' said the dean.

'Yes, my name is to the bills, certainly, but it was to oblige a friend.'

And then the dean, having given his advice, rode away. He could not understand how a clergyman, situated as was Mr. Robarts, could find himself called upon by friendship to attach his name to accommodation bills which he had not the power of liquidating when due! On that evening they were both wretched enough at the parsonage. Hitherto Mark had hoped that perhaps, after all, no absolutely hostile steps would be taken against him with reference to these bills. Some unforeseen chance might occur in his favour, or the persons holding them might consent to take small instalments of payment from time to time; but now it seemed that the evil day was actually coming upon him at a blow. He had no longer any secrets from his wife. Should he go to a lawyer? and if so, to what lawyer? And when he had found his lawyer, what should he say to him? Mrs. Robarts at one time suggested that everything should be told to Lady Lufton. Mark, however, could not bring himself to do that. 'It would seem,' he said, 'as though I wanted her to lend me the money.'

On the following morning Mark did ride into Barchester, dreading, however, lest he should be arrested on his journey, and he did see a lawyer. During his absence two calls were made at the parsonage – one by a very rough-looking individual, who left a suspicious document in the hands of the servant, purporting to be an invitation – not to dinner – from one of the Judges of the land; and the other call was made by Lady Lufton in person.

Mrs. Robarts had determined to go down to Framley Court on that day. In accordance with her usual custom she would have been there within an hour or two of Lady Lufton's return from London, but things between them were not now as they usually had been. This affair of Lucy's must make a difference, let them both resolve to the contrary as they might. And, indeed, Mrs. Robarts had found that the closeness of her intimacy with Framley Court had been diminishing from day to day since Lucy had first begun to be on friendly terms with Lord Lufton. Since that she had been less at Framley Court than usual; she had heard from Lady Lufton less frequently by letter during her absence than she had done in former years, and was aware that she was less implicitly trusted with all the affairs of the parish. This had not made her angry, for she was in a manner conscious that it must be so. It made her unhappy, but what could she do? She could not blame Lucy, nor could she blame Lady Lufton. Lord Lufton she did blame, but she did so in the hearing of no one but her husband. Her mind, however, was made up to go over and bear the first brunt of her ladyship's arguments, when she was stopped by her ladyship's arrival. If it were not for this terrible matter of Lucy's love – a matter on which they could not now be silent when they met – there would be twenty subjects of pleasant, or, at any rate, not unpleasant conversation. But even then there would be those terrible bills hanging over her conscience, and almost crushing her by their weight. At the moment in which Lady Lufton walked up to the drawing-room window, Mrs. Robarts held in her hand that ominous invitation from the Judge. Would it not be well that she should make a clean breast of it all, disregarding what her husband had said? It might be well: only this – she had never done anything in opposition to her husband's wishes. So she hid the slip within her desk, and left the matter open to consideration. The interview commenced with an affectionate embrace, as was a matter of course. 'Dear Fanny,' and 'Dear Lady Lufton,' was said between them with all the usual warmth. And then the first inquiry was made about the children, and the second about the school. For a minute or two Mrs. Robarts thought that, perhaps, nothing was to be said about Lucy. If it pleased Lady Lufton to be silent, she, at least, would not commence the subject. Then there was a word or two spoken about Mrs. Podgens's baby, after which Lady Lufton asked whether Fanny were alone. 'Yes,' said Mrs. Robarts. 'Mark has gone over to Barchester.'

'I hope he will not be long before he lets me see him. Perhaps he can call to-morrow. Would you both come and dine to-morrow?'

'Not to-morrow, I think, Lady Lufton; but Mark, I am sure, will go over and call.'

'And why not come to dinner? I hope there is to be no change among us, eh, Fanny?' and Lady Lufton as she spoke looked into the other's face in a manner which almost made Mrs. Robarts get up and throw herself on her old friend's neck. Where was she to find a friend who would give her such constant love as she had received from Lady Lufton? And who was kinder, better, more honest than she?'

'Change! no, I hope not, Lady Lufton,' and as she spoke the tears stood in her eyes.

'Ah, but I shall think there is if you will not come to me as you used to do. You always used to come and dine with me the day I came home, as a matter of course.' What could she say, poor woman, to this?

'We were all in confusion yesterday about poor Mrs. Crawley, and the dean dined here; he had been over at Hogglestock to see his friend.'

'I have heard of her illness, and will go over and see what ought to be done. Don't you go, do you hear, Fanny? You with your young children! I should never forgive you if you did.' And then Mrs. Robarts explained how Lucy had gone there, had sent the four children back to Framley, and was herself now staying at Hogglestock with the object of nursing Mrs. Crawley. In telling the story she abstained from praising Lucy with all the strong language which she would have used had not Lucy's name and character been at the present moment of peculiar import to Lady Lufton; but nevertheless she could not tell it without dwelling much on Lucy's kindness. It would have been ungenerous to Lady Lufton to make much of Lucy's virtue at this present moment, but unjust to Lucy to make nothing of it.

'And she is actually with Mrs. Crawley now?' asked Lady Lufton.

'Oh, yes; Mark left her there yesterday afternoon.'

'And the four children are all here in the house?'

'Not exactly in the house – that is, not as yet. We have arranged a sort of quarantine hospital over the coach-house.'

'What, where Stubbs lives?'

'Yes; Stubbs and his wife have come into the house, and the children are to remain up there till the doctor says that there is no danger of infection. I have not even seen my visitors myself as yet,' said Mrs. Robarts with a slight laugh.

'Dear me!' said Lady Lufton. 'I declare you have been very prompt. And so Miss Robarts is over there! I should have thought Mr. Crawley would have made a difficulty about the children.'

'Well, he did; but they kidnapped them – that is, Lucy and Mark did. The dean gave me such an account of it. Lucy brought them out by by twos and packed them in the pony-carriage, and then Mark drove off at a gallop while Mr. Crawley stood calling to them in the road. The dean was there at the time and saw it all.'

'That Miss Lucy of yours seems to be a very determined young lady when she takes a thing into her head,' said Lady Lufton, now sitting down for the first time.

'Yes, she is,' said Mrs. Robarts, having laid aside all her pleasant animation, for the discussion which she dreaded was now at hand.

'A very determined young lady,' continued Lady Lufton. 'Of course, my dear Fanny, you know all this about Ludovic and your sister-in-law?'

'Yes, she has told me about it.'

'It is very unfortunate – very.'

'I do not think Lucy has been to blame,' said Mrs. Robarts; and as she spoke the blood was already mounting to her cheeks.

'Do not be too anxious to defend her, my dear, before any one accuses her. Whenever a person does that it looks as though their cause were weak.'

'But my cause is not weak as far as Lucy is concerned; I feel quite sure that she has not been to blame.'

'I know how obstinate you can be, Fanny, when you think it necessary to dub yourself any one's champion. Don Quixote was not a better knight-errant than you are.

But is it not a pity to take up your lance and shield before an enemy is within sight or hearing? But that was ever the way with your Don Quixotes.'

'Perhaps there may be an enemy in ambush.' That was Mrs. Robarts's thought to herself, but she did not dare to express it, so she remained silent.

'My only hope is,' continued Lady Lufton, 'that when my back is turned you fight as gallantly for me.'

'Ah, you are never under a cloud, like poor Lucy.'

'Am I not? But, Fanny, you do not see all the clouds. The sun does not always shine for any of us, and the down-pouring rain and the heavy wind scatter also my fairest flowers – as they have done hers, poor girl. Dear Fanny, I hope it may not be long before any cloud comes across the brightness of your heaven. Of all the creatures I know you are the one most fitted for quiet continued sunshine.' And then Mrs. Robarts did get up and embrace her friend, thus hiding the tears which were running down her face. Continued sunshine indeed! A dark spot had already gathered on her horizon, which was likely to fall in a very water-spout of rain. What was to come of that terrible notice which was now lying in the desk under Lady Lufton's very arm?

'But I am not come here to croak like an old raven,' continued Lady Lufton, when she had brought this embrace to an end. 'It is probable that we all may have our sorrows; but I am quite sure of this, – that if we endeavour to do our duties honestly, we shall all find our consolation and all have our joys also. And now, my dear, let you and I say a few words about this unfortunate affair. It would not be natural if we were to hold our tongues to each other; would it?'

'I suppose not,' said Mrs. Robarts.

'We should always be conceiving worse than the truth – each as to the other's thoughts. Now, some time ago, when I spoke to you about your sister-in-law and Ludovic – I dare say you remember –'

'Oh, yes, I remember.'

'We both thought then that there would really be no danger. To tell you the plain truth I fancied, and indeed hoped, that his affections were engaged elsewhere; but I was altogether wrong then; wrong in thinking it, and wrong in hoping it.' Mrs. Robarts knew well that Lady Lufton was alluding to Griselda Grantly, but she conceived that it would be discreet to say nothing herself on that subject at present. She remembered, however, Lucy's flashing eye when the possibility of Lord Lufton making such a marriage was spoken of in the pony-carriage, and could not but feel glad that Lady Lufton had been disappointed.

'I do not at all impute any blame to Miss Robarts for what has occurred since,' continued her ladyship. 'I wish you distinctly to understand that.'

'I do not see how any one could blame her. She has behaved so nobly.'

'It is of no use inquiring whether any one can. It is sufficient that I do not.'

'But I think that is hardly sufficient,' said Mrs. Robarts, pertinaciously.

'Is it not?' asked her ladyship, raising her eyebrows.

'No. Only think what Lucy has done and is doing. If she had chosen to say that she would accept your son I really do not know how you could have justly blamed her. I do not by any means say that I would have advised such a thing.'

'I am glad of that, Fanny.'

'I have not given any advice; nor is it needed. I know no one more able than Lucy to see clearly, by her own judgement, what course she ought to pursue. I should be afraid to advise one whose mind is so strong, and who, of her own nature, is so self-denying as she is. She is sacrificing herself now, because she will not be the means of bringing trouble and dissension between you and your son. If you ask me, Lady Lufton, I think you owe her a deep debt of gratitude. I do, indeed. And as for blaming her – what has she done that you possibly could blame?'

'Don Quixote on horseback!' said Lady Lufton. 'Fanny, I shall always call you Don Quixote, and some day or other I will get somebody to write your adventures. But the truth is this, my dear; there has been imprudence. You may call it mine, if you will – though I really hardly see how I am to take the blame. I could not do other than ask Miss Robarts to my house, and I could not very well turn my son out of it. In point of fact, it has been the old story.'

'Exactly; the story that is as old as the world, and which will continue as long as people are born into it. It is a story of God's own telling.'

'But, my dear child, you do not mean that every young gentleman and every young lady should fall in love with each other directly they meet! Such a doctrine would be very inconvenient.'

'No, I do not mean that. Lord Lufton and Miss Grantly did not fall in love with each other, though you meant them to do so. But was it not quite as natural that Lord Lufton and Lucy should do so instead?'

'It is generally thought, Fanny, that young ladies should not give loose to their affections until they have been certified of their friends' approval.'

'And that young gentlemen of fortune may amuse themselves as they please! I know that is what the world teaches, but I cannot agree to the justice of it. The terrible suffering which Lucy has to endure makes me cry out against it. She did not seek your son. The moment she began to suspect that there might be danger she avoided him scrupulously. She would not go down to Framley Court, though her not doing so was remarked by yourself. She would hardly go out about the place lest she should meet him. She was contented to put herself altogether in the background till he should have pleased to leave the place. But he – he came to her here, and insisted on seeing her. He found her when I was out, and declared himself determined to speak to her. What was she to do?

She did try to escape, but he stopped her at the door. Was it her fault that he made her an offer?'

'My dear, no one has said so.'

'Yes, but you do say so when you tell me that young ladies should not give play to their affections without permission. He persisted in saying to her, here, all that it pleased him, though she implored him to be silent. I cannot tell the words she used, but she did implore him.'

'I do not doubt that she behaved well.'

'But he – he persisted, and begged her to accept his hand. She refused him then, Lady Lufton – not as some girls do, with a mock reserve, not intending to be taken at their words – but steadily, and, God forgive her, untruly. Knowing what your feelings would be, and knowing what the world would say, she declared to him that he was indifferent to her. What more could she do in your behalf?' And then Mrs. Robarts paused.

'I shall wait till you have done, Fanny.'

'You spoke of girls giving loose to their affections. She did not do so. She went about her work exactly as she had done before. She did not even speak to me of what had passed – not then, at least. She determined that it should all be as though it had never been. She had learned to love your son; but that was her misfortune, and she would get over it as she might. Tidings came to us here that he was engaged, or about to engage himself, to Miss Grantly.'

'Those tidings were untrue.'

'Yes, we know that now; but she did not know it then. Of course she could not but suffer; but she suffered within herself.' Mrs. Robarts, as she said this, remembered the pony-carriage and how Puck had been beaten. 'She made no complaint that he had ill-treated her – not even to herself. She had thought it right to reject his offer; and there, as far as he was concerned, was to be an end of it.'

'That would be a matter of course, I should suppose.'

'But it was not a matter of course, Lady Lufton. He returned from London to Framley on purpose to repeat his offer. He sent for her brother – You talk of a young lady waiting for her friends' approval. In this matter who would be Lucy's friends?'

'You and Mr. Robarts, of course.'

'Exactly; her only friends. Well, Lord Lufton sent for Mark and repeated his offer to him. Mind you, Mark had never heard a word of this before, and you may guess whether or no he was surprised. Lord Lufton repeated his offer in the most formal manner, and claimed permission to see Lucy. She refused to see him. She has never seen him since that day when, in opposition to all her efforts, he made his way into this room. Mark, – as I think very properly, – would have allowed Lord Lufton to come up here. Looking at both their ages and position he could have had no right to forbid it. But Lucy positively refused to see your son, and sent him a message instead, of the purport of which you are now aware – that she would never accept him unless she did so at your request.'

'It was a very proper message.'

'I say nothing about that. Had she accepted him I would not have blamed her; and so I told her, Lady Lufton.'

'I cannot understand your saying that, Fanny.'

'Well; I did say so. I don't want to argue now about myself, – whether I was right or wrong, but I did say so. Whatever sanction I could give she would have had. But she again chose to sacrifice herself, although I believe she regards him with as true a love as ever a girl felt for a man. Upon my word I don't know that she is right. Those considerations for the world may perhaps be carried too far.'

'I think that she was perfectly right.'

'Very well, Lady Lufton; I can understand that. But after such sacrifice on her part – a sacrifice made entirely to you – how can you talk of "not blaming her"? Is that the language in which you speak of those whose conduct from first to last has been superlatively excellent? If she is open to blame at all, it is – it is –' But here Mrs. Robarts stopped herself. In defending her sister she had worked herself almost into a passion; but such a state of feeling was not customary to her, and now that she had spoken her mind she sank suddenly into silence.

'It seems to me, Fanny, that you almost regret Miss Robarts's decision,' said Lady Lufton.

'My wish in this matter is for her happiness, and I regret anything that may mar it.'

'You think nothing then of our welfare, and yet I do not know to whom I might have looked for hearty friendship and for sympathy in difficulties, if not to you?' Poor Mrs. Robarts was almost upset by this. A few months ago, before Lucy's arrival, she would have declared that the interests of Lady Lufton's family would have been paramount with her, after and next to those of her own husband. And even now, it seemed to argue so black an ingratitude on her part – this accusation that she was indifferent to them! From her childhood upwards she had revered and loved Lady Lufton, and for years had taught herself to regard her as an epitome of all that was good and gracious in woman. Lady Lufton's theories of life had been accepted by her as the right theories, and those whom Lady Lufton had liked she had liked. But now it seemed that all these ideas which it had taken a life to build up were to be thrown to the ground, because she was bound to defend a sister-in-law whom she had only known for the last eight months. It was not that she regretted a word that she had spoken on Lucy's behalf. Chance had thrown her and Lucy together, and, as Lucy was her sister, she should receive from her a sister's treatment. But she did not the less feel how terrible would be the effect of any disseverance from Lady Lufton. 'Oh, Lady Lufton,' she said, 'do not say that.'

'But Fanny, dear, I must speak as I find. You were talking about clouds just now, and do you think that all this is not a cloud in my sky? Ludovic tells me that he is attached to Miss Robarts, and you tell me that she is attached to him; and I am called upon to decide between them. Her very act obliges me to do so.'

'Dear Lady Lufton,' said Mrs. Robarts, springing from her seat. It seemed to her at the moment as though the whole difficulty were to be solved by an act of grace on the part of an old friend.

'And yet I cannot approve of such a marriage,' said Lady Lufton. Mrs. Robarts returned to her seat saying nothing further.

'Is not that a cloud on one's horizon?' continued her ladyship. 'Do you think that I can be basking in the sunshine while I have such a weight upon my heart as that? Ludovic will soon be home, but instead of looking to his return with pleasure I dread it. I would prefer that he should remain in Norway. I would wish that he should stay away for months. And, Fanny, it is a great addition to my misfortune to feel that you do not sympathize with me.' Having said this, in a slow, sorrowful, and severe tone, Lady Lufton got up and took her departure. Of course Mrs. Robarts did not let her go without assuring her that she did sympathize with her, – did love her as she ever had loved her. But wounds cannot be cured as easily as they may be inflicted, and Lady Lufton went her way with much real sorrow at her heart. She was proud and masterful, fond of her own way, and much too careful of the worldly dignities to which her lot had called her: but she was a woman who could cause no sorrow to those she loved without deep sorrow to herself

CHAPTER XLII

Touching Pitch

IN these hot midsummer days, the end of June and the beginning of July, Mr. Sowerby had but an uneasy time of it. At his sister's instance, he had hurried up to London, and there had remained for days in attendance on the lawyers. He had to see new lawyers, Miss Dunstable's men of business, quiet old cautious gentlemen whose place of business was in a dark alley behind the Bank, Messrs. Slow & Bideawhile by name, who had no scruple in detaining him for hours while they or their clerks talked to him about anything or about nothing. It was of vital consequence to Mr. Sowerby that this business of his should be settled without delay, and yet these men, to whose care this settling was now confided, went on as though law processes were a sunny bank on which it delighted men to bask easily. And then, too, he had to go more than once to South Audley Street, which was a worse infliction; for the men in South Audley Street were less civil now than had been their wont. It was well understood there that Mr. Sowerby was no longer a client of the duke's, but his opponent; no longer his nominee and dependant, but his enemy in the county. 'Chaldicotes,' as old Mr. Gumption remarked to young Mr. Gagebee; 'Chaldicotes, Gagebee, is a cooked goose, as far as Sowerby is concerned. And what difference could it make to him whether the duke is to own it or Miss Dunstable? For my part I cannot understand how a gentleman like Sowerby can like to see his property go into the hands of a gallipot wench whose money still smells of bad drugs. And nothing can be more ungrateful,' he said, 'than Sowerby's conduct. He has held the county for five-and-twenty years without expense; and now that the time for payment has come, he begrudges the price.' He called it no better than cheating, he did not – he, Mr. Gumption. According to his ideas Sowerby was attempting to cheat the duke. It may be imagined, therefore, that Mr. Sowerby did not feel any very great delight in attending at South Audley Street. And then rumour was spread about among all the bill-discounting leeches that blood was once more to be sucked from the Sowerby carcass. The rich Miss Dunstable had taken up his affairs; so much as that became known in the purlieus of the Goat and Compasses. Tom Tozer's brother declared that she and Sowerby were going to make a match of it, and that any scrap of paper with Sowerby's name on it would become worth its weight in bank-notes; but Tom Tozer himself – Tom, who was the real hero of the family – pooh-poohed at this, screwing up his nose, and alluding in most contemptuous terms to his brother's softness. He knew better – as was indeed the fact. Miss Dunstable was buying up the squire, and by Jingo she should buy them up – them, the Tozers, as well as others! They knew their value, the Tozers did; – whereupon they became more than ordinarily active. From them and all their brethren Mr. Sowerby at this time endeavoured to keep his distance, but his endeavours were not altogether effectual. Whenever he could escape for a day or two from the lawyers he ran down to Chaldicotes; but Tom Tozer in his perseverance followed him there, and boldly sent in his name by the servant at the front door.

'Mr. Sowerby is not just at home at the present moment,' said the well-trained domestic.

'I'll wait about then,' said Tom, seating himself on an heraldic stone griffin which flanked the big stone steps before the house. And in this way Mr. Tozer gained his purpose. Sowerby was still contesting the county, and it behoved him not to let his enemies say that he was hiding himself. It had been a part of his bargain with Miss Dunstable that he should contest the county. She had taken it into her head that the duke had behaved badly, and she had resolved that he should be made to pay for it. 'The duke,' she said, 'had meddled long enough;' she would now see whether the Chaldicotes interest would not suffice of itself to return a member for the county, even in opposition to the duke. Mr. Sowerby himself was so harassed at the time, that he would have given way on this point if he had had the power; but Miss Dunstable was determined, and he was obliged to yield to her. In this manner Mr. Tom Tozer succeeded and did make his way into Mr. Sowerby's presence – of which intrusion one effect was the following letter from Mr. Sowerby to his friend Mark Robarts:—

'CHALDICOTES, July, 185—.

'My dear Robarts,

'I am so harassed at the present moment by an infinity of troubles of my own that I am almost callous to those of other people. They say that prosperity makes a man selfish. I have never tried that, but I am quite sure that adversity does so. Nevertheless I am anxious about those bills of yours' –

'Bills of mine!' said Robarts to himself, as he walked up and down the shrubbery path at the parsonage, reading this letter. This happened a day or two after his visit to the lawyer at Barchester.

'– and would rejoice greatly if I thought that I could save you from any further annoyance about them. That kite, Tom Tozer, has just been with me, and insists that both of them shall be paid. He knows – no one better – that no consideration was given for the latter. But he knows also that the dealing was not with him, nor even with his brother, and he will be prepared to swear that he gave value for both. He would swear anything for five hundred pounds – or for half the money, for that matter. I do not think that the father of mischief ever let loose upon the world a greater rascal than Tom Tozer.

'He declares that nothing shall induce him to take one shilling less than the whole sum of nine hundred pounds. He has been brought to this by hearing that my debts are about to be paid. Heaven help me! The meaning of that is that these wretched acres, which are now mortgaged to one millionaire, are to change hands and be mortgaged to another instead. By this exchange I may possibly obtain the benefit of having a house to live in for the next twelve months, but no other. Tozer, however, is altogether wrong in his scent; and the worst of it is that his malice will fall on you rather than on me.

'What I want you to do is this: let us pay him one hundred pounds between us. Though I sell the last sorry jade of a horse I have, I will make up fifty; and I know you can, at any rate, do as much as that. Then do you accept a bill, conjointly with me, for eight hundred. It shall be done in Forrest's presence, and handed to him; and you shall receive back the two old bills into your own hands at the same time. This new bill should be timed to run ninety days; and I will move heaven and earth, during that time, to have it included in the general schedule of my debts which are to be secured on the Chaldicotes property.'

The meaning of which was that Miss Dunstable was to be cozened into paying the money under an idea that it was a part of the sum covered by the existing mortgage.

'What you said the other day at Barchester, as to never executing another bill, is very well as regards future transactions. Nothing can be wiser than such a resolution. But it would be folly – worse than folly – if you were to allow your furniture to be seized when the means of preventing it are so ready to your hand. By leaving the new bill in Forrest's hands you may be sure that you are safe from the claws of such birds of prey as these Tozers. Even if I cannot get it settled when the three months are over, Forrest will enable you to make any arrangement that may be most convenient.

'For Heaven's sake, my dear fellow, do not refuse this. You can hardly conceive how it weighs upon me, this fear that bailiffs should make their way into your wife's drawing-room. I know you think ill of me, and I do not wonder at it. But you would be less inclined to do so if you knew how terribly I am punished. Pray let me hear that you will do as I counsel you.

'Yours always faithfully,

'N. Sowerby.'

In answer to which the parson wrote a very short reply:—

'FRAMLEY, July, 185–.

'My dear Sowerby,

'I will sign no more bills on any consideration.

'Yours truly,

'Mark Robarts.'

And then having written this, and having shown it to his wife, he returned to the shrubbery walk and paced it up and down, looking every now and then to Sowerby's letter as he thought over all the past circumstances of his friendship with that gentleman. That the man who had written this letter should be his friend – that very fact was a disgrace to him. Sowerby so well knew himself and his own reputation, that he did not dare to suppose that his own word would be taken for anything, – not even when the thing promised was an act of the commonest honesty. 'The old bills shall be given back into your own hands,' he had declared with energy, knowing that his friend and correspondent would not feel himself secure against further fraud under less stringent guarantee. This gentleman, this county member, the owner of Chaldicotes, with whom Mark Robarts had been so anxious to be on terms of intimacy, had now come to such a phase of life that he had given over speaking of himself as an honest man. He had become so used to suspicion that he argued of it as of a thing of course. He knew that no one could trust either his spoken or his written word, and he was content to speak and to write without attempt to hide this conviction. And this was the man whom he had been so glad to call his friend; for whose sake he had been willing to quarrel with Lady Lufton, and at whose instance he had unconsciously abandoned so many of the best resolutions of his life. He looked back now, as he walked there slowly, still holding the letter in his hand, to the day when he had stopped at the school-house and written his letter to Mr. Sowerby, promising to join the party at Chaldicotes. He had been so eager then to have his own way, that he would not permit himself to go home and talk the matter over with his wife. He thought also of the manner in which he had been tempted to the house of the Duke of Omnium, and the conviction on his mind at the time that his giving way to that temptation would surely bring him to evil. And then he remembered the evening in Sowerby's bedroom, when the bill had been brought out, and he had allowed himself to be persuaded to put his name upon it – not because he was willing in this way to assist his friend, but because he was unable to refuse. He had lacked the courage to say, 'No,' though he knew at the time how gross was the error which he was committing. He had lacked the courage to say, 'No,' and hence had come upon him and on his household all this misery and cause for bitter repentance.

I have written much of clergymen, but in doing so I have endeavoured to portray them as they bear on our social life rather than to describe the mode and working of their professional careers. Had I done the latter I could hardly have steered clear of subjects on which it has not been my intention to pronounce an opinion, and I should either have laden my fiction with sermons or I should have degraded my sermons into fiction. Therefore I have said but little in my narrative of this man's feelings or doings as a clergyman. But I must protest against its being on this account considered that Mr. Robarts was indifferent to the duties of his clerical position. He had been fond of pleasure and had given way to temptation, – as is so customarily done by young men of six-and-twenty, who are placed beyond control and who have means at command. Had he remained as a curate till that age, subject in all his movements to the eye of a superior, he would, we may say, have put his name to no bills, have ridden after no hounds, have seen nothing of the iniquities of Gatherum Castle. There are men of twenty-six as fit to stand alone as ever they will be – fit to be prime ministers, heads of schools, Judges on the Bench – almost fit to be bishops; but Mark Robarts had not been one of them. He had within him many aptitudes for good, but not the strengthened courage of a man to act up to them. The stuff of which his manhood was to be formed had been slow of growth, as it is with many men; and, consequently, when temptation was offered to him, he had fallen. But he deeply grieved over his own stumbling, and from time to time, as his periods of penitence came upon him, he resolved that he would once more put his shoulder to the wheel as became one who fights upon earth that battle for which he had put on the armour. Over and over again did he think of those words of Mr. Crawley, and now as he walked up and down the path, crumpling Mr. Sowerby's letter in his hand, he thought of them again – 'It is a terrible falling off; terrible in the fall, but doubly terrible through that difficulty of returning.' Yes; that is a difficulty which multiplies itself in a fearful ratio as one goes on pleasantly running down the path – whitherward? Had it come to that with him that he could not return – that he could never again hold up his head with a safe conscience as the pastor of his parish! It was Sowerby who had led him into this misery, who had brought on him this ruin? But then had not Sowerby paid him? Had not that stall which he now held in Barchester been Sowerby's gift? He was a poor man now – a distressed, poverty-stricken man; but nevertheless he wished with all his heart that he had never become a sharer in the good things of the Barchester chapter. 'I shall resign the stall,' he said to his wife that night. 'I think I may say that I have made up my mind as to that.'

'But, Mark, will not people say that it is odd?'

'I cannot help it – they must say it. Fanny, I fear that we shall have to bear the saying of harder words than that.'

'Nobody can ever say that you have done anything that is unjust or dishonourable. If there are such men as Mr. Sowerby –'

'The blackness of his fault will not excuse mine.' And then again he sat silent, hiding his eyes, while his wife, sitting by him, held his hand.

'Don't make yourself wretched, Mark. Matters will all come right yet. It cannot be that the loss of a few hundred pounds should ruin you.'

'It is not the money – it is not the money!'

'But you have done nothing wrong, Mark.'

'How am I to go into the church, and take my place before them all, when every one will know that bailiffs are in the house?' And then, dropping his head on to the table, he sobbed aloud.

Mark Robarts's mistakes had been mainly this, – he had thought to touch pitch and not to be defiled. He, looking out from his pleasant parsonage into the pleasant upper ranks of the world around him, had seen that men and things in those quarters were very engaging. His own parsonage, with his sweet wife, were exceedingly dear to him, and Lady Lufton's affectionate friendship had its value; but were not these things rather dull for one who had lived in the best sets at Harrow and Oxford; – unless, indeed, he could supplement them with some occasional bursts of more lively life? Cakes and ale were as pleasant to his palate as to the palates of those with whom he had formerly lived at college. He had the same eye to look at a horse, and the same heart to make him go across a country, as they. And then, too, he found that men liked him, – men and women also; men and women who were high in worldly standing. His ass's ears were tickled, and he learned to fancy that he was intended by nature for the society of high people. It seemed as though he were following his appointed course in meeting men and women of the world at the houses of the fashionable and the rich. He was not the first clergymen that had so lived and had so prospered. Yes, clergymen had so lived, and had done their duties in their sphere of life altogether to the satisfaction of their countrymen – and of their sovereigns. Thus Mark Robarts had determined that he would touch pitch, and escape defilement if that were possible. With what result those who have read so far will have perceived. Late on the following afternoon who should drive up to the parsonage door but Mr. Forrest, the bank manager from Barchester – Mr. Forrest, to whom Sowerby had always pointed as the *Deus ex machina* who, if duly invoked, could relieve them all from their present troubles, and dismiss the whole Tozer family – not howling into the wilderness, as one would have wished to do with that brood of Tozers, but so gorged with prey that from them no further annoyance need be dreaded? All this Mr. Forrest could do; nay, more, most willingly would do! Only let Mark Robarts put himself into the banker's hand, and blandly sign what documents the banker might desire. 'This is a very unpleasant affair,' said Mr. Forrest as soon as they were closeted together in Mark's book-room. In answer to which observation the parson acknowledged that it was a very unpleasant affair.

'Mr. Sowerby has managed to put you into the hands of about the worst set of rogues now existing in their line of business in London.'

'So I suppose! Curling told me the same.' Curling was the Barchester attorney whose aid he had lately invoked.

'Curling has threatened them that he will expose their whole trade; but one of them who was down here, a man named Tozer, replied, that you had much more to lose by exposure than he had. He went further, and declared that he would defy any jury in England to refuse him his money. He swore that he discounted both bills in the regular way of business; and, though this is of course false, I fear that it will be impossible to prove it so. He well knows that you are a clergyman, and that, therefore, he has a stronger hold on you than on other men.'

'The disgrace shall fall on Sowerby,' said Robarts, hardly actuated at the moment by any strong feeling of Christian forgiveness.

'I fear, Mr. Robarts, that he is somewhat in the condition of the Tozers. He will not feel it as you will do.'

'I must bear it, Mr. Forrest, as best I may.'

'Will you allow me, Mr. Robarts, to give you my advice? Perhaps I ought to apologize for intruding it upon you; but as the bills have been presented and dishonoured across my counter, I have, of necessity, become acquainted with the circumstances.'

'I am sure I am very much obliged to you,' said Mark.

'You must pay this money, at any rate, the most considerable portion of it; – the whole of it, indeed, with such deduction as a lawyer may be able to induce these hawks to make on the sight of the ready money. Perhaps £750 or £800 may see you clear of the whole affair.'

'But I have not a quarter of that sum lying by me.'

'No, I suppose not; but what I would recommend is this: that you should borrow the money from the bank, on your own responsibility, – with the joint security of some friend who may be willing to assist you with his name. Lord Lufton probably would do it.'

'No, Mr. Forrest –'

'Listen to me first, before you make up your mind. If you took this step, of course you would do so with the fixed intention of paying the money yourself, – without any further reliance on Sowerby or on any one else.'

'I shall not rely on Mr. Sowerby again; you may be sure of that.'

'What I mean is that you must teach yourself to recognize the debt as your own. If you can do that, with your income you can surely pay it, with interest, in two years. If Lord Lufton will assist you with his name, I will so arrange the bills that the payments shall be made to fall equally over that period. In that way the world will know nothing about it, and in two years' time you will once more be a free man. Many men, Mr. Robarts, have bought their experience much dearer than that, I can assure you.'

'Mr. Forrest, it is quite out of the question.'

'You mean that Lord Lufton will not give you his name.'

'I certainly shall not ask him; but that is not all. In the first place, my income will not be what you think it, for I shall probably give up the prebend at Barchester.'

'Give up the prebend! give up six hundred a year!'

'And, beyond this, I think I may say that nothing shall tempt me to put my name to another bill. I have learned a lesson which I hope I may never forget.'

'Then what do you intend to do?'

'Nothing!'

'Then those men will sell every stick of furniture about the place. They know that your property is enough to secure all that they claim.'

'If they have the power, they must sell it.'

'And all the world will know the facts.'

'So it must be. Of the faults which a man commits he must bear the punishment. If it were only myself!'

'That's where it is, Mr. Robarts. Think what your wife will have to suffer in going through such misery as that! You had better take my advice. Lord Lufton, I am sure –' But the very name of Lord Lufton, his sister's lover, again gave him courage. He thought, too, of the accusations which Lord Lufton had brought against him on that night, when he had come to him in the coffee-room of the hotel, and he felt that it was impossible that he should apply to him for such aid. It would be better to tell all to Lady Lufton! That she would relieve him, let the cost to herself be what it might, he was very sure. Only this; – that in looking to her for assistance he would be forced to bite the dust in very deed.

'Thank you, Mr. Forrest, but I have made up my mind. Do not think that I am the less obliged to you for your disinterested kindness, – for I know that it is disinterested; but this I think I may confidently say, that not even to avert so terrible a calamity will I again put my name to any bill. Even if you could take my own promise to pay without the addition of any second name, I would not do it.' There was nothing for Mr. Forrest to do under such circumstances but simply to drive back to Barchester. He had done the best for the young clergyman according to his lights, and perhaps, in a worldly view, his advice had not been bad. But Mark dreaded the very name of a bill. He was as a dog that had been terribly scorched, and nothing should again induce him to go near the fire.

'Was not that the man from the bank?' said Fanny, coming into the room when the sound of the wheels had died away.

'Yes; Mr. Forrest.'

'Well, dearest?'

'We must prepare ourselves for the worst.'

'You will not sign any more papers, eh, Mark?'

'No; I have just now positively refused to do so.'

'Then I can bear anything. But, dearest, dearest Mark, will you not let me tell Lady Lufton?'

Let them look at the matter in any way the punishment was very heavy.

CHAPTER XLIII

Is She Not Insignificant?

AND now a month went by at Framley without any increase of comfort to our friends there, and also without any absolute development of the ruin which had been daily expected at the parsonage. Sundry letters had reached Mr. Robarts from various personages acting in the Tozer interest, all of which he referred to Mr. Curling, of Barchester. Some of these letters contained prayers for the money, pointing out how an innocent widow lady had been induced to invest her all on the faith of Mr. Robarts's name, and was now starving in a garret, with her three children, because Mr. Robarts would not make good his own undertakings. But the majority of them were filled with threats; – only two days longer would be allowed, and then the sheriff's officers would be enjoined to do their work; then one day of grace would be added, at the expiration of which the dogs of war would be unloosed. These, as fast as they came, were sent to Mr. Curling, who took no notice of them individually, but continued his endeavour to prevent the evil day. The second bill Mr. Robarts would take up – such was Mr. Curling's proposition; and would pay by two instalments of £250 each, the first in two months, and the second in four. If this were acceptable to the Tozer interest – well; if it were not, the sheriff's officers must do their worst and the Tozer interest must look for what it could get. The Tozer interest would not declare itself satisfied with these terms, and so the matter went on. During which the roses faded from day to day on the cheeks of Mrs. Robarts, as under such circumstances may easily be conceived. In the meantime Lucy still remained at Hogglestock, and had there become absolute mistress of the house. Poor Mrs. Crawley had been at death's door; for some days she was delirious, and afterwards remained so weak as to be almost unconscious; but now the worst was over, and Mr. Crawley had been informed, that as far as human judgement might pronounce, his children would not become orphans nor would he become a widower. During these weeks Lucy had not once been home nor had she seen any of the Framley people. 'Why should she incur the risk of conveying infection for so small an object?' as she herself argued, writing by letters, which were duly fumigated before they were opened at the parsonage. So she remained at Hogglestock, and the Crawley children, now admitted to all the honours of the nursery, were kept at Framley. They were kept at Framley, although it was expected from day to day that the beds on which they lay would be seized for the payment of Mr. Sowerby's debts. Lucy, as I have said, became mistress of the house at Hogglestock, and made herself absolutely ascendant over Mr. Crawley. Jellies, and broth, and fruit, and even butter, came from Lufton Court, which she displayed on the table, absolutely on the cloth before him, and yet he bore it. I cannot say that he partook of these delicacies with any freedom himself, but he did drink his tea when it was given to him although it contained Framley cream; – and, had he known it, Bohea itself from the Framley chest. In truth, in these days, he had given himself over to the dominion of this stranger; and he said nothing beyond, 'Well, well,' with two uplifted hands, when he came upon her as she was sewing the buttons on to his own shirts – sewing on the buttons and perhaps occasionally applying her needle elsewhere, – not without utility. He said to her at this period very little in the way of thanks. Some protracted conversations they did have, now and again, during the long evenings; but even in these he did not utter many words as to their present state of life. It was on religion chiefly that he spoke, not lecturing her individually, but laying down his ideas as to what the life of a Christian should be, and especially what should be the life of a minister. 'But though I can see this, Miss Robarts,' he said, 'I am bound to say that no one has fallen off so frequently as myself. I have renounced the devil and all his works; but it is by word of mouth only – by word of mouth only. How shall a man crucify the old Adam that is within him, unless he throw himself prostrate in the dust and acknowledge that all his strength is weaker than water?' To this, often as it might be repeated, she would listen patiently, comforting him by such words as her theology would supply; but then, when this was over, she would again resume her command and enforce from him a close obedience to her domestic behests.

At the end of the month Lord Lufton came back to Framley Court. His arrival there was quite unexpected; though, as he pointed out when his mother expressed some surprise, he had returned exactly at the time named by him before he started.

'I need not say, Ludovic, how glad I am to have you,' said she, looking to his face and pressing his arm; 'the more so, indeed, seeing that I hardly expected it.'

He said nothing to his mother about Lucy the first evening, although there was some conversation respecting the Robarts family.

'I am afraid Mr. Robarts has embarrassed himself,' said Lady Lufton, looking very seriously. 'Rumours reach me which are most distressing. I have said nothing to anybody yet – not even to Fanny; but I can see in her face, and hear in the tones of her voice, that she is suffering some great sorrow.'

'I know all about it,' said Lord Lufton.

'You know all about it, Ludovic?'

'Yes; it is through that precious friend of mine, Mr. Sowerby, of Chaldicotes. He has accepted bills for Sowerby; indeed, he told me so.'

'What business had he at Chaldicotes? What had he to do with such friends as that? I do not know how I am to forgive him.'

'It was through me that he became acquainted with Sowerby. You must remember that, mother.'

'I do not see that that is any excuse. Is he to consider that all your acquaintances must necessarily be his friends also? It is reasonable to suppose that you in your position must live occasionally with a great many people who are altogether unfit companions for him as a parish clergyman. He will not remember this, and he must be taught it. What business had he to go to Gatherum Castle?'

'He got his stall at Barchester by going there.'

'He would be much better without his stall, and Fanny has the sense to know this. What does he want with two houses. Prebendal stalls are for older men than he – for men who have earned them, and who at the end of their lives want some ease. I wish with all my heart that he had never taken it.'

'Six hundred a year has its charms all the same,' said Lufton, getting up and strolling out of the room.

'If Mark really be in any difficulty,' he said, later in the evening, 'we must put him on his legs.'

'You mean, pay his debts?'

'Yes; he has no debts except these acceptances of Sowerby's.'

'How much will it be, Ludovic?'

'A thousand pounds, perhaps, more or less. I'll find the money, mother; only I shan't be able to pay you quite as soon as I intended.' Whereupon his mother got up, and throwing her arms round his neck declared that she would never forgive him if he ever said a word more about her little present to him. I suppose there is no pleasure a mother can have more attractive than giving away her money to an only son.

Lucy's name was first mentioned at breakfast the next morning. Lord Lufton had made up his mind to attack his mother on the subject early in the morning – before he went up to the parsonage; but as matters turned out, Miss Robarts's doings were necessarily brought under discussion without reference to Lord Lufton's special aspirations regarding her. The fact of Mrs. Crawley's illness had been mentioned, and Lady Lufton had stated how it had come to pass that all the Crawleys' children were at the parsonage.

'I must say that Fanny has behaved excellently,' said Lady Lufton. 'It was just what might have been expected from her. And indeed,' she added, speaking in an embarrassed tone, 'so has Miss Robarts. Miss Robarts has remained at Hogglestock and nursed Mrs. Crawley through the whole.'

'Remained at Hogglestock – through the fever!' exclaimed his lordship.

'Yes, indeed,' said Lady Lufton.

'And is she there now?'

'Oh, yes; I am not aware that she thinks of leaving just yet.'

'Then I say that it is a great shame – a scandalous shame!'

'But, Ludovic, it was her own doing.'

'Oh, yes; I understand. But why should she be sacrificed? Were there no nurses in the country to be hired, but that she must go and remain there for a month at the bedside of a pestilent fever? There is no justice in it.'

'Justice, Ludovic? I don't know about justice, but there was great Christian charity. Mrs. Crawley has probably owed her life to Miss Robarts.'

'Has she been ill? Is she ill? I insist upon knowing whether she is ill. I shall go over to Hogglestock myself immediately after breakfast.' To this Lady Lufton made no reply. If Lord Lufton chose to go to Hogglestock she could not prevent him. She thought, however, that it would be much better that he should stay away. He would be quite as open to the infection as Lucy Robarts; and, moreover, Mrs. Crawley's bedside would be as inconvenient a place as might be selected for any interview between two lovers. Lady Lufton felt at the present moment that she was cruelly treated by circumstances with reference to Miss Robarts. Of course it would have been her part to lessen, if she could do so without injustice, that high idea which her son entertained of the beauty and worth of the young lady; but, unfortunately, she had been compelled to praise her and to load her name with all manner of eulogy. Lady Lufton was essentially a true woman, and not even with the object of carrying out her own views in so important a matter would she be guilty of such deception as she might have practised by simply holding her tongue; but nevertheless she could hardly reconcile herself to the necessity of singing Lucy's praises.

After breakfast Lady Lufton got up from her chair, but hung about the room without making any show of leaving. In accordance with her usual custom she would have asked her son what he was going to do; but she did not dare so to inquire now. Had he not declared, only a few minutes since, whither he would go? 'I suppose I shall see you at lunch?' at last she said.

'At lunch? Well, I don't know. Look here, mother. What am I to say to Miss Robarts when I see her?' and he leaned with his back against the chimney-piece as he interrogated his mother.

'What are you to say to her, Ludovic?'

'Yes, what am I to say, – as coming from you? Am I to tell her that you will receive her as your daughter-in-law?'

'Ludovic, I have explained all that to Miss Robarts herself.'

'Explained what?'

'I have told her that I did not think that such a marriage would make either you or her happy.'

'And why have you told her so? Why have you taken upon yourself to judge for me in such a matter, as though I were a child? Mother, you must unsay what you have said.' Lord Lufton, as he spoke, looked full into his mother's face; and he did so, not as though he were begging from her a favour, but issuing to her a command. She stood near him, with one hand on the breakfast-table, gazing at him almost furtively, not quite daring to meet the full view of his eye. There was only one thing on earth which Lady Lufton feared, and that was her son's displeasure. The sun of her earthly heaven shone upon her through the medium of his existence. If she were driven to quarrel with him, as some ladies of her acquaintance were driven to quarrel with their sons, the world to her would be over. Not but what facts might be so strong as to make it absolutely necessary that she should do this. As some people resolve that, under certain circumstances, they will commit suicide, so she could see that, under certain circumstances, she must consent even to be separated from him. She would not do wrong, – not that which she knew to be wrong, – even for his sake. If it were necessary that all her happiness should collapse and be crushed in ruin around her, she must endure it, and wait God's time to relieve her from so dark a world. The light of the sun was very dear to her, but even that might be purchased at too dear a cost.

'I told you before, mother, that my choice was made, and I asked you then to give your consent; you have now had time to think about it, and therefore I have come to ask you again. I have reason to know that there will be no impediment to my marriage if you will frankly hold out your hand to Lucy.'

The matter was altogether in Lady Lufton's hands, but, fond as she was of power, she absolutely wished that it were not so. Had her son married without asking her, and then brought Lucy home as his wife, she would undoubtedly have forgiven him; and much as she mightt have disliked the match, she would, ultimately, have embraced the bride. But now she was compelled to exercise her judgement. If he married imprudently, it would be her doing. How was she to give her expressed consent to that which she believed to be wrong? 'Do you know something against her; any reason why she should not be my wife?' continued he.

'If you mean as regards her moral conduct, certainly not,' said Lady Lufton. 'But I could say as much as that in favour of a great many young ladies whom I should regard as very ill suited for such a marriage.'

'Yes; some might be vulgar, some might be ill-tempered, some might be ugly; others might be burdened with disagreeable connexions. I can understand that you should object to a daughter-in-law under any of these circumstances. But none of these things can be said of Miss Robarts. I defy you to say that she is not in all respects what a lady should be.'

But her father was a doctor of medicine, she is the sister of the parish clergyman, she is only five feet two in height, and is so uncommonly brown! Had Lady Lufton dared to give a catalogue of her objections, such would have been its extent and nature. But she did not dare to do this.

'I cannot say, Ludovic, that she is possessed of all that you should seek in a wife.' Such was her answer.

'Do you mean that she has not got money?'

'No, not that; I should be very sorry to see you making money your chief object, or indeed any essential object. If it chanced that your wife did have money, no doubt you would find it a convenience. But pray understand me, Ludovic; I would not for a moment advise you to subject your happiness to such a necessity as that. It is not because she is without fortune –'

'Then why is it? At breakfast you were singing her praises, and saying how excellent she is.'

'If I were forced to put my objection into one word, I should say –' and then she paused, hardly daring to encounter the frown which was already gathering itself on her son's brow.

'You would say what?' said Lord Lufton, almost roughly.

'Don't be angry with me, Ludovic; all that I think, and all that I say on this subject, I think and say with only one object – that of your happiness. What other motive can I have for anything in this world?' And then she came close to him and kissed him.

'But tell me, mother, what is this objection; what is this terrible word that is to sum up the list of all poor Lucy's sins, and prove that she is unfit for married life?'

'Ludovic, I did not say that. You know that I did not.'

'What is the word, mother?'

And then at last Lady Lufton spoke it out.' 'She is—insignificant. I believe her to be a very good girl, but she is not qualified to fill the high position to which you would exalt her.'

'Insignificant!'

'Yes, Ludovic, I think so.'

'Then, mother, you do not know her. You must permit me to say that you are talking of a girl whom you do not know. Of all the epithets of opprobrium which the English language could give you, that would be nearly the last which she would deserve.'

'I have not intended any opprobrium.'

'Insignificant!'

'Perhaps you do not quite understand me, Ludovic.'

'I know what insignificant means, mother.'

'I think that she would not worthily fill the position which your wife should take in the world.'

'I understand what you say.'

'She would not do you honour at the head of your table.'

'Ah, I understand. You want me to marry some bouncing Amazon, some pink and white giantess of fashion who would frighten the little people into their proprieties.'

'Oh, Ludovic! you are intending to laugh at me now.'

'I was never less inclined to laugh in my life – never, I can assure you. And now I am more certain than ever that your objection to Miss Robarts arises from your not knowing her. You will find, I think, when you do know her, that she is as well able to hold her own as any lady of your acquaintance – aye, and to maintain her husband's position, too. I can assure you that I shall have no fear of her on that score.'

'I think, dearest, that perhaps you hardly –'

'I think this, mother, that in such a matter as this I must choose for myself. I have chosen; and I now ask you, as my mother, to go to her and bid her welcome. Dear mother, I will own this, that I should not be happy if I thought that you did not love my wife.' These last words he said in a tone of affection that went to his mother's heart, and then he left the room.

Poor Lady Lufton, when she was alone, waited till she heard her son's steps retreating through the hall, and then betook herself upstairs to her customary morning work. She sat down at last as though about so to occupy herself; but her mind was too full to allow of her taking up her pen. She had often said to herself, in days which to her were not as yet long gone by, that she would choose a bride for her son, and that then she would love the chosen one with all her heart. She would dethrone herself in favour of this new queen, sinking with joy into her dowager state, in order that her son's wife might shine with the greater splendour. The fondest day-dreams of her life had all the reference to the time when her son should bring home a new Lady Lufton, selected by herself from the female excellence of England, and in which she might be the first to worship her new idol. But could she dethrone herself for Lucy Robarts? Could she give up her chair of state in order to place thereon the little girl from the parsonage? Could she take to her heart, and treat with absolute loving confidence, with the confidence of an almost idolatrous mother, that little chit who, a few months since, had sat awkwardly in one corner of her drawing-room, afraid to speak to any one? And yet it seemed that it must come to this – to this – or else those day-dreams of hers would in nowise come to pass. She sat herself down, trying to think whether it were possible that Lucy might fill the throne; for she had begun to recognize it as probable that her son's will would be too strong for her; but her thoughts would fly away to Griselda Grantly. In her first and only matured attempt to realize her day-dreams, she had chosen Griselda for her queen. She had failed there, seeing that the Fates had destined Miss Grantly for another throne; for another and a higher one, as far as the world goes. She would have made Griselda the wife of a baron, but fate was about to make that young lady the wife of a marquis. Was there cause of grief in this? Did she really regret that Miss Grantly, with all her virtues, should be made over to the house of Hartletop? Lady Lufton was a woman who did not bear disappointment lightly; but nevertheless she did almost feel herself to have been relieved from a burden when she thought of the termination of the Lufton-Grantly marriage treaty.

What if she had been successful, and, after all, the prize had been other than she had expected? She was sometimes prone to think that the prize was not exactly all that she had once hoped. Griselda looked the very thing that Lady Lufton wanted for a queen; but how would a queen reign who trusted only to her looks? In that respect it was perhaps well for her that destiny had interposed. Griselda, she was driven to admit, was better suited to Lord Dumbello than to her son. But still—such a queen as Lucy! Could it ever come to pass that the lieges of the kingdom would bow the knee in proper respect before so puny a sovereign? And then there was that feeling which, in still higher quarters, prevents the marriage of princes with the most noble of their people. Is it not a recognized rule of these realms that none of the blood royal shall raise to royal honours those of the subjects who are by birth unroyal? Lucy was a subject of the house of Lufton in that she was the sister of the parson and a resident denizen of the parsonage. Presuming that Lucy herself might do for queen – granting that she might have some faculty to reign, the crown having been duly placed on her brow – how, then, about that clerical brother near the throne? Would it not come to this, that there would no longer be a queen at Framley? And yet she knew that she must yield. She did not say so to herself. She did not as yet acknowledge that she must put out her hand to Lucy, calling her by her name as her daughter. She did not absolutely say as much to her own heart – not as yet. But she did begin to bethink herself of Lucy's high qualities, and to declare to herself that the girl, if not fit to be a queen, was at any rate fit to be a woman. That there was a spirit within that body, insignificant though the body might be, Lady Lufton was prepared to admit. That she had acquired the power – the chief of all powers in this world – of sacrificing herself for the sake of others; that, too, was evident enough. That she was a good girl, in the usual acceptation of the word good, Lady Lufton had never doubted. She was ready-witted, too, prompt in action, gifted with a certain fire. It was that gift of fire which had won for her, so unfortunately, Lord Lufton's love. It was quite possible for her also to love Lucy Robarts; Lady Lufton admitted that to herself; but then who could bow the knee before her, and serve her as a queen? Was it not a pity that she should be so insignificant?

But, nevertheless, we may say that as Lady Lufton sate that morning in her own room for two hours without employment, the star of Lucy Robarts was gradually rising in the firmament. After all, love was the food chiefly necessary for the nourishment of Lady Lufton – the only food absolutely necessary. She was not aware of this herself, nor probably would those who knew her best have so spoken of her. They would have declared that family pride was her daily pabulum, and she herself would have said so too, calling it, however, by some less offensive name. Her son's honour, and the honour of her house! – of those she would have spoken as the things dearest to her in this world. And this was partly true, for had her son been dishonoured, she would have sunk with sorrow to the grave. But the one thing necessary to her daily life was the power of loving those who were near to her. Lord Lufton, when he left the dining-room, intended at once to go up to the parsonage, but he first strolled round the garden in order that he might make up his mind what he would say there. He was angry with his mother, having not had the wit to see that she was about to give way and yield to him, and he was determined to make it understood that in this matter he would have his own way. He had learned that which it was necessary that he should know as to Lucy's heart, and such being the case he would not conceive it possible that he should be debarred by his mother's opposition. 'There is no son in England loves his mother better than I do,' he said to himself; 'but there are some things which a man cannot stand. She would have married me to that block of stone if I would have let her; and now, because she is disappointed there – Insignificant! I never in my life heard anything so absurd, so untrue, so uncharitable, so – She'd like me to bring a dragon home, I suppose. It would serve her right if I did – some creature that would make the house intolerable to her.' 'She must do it though,' he said again, 'or she and I will quarrel,' and then he turned off towards the gate, preparing to go to the parsonage.

'My lord, have you heard what has happened?' said the gardener, coming to him at the gate. The man was out of breath and almost overwhelmed by the greatness of his own tidings.

'No; I have heard nothing. What is it?'

'The bailiffs have taken possession of everything at the parsonage.'

CHAPTER XLIV

The Philistines at The Parsonage

IT has been already told how things went on between the Tozers, Mr. Curling, and Mark Robarts during that month. Mr. Forrest had drifted out of the business altogether, as also had Mr. Sowerby, as far as any active participation in it went. Letters came frequently from Mr. Curling to the parsonage, and at last came a message by special mission to say that the evil day was at hand. As far as Mr. Curling's professional experience would enable him to anticipate or foretell the proceedings of such a man as Tom Tozer he thought that the sheriff's officers would be at Framley parsonage on the following morning. Mr. Curling's experience did not mislead him in this respect. 'And what will you do, Mark?' said Fanny, speaking through her tears, after she had read the letter which her husband handed to her.

'Nothing. What can I do? They must come.'

'Lord Lufton came to-day. Will you not go to him?'

'No. If I were to do so it would be the same as asking him for the money.'

'Why not borrow it of him, dearest? Surely it would not be so much for him to lend.'

'I could not do it. Think of Lucy, and how she stands with him. Besides, I have already had words with Lufton about Sowerby and his money matters. He thinks that I am to blame, and he would tell me so; and then there would be sharp things said between us. He would advance me the money if I pressed for it, but he would do so in a way that would make it impossible that I should take it.'

There was nothing more, then, to be said. If she had had her own way Mrs. Robarts would have gone at once to Lady Lufton, but she could not induce her husband to sanction such a proceeding. The objection to seeking assistance from her ladyship was as strong as that which prevailed as to her son. There had already been some little beginning of ill-feeling, and under such circumstances it was impossible to ask for pecuniary assistance. Fanny, however, had a prophetic assurance that assistance out of these difficulties must in the end come to them from that quarter, or not come at all; and she would fain, had she been allowed, make everything known at the big house. On the following morning they breakfasted at the usual hour, but in great sadness. A maid-servant, whom Mrs. Robarts had brought with her when she married, told her that a rumour of what was to happen had reached the kitchen. Stubbs, the groom, had been in Barchester on the preceding day, and, according to his account – so said Mary – everybody in the city was talking about it. 'Never mind, Mary,' said Mrs. Robarts, and Mary replied, 'Oh, no, of course not, ma'am.' In these days Mrs. Robarts was ordinarily very busy, seeing that there were six children in the house, four of whom had come to her but ill supplied with infantine belongings; and now, as usual, she went about her work immediately after breakfast. But she moved about the house very slowly, and was almost unable to give her orders to the servants, and spoke sadly to the children who hung about her wondering what was the matter. Her husband at the same time took himself to his book-room, but when there he did not attempt any employment. He thrust his hands into his pockets, and, leaning against the fire-place, fixed his eyes upon the table before him without looking at anything that was on it; it was impossible for him to betake himself to his work. Remember what is the ordinary labour of a clergyman in his study, and think how fit he must have been for such employment! What would have been the nature of a sermon composed at such a moment, and with what satisfaction could he have used the sacred volume in referring to it for his arguments? He, in this respect, was worse off than his wife; she did employ herself, but he stood there without moving, doing nothing, with fixed eyes, thinking what men would say of him. Luckily for him this state of suspense was not long, for within half an hour of his leaving the breakfast-table, the footman knocked at his door – that footman with whom, at the beginning of his difficulties, he had made up his mind to dispense, but who had been kept on because of the Barchester prebend.

'If you please, your reverence, there are two men outside,' said the footman. Two men! Mark knew well enough what two men they were, but he could hardly take the coming of two such men to his quiet country parsonage quite as a matter of course.

'Who are they, John?' said he, not wishing any answer, but because the question was forced upon him.

'I'm afeard they're – bailiffs, sir.'

'Very well, John; that will do; of course they must do what they please about the place.' And then, when the servant left him, he still stood without moving, exactly as he had stood before. There he remained for ten minutes, but the time went by very slowly. When about noon some circumstance told him what was the hour, he was astonished to find that the day had not nearly passed away. And then another tap was struck on the door – a sound which he well recognized – and his wife crept silently into the room. She came close up to him before she spoke, and put her arm within his:

'Mark,' she said, 'the men are here; they are in the yard.'

'I know it,' he answered gruffly.

'Will it be better that you should see them, dearest?'

'See them; no; what good can I do by seeing them? But I shall see them soon enough; they will be here, I suppose, in a few minutes.'

'They are taking an inventory, cook says; they are in the stable now.'

'Very well; they must do as they please; I cannot help them.'

'Cook says that if they are allowed their meals and some beer, and if nobody takes anything away, they will be quite civil.'

'Civil! But what does it matter! Let them eat and drink what they please, as long as the food lasts. I don't suppose the butcher will send you more.'

'But, Mark, there's nothing due to the butcher, – only the regular monthly bill.'

'Very well; you'll see.'

'Oh, Mark, don't look at me in that way. Do not turn away from me. What is to comfort us if we do not cling to each other now?'

'Comfort us! God help you! I wonder, Fanny, that you can bear to stay in the room with me.'

'Mark, dearest Mark, my own dear, dearest husband! who is to be true to you, if I am not? You shall not turn from me. How can anything like this make a difference between you and me?' And then she threw her arms round his neck and embraced him. It was a terrible morning to him, and one of which every incident will dwell on his memory to the last day of his life. He had been so proud in his position – had assumed to himself so prominent a standing – had contrived, by some trick which he had acquired, to carry his head so high above the heads of neighbouring parsons. It was this that had taken him among great people, had introduced him to the Duke of Omnium, had procured for him the stall at Barchester. But how was he to carry his head now? What would the Arabins and Grantlys say? How would the bishop sneer at him, and Mrs. Proudie and her daughters tell of him in all their quarters? How would Crawley look at him – Crawley, who had already once had him on the hip? The stern severity of Crawley's face loomed upon him now. Crawley, with his children half naked, and his wife a drudge, and himself half starved, had never had a bailiff in his house at Hogglestock. And then his own curate, Evans, whom he had patronized, and treated almost as a dependant – how was he to look his curate in the face and arrange with him for the sacred duties of the next Sunday? His wife still stood by him, gazing into his face; and as he looked at her and thought of her misery, he could not control his heart with reference to the wrongs which Sowerby had heaped on him. It was Sowerby's falsehood and Sowerby's fraud which had brought upon him and his wife this terrible anguish.

'If there be justice on earth he will suffer for it yet,' he said at last, not speaking intentionally to his wife, but unable to repress his feelings.

'Do not wish him evil, Mark; you may be sure he has his own sorrows.'

'His own sorrows! No; he is callous to such misery as this. He has become so hardened in dishonesty that all this is mirth to him. If there be punishment in heaven for falsehood –'

'Oh, Mark, do not curse him!'

'How am I to keep myself from cursing when I see what he has brought upon you?'

'"Vengeance is mine, saith the Lord,"' answered the young wife, not with solemn, preaching accent, as though bent on reproof, but with the softest whisper into his ear. 'Leave that to Him, Mark; and for us, let us pray that He may soften the hearts of us all; – of him who has caused us to suffer, and of our own.' Mark was not called upon to reply to this, for he was again disturbed by a servant at the door. It was the cook this time herself, who had come with a message from the men of the law. And she had come, be it remembered, not from any necessity that she as cook should do this line of work; for the footman, or Mrs. Robarts's maid, might have come as well as she. But when things are out of course servants are always out of course also. As a rule, nothing will induce a butler to go into a stable, or persuade a housemaid to put her hand to a frying-pan. But now that this new excitement had come upon the household – seeing that the bailiffs were in possession, and that the chattels were being entered in a catalogue, everybody was willing to do everything – everything but his or her own work. The gardener was looking after the dear children; the nurse was doing the rooms before the bailiffs should reach them; the groom had gone into the kitchen to get their lunch ready for them; and the cook was walking about with an inkstand, obeying all the orders of these great potentates. As far as the servants were concerned, it may be a question whether the coming of the bailiffs had not hitherto been regarded as a treat.

'If you please, ma'am,' said Jemima cook, 'they wishes to know in which room you'd be pleased to have the inmintory took fust. 'Cause, ma'am, they wouldn't disturb you nor master more than can be avoided. For their line of life, ma'am, they is very civil – very civil indeed.'

'I suppose they may go into the drawing-room,' said Mrs. Robarts, in a sad low voice. All nice women are proud of their drawing-rooms, and she was very proud of hers. It had been furnished when money was plenty with them, immediately after their marriage, and everything in it was pretty, good, and dear to her. O ladies, who have drawing-rooms in which the things are pretty, good, and dear to you, think of what it would be to have two bailiffs rummaging among them with pen and inkhorn, making a catalogue preparatory to a sheriff's auction; and all without fault or extravagance of your own! There were things there that had been given to her by Lady Lufton, by Lady Meredith, and other friends, and the idea did occur to her that it might be possible to save them from contamination; but she would not say a word, lest by so saying she might add to Mark's misery.

'And then the dining-room,' said Jemima cook, in a tone almost of elation.

'Yes; if they please.'

'And then master's book-room here; or perhaps the bed-rooms, if you and master be still here.'

'Any way they please, cook; it does not much signify,' said Mrs. Robarts. But for some days after that Jemima was by no means a favourite with her.

The cook was hardly out of the room before a quick footstep was heard on the gravel before the window, and the hall door was immediately opened.

'Where is your master?' said the well-known voice of Lord Lufton; and then in half a minute he also was in the book-room.

'Mark, my dear fellow, what's all this?' said he, in a cheery tone and with a pleasant face. 'Did not you know that I was here? I came down yesterday; landed from Hamburg only yesterday morning. How do you do, Mrs. Robarts? This is a terrific bore, isn't it?' Robarts, at the first moment, hardly knew how to speak to his old friend. He was struck dumb by the disgrace of his position; the more so as his misfortune was one which it was partly in the power of Lord Lufton to remedy. He had never yet borrowed money since he had filled a man's position, but he had had words about money with the young peer, in which he knew that his friend had wronged him; and for this double reason he was now speechless.

'Mr. Sowerby has betrayed him,' said Mrs. Robarts, wiping the tears from her eyes. Hitherto she had said no word against Sowerby, but now it was necessary to defend her husband.

'No doubt about it. I believe he has always betrayed every one who has ever trusted him. I told you what he was, some time since; did I not? But, Mark, why on earth have you let it go so far as this? Would not Forrest help you?'

'Mr. Forrest wanted him to sign more bills, and he would not do that,' said Mrs. Robarts, sobbing.

'Bills are like dram-drinking,' said the discreet young lord: 'when one once begins, it is very hard to leave off. Is it true that the men are here now, Mark?'

'Yes, they are in the next room.'

'What, in the drawing-room?'

'They are making out a list of the things,' said Mrs. Robarts.

'We must stop that at any rate,' said his lordship, walking off towards the scene of the operations; and as he left the room Mrs. Robarts followed him, leaving her husband by himself.

'Why did you not send down to my mother?' said he, speaking hardly above a whisper, as they stood together in the hall.

'He would not let me.'

'But why not go yourself? or why not have written to me, – considering how intimate we are!' Mrs. Robarts could not explain to him that the peculiar intimacy between him and Lucy must have hindered her from doing so, even if otherwise it might have been possible; but she felt such was the case.

'Well, my men, this is bad work you're doing here,' said he, walking into the drawing-room. Whereupon the cook curtsied low, and the bailiffs, knowing his lordship, stopped from their business and put their hands to their foreheads. 'You must stop this, if you please, – at once. Come, let's go out into the kitchen, or some place outside. I don't like to see you here with your big boots and the pen and ink among the furniture.'

'We ain't a-done no harm, my lord, so please your lordship,' said Jemima cook.

'And we is only a-doing our bounden dooties,' said one of the bailiffs.

'As we is sworn to do, so please your lordship,' said the other.

'And is wery sorry to be so inconwenient, my lord, to any gen'leman or lady as is a gen'leman or lady. But accidents will happen, and then what can the likes of us do?' said the first.

'Because we is sworn, my lord,' said the second. But, nevertheless, in spite of their oaths, and in spite also of the stern necessity which they pleaded, they ceased their operations at the instance of the peer. For the name of a lord is still great in England.

'And now leave this, and let Mrs. Robarts go into her drawing-room.'

'And, please your lordship, what is we to do? Who is we to look to?' In satisfying them absolutely on this point Lord Lufton had to use more than his influence as a peer. It was necessary that he should have pen and paper. But with pen and paper he did satisfy them; – satisfy them so far that they agreed to return to Stubbs's room, the former hospital, due stipulation having been made for the meals and beer, and there await the order to evacuate the premises which would no doubt, under his lordship's influence, reach them on the following day. The meaning of all which was that Lord Lufton had undertaken to bear upon his own shoulder the whole debt due to Mr. Robarts. And then he returned to the book-room where Mark was still standing almost on the spot in which he had placed himself immediately after breakfast. Mrs. Robarts did not return, but went up among the children to counter-order such directions as she had given for the preparation of the nursery for the Philistines. 'Mark,' he said, 'do not trouble yourself about this more than you can help. The men have ceased doing anything, and they shall leave the place tomorrow morning.'

'And how will the money – be paid?' said the poor clergyman.

'Do not bother yourself about that at present. It shall so be managed that the burden shall fall ultimately on yourself – not on any one else. But I am sure it must be a comfort to you to know that your wife need not be driven out of her drawing-room.'

'But, Lufton, I cannot allow you – after what has passed – and at the present moment –'

'My dear fellow, I know all about it, and I am coming to that just now. You have employed Curling, and he shall settle it; and upon my word, Mark, you shall pay the bill. But, for the present emergency, the money is at my banker's.'

'But, Lufton –'

'And to deal honestly, about Curling's bill I mean, it ought to be as much my affair as your own. It was I that brought you into this mess with Sowerby, and I know now how unjust about it I was to you up in London. But the truth is that Sowerby's treachery had nearly driven me wild. It has done the same to you since, I have no doubt.'

'He has ruined me,' said Robarts.

'No, he has not done that. No thanks to him though; he would not have scrupled to do it had it come in his way. The fact is, Mark, that you and I cannot conceive the depth of fraud in such a man as that. He is always looking for money; I believe that in all his hours of most friendly intercourse, – when he is sitting with you over your wine, and riding beside you in the field, – he is still thinking how he can make use of you to tide him over some difficulty. He has lived in that way till he has a pleasure in cheating, and has become so clever in his line of life that if you or I were with him again to-morrow he would again get the better of us. He is a man that must be absolutely avoided; I, at any rate, have learned to know so much.' In the expression of which opinion Lord Lufton was too hard upon poor Sowerby; as indeed we are all apt to be too hard in forming an opinion upon the rogues of the world. That Mr. Sowerby had been a rogue, I cannot deny. It is roguish to lie, and he had been a great liar. It is roguish to make promises which the promiser knows he cannot perform, and such had been Mr. Sowerby's daily practice. It is roguish to live on other men's money, and Mr. Sowerby had long been doing so. It is roguish, at least so I would hold it, to deal willingly with rogues; and Mr. Sowerby had been constant in such dealings. I do not know whether he had not at times fallen even into more palpable roguery than is proved by such practices as those enumerated. Though I have for him some tender feeling, knowing that there was still a touch of gentle bearing round his heart, an abiding taste for better things within him, I cannot acquit him from the great accusation. But, for all that, in spite of his acknowledged roguery, Lord Lufton was too hard upon him in his judgement. There was yet within him the means of repentance, could a *locus penitentiæ* have been supplied to him. He grieved bitterly over his own ill-doings, and knew well what changes gentlehood would have demanded from him. Whether or no he had gone too far for all changes – whether the *locus penitentiæ* was for him still a possibility – that was between him and a higher power.

'I have no one to blame but myself,' said Mark, still speaking in the same heart-broken tone and with his face averted from his friend.

The debt would now be paid, and the bailiffs would be expelled; but that would not set him right before the world. It would be known to all men – to all clergymen in the diocese, that the sheriff's officers had been in charge of Framley parsonage, and he could never again hold up his head in the close of Barchester. 'My dear fellow, if we were all to make ourselves miserable for such a trifle as this, – ' said Lord Lufton, putting his arm affectionately on his friend's shoulder.

'But we are not all clergymen,' said Mark, and as he spoke he turned away to the window and Lord Lufton knew that the tears were on his cheek.

Nothing was then said between them for some moments, after which Lord Lufton again spoke, –

'Mark, my dear fellow!'

'Well,' said Mark, with his face still turned towards the window.

'You must remember one thing; in helping you over this stile, which will be really a matter of no inconvenience to me, I have a better right than that even of an old friend; I look upon you now as my brother-in-law.' Mark turned slowly round, plainly showing the tears upon his face.

'Do you mean,' said he, 'that anything more has taken place?'

'I mean to make your sister my wife; she sent me word by you to say that she loved me, and I am not going to stand upon any nonsense after that. If she and I are both willing no one alive has a right to stand between us, and, by heavens, no one shall. I will do nothing secretly, so I tell you that, exactly as I have told her ladyship.'

'But what does she say?'

'She says nothing; but it cannot go on like that. My mother and I cannot live here together if she opposes me in this way. I do not want to frighten your sister by going over to her at Hogglestock, but I expect you to tell her so much as I now tell you, as coming from me; otherwise she will think that I have forgotten her.'

'She will not think that.'

'She need not; good-bye, old fellow. I'll make it all right between you and her ladyship about this affair of

Sowerby's.' And then he took his leave and walked off to settle about the payment of the money.

'Mother,' said he to Lady Lufton that evening, 'you must not bring this affair of the bailiffs up against Robarts. It has been more my fault than his.'

Hitherto not a word had been spoken between Lady Lufton and her son on the subject. She had heard with terrible dismay of what had happened, and had heard also that Lord Lufton had immediately gone to the parsonage. It was impossible, therefore, that she should now interfere. That the necessary money would be forthcoming she was aware, but that would not wipe out the terrible disgrace attached to an execution in a clergyman's house. And then, too, he was her clergyman, – her own clergyman, selected and appointed, and brought to Framley by herself, endowed with a wife of her own choosing, filled with good things by her own hand! It was a terrible misadventure, and she began to repent that she had ever heard the name of Robarts. She would not, however, have been slow to put forth the hand to lessen the evil by giving her own money, had this been either necessary or possible. But how could she interfere between Robarts and her son, especially when she remembered the proposed connexion between Lucy and Lord Lufton?

'Your fault, Ludovic?'

'Yes, mother. It was I who introduced him to Mr. Sowerby; and, to tell the truth, I do not think he would ever have been intimate with Sowerby if I had not given him some sort of a commission with reference to money matters then pending between Mr. Sowerby and me. They are all over now, – thanks to you, indeed.'

'Mr. Robarts's character as a clergyman should have kept him from such troubles, if no other feeling did so.'

'At any rate, mother, oblige me by letting it pass by.'

'Oh, I shall say nothing to him.'

'You had better say something to her, or otherwise it will be strange; and even to him I would say a word or two, – a word in kindness, as you so well know how. It will be easier to him in that way, than if you were to be altogether silent.'

No further conversation took place between them at the time, but later in the evening she brushed her hand across her son's forehead, sweeping the long silken hairs into their place, as she was wont to do when moved by any special feeling of love. 'Ludovic,' she said, 'no one, I think, has so good a heart as you. I will do exactly as you would have me about this affair of Mr. Robarts and the money.' And then there was nothing more said about it.

CHAPTER XLV

Palace Blessings

AND now, at this period, terrible rumours found their way into Barchester, and flew about the cathedral towers and round the cathedral door; aye, and into the canons' houses and the humbler sitting-rooms of the vicars choral. Whether they made their way from thence up to the bishop's palace, or whether they descended from the palace to the close, I will not pretend to say. But they were shocking, unnatural, and no doubt grievous to all those excellent ecclesiastical hearts which cluster so thickly in those quarters. The first of these had reference to the new prebendary, and to the disgrace which he had brought on the chapter; a disgrace, as some of them boasted, which Barchester had never known before. This, however, like most other boasts, was hardly true; for within but a very few years there had been an execution in the house of a late prebendary, old Dr. Stanhope; and on that occasion the doctor himself had been forced to fly away to Italy, starting in the night, lest he also should fall into the hands of the Philistines, as well as his chairs and tables. 'It is a scandalous shame,' said Mrs. Proudie, speaking not of the old doctor, but of the new offender; 'a scandalous shame: and it would only serve him right if the gown were stripped from his back.'

'I suppose his living will be sequestrated,' said a young minor canon who attended much to the ecclesiastical injunctions of the lady of the diocese, and was deservedly held in high favour. If Framley were sequestrated, why should not he, as well as another, undertake the duty – with such stipend as the bishop might award?

'I am told that he is over head and ears in debt,' said the future Mrs. Tickler, 'and chiefly for horses which he has bought and not paid for.'

'I see him riding very splendid animals when he comes over for the cathedral duties,' said the minor canon.

'The sheriff's officers are in the house at present, I am told,' said Mrs. Proudie.

'And is not he in jail?' said Mrs. Tickler.

'If not, he ought to be,' said Mrs. Tickler's mother.

'And no doubt soon will be,' said the minor canon; 'for I hear that he is linked up with a most discreditable gang of persons.'

This was what was said in the palace on that heading; and though, no doubt, more spirit and poetry was displayed there than in the houses of the less gifted clergy, this shows the manner in which the misfortune of Mr. Robarts was generally discussed. Nor, indeed, had he deserved any better treatment at their hands. But his name did not run the gauntlet for the usual nine days; nor, indeed, did his fame endure at its height for more than two. This sudden fall was occasioned by other tidings of a still more distressing nature; by a rumour which so affected Mrs. Proudie that it caused, as she said, her blood to creep. And she was very careful that the blood of others should creep also, if the blood of others was equally sensitive. It was said that Lord Dumbello had jilted Miss Grantly. From what adverse spot in the world these cruel tidings fell upon Barchester I have never been able to discover. We know how quickly rumour flies, making herself common through all the cities. That Mrs. Proudie should have known more of the facts connected with the Hartletop family than any one else in Barchester was not surprising, seeing that she was so much more conversant with the great world in which such people lived. She knew, and was therefore correct enough in declaring, that Lord Dumbello had already jilted one other young lady – the Lady Julia Mac Mull, to whom he had been engaged three seasons back, and that therefore his character in such matters was not to be trusted. That Lady Julia had been a terrible flirt and greatly given to waltzing with a certain German count, with whom she had since gone off – that, I suppose, Mrs. Proudie did not know, much as she was conversant with the great world, – seeing that she said nothing about it to any of her ecclesiastical listeners on the present occasion.

'It will be a terrible warning, Mrs. Quiverful, to us all; a most useful warning to us – not to trust to the things of this world. I fear they made no inquiry about this young nobleman before they agreed that his name should be linked with that of their daughter.' This she said to the wife of the present warden of Hiram's Hospital, a lady who had received favours from her, and was therefore bound to listen attentively to her voice.

'But I hope it may not be true,' said Mrs. Quiverful, who, in spite of the allegiance due by her to Mrs. Proudie, had reasons of her own for wishing well to the Grantly family.

'I hope so, indeed,' said Mrs. Proudie, with a slight tinge of anger in her voice; 'but I fear that there is no doubt. And I must confess that it is no more than we had a right to expect. I hope that it may be taken by all of us as a lesson, and an ensample, and a teaching of the Lord's mercy. And I wish you would request your husband – from me, Mrs. Quiverful – to dwell on this subject in morning and evening lecture at the hospital on Sabbath next, showing how false is the trust which we put in the good things of this world;' which behest, to a certain extent, Mr. Quiverful did obey, feeling that a quiet life in Barchester was of great value to him; but he did not go so far as to caution his hearers, who consisted of the aged bedesmen of the hospital, against matrimonial projects of an ambitious nature. In this case, as in all others of the kind, the report was known to all the chapter before it had been heard by the archdeacon or his wife. The dean heard it, and disregarded it; as did also the dean's wife – at first; and those who generally sided with the Grantlys in the diocesan battles pooh-poohed the tidings, saying to each other that both the archdeacon and Mrs. Grantly were very well able to take care of their own affairs. But dripping water hollows a stone; and at last it was admitted on all sides that there was ground for fear, – on all sides, except at Plumstead.

'I am sure there is nothing in it; I really am sure of it,' said Mrs. Arabin, whispering to her sister; 'but after turning it over in my mind, I thought it right to tell you. And yet I don't know now but I am wrong.'

'Quite right, dearest Eleanor,' said Mrs. Grantly. 'And I am much obliged to you. But we understand it, you know. It comes, of course, like all other Christian blessings, from the palace.' And then there was nothing more said about it between Mrs. Grantly and her sister. But on the following morning there arrived a letter by post, addressed to Mrs. Grantly, bearing the postmark of Littlebath. The letter ran: –

'Madam,

'It is known to the writer that Lord Dumbello has arranged with certain friends how he may escape from his present engagement. I think, therefore, that it is my duty as a Christian to warn you of this.

'Yours truly,
'A Wellwisher.'

Now it had happened that the embryo Mrs. Tickler's most intimate bosom friend and confidante was known at Plumstead to live at Littlebath, and it had also happened – most unfortunately – that the embryo Mrs. Tickler, in the warmth of her neighbourly regard, had written a friendly line to her friend Griselda Grantly, congratulating her with all female sincerity on her splendid nuptials with the Lord Dumbello.

'It is not her natural hand,' said Mrs. Grantly, talking the matter over with her husband, 'but you may be sure it has come from her. It is a part of the new Christianity which we learn day by day from the palace teaching.' But these things had some effect on the archdeacon's mind. He had learned lately the story of Lady Julia Mac Mull, and was not sure that his son-in-law – as ought to be about to be – had been entirely blameless in that matter. And then in these days Lord Dumbello made no great sign. Immediately on Griselda's return to Plumstead he had sent her a magnificent present of emeralds, which, however, had come to her direct from the jewellers, and might have been – and probably was – ordered by his man of business. Since that he had neither come, nor sent, nor written. Griselda did not seem to be in any way annoyed by this absence of the usual sign of love, and went on steadily with her great duties. 'Nothing,' as she told her mother, 'had been said about writing, and, therefore, she did not expect it.' But the archdeacon was not quite at his ease. 'Keep Dumbello up to his p's and q's, you know,' a friend of his had whispered to him at his club. By heavens, yes. The archdeacon was not a man to bear with indifference a wrong in such a quarter. In spite of his clerical profession, few men were more inclined to fight against personal wrongs – and few men more able.

'Can there be anything wrong, I wonder?' said he to his wife. Is it worth while that I should go up to London?' But Mrs. Grantly attributed it all to the palace doctrine.

What could be more natural, looking at all the circumstances of the Tickler engagement? She therefore gave her voice against any steps being taken by the archdeacon. A day or two after that Mrs. Proudie met Mrs. Arabin in the close and condoled with her openly on the termination of the marriage treaty; – quite openly, for Mrs. Tickler – as she was to be – was with her mother, and Mrs. Arabin was accompanied by her sister-in-law, Mary Bold.

'It must be very grievous to Mrs. Grantly, very grievous indeed,' said Mrs. Proudie, 'and I sincerely feel for her. But, Mrs. Arabin, all these lessons are sent to us for our eternal welfare.'

'Of course,' said Mrs. Arabin. 'But as to this special lesson, I am inclined to doubt that it –'

'Ah-h! I fear it is too true. I fear there is no room for doubt. Of course you are aware that Lord Dumbello is off for the Continent.' Mrs. Arabin was not aware of it, and she was obliged to admit as much.

'He started four days ago, by way of Boulogne,' said Mrs. Tickler, who seemed to be very well up in the whole affair. 'I am so sorry for poor dear Griselda. I am told she has got all her things. It is such a pity, you know.'

'But why should not Lord Dumbello come back from the Continent?' said Miss Bold, very quietly.

'Why not, indeed? I'm sure I hope he may,' said Mrs. Proudie. 'And no doubt he will, some day. But if he be such a man as they say he is, it is really well for Griselda that she should be relieved from such a marriage. For, after all, Mrs. Arabin, what are the things of this world? – dust beneath our feet, ashes between our teeth, grass cut for the oven, vanity, vexation, and nothing more!' – well pleased with which variety of Christian metaphors Mrs. Proudie walked on, still muttering, however, something about worms and grubs, by which she intended to signify her own species and the Dumbello and Grantly sects of it in particular. This now had gone so far that Mrs. Arabin conceived herself bound in duty to see her sister, and it was then settled in consultation at Plumstead that the archdeacon should call officially at the palace and beg that the rumour might be contradicted. This he did early on the next morning and was shown into the bishop's study, in which he found both his lordship and Mrs. Proudie. The bishop rose to greet him with special civility, smiling his very sweetest on him, as though of all his clergy the archdeacon were the favourite; but Mrs. Proudie wore something of a gloomy aspect, as though she knew that such a visit at such an hour must have reference to some special business. The morning calls made by the archdeacon at the palace in the way of ordinary civility were not numerous. On the present occasion he dashed at once into his subject. 'I have called this morning, Mrs. Proudie,' said he, 'because I wish to ask a favour from you.' Whereupon Mrs. Proudie bowed.

'Mrs. Proudie will be most happy, I am sure,' said the bishop.

'I find that some foolish people have been talking in Barchester about my daughter,' said the archdeacon; 'and I wish to ask Mrs. Proudie –'

Most women under such circumstances would have felt the awkwardness of their situation, and would have prepared to eat their past words with wry faces. But not so Mrs. Proudie. Mrs. Grantly had had the imprudence to throw Mr. Slope in her face – there, in her own drawing-room, and she was resolved to be revenged. Mrs. Grantly, too, had ridiculed the Tickler match, and no too great niceness should now prevent Mrs. Proudie from speaking her mind about the Dumbello match.

'A great many people are talking about her, I am sorry to say,' said Mrs. Proudie; 'but, poor dear, it is not her fault. It might have happened to any girl; only, perhaps, a little more care –; you'll excuse me, Dr. Grantly.'

'I have come here to allude to a report which has been spread about in Barchester, that the match between Lord Dumbello and my daughter has been broken off; and –'

'Everybody in Barchester knows it, I believe,' said Mrs. Proudie.

– 'and', continued the archdeacon, 'to request that that report may be contradicted.'

'Contradicted! Why, he has gone right away, – out of the country!'

'Never mind where he has gone to, Mrs. Proudie; I beg that the report may be contradicted.'

'You'll have to go round to every house in Barchester then,' said she.

'By no means,' replied the archdeacon. 'And, perhaps, it may be right that I should explain to the bishop that I came here because –'

'The bishop knows nothing about it,' said Mrs. Proudie.

'Nothing in the world,' said his lordship. 'And I am sure I hope that the young lady may not be disappointed.'

'– because the matter was so distinctly mentioned to Mrs. Arabin by yourself yesterday.'

'Distinctly mentioned! Of course it was distinctly mentioned. There are some things which can't be kept under a bushel, Dr. Grantly; and this seems to be one of them. Your going about in this way won't make Lord Dumbello marry the young lady.' That was true; nor would it make Mrs. Proudie hold her tongue. Perhaps the archdeacon was wrong in his present errand, and so he now began to bethink himself. 'At any rate,' said he, 'when I tell you that there is no ground whatever for such a report you will do me the kindness to say that, as far as you are concerned, it shall go no further. I think, my lord, I am not asking too much in asking that.'

'The bishop knows nothing about it,' said Mrs. Proudie again.

'Nothing at all,' said the bishop.

'And as I must protest that I believe the information which has reached me on this head,' said Mrs. Proudie, 'I do not see how it is possible that I should contradict it. I can easily understand your feelings, Dr. Grantly.

Considering your daughter's position the match was, as regards earthly wealth, a very great one. I do not wonder that you should be grieved at its being broken off; but I trust that this sorrow may eventuate in a blessing to you and to Miss Griselda. These worldly disappointments are precious balms, and I trust you know how to accept them as such.' The fact was that Dr. Grantly had done altogether wrong in coming to the palace. His wife might have some chance with Mrs. Proudie, but he had none. Since she had come to Barchester he had had only two or three encounters with her, and in all of these he had gone to the wall. His visits to the palace always resulted in his leaving the presence of the inhabitants in a frame of mind by no means desirable, and he now found that he had to do so once again. He could not compel Mrs. Proudie to say that the report was untrue; nor could he condescend to make counter hits at her about her own daughter, as his wife would have done. And thus having utterly failed, he got up and took his leave. But the worst of the matter was, that, in going home, he could not divest his mind of the idea that there might be some truth in the report. What if Lord Dumbello had gone to the Continent resolved to send back from thence some reason why it was impossible that he should make Miss Grantly his wife? Such things had been done before now by men in his rank. Whether or no Mrs. Tickler had been the letter-writing wellwisher from Littlebath, or had induced her friend to be so, it did seem manifest to him, Dr. Grantly, that Mrs. Proudie absolutely believed the report which she promulgated so diligently. The wish might be father to the thought, no doubt; but that the thought was truly there, Dr. Grantly could not induce himself to disbelieve. His wife was less credulous, and to a certain degree comforted him; but that evening he received a letter which greatly confirmed the suspicions set on foot by Mrs. Proudie, and even shook his wife's faith in Lord Dumbello. It was from a mere acquaintance, who in the ordinary course of things would not have written to him. And the bulk of the letter referred to ordinary things, as to which the gentleman in question would hardly have thought of giving himself the trouble to write a letter. But at the end of the note he said, – 'Of course you are aware that Dumbello is off to Paris; I have not heard whether the exact day of his return is fixed.'

'It is true, then,' said the archdeacon, striking the library table with his hand, and becoming absolutely white about the mouth and jaws.

'It cannot be,' said Mrs. Grantly; but even she was now trembling.

'If it be so I'll drag him back to England by the collar of his coat, and disgrace him before the steps of his father's hall.' And the archdeacon as he uttered the threat looked his character as an irate British father much better than he did his other character as a clergyman of the Church of England. The archdeacon had been greatly worsted by Mrs. Proudie, but he was a man who knew how to fight his battles among men – sometimes without too close a regard to his cloth.

'Had Lord Dumbello intended any such thing he would have written, or got some friend to write by this time,' said Mrs. Grantly. 'It is quite possible that he might wish to be off, but he would be too chary of his name not to endeavour to do so with decency.'

Thus the matter was discussed, and it appeared to them both to be so serious that the archdeacon resolved to go at once to London. That Lord Dumbello had gone to France he did not doubt; but he would find some one in town acquainted with the young man's intentions, and he would, no doubt, be able to hear when his return was expected. If there were real reason for apprehension he would follow the runagate to the Continent, but he would not do this without absolute knowledge. According to Lord Dumbello's present engagements he was bound to present himself in August next at Plumstead Episcopi, with the view of then and there taking Griselda Grantly in marriage; but if he kept his word in this respect no one had a right to quarrel with him for going to Paris in the meantime. Most expectant bridegrooms would, no doubt, under such circumstances, have declared their intentions to their future brides; but if Lord Dumbello were different from others, who had a right on that account to be indignant with him? He was unlike other men in other things; and especially unlike other men in being the eldest son of the Marquess of Hartletop. It would be all very well for Tickler to proclaim his whereabouts from week to week; but the eldest son of a marquess might find it inconvenient to be so precise! Nevertheless the archdeacon thought it only prudent to go up to London. 'Susan,' said the archdeacon to his wife, just as he was starting; – at this moment neither of them were in the happiest spirits – 'I think I would say a word of caution to Griselda.'

'Do you feel so much doubt about it as that?' said Mrs. Grantly. But even she did not dare to put a direct negative to this proposal, so much had she been moved by what she had heard!

'I think I would do so, not frightening her more than I could help. It will lessen the blow if it be that the blow is to fall.'

'It will kill me,' said Mrs. Grantly; 'but I think that she will be able to bear it.' On the next morning Mrs. Grantly, with much cunning preparation, went about the task which her husband had left her to perform. It took her long to do, for she was very cunning in the doing of it; but at last it dropped from her in words that there was a possibility – a bare possibility – that some disappointment might even yet be in store for them.

'Do you mean, mamma, that the marriage will be put off?'

'I don't mean to say that I think it will; God forbid! but it is just possible. I dare say that I am very wrong to tell you this, but I know that you have sense enough to bear it. Papa has gone to London, and we shall hear from him soon.'

'Then, mamma, I had better give them orders not to go on with the marking.'

CHAPTER XLVI

Lady Lufton's Request

THE bailiffs on that day had their meals regular – and their beer, which state of things, together with an absence of all duty in the way of making inventories and the like, I take to be the earthly paradise of bailiffs; and on the next morning they walked off with civil speeches and many apologies as to their intrusion. 'They was very sorry,' they said, 'to have troubled a gen'leman as were a gen'leman, but in their way of business what could they do?' To which one of them added a remark that, 'business is business.' This statement I am not prepared to contradict, but I would recommend all men in choosing a profession to avoid any that may require an apology at every turn; either an apology or else a somewhat violent assertion of right. Each younger male reader may, perhaps, reply that he has no thought of becoming a sheriff's officer; but then are there not other cognate lines of life to which, perhaps, the attention of some such may be attracted? On the evening of the day on which they went Mark received a note from Lady Lufton begging him to call early on the following morning, and immediately after breakfast he went across to Framley Court. It may be imagined that he was not in a very happy frame of mind, but he felt the truth of his wife's remark that the first plunge into cold water was always the worst. Lady Lufton was not a woman who would continually throw his disgrace into his teeth, however terribly cold might be the first words with which she spoke of it. He strove hard as he entered her room to carry his usual look and bearing, and to put out his hand to greet her with his customary freedom, but he knew that he failed. And it may be said that no good man who has broken down in his goodness can carry the disgrace of his fall without some look of shame. When a man is able to do that, he ceases to be in any way good.

'This has been a distressing affair,' said Lady Lufton, after her first salutation.

'Yes, indeed,' said he. 'It has been very sad for poor Fanny.'

'Well; we must all have our little periods of grief; and it may perhaps be fortunate if none of us have worse than this. She will not complain, herself, I am sure.'

'She complain!'

'No, I am sure she will not. And now all I've got to say, Mr. Robarts, is this: I hope you and Lufton have had enough to do with black sheep to last you your lives; for I must protest that your late friend Mr. Sowerby is a black sheep.' In no possible way could Lady Lufton have alluded to the matter with greater kindness than in thus joining Mark's name with that of her son. It took away all the bitterness of the rebuke, and made the subject one on which even he might have spoken without difficulty. But now, seeing that she was so gentle to him, he could not but lean the more hardly on himself.

'I have been very foolish,' said he, 'very foolish, and very wrong, and very wicked.'

'Very foolish, I believe, Mr. Robarts – to speak frankly and once for all; but, as I also believe, nothing worse. I thought it best for both of us that we should just have one word about it, and now I recommend that the matter be never mentioned between us again.'

'God bless you, Lady Lufton,' he said, 'I think no man ever had such a friend as you are.' She had been very quiet during the interview, and almost subdued, not speaking with the animation that was usual to her; for this affair with Mr. Robarts was not the only one she had to complete that day, nor, perhaps, the one most difficult of completion. But she cheered up a little under the praise now bestowed on her, for it was the sort of praise she loved best. She did hope, and perhaps flatter herself, that she was a good friend.

'You must be good enough, then, to gratify my friendship by coming up to dinner this evening; and Fanny, too, of course. I cannot take any excuse, for the matter is completely arranged. I have a particular reason for wishing it.' These last violent injunctions had been added because Lady Lufton had seen a refusal rising in the parson's face. Poor Lady Lufton! Her enemies – for even she had enemies – used to declare of her, that an invitation to dinner was the only method of showing itself of which her good-humour was cognizant. But let me ask of her enemies whether it is not as good a method as any other known to be extant? Under such orders as these obedience was of course a necessity, and he promised that he, with his wife, would come across to dinner. And then, when he went away, Lady Lufton ordered her carriage.

During these doings at Framley, Lucy Robarts still remained at Hogglestock, nursing Mrs. Crawley. Nothing occurred to take her back to Framley, for the same note from Fanny which gave her the first tidings of the arrival of the Philistines told her also of their departure – and also of the source from whence relief had reached them. 'Don't come, therefore, for that reason,' said the note, 'but, nevertheless, do come as quickly as you can, for the whole house is sad without you.' On the morning after the receipt of this note Lucy was sitting, as was now usual with her, beside an old arm-chair to which her patient had lately been promoted. The fever had gone, and Mrs. Crawley was slowly regaining her strength – very slowly, and with frequent caution from the Silverbridge doctor that any attempt at being well too fast might again precipitate her into an abyss of illness and domestic inefficiency.

'I really think I can get about to-morrow,' said she; 'and then, dear Lucy, I need not keep you longer from your home.'

'You are in a great hurry to get rid of me, I think. I suppose Mr. Crawley has been complaining again about the cream in his tea.'

Mr. Crawley had on one occasion stated his assured conviction that surreptitious daily supplies were being brought into the house, because he had detected the presence of cream instead of milk in his own cup. As, however, the cream had been going for sundry days before this, Miss Robarts had not thought much of his ingenuity in making the discovery.

'Ah, you do not know how he speaks of you when your back is turned.'

'And how does he speak of me? I know you would not have the courage to tell me the whole.'

'No, I have not; for you would think it absurd coming from one who looks like him. He says that if he were to write a poem about womanhood, he would make you the heroine.'

'With a cream-jug in my hand, or else sewing buttons on to a shirt-collar. But he never forgave me about the mutton broth. He told me, in so many words, that I was a – story-teller. And for the matter of that, my dear, so I was.'

'He told me that you were an angel.'

'Goodness gracious!'

'A ministering angel. And so you have been. I can almost feel it in my heart to be glad that I have been ill, seeing that I have had you for my friend.'

'But you might have had that good fortune without the fever.'

'No, I should not. In my married life I have made no friends till my illness brought you to me; nor should I ever really have known you but for that. How should I get to know any one?'

'You will now, Mrs. Crawley; will you not? Promise that you will. You will come to us at Framley when you are well? You have promised already, you know.'

'You made me do so when I was too weak to refuse.'

'And I shall make you keep your promise, too. He shall come, also, if he likes; but you shall come whether he likes or no. And I won't hear a word about your old dresses. Old dresses will wear as well at Framley as at Hogglestock.' From all which it will appear that Mrs. Crawley and Lucy Robarts had become very intimate during this period of the nursing; as two women always will, or, at least, should do, when shut up for weeks together in the same sick room.

The conversation was still going on between them when the sound of wheels was heard upon the road. It was no highway that passed before the house, and carriages of any sort were not frequent there.

'It is Fanny, I am sure,' said Lucy, rising from her chair.

'There are two horses,' said Mrs. Crawley, distinguishing the noise with the accurate sense of hearing which is always attached to sickness; 'and it is not the noise of the pony-carriage.'

'It is a regular carriage,' said Lucy, speaking from the window, 'and stopping here. It is somebody from Framley Court, for I know the servant.' As she spoke a blush came to her forehead. Might it not be Lord Lufton, she thought to herself – forgetting, at the moment, that Lord Lufton did not go about the country in a close chariot with a fat footman. Intimate as she had become with Mrs. Crawley she had said nothing to her new friend on the subject of her love affair. The carriage stopped, and down came the footman, but nobody spoke to him from the inside.

'He has probably brought something from Framley,' said Lucy, having cream and such-like matters in her mind; for cream and such-like matters had come from

Framley Court more than once during her sojourn there. 'And the carriage, probably, happened to be coming this way.' But the mystery soon elucidated itself partially, or, perhaps, became more mysterious in another way. The red-armed little girl who had been taken away by her frightened mother in the first burst of the fever had now returned to her place, and at the present moment entered the room, with awestruck face, declaring that Miss Robarts was to go at once to the big lady in the carriage.

'I suppose it's Lady Lufton,' said Mrs. Crawley. Lucy's heart was so absolutely in her mouth that any kind of speech was at the moment impossible to her. Why should Lady Lufton have come thither to Hogglestock, and why should she want to see her, Lucy Robarts, in the carriage? Had not everything between them been settled? And yet –! Lucy, in the moment for thought that was allowed to her, could not determine what might be the probable upshot of such an interview. Her chief feeling was a desire to postpone it for the present instant. But the red-armed little girl would not allow that.

'You are to come at once,' said she.

And then Lucy, without having spoken a word, got up and left the room. She walked downstairs, along the little passage, and out through the small garden, with firm steps, but hardly knowing whither she went or why. Her presence of mind and self-possession had all deserted her. She knew that she was unable to speak as she should do; she felt that she would have to regret her present behaviour, but yet she could not help herself. Why should Lady Lufton have come to her there? She went on, and the big footman stood with the carriage door open. She stepped up almost unconsciously, and, without knowing how she got there, she found herself seated by Lady Lufton. To tell the truth her ladyship also was a little at a loss to know how she was to carry through her present plan of operations. The duty of beginning, however, was clearly with her, and therefore, having taken Lucy by the hand, she spoke. 'Miss Robarts,' she said, 'my son has come home. I don't know whether you are aware of it.' She spoke with a low, gentle voice, not quite like herself, but Lucy was much too confused to notice this.

'I was not aware of it,' said Lucy. She had, however, been so informed in Fanny's letter, but all that had gone out of her head.

'Yes; he has come back. He has been in Norway, you know, – fishing.'

'Yes,' said Lucy.

'I am sure you will remember all that took place when you came to me, not long ago, in my little room upstairs at Framley Court.' In answer to which, Lucy, quivering in every nerve, and wrongly thinking that she was visibly shaking in every limb, timidly answered that she did remember. Why was it that she had then been so bold, and now was so poor a coward?

'Well, my dear, all that I said to you then I said to you thinking that it was for the best. You, at any rate, will not be angry with me for loving my own son better than I love any one else.'

'Oh, no,' said Lucy.

'He is the best of sons, and the best of men, and I am sure that he will be the best of husbands.'

Lucy had an idea, by instinct, however, rather than by sight, that Lady Lufton's eyes were full of tears as she spoke. As for herself she was altogether blinded, and did not dare to lift her face or to turn her head. As for the utterance of any sound, that was quite out of the question.

'And now I have come here, Lucy, to ask you to be his wife.'

She was quite sure that she heard the words. They came plainly to her ears, leaving on her brain their proper sense, but yet she could not move or make any sign that she had understood them. It seemed as though it would be ungenerous in her to take advantage of such conduct and to accept an offer made with so much self-sacrifice. She had not time at the first moment to think even of his happiness, let alone her own, but she thought only of the magnitude of the concession which had been made to her. When she had constituted Lady Lufton the arbiter of her destiny she had regarded the question of her love as decided against herself. She had found herself unable to endure the position of being Lady Lufton's daughter-in-law while Lady Lufton would be scorning her, and therefore she had given up the game. She had given up the game, sacrificing herself, and, as far as it might be a sacrifice, sacrificing him also. She had been resolute to stand to her word in this respect, but she had never allowed herself to think it possible that Lady Lufton should comply with the conditions which she, Lucy, had laid upon her. And yet such was the case, as she so plainly heard. 'And now I have come here, Lucy, to ask you to be his wife.' How long they sat together silent, I cannot say; counted by minutes the time would not probably have amounted to many, but to each of them the duration seemed considerable. Lady Lufton, while she was speaking, had contrived to get hold of Lucy's hand, and she sat, still holding it, trying to look into Lucy's face, – which, however, she could hardly see, so much was it turned away. Neither, indeed, were Lady Lufton's eyes perfectly dry. No answer came to her question, and therefore, after a while, it was necessary that she should speak again.

'Must I go back to him, Lucy, and tell him that there is some other objection – something besides a stern old mother; some hindrance, perhaps, not so easily overcome?'

'No,' said Lucy, and it was all which at the moment she could say.

'What shall I tell him then? Shall I say yes – simply yes?'

'Simply yes,' said Lucy.

'And as to the stern old mother who thought her only son too precious to be parted with at the first word – is nothing to be said to her?'

'Oh, Lady Lufton!'

'No forgiveness to be spoken, no sign of affection to be given? Is she always to be regarded as stern and cross, vexatious and disagreeable?' Lucy slowly turned round her head and looked up into her companion's face. Though she had as yet no voice to speak of affection she could fill her eyes with love, and in that way make to her future mother all the promises that were needed. 'Lucy, dearest Lucy, you must be very dear to me now.' And then they were in each other's arms, kissing each other. Lady Lufton now desired her coachman to drive up and down for some little space along the road while she completed her necessary conversation with Lucy. She wanted at first to carry her back to Framley that evening, promising to send her again to Mrs. Crawley on the following morning – 'till some permanent arrangement could be made,' by which Lady Lufton intended the substitution of a regular nurse for her future daughter-in-law, seeing that Lucy Robarts was now invested in her eyes with attributes which made it unbecoming that she should sit in attendance at Mrs. Crawley's bedside. But Lucy would not go back to Framley on that evening; no, nor on the next morning. She would be so glad if Fanny would come to her there, and then she would arrange about going home. 'But, Lucy, dear, what am I to say to Ludovic? Perhaps you would feel it awkward if he were to come to see you here.'

'Oh, yes, Lady Lufton; pray tell him not to do that.'

'And is that all that I am to tell him?'

'Tell him – tell him – he won't want you to tell him anything; – only I should like to be quiet for a day, Lady Lufton.'

'Well, dearest, you shall be quiet; the day after tomorrow then. – Mind, we must not spare you any longer, because it will be right that you should be at home now. He would think it very hard if you were to be so near, and he was not to be allowed to look at you. And there will be some one else who will want to see you. I shall want to have you very near to me, for I shall be wretched, Lucy, if I cannot teach you to love me.' In answer to which Lucy did find voice enough to make sundry promises. And then she was put out of the carriage at the little wicket gate, and Lady Lufton was driven back to Framley. I wonder whether the servant when he held the door for Miss Robarts was conscious that he was waiting on his future mistress. I fancy that he was, for these sort of people always know everything, and the peculiar courtesy of his demeanour as he let down the carriage steps was very observable.

Lucy felt almost beside herself as she returned upstairs, not knowing what to do or how to look, and with what words to speak. It behoved her to go at once to Mrs. Crawley's room, and yet she longed to be alone. She knew that she was quite unable either to conceal her thoughts or express them; nor did she wish at the present moment to talk to any one about her happiness, – seeing that she could not at the present moment talk to Fanny Robarts. She went, however, without delay into Mrs. Crawley's room, and with that little eager way of speaking quickly which is so common with people who know that they are confused, said that she feared she had been a very long time away. 'And was it Lady Lufton?'

'Yes; it was Lady Lufton.'

'Why, Lucy; I did not know that you and her ladyship were such friends.'

'She had something particular she wanted to say,' said Lucy, avoiding the question, and avoiding also Mrs. Crawley's eyes; and then she sat down in her usual chair.

'It was nothing unpleasant, I hope.'

'No, nothing at all unpleasant; nothing of that kind. – Oh, Mrs. Crawley, I'll tell you some other time, but pray do not ask me now.' And then she got up and escaped, for it was absolutely necessary that she should be alone.

When she reached her own room – that in which the children usually slept – she made a great effort to compose herself, but not altogether successfully. She got out her paper and blotting-book, intending, as she said to herself, to write to Fanny, knowing, however, that the letter when written would be destroyed; but she was not able even to form a word. Her hand was unsteady and her eyes were dim and her thoughts were incapable of being fixed. She could only sit, and think, and wonder and hope; occasionally wiping the tears from her eyes, and asking herself why her present frame of mind was so painful to her? During the last two or three months she had felt no fear of Lord Lufton, had always carried herself before him on equal terms, and had been signally capable of doing so when he made his declaration to her at the parsonage; but now she looked forward with an undefined dread to the first moment in which she should see him. And then she thought of a certain evening she had passed at Framley Court, and acknowledged to herself that there was some pleasure in looking back to that. Griselda Grantly had been there, and all the constitutional powers of the two families had been at work to render easy a process of love-making between her and Lord Lufton. Lucy had seen and understood it, and had, in a certain degree, suffered from beholding it. She had placed herself apart, not complaining – painfully conscious of some inferiority, but, at the same time, almost boasting to herself that in her own way she was the superior. And then he had come behind her chair, whispering to her, speaking to her his first words of kindness and good-nature, and she had resolved that she would be his friend – his friend, even though Griselda Grantly might be his wife. What those resolutions were worth had soon become manifest to her. She had soon confessed to herself the result of that friendship, and had determined to bear her punishment with courage. But now –

She sate so far about an hour, and would fain have so sat out the day. But as this could not be, she got up, and having washed her face and eyes returned to Mrs. Crawley's room. There she found Mr. Crawley also, to her great joy, for she knew that while he was there no questions would be asked of her. He was always very gentle to her, treating her with an old-fashioned, polished respect – except when compelled on that one occasion by his sense of duty to accuse her of mendacity respecting the purveying of victuals –, but he had never become absolutely familiar with her as his wife had done; and it was well for her now that he had not done so, for she could not have talked about Lady Lufton. In the evening, when the three were present, she did manage to say that she expected Mrs. Robarts would come over on the following day. 'We shall part with you, Miss Robarts, with the deepest regret,' said Mr. Crawley; 'but we would not on any account keep you longer. Mrs. Crawley can do without you now. What she would have done, had you not come to us, I am at a loss to think.'

'I did not say that I should go,' said Lucy.

'But you will,' said Mrs. Crawley. 'Yes, dear, you will. I know that it is proper now that you should return. Nay, but we will not have you any longer. And the poor dear children, too, – they may return. How am I to thank Mrs. Robarts for what she has done for us?' It was settled that if Mrs. Robarts came on the following day Lucy should go back with her; and then, during the long watches of the night – for on this last night Lucy would not leave the bedside of her new friend till long after the dawn had broken, she did tell Mrs. Crawley what was to be her destiny in life. To herself there seemed nothing strange in her new position; but to Mrs. Crawley it was wonderful that she – she, poor as she was – should have an embryo peeress at her bedside, handing her her cup to drink, and smoothing her pillow that she might be at rest. It was strange, and she could hardly maintain her accustomed familiarity. Lucy felt this at the moment.

'It must make no difference, you know,' said she, eagerly; 'none at all, between you and me. Promise me that it shall make no difference.' The promise was, of course, exacted; but it was not possible that such a promise should be kept. Very early on the following morning – so early that it woke her while still in her first sleep – there came a letter for her from the parsonage. Mrs. Robarts had written it, after her return home from Lady Lufton's dinner. The letter said: –

'My own own Darling,

'How am I to congratulate you, and be eager enough in wishing you joy? I do wish you joy, and am so very happy. I write now chiefly to say that I shall be over with you about twelve to-morrow, and that I *must* bring you away with me. If I did not some one else, by no means so trustworthy, would insist on doing it.'

But this, though it was thus stated to be the chief part of the letter, and though it might be so in matter, was by no means so in space. It was very long, for Mrs. Robarts had sat writing it till past midnight.

'I will not say anything about him,' she went on to say, after two pages had been filled with his name, 'but I must tell you how beautifully she has behaved. You will own that she is a dear woman; will you not?'

Lucy had already owned it many times since the visit of yesterday, and had declared to herself, as she has continued to declare ever since, that she had never doubted it.

'She took us by surprise when we got into the drawing-room before dinner, and she told us first of all that she had been to see you at Hogglestock. Lord Lufton, of course, could not keep the secret, but brought it out instantly. I can't tell you now how he told it all, but I am sure you will believe that he did it in the best possible manner. He took my hand and pressed it half a dozen times, and I thought he was going to do something else; but he did not, so you need not be jealous. And she was so nice to Mark, saying such things in praise of you, and paying all manner of compliments to your father. But Lord Lufton scolded her immensely for not bringing you. He said it was lackadaisical and nonsensical; but I could see how much he loved her for what she had done; and she could see it too, for I know her ways, and know that she was delighted with him. She could not keep her eyes off him all the evening, and certainly I never did see him look so well.

'And then while Lord Lufton and Mark were in the dining-room, where they remained a terribly long time, she would make me go through the house that she might show me your rooms, and explain how you were to be mistress there. She has got it all arranged to perfection, and I am sure she has been thinking about it for years. Her great fear at present is that you and he should go and live at Lufton. If you have any gratitude in you, either to her or me, you will not let him do this. I consoled her by saying that there are not two stones upon one another at Lufton as yet; and I believe such is the case. Besides, everybody says that it is the ugliest spot in the world. She went on to declare, with tears in her eyes, that if you were content to remain at Framley, she would never interfere in anything. I do think that she is the best woman that ever lived.'

So much as I have given of this letter formed but a small portion of it, but it comprises all that it is necessary that we should know. Exactly at twelve o'clock on that day Puck the pony appeared, with Mrs. Robarts and Grace Crawley behind him, Grace having been brought back as being capable of some service in the house. Nothing that was confidential, and very little that was loving, could be said at the moment, because Mr. Crawley was there, waiting to bid Miss Robarts adieu; and he had not as yet been informed of what was to be the future fate of his visitor. So they could only press each other's hands and embrace, which to Lucy was almost a relief; for even to her sister-in-law she hardly as yet knew how to speak openly on this subject.

'May God Almighty bless you, Miss Robarts,' said Mr. Crawley, as he stood in his dingy sitting-room ready to lead her out to the pony-carriage. 'You have brought sunshine into this house, even in the time of sickness, when there was no sunshine; and He will bless you. You have been the Good Samaritan, binding up the wounds of the afflicted, pouring in oil and balm. To the mother of my children you have given life, and to me you have brought light, and comfort, and good words, – making my spirit glad within me as it had not been gladdened before. All this hath come of charity, which vaunteth not itself and is not puffed up. Faith and hope are great and beautiful, but charity exceedeth them all.' And having so spoken, instead of leading her out, he went away and hid himself. How Puck behaved himself as Fanny drove him back to Framley, and how those two ladies in the carriage behaved themselves – of that, perhaps, nothing further need be said.

CHAPTER XLVII

Nemesis

BUT in spite of all these joyful tidings it must, alas! be remembered that Pœna, that just but Rhadamanthine goddess, whom we moderns ordinarily call Punishment, or Nemesis when we wish to speak of her goddess-ship, very seldom fails to catch a wicked man though she have sometimes a lame foot of her own, and though the wicked man may possibly get a start of her. In this instance the wicked man had been our unfortunate friend Mark Robarts; wicked in that he had wittingly touched pitch, gone to Gatherum Castle, ridden fast mares across the country to Cobbold's Ashes, and fallen very imprudently among the Tozers; and the instrument used by Nemesis was Mr. Tom Towers of the *Jupiter,* than whom, in these our days, there is no deadlier scourge in the hands of that goddess. In the first instance, however, I must mention, though I will not relate, a little conversation which took place between Lady Lufton and Mr. Robarts. That gentleman thought it right to say a few words more to her ladyship respecting those money transactions. He could not but feel, he said, that he had received that prebendal stall from the hands of Mr. Sowerby; and under such circumstances, considering all that had happened, he could not be easy in his mind as long as he held it. What he was about to do would, he was aware, delay considerably his final settlement with Lord Lufton; but Lufton, he hoped, would pardon that, and agree with him as to the propriety of what he was about to do.

On the first blush of the thing Lady Lufton did not quite go along with him. Now that Lord Lufton was to marry the parson's sister it might be well that the parson should be a dignitary of the Church; and it might be well, also, that one so nearly connected with her son should be comfortable in his money matters. There loomed, also, in the future, some distant possibility of higher clerical honours for a peer's brother-in-law; and the top rung of the ladder is always more easily attained when a man has already ascended a step or two. But, nevertheless, when the matter came to be fully explained to her, when she saw clearly the circumstances under which the stall had been conferred, she did agree that it had better be given up. And well for both of them it was – well for them all at Framley – that this conclusion had been reached before the scourge of Nemesis had fallen. Nemesis, of course, declared that her scourge had produced the resignation; but it was generally understood that this was a false boast, for all clerical men at Barchester knew that the stall had been restored to the chapter, or, in other words, into the hands of the Government, before Tom Towers had twirled the fatal lash above his head. But the manner of the twirling was as follows: –

'It is with difficulty enough,' said the article in the *Jupiter,* 'that the Church of England maintains at the present moment that ascendancy among the religious sects of this country which it so loudly claims. And perhaps it is rather from an old-fashioned and time-honoured affection for its standing than from any intrinsic merits of its own that some such general acknowledgement of its ascendancy is still allowed to prevail. If, however, the patrons and clerical members of this Church are bold enough to disregard all general rules of decent behaviour, we think we may predict that this chivalrous feeling will be found to give way. From time to time we hear of instances of such imprudence, and are made to wonder at the folly of those who are supposed to hold the State Church in the greatest reverence.

'Among those positions of dignified ease to which fortunate clergymen may be promoted are the stalls of the canons or prebendaries in our cathedrals. Some of these, as is well known, carry little or no emolument with them, but some are rich in the good things of this world. Excellent family houses are attached to them, with we hardly know what domestic privileges, and clerical incomes, moreover, of an amount which, if divided, would make glad the hearts of many a hard-working clerical slave. Reform has been busy even among these stalls, attaching some amount of work to the pay, and paring off some superfluous wealth from such of them as were over full; but reform has been lenient with them, acknowledging that it was well to have some such places of comfortable and dignified retirement for those who have worn themselves out in the hard work of their profession. There has of late prevailed a taste for the appointment of young bishops, produced no doubt by a feeling that bishops should be men fitted to get through really hard work; but we have never heard that young prebendaries were considered desirable. A clergyman selected for such a position should, we have always thought, have earned an evening of ease by a long day of work, and should, above all things, be one whose life has been, and therefore in human probability will be, so decorous as to be honourable to the cathedral of his adoption.

'We were, however, the other day given to understand that one of these luxurious benefices, belonging to the cathedral of Barchester, had been bestowed on the Rev. Mark Robarts, the vicar of a neighbouring parish, on the understanding that he should hold the living and the stall together; and on making further inquiry we were surprised to learn that this fortunate gentleman is as yet considerably under thirty years of age. We were desirous, however, of believing that his learning, his piety, and his conduct, might be of a nature to add peculiar grace to his chapter, and therefore, though almost unwillingly, we were silent. But now it has come to our ears, and, indeed, to the ears of all the world, that this piety and conduct are sadly wanting; and judging of Mr. Robarts by his life and associates, we are inclined to doubt even the learning. He has at this moment, or at any rate had but a few days since, an execution in his parsonage house at Framley, on the suit of certain most disreputable bill discounters in London; and probably would have another execution in his other house in Barchester close, but for the fact that he has never thought it necessary to go into residence.'

Then followed some very stringent, and, no doubt, much-needed advice to those clerical members of the Church of England who are supposed to be mainly responsible for the conduct of their brethren; and the article ended as follows:

'Many of these stalls are in the gift of the respective deans and chapters, and in such cases the dean and chapters are bound to see that proper persons are appointed;

but in other instances the power of selection is vested in the Crown, and then an equal responsibility rests on the Government of the day. Mr. Robarts, we learn, was appointed to the stall in Barchester by the late Prime Minister, and we really think that a grave censure rests on him for the manner in which his patronage has been exercised. It may be impossible that he should himself in all such cases satisfy himself by personal inquiry. But our Government is altogether conducted on the footing of vicarial responsibility. *Quod facit per alium, facit per se*, is in a special manner true of our ministers, and any man who rises to high position among them must abide by the danger thereby incurred. In this peculiar case we are informed that the recommendation was made by a very recently admitted member of the Cabinet, to whose appointment we alluded at the time as a great mistake. The gentleman in question held no high individual office of his own; but evil such as this which has now been done at Barchester, is exactly the sort of mischief which follows the exaltation of unfit men to high positions, even though no great scope for executive failure may be placed within their reach.

'If Mr. Robarts will allow us to tender to him our advice he will lose no time in going through such ceremony as may be necessary again to place the stall at the disposal of the Crown!'

I may here observe that poor Harold Smith, when he read this, writhing in agony, declared it to be the handiwork of his hated enemy, Mr. Supplehouse. He knew the mark; so, at least, he said; but I myself am inclined to believe that his animosity misled him. I think that one greater than Mr. Supplehouse had taken upon himself the punishment of our poor vicar. This was very dreadful to them all at Framley, and, when first read, seemed to crush them to atoms. Poor Mrs. Robarts, when she heard it, seemed to think that for them the world was over. An attempt had been made to keep it from her, but such attempts always fail, as did this. The article was copied into all the good-natured local newspapers, and she soon discovered that something was being hidden. At last it was shown to her by her husband, and then for a few hours she was annihilated; for a few days she was unwilling to show herself; and for a few weeks she was very sad. But after that the world seemed to go on much as it had done before; the sun shone upon them as warmly as though the article had not been written; and not only the sun of heaven, which, as a rule, is not limited in his shining by any display of pagan thunder, but also the genial sun of their own sphere, the warmth and light of which were so essentially necessary to their happiness. Neighbouring rectors did not look glum, nor did the rectors' wives refuse to call. The people in the shops at Barchester did not regard her as though she were a disgraced woman, though it must be acknowledged that Mrs. Proudie passed her in the close with the coldest nod of recognition.

On Mrs. Proudie's mind alone did the article seem to have any enduring effect. In one respect it was, perhaps, beneficial; Lady Lufton was at once induced by it to make common cause with her own clergyman, and thus the remembrance of Mr. Robarts's sins passed away the quicker from the minds of the whole Framley Court household. And, indeed, the county at large was not able to give to the matter that undivided attention which would have been considered its due at periods of no more than ordinary interest. At the present moment preparations were being made for a general election, and although no contest was to take place in the eastern division, a very violent fight was being carried on in the west; and the circumstances of that fight were so exciting that Mr. Robarts and his article were forgotten before their time. An edict had gone forth from Gatherum Castle directing that Mr. Sowerby should be turned out, and an answering note of defiance had been sounded for Chaldicotes, protesting on behalf of Mr. Sowerby, that the duke's behest would not be obeyed.

There are two classes of persons in this realm who are constitutionally inefficient to take any part in returning members to Parliament – peers, namely, and women; and yet it was soon known through the whole length and breadth of the county that the present electioneering fight was being carried on between a peer and a woman. Miss Dunstable had been declared the purchaser of the Chace of Chaldicotes, as it were, just in the very nick of time; which purchase – so men in Barsetshire declared, not knowing anything of the facts – would have gone altogether the other way, had not the giants obtained temporary supremacy over the gods. The duke was a supporter of the gods, and therefore, so Mr. Fothergill hinted, his money had been refused. Miss Dunstable was prepared to beard this ducal friend of the gods in his own county, and therefore her money had been taken. I am inclined, however, to think that Mr. Fothergill knew nothing about it, and to opine that Miss Dunstable, in her eagerness for victory, offered to the Crown more money than the property was worth in the duke's opinion, and that the Crown took advantage of her anxiety, to the manifest profit of the public at large. And it soon became known also that Miss Dunstable was, in fact, the proprietor of the whole Chaldicotes estate, and that in promoting the success of Mr. Sowerby as a candidate for the county, she was standing by her own tenant. It also became known, in the course of the battle, that Miss Dunstable had herself at last succumbed, and that she was about to marry Dr. Thorne of Greshamsbury, or the 'Greshamsbury apothecary,' as the adverse party now delighted to call him. 'He has been little better than a quack all his life,' said Dr. Fillgrave, the eminent physician of Barchester, 'and now he is going to marry a quack's daughter.' By which, and the like to which, Dr. Thorne did not allow himself to be much annoyed. But all this gave rise to a very pretty series of squibs arranged between Mr. Fothergill and Mr. Closerstill, the electioneering agent. Mr. Sowerby was named 'the lady's pet,' and descriptions were given of the lady who kept this pet, which were by no means flattering to Miss Dunstable's appearance, or manners, or age. And then the western division of the county was asked in a grave tone – as counties and boroughs are asked by means of advertisements stuck up on blind walls and barn doors – whether it was fitting and proper that it should be represented by a woman. Upon which the county was again asked whether it was fitting and proper that it should be represented by a duke. And then the question became more personal as against Miss Dunstable, and inquiry was urged whether the county would not be indelibly disgraced if it were not only handed over to a woman, but handed over to a woman who sold the oil of Lebanon. But little was got by this move, for an answering placard explained to the unfortunate county how deep would be its shame if it allowed itself to become the appanage of any peer, but more especially of a peer who was known to be the most immoral lord that ever disgraced the benches of the Upper House. And so the battle went on very prettily, and, as money was allowed to flow freely, the West Barsetshire world at large was not ill satisfied. It is wonderful how much disgrace of that kind a borough or county can endure without flinching; and wonderful, also, seeing how supreme is the value attached to the Constitution by the realm at large, how very little the principles of that Constitution are valued by the people in detail. The duke, of course, did not show himself. He rarely did on any occasion, and never on such occasions as this; but Mr. Fothergill was to be seen everywhere. Miss Dunstable, also, did not hide her light under a bushel; though I here declare, on the faith of an historian, that the rumour spread abroad of her having made a speech to the electors from the top of the porch over the hotel-door at Courcy was not founded on fact. No doubt she was at Courcy, and her carriage stopped at the hotel; but neither there nor elsewhere did she make any public exhibition. 'They must have mistaken me for Mrs. Proudie,' she said, when the rumour reached her ears. But there was, alas! one great element of failure on Miss Dunstable's side of the battle. Mr. Sowerby himself could not be induced to fight it as became a man. Any positive injunctions that were laid upon him he did, in a sort, obey. It had been a part of the bargain that he should stand the contest, and from that bargain he could not well go back; but he had not the spirit left to him for any true fighting on his own part. He could not go up on the hustings, and there defy the duke. Early in the affair Mr. Fothergill challenged him to do so, and Mr. Sowerby never took up the gauntlet.

'We have heard,' said Mr. Fothergill, in that great speech which he made at the Omnium Arms at Silverbridge – 'we have heard much during this election of the Duke of Omnium, and of the injuries which he is supposed to have inflicted on one of the candidates. The duke's name is very frequent in the mouths of the gentlemen – and of the lady – who support Mr. Sowerby's claims. But I do not think that Mr. Sowerby himself has dared to say much about the duke. I defy Mr. Sowerby to mention the duke's name upon the hustings.' And it so happened that Mr. Sowerby never did mention the duke's name.

It is ill fighting when the spirit is gone, and Mr. Sowerby's spirit for such things was now wellnigh broken. It is true that he had escaped from the net in which the duke, by Mr. Fothergill's aid, had entangled him; but he had only broken out of one captivity into another. Money is a serious thing; and when gone cannot be had back by a shuffle in the game, or a fortunate blow with the battledore, as may political power, or reputation, or fashion. One hundred thousand pounds gone, must remain as gone, let the person who claims to have had the honour of advancing it be Mrs. B. or my Lord C. No lucky dodge can erase such a claim from the things that be – unless, indeed, such dodge be possible as Mr. Sowerby tried with Miss Dunstable. It was better for him, undoubtedly, to have the lady for a creditor than the duke, seeing that it was possible for him to live as a tenant in his own old house under the lady's reign. But this he found to be a sad enough life, after all that was come and gone.

The election on Miss Dunstable's part was lost. She carried on the contest nobly, fighting it to the last moment, and sparing neither her own money nor that of her antagonist; but she carried it on unsuccessfully. Many gentlemen did support Mr. Sowerby because they were willing enough to emancipate their county from the duke's thraldom; but Mr. Sowerby was felt to be a black sheep, as Lady Lufton had called him, and at the close of the election he found himself banished from the representation of West Barsetshire; – banished for ever, after having held the county for five-and-twenty years. Unfortunate Mr. Sowerby! I cannot take leave of him here without some feeling of regret, knowing that there was that within him which might, under better guidance, have produced better things. There are men, even of high birth, who seem as though they were born to be rogues; but Mr. Sowerby was, to my thinking, born to be a gentleman. That he had not been a gentleman – that he had bolted from his appointed course, going terribly on the wrong side of the posts – let us all acknowledge. It is not a gentlemanlike deed, but a very blackguard action, to obtain a friend's acceptance to a bill in an unguarded hour of social intercourse. That and other similar doings have stamped his character too plainly. But, nevertheless, I claim a tear for Mr. Sowerby, and lament that he has failed to run his race discreetly, in accordance with the rules of the Jockey Club. He attempted that plan of living as a tenant in his old house at Chaldicotes, and of making a living out of the land which he farmed; but he soon abandoned it. He had no aptitude for such industry, and could not endure his altered position in the county. He soon relinquished Chaldicotes of his own accord, and has vanished away, as such men do vanish – not altogether without necessary income; to which point in the final arrangement of their joint affairs, Mrs. Thorne's man of business – if I may be allowed so far to anticipate – paid special attention. And thus Lord Dumbello, the duke's nominee, got in, as the duke's nominee had done for very many years past. There was no Nemesis here – none as yet. Nevertheless, she with the lame foot will assuredly catch him, the duke, if it be that he deserve to be caught. With us his grace's appearance has been so unfrequent that I think we may omit to make any further inquiry as to his concerns.

One point, however, is worthy of notice, as showing the good sense with which we manage our affairs here in England. In an early portion of this story the reader was introduced to the interior of Gatherum Castle, and there saw Miss Dunstable entertained by the duke in the most friendly manner. Since those days the lady has become the duke's neighbour, and has waged a war with him, which he probably felt to be very vexatious. But, nevertheless, on the next great occasion at Gatherum Castle, Doctor and Mrs. Thorne were among the visitors, and to no one was the duke more personally courteous than to his opulent neighbour, the late Miss Dunstable.

CHAPTER XLVIII

How They Were All Married, Had Two Children, and Lived Happy Ever After

DEAR, affectionate, sympathetic readers, we have four couple of sighing lovers with whom to deal in this our last chapter, and I, as leader of the chorus, disdain to press you further with doubts as to the happiness of any of that quadrille. They were all made happy, in spite of that little episode which so lately took place at Barchester; and in telling of their happiness – shortly, as is now necessary – we will take them chronologically, giving precedence to those who first appeared at the hymeneal altar. In July, then, at the cathedral, by the father of the bride, assisted by his examining chaplain, Olivia Proudie, the eldest daughter of the Bishop of Barchester, was joined in marriage to the Rev. Tobias Tickler, incumbent of the Trinity district church in Bethnal Green. Of the bridegroom in this instance, our acquaintance has been so short, that it is not, perhaps, necessary to say much. When coming to the wedding he proposed to bring his three darling children with him; but in this measure he was, I think prudently, stopped by advice, rather strongly worded, from his future valued mother-in-law. Mr. Tickler was not an opulent man, nor had he hitherto attained any great fame in his profession; but, at the age of forty-three he still had sufficient opportunity before him, and now that his merit has been properly viewed by high ecclesiastical eyes the refreshing dew of deserved promotion will no doubt fall upon him. The marriage was very smart, and Olivia carried herself through the trying ordeal with an excellent propriety of conduct. Up to that time, and even for a few days longer, there was doubt at Barchester as to that strange journey which Lord Dumbello undoubtedly did take to France. When a man so circumstanced will suddenly go to Paris, without notice given even to his future bride, people must doubt; and grave were the apprehensions expressed on this occasion by Mrs. Proudie, even at her child's wedding breakfast. 'God bless you, my dear children,' she said, standing up at the head of her table as she addressed Mr. Tickler and his wife; 'when I see your perfect happiness – perfect, that is, as far as human happiness can be made perfect in this vale of tears – and think of the terrible calamity which has fallen on our unfortunate neighbours, I cannot but acknowledge His infinite mercy and goodness. The Lord giveth and the Lord taketh away.' By which she intended, no doubt, to signify that whereas Mr. Tickler had been given to her Olivia, Lord Dumbello had been taken away from the archdeacon's Griselda. The happy couple then went in Mrs. Proudie's carriage to the nearest railway station but one, and from thence proceeded to Malvern, and there spent the honeymoon. And a great comfort it was, I am sure, to Mrs. Proudie when authenticated tidings reached Barchester that Lord Dumbello had returned from Paris, and that the Hartletop-Grantly alliance was to be carried to its completion. She still, however, held her opinion – whether correctly or not who shall say? – that the young lord had intended to escape. 'The archdeacon has shown great firmness in the way in which he has done it,' said Mrs. Proudie; 'but whether he has consulted his child's best interests in forcing her into a marriage with an unwilling husband, I for one must take leave to doubt. But then, unfortunately, we all know how completely the archdeacon is devoted to worldly matters.'

In this instance the archdeacon's devotion to worldly matters was rewarded by that success which he no doubt desired. He did go up to London, and did see one or two of Lord Dumbello's friends. This he did, not obtrusively, as though in fear of any falsehood or vacillation on the part of the viscount, but with that discretion and tact for which he has been so long noted. Mrs. Proudie declares that during the few days of his absence from Barsetshire he himself crossed to France and hunted down Lord Dumbello at Paris. As to this I am not prepared to say anything; but I am quite sure, as will be all those who knew the archdeacon, that he was not a man to see his daughter wronged as long as any measure remained by which such wrong might be avoided. But, be that as it may – that mooted question as to the archdeacon's journey to Paris – Lord Dumbello was forthcoming at Plumstead on the 5th of August, and went through his work like a man. The Hartletop family, when the alliance was found to be unavoidable, endeavoured to arrange that the wedding should be held at Hartletop Priory, in order that the clerical dust and dinginess of Barchester Close might not soil the splendour of the marriage gala doings; for, to tell the truth, the Hartletopians, as a rule, were not proud of their new clerical connexions. But on this subject Mrs. Grantly was very properly inexorable; nor when an attempt was made on the bride to induce her to throw over her mamma at the last moment and pronounce for herself that she would be married at the priory, was it attended with any success. The Hartletopians knew nothing of the Grantly fibre and calibre, or they would have made no such attempt. The marriage took place at Plumstead, and on the morning of the day Lord Dumbello posted over from Barchester to the rectory. The ceremony was performed by the archdeacon, without assistance, although the dean, and the precentor, and two other clergymen, were at the ceremony. Griselda's propriety of conduct was quite equal to that of Olivia Proudie; indeed, nothing could exceed the statuesque grace and fine aristocratic bearing with which she carried herself on the occasion. The three or four words which the service required of her she said with ease and dignity; there was neither sobbing nor crying to disturb the work or embarrass her friends, and she signed her name in the church books as 'Griselda Grantly' without a tremor – and without a regret.

Mrs. Grantly kissed her and blessed her in the hall as she was about to step forward to her travelling carriage leaning on her father's arm, and the child put up her face to her mother for a last whisper. 'Mamma,' she said, 'I suppose Jane can put her hand at once on the moire antique when we reach Dover?' Mrs. Grantly smiled and nodded, and again blessed her child. There was not a tear shed – at least, not then – nor a sign of sorrow to cloud for a moment the gay splendour of the day. But the mother did bethink herself, in the solitude of her own room, of those last words, and did acknowledge a lack of something for which her heart had sighed. She had boasted to her sister that she had nothing to regret as to her daughter's education; but now, when she was alone after her success, did she feel that she could still support herself with that boast? For, be it known, Mrs. Grantly had a heart within her bosom and a faith within her heart. The world, it is true, had pressed upon her sorely with all its weight of accumulated clerical wealth, but it had not utterly crushed her – not her, but only her child. For the sins of the father, are they not visited on the third and fourth generation? But if any such feeling of remorse did for awhile mar the fullness of Mrs. Grantly's joy, it was soon dispelled by the perfect success of her daughter's married life. At the end of the autumn the bride and bridegroom returned from their tour, and it was evident to all the circle at Hartletop Priory that Lord Dumbello was by no means dissatisfied with his bargain. His wife had been admired everywhere to the top of his bent. All the world at Ems, and Baden, and at Nice, had been stricken by the stately beauty of the young viscountess. And then, too, her manner, style, and high dignity of demeanour altogether supported the reverential feeling which her grace and form at first inspired. She never derogated from her husband's honour by the fictitious liveliness of gossip, or allowed any one to forget the peeress in the woman. Lord Dumbello soon found that his reputation for discretion was quite safe in her hands, and that there were no lessons as to conduct in which it was necessary that he should give instruction. Before the winter was over she had equally won the hearts of all the circle at Hartletop Priory. The duke was there and declared to the marchioness that Dumbello could not possibly have done better. 'Indeed, I do not think he could,' said the happy mother. 'She sees all that she ought to see, and nothing that she ought not.'

And then, in London, when the season came, all men sang all manner of praises in her favour, and Lord Dumbello was made aware that he was reckoned among the wisest of his age. He had married a wife who managed everything for him, who never troubled him, whom no woman disliked, and whom every man admired. As for feast of reason and for flow of soul, is it not a question whether any such flows and feasts are necessary between a man and his wife? How many men can truly assert that they ever enjoy connubial flows of soul, or that connubial feasts of reason are in their nature enjoyable? But a handsome woman at the head of your table, who knows how to dress, and how to sit, and how to get in and out of her carriage – who will not disgrace her lord by her ignorance, or fret him by her coquetry, or disparage him by her talent – how beautiful a thing it is! For my own part I think that Griselda Grantly was born to be the wife of a great English peer.

'After all, then,' said Miss Dunstable, speaking of Lady Dumbello – she was Mrs. Thorne at this time – 'after all, there is some truth in what our quaint latter-day philosopher tells us – "Great are thy powers, O Silence!"' The marriage of our old friends, Dr. Thorne and Miss Dunstable, was the third on the list, but that did not take place till the latter end of September. The lawyers on such an occasion had no inconsiderable work to accomplish, and though the lady was not coy, nor the gentleman slow, it was not found practicable to arrange an earlier wedding. The ceremony was performed at St. George's, Hanover Square, and was not brilliant in any special degree. London at the time was empty, and the few persons whose presence was actually necessary were imported from the country for the occasion. The bride was given away by Dr. Easyman, and the two bridesmaids were ladies who had lived with Miss Dunstable as companions. Young Mr. Gresham and his wife were there, as was also Mrs. Harold Smith, who was not at all prepared to drop her old friend in her new sphere of life. 'We shall call her Mrs. Thorne instead of Miss Dunstable, and I really think that will be all the difference,' said Mrs. Harold Smith. To Mrs. Harold Smith that probably was all the difference, but it was not so to the persons most concerned.

According to the plan of life arranged between the doctor and his wife she was still to keep up her house in London, remaining there during such period of the season as she might choose, and receiving him when it might appear good to him to visit her; but he was to be the master in the country. A mansion at the Chace was to be built, and till such time as that was completed, they would keep on the old house at Greshamsbury. Into this, small as it was, Mrs. Thorne, – in spite of her great wealth, – did not disdain to enter. But subsequent circumstances changed their plans. It was found that Mr. Sowerby could not or would not live at Chaldicotes; and, therefore, in the second year of their marriage, that place was prepared for them. They are now well known to the whole county as Dr. and Mrs. Thorne of Chaldicotes, – of Chaldicotes, in distinction to the well-known Thornes of Ullathorne in the eastern division. Here they live respected by their neighbours, and on terms of alliance both with the Duke of Omnium and with Lady Lufton. 'Of course those dear old avenues will be very sad to me,' said Mrs. Harold Smith, when at the end of a London season she was invited down to Chaldicotes; and as she spoke she put her handkerchief up to her eyes.

'Well, dear, what can I do?' said Mrs. Thorne. 'I can't cut them down; the doctor would not let me.'

'Oh, no,' said Mrs. Harold Smith, sighing; and in spite of her feeling she did visit Chaldicotes.

But it was October before Lord Lufton was made a happy man; – that is, if the fruition of his happiness was a greater joy than the anticipation of it. I will not say that the happiness of marriage is like the Dead Sea fruit – an apple which, when eaten, turns to bitter ashes in the mouth. Such pretended sarcasm would be very false. Nevertheless, is it not the fact that the sweetest morsel of love's feast has been eaten, that the freshest, fairest blush of the flower has been snatched and has passed away, when the ceremony at the altar has been performed, and legal possession has been given? There is an aroma of love, an undefinable delicacy of flavour, which escapes and is gone before the church portal is left, vanishing with the maiden name, and incompatible with the solid comfort appertaining to the rank of wife. To love one's own spouse, and to be loved by her, is the ordinary lot of man, and is a duty exacted under penalties. But to be allowed to love youth and beauty that is not one's own – to know that one is loved by a soft being who still hangs cowering from the eye of the world as though her love were all but illicit – can it be that a man is made happy when a state of anticipation such as this is brought to a close? No; when the husband walks back from the altar, he has already swallowed the choicest dainties of his banquet. The beef and pudding of married life are then in store for him; – or perhaps only the bread and cheese. Let him take care lest hardly a crust remain – or perhaps not a crust. But before we finish, let us go back for one moment to the dainties – to the time before the beef and pudding were served – while Lucy was still at the parsonage, and Lord Lufton still staying at Framley Court. He had come up one morning, as was now frequently his wont, and, after a few minutes' conversation, Mrs. Robarts had left the room – as not unfrequently on such occasions was her wont. Lucy was working and continued her work, and Lord Lufton for a moment or two sat looking at her; then he got up abruptly, and, standing before her, thus questioned her:–

'Lucy,' said he.

'Well, what of Lucy now? Any particular fault this morning?'

'Yes, a most particular fault. When I asked you here, in this room, on this very spot, whether it was possible that you should love me – why did you say that it was impossible?'

Lucy, instead of answering at the moment, looked down upon the carpet, to see if his memory were as good as hers. Yes; he was standing on the exact spot where he had stood before. No spot in all the world was more frequently clear before her own eyes.

'Do you remember that day, Lucy?' he said again.

'Yes, I remember it,' she said.

'Why did you say it was impossible?'

'Did I say impossible?' She knew that she had said so. She remembered how she had waited till he had gone, and that then, going to her own room, she had reproached herself with the cowardice of the falsehood. She had lied to him then; and now – how was she punished for it?

'Well, I suppose it was possible,' she said.

'But why did you say so when you knew it would make me so miserable?'

'Miserable! nay, but you went away happy enough! I thought I had never seen you look better satisfied.'

'Lucy!'

'You had done your duty, and had had such a lucky escape! What astonishes me is that you should have ever come back again. But the pitcher may go to the well once too often, Lord Lufton.'

'But will you tell me the truth now?'

'What truth?'

'That day, when I came to you – did you love me at all then?'

'We'll let bygones be bygones, if you please.'

'But I swear you shall tell me. It was such a cruel thing to answer me as you did, unless you meant it. And yet you never saw me again till after my mother had been over for you to Mrs. Crawley's.'

'It was absence that made me – care for you.'

'Lucy, I swear I believe you loved me then.'

'Ludovic, some conjurer must have told you that.' She was standing as she spoke, and, laughing at him, she held up her hands and shook her head. But she was now in his power, and he had his revenge – his revenge for her past falsehood and her present joke. How could he be more happy when he was made happy by having her all his own, than he was now? And in these days there again came up that petition as to her riding – with very different result now than on that former occasion. There were ever so many objections, then. There was no habit, and Lucy was – or said that she was – afraid; and then, what would Lady Lufton say? But now Lady Lufton thought it would be quite right; only were they quite sure about the horse? Was Ludovic certain that the horse had been ridden by a lady? And Lady Meredith's habits were dragged out as a matter of course, and one of them chipped and snipped and altered, without any compunction. And as for fear, there could be no bolder horsewoman than Lucy Robarts. It was quite clear to all Framley that riding was the very thing for her. 'But I never shall be happy, Ludovic, till you have got a horse properly suited for her,' said Lady Lufton. And then, also, came the affair of her wedding garments, of her trousseau – as to which I cannot boast that she showed capacity or steadiness at all equal to that of Lady Dumbello. Lady Lufton, however, thought it a very serious matter; and as, in her opinion, Mrs. Robarts did not go about it with sufficient energy, she took the matter mainly into her own hands, striking Lucy dumb by her frowns and nods, deciding on everything herself, down to the very tags of the boot-ties.

'My dear, you really must allow me to know what I am about;' and Lady Lufton patted her on the arm as she spoke. 'I did it all for Justinia, and she never had reason to regret a single thing that I bought. If you'll ask her, she'll tell you so.' Lucy did not ask her future sister-in-law, seeing that she had no doubt whatever as to her future mother-in-law's judgement on the articles in question. Only the money! And what could she want with six dozen pocket-handkerchiefs all at once? There was no question of Lord Lufton's going out as Governor-General to India! But twelve dozen pocket-handkerchiefs had not been too many for Griselda's imagination. And Lucy would sit alone in the drawing- room at Framley Court, filling her heart with thoughts of that evening when she had first sat there. She had then resolved, painfully, with inward tears, with groanings of her spirit, that she was wrongly placed in being in that company. Griselda Grantly had been there, quite at her ease, petted by Lady Lufton, admired by Lord Lufton; while she had retired out of sight, sore at heart, because she felt herself to be no fit companion to those around her. Then he had come to her, making matters almost worse by talking to her, bringing the tears into her eyes by his good-nature, but still wounding her by the feeling that she could not speak to him at her ease. But things were at a different pass with her now. He had chosen her – her out of all the world, and brought her there to share with him his own home, his own honours, and all that he had to give. She was the apple of his eye, and the pride of his heart. And the stern mother, of whom she had stood so much in awe, who at first had passed her by as a thing not to be noticed, and had then sent out to her that she might be warned to keep herself aloof, now hardly knew in what way she might sufficiently show her love, regard, and solicitude.

I must not say that Lucy was not proud in these moments – that her heart was not elated at these thoughts. Success does beget pride, as failure begets shame. But her pride was of that sort which is in no way disgraceful to either man or woman, and was accompanied by pure true love, and a full resolution to do her duty in that state of life to which it had pleased her God to call her. She did rejoice greatly to think that she had been chosen, and not Griselda. Was it possible that having loved she should not so rejoice, or that, rejoicing, she should not be proud of her love? They spent the whole winter abroad, leaving the dowager Lady Lufton to her plans and preparations for their reception at Framley Court; and in the following spring they appeared in London, and there set up their staff. Lucy had some inner tremblings of the spirit, and quiverings about the heart, at thus beginning her duty before the great world, but she said little or nothing to her husband on the matter. Other women had done as much before her time, and by courage had gone through with it. It would be dreadful enough, that position in her own house with lords and ladies bowing to her, and stiff members of Parliament for whom it would be necessary to make small talk; but, nevertheless, it was to be endured. The time came, and she did endure it. The time came, and before the first six weeks were over she found that it was easy enough. The lords and ladies got into their proper places and talked to her about ordinary matters in a way that made no effort necessary, and the members of Parliament were hardly more stiff than the clergymen she had known in the neighbourhood of Framley. She had not been long in town before she met Lady Dumbello. At this interview also she had to overcome some little inward emotion. On the few occasions on which she had met Griselda Grantly at Framley they had not much progressed in friendship, and Lucy had felt that she had been despised by the rich beauty. She also in her turn had disliked, if she had not despised, her rival. But how would it be now? Lady Dumbello could hardly despise her, and yet it did not seem possible that they should meet as friends. They did meet, and Lucy came forward with a pretty eagerness to give her hand to Lady Lufton's late favourite. Lady Dumbello smiled slightly – the same old smile which had come across her face when they two had been first introduced in the Framley drawing-room; the same smile without the variation of a line, – took the offered hand, muttered a word or two, and then receded. It was exactly as she had done before. She had never despised Lucy Robarts. She had accorded to the parson's sister the amount of cordiality with which she usually received her acquaintance; and now she could do no more for the peer's wife. Lady Dumbello and Lady Lufton have known each other ever since, and have occasionally visited at each other's houses, but the intimacy between them has never gone beyond this.

The dowager came up to town for about a month, and while there was contented to fill a second place. She had no desire to be the great lady in London. But then came the trying period when they commenced their life together at Framley Court. The elder lady formally renounced her place at the top of the table, – formally persisted in renouncing it though Lucy with tears implored her to resume it. She said also, with equal formality – repeating her determination over and over again to Mrs. Robarts with great energy, – that she would in no respect detract by interference of her own from the authority of the proper mistress of the house; but, nevertheless, it is well known to every one at Framley that old Lady Lufton still reigns paramount in the parish.

'Yes, my dear; the big room looking into the little garden to the south was always the nursery; and if you ask my advice, it will still remain so. But, of course, any room you please –'

And the big room looking into the little garden to the south is still the nursery at Framley Court.

THE END

Everyman's Library, founded in 1906 and relaunched in 1991, aims to offer the most complete library in the English language of the world's classics. Each volume is printed in a classic typeface on acid-free, cream-wove paper with a sewn full cloth binding.